D1453725

Tyrant Books
9 Clinton St
Upper North Store
NY, NY 10002

Via Piagge Marine 23
Sezze (LT) 04018
Italy

www.NYTyrant.com

Cover design by Nicole Caputo

Book design by Adam Robinson

LIVEBLOG

MEGAN BOYLE

tyrant books

STARTING TODAY, MARCH 17, 2013, I WILL BE LIVEBLOGGING everything i do, think, feel, and say, to the best of my ability. right now there is no one i talk to frequently enough to affect by my failure to follow through with tasks i said i'd do. the only person 'keeping tabs' on my life is me. as time has been passing, i have been feeling an equally uncontrollable sensation of my life not belonging to me or something. like it's just this event i don't seem to be participating in much, and so could be attending by mistake. maybe i wasn't invited. clerical error. i witness myself willfully allowing opportunities to fade away, because sometimes, for whatever reason, it is hard for me to do things that i know will make me happy.

i can't control getting older but i can control what i do as i age. also, i feel like my memory is deteriorating. i used to like documenting my daily activities. that seemed to help me remember more. lately the things i've been doing haven't felt worth remembering, but i feel like that could just be a mind trick, and if i start writing more again, i'll convince myself everything is basically the same as however many years ago it was when i felt more satisfied or hopeful or whatever it is i don't feel now.

THIS IS NOT GOING TO BE INTERESTING **I AM NOT GOING TO TRY TO MAKE THIS SOUND INTERESTING OR TRY TO MAKE YOU LIKE ME OR THINK ABOUT IF YOU ARE READING THIS OR ENJOYING READING THIS, IT'S JUST GOING TO BE WHAT IT IS: A FUNCTIONAL THING THAT WILL HOPEFULLY HELP ME FEEL MORE LIKE IMPROVING MYSELF**

going to start a little earlier, with what happened earlier tonight:

2:00AM: pushed orange peel down garbage disposal and walked to my room. heard garbage disposal turn on, then dad's voice announcing 'oranges smell good' to empty kitchen and living room.

2:30AM: walked to mom's room to show parents youtube video of 'the meaning of life' by don hertzfelt. during opening credits dad said 'oh wow, the sundance film festival,' and 'a long trip down a birth canal.' mom gently quieted him. focused on eating my orange. parents laughed in a manner like they felt pressured, maybe, when the cartoons started talking. stars replaced the talking cartoons and dad said 'oh, well now that made me like it,' stressing 'that.' near the end of the video, a small alien is left alone to look at the stars. mom sounded teary and like she might be smiling. dad talked excitedly about not understanding what the video was trying to say but he really, really liked it, like 'hoo boy did i ever like that.' mom said 'it's not over yet, mike.' dad adjusted his posture and said 'oh! oh no, hush, let's hush and see what else happens.' i didn't look at either parent. the poignant part of the video had passed. i said 'yeah, so.' credits scrolled over pretty galaxy-like orbs. i said 'yeah, the guy, he didn't use computers to make it.' dad said 'oh, no computers? oh wow it was just great, wow, really great, is there some kind of website i can get to, to get to this guy? i really didn't quite get it but the flavor of it is just so, wow. it's really something.' i said 'i don't know his website.' it was hard to look at dad. i said goodnight. mom smiled and dad thanked me again for showing him the movie. i walked back to my room, feeling like i had just missed a crucial, seemingly easily-made three-pointer and the other team had taken possession of the ball.

3:12AM: plugged drain and turned faucets. sat in my room, waiting for tub to fill. dad stood in hallway between bathroom and my room and asked about my symptoms, which stopped a few days ago, and i'm pretty sure were caused by drugs i did in new york. i haven't wanted parents to worry so i've been feigning a slow recovery from a stomach flu. told dad i'm feeling better. he reminded me xanax would help me sleep and i thanked him. placed macbook on chair in front of tub, for 'bathtub internet viewing station.' retrieved papaya from fridge. snorted medium-large amount of heroin from cute box given to me by tao, from a recent trip to taiwan. it's a square made of four smaller squares with lids. almost transparent blue color. tapped baggie until 'heroin quadrant' was filled with an amount of powder, for next time. undressed and got in tub.

4:00AM: sort of ignored gchat from ex-boyfriend, then responded. he hasn't yet. washed and conditioned hair. submerged all but eyes and nose under water. felt anemone-like. rubbed fingernails up and down legs and watched grayish flecks of skin float around body. thought about things i said i'd do by monday. replied to two emails with difficulty, typing with one hand and covering an eye with the other. rinsed with fresh water, unplugged drain, toweled dry. ate 1mg xanax.

4:10AM: peeled orange over kitchen sink, feeling calm and warm but also 'is this…too much…does 'too much' feel like this?' pictured dad in the morning, using garbage disposal and announcing 'oranges smell good' like he did earlier tonight, only i'm dead in my bed.

4:30AM: researched heroin/xanax interactions. seems like i'll probably just sleep a lot tonight. probably wouldn't hurt to vomit.

4:42AM: used variety of finger pressures/speeds to encourage chunks of mostly undigested fruit into toilet bowl. saw a little fresh blood on thumb. used to be able to vomit by like, tickling the back of my tongue. drank water and jumped/twisted abdomen, to stir anything that had settled, then kneeled for 'the final emptying.' legs felt weak. vomit was pretty, shades of orange. realized i was looking at it without thoughts/emotions, but some similarly dominant level of brain activity. flushed toilet. brushed teeth, washed face. ate raw 'go pecan pie' granola bar.

5:36AM: the things i've done tonight are not things i would normally tell people i did, i think.

6:11AM: stomach is making whale noises. starting to hear distant cars. it's always bad when you start to hear cars. wish i wanted to masturbate. i feel like, 5000 years old, like leto ii in 'god emperor of dune.'

6:35AM: drinking unpasteurized milk mom said 'comes right from the cow.' holding four raspberry cookies. probably going to get seconds.

6:56AM: looked at facebook and felt sad and bewildered and like 'shit, what did i do' about a person i like, who has indirectly communicated negative feelings about me. 'in my younger, wilder days' i probably would've tried harder to make amends. now i accept not being liked. that's depressing, seems like faulty logic. when you resign, you think you're being open-minded because you're accepting something you'd rather not, but really you're just less open to possibilities other than 'i will feel disappointed.' i could type more about this but it feels better not to. interesting. want to eat two egg mcmuffins and hash browns and orange juice and for it to be night all tomorrow.

8:25AM: woke feeling as bad but not worse than yesterday. ate 1mg xanax 'for medicinal purposes.' toasted 'bagel thin' condensed bagel. spread chive cream cheese on half that didn't burn. want more sleep. smells like burning.

8:45AM: unplugged toaster. troubled by 'sleeping at sunrise then waking every two or three hours until early evening' routine. going to look at internet and wait for xanax to kick in.

11:00AM: woke to muffled talking sounds punctuated by basso voice of dad, who seemed to be agreeing with something a lot. covered head and macbook with blanket.

3:15PM: my job was to paint the freshmen's tents pink. i knew earth would explode in a few minutes, because the universe was resetting. this had been shown to me in a kind of pre-flight safety video. the freshman looked human but acted like feral cats. they shared a brain with 'feral cat concerns.' i was their caretaker, kind of. they wanted sex with me. told dream to mom. she said 'are you sure you want to be moving to new york right now?' i said 'i don't know what else to do, i need to do something, i feel like i'm dying.' put spinach, avocado, cucumber, coconut water, banana in blender. mom described plot of murder mystery novel. i looked for another banana or a suitable second banana substitute. mom said 'i'm so glad you don't want to be an F.B.I. agent.' i said 'yeah, i thought about being one, back when i watched 'silence of the lambs.' they don't let you do drugs though.' she said 'what?' i said 'it seems too hard.'

3:53PM: mom said 'meggie do you want dad to bring home some bananas? he should be home soon.' i said 'no thank you, that's okay, i'll get them.' she said 'it really wouldn't be a problem.' i said 'i know, i know, i just feel like i want to take a drive,' like napoleon dynamite. ate 10mg adderall.

things i need to do today:

- write letter recommending myself as if i am tao and he is my employer

- ask keith (friend/former boss) if he'll write short letter recommending me, or if he'll endorse letter i'll write as him

- ask colin (real estate agent) what time and where in NYC he wants to meet tomorrow

- write cover letter for apartment application binder

- buy binder for apartment application binder

- write article for vice column

4:11PM: texted keith, asked if he wants to get drinks tonight. texted colin. colin is three years younger than me, owns a small business, works tech support for cable company he might also own, has served in military, has yet to but will most surely definitely graduate college. dwarves me with his success. lives in the apartment across the hall from the one i want.

4:17PM: watching video of sam pink reading at KGB. he looks handsome, like grecian god style. he's said 'sour cream' twice, so far. people laughed onscreen. the lighting is making his face look like 'what the other hitman would've been told not to remember.' sort of remember where i stood in relation to camera that night. would be crazy if i knew where i stood in relation to camera at all times. need to get my ass out the door to buy bananas. he said 'sour cream' again.

4:26PM: skipped to kitchen, making a noise like 'blreelerleeloobleelooloooloo.' opened four-pack steaz energy drinks and took one as a reward for 'being so productive so far.' skipped back to room thinking 'how will i type 'blreelerloorlooleeloo' noise?' no responses from keith or colin yet. going to read liveblog i've written as a reward. this is not a reward. shit. i should just get moving instead. no, allow yourself small rewards, otherwise this won't work. small rewards. shit.

4:32PM: keith texted 'Dang. Id love to madge, but I'm afraid I can't.'

**IF ANYONE READING THIS WOULD LIKE TO WRITE A SHORT LETTER RECOMMENDING ME, LIKE, PRETENDING YOU KNOW ME AS AN EMPLOYEE BUT HAVE COME TO THINK OF ME AS A FRIEND YOU TRUST THE WAY YOU TRUST A NEIGHBOR OR TENANT WHICH ARE BOTH AREAS YOU THINK I COULD EXCEL—COLIN SAID IT WOULD BE GOOD TO INCLUDE THE WORD 'INTEGRITY'—PLEASE EMAIL ME, WILL PAY YOU, NEEDS TO SOUND LIKE WE'VE KNOWN EACH OTHER FOR YEARS **

**MY LIFE IS……………………………….JESUS………..FEEL….. JESUS…………….

5:26PM: matthew donahoo has come to my rescue with a sweet letter of recommendation and writing topic lists. masha has started liveblog project. sam cooke emailed list too. my crotch smells like coconut oil.

6:02PM: mom brought a big beige 'industrial strength'-looking blanket to my room and said 'do you want this, for emergencies? for the trunk of your car? you can fold it.' i said 'sure' and she walked away, leaving the obviously-not-her-style blanket. ate b-vitamin, zeolite supplement. sent two emails. paid matthew. have been feeling, like, waiting for something, and ready, like in 'a farewell to arms' where they're in the trench and haven't eaten and ernest hemingway brings them moldy cheese and pasta and then they get bombed. going to leave for whole foods now.

6:17PM: when i passed mom's room she covered the talking part of her phone, said 'meggie? oh nevermind, i was going to ask dad to bring bananas but you want fresh air.' walked downstairs saying, 'yeah, yeah, i want that, fresh air,' accidentally like how terry gross says it on NPR, like, 'FRRRR-RResh air.'

6:39pm: Driving to Wegman's instead, to buy mom special Wegman's eggplant dip. Smoking second American spirit menthol cigarette. Listening to iPod on shuffle mode. Feel like I'm launching or something. Liveblog is helping. There are higher stakes if I fail to complete tasks today. Others will know. Saw that Elizabeth Ellen 'liked' liveblog tumblr post. Swerved into other lane. Feeling capable and optimistic and like lame and fragile parts of me are being exposed, but am strangely positive about that. 'Rubber traits' by Why? is playing. About to turn left, to Wegman's parking lot. Sky looks like the sky of a day in July 2008, when I had just broken up with boyfriend and walked around 24-hour grocery store, didn't buy anything, cried driving home, went on cruise to Alaska with family the next day. Parked. Typing is making me equally more attentive and detached about what I'm doing/thinking, like I'm narrating myself from a distance.

6:52pm: zero non-green bananas in Wegman's. Recognized 'All the way to Reno' by R.E.M. on loudspeaker after wandering around produce section for some time. Bought eggplant dip and green probiotic drink. Going to whole foods for bananas, kale and kombucha for 'flushing green stuff through me' smoothie. Forget why I'm doing this. Have never tried to live somewhere with an application process involving a 'committee of apartment people' reading cover letters. Stressful. Would not be doing this if apartment was not a sweet ass studio on the beach, $750/month. Feeling nonspecifically discouraged, maybe due to adderall wearing off.

7:03pm: drank probiotic drink too fast to taste. Car idling in parking spot.

7:07pm: 'earth intruders' by bjork came on iPod shuffle. Chuckled imagining being the emperor of the universe and banishing Brandon Scott Gorrell to a small white room where he has to do…something…for eternity, while this song plays on repeat (I feel positive things about bsg and wouldn't do that if I was emperor of universe). Considering eating one Molly pill but that'd maybe…I don't know. Does not bode well.

7:15pm: less than 12 hours until I should leave for NYC. Might email Colin that I'll come Tuesday, not tomorrow.

7:28pm: pulling in to whole foods parking lot. Texted adderall dealer. Do not anticipate response.

7:33pm: jogged from car to store. Selected kale bunch, bananas, citrus kombucha. Waiting to pay now. Intense neurotic 'time is running out' feeling. Jealous of all the people waiting in other lines who don't have my life. Want to be cradled by something. Thought I saw a 'new message' alert flash on kombucha bottle and panicked. Impulsively selected organic energy shot from box labeled 'try me.'

7:43pm: read supportive emails from Andrea Coates, Masha, more article ideas from Sam Cooke. Responded while driving. Felt something in stomach change after checking email. Drinking organic energy shot.

8:41PM: security alarm beeped once as i closed door to mom's. apartment smelled like bacon. mom said 'i'm making chicken BLT's, i can make you one' and i said 'no thanks mom, i'm on a roll.' unloaded whole foods bag near two plates containing loosely assembled sandwiches. stared at a square of yellow cheese complexly, like i was downloading a message from it. blended smoothie. ate 20mg XR adderall. texted colin a lie about not receiving .pdf of lease, so i'll be coming tuesday. wrote short recommendation for him on trulia.com. sitting at my desk. robotic and panicky. stomach doing acid reflux things.

8:52PM: spelled 'mexican' as 'mescxican' in tweet about my book being available as an ebook. proofread correctly-spelled tweet until words seemed more like 'alphabet-shaped lines' than language.

9:09PM: worried apartment building committee people will google my name. might make liveblog private. printing keith-approved recommendation letter. two out of three recommendations complete. emailed matthew donahoo to outsource writing 'tao' recommendation. should've considered how un-recommendable i feel before offering to write recommendations, so others wouldn't have to. i am learning from this. keep thinking 'i am learning.' my breath smells a way i've smelled on others and avoided saying 'your breath smells.' musty/basement-y. going to brush teeth then walk outside, thinking about. something. thinking 'keep moving.'

9:48PM: used two strings of dental floss. spit blood. felt vengeful against everyone who doesn't floss regularly, including myself, inflicting their bad breath on me, 'forcing me' into polite silence as i flossed. remembered nervously asking first boyfriend to show me his brushing method, then introducing him (carefully and mindfully of his feelings and limited hygiene experience) to concepts like 'doing this once a day' and 'molars' and 'using enough paste to create a lather,' saying like, 'maybe you should press a little harder' and experiencing a new kind of interpersonal anxiety at his 'it feels weird, i don't think i need to' response. remembered another ex-boyfriend's concerns about my hygiene and thought 'goddamnit megan, you know how it feels, it's not an emotional attack or critique of you, it's practical: you don't want to smell bad.' felt like i was performing the humanitarian task of flossing in front of a large and interested audience who would never be the same, 'after this.' felt like matthew broderick at the end of 'glory,' when he's about to lead denzel and the rest of the troop into a battle they'll clearly lose and have been preparing to fight for the entire movie—but my fight is with a nonspecific audience in my memory, or who is reading this now and doesn't care. 'this is what happens sometimes, if you consider other people, sometimes your gums will bleed so people won't have to think about how your mouth smells, let me show you the way my children: you will be better for this.' i am being insane right now i am aware of being neurotic and insane.

10:14PM: mom sat in the chair closest to my desk and asked if she could do anything to help. struggled to say something like 'could you maybe just jot some things down about me, like, as someone who likes my writing and thinks i'm…i don't know, responsible.' think i said 'jot' more than once, something about tao discovering my blog in 2008. mom said 'so i should say i started reading you in two-thousand eight?' i said 'no no no, no don't worry about the scheduling or two-thousand eight.' she said 'what do you mean, 'the scheduling?'' i said 'like the events. of like. don't worry about the events in time. i'm just having a hard time thinking of nice things to say about myself, i think it is, that's it. could you just write a thing as if you're someone who thinks nice things about me and like, likes my writing? what a person like that would say?' she nodded and stood, said 'oh honey of course.' i touched part of her bathrobe and said 'thank you so much mom,' nodding fast.

10:27PM: mom's head poked cheerfully into hallway, said 'can i say i've liked your writing since you were a little girl?' i waved dismissively but not unsociably and said 'just say whatever you want, just, whatever is good.'

10:29PM: jogged to kitchen in 'sprinkling' manner. drank big swig of liquid antacid. said 'you're the best mom' in a voice that sounded less childlike in my head. brought can of steaz energy drink to my room. something about now feels like christmas. can hear papers rustling. mom just entered, smiling, said 'this is a draft, this is a draft, i wrote it as a letter, it's not perfect,' handed me a paper. her handwriting was on both sides. i said 'this is perfect, thank you.' mom said 'i think i may have said two or three things two or three times' and left without looking back. i stood and tripped over basket of pencils, then caught up to hug her before she was gone. she is wearing a green bathrobe. feeling something indescribable about ending up in mom, getting born by mom, knowing mom all of this time.

10:37PM: read 'megan has shown a touching, intelligent sense of the absurd and at the same time, the real—sometimes sad, sometimes funny, sometimes purely existential experience of being human.' read 'fearless.' walked to mom's room. on the bed dad was leaning diagonally towards a recumbent mom, looking at her kindle. they were under the covers and smiling. dad had a towel on his head. said goodnight, hugged them, started walking back to my room. in the doorway i said 'it's nice to know you guys are around,' knowing this was not what i wanted to say, not knowing what i wanted to say, but that i wanted to say something.

MARCH 18, 2013

12:58AM: used only the word 'approach,' i think, from mom's fake tao letter. dad walked out to hallway while brushing his teeth. a friend of a friend of his lived in rockaway park, near my potential future address, in the only house on the block undamaged by hurricane sandy. he asked if my building was by the bay or the ocean. doing something with my arms, i said 'there's one on each side, like, it's five blocks wide, about five blocks.' he repeated 'five blocks' and my arm motion, displaying the non-judgmentally proud face behind g.p.s. direction. the bathroom door opened after an amount of time i was retroactively embarrassed for having considered myself alone. for some reason suspected dad felt obligated to talk as he stood in the hall, describing a kind of therapy where the main thing is you scream in a room. he repeated 'the release technique' several times, with hair fluffily protruding in all directions, as if electrically charged.

1:15AM: small crisis. thought i'd lost security deposit check. sitting on the floor in the center of scattered apartment application-related papers, that colin recommended i organize in a binder for the selection committee people. typed 'sup ipad' in a long-un-responded-to gchat from ex-boyfriend. going to drive somewhere. 24-hour grocery store. buy folders and a stapler. brainstorm article ideas in car. seems important to stay in motion. 'stay' is funny/cute. that you can be 'staying.' imagining people in their rooms like how i'm in my room. anxiously imagined ex-boyfriend reading this. he wouldn't want to read this much from me ever, i don't think, and if he did it wouldn't matter.

1:35AM: something that sounds like a piano playing notes at almost not-random, cinematic intervals is coming from either directly under me or behind my closet. sometimes it stops. feeling. i don't know. i have a relationship with this liveblog now. everyone i've interacted with today has been so helpful and seemingly selfless. feel like reaching out to…something…thought 'if there was something i could do with my arms.'

3:01AM: want sex badly. heard somewhere that if your cat is in heat and you put a q-tip up to her ass, she'll back into it and be happy. i am so many miles from anyone i want to have sex with. currently enjoying sitting on heel and tentatively rolling. jesus. not horny enough to masturbate. missing something. everything is in order: the engine checks are finished, all passengers accounted for, weather and runway are clear, but this plane can't fly without a co-pilot. actually i'm the co-pilot. yeah, it's just the co-pilot here, i'm waiting on denzel, he's still sleeping next to the pretty naked lady in a trashed motel room and it says 'directed by: robert zemeckis' at the bottom of the screen and slowly we learn the lady and denzel have been partying on alcohol and cocaine all night and soon denzel needs to fly an airplane. we do not yet know the lady is a stewardess who dies. at this point in the movie i didn't know it wasn't a true story. the movie is 'flight.' getting carried away. stopped being horny. thought 'it all comes back to denzel.'

3:47AM: have not moved much. forgot i still need to write cover letter. pasted liveblog up until this update in microsoft word document, 'LIVE-BLOG.doc.' i could easily write this much or more every day, i think. have been enjoying this. immediate plans: reapply sweater, drink energy drink, drive to 24-hour grocery store, buy stapler and folder, *have happy goodtime thinky thoughts on drive home get oh so inspired teehee*, eat adderall, write cover letter, write article.

considering eating a molly to make the time before cover letter more interesting. inspiration. goddamnit. should i…

4:10AM: 'nah cause last time i did molly after addy binge it wasn't that great from cross tolerance…but u know, u r the master of ur domain,' masha tweeted. looked at 'cross tolerance' and thought something about bees that did not bode well. not going to eat the molly. will be less functional tomorrow if i eat the molly. want to eat the molly. pictured baby animatronic dinosaur from 90's TV show saying 'not the molly,' freezing for a horror movie interval, shaking something at me antagonistically.

4:34AM: short gchat with ex-boyfriend. something felt upsetting but neither of us explicitly said what. maybe he wasn't upset. he's at our apartment in philadelphia. feel like he thinks i forgot him or something. leaving mom's now.

5:05am: opened/closed kitchen cabinets quietly. Drank swigs of antacid while responding to texts from Mira, Sam Cooke, Willis, Alex. Willis is responding.

5:10am: thought 'at least it's warm outside' walking down stairs. Opened door and was struck with coldness and overpowering 'wet dog nose'/saliva-like smell that trailed into car a little. Turned key in ignition. Texted Willis about the smell, thinking we'd riff about it to better endure it together. He responded normally. Texted 'Going to concentrate on driving now.' Car feels lower to the ground than normal. Merging onto 695E. Checked email. Irritated at mass 'Matt Monarch' raw food newsletter. Remembered tweet by Ellen Kennedy like 'I am responsible for the zero emails in my inbox,' I feel that.

6:00am: read liveblog from beginning while driving full circle around the Baltimore-Washington beltway. Tired, physically. Inner monologue is whining things like 'this is easy for other people, other people just do things, other people would've had a folder and a stapler by now.' Replaying memories of Sam Pink from a few days ago: somewhere in Brooklyn, looking for my car. Talking about how it's stupid when people freak out when they're late and already on the way to the destination, so there's nothing to do but wait to arrive—which is relaxing, and feels kind of special. Me saying 'wish I had a voodoo grandma,' him saying something indicating he understood, or at least didn't want to stop talking. Seeing him in 'distractingly free of associations shirt' and noticing the color of his eyes for maybe the first time before the Housing Works reading, thinking 'what do I say,' doing some kind of brief physical greeting with him and feeling wetness on my face, but not near parts that normally become wet. Eyes looked gray, then more brown. I don't notice eyes unless it looks like someone is behind them, controlling where they look. Sam has eyes like that. Wonder if he's reading this. Seems 15-60% likely. The sky is dark and morning commute cars are on the road. I never assume people like me are on the road. Lost wandering shitheads. Wish there was a Grindr-like iPhone app for lost wandering shitheads, so you could locate others. I probably wouldn't use it.

6:14am: removed foot from gas pedal 'for fun.' Nearing 24-hour grocery store and house where I lived, ages 10-22. At stoplight heard birds tweeting stereotypically. Still dark outside. Large bald man with reflective tape on his back is walking on shoulder of road.

6:20am: braked to let truck merge in front of me, feeling a familiar pang of loss/envy/regret. Like, 'there goes the life of adventure and financial and temporary existential certainty I was too much of a drifting loser to attain.' Feel like truck drivers know this about me and can sense waves of inefficiency evaporating through my roof. I thought I wanted to drive trucks. I have a Class-A commercial driver's license. At my first and only interview drugs showed in my pee test and I didn't have an excuse and I got scared and gave up. There. I said it. Unsure if I'll drive trucks in the future. Maybe I haven't failed completely yet. I don't know what I want. Life is so long. I just want to be okay. Feel close to crying now, in car parked in grocery store parking lot. Thinking about how to type location replaced urge to cry. Car parked near me has had its headlights on this entire time. Achy body. Okay. Going inside store.

6:37am: still sitting here. Getting colder. Headlights car has 'finally' left. Afraid to go inside for some reason. Might just drive home, come back later. Yes I feel good thinking that: going to come back later. Stomach is burning again goddamnit.

6:46am: street lights against navy blue sky are making trees look orange. Pretty. Still sitting here. Temperature in car feels the same as outside. Focusing too much on liveblog. Need to refocus.

6:48am: turned head and caught a whiff of me. Thought 'hey I smell okay' like it was the catchphrase of a Saturday morning kids TV show theme song. The music would take a sudden turn and almost stop, then a balding man in a sweatshirt would pop out from behind a cardboard tree and say 'hey I smell okay.' After a 'crucial pause,' the offscreen characters would gather in a circle to sing the refrain and the sweatshirt man would like, run to join them, 'late as usual,' trailed by an animation that becomes an exclamation point at the end of the title graphic. This would happen before every episode.

6:53am: need to refocus.

6:56am: driving out of the parking lot now, can't believe I just did this, I just sat there the whole time oh my god. Lawdy lawdy honeychile, shoot. Sittin' there. Shoot. Peace be witchoo honeychile.

7:04am: would be funny if that was the last thing I'd type before a fatal car collision. Or if this was the last thing. Or this. Or this. Or this. Or this. Okay guess it's not going to happen.

7:08am: OR THIS!!!!!!!!!

7:09am: laughed really loud. For maybe three seconds.

7:11am: 'three seconds' is not a comment on…nevermind…

7:18am: Maybe I am ready for the grocery store now. I might just be. Pictured a chuckling Barack Obama finding my eyes in a crowd, saying 'yes you can' to America, moving closer to me with a concerned face, placing his hand on my shoulder, saying 'yes. You can,' gesturing to his watch and mouthing 'it's time' with a wink.

7:36am: I am turning around. I am not ready for the grocery store yet. It is wise that I know this. I don't want to waste my time. Oh my god. Laughing silently at me, retreating home, this needs to stop, almost out of gas.

7:39am: realized I've been taking this 'time is valuable and I am wasting it' thing too seriously, which seems related to why I yearn for long stretches of zero obligations. This is not new information. Nothing I do means anything, like in the spectrum of things…all possible outcomes are ultimately death. Nothing is permanent. For me to want to stay alive I have to forget that, otherwise I won't feel motivated to do things. That always feels like lying, a little. Think I just want to be a kid forever, that's what I really want. Doesn't make sense to do all this other shit. Would like to be a 'kept woman.' I forget what that means. I think it's what I want.

7:47am: turned left onto street of childhood house. Interesting timing. In someone's yard, a small white dog running to the end of a leash tied to a pole. Walking towards bus stop, a girl who seems cooler and prettier and somehow older than I was when I was however old she is, touching her long straight blonde hair. Thought I'd be feeling something poignant related to childhood by now.

7:57am: would be funny to buy a cop car and just like, drive it.

8:20am: pulled next to the only free pump at BP. Squeezed/shimmied to exit car, due to parking too close to hard-to-describe fixture I see a lot at gas stations. Felt certain I'd locked keys in car. Pictured impending future where I'd need to call a locksmith, with my phone locked in the car. Across the street is the Jiffy Lube where a few weeks ago I got my oil changed before driving to New York to hang out with ex-boyfriend—cat-sitting for Adam and Lauren—and maybe look for apartments. Feels like I've had multiple birthdays since then. Three men in one-piece Jiffy Lube uniforms are smoking cigarettes by the garage. Looks like an Edward Hopper painting. Wish I was one of them.

8:28am: I have been smoking the shit out of this pack of cigarettes. Five remain from pack I opened earlier tonight.

8:31am: I don't know why I always dread pulling into a driveway or seeing my apartment building when walking or any of the other ways I've arrived home. Always feel better when I'm on the way to somewhere.

8:36am: made fun of myself in a mean-spirited way while watching fingers type '8:36am.'

8:38am: 'in case you are just tuning in,' here is what happened: around 2AM I started enjoying writing to generate content for a liveblog designed to stop me from getting in my own way. I guess at least I feel like I've been doing something, which is better than how I usually feel.

9:02AM: walked inside. retrieved green juice from fridge and drank more liquid antacid. ate 20mg adderall and scanned for small edits. feels okay to be doing this, like i'm preparing for something.

9:47AM: heard dad move around and coffee start dripping. want another cigarette. want to just turn this in as my 'everything i owe to everyone.' just remembered title of everclear song incorrectly as 'everything to everyone.' no wait, that's right i think. maybe it is time to try the grocery store again. feel like if it were sunny outside and i was waking to my cats walking on my stomach on a mattress near the smell of a person i like, things would be different. think that's all i want. i don't even want sex that much, i just want to always be near the smell of someone i like, whose presence is like equal parts 'hallucinogen' and 'antidepressant' and 'anxiolytic,' like i can just look at them and think 'great, now they're here, time for me to sit back and listen to all the surprises.' that sounds lazy maybe. i want them to want a person like that too so i can be like that for them too. doesn't seem real or possible. think i'm always on the verge of experiencing one of two extremes about other people. have experienced these rare insane manic connections, like 'beyond my wildest dreams'-style connections, which i've probably only felt so intensely because i've wanted to feel that way (often remember things and think 'you were just ignoring something so you could feel something else'). on a chart about how i feel most of the time most of my dots would be in the middle-to-'opposite of intensely connected to people' spectrum. when the opposite thing feels extreme it also seems attributable to disappointments about close relationships, but think it for real only involves other people to the extent that my ideas about their intentions are caused by this arcane primal fear that always seems to be experiencing itself over and over from some hidden location in me, syncing infrequently with my awareness, more often surfacing as a vague and near-ly-constant desire to apologize for something i've done, will probably do, or have already and unstoppably been doing 'this whole time,' just by being alive. but neither of those feelings, even the extreme connection thing, have anything to do with other people, i don't think. they are both supposed to be feelings about other people but they are both about me. think it's impossible for me to be close with someone in the way i think i want to be, or that most people are, or that i've thought i've been or something. the 'sit back and listen to all the surprises' thing seems more hopeful than the 'maintaining extreme closeness over time' thing, for me. like, if there's going to be anything. actually it might be the same thing. i don't know. like 'even when i'm so connected i'm always so alone and so tortured by a fear which cannot be expressed clearly' or whatever it is i'm saying with this bullshit—like, what is the point? would it logically follow that the the point of 'feeling connected' to someone would be to just continue feeling so similar that you eventually sort of become them, but then you'd just be the same thing, which is the same thing as being alone? MAN FUCK THIS SHIT MAN LISTEN TO THIS BITCH OVER HERE, ACTIN

ALL LIKE IT'S 9:47AM BUT IT'S 1:51PM AND SHE TWERKIN ON ADDERALL AND NO SLEEP TRYNA MAKE A FUCKIN SHIT ASS SENTENCE MAKE SENSE THAT DON'T EVEN MATTER LIKE WHAT'S GONNA HAPPEN NOW BITCH, NICE SENTENCE, WHERE THAT $1,000,000,000,000 CHECK? WHERE THAT PENT-HOUSE AT? AIN'T YOU SUPPOSED TO WIN THE GRAMMYS OR SOME SHIT NOW YOU BITCH ASS WRITIN THIS GODDAMNED SENTENCE FOR TWO HOURS? HM? SMELL YOUR GOD-DAMN ARMPIT. THAT'S RIGHT. SMELL ON THAT A MINUTE. MMHMM. THAT'S RIGHT. THAT'S WHAT I THOUGHT. YEAH I THINK IT'S TIME TO GO TO THAT GROCERY STORE. I THINK IT'S TIME TO GO TO THAT FUCKIN GROCERY STORE FUCKIN SEVEN HOURS AGO WHEN YOU WAS ALL 'TEEHEE GOING TO GET A STAPLER AND A FOLDER NOW BECAUSE THOSE ARE THINGS THAT I WANT AND NEED OH BOY LOOK AT ME GO!' YOU BETTER HOPE I DON'T LOOK IN A MIRROR SOON BECAUSE BITCH, IF I SEE YOU LOOKIN BACK AT ME, YOU AND ME IS BOTH IN PIECES. P-I-E-C-E-S. I THINK YOU KNOW I AIN'T TALKING REESES BUT NOW THAT YOU MENTION IT, FUCK YOU YOU STUPID SKINNY ASS HO, GETTIN ALL PROUD WHEN YOU BE STARVIN YOUR SKINNY ASS SAYIN 'IT'S HEALTHY' OR SOME SHIT. I WANNA STRAIGHT UP X-RAY THE SHIT OUT YOUR HEALTHY ASS ROTTEN ASS DIGESTIVE TRACK, SHOW A BITCH WHAT HEALTHY IS. GET Y'ALL FUCKED UP STOMACH AND 'TESTINES UP HERE ON THE COUCH WITH ME SO YOU CAN SEE FOR YOURSELF ALL THEM HOLES YOU BE MAKIN THAT GOT YOU SIPPIN ON THAT ANTACID! BITCH—NOW I KNOW YOUR ASS GOT NO PLACE TO GO BUT THE FLOOR AND NOT CAUSE YOU AT THE CLUB—AND YEAH, SOMETHIN BOUT YOUR LEGS UH, THEY JUST NASTY, UH, I DON'T KNOW, SHIT DON'T LOOK HUMAN TO ME PERSONALLY—BUT GET THAT SHIT TOGETHER! THAT SHIT'S THE ONLY SHIT YOU GOT! YOU STUCK IN THIS SHIT! OH YOU WHININ WITH SOME LONG SENTENCES BOUT HOW YOU SO LONELY OH YOU SO SAD AND ALONE I SEE UH WELL UH, UH, SEE HERE M'AM, YOU ARE USING DRUGS TO THE EXTENT, UH, M'AM, ALSO WITH THIS UH, YOU SEE, THIS UH, M'AM YOU EAT THIS FOOD AND THEN YOU VOMIT, THEN UH, THE LAXATIVES, YOU SEE? M'AM, AND THE CIGARETTES? UH, M'AM, AND FOR HOW MANY YEARS? YOU SEE WHERE I'M GOING WITH THIS M'AM? M'AM? OKAY GREAT GLAD YOU SEE, GLAD YOU SEE, OKAY. GREAT. GREAT, WELL THIS IS GREAT BECAUSE ALL OF

THIS HAS BEEN IN AN EFFORT TO TELL YOU THAT IT WAS ALL A MISUNDERSTANDING. WE HAVE ALL BEEN WAITING FOR THIS DAY. IF YOU LOOK OUT THE WINDOW YOU WILL SEE THE CAR WE HAVE PREPARED. REMEMBER WHO YOU ARE? THIS JOB? YOU TOOK THIS JOB, REMEMBER? YOU ARE A PRO-FESSIONAL FAMOUS ACTOR? YEAH MAN. HELL YEAH MAN! FIVE YEARS MAN, WELCOME BACK! YOU JUST GOT SO DEEP INTO THIS ROLE. METHOD ACTING. YEAH. YOU GOT SO DEEP INTO METHOD ACTING 'THE TERRIBLE TRAGEDY OF MEGAN BOYLE' THAT YOU FORGOT YOUR OWN IDENTITY. RELENTLESS, MAN. YOU. ARE. RELENTLESS. YOU EVEN CON-VINCED YOURSELF YOU OVERDOSED AND KILLED YOURSELF IN SOME APARTMENT IN MANHATTAN—TO IDENTIFY WITH HER, WE THINK. WE THINK THAT'S WHY YOU DID THAT. YEAH, IT'S BEEN YEARS SINCE YOU'VE TALKED TO ANYONE. YOU THOUGHT YOU WERE IN A 'BATMAN' MOVIE. NO, NO, THAT OTHER GUY ISN'T REAL, WE DON'T KNOW WHY YOU DID THAT, SOME PEOPLE ARE SAYING YOU MADE UP THIS OTHER VERSION OF YOURSELF—THIS ALTERNATE MEDIA REALITY OR SOMETHING—IT'S COMPLICATED, I DON'T FULLY UNDERSTAND THIS—YOU CONVINCED YOURSELF YOU WERE THE 'YOU' YOU THOUGHT YOUR CHARACTER WANTED TO SEE. RELENTLESS. AND I MEAN, SAD STORY AND ALL BUT SHE REALLY DIDN'T SEE THINGS TOO UH, HOW DO YOU SAY, 'CLEARLY,' HAHA, AM I RIGHT? YOU JUST NEEDED TO UNDERSTAND. YEAH MAN. THERE'S A LINE IN THE MOVIE, SHE SAYS SOMETHING LIKE 'WHY ARE YOU SO SERIOUS?' YOU REALLY TOOK OFF WITH THAT. YOU DIDN'T GET WHY SHE SAID THAT, YOU KNOW, WITH HER BEING SO SERIOUS ALL THE TIME. SO THEN YOU MADE UP THIS THING ABOUT HOW THERE WAS A NEW 'BATMAN' MOVIE AND HER REAL MOTIVATION IN THE SCENE WAS ALL ABOUT HOW SHE THOUGHT SHE SOUNDED LIKE AN IDIOT MISQUOTING THE JOKER, PLAYED BY YOU, WHO WAS ALSO HER, IN HER MIND, AND NONE OF YOU WERE ACTING ANYTHING LIKE JACK NICHOLSON. MAN IT'S SOME CRAZY SHIT. YOU GOTTA SEE THE TAPES. FUCKING 2008 MAN, IT'S BEEN A LONG ASS TIME! GOOD TO HAVE YOU BACK!

10:32AM: heard dad's slippers approaching on carpet. he asked if i wanted coffee. i said 'not right now, thank you though.' he said something about it being very fresh as the sound of his slippers reversed direction. mom also asks if i want coffee whenever she makes it. i've responded with 'i'll get it if i want it' in varying tones of annoyance, sometimes leading to a heightened argument about 'being considerate.' a few months ago i decided it's better for everyone if i just say 'not right now, thank you' or 'smells good, thank you, maybe later.' for some reason i never want it when they ask me, but sometimes less than a minute later i'll get it myself, stepping as softly as i can, trying to be unnoticeable as i pour a cup of 'my little secret' which i carry back to my room, where i feel about six years old. this happens every time. i don't know how to stop it unless people stop asking me if i want coffee but no one is ever going to stop.

10:51AM: walked softly to kitchen. drank liquid antacid. mimed pouring capped antacid container into coffee mug and said 'do you think it'd be good if i used it, you know, used it like this, for coffee' to dad, nowhere to be seen. started to say more and was stopped by a rustling noise. dad emerged from a hidden corner-area, holding a newspaper. he said 'what now?' i said 'oh like, used this for cream? it'd be a creamer substitute, this stuff, you know.' dad looked confused. i said 'i don't even like cream, so. this would be especially bad,' gesturing to the antacid. he didn't move for a moment, then seemed to 'get it' and made a joke. a little later he asked for my permission to show me an article about how irish people behave in the morning. he said 'your ancestors, you know. irish heritage. it's here if you want it.' withheld urge to remind him he doesn't need to ask my permission. knew i wouldn't read article, felt guilty/sad. i said 'maybe later, i'm on a roll now, doing things.' he asked what things. i told him i'd been writing in this liveblog for most of the night and now i wanted to 'knuckle down' and do other things. felt really guilty. it was hard to walk back to my room. we kept saying things. i said 'but i think first i need to rest, you know, rest before i knuckle down.' dad said 'of course.' felt really, really guilty.

11:07AM: peed and thought things like 'did i respond to colin's texts' in the same neutrally focused 'tone' of the pee, which stopped when the pee stopped.

11:12AM: can't find liquid antacid. keep wretching and swallowing pre-vomit stomach acid. last food eaten was raspberry cookies, over 24 hours ago.

3:19PM: want to be talking in insane unprecedented 9:47AM update voice all the time. funny to read 11:12AM update after writing insane update.

4:29PM: sitting on bed. liveblog seems unhealthy. afraid to re-read things that aren't the all-caps thing. all-caps thing seems like the only 'good thing' about this, maybe, right now, to me. i don't know.

REMINDER OF MY GOAL: TO LIVEBLOG DAILY ACTIVITIES WITHOUT PRIVACY AS A FORM OF NEGATIVE REINFORCEMENT, TO 'ACT BETTER'

don't really know what i meant by 'act better.' 'get things done?' i don't know. i don't know. it is raining. i am going to the grocery store. WHEN I GO TO THE GROCERY STORE I WILL WALK IN THE DOOR AND BUY THE THINGS I SAID I WOULD BUY, THEN I WILL LEAVE. MY DEAR CHILD, WHAT EVER STOPPED YOU FROM DOING SUCH PRACTICAL THINGS? seems so pointless…this entire thing… entire…jesus…laughing…wish someone would call me on the phone… kind of…

4:45PM: looked at phone, which has five missed calls, one voicemail, two texts. 'rimshot.'

5:35PM: heard shower water stop running, then shower head made a hilarious long noise that i could probably imitate if you called me. email me for my phone number. would hang up immediately after making the noise. serious inquiries only. hope some compassionate person from the year 6013 finds and reads all of this and comes back in time to kill me relatively painlessly when i leave the house in a few minutes. wrote this paragraph to prove 'you can still sound a certain way if you try, you don't feel as bad as you thought' to myself. making the shower noise at people on the phone then hanging up would also improve mood

if you're going to do it, when i pick up the phone say 'shower' so i won't make the noise to colin or someone else who's supposed to call me about the apartment

no one is going to do this

just made the noise really quietly, i'm laughing, i'm practicing it for you shitheads, come at me

doing it again

did not laugh at all that time

6:19PM: someone called. this is what was said:

> me: hello?

> person: hi megan, i was wondering if you could do the shower noise at me?

> me: oh man i think i kind of forget. i'm going to hang up right after.

> person: ok
>
> me: [makes noise, hangs up]

i'm still shaking from laughing from getting to do this. thank you, whoever called.

6:23PM: phone rang as i was typing previous update. i got really excited. it was dad. unknown number from portland oregon called and i said 'hello' in a playful way, extending 'lo.' docile confused older woman's voice asked about my health insurance. seems like someone is giving my phone number to telemarketers and saying i was born 3/29/72. COME AT ME BRO I LIKE PHONE CALLS I'LL CORRECT TELEMARKETERS ON THE PHONE ALL DAY LONG WATCH ME.

6:29PM: responded to texts from mira and masha. stored masha's number in my phone. person who called me asking for shower noise texted 'how many people have called for the noise.' i replied 'just you.' wanted to keep going like, 'just you, just you baby, it's always been you, only you, this entire time, you know it's true' but have them read it and it sounds like elvis.

6:49PM: something just happened. mom showed me this thing. apparently dad had ordered her this thing, it just showed up in the mail. she asked me to guess what it was. then it seemed like she wasn't going to wait for me to guess. wanted badly to guess. could tell guessing what this thing was would be the highlight of my day. mom kept squeezing its handle at me and this little rubber mouth would move. it was a sphincter-like movement. then this happened:

> mom: [comes at me with thing, pressing handle, cackling]
>
> me: no get the jebadoh away
>
> mom: what?
>
> me: i said jebadoh, but i meant 'jedi'
>
> mom: oh my god

[somehow deduced this thing is used for something pertaining to the toilet, goddamnit now i forget, was laughing in a manner like i was gasping for air this whole time, i asked 'if you don't wash your hands before you use it, will people stop being your friend' and mom said 'yes' and i laughed more, somehow deduced this thing is designed to grasp toilet paper and aid in ass wiping, it's an ass wiper, couldn't stop laughing] mom: your dad saw it in one of those tacky catalogs he likes, you know, like 'robin wright…'

me: are you going to say 'robin wright penn'

mom: well or you know, it's something like that, 'wright'

me: sean penn's wife, robin wright penn

mom: there's a catalog called 'robin wright'

me: asswipes, robin wright penn [can't stop laughing]

mom: it's 'walter drake'

me: walter drake, harriet carter [can't stop laughing]

i know the feeling of reading about how someone laughed. i hate that feeling but too bad. going to read this over and over again all by myself and laugh forever and ever.

8:52pm: stood in kitchen leaning on counter, looking at phone. Mom said 'what are you doing? Are you just standing quietly?'

8:55pm: asked mom what the movie she wanted to watch at 9pm was called. She didn't remember. Said 'I bet you'll remember when I get back' in a strange voice as I descended stairs. Locked door. Those would be really good last words. 'I bet you'll remember when I get back.' Actually might be better for murdering, in murder situations, murder-specific.

8:56pm: trying to see through rainy windshield. Driving to dad's to procure Adderall. Squinted and felt like Wayne knight when his Jeep breaks down in 'Jurassic Park.' Mistaking a lot of things for other things. I know people like to shittalk how people say 'feel like' and 'seems like.' That's all. Just, know that I know that. I know you do that. I'm watching you.

9:08pm: haven't slept in so long. Feel like I'm dying. Pictured annoying Zen figure hitting my head with a stick and saying 'you are.'

9:34pm: mental functions seems rapidly deteriorating. Van in front of me says 'your next car: PenskeCar.com' but I mean is that really my next car gotta give them a call

9:42pm: got lost somehow. going to dad's apartment is what i'm doing, on the way to do. pulled into CVS parking lot to re-calibrate GPS. Thinking things like 'certains' and 'chumly' and 'fiendish' and 'barnaby the string eater' looking at apple right now how'd this apple get here

9:44pm: ended voicemail to Colin with 'okay, bye-bye.'

9:52pm: going to type what I'm thinking in rapid succession: I'm losing it, my marbles, off my rocker, rocking out, heavy metal garage band, toy boat, where my dads, blinky buttress, that show on MTV with Matt Pinfield, did I ever mow the lawn completely, mow mow, mowrats, the momeraths out grabe, powpowpower wheels, dicey jukebox, the hellish landscapes of a Peruvian metal crisis, financial distress

11:36pm: somehow was capable of having heated vague two-hour conversation with dad about problems with our interactions, which ended with us hugging a few times and making jokes. When I walked through door dad almost immediately presented me with 'Mindfulness and Depression' CD and other things in a hurried manner, repeating himself a lot, pointing to his credit report and explaining things as if I was the person who would be assessing it, but it was like he thought he was 'in trouble' with me and forgot who I was. Instead of nodding and being quiet so it would be over soon, I said 'when you explain and repeat things and give unsolicited help I feel like it means you think I don't understand and need to be fixed, so I'm sort of a failure, and since I'm a failure it might mean you think you failed at parenting me or something. I worry about that, I feel guilty or something.' Remember saying 'when I can tell someone is anxious about talking with me and seems to mostly want my approval, I don't feel comfortable, I act fake and nod my head, I wish I didn't feel like doing that with you.' Talked about how I don't like it when he asks for 'permission to interrupt me' before he comes into whatever room I'm in, even though I say 'just always come in, it's always okay' and have been telling him this for years. Said 'I feel like if someone I liked told me I didn't need to be anxious around them I'd be happy.' Told him his asking permission sometimes seems sarcastic because I thought he knew I was never doing anything important. He denied the sarcasm strongly. He has always thought I've been doing something important. How could he think that. I believe him, but. What a disappointment I must be. He was generally receptive, asked questions, and voiced problems with me too (mostly related to my problems with him, which is a similar dynamic I've experienced in relationships, which is...I don't know). Feel like a little tyrant or something, typing this—like he is kind and generous and wants good things for me, so I shouldn't have problems. Told him that and he expressed a strong preference for me not keep problems to myself. It's always sort of hard to remember exactly what dad says. He uses a lot of generalizations and nonspecific buzzword-style language, like 'the self' and 'being for the sake of being' and pronounces some pronouns with capital letters.

At one point he said something about how mom is emotional but he feels flat all of the time. Without looking away, I said 'you seem sad to me.' He nodded slowly, shrugged and pressed his lips together. I wanted to do something to help. Looked around his apartment and thought about how he has thought about places for all his things to go and has arranged them on purpose. Like an area of slightly different Harley Davidson and Beatles gift-y things given to him by the same people, little statues and toys in a line on a mantle, unopened snack boxes in a line and back-ups of the snacks in the pantry, copies of CDs and self-help books and manila folders stacked carefully in neat piles, affirmations and phone numbers on post-its stuck in unusual places, a large variety of pens, an expensive-looking TV which I think he bought because he thinks mom likes TV and we used to watch movies as a family, when we lived in the same house. He sometimes refers to it as 'the entertainment center' and talks about how good the sound is. On a bookcase in his bedroom, too large to fit on the shelves, there is a professionally colored-in, formerly black-and-white photo of him smiling in a Navy uniform in 1957 or 1958, I think, between two bouquets of fake flowers all touching the ceiling, which feels especially sad to me—not in a pitiful way—in a way that makes me want to make his life better for him and wish that things could've been better.

MARCH 19, 2013

12:16am: have returned to parking lot of 24-hour grocery store. Driving here I felt strongly that I wouldn't go inside. People are sitting by the inoperable entrance smoking and talking. Can hear them as if they were a radio station in my car. Just thought it was possible to press something on my phone to immediately 'show you this.'

12:18am: more employees have come to sit at the operable entrance, at tables under umbrellas. I'm shivering. I'm inside the store. I need to find folders and a stapler. A hole punch. Energy drink. Shivering. I haven't eaten today or slept since whenever I last mentioned it in liveblog. Pronounced it 'live-[rhymes with boaje]' in my head, like, French. French-Canadian.

12:24am: a Paula Abdul song is playing. Have been holding this folder option and staring at it in disbelief, sometimes making little noises, for as long as song has been playing. About 90 seconds into the song now, safe estimate. Paralyzed by the hilarity of this thing. It says 'title page pocket' about the title page pocket and it shows you a picture of it too. Unbelievable. My hands holding a picture of hands holding the folder I'm about to buy. Look at the all the hands. Oh my god…

12:30am: now 'Simply the Best' by Tina Turner is playing. Keep gawking and laughing at things, like, how is this what I'm seeing—'party time,' 'married for life,' 'go for it.' All of this seems specifically arranged just for me, right now. Aware of being store's only observable customer, who appears more concerned with her phone than shopping. Moving only to avoid looking suspicious. Trying to walk with purpose. Sensed a person nearing me and narrowed my eyes ceiling-ward, like the lyrics of 'Simply the Best' were making me look elsewhere to more seriously contemplate them, because this is something I thought 'normal people' would do.

12:33am: old man pushing large wheeled machine looked me in the eye like he was thinking 'Christ, I'd wish you well but what's the use' as we passed each other. Selected a Monster 'Absolutely Zero' energy drink. Absolutely zero. Simply the best.

12:35am: used automated self-checkout to pay.

12:36am: a shitty philosophy class would have 'photo of barcode on red bull can next to actual barcode: which is more real?' on the syllabus. I could teach the shit out of that class right now.

12:38am: an example of something 'basic' that isn't widely regarded as 'basic' yet: the set-up of pressing the 'no, that's not ok' option on an ATM screen and instead of printing your receipt the ATM responds by arguing with you.

12:40am: sitting in parking lot again. Forgot to mention I've been eating a birth control pill every night around this time. Seems like a weird time to mention my coat smells like dad's cologne but hey I don't make this shit happen I just write it down.

12:52am: driving to mom's. Seems highly unlikely that I'll sleep tonight if I don't eat Xanax. If I eat the Xanax I will sleep really hard and probably hit 'snooze' too many times and miss appointment with Colin tomorrow in NYC. We're meeting so I can give him my apartment-garnering portfolio binder thing at 12:30pm. That is less than 12 hours from now. Four of those hours will be driving. Traffic. Consider showering and dressing, that takes time also. Should I eat the Molly now. Goddamnit. I have six Mollies. Should I eat one, then eat remaining adderall to drive? Seems like a good conservation of uppers. Megan Boyle: noted uppers conservationist. Uppers activist. Sleepless shivering retard. Molly-eating seems so inevitable now, like being secretly gay and locked in an elevator with the man you've loved since 'the war,' who you know loves you too.

1:04am: when my body aches like this I feel like it's getting stronger. Does anyone know anyone know if being awake for a long time counts as exercise? Should I keep driving so I can smoke another cigarette? Shit. No it's time to end this hell.

1:24AM: arrived home. pooped twice. washed face and brushed teeth and did more boring things. hugged mom, who was watching 'the mary tyler moore show' in bed. tried on t-shirt dad gave me. dad said he donated money to some people so they could arrange a memorial concert for a dead friend and they made t-shirts and gave him one. i like everything about the shirt.

1:35AM: counted only five molly pills in light blue pill container. paced between the kitchen and bedroom, not taking time to look at anything. counted again. rampant molly outbreak. rampant. keep thinking 'rampant.' in order to be in new york by 12:30PM i should be awake by 7AM and out the door by 7:30AM.

1:45AM: blended kale with citrus kombucha. the cord kept falling out of the plug. blender sounded louder with each subsequent plug-in. took smallish sips and felt healthier. stopped being able to drink it without wretching. poured remaining 15-20% down the drain and remembered inside joke with former best friend. we'd raise our hands in a surrendering motion while shaking our heads and matter-of-fact-ly saying 'can't do it,' imitating colin farrell's character in a recent but seemingly widely forgotten woody allen movie about boats. we saw it in a theater. can't remember anything else about movie. 'can't do it.' slight british accent.

2:00AM: experimentally used porky pig voice to say 'ba-theeba-theeba-th-eeba that's all folks' to mom, indicating the end of loud blender noises. she said 'what?' walked to her bedroom door and stood, using my hand to mime a diminishing circle, which i then poked my head through (like at the end of looney tunes), then repeated 'ba-theeba-theeba-theeba that's all folks,' enunciating the sounds slower. unsure if she 'got it.' had thought 'surely she would 'get this'' but now it's hard to say. refilled kombucha bottle with water.

2:26AM: responded to text from mira. swallowed the molly. 'here we go.' okay.

2:53AM: felt heart beating extremely hard all of a sudden. palms are sweating. was typing/elaborating on earlier thing about dad's apartment and thought my body was having a physical reaction to emotions but then remembered eating molly. shivering. shit. shit. shit. feel. shit. unable to. shit. what do i have to do. it's going to be hard or something, the thing i have to do. looked around room suspiciously, like, expecting it to answer me, then eyes landed on unopened sugar-free red bull propped against my crotch, looking up at me sexily. doolooodobbooboob.

if 8oz sugar-free red bull can was a person: would look like the guy from that band handsome furs. just picked it up. it is very feathery and light. it might be lurch from 'the addams family.' do you guys get it, the person i'm trying to say it's like? heart is beating definitely faster.

can't tell if i'm supposed to be capitalizing things anymore. molly. thought 'molly' and laughed self-consciously, like i was supposed to be laughing, like someone was watching me be on molly and contemplate 'molly.'

if my hands were a person: jesus.

jesus.

they would be a wet person.

made all ten fingers do 'the wave.' the sound is like…pictured a well, like what kids get thrown down into, and like, a cave with a low grassy entrance with white flowers around it like where i used to imagine they kept jesus before he came back to life.

feel afraid of religious things right now. imagining hell, actual hell. no. i just wrote that, i'm not going to imagine it. shit. starting to imagine. idea virus of imagining hell infecting my head. no, doing this is warding it off. just say things as you think them to ward off hell thoughts: blake butler article about video game liveblogging, megabus, sears bra rack, baja, bajajajaja, lido deck, man overboard, polecat, cactus pop-up book, helpful secretary, Nicholson baker, egregious capitalization, gian's apartment, soft heads of [nothing], grandpa luna moth, lunesta, backyard, deck, summer 1992, it was all 1992 when you were a baby and a kid there were never other years then it was 1998, copper pots hanging rustically from a kitchen ceiling, roller rink, no, like, an arcade, arcade where i won tiny erasers, eraserhead, begotten, shit no not begotten the movie that movie is like hell, remembered why i was doing this, curious about why begotten seemed so scary, i'm not scared anymore, if had an intern i would pay them to tell me exactly what my crotch smelled like right now

god

can't not do this

what my crotch smells like: i don't know. honestly don't know. pictured my detached head and flummoxed curious face spinning down an endless tunnel saying 'honestly don't know' in every accent, mostly british accents.

seems like there is a country called 'crotch'

pictured throwing my hands up in surrender and shaking my head, no wait

going out onstage for an open-mic at stand-up comedy thing, saying 'seems like there is a country called crotch' with almost no facial or vocal expression

goddamnit women aren't funny no one would laugh

sorry women, sorry me

gotta try to make this one work for all of us. make it up to us. hoo. chalking up my hands. jumping in the corner. coach is putting in my mouth guard. hoo

let me try this again, disregard the first time: going out onstage for an open-mic at stand up comedy thing, saying 'seems like there is a country called crotch' with almost no facial or vocal expression, then being completely silent for like three minutes, staring intensely into the audience and urgently nodding head sometimes, then raising hands in surrender and matter-of-factly saying 'can't do it'

i can't tell if i'm horrible

honestly enjoy the company of myself

this whole time i've been awake, yeah, hey. enjoying myself. well. not the whole time, we've. there were ups and downs. had some ins and outs but you know. strong ins and strong outs. the main thing is keeping a strong defense, delivering for the team

wish i was talking like an athlete after a big game right now, seems so sweet to be able to talk like that

stand-up comedian who gives earnest mumbled post-game commentary and never looks at the audience and it's never clear what sport he plays

wonder how many blowjobs the guy who thought of using 'fly like an eagle' for the usps ad campaign in 1998 has gotten from then until now

TO THIS DAY

remembered imagining jesus storage cave earlier and pictured it again and jesus pushed back a big boulder at the entrance and blushed and 'twinkled' his fingers at me

seems like…endless ideas…am i going to regret this…

video game called 'what thing in my room is a nut sack' or 'where is the nut sack' which is actually just like, halo 10

lovingly cradled formerly crotch-leaning sugar-free red bull, looking down at it like mary mother of jesus. but then suddenly it would shoot upwards fast and i'd still be holding onto it. then i would let go. it would try to bang its head on the ceiling to a make a hole so it could go live out its calling, which is to stop denzel's plane from crashing, it received an email about its calling even before i bought it and it was in my crotch, it's known this all along but has not wanted to spoil something about how things have been going with us by telling me it wouldn't always be here, and as soon as i find this out i am more able to be happy that it's gone

i am the only person i know who says 'denzel' and talks about 'flight' a lot, feel i do those things a lot

remembered broccoli 'wall' on bottom level of union square whole foods and pointing to it and saying 'is it breathing' to tao can't remember if numbers go like '11,200, 12,000,

jesus way too boring, 'can't do it'

heart is normal now

feeling less peaking am no longer peaking

forgot about feeling despair or obligation or overtired things earlier, didn't expect that, thought i'd just tiredly go on

4:09AM: i felt all of that so intensely. now i'm back to normal, mostly. still shivering. going to get in bathtub.

6:36AM: have been stalling assembly of apartment-garnering portfolio.

7:09AM: printed free credit report for portfolio. my hand smells like wet cat food. my credit is 'medium.' having credit cards that aren't attached to your bank account…i can't believe that idea caught on…like, even i wouldn't fall for that…of course places will go after you…listen: when someone or something lends you money, you revoke the right to pay it back whenever you want. you'll owe the total amount you borrowed, if not more, until you pay it back on their terms. credit cards seem like mafia business. i feel like 'old woman rickets' or something, ranting to no one from my porch. maybe i should get a mafia credit card. i'm stalling cover letter-writing and showering.

7:16AM: shit 14 minutes.

7:21AM: you can tell your adderall is extended-release because it will have the 'deluxe transparent addy ball visualizer' bottom-half. i don't really have to leave until 8:30. saying i had to leave by 7:30 is an example of a trick i do to avoid being late when i know i'll want to be late for fun but the stakes are high and if i drag my feet there will be consequences. fake early deadline. classic stakes-raiser. high stakes mental clock readjustment. just another trick up the sleeve of old woman rickets.

my friend brian and i used to do this lumbering, dopey, innocent-sounding voiceover for lady, my family's potato-shaped food-loving dog. it started when lady was watching the fridge. brian said 'oh, fiddlesticks. why won't they ever let me go in the big white box?' that's what my brain sounds like right now.

8:18AM: thought 'give us this day, our daily [michael kimball's smiling head engulfing entire computer screen, gradually windchimes can be heard]' as

a flash intro to some kind of website, a marketing thing…a union thing…
presidential campaign…

9:14AM: not going to make it to NYC. i shouldn't have talked about my
high stakes consequences trick, that invalidated it. i would not rent an apartment to me. i would be able to tell i'm a nasty slumlord good-for-nothing.
i would google the shit out of anyone who applied to live in my building. i
want to own a parking garage. i need mafia credit cards to get credit to get
loans to buy a parking garage. when have you ever heard of a parking garage
going out of business? nasty slumlord. keep picturing the michael kimball
head thing and laughing in forceful bursts. wish i could make that the cover
of my huge ass binder of everything there is to know about me, that i'm giving to apartment building/company/committee/i don't know who or what
i'm giving it to, exactly. maybe i am being scammed. would feel relieved,
i think, if this turns out to be a scam. i could just do something else then.

9:22AM: for the past week i've semi-frequently been thinking about how
i said something like 'i feel like a richard yates character all the time lately,
when i am older this will not be 'cute'' in my book. now feel like i am the
'older' age where it is no longer 'cute.' most people i hang out with are
under 24. wonder if they think of me as 'older person' now. the only people
i've thought seemed older than me have also been substantially larger than
me in size. it would make sense if as people got older, they never stopped
accumulating height and mass. people would measure death in height
instead of age, like you'd die at 46'9" tall instead of 80 years old. age is
harder to see than height.

9:32AM: sat on floor to continue organizing apartment-garnering portfolio. heard loud plangent basketball-like banging coming from the area
behind my closet. the noise went away. it started again. irritated by this
noise. the starting and stopping of it. it's the same every time. mom walked
to my room and when she saw me sitting beside computer i knew she'd
know i'd been up all night again. she started expressing mom-like concerns,
abruptly stopped talking, tilted head and looked alert. i said 'yeah, the
noise, it's extremely irritating.' she asked when it started. i said 'just before
you walked in' and irrationally blamed her for the noise. she said something about pipes or leaks, then 'i'm supposed to call someone if it's…if
there's a leak, if the noises are coming from the roof. this has happened, the
banging,' sounding like she was struggling to access her network's default
'emergency broadcast' message. i said 'it's not coming from the roof, it's
coming from where i hear the baby crying,' and pointed to the closet. mom
seamlessly transitioned back into worrying about me.

9:52AM: kneeled in front of fridge and ate bites of raw spirulina pie thing. tasted too rich. put it back. thought 'catch and release.' currently eating a banana to quell whale noises in stomach. really taking my time with this banana too, like, showing it a good time, being careful not to make any sudden movements while it rests on my calf.

9:57AM: i pointed and said 'it's coming from there.' mom stood with surprising quickness and i followed her out to the balcony. she asked 'when do you hear the sounds the baby makes?' i said 'not regularly, not lately. that's a scary question.' she said 'oh no! no, no, no.' i said 'no, no, no, i mean like scary like david lynch, like he'd have someone say what you just said and then disappear or something.' there was a noise. mom's head darted in meerkat-like manner. i said 'maybe it's a burglar who has come to give us the lottery, wouldn't that be exciting?' mom smiled and made a face. felt attentive to silences between noises. i said 'it'd be an 'opposite' kind of burglar.'

10:23AM: interested in never sleeping again maybe, dying…somehow… from that?

12:12PM: fedex-ing my tenant application form instead of giving to colin in person. doesn't make sense to drive to NYC with incomplete portfolio. 24-year-old real estate mogul neighbor. 'mogul' is weird. feel like my hands are skeletal and 'mogul' right now. the capillaries or something look purple and webby and close to being on the other side of my skin with the rest of the world. think i'm thinking of 'gollum.'

12:21PM: almost always have itunes open and almost never play music. i don't know anyone who listens to less music than me. remember telling that to tao in a car, hearing 'seems…depressing…' after a few moments.

12:24PM: pictured the annoying hot girl from 'girls' saying 'i LOOOOOVE old woman rickets.' she'd go global with old woman rickets. take that shit global. that girl has nice teeth. if i were a guy and i saw her across a room i'd say 'i'd like to take her out back, if you know what i mean' to the guy next to me. he would know. people are always knowing things. they're always saying things like that and understanding each other.

12:39PM: laying under blankets. can't believe i took so long to do 'laying' or 'blankets.'

12:48PM: banging noises have been replaced by bumping at a rhythm similar to this thing in the song. hm. i would pay someone to figure out what the song is, maybe. i almost can remember words.

12:53PM: the song is 'a sweet summer's night on hammer hill.' listening now. it's horrible when they say 'boom-ba-boom.' eyes watered when i felt like i couldn't continue typing something as embarrassing as the last 'boom' of the rhythm sequence. it out-embarrassed me. i don't think i've ever felt this intensely negative about a song, or felt too embarrassed to finish typing something. i kind of like how awful listening to it feels.

i can imagine someone reading this and being really annoyed by me. seems harder to imagine people being annoyed with me in person. i'm confident about my chill, attentive presence. oh gross. imagine some 18-22 year old guy smiling sexily, taking his shirt off as he scoots himself close to you on your beach towel—you are mostly in the sand and he is taking up most of the beach towel—squinting his eyes and nodding and saying 'i'm confident about my chill, attentive presence' at you.

1:04PM: jens lekman has been playing since other song. this is my ex-boy-friend's computer, it has all his music on it. going to try to listen to music. randomly selected 'i'm your boogie man' by kc and the sunshine band and fast-forwarded to a middle part where it's. i can't describe. you would recognize it, probably. i recognized it. i laughed. oh god. 'here we go:'

it seems like a club. the lights come on. it is a club. no one is there yet. after a moment a james brown-like voice says 'give us this day, our daily[not heard over sounds of immense unseen hydraulic power lowering 100' diameter disco ball that looks like michael kimball's smiling head, spinning slowly. when the hydraulics stop making noise 'i'm your boogie man' by kc and the sunshine band can be heard faintly, but something went wrong, it was sent to the wrong address and is playing next door instead].'

that's what the release party for the flash intro to the marketing website would be. i'm crying laughing so hard. i never believe people when they say that.

1:17PM: i want everyone to be doing this too, liveblogging all the time. a future where no one talks and. damnit. i used to picture this bleak all-white 'matrix'-like people-harvesting room. the entire earth had changed into this white room where everyone just sat silently, and that was the future. thought 'maybe that would be good if everyone was liveblogging' and i guess worse things could happen than that, but i'm definitely not as excited about it anymore.

1:29PM: i'm not even trying to do anything but just lay here anymore. until further notice i will be laying here. good. the banging noise seems insane, definitely directed at me.

1:31PM: people think multitasking is distracting and it's not good to get sidetracked but what if that's actually how our brains want to evolve? like they want to process a larger and less-related variety of information and do this as fast as possible, eventually achieving infinity or something, perceiving infinite things at infinite speed. seems like i may have not been the first person to think this, vague memories of tao describing something like this in 'taipei.'

1:46PM: approaching 48ᵗʰ hour awake. i'm going to have nothing to say for like two weeks after i finish this. i love anyone who has made it to this sentence. pictured ricky fitts with bloody nose, saying 'don't give up on me, dad' as a kind of warning or command to chris cunningham, who has just punched him, i think, in 'american beauty.' that part.

2:12PM: here is an 'other people' update:

- mom asked if i wanted anything from whole foods. i said 'no thanks' then 'chim chim' quietly, half-hoping i had actually just repeated 'no thanks'

- read supportive texts from gian and stephen dierks and felt good and like texts are one of the things influencing me to write more today

- last night friend of 'shower noise requester caller' texted me and sent a picture but i haven't responded

- colin the real estate mogul texted 'ASAP' regarding something i forgot around 10AM

- moved car from driveway to new parking spot so mom could drive out of garage. held apple i found on my car's floor as i walked to condo, thinking 'mom will feel good if she sees me eating the apple.' made plans to take first bite of apple once i saw 'the whites of mom's eyes.' saw that i'd left condo's door wide open but walked inside confidently and nonchalantly, bumping into mom, who i reflexively said 'night night' to, then hurriedly bit apple to 'make up for lost time.' mom smiled and shook her head a little. i laughed and said 'night night sorry hello goodbye.'

imagine all of the homeless people who have hotmail accounts. in the year 4000 all homeless people will have emails but somehow it's going to be worse.

2:54PM: experiencing weird light and depth/size hallucinations. the thing i'm mostly seeing seems like it's everywhere also. it's sort of weak in that i'm mostly seeing stuff i normally see, but if i focus harder/almost cross my eyes there is this other layer of stuff like, spinning fast, underneath everything i normally see. the layer kind of looks like a patterned neon turtle shell, spinning very fast. it has a still center-point with a concave half-sphere behind it that seems to be 'wagging.' the 'wags' become smaller and appear more 'vibrating' as my focus shifts further from the center point. the thing seems to be gaining other parts with more opacity that move faster. feel like the shape is intelligent, it's like, an intelligent DMT lifeform that i'm kind of afraid of and interested in watching. have seen/experienced something similar to this on DMT. like underneath the reality i normally experience there is another version of everything—maybe infinite multiple layers of concurrent realities, similar to ours in that they're also 'realities,' where things exist that are similarly conscious but in vastly different ways than humans are, like, unknowable to humans not on DMT, given our limit of only regularly experiencing one consicousness at a time. i sound like i'm on hallucinogens. feel worried a little, about my brain, like this is how the beginning of naturally occurring brain damage feels. i don't know.

3:17PM: you know when you look up from underwater in a pool? or see like, heat rising from the ground? that wavy thing? maybe that wavy thing happens on your eyeballs all the time, and that's what i'm seeing. the patterns aren't just the wavy thing though.

this must be so boring for anyone not me right now, jesus. imagining 'i'm chill and approachable' 18-22 year old beach blanket guy saying all of this shit to me without stopping and i'm just staring in the other direction and i can feel him smiling or something. yuck. there are people like that. i've talked to them. you might be one of them. you are probably one of them. maybe i am also, shit. how can a person talk continuously at another person staring in the opposite direction, like, willfully away. how could you keep talking, then…or like…ever.

think i only do that when i'm on cocaine. feel like that's what motivates most people to talk: a desire to find a less-talkative human source to smile and be a repository for their endless talking. something they can really empty themselves into that churns and re-forms all the things they said into minimal blips of encouraging feedback. depressing.

it might seem like i'm being the 'talking person' to you now but it's different because you are choosing to read this and…i can't sense you being there… or something…i feel like i'm alone, transcribing my thoughts onto something with RAM. have felt consumed by the menial task of downloading my thoughts onto this document since 9AM, maybe. i know i'm not really saying anything and there has been a lot of it but it feels good. like some kind of exercise.

6:25PM: mom made a frozen stir-fry thing of general tso's chicken. smelled heavenly. the chicken was cubed. felt excited, putting 'only the best' scoops on my plate. 'simply the best.' freely discarded entire scoops that were 'not as good' as others. red bell peppers were not included in any scoops that made it to my plate. fuck no. mom scooped things onto her plate and we used probably six accents to say nonsense stuff in a rapid-fire joke thing i don't remember, which then petered out. i said 'i'm from france' without an accent.

6:38PM: seems like it's actually going to be hard to sleep. body feels too weird to sleep. watching 'negatives'/inverse images of silhouettes moving at a different speed than the rest of my vision. keep thinking about parts of 'nothing' by blake butler, wish i had it here. feel like i could match or beat blake in a 'no sleeping' contest. i could probably do a week. would be good to be on a reality show with him where the object of the game is to stay awake the longest, but the night before the game starts, you are flown to your opponent's house, to booby-trap it. then you are flown back to your house. the commercial for the show would have a voiceover that would be like (when it's capitalized it means it's an echo): 'two people TWO TWO TWO. who have met once ONCE ONCE [man yells 'two-thousand eleven'] [man yells 'the internet' and sounds like he is falling off a cliff] [no audio or visual for several seconds, then a rumbling, then something emerges in the distance. it is a monster truck driven by an extremely muscular man screaming 'AT AWP WHEN BLAKE WAS DRUNK' as the truck roars and jumps over the camera and crashes offscreen] [this is replaced with long, panning shots of a desert at night and desert noises, like desert loons and coyotes. barely audible gregorian chanting can also be heard.] johnny cash's voice wryly says: 'what happens when you gotta spend a week in your own house?' [the desert is replaced with black and white slow-motion footage of a young johnny cash walking offstage.] 'no-ho-ho rules, my friend. except you snooze? you lose.' [he is gone. the mic stand remains. a giant can of foster's beer materializes over the still-cheering crowd. next, the text: 'foster's: australian for beer.'] [screen is black] [man's voice from beginning yells 'sponsored by foster's' and it sounds like he is falling off a cliff again].' so that would be the commercial. want johnny cash to say 'the man of the house' at some point. maybe the show is just called 'the man of the house.' i don't know what the booby-trapping…like, am i thinking the booby-traps would be…? so in order to defeat the other person the traps would need to make them fall asleep. how do you do that. boring comfortable booby-trapped house. seems shitty. you have to make them fall asleep without killing them. no wait you can kill them. if you want. you would still get arrested though it would not be 'hunger games' style. then after you murder the other person and win, it becomes another reality show where you're running from the cops. or no, it's just the next season of the first show. then i guess you die too, eventually. there will be a lot of seasons. there would be one season where the winner of the no-sleep thing escapes the cops so many times that they actually convince everyone that they're the president. then it becomes a government reality show. no, they don't need to lie, they actually run for president and win. because the cops like them. even though they killed the other person. they're just really good, loved by all. they are followed by cameras until their groundbreaking record-setting death of old age. it turns out they are the oldest person. they were actually the oldest person the entire time. even in the beginning, before they even knew the show was really about being the oldest, they were still the oldest. they did not back down in the face of adversity. they remained older than everyone the entire time. which is really the message of the show. the lesson to be learned: the oldest person wins the race. oh my god. 'mafia credit card,' remember that. 'hunger games' was stupid.

11:05PM: right hand smelled like garlic for a long time after touching checkbook. hard to do things that aren't 'staring.' going to scope out the scene in mom's room.

11:52PM: laid on mom's bed while she tried to explain plot of 'downton abbey.' seemed like the most impossible thing to pay attention to and she seemed to agree, but would also interject 'oh i know who that guy is' comments. she said 'it's the only thing on TV, it'll make you fall asleep.' i dipped rice cakes in baba ganoush and think i was annoying and interruptive. eventually slid off the bed, like, laughing, feet-first. it happened a little then i ran with it. i said 'beddy bye.'

MARCH 20, 2013

12:22AM: bathwater is running. i'm just going ot do this until forever. ate half of some kind of pill, 1mg Xanax ithink. ate other one . just thought 'willis is just in the other room, he said he watned to show me something.

123331

ookkk anoth athter xaanxn at som e oo==ibe, ijay sruffl is going to better e=vetter i know

1:12AM: woke in mostly empty bathtub. very cold. drain wouldn't close so i just sat on it and refilled tub with hot water. when i woke felt obsessed with finding candy i had been eating but guess i ate it all. flopped around trying to always be covered in hot water, thinking 'sexy seal' and 'sprinkle princess' and pictured someone tossing me a fish and this is what would get me into the maxim top 100 hottest women or whatever. because enough seals voted me in.

1:18AM: looked at emotional gchats from ex-boyfriend.

1:23AM: pictured emerging rapper, he's like, only been in videos hanging out before but he just got to say this line in this song...he's short and wears this giant shiny thing...i don't know what it is, maybe a suit or a special kind of lakers jersey, and his mouth has so much grill it that it weighs his neck down a little but he still tries to keep his face up so people call him 'sunnyside.' he's like, sitting at one of those sweet ass round leather sofas in a dark club with decanters on the table which is also a platform/light thing where sexy women's legs in pumps are walking around and then beat drops and camera focuses on 'sunnyside' and he says 'luhdda see em fart bubbles plip plop in the hot tub.'

1:27AM: think i'm thinking of that song where the one ying yang twin is like 'i'd rather see yo ass clap clap in them shoes'

1:35AM: earlier tonight i was listening to r. stevie moore thinking it was stevie wonder for a long time and feeling like something wasn't right.

3:37AM: still in bathtub. exfoliating skin with nails. there is a lot of 'dead me' in here. skin. re-filling sugar-free red bull can with cold water. fantasizing about living in some tropical town where you get drinking water in cans every morning. water in cans. seems so good. the way the air would smell.

3:39AM: afraid to sleep, i think. i don't feel tired at all. like i don't want to sleep unless i go to sleep at 11PM but i keep missing my '11PM train.' right now i could be sleeping or i could be doing anything else but sleeping. sleeping does feel good. it sucks that you can only sort of re-play dreams but you can never re-play sleep. er. meditation, kind of. not really. you know what i mean.

interesting thing: around midnight i felt sudden dawning horror that the 'turtle shell'/wavy heat rising effect/cross-eyed focus on convex part of the eyeball—like the pattern that was really moving were all of these disgusting boomberang shapes, it was so crowded, they were taking up everything and moving in a sickly maggot way. and. AND! you know what they were? i think? i think they were my rods and cones. i think. i don't know if you can see those. oh my god though thinking about seeing them, no, stop it, disgusting. i experience this thing 'tryptophobia' which is like this dizzying sickness at seeing small holes close together. found out rods and cones aren't on your cornea, they're like, back near the optic nerve or something, so maybe i was seeing some kind of inverse image of…i don't know. if anyone knows about this stuff i'm curious about it.

4:15AM: 'liked' a lot of mallory whitten's photos from young americans tour facebook album. hard-to-identify positive emotions. everyone keeps looking different. emotions. keep draining then filling tub with hot water and scrubbing tub with yellow sponge and dr. bronner's soap before tub fills and the sides look clean again. keep pulling off skin. the skin is gray and floating and won't drain all the way. i don't feel gross or anything, sitting with it. i was sitting with it before i was in the tub too. have never felt that 'sitting in your own filth' aversion people have to baths. you were just…you're always going to be doing that…baths…i don't know, rinse off afterwards. man the fuck up.

ate another xanax to make me tired again. listening to buddy holly. want to like buddy holly. i'm going to try to listen to more music, i used to be a listener and seeker of new music. 2003-2008. 'music person' days. hell yeah. have been scrolling through ex-boyfriend's eclectic selection. he has a lot of butthole surfers. listening to 'pepper.' if you are someone who knows 'pepper' by butthole surfers and knows that primitive radio gods song with the long title and knows that bran van 3000 song 'drinking in l.a.' and knows that placebo song that people think is 'pepper' by butthole surfers but is like 'pure morning' or something—it will be like 'teehee we have secrets' and i will always feel this warm thing and talk about you to people years after we stop talking. i'll say, like, 'yeah we both knew all of those songs' and i'll miss you deeply but i won't know what to say to you anymore. it won't make any sense.

4:50AM: this soap just seems so versatile…how it makes this tub so clean, makes me clean…soft skin…years…dr.bronner's. extremely effected by Xanax all of a suddn. 51 hours no sleep. actually slept for like a half an hour in tub.

5:06AM: no i just fell asleep letting hot water pour on my head. i woke thinking i was surrounded by ambulances on a highway but that i was not part of the accident, i was just looking at it. put towel on my head. no, i put a towel no my haed. no just tyed it up. the water is hot again.

5:20AM: copied all of this text and opened flickr but there was no where to paste it.

5:21AM: imovie is opening again.

5:23AM: just realized wolf voices, coming from the ktchen in Philadelphia na seeing ex-bourfreidn there at kitchen table, sat next to him 'there is something wrong with your imovie, it's only playing wolf things.' then like, flashing in and out of being in a bathtub, a really alert/aware state where i'm thinking 'write that dream or whatever down, what is going on' but think i am forgetting crucial parts. except for nap from 12:30-1 or whenever. so since. woke 3:15PM 3/17 and now it's 5:15AM march 20th

just slid ti catch something from falling into the water. it was like, one of those things parents have , a sony…you like watch slideshows of difital images on its frme.

5:18(???)AM: now it says 5:18. i want food more. need to wash conditioner out ooooohok. i think there is a nother eperson in here with me. i can feel them. like it's Jordan or something. damnit. i'm feeling eyeball things. optic things. imovie closed but i don't know why opened it. okay.

5:26AM: feel like i am supposed to tel my parents somethingn soon, like my mom wanted me to reminder her something to r. stevie moore is like wesley willis to me in some way. i am forgetting something about why typing this now. i thikn it was to get ou tof the tub. seems hard. feel like there are bandmates here. i am not quite awake. let water out of tub. damn. water in cans. feel so good abou water in cans, my water in a can. wish cans had tops you could put ack on. take them on the go. there is an ear what is this shit.

5:32AM: uploading…doing all of this stuff is so. the water is all out of the tub and conditioner is still on my hair. i feel soft. earlier i looked down at my abdomen and vag and pictured a for real person in there, like growing, felt excited, someday!!! get to…yeah…jesus, if you ever feel sad just think about how you can always do this crazy thing to your body and know someone all your life or theirs, rather. can't talking about it well. want to make breakfast for my kids like michelle illiams in blue valentine only i'd LOVE MY KIDS and play with them because they do say the darndest things, truly, i feel. i'm just one of them too. we gon have fun. shit man. get ready for my baby squad. gonna reshape the game man. or like. what i mean to say is it will be different. ir. what the hell am i talking about

6:33PM: there is this good feeling you have when you're younger, like a teenager to maybe 25 years old, that the world is ready for the possibility you have to offer it. there are schools giving you tours, meetings with little committees, loans from people investing in what they think you will bring to the world. people are depending on you, sort of. passively monitoring you, in hopes that the good thing they thought would happen to them will happen to you instead.

you have all of these ideas about what you want to do with 'your life,' which is hard to imagine because it seems so far away. it feels like you can do anything. feeling like you can do anything makes you feel like doing nothing, which is okay, or…what else could it be but okay. they must be preparing another 'you' with the training you didn't receive, to guide and someday replace you, and however you fill your life while you wait is inconsequential. maybe you do too many drugs or have bad relationships or get in trouble with money or police. i don't know. so you think 'there is still time, i will take a break. after the break the bad thing will feel over. people will have forgotten and maybe i will have changed or forgotten. then i'll get back to all of those other exciting things i was going to do.' there is so much time.

but the break thing.

i don't know.

you end up 27 waking at 4PM feeling like some kind of experiment. like you have switched from the thing you used to be to a new thing that's being studied. but you don't feel important enough to be studied, no one is actually studying you. you have just allowed yourself so many 'breaks' after so many 'bad things' that you feel the best thing is to isolate yourself from the possibility of more bad things, and sort of hope no one knows this, or. people wonder where you went, you think, but you hope no one is really paying attention, and they aren't really.

the 'experiment' thing is more like this sensation that the people who talk to you feel like they need to be careful. they are aware of the things you thought you would be. they want to be careful not to remind you of those things, or pretend you are still capable of those things. you can see when they are being kind to you, just in little ways, like you are way more aware of when anyone is kind to you accidentally, and it fills you with thing, this sadness for yourself and for person who did the kind thing and for everyone who wants a better life. you don't actually feel the 'everyone' but you have this idea that it's probably everyone, and the feeling…the wanting feeling after the accidental kind thing…the feeling is big enough in your body that you feel confident saying things like 'everyone.'

7:14PM: i don't really know what i mean by all of that. i'm a little bitch.

WHAT'S HAPPENED SINCE BATHTUB LAST NIGHT:

- dried off and put on pajamas
- ate 1mg xanax (2.5-3.5mg total, i think)
- toasted 'everything' bagel, spread chive cream cheese on both sides
- ate half the bagel in bed, looked at internet, probably fell asleep around 6AM
- woke around 12PM to text from colin asking if i'd fedex-ed him my tenant application yet (application process feels less time-sensitive since i flaked on driving to NYC) and texted 'i'm on my way, will do fastest shipping option'
- found the other bagel half, ate it
- ate three small sugar-free sprouted cookies, one glass raw/unpasteurized milk
- set alarm for 3PM with plans to wake, write cover letter, go to fedex
- dreamed something about being an orphan child with sam pink and living in a cement room where we collected things we stole and… seemed to 'party'…it was fun…we lived in a room in one of those horseshoe-shaped two-story buildings with a courtyard that you see in florida a lot
- woke around 4PM. colin had texted 'ok good'
- ate another sprouted cookie thing and felt xanax things like i wanted to eat more

- ate half an apple, handful raw sugar snap peas

- mom made me a tuna melt and we stood talking in the kitchen

- told mom about hallucinations and how i thought they were eye-ball-related

- talked with mom and ate tuna melt at dining room table

- drank a glass of 'hot lips no sugar added pear soda' over ice

- looked at internet, re-read parts of this, read emails, read texts from keith and mira. feels hard to interact with people right now which is why i haven't talked/responded to you (if i haven't), i have plans to respond to everyone at some point

- looked at gchats i haven't responded to from ex-boyfriend

- typed 6:46PM update

- wanted another 'hot lips no sugar added pear soda,' drank melted ice, thought 'flavorless but cold is enough,' filled glass with ice and water

- asked mom what she planned to do tonight. she said she'd watch 'downton abbey' again. i said 'i thought you thought it was boring' and she said, sounding a little like george costanza, something like, 'well, the characters...you get to watching and...i don't know. it's really a little interesting!'

- said 'i might go to yoga or something...my body...i'm barely moving' and mom said something consoling i wish she hadn't

- walked back to room feeling hellish about seeing the same things for so many days in a row

- imagined several tasks i could do today that already seem harder/less realistic to accomplish because of eating the tuna melt and bagel

considering doing more heroin to improve mood. might feel like exercising lightly or taking a walk if i do that. out of adderall.

7:40PM: under blankets. propped body on pillows. want to drive to washington d.c., maybe. i could see a movie or something. i might do that. yeah. walking around washington d.c. alone tonight, why not. i like driving there. the george washington parkway is pretty but it'll be too dark to see tonight. excited for warm weather, reliving idyllic 2007 drives to d.c. fully reliving idyllic-ness would require the company of another person who i could joke and have sex and be in love with like i was with the person in 2007. man i am tired of that 'we get excited about each other and…' routine. i don't know. have felt so hopeful so many times. old woman rickets over here.

10:50PM: have been looking at internet and listening to 'last days of disco' by yo la tengo. responded to ex-boyfriend's g-chats. our lease expires in 11 days. he showed me this song. last night he said:

'honeychile

ive been pronouncing the ultimate E as a long E

member when we walked over that bridge'

the bridge lead to atlantic city, i think. maybe we just ended up in atlantic city later that night. i had started living in the apartment again. this was during the 'less arguing than joking but usually one or the other, before it got sad' time. sometimes i'd want to talk about why we broke up or what we were doing together if we weren't together anymore. then we'd talk more and i'd remember why.

typed this in phone the morning after 'bridge day:'

'Light moving through windows seemed fast, flickery/sparkly, Z's face smiling, the thing I said or read: people's faces when they're sleeping or just waking are always honest

Remembering walking over bridge and how clear and expansive and low to the ground sky was, wanting to hold onto that memory and in that memory how much I wanted to hold onto Z, all yesterday feeling his presence as a kind of absence that must be urgently protected, like when all of a sudden I know I'm dreaming and the dream becomes about how to prevent waking, simultaneously touching and missing him, how easy it was to talk until the drive home from AC, it was almost perfect, then things we've done to hurt each other seemed louder and more present than the music, scenery, my hand on his thigh, etc.

Watching shadows of branches making the light move fast and smelling how he smells, thinking "none of this will stay," watching his eyeballs move under his eyelids while he slept like they were looking at fast moving things too, finding spaces in his body for my body to fit even though it was uncomfortably sweaty, now im gone in a car with nothing to hold onto

Now merging onto 95n, a feeling of ghostly temporary deafness/blindness in right side of face, like right now in a parallel universe I'm having a stroke'

11:08PM: snorted a little more than half the powder heroin quadrant of light blue pill container. forgot i'd preemptively divvied out an amount 'for next time,' as a friendly gesture to 'future me who doesn't want to decide how much heroin she wants or find a surface to snort it.' laid in bed and closed eyes.

just saw mental picture of sitting in my car behind a pick-up truck with an american flag decal that took up the entire back window, on left side shoulder of highway, police lights, i was in the cop car

pental picture of four of my driver's licenses falling from a white paper that had been folded in half

mental picture of the itunes visualizer as just a black spinning oval over a slightly less black background

what if the itunes visualizer was

mental picture of…damn…no way to describe, it wase

mental picture of something about…like…jeusu. forgetting things so fast.

11:38PM: it really took 30 minutes to type from 'just saw…' to '11:38PM.' leaving typos to show struggle. keep doing stereotypical 'head drops slowly groundward then jerks up' thing like that sleepy kitten viral video on you-tube. the first viral kitten video thing. annoyed by difficulty to focus eyes and urge to lay motionless. enjoyed watching all of the image thingies. probably saw/imagined 20-25 things total. some of them seemed hyper-de-tailed the way dreams can be, like, entire rooms and life contexts/sets of memories.

11:42PM: got ice water and four chocolate-covered cherry and orange candies. sat at desk to discourage laying down. somehow thought heroin would make me feel less sedentary.

11:50PM: mom approached my room, talking fast and almost affectedly cheerfully about how she was going to be a person on 'downton abbey,' from now on. picture of pill container was visible. panicked and forgot how to minimize things but didn't want to draw attention to computer. knew my eyes would probably look unfocused and suspicious if i looked at mom. she was still talking. clutched computer to body and turned so screen faced only me. mom said 'are you crying?' i said 'no.' she said 'i came in here because your face looked like it was crying.' i said 'i'm not' and she said more things about the show and what she thought i looked like and i looked for other places to look and concentrated on discreetly holding the computer. seemed like it would never end.

11:57PM: can feel pulse in heels, arms, face. it's not beating at the same time. all places receive pulse at slightly different speeds. seems crazy to think about where in body speeds are faster than others because that would like…involve…that they all started at a time…i guess i did technically have 'one first beat of pulse' but…

MARCH 21, 2013

12:16PM: feel heroin effects less. forgot about unfocusable eyes thing. wanted to drive to d.c. will still do that, i think. or no. i don't know. nothing at all today.

12:30AM: intense urge to be on a couch, like one of those really ugly, brown, deep couches that have holes patched with duct tape and an afghan draping on it, that don't look like they have origins in any specific time period…like the couch from 'roseanne!' yeah, exactly the 'roseanne' couch. making out with sam pink and one of his hands would be on my jawline. the couch. fuck yeah. canned water. drinking canned water. damn. being his female cat who he never got spayed and backing into a q-tip he held up to me. maybe a little vaseline on the tip of the q-tip. seems 'risky' putting this out there but fuck it.

12:38AM: a good alternative to the 'house arrest ankle band' would be that you have to accidentally over-hear someone saying 'the wimbledon bounty.' you would have to wear a similar device as the ankle band but you could leave your house. there would be a camera on the ankle device and it would be able to sense whenever you started thinking of ways to steer conversations towards 'the wimbledon bounty.' every time you'd do that the device would make your death row sentence five minutes earlier.

12:49AM: have probably chewed 40-55 ice cubes since 9PM. ate a tangerine and pringles 'light' dipped in baba ganoush.

1:49AM: dipped a pringle in baba ganoush and walked to mom's room. she was watching 'downton abbey.' said 'close your eyes' to mom and fed it to her and she made noises of non-sexual pleasure.

2:04AM: last night a person offered me $100 for a printed, signed manuscript of this liveblog. around 30 minutes ago he upped the offer to $125. in his email he gave suggestions for easier-to-read layout colors and said he wanted me to eat and sleep more. he seems nice. including this because i'm pumped someone would offer me money for this and now he will be in the manuscript i send him.

3:06AM: sudden memory of 'wash 'n' curl' pink square shampoo bottle after swim practice at the YMCA.

4:05AM: sitting cross-legged on bed. listening to balam acab playlist. eyes keep unfocusing. reclined and 'spanked' crotch rapidly, like three measures of 32nd notes.

4:39AM: turned lights off and laid with computer on stomach. thought i saw man in blue shirt and khaki pants glide to center of room and vanish.

4:42AM: closed eyes for a moment, heard female commercial voice say 'duracell advanced heat.'

4:48AM: saw gliding khaki man do the thing again. whispered 'get the fuck out' and turned on light next to bed. what is actually scary about a gliding khaki man. if i saw a man in khakis gliding by radio shack it would be good.

4:51AM: thought i heard man's voice on phone (like how the other person sounds on the phone when you're on the receiving end) say 'horse.' when i haven't slept for a long time i sometimes hear voices and see things, curious if other people experience this.

6:24AM: smoking cigarette on balcony. there is a noise like feet moving tentatively in the woods 20'-30' away from me. can't see anything there. just made forceful 'FFFF' sound and the feet noise stopped abruptly then sounded like it was backing up really fast. then it resumed normal walking pace. i went 'FFFFFF' louder but nothing changed about the feet noise that time.

6:54AM: smoked another cigarette on balcony. nauseated. keep hiccuping and feeling burning stomach thing. before i was seeing/hearing weird stuff i listened to 'getting by with its' by reggie and the full effect and remembered senior year of high school and ate two 'weight watchers english toffee' pop-sicle-like ice cream bars. typed everything from 'weight watchers' to end of sentence with eyes closed. eues are closed now. saw imafe of a man's forearm with blonde hair moving like it was doing 'poi' without lightsticks. eyes are closed. peeked a little to write 'poi' but they are closed now. so sleepy. going to sleep. eyes are stil closed.

6:11PM: i was at a philadelphia steakhouse/movie theater with ex-boyfriend and a group of guys i knew in high school. i didn't want to be there. felt myself actively making a compromise for ex-boyfriend, enduring the steak-house instead of leading our group to a pizza place across the street. it was one of those places with two tables and a counter and plastic letters missing from a menu of backlit panels that says like, 'sm med lar x-lar' and 'shrimp (not pizza)' and there's a really old pepsi decal somewhere. food was taking too long at the steakhouse and i didn't think anyone at the table would notice, so i walked to the pizza place. ordered a small slice. the guys behind the counter spoke another language and were laughing and play-fighting. all of them were in the process of eating huge slices. sometimes one of them would say how much they loved the pizza, in english, and everyone would laugh and hit each other. brotherly hitting. i wanted a bigger slice, like theirs. ex-boyfriend walked in and took me back to the steakhouse/movie theater, where everyone had finished their food, eaten my food, and moved to a smaller booth. collected scraps of food from everyone's uneaten food on a plate i carried boastfully to the small booth. everyone was like 'damn i want that food' and i was like 'you coulda had that food.'

then i was standing beside ex-boyfriend, facing a ticket kiosk machine near a life-sized cardboard cut-out of daniel stern pulling up his shirt. he was making a 'look ma, i'm nasty' face. his nipples were showing. i said 'we should see the new daniel stern movie, it looks funny.' ex-boyfriend said 'you like him?' i said 'i don't know, isn't he like [tried to think of a funny actor]…that person we like?' he said 'i don't like him.'

sort of sensed mom's face over my bed and her hand touching my head. thought 'it must be early in the morning.' opened eyes again and mom was gone. looked for my phone. it made the 'not enough battery to work' graphic when i tried turning it on. looked at computer screen, read '6:00PM.' computer started to fall off the bed but i caught it by slapping my hand hard on the keyboard.

6:11PM: poured glass of milk and ate three cookies while talking to grocery-unloading mom. she expressed worry about hearing me on the balcony this morning and sleeping so late. i said 'i'm sorry, i'm okay, don't worry.' she unloaded a cardboard cylinder that said 'plum amazings' and said 'doesn't this look good?' i said 'oh yeah i almost bought you that one time when i couldn't find raisins. plum amazins. amazings.' mom said something about how she bought a big corned beef to cook for my dad because she felt bad about forgetting st. patrick's day. walked to bedroom to check if it was too late to fedex tenant application to colin. it felt too late. heard mom say 'i keep thinking, in andrea boccelli's voice, 'bonna fortuna!" and laugh.

6:15PM: mom said 'want to try something really nummy?' felt irritated as i walked to kitchen. the fridge door was open, condiments had fallen. mom was on her hands and knees, looking for something. an opened circular mint green bottle was on the table. mom said 'have you ever had this stuff that's not—it's not the green thing—it's wasabi something? it's not wasabi. oh jeez, because they were giving it out on shrimp and AH!' she held an almost empty bottle that said 'dijon wasabi marinade,' i think. i said 'oh you already had it?' she said 'yeah but wait'll you see what—oh boy. i want to see if you'll like this.' from the freezer, she procured a plastic tray of shrimp arranged in three lines around a cocktail sauce container center-point. i said 'you got shrimpies!' she said 'shrimpies shrimpies! i wanted to make them nice and cold.' i said 'oh they're not all the way frozen?' she said 'no, no, i was just trying to make them nice and cold.' she looked for something in the cabinet and said 'yeah! but, and now—i want to see if you'll like it without cocktail sauce. with this stuff, instead. they were giving it out in this way. it was just heavenly, to me. now where is this, i had a dish?' i tried the shrimp in the mustard. it was really good. mom ate a shrimp too. i said 'oh no, it's so good' and peeled the tail off my shrimp. mom tossed a shrimp tail with meat in it into the sink. i said 'mom, the shrimpy tail! you know what you have to do!' she said 'oh, am i wasting the tail? i have to eat it without peeling?' (dad and i used to eat fried shrimp tails when i was little to gross out mom). i said 'no you can peel. or. no, i will. you can't waste the shrimpy' then felt weird about…i was being serious, to some extent, i felt weird about the seriousness…i said 'no don't peel it, you can throw it out, i don't care.' she said 'no, i'll peel it for you. i won't waste the shrimpy.' we talked about when i went to taiwan with tao, all the 'hot pot' restaurants his parents took us to. pictured his dad doing 'the rubber pencil trick,' gently shaking a large uncooked shrimp to give it the illusion of hovering, saying 'you see? it's good.'

6:34PM: mom stood in my door and said she was going to watch all of the 'downton abbey' episodes she'd missed. i said 'ohhh' and nodded conspiratorially. she sort of guiltily talked about how there were 'hours' she had missed. i said 'well, i think you'll have fun' or something as she walked away, grinning guiltily.

6:40PM: looked at twitter and other websites. remembered i was supposed to see when fedex closed. figured it was too late and gave up. will just do it tomorrow. the apartment is slipping away from me. i don't care if i move in april 1st, why does colin think that matters to me. he's just trying to be a good agent, maybe. it's okay. no wait, yeah. it's okay. it shouldn't take the apartment committee people a week to review an application for somewhere no one else is applying to live (colin said i was the only one). goddamnit. world is dysfunctional and i am part of that dysfunction. integral shitty isolated dysfunctional cog in the workings of the giant barely functional rube goldberg machine that is the earth. good thing i'm here…i mean…jesus.

6:45PM: went to the kitchen for more coffee. heard 'downton abbey' sounds coming from mom's room. i said 'i hate how it's not 'downtown abbey.' i hate it.' mom said 'you're not british.'

7:25PM: produced two long thin turds. thought 'why hello mr. green, we meet again' at them while wiping. flushed toilet. felt james bond-like.

7:48PM: i've been listening to 'metro (brooklyn mix)' by i am the world trade center, on repeat. ex-boyfriend showed it to me. it sounds like shirley, his cat, like she's singing it. also playing all the instruments. sounds so much like shirley. i 'go to pieces' when i imagine shirley singing this, like. it's too cute to be real. 'cute' isn't the right word. it's just too…i don't know. something about how the person in this band is singing is like, exactly in shirley's tone when she meows. pretend it's not a person singing words, pretend it's a fluffy little shirley cat letting you pet her really hard, making noises like 'huh, okay, i don't know what's going on, please continue.' it makes more sense. shirley has long gray hair (like alvie, my cat. both cats are currently with ex-boyfriend at our apartment in philadelphia) but the fur on her legs puffs out. i call her leg fur her 'pantalons' or sometimes her 'culottes.' they are so good. you have to say 'panta-lonz' when you call them her 'pantalons.' her little face. jesus. i'm 'going to pieces' right now. hope ex-boyfriend lets me keep shirley when i move. i love shirley more than he does.

8:00PM: mom peeked head in room, said 'am i being too loud?' i said 'no, you're fine, everything's okay.' she said 'because i can move to my bedroom, i don't have to be in the living room.' i said 'no it's really okay, i just closed the door for. i don't know why. everything's okay.' she said 'okay, well, okay. you know what would make me stop watching 'downton abbey?' is if you wanted to watch 'les miserables' with me.' i have been afraid of watching emotionally-faced poor french people sing (which seems so weird to me, in general: watching people sing…people singing, in general…why are they singing…sustaining talking-notes at unnatural pitches…but now, poverty…france…thought 'and ann beattie, crying horrifically' but meant 'ann hathaway'). hope she forgets she suggested it and so we can watch something else. going to try to steer things towards watching anything else. not going to even pretend to do anything but be a complete unproductive shithead today. if i embrace it maybe it will go away. when i like things they go away.

9:15PM: i've been gleefully re-reading this, laughing at parts. jogged into kitchen to take kettle off stove for tea. said 'spot of tea, hehehehehe, oh no mom, my ass is so bouncy.' mom made a noise. heard 'downton abbey' noises. i said 'i'm going to be healthy tomorrow. i'm going to go to yoga and fedex my application and mail packages. do you want tea a too?' she said 'it's a very sad moment right now. they're about. to…' i said 'oh no, sorry, i'll. good,' and walked with tea to my bedroom. eating baba ganoush rice cakes.

9:23PM: checked email. read inaugural liveblog comment by sam cooke. i like sam more than i like most people i don't know well but 'like.' his parents were aware of the singer when they named sam and, i think, didn't have strong feelings about him. there is less of a gray area with our mutual acquaintances. people either like or dislike sam cooke. more often men don't like him. they view him as a threat or something, because he talks easily to girls and makes politically incorrect comments and like, pushes people to act 'extreme' in social situations, but for…unconventional reasons…i forget, figured this out on cocaine with sam and mira. people think he just wants attention. but to me, his motivations seem to come from some place of egoless nihilistic boredom, like some feeble attempt to…something. last ditch effort to amuse the universe. sam is easy to talk to and down to do anything, which are the most important things i consider when deciding 'can i be friends with this person.'

9:32PM: emailed masha email re xanax/addy exchange rates. bought noopept from a website she recommended. 'noo' is a soothing ass prefix. remember in psychology class there was a brain chemical…'noo' something…loved listening to teacher say 'noo[something].'

10:04PM: mom said something about watching 'les miserables' i said 'in a half hour?' she said 'yeah but knowing you, it probably won't be a half an hour.' thought 'perceptive, mom.' she is right. no, i'm going to prove her wrong. i'm excluding a 'totally fascinating, integral' conversation about pizza, just to prove mom wrong. i will watch the movie on time. hope you're happy, mom. you are depriving all four people still reading liveblog of hearing all of those hilarious things we said about pizza.

10:23PM: seems like i'm getting carried away with typing in liveblog. what if i just did this forever. that's exciting. has anyone done that? might be hard to sustain if/when i become more social.

10:31PM: entered kitchen to look for snacks i knew i didn't want. mom said 'there's always downton, we always must think of downton, it's all we have' in a british accent. i said 'oh my god. you're so right.' stopped what we were doing and looked at each other and laughed. i said 'it's all we have.'

10:33PM: ate 1mg xanax. handled pear that had been cut strangely. said 'are you going to eat this pear?' in a strange voice i didn't plan on using. mom said 'well i think we should watch it in the bedroom, because of the HD.' i said 'no, i said 'can i have this pear? are you done eating it?"

10:39PM: sitting beside mom on her bed. man on TV in a butler outfit said 'i want to please lady mary,' extending and retracting his hands several times, palms facing upward, as if holding invisible melons.

10:41PM: mom said 'we must always talk like this. OOOOH' in british accent. i said 'BLOOOOOR' in…britishly, i think. man on TV said 'before the war i believed my life had value. i would like to feel that way again, i suppose.'

10:42PM: started laughing really hard typing 'BLOOOOOR.' mom said 'don't laugh, they've been in love for twenty years.'

11:02PM: 'les miserables' cannot be ordered 'on demand.' something is wrong with 'on demand.' crisis.

11:12PM: mom is calling comcast. we are eating from a plastic bag of lemon jelly beans from whole foods. interested in watching 'the master.' mom says it's 'too depressing.' remembered text from keith about 'the master.' phone has been dead since yesterday. enjoying leaving it dead for now. secretly recording a video of mom talking to comcast.

11:20PM: ate handful lemon jelly beans and said 'after this i'm going to stop.' mom said 'i think it's the sugar that keeps us coming back.' i said 'well. you know. whatever you can get, you know. you gotta take whatever keeps you coming back.'

11:26PM: we have decided to watch 'the master.' feel i convinced…this was a product of my convincing. i get guilty when things feel like products of my convincing.

MARCH 22, 2013

1:25AM: an intense vague thing is happening with a wall. people are watching an increasingly frustrated joaquin phoenix pace from a window to a wall, saying 'it's a wall.' seems like he was instructed to do this by philip seymour hoffman. philip seymour hoffman just embraced joaquin phoenix. i said 'this is a really weird episode of 'the office' you're showing me, mom.'

1:40AM: mom paused the movie. oh man, before the movie i had eaten another 1mg xanax. then i made and ate an entire frozen pizza (to be fair, it was only like eight inches in diameter). while the pizza was baking mom and me listed all the places we've ever lived. i wrote a list of the places.

2:46AM: ate two pieces of buttered toast (one with raspberry jam, one cinnamon sugar). i don't feel xanax effects anymore. i liked 'the master' in that i like all movies, i think. joaquin phoenix's character reminded me of someone i was obsessed with in high school and would later have casual sex with for a few years. sometimes the sex felt less casual than other times. he also looked a little like joaquin phoenix. set alarm for 11:30AM.

4:09AM: ate 1mg xanax. searched gmail for '3/21/12.' several emails from rite aid. some 'how will we move apartment' or 'hey meet me here at this time' gchats from ex-boyfriend. stopped looking at gmail. walked to kitchen and opened a coconut as quietly as possible. going to…fucking…watch the last episode of 'girls'…fall asleep…phone died, will have no alarm tomorrow morning. oh well. something about the movie made me think about babies. or no, mom. talking with mom about all the places she lived when she was around my age. she was doing all these things with a child around. wish i could've been there, helping them. she said having my sister with her was the only thing stopping her from killing herself sometimes. if i had a baby i wouldn't kill myself, i don't think. unless it was suffering and i thought we both wanted to die. i'd just wait for it to die and then kill myself. want to talk to my sister more. soothing ass coconut water.

5:04AM: if i eat a bagel it might help me sleep.

5:51AM: ate bagel, three cookies, 1mg xanax. watched 'girls.' not sleepy. feel like my job is to wrangle herd of thoughts by thinking 'the fluffier comforter is always under the heavier one, you are under both.' feel shitty.

6:05AM: gotta be real witchall. i sleep with a stuffed dragon every night. his name is 'ta ta.'

12:00PM: mom woke me. felt like a small child, unprepared. drank glass of milk. ate two cookies.

1:28PM: mom tried to say something like 'it doesn't seem like you really want to live in new york' and felt irritated. tao is doing a poetry presentation in chicago tonight and invited people to party in his room, it says on twitter. nostalgic for the beginning of our relationship, when i went along on his book tour. read all about it in 'taipei,' look out for 'taipei,' which reading will likely make you sad and laugh and think interesting things about life the way tao's books do only this one is my favorite.

plugged phone into charger and hit snooze alarm for 30 minutes. saw barrage of texts and felt good.

1:30–5:30PM: hit snooze several times. made 'the least you can do' smoothie for energy/motivation to be healthy today.

THE LEAST YOU CAN DO SMOOTHIE:

- 2 bananas

- 1 large bunch spinach

- ice

it's the least you can do. it tastes good. continued napping.

at some point i talked with ex-boyfriend on the phone. he's at his parents' house in new jersey. sad about things. no more apartment. this is how it went. all that hope in the beginning, and this is how it went. on the phone i said, 'our lease expires in like a week, then i'll like, never talk to you again' and we laughed a little, but i think that's mostly true. made plans to hang out tomorrow…there is some movie…i don't know. the last little dingle-berry hangings-on of a relationship. being nice all of a sudden to honor some thing. the hope you had, maybe. the other day he said 'isn't it weird that no matter what, we're always going to remember each other, like, we are the people we are going to remember?' it was funny.

5:30–6:17PM: later something was said about drugs, dad giving me adderall. mom said 'you don't want to have your dad's mind when you're his age, be careful' with an honestly concerned-to-the-point-of-fear face. i said 'i won't, i won't' unconvincingly.

fed-ex is open until 9PM.

mom said 'will it bother you if i go play piano in the other room?' i said it wouldn't at all. she is playing 'when you wish upon a star.'

8:36PM: printed 115-page liveblog manuscript. satisfying to hold. happy. happy little shithead deluxe edition idiot deadbeat dad megan boyle (have been referring to myself as a 'deadbeat dad' a lot lately).

9:07pm: FedEx was closed. Yoga is done for the day. Did not write cover letter. On the way to get adderall I left at dad's apartment. Smoking cigarette. Ran over a gray lump. Want to pay someone to read this and diagnose me. Nagging prescience that there is something I can't see, an obvious problem outsiders can see clearly, that knowing would help change. Feel that thing I'd feel on Sundays, knowing school is tomorrow and I haven't done my homework. Disappointed in me.

9:21pm: Think I'm less likely to complete tasks now because I used to make more of an effort, things would be completed, but nothing has ever really changed about how I feel. Like all of the things I've tried…still feel this directionless…here I am, no matter what.

9:32pm: dad was wearing '#1 father' sweatshirt. I hugged him and said 'number one dad.' Saw two security cameras near kitchen. I said 'are they real?' he said they were fake, 'with little red dots' to discourage burglars, then described scenarios where a burglar would see each camera. He said 'they'd see one there, but then they'd see the other one there.' he gave me 2x 30mg adderall xr, hugged him again, left.

9:54pm: passed whole foods parking lot. It was too late. Going to Wegman's to buy kale and cantaloupe for a smoothie. Might exercise in mom's gym. I don't feel funny or interesting or capable of writing anything but robotic 'this is what happened' thoughts. This is the boring hell portion of liveblog. Boring low-point.

10:06pm: trying to think of things I want to listen to but feel deadly 'there is nothing to want at all, about anything' thing. Trying to conjure romantic fantasies but feel overpowered with 'none of that is going to happen, too many factors pulling in other directions, plus you are bad to be in relationships with, it is kinder not to inflict yourself on another person. Plus, remember what happens with every person you've ever felt happy around. It's just going to end up the same thing.'

Aware that these feelings will pass on their own, as soon as I feel them enough or whatever, and I'll feel completely different things soon. Just want to sleep. Thought 'sleep under the armpit of someone.' That seems hopeful. Slow return of hope. In the hope-launching process now. Denzel's voice calmly saying 'we are inverted now, fully inverted, we are now in the hope launching process' to air traffic control.

10:23pm: listened to 'ruins' by Aloha. I've seen them play many times. My 'can't do it' surrendering-arms gesture friend and I were obsessed with the drummer, Cale Parks. He moves his arms so fast and effortlessly and does really sweet fills. Feel stupid saying 'really sweet fills' but that's what they are. Listened to lyrics, which I know most of, and sat in parking spot, crying a little. At the end there's this part like, 'at the end of the story I was just beyond camera. Right outside the frame. Waiting for a getaway car that never came.' Wanted to cry more than I was able to. Cried a little again typing lyrics just now, sitting in pee stall at Wegman's.

10:31pm: male voice said 'maintenance.' I said 'okay' from bathroom stall. Female voice said 'is anyone in here' as I flushed toilet and exited stall. I smiled and said 'sorry' to a woman's head, peeking in. I was at the hands-washing station. She smiled and said 'it's fine take you time,' closing the door.

10:37pm: selected kale, cantaloupe, green probiotic drink, b-vitamins. Stood in line with least people. The woman from the bathroom rang me up. Selected earbuds from the impulse buy rack. Wondered if woman and I would talk about bathroom thing. Customer in front of me left. I said 'hi-iiiii' and smiled. She didn't look at me and said 'hi how are you tonight' I said 'goo-oooood, how are you' with the last part mumbled. She scanned my items. I entered my phone number in the credit card pay device thing. She held up a brown and mustard-yellow hippie-looking beanie and said 'mark is this Dylan's? It's been here all day.' I smiled and nodded and made a face/noise of 'I know how that goes, man. Dylan, man' but she didn't see. I finished paying on the device. She said 'someone gotta up and take that hat, I'm not about to...' but I had taken my bags and left at that point.

11:03pm: ex-boyfriend called when I was peeing. Not going to say details. Seems apparent that he's read this, or at least part of it. He's not at his parents' house. Has been in Philadelphia for some days. Corrected me in a funny way. Said I should come tonight instead. Think I will. I don't know. If I go I can go to the library and write article tomorrow. I like that library. Conflicted knowing he reads this. Will be inhibited when I type now, to some degree, knowing it could lead to hearing him say something like 'oh you included that, I see. Huh. That's interesting,' and I'll feel bad. Fuck that. Fuck that [name omitted by request] you know this is the end of it. Fuck me for letting things effect me. What I just wrote leads me to believe there is no reason for me to go, if my goal is to feel good. I want to go though. Maybe it will be nice. Used to be nice. It's actually always nice and kind of bad-feeling, seeing him. Equal amounts. The library. Using the library and 'wanting change of scenery' as my rational excuses for going.

Desire to go is mostly fueled by emotion, though. Okay at least I know that, both of those things. Parked in mom's driveway right now. Coat smells like from hugging dad. If it starts to feel more bad than good I'll just leave.

11:47PM: entered mom's. blender difficulty. coaxed kale and cantaloupe together with a spoon, which required physical effort, like, pushing. allowed eyes to unfocus. imagined spoon colliding with blade, causing blender to explode, glass flying into my throat, blood everywhere, nearly instant death.

11:30-11:59pm: drank smoothie. Called ex-boyfriend to say I wasn't coming. Left him a voicemail like 'hey-a thissa the pizza guy, manny, you ordera errr uh pick up your phone.' called again. He said he was sad to hear I wasn't coming. I said something about not wanting to think about what to bring. He reminded me most of my stuff is there. I said 'if I come can we go to the library tomorrow morn—er, afternoon?' he said yes and that he had written 4500 words today and felt good. I said 'I've been doing that too, it feels good.' he said something about being focused on words like…'high' but he didn't say 'high'…but then that he had gone, alone, to 3G—a bar we joke about because of its presentation as 'extreme hot spot,' located on the corner of 3rd st. and Girard st., that when I first saw over a year ago, made me think 'we'll be living in the neighborhood where 'things happen,' this is the 'happening' neighborhood.' we've never gone inside. Tonight when he left, a group of people asked him to take a picture with them, and were like 'why are you going so soon?' he seemed drunk talking to me in the first conversation leaving Wegman's and drunk in the conversation just before midnight. But. Seems too complicated to talk about this, the dynamic between us, my wants for going, my 'knowing better' but not really, how…you know a person over time…there is sadness… you cause sadness and disappointment in each other but you don't stop, or like, you almost stop, you're basically completely stopped until your lease expires. And then you know you won't know them anymore. You know you will forget most of it. But they've been the most consistent thing in your progressively insignificant life for 18 months. You've done and said everything mean and bad you can say to each other but it's also never been hard to laugh. Yeah I've laughed the most in this one. Relationship. But also felt the least similar to…the person…a fatal dissimilarity we're both aware of…goddamnit.

12:54am: mom followed me downstairs and for the maybe 90 seconds it took to arrange objects in 'voyage ready' car positions, stood in doorway, watching me. She said 'I almost want to tell you to give him a hug for me but…' I said 'no he's fine, he's just, don't not want to hug him, it's complicated' and didn't know what to say. Driving now.

1:41am: have been listening to 'ruins' on repeat. Read lyrics and had goosebumps. Thought I was going to cry full-out and didn't. Words sound newly poignant, like what I can't put to words right now. The end part. Jesus. Fuck it, I considerately withheld lyrics before but now you must endure (or skip ahead):

> We were giants on a plywood stage
> In evenings I was your household name
> And for a little while, I knew all the words you'd say
> Cut me from the movie
> Hold me for the credits
> I was just beyond camera
> Right outside the frame
> Waiting for a getaway car that never came
> At the end of the story I was just beyond camera
> Right outside the frame
> Waiting for a getaway car that never came
> Waiting for a getaway car that never came

1:58am: passing Newark, Delaware. Predict I will not update liveblog as frequently when I'm interacting with ex-boyfriend. Predict feelings of self-consciousness and wanting to avoid saying or doing things that will elicit a negative response from him. This is fucked up about me, I think.

2:17am: commented on Sam Pink's thing he just posted about a candy ass racist reviewer. Wish I was driving to Sam Pink's house instead of where I'm going. Should I not include things like this. No I'm including everything, fuck it, fuck me fuck it. I don't really wish I was anything at the moment actually. Wish I was a…just…something alive but unconscious. Or like, anything else. Wish I was anything else. Good epitaph for me: 'she was never anything else.'

2:22am: passed billboard advertising a 'lifestyle salad.' Want to eat a 'Fleetwood Mac 'rumors' tour lifestyle salad.'

2:30AM: parked outside apartment. entered building. saw giant nesquick container on top of our mailbox. walked up the stairs to apartment, through door, up more stairs to first level of apartment. lights were off. thought 'shit, i won't be able to sleep.' put vegetables i brought in fridge, then took my coat with me to the bathroom. took 2mg xanax from coat pocket and chewed with front teeth while peeing. coat was propped on the shower. heard footsteps. said 'that's too heavy to be shirley' and saw ex-boyfriend standing in the bathroom doorway, wearing glasses and pajama pants and a giant blue knee-length t-shirt (i have the same one in pink, we bought them at a thrift store shortly after moving in together, but have rarely worn them). he was holding a water bottle and looked sad and faraway and tired and maybe drunk. i wiped and walked to him without flushing toilet. i said 'hi mingus' or something, then 'how about that nesquick?' he didn't say anything. it seemed hard to adjust to seeing his body in front of me, like he seemed shorter maybe, or his head was larger. his hair was wet. he held me really close to him and i held him really close back. touched each other's bodies in places while hugging. felt effected by how he seemed to be affected. smelled by his ear and it smelled like him. on the drive over i wasn't thinking about…something…that now i seemed to be thinking about, which seemed important, but is hard to articulate. the thing caused by just physically-being-around someone. walked to the bedroom and kissed and took off each other's clothes. not going to describe sex. hadn't planned on having sex and sort of didn't want to but knew i would and we would if i went and wanted to as it happened.

4–5AM: wanted a sandwich badly. drove us to aramingo diner. the waitress said 'hey ladies' then realized ex-boyfriend was a boy (he has very long hair) and apologized. this has happened before. i said 'they think that because of your face also, your face is also very pretty.' at some point he asked me to change his name to 'ex-boyfriend' completely, in liveblog, but this may have happened at some other time. talked about person who i like but i don't think likes me anymore. he said something about it being because i had introduced the person to drugs. i said i didn't think so, that i wasn't the first person to do drugs with them, and that they didn't seem like the kind of person who would 'blame' or hold anyone responsible for their decisions anyway, that they probably didn't like me anymore because of other things, which i felt i sort of understood and didn't want to talk about. he seemed insistent on the drug thing. feeling very irritated, typing this now, stupidly obsessively unstoppably irritated. resisting urge to talk about argument in detail. enjoyed the sandwich very much. things seemed better, eventually. it seemed apparent that neither of us wanted to argue but were aware of argu-ing, so one or both of us stopped or changed the subject. i don't remember other things we talked about at the diner. remember joking about music in the car. went to bed feeling good.

12:30PM: woke and had sex. felt not fully awake, the entire time. after sex we laid with no covers on. our apartment has never had heat, which is okay, but i'm always cold. i said something about wanting a blanket and ex-boyfriend said 'you don't need that.' i sort of lazily wrestled with him to pull the smaller blanket onto me and he said 'you don't need that' again. blanket didn't seem to warm me. laid like that for a while, saying small things, some jokes, i think. i said 'i'm making a smoothie,' dressed in pajamas, and walked to kitchen area, with ex-boyfriend following shortly behind.

1:15PM: ex-boyfriend played the 'shirley song' i referenced earlier and said 'is this the shirley song?' i said 'yes' and tried to show him, like, sing it as if it was shirley, while assembling smoothie ingredients and blending. in the blending process, a 'cracked egg mid-falling into a bowl' sculpture i like but ex-boyfriend has always hated broke from the vibrations on the table. made an 'incredulous, losing the most obvious bet on 'the price is right'' face and he made the same face and then a fake-villain 'hand rub.' we said 'oh no' a few times. i said 'you think it's broken, but it's happened before, and i've fixed it' in a...some kind of tone...fake-mad. smoothie was extremely cold. i said 'i'm going back to the bedroom to drink this under the covers.' he said 'then i'll go take my shower my favorite way: alone.' i said 'fine. then after that i'll take my shower my favorite way: alone.' we sounded like children doing that competitive angry thing, only that we were aware of it and making fun of ourselves, maybe, or at least i was. i went to the bedroom and am under blankets. alive is kneading near me. drinking spinach, avocado, coconut water, frozen banana smoothie.

1:26PM: heard shower water run, stop, and radiator switch click on and off, which means there is no hot water. ex-boyfriend appeared in doorway, wearing giant knee-length t-shirt from last night, shrugging exaggeratedly with a crazed face. i said 'oh, you had to do the thing.'

1:30PM: ex-boyfriend entered shower and i peed. removed clothes. ex-boyfriend sang 'i'm your boogie man' in the shower and i sang part of 'boogie nights.' he said 'that's not the same song.' i said 'i know.' was hard to remember anything but the part of 'boogie nights' that's like 'dance to the boogie, get down.' i sang that, then the next part, which is like, 'cause boogie nights are a-dundun dun [low voice] keep on dancing, keep on dancin'.' joined him in the shower and sang parts of 'i'm your boogie man' and 'boogie nights' together.

stood under hot water. at some point ex-boyfriend said something about how i've been living in 'the luxury of your mom's condo, where you can just order thai food and say 'hey can you guys just please bring it to my bedroom? i don't want to get the door, can you just bring it upstairs to my bed?" i laughed a little and like, jokingly defended myself. i said 'i haven't even ordered food once since i've been there.' continued to make mild complaints about the water, coldness, each other. i said 'DONE' and felt like a child and turned off the water. looked at ex-boyfriend's face, which was displaying a helplessly uncomfortable expression, looking somewhere in the distance. handed him the thicker/'nicer' towel. he stepped out of shower while i toweled off standing in the bathtub. felt myself shivering and unable to focus on anything but how it would be cold until my hair was dry, minutes away, 'long sets' of minutes, like at least 15. didn't feel seriously irritated by anything that was going on. unsure if ex-boyfriend did. ex-boyfriend left bathroom and turned on the kitchen radio. i re-applied pajamas for 'the cold walk to the bedroom,' where i turned the radio to the same station, playing tom waits.

1:49PM: ex-boyfriend said 'meg i won't even have to keep you away from me cause tom waits is on.' i said 'noooooooo.' jogged to bed and burrowed under the covers. tom waits made horrible noises, then the DJ asked him about pirates. i said 'has any rapper ever been like, 'i'm rap's scallion?" ex-boyfriend said 'that's good' and went to make coffee.

1:53PM: dressed in black leggings, black american apparel dress, black cardigan, two long gold necklaces. this is a 'look' i see mira and chelsea wearing. unsure if i can do this look. i like trying. i like 'all black.'

2:20PM: entered dining room with picnic table, where ex-boyfriend was sitting with two mugs. he said 'well, look at you,' narrating himself in tonally oblique way, like some kind of feigned act of appraisal. i snort-laughed and said 'yeah,' not knowing why. emotional music was playing. i asked what he'd do after we'd moved. he didn't want to talk about it.

i told him when i met him in 2009 and he was living with his girlfriend in this really nice apartment in brooklyn, i'd thought 'whoa, that's what life can be like? every day they just wake together in this place, and do these things, and talk to these people they like, and this is just normal?' he said that even then he felt bad. he said 'i remember like, drinking beers on the porch before work and feeling bad. i was just starting to be disillusioned or something, now i'm fully…whatever.' i thought about him and me and how our lives have changed since we met. felt hotness and water behind my eyes. he picked up a long, white, rolled paper and said 'look at this thing.' i said 'whoa, look at it,' hearing my voice trying to sound okay. with a defeated expression, he said 'i don't know, maybe i'll move to new york again.' we were quiet for a few moments. i said 'i'm going to do something potentially alienating right now,' as i moved to sit beside him. i hugged him and said 'i'm glad i at least got to know you for a little while.' i don't like that i said the alienating thing, i should've just. or. i don't know. i don't like that i did that, any of that.

2:20PM: debated walking to library. i said we should drive because we need to buy cat food, because the cats 'are depending on us.' ex-boyfriend said 'they have dry, look,' pointing to uneaten dry and crusted-over wet food. i said 'you know they're not going to eat that.'

driving to operation ava for cat food, i said 'do you think either of us are going to find, like, true love?' he said 'i am.' i said 'do you think i am?' he said 'maybe with someone gay. in some kind of, like, alternative set-up.' i said 'what do you mean, like an actual gay person?' he said 'i don't know. it's going to be an alternative set-up.' i said 'i think i found it before.' he said 'oh, with that idiot?' i said 'no i think i had it with [person]. and maybe. like. there could be again. i don't know.' i felt bad saying all of this and like i was hating myself for saying it but was unable to stop. i said 'so, i wonder what she's going to be like: your person. okay. she's going to have to read john o'hara, and know as many books as you know, and be really pretty but not wear make-up, have a steady job.' he said 'you're being stupid right now.' i said 'i know, i'm sorry.' a reggae station was on the radio the whole time. i parked next to kaplan's deli and operation ava. i said 'oh no, i can't go in there, they know about the annie thing' (gave annie, my other cat, to a shelter after taking her to the vet at operation ava).

2:30PM: ex-boyfriend entered kaplan's carrying blue plastic bag. i said 'they didn't have everything bagels so i got you a poppy one.' he said 'they didn't have cat food so i got dog food.' i said 'are you serious' and tried to look in the bag, which he kept jerking away. i said 'you got…you really got…' and he was smiling and said 'yes' and i said 'we need to return—or, i mean. wait.' he said 'they were out of cat food. really. you honestly, really think they were out of cat food. over there. there was no cat food.' i smiled and said 'oh jeez' or something but felt a little bad.

3:30PM: parked on 15th street. ex-boyfriend said 'look at the bud light eagles can, oh my god.' i could barely see it was 'eagles'-themed. he said 'it looks so small, around the other things, oh my god.' i loved the can and loved ex-boyfriend and that this was happening. i said 'yeah, it's like—the label is facing out, it's showing us.' he said 'yeah. i can't believe it's there.' it looked like it was a person on the street, lost, maybe selling something. i said 'i want a picture,' meaning just the can. ex-boyfriend jogged to pose by it. he gestured to the can, i took a picture without him gesturing. put picture on instagram. felt excited for other things like the can, that we could find. felt my brain gearing up in a certain way…to look for interesting things with a person…that i like to do, but know i can sometimes 'go overboard' and annoy people. i think it's usually one of the first things people like and grow to hate about me, in romantic situations, because i'm like…always doing that, always wanting to do that…just say stuff… like 'look at that thing, it's like that thing is something else' then invent 'something else' scenarios, ideally together, but. yeah this seems to annoy people eventually, always. people always want to stop doing that. it's like they get the joke but i like the things that…it can stop being a joke of 'it's something else' and evolve into even more ridiculous things…untapped potential for everything to become ridiculous scenarios, always…so. i can see myself being annoyed with a person who does it as relentlessly and sometimes insensitively, to like, other dynamics, as i do it. like if i can sense the person feels bad but i feel good i'll still want to do it—sometimes because i think it can make them feel better, more often because i'm bored with them feeling bad.

3:32PM: walked to 'fresh grocer.' ex-boyfriend said 'entrance and exit. when you go to the exit you also exit, but when you go to the entrance you enter. enter.' i laughed and said things. he said 'this is where the energy things are' and i rubbed my hands together fiendishly, knowing he doesn't like energy drinks. i like to jokingly exaggerate things he doesn't like. i saw 'xyience xenergy drink: official energy drink of the UFC,' which is my favorite, not only because its name is so ridiculous and it's the official drink of the UFC, but it tastes really good. i selected one of each flavor (cran razz, blue pom, mango guava—most places usually just have two flavors but fresh grocer had all three, i was excited) like a madman. i laughed like a madman, i think, fake madman-laughed.

said casual things about our surroundings while walking to the self-checkout line with the least people. ex-boyfriend said 'a lot of people buying things today. this is the day they want the stuff.' i said 'yeah. remember when we were here with atcolv [what we call andrew colville]? and the cheese-its?' he said 'yeah. he seems to snack a lot.' i said 'yeah. i can see him snacking a lot. it's what keeps him so tall.' ex-boyfriend laughed. there was a big box of discounted books. i said 'do you think there's a john o'hara book in there?' he said 'maybe, probably. i wouldn't want to date a girl who liked john o'hara. he's like. it's nasty to like that.' i said 'i thought that was the thing about me. or like, or one of them. that i never wanted to read john o'hara.' he said 'no, no' and shook his head, then made a comedian-like face and said 'that was definitely not it,' referencing all of the other things 'it' was, i think, maybe seriously.

i scanned the energy drinks on the self-scanner and put them in a bag. ex-boyfriend inserted coins into the machine before i could. i inserted a five dollar bill and the overhead music changed to, like, old timey vaudeville music, like 'speakeasy' music. i struggled with inserting the one dollar bill. i said 'the music is perfect for what i'm doing.' the machine printed my receipt and a nickel flew out into the coin return area. i made a groucho marx face and pointed at the coin dispenser and said 'keep the change.' ex-boyfriend ran to get the nickel, fueled by his (what i consider) neurotic want to not waste things.

3:37PM: walking to temple university campus, out of nowhere, ex-boyfriend said "forty going on sixty' would be a much more interesting concept, to me.' i smiled and said 'yeah.' passed a building, the entire back of which seemed missing. sheets in its windows were like, blowing in the wind. i said 'that building is so good, i want a picture,' and took one. ex-boyfriend said 'yeah, like. jail is the only place where you're not supposed to leave. you're supposed to leave, like, city halls or libraries. everywhere wants you to leave. but not jail. it's the only place where they won't let you leave.' i smiled, said something in agreement. felt good things about him, like, 'shit i'm going to miss being around someone who thinks like this.'

said things about people going to school at temple. a man was running. one of us said 'yeah, better run to that place you're going,' and we said things like 'yeah get there fast, guy, the faster you get there the better, you don't want to be late for that thing you're going to.' there was some building, like, a dorm-like building. i said 'temple commons, party in temple commons tonight, don't forget your busch light,' then paused and said 'no one has ever said that, i'm the first one.' ex-boyfriend said 'oh, really?' i sensed he sensed i was starting to do the thing were i get carried away with trying to find interesting things to say.

3:40PM: entered a student center-like building to find ex-boyfriend's bank. he said 'do you think the bank will be open?' not knowing or caring if it would, i said it would. he walked ahead. the only others in the building seemed much older than us, seated in scattered gatherings of chairs. almost took a picture of an extremely, cartoonishly old-looking man who i pointed to discreetly and said 'albert einstein' about, to ex-boyfriend as he withdrew money from an ATM. ex-boyfriend seemed mildly irritated. i thought 'just be quiet for a while, don't be the first to say something for a while, maybe show him you don't need to be around him, it'll get better,' and walked to a glass window completely covered in a modern-looking decal about office supplies. i stared at a box that said 'LAMIN' above 'ATION.' thought about taking a picture. two people sat near the decal. i thought they'd see me taking the picture and. something. they seemed to be communicating with each other non-verbally, not noticing me. one of them stood and the other began gathering things. ex-boyfriend waved from the ATM, about 30 feet away. i walked to him. i said 'it's depressing in here.'

3:41PM: walked through a set of library doors to an area where the ceiling seemed high, and looked like it could've contained some kind of security device, though i somehow knew it didn't. saw a man in a suit. ex-boyfriend said 'let's go in the other way,' and we walked out the doors. i said 'yeah, seemed too official.' walked to the other entrance. saw closed-looking 'food station' with interesting use of ellipsis.

3:45PM: sat in wheel-y office chair among open-looking 'quiet zone' of cubicle-like fixtures that i said looked 'better for computers.' ex-boyfriend said he was going to work upstairs, where he went last time.

4:50PM: minimized screen when i sensed ex-boyfriend approaching my computer station. he nodded like 'whoa, okay, you crazy person' and i smiled and tugged his arm and said 'hi bingo.' i didn't let go of his arm and he spun me around in the chair. he kept looking like 'you crazy person' at me and i kept smiling. i said 'what, do you want to read what i wrote?' and made screen visible again. he shook his head 'definitely no' and backed away. felt aware of silence. i said 'how long do you want to stay here?' and he shrugged, now seemingly intentionally not saying words, and i kind of pulled his lower arm and said 'i want to stay here a long time.' he nodded slowly and walked away, making a face like he had just heard someone say 'i'm going to burn my lottery winnings and jump off a cliff.' i made little laughing nose-sounds as i watched him walk away. it feels like we're both kidding all of the time, acting the parts of something. hard to discern when one of us is serious, unless we're arguing or i'm crying.

5:36PM: peed. i like using the same stall every time. it's like 'hello again, old friend.'

6:18PM: feeling guilty for typing so much about what we're doing.

6:32PM: going to work on cover letter now.

7:03PM: ex-boyfriend approached, saying something about library closing three minutes ago. he stood by me while i gathered my things, said 'you can pee in fresh grocer, come on, let's go,' continued walking. i gathered my things and jogged to him, noticing people still seated at cubicles.

he said he didn't do much at library. i said 'i've just been writing about everything since last night,' aware of walking fast to match his pace. he said 'good.' we passed the temple commons building. he said 'busch light' and i said 'busch light headquarters.' sometimes he acts impatient like this. i wanted to be like 'where are you going, what's the urgency,' and benignly negatively compared him to the running man we joked about earlier.

8:00PM: near the fresh grocer sign were smaller signs for 'deli,' 'produce,' 'frogro: sushi.' i said "frogro,' like how people say 'rofo' about royal farms.' ex-boyfriend said 'frogro…' i said 'rofo.' he said "deli' means…' placing my hand on his shoulder, i said "deli' means never having to say you're sorry.' he said 'oh god,' looking up and to the left, as if for an answer to 'when will it stop.' the automated doors opened and we walked inside. he said 'would it be better if atcolv was around right now, to just. it would be another person? would that make me feel better?' i said 'i can go home, i don't have to be here.' he said 'no, i'm sorry, we're having a nice time, i'm sorry.' i said 'i don't want to make you feel bad just by being here, it's really no problem for me to go.' he said 'no honey, i'm sorry,' pointing to an ambiguously restricted bathroom area.

there was an increasingly bad feeling as we walked around the produce section, talking about what to buy for dinner. didn't agree on much other than 'i wish i never had to think about what to eat.' i wanted to make food together or go to a restaurant, which he didn't want, so then i mostly didn't want to be in the grocery store. i said 'i'll just eat whatever's left of my smoothie and buy fruit,' sounding petulant. he said 'there's no point in buying more olive oil, i'm only going to live here for another week.' we looked at bagels. he said he would just make rice and beans. i said 'i want a bagel for later. no i don't.' he said 'you want this, this egg bagel?' i said 'no that shit's yellow, fuck that shit.' felt increasingly bad, wandering produce aisles, watching him walk fast. i paused aimlessly in front of a melon display. watched ex-boyfriend select a green pepper, then walked to him to resume walking together. he said 'i feel like i'm going to cry,' smiling a little. 'me too, i feel so bad,' i said.

in the car he said 'i just had a bad day at the library. you had a good day.' i said 'yeah but i didn't actually do anything like, important, that i said i'd do. what are the actual things that are making you feel bad right now?' he expressed a vague sense of unrest and underlying futility about a lack of motivation to do anything creative, let alone life's more practical daily demands, managed easily by others. he asked why i felt bad. i was surprised he asked, in a way that distracted me from answering the question.

i said something like 'worried about my future, sad about now, i don't have anything to look forward to anymore.' he said 'i don't even get the concept of 'looking forward to' anymore, like, what will happen? it's just temporary comforting things until the inevitable thing.' i said 'yeah, that's what i mean by 'nothing to look forward to.''

parked by our apartment. seemed hard to exit, to want to go inside. the car in front of us had a funny permanent-looking 'for sale' decal on the back window, like 'for sale' almost in cursive. i turned off the car. it was quiet. i said 'we have to go inside now.' he said 'do we?' i leaned over and hugged him. he said 'a hug is just like, being outbid on ebay.'

inside we seemed to feel worse and worse, saying things to each other that indicated vaguely, some kind of hopelessness. in the kitchen i hugged him from behind and said 'now your back will be warm.' he said 'i'm being outbid on ebay.'

i opened the fridge door. there's a watermelon in there that's been there for months, i think. seemingly months. it's what has been smelling bad about the kitchen. earlier one of us had said we thought the watermelon was what's been making the kitchen smell bad. i said 'i want to throw it out the window.' ex-boyfriend said 'like where i threw up' (before the library, he had shown me that he vomited macaroni and cheese out the bedroom window onto part of our roof—the apartment is such that...we have two floors, kind of. there is an area where you can vomit out the window and it will land on our roof).

i said 'no, like, right out here, throw it out this window.' he said 'we can't do that.' he said 'should we take it to the park?' i grinned and said 'yeah.' somehow...we became committed to this. taking the watermelon some-where. he said 'here, put it in this shitty bag,' and handed me an urban out-fitters tote bag. he said 'was that...did that come with like, a thirty dollar purchase or something?' i kneeled by the fridge and said 'no, fuck, i don't know,' breathing through my mouth to avoid the rotten smell. holding a whiskey bottle, he said 'i'm bringing this, so we can have a toast, after we throw it. toast it after we throw it.' he placed the whiskey in a plastic bag. i said 'yeah, yeah, good idea.' i stood and held the bag. he said 'what park should we take it to?' i felt a new kind of energy in the space between my eyes and his. i said 'penn treaty?' he said 'yeah, penn treaty, good. i'm feeling better already.' i said 'me too.'

he said 'i'm not even bringing my keys, i'm not even...turning off the music, i'm not turning off the lights.' i was grinning really big, breathing through my mouth, moving fast, getting my keys. we left hurriedly. i thought for a minute we'd walk then he said 'we're taking the car, right?' and i said 'yeah, yeah, the car, yeah, fast.' on the way there we decided to hurl it into the river. i said 'maybe it will grow like, a thing. bounty. fortune.'

parked. walked towards the water with the watermelon bag and whiskey bag. pointed at a cloud and said 'look, it looks pink.' he said 'yeah, it does.' the lights looked really pretty. reminded me of a night in ohio with tao, when we did mushrooms before we were dating, walked along a beach by a city. i pointed at the bridge and said 'i can't believe the lights are really changing color, that's really what...' ex-boyfriend said 'yeah, that's what they did with that money.' a group of people were standing by the water. ex-boyfriend said 'oh no' and i said 'no, they're doing bad things too.'

i said 'take a picture of me.' he said 'what is this, hipstermatic? wasn't there a thing called that?' i said 'hipstamatic, yeah, i had that,' climbing over more rocks than i thought there would be. there was confusion about whether the bag would be thrown. the bag was not to be used. i lifted the watermelon out of the bag and threw it as hard as i could. when it landed it made an 'UFF' sound. ex-boyfriend said 'UFF' like how rick ross says it, in a way we've referenced a lot, that i think started because of something victoria trott tweeted about how her dog sometimes makes an 'UFF' sound like rick ross.

investigated watermelon landing area. took another picture. ex-boyfriend poured whiskey into two 'florida' shot glasses we found in abandoned trailer months ago. we drank the shots. i threw mine at my face more than i drank it. a lot dripped down the sides of my face. i was laughing. ex-boyfriend said something and i said about 11% of it didn't make it in my mouth.

i said 'we did it, it's over.' ex-boyfriend said 'it can be better now peg, see? see, now we can make other stuff for dinner: i'll buy mushrooms and avocado, because lately when i've been making rice and beans i find it's nice to have a bite of cooked vegetables and rice AND avocado' and i was touching his arm and being like 'yeah yeah!' and jumping/jogging a little as we walked to the car.

at fine wine & good spirits, someone had spilled something and they were mopping it up. i said 'that would be a good game, 'guess that smell of that alcohol.'' ex-boyfriend said it was white wine. i said 'no, it's one of those weird cupcake-y things. one of those things i always say i'm going to buy. i'm going to actually buy one of those things this time.' he said 'okay' excitedly, kind of. i selected a bottle of something apparently brandless, with a beach graphic on a label that said 'i'm coconuts for you.' ex-boyfriend said he had tried it at an in-store tasting and liked it. there was a long line.

returned to apartment. ex-boyfriend fixed dinner while i typed most of this. ate around 9:15PM.

during dinner we listened to hall & oates and said things about the 'i'm coconuts for you' bottle. read everything on the bottle. the bottle seems insane.

10:18PM: can hear him reading, drinking whiskey, sighing sometimes in bedroom. i'm in the next room, 'the living room,' where we keep the TV and a couch. the rooms are small, like 13' x 6', just narrow enough to maneuver around furniture. looks like they were just squeezed in to the renovations or something. hastily separated doors. maximum tiny room tolerance. someone thought it would make more money as a 'technically' two-bedroom apartment, for families.

there is a lot more i want to be saying...a lot i'm leaving out...distracted. i'm downloading 'the fighter.' we have plans to watch 'the fighter.'

2:02AM: kept pausing movie to say funny things to each other. am sort of drunk now. just had heated argument with ex-boyfriend about things like the show 'girls' and thought catalog being 'bad art' or something. felt something big in my chest now saying like, 'it doesn't matter what you do, just, no matter what you do, as long as you find something you like, you're going to die, everyone's just trying to do the best they can, it doesn't matter,' (don't remember what i said). he said 'i drank beer in brooklyn, i know what it's like, that show is made for people who are afraid of something (…), it caters to people's ideas and fears about post-college life' and i said 'it doesn't matter, enough people like it, i've felt stuff like the people on the show feel, maybe it's stupid but maybe for some people that's real, it doesn't matter, if it entertains people then so what, we're just all trying to do the best we can.' repeated 'we're all just trying to do the best we can' maybe three times. said 'i've had enough of this, this is stupid, i can't talk to you if you think like this' and left and am in living room now.

i said…earlier in the movie we paused it, via me saying something about how the cops were being fucked up to mickey and dickey, like it was fucked up that the cops didn't get in trouble for breaking mickey's hand. then that lead to a conversation about government and anarchy. i said 'it's all just always the same thing, people are just always afraid of each other.' ex-boyfriend seemed to agree and said things about jesus and believing jesus was saying nice things and he was crying a little. i agreed with everything he was saying. i kissed his face and he said 'don't do that because…' i said 'i'm doing it because i want to do it, not because i think you're trying to get me to do it.'

referenced jesus in argument just now. like. i said something really stupid. i don't know much about jesus. i said 'jesus would be like: love people, people will never think the same things, it's okay, don't hurt each other, you're all still people, you all ended up in bodies one day, the best thing to do is be nice to each other and not make each other feel bad.' forget what he said, i don't think i gave him a chance to respond. went to kitchen for water, then to our room to get a bigger bottle, which he seemed ready to volunteer. i said 'what you're saying is fucked up, like, you think one person's experience of life or art or whatever is inherently better than another person's, i think that's so fucked up, that's like, the same line of thinking as nazis or whatever.' something on his phone was making a noise. collected computer cord to take with me to the living room. he said 'where are you going?' seemed like if i said i was going home he would've gotten upset the way he does when i've driven back to baltimore after drinking and arguments.

heard him hovering by living room door. i locked it. he said 'oh, okay.' i'm not mad at him. this idea he has just seems shitty, has always seemed shitty…we argue about 'my writing' and this…related things…how i'm producing shitty things…seems so…goddamnit. it makes me like. i'm. wish i could…make something come out of me. shit a giant shit or shit bullets out my ass into nothing.

want to make something clear.

i don't give a fuck if you think there is good or bad art.

i give a MAJOR FUCK if you think other people are more entitled to make art, or that more people deserve to exist than others.

i'm crying right now…thinking…of people…no, i'm not crying. almost. i almost did. YOU HONESTLY THINK ONE PERSON HAS MORE OF A RIGHT TO MAKE SOMETHING, AN ART PRODUCT, FOR ENTERTAINMENT, THAT TELLS THE WORLD WHAT IT FEELS LIKE TO BE THEM, THAN ANYONE ELSE?!?!

HONESTLY????

CAN ANYONE HONESTLY…

you're just bitter because you think you're so great but you don't have an audience—and that's the thing. the most fucked up thing. is that you want attention WAY MORE than 'girls'…HBO…fucking…thought catalog… whatever…the things you think people just make for attention. or that no, you think you're DESERVING of attention. like, a smarter kind of atten- tion. because your 'art' is better, because you don't make it for attention, which is why you think anyone who gets attention for art must've made it, but you don't even make it anymore because we're all too stupid to like 'appreciate' it, because you don't want people to read something by you and think 'any idiot could say that' and forget you, you want them to think 'not just any idiot could say that, wow, will i ever be the same again? will the world?' it's the same thing. attention. that is so idiotic, especially factoring in other shit you say about meaninglessness and…goddamnit. i'm drunk. what i'm saying right now is not accurate. can hear music from his ipad. i'm abusing liveblog. just heard him say 'STOPPPPP,' from bedroom. makes me want to make more typing sounds type more sdkjsd sdfj osdijf osos os jduiu fosidoi fl s dsoi s di fid jjjdf osih ih hdjdjd hjiffd kjdkdk fkd k dkf dkfjsldfjsoj sk jd f dijf so ij sd fos difj oijdfoi ii j oisd fo oijd id fijoijoid di id di oijoijoisjdfoij ij idjfidjifjdosif oisjoidfjsodifj oij sd oijijifdfd d d d shd oiio,,,, dddd sdfjdsio sos jsodifjsoifj s ddjfdifj osdijfs dd d e ejskjdohf s d df os s dnf s doihfoid sliek i am fsell soinf sit sodesnt matter i'sms just typing this gto make him angry because he io = ois think ih e no want no hear typy etype tyepetype!!!!!!!!

2:34AM: he g-chatted in ambiguously friendly manner about finishing the movie. maybe i'm misreading something. this has been a major disagreement, like, an argument we have repeatedly. there is no reason for me to be here. no matter how many jokes we make…like…i don't know. still going to feel bad, to be around someone who thinks like this, and that things i've written, or things i want to say…is…that basically my experience of life is 'bad art.' drunk. ranting. going to my car to smoke a non-judgmental cigarette.

2:39AM: feels bad out here, alone over here. 1504 north 4th street. philadelphia. nothing to do but this. type into a computer. fear getting cigarettes because if the guy in the room next to you hears you walk outside, he'll think you're leaving 'for good.' you'll have to say 'no i just want to get cigarettes,' when you don't want to say anything or do anything ever, at all. the end. i liked watching 'the fighter,' though.

3-5:00AM(?): had another fight. depressed. cried a lot. got better somehow. he came out with me to my car. smoked a cigarette while he sat beside me and we didn't say much. 'heaven or hell' by volbeat came on the radio. it's an 'our song' song, we heard it on the drexel college radio station last spring and were surprised by how stupid it sounded and how much we liked it. ex-boyfriend said 'i would pay eighty dollars to see dipset and volbeat play together, but like…not forty dollars to see dipset play and forty dollars to see volbeat play.' went inside. things felt better. drank picklebacks. he made a point to get water in cans, we were refilling cans with water a lot.

i was crying lightly the whole time i think, saying things about my mom, how my life is stupid. remember asking him to read me a story he liked out loud. he wanted to make a video but stopped reading not long after he started. camera ended up recording us crying, talking about buying a gun, vacationing somewhere nice for a week and then shooting ourselves. have discussed doing this in the past. always feel better after talking about this. at least one thing is in our control, or something. ex-boyfriend vomited a lot, i lined a big stew pot with a garbage bag to put by the bed. think he doesn't want me to include video, i haven't watched.

2:45PM-4:55PM: woke, had sex. acting kind and funny to each other. i'm sitting at kitchen table naked except for a big red cardigan. watched youtube on ex-boyfriend's ipad: guided by voices documentary, videos of people playing 'pokemon wifi,' i think a heems video because i said heems was like blastoise, started to watch howard stern interview with henry rollins but i am hungry. getting ready to go eat pho now.

2:45–10PM: the main events:

- ate pho at 'pho ta' on 11th st

- drove by j.r.'s (bar where party animal would play later tonight)

- parked near south street to see dan at dan's store

- store closed

- walked to essene, bought chocolate chip scone

- walked to 'mostly books'

- walked to whole foods and i shat

- walked to rite aid where i got 'azo standard' (that's my vulnerable reveal of the day: it hurts me to pee after sex sometimes, it's not an STD, i get UTIs a lot, since i was like, eight years old, i don't know. burning urgency, extreme pee pain. think it's related to the distance between my asshole and vagina hole. maybe a flesh tunnel…i don't know. body conspiring against me. azo standard turns your pee bright red. okay. there you have it. secret is out.)

- walked to car

- gave kool a.d. one molly pill after party animal show

11:33PM: writing this about to watch 'da vinci code' will update later

MARCH 25, 2013

2:32AM: fell asleep during 'davinci code.' we kept pausing movie to make funny comments. we did that last night with 'the fighter' also, pausing to comment. i wanted our commentary to be filmed, both nights. ex-boyfriend is so funny. as soon as i posted thing from last night, ex-boyfriend read it in bed. i was getting dressed. seemed to make getting dressed difficult. said things about how it was difficult.

3:13AM: laying beside ex-boyfriend in bed, waiting for 'angels and demons' to download on my computer. he's looking at his ipad. i'm sleepy and not quite sober from nap. he just said 'there are six-hundred eleven-thousand, two-hundred ninety-six living people on wikipedia's 'living people' page.' as i was typing that he left the room.

3:45AM: ex-boyfriend returned with hot sauce and styrofoam box, said 'i put hot sauce on everything' as he got in bed. i picked up the calzone and said 'yeah, why do you always put hot sauce on everything? you're always making things so hot.' he laughed a little and said "why do you always put hot sauce on everything,' she said, holding a thing bigger than her face.'

4:06AM: now we're drinking whiskey, watching 'angels and demons.' shirley jumped onto the bed and started kneading me. i said 'shirley likes her men like she likes her whiskey: neat.' ex-boyfriend said 'i like my women like i like my whiskey: cold.' i said 'i like my women like i like my whiskey: aged for…over many years, in a barrel. an oak barrel. in kentucky,' vaguely aware of referencing a jack handey quote about women and coffee. ex-boyfriend laughed as if he was unaware of the quote.

4:30AM: we weren't making as many funny comments as last night. i said 'can you get me a glass of ice?' in a fran drescher voice. he rolled his eyes. heard the sink running and teeth-brushing sounds. he came back with an ice tray, making an over-the-top annoyed face. i said 'thank you. i'll always be your pope.' he said 'i don't want you, i just want cory,' and pulled over most of the covers. i said 'oh i see you've got your. your blankets, there.' he said 'here take this,' and transferred my computer from his lap onto mine. i was grinning. he said 'i hate you, you're so annoying.' i laughed like 'hehehehehehe.' he said 'hurry up, hurry up, come on.'

5:28AM: started re-reading liveblog after it became clear that ex-boyfriend was sleeping. he stirred in bed and saw 'angels and demons' and liveblog on-screen. i said 'i'll. i can just move this. into the other. i'll move this into the other room.' brushed teeth. ex-boyfriend rarely doesn't brush before bed and i got in the habit.

5:58AM: sitting on couch in living room. renewed interest in updating/ writing. shirley is curled up in a ball by my lower back. thought 'i know you don't know what you want out of life but you're 27 and some people know how to fly helicopters by now.'

7:35AM: i've been drinking 'i'm coconuts for you' out of the bottle and reading this on living room couch, next to a sleeping shirley. it is snowing and no longer nighttime. want a cigarette. not tired. i miss my apartment in baltimore. i was so happy then. there were things i was trying to do, that. i felt i was. trying. hoping. things were happening. there was hope. i was. how did i get so old.

here is what it says, exactly what it says, in the description area on the back of the 'i'm coconuts for you' 'original bartenders premium selection' bottle, reproducing the text exactly right now for you, so you understand:

ORIGINAL BARTENDERS

"I'M COCONUTS OVER YOU"

A Local Caribbean band played a laid-back melody they called "I'm Coconuts Over You." The club bartender loved it. He decided to make a drink which would go with music. Starting with extra fine aged Rum he added all natural coconut. Soon everyone in the club went wild. Hearing the band play and drinking "I'm Coconuts Over You."

Enjoy on ice with Cola.

it's just this thing: here it is. here it is, for anyone. that's how it introduces itself. this, in this way. it's. jesus, there's no way to talk about this without it sounding condescending, but what i feel is affection and sadness, towards a sad thing of the world. i want to be in jordan's car that morning we stayed up all night and picked mal up from work and went to whole foods. it was this fall. i miss them a lot. 'i'm coconuts over you' jesus goddamn fuck. need to be re-baptised or something.

3–4:15PM: woke thinking/dreaming i was talking to ex-boyfriend. asked if he wanted to go to the library and he said 'yes' and i went back to sleep. woke several times, unsure if we had been mid-conversation. saw him drinking whiskey. saw him enter bedroom with leftovers and say 'it's so coagulated' about the cheese. saw him enter bedroom with beer cans maybe twice.

5:40PM: ex-boyfriend walked into living room, where i'm sitting, wearing only gray sort-of boxer briefs with holes in the fabric and barely any elastic. he calls these his 'pretty panties.' he stood facing the window, staring affectedly catatonically with his flaccid penis out, like, tugging it. he said 'look at alvie, how alvie is sitting with his three legs like…he's sitting like in that movie. like the holy trinity.' alvie was leaning sexily on the arm of the chair, letting his legs extend, adding to the sexiness.

ex-boyfriend said things about his 'boner,' referencing a song, then said 'it's really sick when guys talk about boners like that. boners are gross. like, they actually talk about them like.' i said 'yeah it's weird that people…boners… they talk about them like that. you don't have a boner.' one of us said something about going to the library. he said 'yeah but like, jeopardy is going to be on at seven and…' and shrugged. i said 'yeah. jeopardy. let's not go.' i tugged his penis hard. he laughed. i said 'look out, i'm tugging.' he was laughing. i said 'i'm going to pull it off. look out.' he said 'remember when jordan earnestly tried to rip his dick off?' i said 'yeah that was good.' he left the room, saying something about me and nicolas cage and jordan ripping his 'dick… off' like how nicolas cage says 'i want to take his face…off' in 'face/off.'

5:45PM: ex-boyfriend said 'here peg, let me top you off all the way,' filling my mug with coffee that almost started spilling, 'now you'll have to lap at it.' i smiled and said 'lapping' or something. he said 'i'm at the point in my formspring where someone says they had sex with my one true love.' he is reading his old formspring in the bedroom, has been since i woke.

5:49PM: from the bedroom, ex-boyfriend said 'peg, i cut the cat's whisker's off.' i said 'no! on accident?' he said 'yeah. just. one on the right, it like, fell off.' i said 'that's okay, one time when i was little i cut them all off on purpose. my cat couldn't walk around.' he kind of laughed and said 'you're going to have to keep shirley in the little room.' pictured closet-like room at dad's apartment, where i'll stay with cats april 1st until i know where i'll live next. i said 'no, that won't happen, she will roam free. no matter what she will roam free.'

6:47PM: entered bedroom and propped myself against ex-boyfriend's legs. he was drinking and listening to 'fishkind,' a band he was in a few years ago, named after david fishkind. i said something about my liveblog and he made a face and put his hand through my hair but it got stuck. he pulled and i made a yelping noise. he said 'oh, come on.' seemed drunk. his hand returned to the same spot and he said 'let's just be nice.' i said 'yeah i want to be nice, you gotta stop pulling my hair though.' he made a face. i smiled. i felt bad when i was typing in the other room. unsure if i felt worse in the bedroom.

i said 'can you just hold me a minute.' he said 'yes but only if we listen to this.' he played a fishkind song: a few of his friends and him half-talking half-singing 'five-hundred twenty-five thousand people died in nine-eleven' over 'rape me' on acoustic guitar. i've heard it before. seemed sad to me, that he was drinking in bed and listening to it and reading his old formspring. he said 'i just wish i was here with my one true love.' i said 'oh, [person]?' he said 'yeah, [person]' wistfully, drunkenly. i said 'oh.' i looked at his calendar wall-hanging from 1975, made of a some kind of light towel or canvas-like fabric. i said 'i'm sorry i couldn't be better.' he said 'it's okay. you have people you like more too.' i said 'yeah, but. i don't know.' he said 'i need to be with someone who i can like, control more. like, i want to be completely open with the person, but i also want distance from them. your openness seems like an attack on your readers.' i said 'wait, do you mean…are you talking about my writing or me, the person?' he did something with his arms and shook his head and his tone changed and he said 'i mean 'what is a person,' come on, come the fuck on, like…' and i said 'what do you mean, what are you talking about? my openness is…i attack you, you feel?' he said something about him saying things that have hurt me, or something, and wanting to be with someone who he could say those things to more and it not mattering to them. i said 'i understand that…i feel…yeah, i don't like it when you've talked about other people you'd rather be with while you're with me.' he said 'but why not? it's not like you don't have other people.' i said 'i know. it just doesn't feel good. like, it doesn't feel good to hear. i wouldn't want to just, out of nowhere, just like, start talking to you about someone i'm interested in, as if i wished you were them or something.' felt myself about to cry, leaning on my arm, not wanting to cry. i thought 'look at him, it will make you either cry or not cry.' looked and didn't. he said 'well great. good for you' and kind of rolled his eyes. i said 'you…but you just asked me…i only said because you asked me…what?' he said 'we were having this conversation a year ago.' i didn't say anything.

7:15PM: something weird was happening with jeopardy. bad reception. ex-boyfriend said 'i'll put the BASF on it' and propped a VHS tape that says 'BASF' on the antenna. something happened to jeopardy. it was clear that the station had made a mistake, like, with the timing. they showed the beginning of the episode again. ex-boyfriend said 'it's definitely the station, not our TV' and 'i wonder what…what could they possibly do, how can they possibly fix this?' i felt distracted or like…i wasn't as invested in this.

7:30PM: talked about being hungry. i wanted pizza or something we couldn't make with our few remaining food items. ex-boyfriend said things about the 'perfectly good rice and beans' leftovers, which i didn't want, and knew he knew i wouldn't. he said 'but you wouldn't want that now, would you.' he said 'and what is that, uh, you got that cole slaw in there? from last night?' i said 'i don't want to eat it, it was like, sweet. vanilla-y. it was weird, i don't want it.' he seemed disapproving, performing disapproval, argumentative or something, drunk, i don't know. especially competitive during jeopardy, pointed out my 'wrong answers,' like i was stupid, and acted like a sore loser when his answer was wrong.

7:40PM: i said 'you're being drunk, like, antagonistically, i don't like it, i'm going in the other room.' sitting in bedroom now.

7:51PM: ex-boyfriend stood in bedroom doorway, said 'oh. frowning and minimizing the screen.' i said 'what?' he said 'you were frowning, then you minimized something.' i turned the screen to show him a google search result window, and said 'no, i touched this,' then maximized the msword window and said, 'why, do you want to read this?' he said something with the effect of 'hell no.' he tilted his head and kind of did this dancing-in-place thing he does, like, a snaky dance, i call it 'circles' sometimes. he said 'come on peggy. i just want to be nice.' i was smiling, feeling pressured to smile. i said 'i want to be nice too.' he took his underwear off and rubbed his ass on the foot of the bed and used a funny voice to say 'look at me, i'm a casper. casss-per.' watching him doing this was, i felt, intended to suddenly make me feel better, but because it wasn't working, and that i felt pressured to feel better, i felt worse, and stupid for feeling worse. i said 'casper, i see.' he stopped and said '[his name] thinks megan feels uncomfortable, needlessly.' i smiled. i said 'megan thinks sometimes [his name] does things to provoke her when he's drunk and then she wants to be alone.' he said '[his name] doesn't mean to provoke her.' i said 'i know you don't mean to. i think i just feel like. i wish i would've done more today, i don't like hearing about all the other people you like more than me, i don't like how you act when you're drunk and i'm not, we're not on the same. um. i don't know. maybe i'll be drunk later and it'll be okay. i'm having a bad day, i'm just sensitive right now, it's not going to be good if i'm around you right now.' somewhere around 'not going to be good,' he gestured like 'done. i'm done. unreasonable, this situation is unmanageable' and left. unsure what was upsetting: that i agreed and felt the same about him, or. actually can't think of anything else, that must be it.

now he's being loud/heavy with the feet. stomping on purpose.

8:15–9pm: main events:

Heard tv go off and him sit next to me

Talked about moving logistics

He said Sunday is our last day here

Looked at 1975 calendar wall hanging, two tears

'Sunday'

Would move things Thursday

I was stupid for not knowing if he meant we should pack mon tues weds

Said I don't know I didn't plan, how could he expect me to know what he was thinking

Said it was better for me to just go

At some point referenced my period not being here yet

He said 'unless there's…one of our little friends'

Unclear if he meant I was pregnant by someone else, 'a friend,' or that I had another 'friend' in me like I had before

Dressed, feeling bad

'I'm just going to go back to Maryland, it'll be better, I have a printer there'

Asked me to jump over bed to 'show me you're a gug gug'

Better to be away when I'm like this, sensitive, before my period

He said 'oh come on don't you just want to be nice' and I said 'yeah, that's why I'm leaving'

At some point I was laying on top of him and crying and he said 'look at you with your quarter-sized nose holes and your silver dollar eyes. They don't make silver dollars much anymore'

'I want someone to say mean things to me'

I said 'I don't want to do that,' then 'well okay I think you can act insensitive when you're drunk'

He immediately made excuse/seemed to want to argue

'I don't want to do that'

Corrected me about how I said he got girl's phone number IMPORTANT: HE GAVE HER HIS PHONE NUMBER, DID NOT ASK FOR HERS, I MISREMEMBERED that and number of people in car, he said I was exaggerating, I said no I want to be accurate and maybe idea of picking up the mom made me feel like six ppl in five person car, he rolled his eyes and said 'well it certainly makes you seem [something about thinking I was trying to garner sympathy/make him look bad]'

I said 'I want to hear factual corrections, is there anything else like that, like, factually'

I was sitting on top of him

I said 'are there other factual things?'

I said 'it's actually funnier, I forgot you gave her your phone number, so and like, in your line of thinking that makes you look worse or whatever, like in your line of thinking what actually happened would be the thing I'd lie about, to make you look worse'

He said 'oh and let's not forget about good writing, being honest, how it's actually better writing to not manipulate the audience' (IMPORTANT: HE DID NOT SAY THE WORD 'MANIPULATE,' I DON'T REMEMBER WHAT HE SAID EXACTLY, 'MUSN'T MISREPRESENT HIM')

I said 'fuck this don't talk to me about better writing, fycj this shit I don't want to hear this from you again'

Gathered deodorant and phone in rapid comedic succession without looking at him, darting my arm back into room to thing I wanted from dresser

On floor of car: his jacket and water bottle

Walked inside thinking 'he'll think I'm coming back to apologize, I'm not even going to say anything, HA' or something similarly stupid

Silently placed jacket/bottle on table and left

Driving now

9:49pm: suddenly aware of hunger. peeled orange. Might cover up cigarette smell, good. Remember yesterday when ex-boyfriend said he thought it was gross when people ate citrus fruits, and my recent switching to only buying oranges around him when I want fruit because he has said things about how pre-cut fruit in containers was 'poisonous,' because the cutting leading to oxygenating areas of the fruit and them decaying faster.

10:22pm: no one seemed to be in apartment. Combed hair with fingers in full-length mirror. Looked for 'most visible spot' to place ex-boyfriend's phone. Alvie made chirping sounds. He found me and walked in an infinity symbol-pattern between my feet. When I kneeled to pet him he rolled on his back and pushed his body into the areas my hands touched him. Thought 'petting me back.' Stood in kitchen with lights off and drank remaining morning coffee. Ex-boyfriend emailed that he was at the library and I could come if I wanted 'stanky leg' but if not that's fine, thanked me for 'going above and beyond,' bringing back phone. Sitting at kitchen table now, unsure what to do. Took a picture of Shirley on my leg and Alvie looking 'caught in the act.'

10:51pm: called mom to say I'm coming home. Responded to a text message. Fed cats. Snorted most of remaining heroin. Watched little particles puff in the lights and mix with dust.

10:57PM: heard keys and the first floor door and decided that was my cue to leave. listened to a few more people enter building, but none of their sounds felt like the 'lucky sound' to cue me to leave. opened door to ex-boyfriend, grinning and carrying a black plastic bag. exchanged sitcom-y looks and variations of 'well, look at who it is' as neither of us followed nor lead the other, i think, to the spot where it felt right to stop and hug.

he said 'so peg, you peg much while i was gone?' i said 'yeah. i'm pegging you right now. you think that's your dick but that's actually how hard i'm pegging you. you don't even know.'

11–11:30PM: sat side-by-side on kitchen table bench, talking normally but something felt different. one of us joked about my parents making a crucial oversight about birth control—something they could mistakenly, but very possibly truly, think. i said 'the apple doesn't fall far from the tree.' ex-boyfriend paused for a moment. he said 'japanese people don't just say 'apple.' their word for 'apple' is like, 'the most visible apple one sees after it has grown and fallen from apple tree.''

talked about the pricing and label of his miller milwauke's best 40oz. i said 'is the. why is it blue, is it like, supposed to tell us it's an ice thing? cold? arctic?' he smiled and said 'huh. yeah, what the hell is that?'

11:30PM: in the fridge is a plastic container of chicken wing tips ex-boyfriend saved from a night we made hot wings, weeks ago. i said 'i think this is also part of what's been making it stink.' he agreed. he said 'should we just dump it in the water at penn treaty park too?' i said 'yeah' and 'dumping things' or something.

11:34PM: sat on toilet and called mom. saw blood on underpants and said 'i got my period' excitedly to ex-boyfriend, watching me from kitchen. he gave me a head check. licked my lips at him and pretended to be aroused by the period blood while i peed. talked in a normal voice to mom while continuing to make 'nasty porno face.' ex-boyfriend feigned disgust. or, i guess it could've been real disgust at my feigned disgusting behavior. so in either case, a degree of inauthenticity on both our parts. authentically inauthentic.

exited bathroom holding tampon applicator and wrapper. somehow it was decided we would throw the tampon accessories out with the rotten wings. gathered wings and tampon accessories in a black plastic bag. in less of a hurry to leave this time.

MARCH 26, 2013

12:04AM: ex-boyfriend said 'i have to pee.' i said 'pee on me.' he said 'okay' and unzipped his pants. i said 'no, pee on the wings, in the wing container. it'll be sick.' he peed in the wing container until it was full. i re-capped the container. he said 'you have to like, punt it. drop-kick it into the water.' i said 'dropkick murphys.' was grinning a lot. it smelled sour. tried to take pictures but it wasn't working. ex-boyfriend said 'yeah, get a picture of it by like, in front of that sick apartment building. philly is so sick.' he said something about my shoes, offered his shoe instead, said 'i can tie it really tight on your foot.' i said i would just use my shoes, 'my flats.' we said 'flats' a few times, chuckling. he said 'can your phone like, take video?' i said 'no there's not enough room. i could get. my computer? should i do that?' he paused and said 'whatever man, it's your thing.' felt something in me drop. it wasn't as fun, thinking it was 'my thing.' asked him to take a picture of me punting the container. he said 'no, i feel like i want to witness the moment fully.' i said 'yeah. yeah. okay.' he said 'no, stand up here on this thing, so you won't worry about falling over.' i stood next to him on the cement fixture. i said 'okay. this is it.' he said 'okay.' he tried to take a picture of me holding the pee-wings. i dropped the container and missed kicking it. heard it hit the rocks. ex-boyfriend stood. it was quiet. he said 'well. that's it.' i said 'yup. that's it.' he put his 40 back in bookbag.

walking back to the car, i said 'it wasn't as urgent as the watermelon, was it? something was different about this time.' he didn't say anything.

12:30-1AM: expressed desire for 'sparkly drink.' ex-boyfriend played a funny chief keef song. i said there should be a video game like 'street fighter' but with rappers, you fight all the rap feuds. ex-boyfriend said that existed.

passed a 'MARCH MADNESS SPECIALS: BEER WINGS SHRIMP' applebees sign. i said 'close your eyes. guess what three words applebees lists for 'march madness specials." ex-boyfriend said 'coors light draft?' i said 'beer wings shrimp.' pulled into wawa parking lot. ex-boyfriend said 'ah, skrim.' i said 'any time i ask you a question like that, like, a march madness food question: know that one of the answers will always be shrimp.'

ordered a BLT and ex-boyfriend ordered another sandwich. stood by sandwich area, waiting. i said 'there are no video games where you're like, the bad guy. you're just doing bad stuff.' ex-boyfriend said 'yeah, well. you do bad stuff but they always make you relatable.' i said 'yeah. or, no. grand theft auto, kind of. just doing bad stuff.'

he said 'yeah, there's no game where you just like, set stuff on fire for no reason.' i said 'no serial killers.' he said 'yeah, grand theft auto i guess.'

i said 'i was so mad at you earlier.' he said 'i know, why were you so mad?' i said 'you were drunk. or. well.' he said 'when?' i said 'like, all of today.' he kind of laughed and said 'oh yeah' and nodded.

1AM–2:30AM: ate sandwiches. TV froze on an image of a shark. antenna recalibrated. i said 'sharks are like DMX, like, exactly.' ex-boyfriend laughed and said 'yeah, exactly.' i said 'their faces, just, everything. they're so mad.' watched 'the office,' part of 'the simpsons' and 'seinfeld.' went to bedroom and gave blowjob. held him until i think he was asleep.

4:32AM: have been sitting at kitchen table looking at internet for some time. snorted remaining heroin in bathroom. ex-boyfriend has been sleeping since i've been here but i still don't want him to know. he'll know tomorrow, or whenever he reads this. just. don't want him to see me doing this right now.

4:36AM: heard pee wee herman-like groaning, then a water bottle.

5:09AM: eyes droopy. crossing involuntarily sometimes. eating orange.

5:30AM: ex-boyfriend is naked about 15 feet away from me in bathroom, peeing with his hands by his sides. asked if he remembered the apple thing. he said 'birth control apple doesn't fall far from the tree.'

5:57AM: annoyed by loud yawning noises and alvie's chirping and shirley's noises and cats chasing each other noises. want to smoke a cigarette and sleep. 'big day tomorrow.'

5:59AM: tossed orange peel at alvie's head. predictable response. i would've done the same thing.

6:42AM: retrieved keys from bedroom and walked away downstairs. ex-boyfriend said 'peg? where you going?' i said 'out to have a cigarette.' he said 'you done writing?' i said 'no, why, am i keeping you awake?' he said 'no, just wondering.' i paused. i said 'i can go somewhere if i'm keeping you awake.' he said 'no. no. you're not. don't.' i said 'are you sure, you're like, yawning a lot.' he said 'yeah no it's fine.'

6:46AM: smoking cigarette in my car. reversed car to accommodate truck making a delivery to corner store. truck didn't move.

7:34AM: sun rose. macbook resting on storage console near gear shift. second cigarette.

8:35AM: walked inside and updated this. heard ex-boyfriend's phone alarm and went to bedroom. he was naked ontop of the covers, said something about how i was 'smokey robinson,' smoking cigarettes in my car for two hours. i said 'i only had two,' and that i'd been 'making words go type-y type.' he said 'i'm going on my bus to new jersey in an hour' playfully, like a kid bragging about a cavity. in a similar tone i said, 'o-hhh yeah, i forgot. guess i'll stay awake so i can drive you to that bus stop.' he said 'o-hhh yeah.'

started shivering big time. put on knee-length pink t-shirt and got under the covers. ex-boyfriend grinned at me mischievously and started masturbating. i swatted at the penis like how cats swat at things on the floor. he laughed, said 'no, get away' and 'i got this one' or something. watched him for a while, unsure where i was looking, thought things like 'is he joking, should i help or go away, i want sex because i wish he was trying to have sex with me instead.' rested chin on hand, said 'you know? it's just one of those moments. one of those…you want to remember it.' he laughed. eventually helped with my mouth. when he came he made a noise like 'waking mid-laugh from what you didn't know was a dream.'

i went to hold him but it seemed to hurt him to be touched. sometimes he acts like that. he handed me a water bottle and said 'adam humphreys,' then ''woodcutters' by thomas bernhard.' i said 'oh yes, 'watercolors'' thoughtfully. he laughed. he said 'it's really basic when people make fun of nice people. like that painter guy, bob. they make fun of them by making them seem like they're evil. you know?' i said 'bob ross?' he said 'yeah.' i said 'yeah, that's like. that's an SNL thing to do.' he said 'i think they did that on SNL.' laid quietly for a few moments. he sat fast and said 'okay, okay, shower time, shower, come on peg, don't you want to shower,' walking away. i looked at him in interested disbelief, said 'i mean, yeah.' felt like i was watching 'the fisher king,' that movie, for most of this. like i was in a scene from 'the fisher king.'

stood and felt overcome with nausea. walked faster. vomited maybe four big vomit units into toilet. said 'huh. how is that BLT still in there?' ex-boyfriend said 'gross.' i said 'i know.' he asked why i threw up and i said ''cause i did heroin, i think.' he made an insane jim carey smiling face and said 'oh noooooo.' he said 'in your car?' i said 'no-ooo, in here.' he said 'oh nooooo' and clapped and sort of danced in place in a circle. i sat at the kitchen table shivering. it's not actually that cold in here, i don't think. ex-boyfriend turned on the shower and i got in maybe two minutes after him. he rubbed soap on his face and with his eyes mostly closed, said 'i think i have like, they're doing something to me, i'm a social experiment, where i end up pickling my insides because they made the world so bad.' i said 'huh? you're. wait, why are they doing that to you?' he said 'like how they have veal in cages, getting tender and stuff. they're doing that to me but like, my cage is just the badness of the world, and it makes me pickle my insides with alcohol?' i said 'oh, i see. yeah.' one of us started singing the smashing pumpkins song that's like 'despite all my rage i am still just a rat in a cage.' i said 'it's actually: 'despite all my suede, i am still just a rat in a cage.' it's about this rat. he just has so much suede, you see? but he's still' ex-boyfriend laughed. no urges to dominate the hot water stream this time, though he seemed to kind of let me.

9:10am: toweled dry, applied coconut oil and clothes. sat at the kitchen table and typed in liveblog document while ex-boyfriend moved from room to room, packing for new jersey. exchanged casual nonsense-like comments sometimes. he's letting me borrow his library card so i can print things today. watched him write his name and access code on a small piece of paper and thought 'considerate [his name], kind [his name]' in 'giant misunderstood lummox on public display' voice.

i said 'it's impossible to include everything.' he said 'yeah, i mean. you can't.' he said something about not wanting to read liveblog anymore because it was 'a waste of his time.' i said 'do you feel bad reading it?' he said 'well. of course i feel bad when i waste my time.' i said 'what is it that you're wasting exactly, is there anything specific,' aware of his change in posture and lack of eye contact. remembered what i wrote about 'how can people talk to someone willfully looking away' and felt like it would be kind of me to stop talking. was also provoked by his tone. not angry-provoked, curious-provoked. like how it would feel if someone had said, 'there are things about me that are fascinating, that i will never tell you, and i'll never tell you why i won't tell you.'

the way he stressed 'waste.' i don't know. this is related to why we wouldn't have worked. sometimes it feels like he's making a special effort to avoid saying what's bothering him. if changing the subject doesn't work, he'll say something acidic as a kind of warning about how little will be accomplished by talking about whatever it is. his face will look defeated and anguished. i've wondered if maybe he doesn't think i'm smart enough to get it. like it wouldn't be worth his time to condescend to someone not as smart as him. it's less that this causes me to feel 'stupid,' more of a sad reminder that there is a limit to how much i'll ever know about him. have sensed this quality of his since the beginning, but then it was more of an afterthought. he was so warm and bright and fun to talk to and sometimes i'd see this sadness about him, like something i'd learned alone and maybe intentionally forgotten, that i wanted to protect.

9:10-9:30am: ex-boyfriend made 'hurry up' gestures. i said 'oh, that's right, all of those important places you need to be. you're on your way to big things, i forgot.' he ignored or didn't seem to hear me and i was glad.

ex-boyfriend said 'hey peg, thank you in advance,' for driving him, I think. I said 'oh. Hm. Well. I don't actually know if I'm going to want to say 'you're welcome' in advance. So. This might. Hm. Do I?' he made noises like he impatiently understood.

Drove down 4th st. We talked about my first cats, Puffy and Bluebell. He said 'let me get this straight: you had two cats that were named after stuffed animal dragons you already had? You named the cats…because of that?' I said yeah. He asked me other stuffed animal names. I rattled them off like the real 'old sage' in town, who knows all the hot spots and wants to show you a good time. Exbf was laughing a lot. I said 'nooooo, soon you'll be gone and I'll be all alone. Over…there.' He said things I should do: get boxes to 'at least fill them with books, so you can look at that and think: 'I did that,'' go see 'spring breakers' alone. I started telling a story and he sighed. Interrupted myself to say 'don't worry, I'll get to the interesting part.' He said 'oh my god, really?'

Said 'I can't believe I threw up out of nowhere like that. Did you put some-thing in your come?' he raised his eyebrows and tilted his head down and said 'yeah, peg.' I said 'like, more than normal? Did you put more heroin than normal in your come?' parked without paying meter outside Wawa. He wanted orange juice. Said goodbye in Wawa.

10:09am: shivering in whole foods parking garage. Ex-boyfriend is on the bus. Seems like liveblog is deteriorating. My sense of time. Something. Tenses.

10:33am: walking around whole foods. Struggling not to show physical shivering. Teeth are chattering like, unstoppably, it feels good to let them. The vibrating chattering shivering thing is designed to help me somehow. My ideal self is a giant vibrating head vibrating so intensely you cant even tell it's vibrating, it makes you feel like you're vibrating, it's just this giant head floating in another dimension.

Passed a woman freely sampling trail mix from bulk containers, nodding excitedly, like she wanted to say 'that's a great point you just made.' Or that they were a new kind of music performed for the first time in her life, that she would then stop everything and rearrange her life to tour with them.

Bought two green juices, a coconut water, four-pack steaz zero calorie energy drinks, large container papaya. Bought mint green nail polish and a grapefruit candle because I wanted to see the sentence 'bought mint green nail polish and a grapefruit candle.' Thought 'small kindness of consumerism.' In car now, teeth chattering and shivering still.

10:46am: wanted another cigarette three drags into this one. Would it be good to just smoke five simultaneously? Is that what I really want? Is that what…all of this…is that the thing that's going to make me stop wanting anything? It was actually 10:47 when I wrote that, thought 'it's okay, it's accurate, it's always 10:46 somewhere. 10:46: Beer o'clock.'

11:28am: impulsively pulled into Dunkin donuts. Ordered an everything bagel toasted with cream cheese and medium coffee. Remembered meeting Colin at a Dunkin donuts in Rockaway Park and felt ashamed. He was eating a multigrain bagel. Letting things I want skip away from me. Wish I had gotten multigrain, knew everything would have too much flavor for me right now. Have just been driving around since whole foods. Saw Ana Carrete posted a picture of food in a McDonald's bag on instagram and thought 'get chic fil a, it's okay, you deserve it' then passed chic fil a 20 minutes later and knew I didn't want it. Pictured bagel ex-boyfriend had the other day. Looked so good. Dunkin donuts. Sat in parked car. Bit bagel like it was a sandwich. Was correct: it had too much flavor for right now.

Re-read parts of this. I seem more interesting and better adjusted when not around ex-boyfriend. A little worried about this. Feel something crippling me right now, knowing soon I'll be returning 'home' to a place where there are mostly memories, scattered evidence of how I've been malfunctioning the past few days, year. I'm nostalgic for three days ago. In three days I'll feel nostalgic for now. Keep smoking cigarettes just because they're here, they're preventing me from arriving somewhere.

11:34am: seems way too bright outside. the sky looks broken, clouds are like an oily soap film on water or something. nothing looks right. just noticed christmas wreath on a light on my building. seems like the only appropriate thing. like 'what the fuck…' is the only appropriate thing. feeling, as usual, unable to complete tasks i said i'd do. like what is supposed to happen to me today? i'll write a letter about how i'm good and want to live in an apartment building? then i'll…print it? somehow? somewhere? the library? then i'll…find a fed ex? park my car? send it? it's…already this late, the application? yeah? then i'll send a check to the truck school, for my loans, three months of loan payments? then i'll get more birth control? then i'll get boxes? then i'll put all my books and things from this apartment into the boxes? the boxes will be moved out of here on sunday? then i'll write things that aren't this? then i'll…respond to emails? i'll be talking to people, as i'm doing all of these things?

12–2:30PM: extreme tiredness. tried to screenshot the reflection of my face in computer and was shocked a little, to not see myself in the screenshot, like that meant i'm dead maybe. remembered things about 'real life.'

2:30PM: overcome with foreign urge to masturbate. remember sam cooke requesting me to write something about masturbating, was aware of like, 'how will i remember this' as i was looking for things to masturbate to, which maybe effected the length of time i felt it took to find something 'good.' i was also extremely tired. think i fell asleep with eyes open and woke twice via hypnic jerk. didn't feel aroused when masturbating, except when i was about to orgasm, then i'd be like 'what the fuck, my body could do this all along?' masturbated a few times in a row with varied frequencies between the orgasms, to like, test if i had been able to do it all along. i could do it all along.

3:30PM: saw images of things i masturbated to when i closed eyes. a lot of cunnilingus happening behind my eyes. felt annoyed by them, like they were pop-up ads of porn and i wanted to swat them away so i could sleep. set alarm for 4:04PM.

6:17PM: gian was wearing a white robe and speaking at a college graduation. he was also the…like…what do you call the smartest person in the class? they're famous, kind of? for like…their grades are so good…anyway. the college graduation was at a coliseum. i was the only non-college person there, not wearing a robe. gian gave his speech (which wasn't too long, it was really good, there were going to be like, headlines about it like the DFW speech [was going to write 'when DFW graduated college' as if that's when he…just laughed and a snot flew out…still waking, jesus]).

here is the thing.

everyone cheered gian and i watched him walk out of the coliseum with his arms up in the air. he was walking towards me. he was wearing sunglasses. HERE IS THE THING:

as he's walking out, an announcement comes onscreen. the announcement was funded by will smith's family. it showed family video images of will smith's kids, will smith as a kid, his entire family as children, and there was a voiceover that said something to the extent of 'while gian's speech was great, we have come to an agreement that he did not include children enough. we want to say these things about children to our graduates: watch three minutes of any 'twilight' movie every day. if you can't read 'JIF' on your peanut butter you need a new blender' [everyone laughs], [several things i don't remember].'

hugged gian and said 'that was the best thing ever, i can't believe you did that and you aren't like, people aren't mobbing you right now.' he said 'they're not mobbing me because of the will smith thing.' he was also my best friend from high school, katie, like morphing into her sometimes. he asked what i did today and i said while simultaneously recalling this in my memory, like, actually unaware of what i was saying/what i had done that day until i had said it out loud. there is some name for this thing i'm talking about, they do it in movies, i'm doing it to an extent with you right now…maybe there isn't a name for it, i forget. here is what i told gian i did that day: 'i was running, then i started to run faster, then [image of me transforming into a 'fleet' of like 16 cats spinning over and over each other, extremely fast, like a wheel, going faster than traffic and in the opposite direction of traffic].' i said 'this was all on the way here. i thought i was really going to make it, to graduation, on time. then [image of me as the spinning cat-wheel frozen in front of a person on a bike in a lane of traffic between cars, then me dodging out of the way 'matrix'-style slow motion]. then [image of me getting hit by a bus, also like, really feeling that i was dying as this image played. looked for 'ruins of me' under the tires. driver's side door opened. saw my hand open it from the inside with 'comic timing.' i emerged from the driver's side door without any legs. i was just a floating torso and head and arms, floating at my normal height. i waved and smirked like 'that's all folks'].' gian said 'whoa, that's some real shit' and looked affected. i said 'yeah so that's why i was late.' there was something else about people from the internet and sex. i said something in my liveblog, in the dream, about someone from the internet who i want to have sex with, then deleting it really fast in the dream. woke after hitting snooze for around two hours.

6:30PM: woke lightly a few times, like, mentally typing how i'd say the dream, what happened before the dream, how i'd make this list to discreetly include [masturbating thing] and [person i want to have sex with thing]. peed, felt more awake. brought papaya and energy drink to bed. g-chatted ex-boyfriend.

ex-boyfriend and i used to watch 'whitney' and 'jeopardy' when it was slow at his work, and call each other at commercial breaks to talk about the show. will miss this. he g-chatted:

Ex-boyfriend: jeopardy starts soon

me: hell yeah

Ex-boyfriend: might have to eat wih my gates oarents tho
hated parents

94

um
what u do
u skeep?

me: yeah
L
like 3:30-now

Ex-boyfriend: my ne true loves on r u chattin wirh her J

me: ;)
yeah she's sitting next to me
we've been talking about you
and your cool dick
she says 'i miss your cool dick kisskisskisskisskisskiss!!!'
i wanna watch jeop
i eating papaya mon
bati boy
Sent at 6:58 PM on Tuesday

Ex-boyfriend: bati
pennsylvanianlottery
where u gat papi, papi
let itngo bad we can throw it in lake nummy

me: lookin for jeop
fuckin
mexico
one plate at a time
fu kin

Ex-boyfriend: (an actual lake in NJ)
chan 6

me: OH I GOT IT
we got a canadian on our hands
saskatchewan

Ex-boyfriend: canadian girl
regina

me: yeah
yeah
rhymes with…

Ex-boyfriend: ah, green short

luck of the brogue
im gonna focus now peqce

me: kk me too
alex likes to start off the week with a big win, he is nice
Sent at 7:01 PM on Tuesday
me: jesus that text unscrambler thing. 'trout: that's the fish'

Ex-boyfriend: rewindind to catch stuff i missed

me: oic

Ex-boyfriend: im a strug
oh great, got it
worked 7 hours today on doddly affairs
u twlk to dad?

me: nah
i'm a bad dog today
call dad tonight

Ex-boyfriend: o???.
oic

me: i just went gug gug
jeop back

Ex-boyfriend: datong websites peace

me: the guy looks like real estate agent
peace
Sent at 7:07 PM on Tuesday

7:07PM: christine, a contestant from regina, saskatchewan, visited alex trebek's hometown of sudberry, ontario when she was a child. alex asked if she remembered anything. she said 'why yes, alex, i did!' and talked about deciding not to be a miner after visiting a nickel mine, but she enjoyed the science center. alex looked pleased. i think alex is a good person. he said 'i like to start the week with a big win.'

alex said 'christine! you knew this! be audacious! go again!' christine kept flinching when she knew the answer but rachel or the other guy would buzz in first. alex says things he thinks no one hears, i think, like 'the nineties: a decade not far away from now' and 'trout: that's the fish' and 'yes, 'show-boat,' which was filmed right here in this studio.'

christine lost. here is the rest of the gchat:

96

me: knew rachel would only do 1000

Ex-boyfriend: i hate rachel
alex doesnt care about cathedral arches

me: she had to say 'weigh'
'what is weigh'
she was right thoguh
yeah i know, he doesn't
he cares about the big nickel
in sudberry
he just wants to hear about the science center from his hometown
sudberry ontario

Ex-boyfriend: what was about weigh

me: anchors
and decisions
forget category name

Ex-boyfriend: oh yeah
words ending in gh

me: yeah
i liked the scrambled fish
the fish unscrambler
Sent at 7:13 PM on Tuesday
me: imagine how much slower it would be if the audience clapped
after every answer

Ex-boyfriend: lo
l
mom knew Brigadune

me: dayng
mama [mom's name]
big [mom's name] in tht ehouse
knowing brigadune
i knew 'elf'
rachel did 2000 that time

Ex-boyfriend: yeah and got it wrong

me: yeah

Ex-boyfriend: Steamnoat

what a twat

me: hehehe
she's a real steamboat

Ex-boyfriend: kind of hope she wins for a long time

me: she's a real stanley steamer
yeah…
i kind of like her
i like her long neck
and her something
that little somethign she has
medieval arches
that's the pizza i ate
at mom's

Ex-boyfriend: enjoy hating her

me: dr. oetker
yeah
wish there was always the fish unscrambler

Ex-boyfriend: diet stuff and fropiz

me: instead of a 3rd contestant

Ex-boyfriend: same lol

me: fish unscrambler

Ex-boyfriend: Hripms

me: hmmmmm.
SKRIMS
i think the answer is:
mt everest
u?
lol
;p;
oops
thought he made a huge typo
bye rachel
i hate that guy who won
internet dating champ

Ex-boyfriend: imthoight it was ISS too

dimmer
peace

me: pace
Sent at 7:27 PM on Tuesday

Ex-boyfriend: im a charter wchool vice principal
Sent at 7:51 PM on Tuesday

8:02PM: TV has been on at a low volume while i've been typing. people in spandex leotards and face paint are jumping from a high platform into a pool in a neither competitive nor synchronized manner. like, twenty people.

8:48PM: recorded video tour of apartment and uploaded to youtube. now in living room, smoking cigarette. it's okay that i didn't do anything today. i'll do things tomorrow. using today as negative reinforcement for tomorrow.

10:37PM: ate three or four bites of hot ass leftovers. enduring hot ass acid reflux. alvie burned his tail on a candle and ran. phone is making noises. TV is on mute. feel like i'm in a waiting room.

man's voice coming from downstairs just yelled, 'i told you to fucking [muffled] when he [muffled] the goddamned [muffled].' a door slammed.

11:12PM: selected 'more comfortable and so better chances of outrunning whoever's chasing me' shoes instead of 'red shoes' for cigarette-garnering journey from apartment to parking spot and back.

MARCH 27, 2013

1:20AM: going to change up the game. really. um. this is really going to happen. so, in grad school, my dad and his friend motivated themselves to finish their dissertations by agreeing to mail one $100 check to the nixon administration for every day late.

so.

here is what i must do by tomorrow 12AM, this is my 'dissertation:'

- return attorney's phone call about accident settlement i'm receiving

- write and print cover letter at library

- mail apartment application binder

- mail book packages

- call dad about getting keys to storage unit thursday

- refill birth control

- pack one box

- shower

- drink kale smoothie

here is what happens if i fail to complete ONE of these tasks, this is my 'nixon fund:'

when i receive the accident settlement, i will have 50% of the bills printed and set them on fire in a trash can.

the settlement—the last i've heard—is slightly more than what i had in my savings account this fall.

i don't want to talk about how long it took to spend. the sum of money, without 50% of its bills destroyed, is enough to 'start being a person again,' for a comfortable, in my view, amount of time, as i settle into a job, a more stable routine, a life that allows me to envision a future for myself, less commas, etc.

the stakes are very high.

these are very high stakes.

OH SHIT I HAVE TO ADD A STAKE, HEIGHTENED SHORT-TERM STAKE, SO YOU WILL KNOW ABOUT THE LONG-TERM THING IN CASE I STOP LIVEBLOGGING BEFORE THE LONG-TERM THING—

if i fail to complete any task on the list i will post a picture of my naked ass 'as is' on this liveblog.

oh, that's nothing, you say? you say this is mere child's play?

THE ASS CHEEKS WILL BE SPREAD.

now i know people tend to enjoy pictures of women's asses. most people. or. i guess most people would find the pictures interesting, at least. some people, not most people. okay. but consider this: i have my period, so if i fail to shower…that's all. just consider this. i'm sorry in advance. now you will be rooting for me maybe.

i am dreading this so hard and i am so excited. so excited about dreadful tomorrow. such high stakes. jesus. i'm completely serious about both of these things. if i fail to complete the tasks and fail to complete my punishments, any person has the right to kill me. this is my will, i'm saying this, this can be legally binding: if i ever end up murdered by a person, i am hereby decreeing it 'not their fault,' if that does anything—i do not want them to be punished. i wouldn't want that anyway. but. just so the world knows, if it makes any difference—if they killed me it would be less like 'murder' and more like 'performing a civic duty.'

i'm not kidding. i know this sounds funny or whatever but i'm not kidding. GOODNIGHT, INTERNET.

LOOK OUT.

FOR TOMORROW.

BABY'S DAY OUT TOMORROW. A REAL B.D.O. TOMORROW, B.D.O. OF MONUMENTAL PROPORTIONS. TAKING MYSELF TO…TOWN. MAKING MYSELF THE MAYOR. OF THE TOWN. THERE IS A TOWN, BY THE WAY. WHEN EX-BOYFRIEND AND MOM ARE AWAY THE SHITHEAD COMES OUT TO PLAY. UFF. TRY AND MESS. B.D.O. 2013.

SIGNING OFF,
YOUR LITTLE BITCHES FOREVER,
LEGALLY BINDINGLY YOURS,
ME AND DUNKIN DONUTS COFFEE CUP

6:04AM: this is not off to a good start. sometimes if i'm alone and i'm supposed to be going to sleep i get 'the fear.' big reveal thing: i slept in my parents' bed at least once a week until i was maybe 12 years old. if i wasn't sleeping in their bed, they let me sleep on a sleeping bag on the floor. when i was a baby i would cry and not sleep. when i got older i wouldn't cry but still couldn't sleep. remember watching 'mash' re-runs and infomercials on the couch around age 8, with the volume low so my parents wouldn't hear.

remember there being 'events.' after giving up/giving in to me, parents would be like, 'maybe we'll try to make megan sleep in her bed again, wanna try again meg?' i'd be like 'yeah let's do this.' they'd be like 'okay, how about the fifth of july?'

this is the routine that needed to be established for me to be able to sleep in my bed:

1. say goodnight to all my 'friends' (in my memory there was like, a wall of stuffed animals almost, filling half of my bed).

2. either parent reads three storybooks.

3. mom improvises a few stories with magical undertones.

4. dad sits on the floor by bed and we meditate until i'm sleeping.

when i was 12 or 13 my parents gave me a portable TV and i'd watch the home shopping network in bed. think that's part of why i like ASMR videos, would feel ASMR things looking at HSN. have never told anyone all of this the extent i'm typing it now, i think, that it was a rare occasion for me to sleep in my bed. i was a scared little asshole.

tonight i felt 'the fear.' 'the fear' causes me to do ritual/preparation-like things. i don't feel it as much anymore, after living alone for three and a half years in baltimore, but sometimes if there's a small change i still feel it. i didn't do the thing where i check all the places another person can be tonight. here is what happened:

STAGE 1: VAGUE FOREBODING SHIT

*   peed, replaced tampon. saw roach on my conditioner and thought 'this doesn't bode well, the bugs have returned. it's on my conditioner, like what i'll use tomorrow. should i kill it?' then i could see its head being separate from its body, like it had a little neck or something. seemed hard to kill.

- washed face and brushed teeth while feeling the first stages of 'the fear' where i'm like, just looking around differently. looking at things more carefully.

- ate 1mg xanax, via 'it'll lessen [something] about dying.'

- refreshed dry cat food and gave them wet food thinking 'if i die tonight they will have enough to eat until ex-boyfriend returns.'

- rubbed experimental 'nighttime lotion' on my face and neck. think a parent gave it to me. felt like this was 'a protective ritual.'

- made bed and brushed all the crumbs/debris stuff off the sheet. this was just for fun.

- dressed in cherry-printed pajama pants given to me by former baltimore neighbor/co-worker, current close friend and 'will always be one of my favorite people who i love and aspire to be like in some way' person, chelsea. was going to leave on shirt i was wearing today, which chelsea also has but we bought before we knew each other, then thought: 'no. it will be too perfect: 'she died wearing the clothes of someone she wished she was more like,' then it'll definitely happen.' in the past i've thought i could increase probability of airplane landing safely if i'd listen to weird al or other unrealistic music to die to.

- applied protective clothing layer: long-sleeved shirt ex-boyfriend bought the day of his 2010 baltimore reading, when he stayed the night at my apartment and we had fun platonic fun all night and the next day.

STAGE 2: PLAN DEFENSE AND FLEE

- tried different lighting schemes. the best lighting to let someone know there is a person inside, ready to attack. fussing with lighting is what put me into stage 2, where i'll start imagining scenarios where i'll be confronted with the thing that's going to 'get me.'

- gathered all knives and scissors and placed them under pillow (however, this means if whatever has come to 'get me' hasn't brought a weapon, which it would've, i feel, it'd have to find even scarier and probably more painful blunt objects in the house to kill me with. anything in here could kill me). i have sharp things ready though, because i think i'd be better at stabbing than clobbering or [who knows].

- stowed car keys and phone under other pillow.

- in stage 2 i have locked the bedroom door before, but. i don't know. undecided on this one tonight. i want cats to be able to roam freely around apartment, maybe sleep near me.

STAGE 3: WAIT IT OUT

- you just wait it out. that's all you do. either you're awake all night or you beat it.

getting sleepy. alvie is acting especially jumpy, pacing and chirping. does not bode well. told myself i'd be asleep before it was light outside and now it's looking bluer out there goddamnit. actually though, this is good, because now i have more visibility out my window. when it was darker earlier 'knew' the face from 'suspiria' was on the other side of the curtains. goosebumps looking for this picture, like, entire google image search, even now, thinking about looking at it.

fear seems manageable tonight. it helped to type this, like now i'm process-ing faster because i moved stuff to my external hard drive. drinking coconut water. shirley is here. about to sleep, sun is up, okay. 'you got this.' B.D.O. tomorrow.

2:55PM: had set alarm for 1PM. not boding well. B.D.O. got a mean case of the not-boding-wells. drinking yesterday's dunkin donuts coffee. so far i woke, which i guess is more than what i was expecting i'd do today, last night, so...no that's setting the bar low.

3:28PM: finally answered phone to tell telemarketers to stop calling. so. that was not on the list of things i want to accomplish today but it should've been. going to shower and make smoothie now. *NOTIFICATION: THIS WILL BE THE LAST TIME I SAY 'GOING TO DO ___' BECAUSE BOY DOES THAT EVER NOT MAKE ME NOT WANT TO DO THINGS.

4:43PM: woman is yelling 'fuck you you dumbass bitch, you stupid ass ho' out window. man is yelling something back. would've been cool if i'd had an expensive microphone when we moved in, so i could've been keeping an audio scrapbook of the sounds of 4th and jefferson. last night around 3:30AM a rooster was crowing. it kept going until i went to my bedroom a little before 6AM. imagine: a rooster, somewhere out there in the expansive wasteland of a dark philadelphia morning. philly sucks man.

kale smoothie: made and drank that shit. -1 shitter from that list.

thought, while scooping out cantaloupe seeds '...with the strength to open melons with a butter knife, the agility of a blender on ice, and the brute force of a thousand butter sticks, megan [discontinued thought].' heard blender about to fall and ran from toilet to avert a famed 'tao lin smoothie disaster of instagram proportions' (didn't even wipe) (serious about averting that disaster) (disaster averted).

called attorney. he's calling tomorrow with new settlement offer. after that mom and i could go to court, to get more money. the guy who hit us doesn't have to pay, it's all corporations, so. i don't know. i don't really care. court seems hard.

assembled packages to mail. not going to make it to post office before they close. will need to fed-ex everything. fuck it, that's good. the post office would've. stalled. because i need fed-ex for the real estate thing anyway.

i put stickers on two envelopes 'for good luck,' rubbed them in 'special secret pattern,' thinking of the part in 'me and you and everyone we know' where she touches the neon dots on her steering wheel.

horn honked twice and a man said 'hey. i love you. mucho. peace' as car drove away.

have responded to more emails per capita than like, ever, i think. four responses so far without spending 15-90 minutes on them. proud of me. baby's fucking day out.

answered another telemarketer. taking this shit out.

baby's fucking. gonna take this shower. take this shower out. fucking. i want a cigarette first. thought 'no, you can smoke when you're dead.'

no i need the small reward of smoking right now.

so happy i didn't add 'quit smoking' my punishment if i don't get shit done today. i was about to do that. it would be hard to live in a world with a nasty photo of my ass on the internet, not enough money to start being a person again, and without the small reward of smoking.

small rewards: only way things happen.

6:01PM: if i have enough time i want to eat a molly to write a draft of my 'cover letter.' (the letter basically just has to say: i'm a nice person, i'm responsible, i have had jobs before, there are jobs i would like to have in your area, nursing home jobs, i want to help old people dress themselves and eat because they are as close to death as me and i understand feeling that and wanting help, i am going places) (the letter has seemed hard to write because i feel like i can't just say those things, i have to like…prove myself...by vaguely...just writing vaguely). just so i can have 'on molly' letter and 'toned down' letter. seems hilarious: 'two-years-jobless woman with emotional problems takes molly to help her write vaguely-worded letter recommending herself as an apartment building tenant.'

molly-eating might be destructive. fed-ex and library close at 9PM. shower has not been taken but don't worry i have ideas about how to conserve precious shower-time. i responded to another email. seems important, to keep this 'email streak' going. fucking taking it out.

6:14PM: just took out another telemarketer. his name was chris. fucking told chris. he will not soon forget that polite request to take a phone number off a list.

who gave my number to a website where...these health insurance people call you? did i do that, somehow?

6:37PM: took that fucking shower out. here was my secret: i never said i had to wash my hair! OH NO! OH NOOOOOOOOOOOOOOOOOOO!!!! that foreboding roach on that conditioner bottle last night—how little did it know about how much it would bode!!!!!!!!

'boding' seems to be an integral aspect of 'baby's day out'

i am using 'boding' loosely...or...um...think it's just fun to say it...things boding well...my decisions being influenced by 'boding'...being a bode daddy...

thought of a good insult: i wouldn't fuck him with your tampon

shit just re-read list, i forgot about refilling birth control, CVS will still be open i hope SHIT

6:47PM: wearing black flats with twinkly gemstone decorations on the toes. check out fucking twinkle toes over here. baby's day out with the twinkle toes over here. boding all over the place, boding everywhere, in all directions. out of control boding. twinkling it up.

6:53pm: I'm stalling, shit. Why do I stall like this. Pay attention to your stalling Boyle.

6:58pm: drove past a dead kennedys looking guy crossing street lighting a cigarette as I was lighting a cigarette. Better believe I head-checked.

7:00pm: sometimes smoking cigarettes feels physically horrible. pulled into CVS parking lot.

7:04pm: The pharmacist said my address. I said 'yup, that's the one' like how Alex Trebek said 'trout: that's the fish.' I don't have any refills left. Shit. Does this count? Shit…doctor is gone at 5pm. Did not account for 'no refill' variable. Shit. I don't know if this counts yet. I think it doesn't, I didn't know.

7:08pm: not going to eat the Molly. Molly eating does not bode well. Driving to library.

7:10pm: want to watch a YouTube compilation of cars making outrageously unnecessary k-turns.

7:15PM: took picture of sky while waiting for parking meter kiosk to print receipt. stood on a cement thingy for a better view. man's voice from behind me said 'beautiful, isn't it.' he was an old man, maybe in a uniform. i said 'yeah, look at all the colors.' after i said 'colors' he turned his head to look at me.

8:13PM: at library. eyes got watery as hell typing this: 'My family has generously offered to continue supporting me, but I want Beach View Apartments to be the place I launch my new independent life—I want Rockaway Park to be my home for years to come.'

how did i write it. i mean it, but…it looks vulnerable, phrased that way. i feel so fake writing cover letter-type things. that weird subtext of 'if the person reading this suspects i'm writing to influence their decision, which is my only reason for writing this, i will sound disingenuous.'

9:14pm: sometimes hearing snippets of an argument between men who don't seem to know each other.

Suspenseful ass coin dispensing process on library printer.

Discovered 24-hour FedEx hell yeah.

Sat in car, emotionally assembling printed liveblog manuscript in folder formerly containing lease/apartment application, given to me by Colin.

Walked to park by American-looking museum buildings. Started walking vaguely in direction of FedEx. Lit a cigarette while looking somewhere in the distance. Thought 'proud American moment. America.' Realized I didn't know where I was walking and had left phone with directions on it in car. Proud American moment. America: I think I live here.

Do people know when I'm not being serious…

Walking to FedEx. Just passed a man dragging a heavy garbage bag. Would like to say 'we did a modest mutual head-check,' but it was more like 'which one of us is going to hurt the other one, uh oh'

9:26pm: walked a little more then saw welcoming lights of 24-hour FedEx.

9:47pm: wandered around FedEx. Stood at a counter. Another wandering woman stood 'competitively' beside me. A man with a ponytail did things to a machine in a vaguely employees-only area. Wandering woman wandered somewhere and I didn't see her again. A woman with a name tag that said 'Lulu' approached me. She said 'I can help you over here,' not moving her eyebrows much. I non-laid-back-ly said 'oh great thanks, thank you.' Followed her to a shipping counter she stood behind. 'I could see you walking around over there lookin like that,' she said. 'Oh heh, yeah I was doing that,' I said. Since entering it'd occurred to me that they might not ship 24 hours. I said 'shit is it too late to ship things?' Lulu made a face like. Um. Lulu was being this way to me like how I would be to honestly confused customers. Like pleasantly surprised that a person would come in who didn't think they knew all the answers. I was happy to be that person, the not-knowing-all-the-answers-already person, for Lulu. Placed two envelopes on the counter. Lulu said 'you don't need to buy that, we can just do this part for free' and placed two puffy white FedEx envelopes between us. I said 'oh. Oh yeah well that would be great, thanks. The other ones, yeah, no good.' She smiled in her no-eyebrows-moving Lulu way, looking mostly at a computer.

She told me to fill out forms and left me alone to do that. The moment after I'd finished, she returned. She had pastel blue nail polish similar to my mint green, but her nails looked manicured. I wanted to say something about this, like something you would say, like, 'springtime: time for nails' but couldn't think of a normal-person thing to say like that. Lulu said 'I'm cold, it's cold in here, isn't it?' I nodded big and said 'yeah it is, it's really cold in here. And I bet for you…yeah, your short sleeves, man.' I didn't think it was cold. Somehow this did not sound awkward.

Lulu processed the packages and asked me questions. When I answered it felt like we understood something about the customer-employee dynamic like 'no one really knows what's going on, we have to say these words to each other that someone faraway at FedEx invented. We are the people between FedEx and the things we want.' Like I was thinking 'I want this to be mailed but I don't care how and I don't know what's going to happen when I leave' and Lulu was thinking 'I am at work and things about this place are normal to me; maybe ideally I'd be doing something else, but right now I'm helping this person, I know how to help them and after I do my job I don't know what's going to happen.'

Lulu said 'I'm gonna close it now' about my envelope. I said 'oh great, thanks. Yeah, it would've been like 'oh no, big mistake' if it was closed and the wrong package.' Rested my eyes on a box behind the counter with 'IRONLUNG' printed on the side in large letters. Lulu said 'okay you can pay now.' I grabbed the phone, thinking it was the credit card swiping device. Lulu laughed and said 'no you give the card to me.' I laughed a little and handed her my card as I said 'I thought, you know. It looks like one of those things.' She handed me a stapled receipt but didn't let go. I watched the receipt and nodded while she said when the things would arrive in other places, something about a tracking number, going online. Then she let me take the receipt. I smiled, said 'thank you so much' as I walked to the door, studiously looking at the receipt without reading it. I stopped and turned to face where lulu now stood, in the middle of the store. I said 'wait don't I have to sign?' She laughed and said 'no that's it.' I smiled like a big idiot and said 'thanks' as I exited FedEx, feeling mildly like Judd Nelson at the end of 'the Breakfast Club,' raising his hand triumphantly with Molly Ringwald's earring in his ear as the frame freezes before the credits.

10:31pm: Baby took this day out. Now all I have to do is the box of books. And like, what, call dad? Easy. Easy peasy. A rapper could be like '[something easy] I got that shit: kindergarten.'

Hungry. Driving to Wawa to get BLT.

10:48pm: this guy in Wawa…I can't even…it was like a Mike judge movie or something, how much he didn't know what was going on…not even going to try to reproduce…wish I had a stenographer with me…you'd also need to see him though…jesus…

11:20PM: parked outside apartment, talking to dad on phone. good talk. we were both about to eat sandwiches with pickles on them. dad was like 'oh you gotta put the pickles on, it's so nice to take a bite with a pickle.'

11:21PM: entered apartment. fed cats. got sandwich ready for after packing box of books. wawa has some baller type shit going on with their condiments, you can get condiments on the sandwich AND on the side. just by pressing a button. some real baller type shit.

11:30PM: packed books from 'abe' to 'german.' boom. 30 minutes to spare.

11:34PM: someone paypaled me $100 for seemingly nothing, i think. haven't opened email yet. jesus christ, person. thank you. this BLT is gonna taste extra good.

MARCH 28, 2013

1:04AM: ben brooks sent the $100, with instructions to spend it on drugs. light gchat argument with ex-boyfriend about renting a u-haul friday. he thinks it'd would be 'wasteful' because his dad has a pick-up truck. definitely seems like i have more things than my car and a pick-up truck can hold. furniture. shit. agreed to see how it looks when everything is packed, then maybe rent a u-haul. just want to leave it all on the street.

i have clothes with sizes ranging from two to eight. i'm like a 27 or 28 in pants and girl's medium or small or kind of 'whatever' in shirts. 34B. haha. who wants my bras? bras have always looked 'embarrassed' on my body, i feel. like 'jesus, this is where i have to be? after that ad?'

2:25AM: laying in bed. ate 1mg xanax. drinking a beer. the people below me are yelling again. the woman seems more mad tonight. they are slamming things and the walls are vibrating sometimes. i haven't seen this couple, but in the past i have seen the couple who lived there before them. they had one or two small children. they would scream like, insane maniac screaming, like punk band with zero twitter followers and 5000 t-shirts to sell screaming. the children also screamed sometimes but i understood their screaming, they were probably trying to get their parents to hear them, but was hard because there was already so much screaming. it would be like, in the morning, ex-boyfriend and i would wake to the sounds of this couple screaming. one time i stomped hard on the floor, to 'check up' on them. the guy yelled 'the fuck i'm gonna quiet down in my own house' or something. it was funny.

imagine people screaming things like 'LEAVE ME ALONE' or 'I DON'T KNOW WHAT YOU WANT FROM ME'

wait, shit. they do that. it's normal, kind of, to do that. i've done that, i think. haha.

2:33AM: in like 20 years you're going to start meeting people named 'huffington.' then in 300 years you're going to start meeting people named 'huffington post' because people will have forgotten about 'the huffington post.' they will have just, over time, noticed other people walking around named 'huffington' and…maybe…i don't know what accounts for the 'post' being a part of the name 300 years away. there's always some margin of error in these things, isn't there? social gene mutations? the 'random' variable? 'random noise variation' accounting for…adaptation? used to know college stuff. shit. some people just keep knowing that shit after college. ho, ho, ho. not i.

recently i tried replacing typing 'haha' or 'hehe' with 'HO HO HO.' also in high school katie and i tried to replace actually-laughing with saying 'that's funny.' seemed impossible.

4:45AM: since i didn't account for 'no more refills' variable on birth control and i didn't get it refilled i invented an auxiliary, semi-ass-related, lower-level punishment: uploaded two topless 'as-is' photos to flickr. posed a little in the first one, the second is closer to the position i was laying in when i had the idea. this is to punish myself, but also to sort of to show you what i mean about how my breasts look embarrassed in bras. the left one is like. looking down, kind of. always. dejectedly. like 'basketball practice has been over for like 45 minutes, when is dad going to get here?'

it feels so nice being in this bedroom and laying with shirley on the bed. i have this candle going. there are a lot of softly-colored green things in here and dim morning lighting. seems like the perfect size, like just enough room to walk to the bed. feels so good. i wish i felt this more regularly. excited to live alone again. i'm putting all my things in storage in maryland and living with my dad until i hear about the apartment in rockaway park. might make liveblog private tomorrow in case the apartment building people want to google me. seems. not worth it, though. if they're the type. who would not like me because of this.

i'm just fully typing like, fully conversational-style, like imagining i'm talking to a person when i type, not imagining 'what should writing look like.' it feels good. felt like i did that really hard today. i don't think i've done this before, to the extent i'm doing it now. like not worrying about saying 'like' or. ending sentences like that. because that's how i'd say it out loud. okay.

5:12AM: want to wander around to see if any 24-hour places have ice cream to sell to me right now. not tired at all. xanax made headache go away.

the brother of the guy who looked like joaquin phoenix, who also looked like joaquin phoenix, who i had even more formal/less casual sex with a few years later, told me this story:

an ex-girlfriend turned to him in bed and said 'there's something weird on my ass, can you come look at it?' he looked and saw nothing. she said 'no, closer?' he moved closer and saw nothing. she asked him to spread her asscheeks. when he did, she farted. it made a 'pfffff' noise. he thought she was really funny and loved that she did this—they'd make the noise at each other sometimes, as a joke. he said 'but after that, there was no mystery left.' he told me this story to stress wanting to keep 'mystery' in our relationship. think i don't want 'mystery,' ever. feel like this liveblog has removed all possible 'mystery' about me. that's not true. every moment can be mysterious, in its own way. er. i don't know what i'm talking about. ice cream.

5:46AM: ate another 1mg xanax. it is garbage night. taking that shit out. put on black coat from last fall and felt something.

imagine the restaurant that would sell a 'palzone.' it's like a calzone big enough for two people. two pals. you have to eat it in a special area of the restaurant with a big neon flickering sign that says 'the pal zone.'

WHAT I THINK SEX WITH CERTAIN GAME SHOW HOSTS WOULD BE LIKE:

- out of all the game show hosts, i think alex trebek would be the kindest, most generous, but also 'nastiest' lover. he would make jokey comments like 'i'm gonna show you where the daily double is.' oh man. but there would be moments where you'd just look at each other's eyes. you'd see how hard it is to really know him. like, really, really know him. the way you want to. the man who says 'trout: that's the fish.' and you'd have no idea what he was thinking sometimes. he is mostly thinking about your pleasure, i think. then he gets aggressive sometimes. it's just. it'd be really good.

- pat sajak just does missionary i think. he has like. constant other concerns. he's really easily distracted. he's thinking about ebay a lot.

- drew carey…is it public knowledge that drew carey is into some kind of really hardcore s&m? wasn't there some thing about that? i picture him as more of a 'strictly doggie-style' guy, who like, enforces it to annoying degrees.

- howie mandel is…so freaky…he just imitates porn, he says the things the guys holding the cameras say in porn. the camera guys who aren't even doing the porn. when they're like 'oh yeah, look at that.' he does stuff like that. he like, puts baby oil on everything. he'll be like 'are you gonna come for howie?' and she'll be making those really embarrassing noises because she thinks it's making him happy.

- steve harvey has studied the female orgasm. he has a sex swing but he's never used it. his wife just like…really likes having sex with him, she bought it.

- it's hard for me to think about ryan seacrest having sex, they way it's hard for me to imagine sea mammals having sex (not just because his name has 'sea' in it, i don't think). like…how would he even… arrange things…with the way he is…his manner…i mean, i guess it would honestly be like 'on the porn-y side of normal.' the weird thing is thinking about his motives for sex. like, they are purely species-furthering in a weird aryan way that is not quite human. like, he ejaculates and thinks 'YESSSSSSS. MY SEEEEEEEDDDDD.'

7:55AM: just returned home from major unprecedented carb spree. bought an everything bagel with cream cheese from 'the last drop' (cafe i liked when i went to UARTs in 2003). then drove by the place i lived when i went to school there. i only went for a semester. i lived on the fourth floor. wanted to taste something sweet. i drove by whole foods but it was closed. then another health food store was closed. driving home, i passed kaplan's and parked. i approached the counter, made an an invisible square with my hands, and said 'is that thing a raspberry thing?' a woman said 'why, yes.' i said 'i'll take it.' the entire exchange seemed like it was under one minute. heard 'have a happy holiday' behind me as i opened the door to exit. legs and body are achy. i could eat like ten more carb units right now, i feel. so sleepy. not going to set alarm.

8:30AM: was awakened by a door-pounding landlord who seemed to want to argue and i said 'you're not wrong, i'm not wrong' and 'just tell me what you want me to do' and 'that already happened, what is there do to now?' and 'i want this to be easy for everyone.' i'd say something like that and he'd look shocked and like he wanted to argue more. seems like he has already spent the last month's rent (we paid first month, last month, & deposit upon moving in) and is upset about not knowing we were moving out until a few weeks ago. seemed hard to get him to leave, he just wanted to argue. he doesn't speak english well so he was basically saying the same sentences also, only getting madder and madder. he said 'i'll go look over my lease' seeming to know that if he did he would find that ex-boyfriend and i are not in trouble and don't owe him money. heard loud jackhammering coming from downstairs.

looked for lease. texted ex-boyfriend. called dad, he makes copies of everything.

jackhammering continued during sleepy phone conversation with ex-boy-friend. i said 'he seems to be doing it on purpose…suddenly doing things to the building…' he and his wife have been the worst landlords. mostly for things in the beginning. a lot of saying they would do stuff and never doing it.

typed 'Could you please call before you come over next time? I know you're upset but that's no reason to not be polite' in a text message draft i deleted.

called ex-boyfriend again. he is driving back from new jersey tonight.

ate another 1mg xanax and put in earplugs. slept through 1PM alarm.

3:30PM: woke tired and sweaty. remembered the carb run. wanted another bagel. need to pack all my things today. seems hopeless, impossible. drinking energy drink.

4:10PM: my shirt is all sweaty. it's making me colder. scared to take it off and feel momentary 'colder than shirt' cold. feel incapable of doing anything while so cold. so much to do. i'm going to go out to somewhere to get boxes and take a molly to pack.

going to want to be writing/not packing while on molly i think.

would be funny if i was on molly when ex-boyfriend comes home…

'hey peg [sadly, droopily, closing front door]'

'[sound of fast, staggered stomping, then down the stairs, hugging him violently]'

'SO HAPPY TO SEE YOU AUUUGHHHHHHHHHH-HHHH I JUST WANT TO BITE DOWN ON STUFF SO HARDDDDDDDDDDDD I LIKE SEEING YOU, LET'S SCREAM AS LOUD AS WE CAN OKAY'

coming down from molly while packing though…uff. guess i'll save for later.

4:15PM: gotta get out this door to some liquor store for more boxes. gotta get garbage bags. gotta at least look like i did shit today. humorless packing day.

5:53pm: driving now. If you get in a car accident with a horse and carriage are you more in trouble about the horse damage or the carriage damage?

If I'm ever in a wheelchair and I get hit by a car and the thing ends up going to court I'm going to insist it was an 'automobile collision' and sue them for discrimination if they insist I'm a pedestrian.

Driving to whole foods to get green juice and garbage bags and boxes. Gonna pack the shit outta this apartment.

5:57pm: made open, relentless, unforgiving eye contact with an albino man while picking my nose.

6:18pm: liquor store employee went to look for boxes. Placed whiskey on counter and cashier rang it up. She was wearing white plastic gloves. The man brought out five boxes. I thanked him and he said 'I tried to get you, like, the pretty ones' like he was saying 'you have something coming out of your nose.'

6:20pm: boxes had cardboard bottle separators in them. I put all the separators into one box. Only one box could fit inside another box. I fashioned the boxes in front of me for 'optimum easy carrying. Felt like I looked like a miro painting. Or. No. Who does the boxes? Maybe miro painting because my head is a circle and the whiskey bag hanging on my arm below the boxes was kind of circular. Passed an ageless looking man singing like how people sing in musicals. Enunciating the words and with vibrato. He looked like he was thinking 'I'm giving the world a message right now and they don't want to hear it but I'm better for it but I should still be careful because the world is evil and it wants to hurt me.' Tried to make eye contact with him but he wouldn't. Thought he would get a kick out of my boxes, like, I was a stagehand or something, carrying boxes backstage to make his show work for him. When he passed me he was singing 'we could've had one season.'

6:40pm: ex-boyfriend texted that he was in traffic and wouldn't make it back for jeopardy. I said I wouldn't either.

7:00pm: asked beer distributor store for boxes. The guy said 'we're a distributor, remember, we sell everything in boxes.'

7:20pm: got more boxes from another liquor store. Like 12 boxes now, I think. Good.

7:46PM: texted colin and called dad. brought in all the boxes. this white and brown spotted cat has been here since we moved in. i call him 'brad.' he is really sweet and friendly and rubby. i wanted him to be one of our cats, or like, for us to take him to a shelter. talked about that with ex-boyfriend and decided he was better 'on the streets,' since people like us could adopt him, or he'd be killed. here he has people on the block to feed him. i used to feed him every day i think, then saw that the corner store fed him also, then i moved out. then i moved back in and i didn't see brad as much.

brad followed me around while i took trips moving boxes from my car to inside. i pet him for some time. he seemed harder to pet, like, around his head. but he also looked less skinny.

7:52PM: saw the woman who lives under me walk in a little before me and locked the door on one of my 'box trips.' she is pretty, with dyed red hair or hair extensions. entered apartment with 'last trip' of boxes. she seemed to be arguing with boyfriend, heard children also. she said 'i ain't do that in like three months.'

7:55PM: fed cats. lit candles in the apartment for. i don't know. when ex-boyfriend gets back there will be candles, it will feel okay. somehow. fed brad. if you want brad. i. jesus. i hope someone nice will find brad and let him come inside. he's never even tried to come inside.

8–9:21PM: packed books and small things. ex-boyfriend came home. we had both bought whiskey. we packed books together in the main room.

he said 'peg are there markers?' i unwrapped a kotex pad on our bedroom dresser, removed the adhesive, and stuck the pad on my forehead before i walked downstairs. i said 'i didn't see markers.' ex-boyfriend didn't mention forehead pad, he like. he just understood the joke.

MARCH 29, 2013

8:14AM: here are things i remember from last night:

- said 'it would be good if there was like, a band that played all clichés, like, they made it their mission to only do that. like every one of their songs was about a specific cliché.' did not use those words to say that. said it because of something ex-boyfriend said that made me think something about the radio.

- later something simlarly interesting was said. asked ex-boyfriend if he remembered what it was and he said 'it was better than your idea' or something. which it was, i feel.

- used ex-boyfriend's phone then mine, via bad reception, to order this: 'germantown special cheesesteak' (contains mushrooms, peppers, onion, pepperoni), ten hot wings, one large mushroom pizza. funny things happened on the phone when ordering.

- at germantown a guy was on 'the CW' news for saving a man from getting hit by a subway train. the man looked like kenny. ex-boyfriend and i do 'kenny voice' sometimes. i haven't written about kenny yet. from 2010 to 2012, i think, my dad house-sat for his friend, who had moved to hawaii. kenny and his girlfriend, alice, rented the third bedroom in the house. i'd sometimes stay there for weekish-long periods. i've known kenny since i was a child. he's always done work on our houses. kenny brings a lot of joy to my life. he likes to tell this story about how he went to nashville to try to be a country singer. apparently he almost had a record deal. my dad said he would've gotten signed, but he was too drunk when he met with the record label people. the meeting ended with kenny telling them they were stupid, throwing a chair, and maybe being escorted out of the building. for christmas one year he gave me a CD of four songs he wrote: 'okey dokey,' 'man of the house,' 'mother's day,' and 'don't be caught dead without jesus.' the cover of the CD is a photo collage of his face interspersed wih an image of him sitting on a stool, holding a guitar, behind the text 'Kenny Ray Sings.'

writing all of this now…damn. i love kenny. i miss living with him and alice. kenny's brother stayed with us for a week. he shat his pants regularly. alice said he asked if he could have sex with her, with kenny in or out of their room. she was upset by this and by kenny's not-immediately revolted reaction. alice worked at the laundromat less than a block from the house. was jealous of her, for that. she or kenny would stand in my bedroom door or on the porch and talk for long periods of time, probably over ten minutes. i wouldn't mind not saying much back to them. think i recorded some conversations on my other computer. one of the last nights at the house, as we were packing to leave, kenny asked me to marry him. he said i should dye my hair red. that's not why i dyed my hair red, but, or. maybe it is, i don't know. i asked what he was having for dinner. he said 'dinner?' i said 'yeah.' he held up a bag and was like, 'i eat this for dinner. six-pack. eat a six-pack for dinner. heh heh heh.' last night on the phone my dad said kenny is taking another ex-girlfriend's son to court for assault, and taking her to court for stealing food stamps. was sad to hear that. dad said the people at the v.a. hospital give kenny too many drugs and he's 'not himself' anymore, which probably means he's calm and doesn't talk much. dad said kenny has a lot of wrist pain. they still talk regularly.

- i said 'the people on 'king of the hill' must be rich or something, or like, dale's wife, since she's the weather lady.' ex-boyfriend said 'but texas is so big, no one makes much money. especially them. they're like, way out there.'

9:00AM: heard my name and walked to bedroom. ex-boyfriend had an erection, said 'can you help? it's almost ready.' made eye contact while he orgasmed in my mouth. held him from behind. wondered if i could fall asleep and heard the rhythmic clicking of his teeth, indicating he had. sometimes he bites in his sleep. the clicking stopped and we laid quietly for some time. felt him inching closer to the wall, usually after a microscopic muscle adjustment or slightly deeper inhalation or exhalation coming from one of us. sometimes i'd hear a noise or one of us would move and i'd think 'no, then another thing will change and soon i'll be doing something else.' indirectly attempted to downgrade 'period of interminable silent wall-scooching' to 'period of interminable snuggling and napping' by asking if this was 'the last time we're going to wake up together, in this bed?' i knew we both knew it was, but wasn't sure how much either of us wanted for it to be. he sat upright and said 'yes' decisively, using a new impersonal tone of voice that seemed to surprise both of us, aiding his speedy departure from the room with limited eye contact. moved to fill the space he left, wanting to continue laying before i knew he was awake. his arms had been too tense to fit mine under his, against his body. felt like i was forcing myself on him. thought 'okay. that's all it's going to be, that's all it ever was, really, okay.'

9:28AM: looked at new watch. ex-boyfriend started ordering watches from the internet this fall. they're always breaking and he's always wearing a new one. i think he's bought more than i've known about. recently learned the watches were incentives/motivation to quit or drink less alcohol. now he likes these cheap european ones, 'breo luminex.' last night he held out his wrist and said 'i got these watches, they're the same as casio.' i said 'oh yeah, those ones. i want the all-white one.' he said 'i got that one too, you can have it.' have been wearing all-white one. that's what i looked at that said '9:28am.'

9:45AM: ex-boyfriend was sitting naked on the blue chair where i was sitting when i had the idea to do baby's day out. now he's in the bedroom. i said 'can't we go to the dew inn?' he said 'no. just fight through the hunger.' i said 'fine. i'm going to whole foods in like. thirty minutes. like, a half an,' he rolled his eyes, 'hour.' he had eaten the leftovers sometime after i had fallen asleep. he said he had a hard time falling asleep, didn't until 5AM or something.

continued 'things i remember from last night:'

- watched 'love you, mean it' pilot episode while eating. whitney's presence seemed terrible. i related to her fragileness and wanting-to-try-ness. i said her presence was so uncomfortable. ex-boyfriend said he loved it, and, with delight, 'she's just not a funny person. i wish it was on mute, just her presence, or someone else saying jokes over her on mute.'

- ex-boyfriend missed a call from his ex-girlfriend and turned off phone. a little later he turned it back on and i said something about how he was 'getting in on' her voicemail, wanting to know what she said. he said 'i'll just tell her we're packing' and left the room to talk. we were about to watch 'king of the hill' when she called, thought he wouldn't call back. heard him talking in the other room. after the phone call we argued a little. i felt like i was acting like him. it was like, clear that i was upset, but i was saying 'i don't want to talk about it, let's just watch 'king of the hill'' in an unconvincingly unbothered voice.

- watched a recent episode of 'king of the hill.' i said 'i've never seen a full one, i think.' asked to watch another one. we watched the first episode. i was like 'i can't believe i've never seen this, this is so good.' ex-boyfriend was like 'yeah, you're stupid for never seeing this.' searched for pictures of mike judge on google image. i said 'he's really handsome.' ex-boyfriend said something about him looking normal. i kept stressing that he was 'so handsome' and looked like a guy i sort of dated. was aware of acting in a way i don't like. looked at the wikipedia page of a movie called 'extract.' i said 'i think i've seen that, if i saw a preview i'd be able to say if i've seen it.' talked about jason bateman. ex-boyfriend said 'he was the bad dad in 'juno.'" i didn't remember. ex-boyfriend was like 'how could you not remember.' i said 'he's on that show i don't like. he's most famous for that.' ex-boyfriend said 'feel like i don't know who he is, at all.' i said "arrested development.' that show is so stupid and not funny.' ex-boyfriend said 'he's the straight man on that show. like he's the normal guy.' remembered bonding about not liking 'arrested development' at an easier, earlier time in our relationship. i said 'do you think mike judge has like, a mansion?' ex-boyfriend said 'definitely' and something about a 'creator credit' and money. i said 'you could do that, you have so many ideas. just move to l.a. and do that.' he made a noise like 'alright, already,' like he did not want to hear the thing i was saying, or didn't believe me, or was irritated i'd think that about him. he could do what mike judge does and get a mansion, though. he is so funny. his brain is like, always generating funny interesting ideas. i said 'it seems like a lot of people probably think mike judge is making fun of the people he makes shows about but i feel like he's just. like. what i like about it is that he's not making fun of anyone.' ex-boyfriend said 'yeah. he came from that. it's about what he came from.'

9:50AM: learned, in the hallway, i fell asleep at 2AM after requesting sex. i said 'was there blood?' ex-boyfriend said 'you would know more than i,' grinning and kind of laughing, referencing blowjob. i said 'was it. did i fall asleep in a 'king of the hill?" zero memory of sex. ex-boyfriend said i was 'begging for it.' i believe it. just felt around for my tampon. not there.

10:05AM: sitting in the living room now. leopard-print snuggie i bought on 'fun platonic fun day after ex-boyfriend's 2010 baltimore reading' is draped on his nude body like tarzan. i am on the couch. he is holding a water bottle and doing snaky 'circles' dance and smiling like jim carrey, seeming to tread water before we talk again, pleasantly treading water.

took pictures of alvie's insane iconic lazy cat pose. ex-boyfriend is visible in some. said 'i know you're just embarrassed for…people to know you were with me…i know that's why you don't want me to say your name,' sounding shakier than i felt. finished strong with a grin and 'don't think i have feelings about it because i don't.' he rolled his eyes and said 'you're making me want to start doing things.' i thought 'shit, he remembers,' and said 'that's good, that's good. anything to make you feel like wanting to do your things.' wished i hadn't said anything, like maybe i could've continued to distract us from packing all day.

10:31AM: i said 'if you take it apart you can just keep it, i don't want to put it back together' about a bookcase. a little later i was irritated to still be talking about this, said something like 'you have to find ways for everything to fit in your car. i'm not responsible for that. i wanted a u-haul.' we talked a little about moving plans. i said 'okay, so. no dew inn. you're going to do your things. i'll do this thing. then i'll go to whole foods. then i'll do the stuff you'll be doing. packing.'

10:43AM: ex-boyfriend entered room dressed and with wet hair, looking for tape. feeling extremely…still…like, half-drunk from last night and effected by 1mg xanax i ate thinking it would help me return to sleep sooner. commented on a lot of facebook photos of my close friend and former roommate and 'person i will always love and strive to be like in some way, probably always from a distance but hopefully up-close again someday,' christiana, who lives in chicago. mattie, if you remember me mentioning mattie, is also a person like this, and a person like chelsea. former best friends who seem upset with me not talking to them but i'm upset about not talking to them as much also. know it's my fault. they all seem successful now, teaching or working at museums or getting doctorates, in relationships i've perceived from a distance to be 'healthy.' wish i lived with mattie and christiana again. wish i lived next to chelsea again.

11:14AM: ex-boyfriend has been packing my records and graphic novels as i've been typing. want to go to whole foods now. he re-entered room and said 'or dew inn is fine. or whole foods. yeah whatever.' i said 'no, yeah i want whole foods.' he said 'yeah, get out of this place. in a car, for a while.' i asked if he wanted me to bring back anything from whole foods. then it was confusing, we had thought different things about who would be going to whole foods. he said 'whatever is fine,' not using those words exactly.

12:48PM: handed phone to zachary (tired of calling him 'ex-boyfriend,' doesn't seem to matter anymore), so he and my dad could sort out money things and i wouldn't be 'middle person' in the conversation anymore. uploaded video of this to youtube. feeling xanax. feeling loose. zachary has been packing really well. i have been sitting here, mostly not caring about if he sees screen.

said 'usually i try to not act like i'm on xanax when i'm on xanax around you.' he said 'yeah, now you're just not making as much sense.' lighthearted tone today. nice stuff. took pictures of the living room for like, three minutes i think. getting them and a 'fun saver' camera i found developed at CVS and hopefully birth control refill. um. we are returning a modem. to CVS? this shit is long. feeling 'out of it' in funny way…like…not attached to anything that's going on around me, everything seems funny.

12:48PM–10:19PM: most of this was spent packing. loaded most things into zachary's dad's pick-up truck but i still have more. here's what i remember happening today:

1–2PM: remember un-self-consciously saying things in the living room before we left for whole foods, like we both wanted to stall leaving. ate another 1mg xanax. forget why i wanted it.

i drove us to comcast so we could return our modem. remember laughing a lot, mostly about things that entertained me about me, like, not things that were going on with zachary, feeling confident enough to tweet 'said 'fuck yeah i'm a customer fuck yeah i like your jeep cherokee i really do' to a man in jeep nodded as i parked behind him at comcast,' and say/do those things.

there was a long line at comcast, and like, bullet-proof glass and 'exchange objects and money using this clear turning-thing without having to touch another person' devices. zachary said 'if they ask why you're cancelling your service you should tell them it's because you're moving to texas.' i said it would also be good to say if they didn't ask me. laughed a lot picturing myself using a straight face to unsolicitedly tell a comcast person 'i'm moving to texas.' i ended up doing it. think i did it really well. convincing. remember saying 'texas' twice. zachary left prematurely i think, because of laughing.

2–10PM: zachary said i shouldn't drive so he drove. earlier at the apartment i said i didn't want whole foods, i wanted el jarocho (mexican restaurant where we went a lot when we started dating, but haven't been to much since).

doing the times of things seems hard. here is just…everything i remember from yesterday, in the order i remember it happening:

- think we went to CVS before comcast. i barely remember CVS. i said something atypically cavalier to the cashier.

- on the way to el jarocho, gynecologist's office returned my call. doctor doesn't want to refill my birth control because i haven't sent her a letter saying 'my doctor has explained to me the risks of not doing a colposcopy, i do not want to have it.' a colposcopy is this thing gynecologists seem to have been doing a lot recently, which i think is a scam. a colposcopy is where they scrape your cervix for a mini-biopsy of cells. you're awake. seems to take a very long time. i don't know. this was in 2007, when i had 'pre-cancerous cells,' but my gyno couldn't tell if they were 'cancer-y' enough from the results and strongly recommended i have this surgery to burn a layer of my cervix off, so i did that, and all of it sucked ass. the colposcopy was the worst part, not the surgery. after the surgery my gyno got the more detailed biopsy results, which said there was nothing wrong with me, my body had taken care of the problem by itself, none of that needed to happen. i told the gynecologist's secretary i'd write and mail the letter saying 'i give consent to not have this thing done to me.' then i can have birth control again. great. birth will soon be under my control. until then it's just going to have to be out of control birthing.

- think all day i was complaining relentlessly about being tired. took a nap.

- zachary woke me around 5pm. he had made coffee. the landlords wanted to show the place to a prospective tenant at 7pm. seemed really hard to wake. i packed at a lethargic pace. didn't understand why zachary was hurrying, would've been willing to switch from 'lethargy' to 'hurry' if i knew more about the situation.

- electricity went out but not due to bad weather. outside, voices were yelling things like 'you got lights?' i stuck my head out the window and yelled 'no lights' to a man in a hoodie. he seemed to be the MC of the 'does this block have lights' thing. texted landlord that there might not be electricity when she and prospective tenant arrive. she texted 'it went out on my block too lol.'

- travis and kat came over. travis is close friends with zachary and i've hung out and talked about him with zachary enough to feel like i sort of know him. this was the first time i met kat, who travis has recently started dating. felt like i could be friends with kat. we had like, an instant 'riff' connection or something. i was packing shoes and trying to give her shoes. she stepped into a pair of high heels and said 'i don't think i can do them, my legs are like, [i forget].' we stared at her legs quietly in the mirror. i said 'you look fly. you know, how people can look 'fly.'' she said 'yeah, sometimes they look 'fly.'' i said 'that's how you look. 'fly.'' travis entered and said things, pausing irregularly. kat walked to him and said 'it's the first time you've seen me in heels.' i didn't see what travis did or remember what he said but i liked both of them a lot in that moment.

- while zachary and travis moved things down to the pick-up truck, kat would sometimes enter whatever room i was in and we'd talk. shirley hid in this radiator/tunnel area and wouldn't come out, so i'm returning to philadelphia to get her sometime before sunday. it'll just be me.

- zachary said 'peg can i give travis a pack of your cigarettes from your carton?' i have a carton. it's cool. i haven't bought cigarettes in a long time.

- mechanically, but like, a very slow machine, helped carry things down-stairs and load cars. as i was going inside, kat said something about 'sensing raptors.' i said 'i can sense them too, since like, i was little.' she said 'me too, since i was little. you can feel it in your ears.' we were smiling. i wasn't sure what we were talking about but i wanted to say more. felt aware of 'just standing there,' then overcome by the exciting terrible certainty that 'this is it, the thought to finally stop me from ever thinking about anything else, it's already working because all i remember is not knowing what to say a few moments ago, this is like the first step, soon i won't be able to move.' then i was inside again.

- a woman appeared in the hallway, followed by landlord, and walked towards me in the living room. they looked like they'd been 'doing this for years,' but neither had known what 'this' was and had each trusted the other did. the woman said 'i'm sorry, i shouldn't be here now,' looking mostly at the ceiling. i said 'me neither, sorry.' she turned to leave without looking at the living room. landlord waved, looking uncharacteristically friendly.

- stood with travis and kat and zachary after cars were packed. zachary told a joke with a long build-up, then said 'it's funny because of all the build-up.' we gave him suggestions for improving the joke. he started another joke. i had heard both earlier. he seemed to be avoiding look-ing at/addressing me.

- the man i said 'no lights' to stood by the corner store, in a group of peo-ple who periodically said 'don't go' to us, with exaggerated fake-crying gestures. i saw a bottle of gin on the hood of my car. the man saw that i saw it and took it and apologized. i said 'no, it's like. feel free.' zachary said 'he has your kind of gin, peg, look! new amsterdam!' felt scared, like next zachary would ask me to give the guy a blowjob. i was trying to maintain 'smiling to silently convey that it's okay to put shit on my car, i don't care, i like that you did it, please don't say any more to me' with the group of people while i 'managed' zachary's comment, which they probably heard, and after hearing meant they knew more about me, but not enough to know that i had found a mostly empty new amsterdam gin bottle in my underwear drawer a few minutes earlier, which is what made him say anything, i think. discrepancies in the amount of information people know about you. highly unpleasant sen-sation. no matter how well i know the people who know things about me, or however trivial the 'things to know' are, i'm always going to feel uncomfortable when someone seems to know more about me than the other person/people. i'm suddenly the middle man in a situation that wouldn't exist without me, and my task is to make sure everyone knows the same amount of things about me, and i hate doing that. this is the kind of thing that makes me not like people and not like myself. the endless. this thing. the urge to do it is insane. big dick boyle dishing out all the spiciest facts about herself. all that important information. to those interested people. whom she will know, for years to come, in her beautiful studio apartment in rockaway park. 'for years to come.' jesus. hate myself. years to come.

• asked zachary if he brought down the laundry and he said 'no.' walked to our building, where a man stood at the door, finagling with keys. he was moving slowly, holding a green palmolive bottle. i wanted to say 'that's palmolive for ya, sure does make it hard to put the key in,' or something. i wanted to say anything. felt happy and good-willed. the man opened the door and i silently followed him up a flight of stairs. he took out his keys. he's the yelling man who lives downstairs. i said 'it would be funny if i didn't live here and i just kept following you into your house.' he turned around and was smiling big and said 'yeah.' surprised i said that without hesitation. seemed like i 'needed' to say it.

• at some point it was just travis and me outside, finishing our cigarettes. he said 'can i say something? i'm really sad you guys are moving.' he looked like he meant it. i said 'me too. the whole thing. yeah. i wish it would've worked out. it would've been good too, because now you live so close,' aware that i had been to his new apartment probably less than five times since he moved, and that people who miss each other usually see each other more than that. i like him a lot, though, he's funny and easy to be around. he is a person i could've missed more. there were opportunities for me to have missed him more. that's what it's like with most people and me, i think. i'm always aware of missing opportunities to miss people more.

10:20pm: before merging onto 95, Zachary called to ask if we could pull over to check the tarp. I said 'yeah, the first rest stop.' he said 'no like as soon as possible.' Pulled over. Re-tied the tarp. He said 'I'm so sorry peg, doing all this to save a guy I don't like a few bucks.' I said 'it's nice that you want to save him money. Plus I feel less dependent on him for money, because of this. It's good.' he looked unusually serious/concerned. Like he was having lot of thoughts. I said 'if my stuff falls out I don't care, it's all stupid.' Zachary looked lost in thought, gestured to the tarp, said 'It would be helpful.' I said 'it's okay. I'll follow you and call if anything happens'

10:28pm: the tarp became mostly detached. I called and said 'pull over' then saw a black thing and said 'pull over pull over my stuff is falling out' in a frantic way I didn't like. Zachary looked defeated. He said 'I'm so sorry peg. I thought it would work.' I said it was okay and hugged him. Felt good that we both knew it would've been easier to rent a u-haul, and used that to justify not helping Zachary re-tie tarp, like I wanted to 'let him live with the consequences' of not following my good u-haul idea. Giving up and getting a motel was discussed. That would be exciting. Sat in my car and found a nearby best western. Wrote directions on the back of a Cvs receipt. Walked to Zachary. He said he still wanted to try. We were at the halfway point between Philadelphia and Baltimore.

10:30pm: tarp detached and we pulled over again.

10:48pm: Zachary called and said 'lets listen to the same radio station. 90.5.' I turned to the station and said 'oh, Johnny cash.' it was the cover of 'personal Jesus.' he said 'is this good?' I said 'yeah yeah. This is good. I like this.' Thought warmly about listening to the same station in separate cars. Seems to be a religious station. Want to change channel kind of.

10:50pm: radio person said the previous song was by temple of the dog. Then he said something about an upcoming block 'taking us up until a little after eleven, if you don't mind. Do you consider yourself a theologian? I sure as hell don't.' now a song is playing where they say 'theologians don't know nothing.'

10:55pm: tarp looked like it was detaching. Called Zachary and pulled over. He is adjusting tarp. I said 'it's like. Is it a religious station?' he said 'I don't think so. I really don't think so.' I said 'yeah it's like good Friday something. 'Do you consider yourself a theologian?" he said "I sure as hell don't." I said 'did he really say 'sure as hell don't?" he said 'I think so.' looked under the tarp. Didn't seem like I could help. Walked back to car. Tried to take a picture then Zachary was at my window and said 'let's just be on speakerphone. I'll call you.'

11:09pm: insane remix of a strokes song is on radio. I was like, singing the words without knowing what I was singing. Seemed interesting. Interesting combination of knowing and not knowing. Dj just said it was the song 'barely legal.'

MARCH 30, 2013

12:53am: went wrong way on the way to storage unit. Turned around. Tarp looked bad. Called Zachary to say we need to readjust. After situational details he said 'this is what life is' and laughed. I laughed and said 'love it, love life, live your life fucking fuck.' Stopped to readjust tarp again. I said 'we're going to have to untie all the rope.' Zachary said 'that'll be the least of our problems.' I said 'yeah, that'll be the start of more problems.'

1:09am: read Jesse prado's thoughts re my liveblog. A person on twitter said 'how many well-known alt lit writers hasn't she blown.' I replied 'like 3-5 not blown so far.'

1:24am: got lost looking for storage unit. Held access-swiper key up to a gate-opening device. Gate would not open. Sign under swipe device said 'closed for good Friday.' a more permanent looking sign on gate said 'access hours: [morning hours] - 9pm.' Walked defeatedly to Zachary's car and told him. Felt lack of energy in my voice. Talked about what to do. A lot of pauses and staring. Decided to go back to dad's despite zero garage and all my stuff being exposed and ready to steal. Zachary seemed more concerned with the stuff not getting stolen. I'd feel good if things got stolen. Less things. I want less things.

1:40am: seems like my body is falling apart, like constantly aching. Want to complain but can't think of things to complain about. Just. Drained. Feel like I've been in that machine from 'the princess bride' that takes years off of the blonde guy's life. Like in my sleep, someone hooks that machine up to me.

1:50am: pictured myself on highway suddenly accelerating to like 100mph and driving off a cliff. Actually first pictured crashing into some car head-on but that would effect Zachary who is following me. Like he probably wouldn't die and his life would just be worse. So cliff thing would be ideal.

1:53am: A man on the radio is earnestly singing 'so pile on the mashed potatoes and another chicken wing, I'll have a little bit of everything.' sounds like a Dawson's Creek-type theme song.

2:11am: royal farms closed. Going to…try….another one…this is life…

2:13am: Just remembered old woman rickets. So far away in time. And yeah I was right: I'm nostalgic for three days ago. I think Dunkin donuts was three days ago. Feels like three days ago. Feels like the first time, baby, feels like the very first time. That's a song, right?

2:27am: whenever I pass over a sewer thing or bump in the road without letting it touch my tires I feel like I am getting 'bonus points' or 'health points.' If I do it a certain number of times in a row or in some kind special pattern it's going to launch me into another dimension.

2:30–4AM: arrived at dad's. The back door of the truck had opened but nothing fell out. Brought whiskey, gin, el jarocho leftovers inside. Zachary said we should put the food on plates and heat them in the microwave. I said, like, 'but…we…in the frying pan…don't you want…heat it in the pan?' He looked at me like 'you dopey loveable lummox' and said, like how you would talk to a kid, 'just think of how much easier it will be. To heat it in the microwave. Think of the easiness.' I continued the lummox-talking, pretending not to understand anything, which progressed into audibly dragging my feet as I walked, running into cabinets, putting a fork in the toaster, trying to eat inedible things, all very slowly and with Zachary's 'gentle assistance.' He started guiding me away from things and saying 'no, no, you don't do that!' Seemed very hard not to laugh. He said 'you tell me 'I hide being on Xanax from you' like you think I don't know you're just saying slightly different things. But like. This? I know this is what you're really like, underneath it all.' We ate our things and watched TV and went to sleep.

11:32AM: preoccupied with moving. stayed overnight at dad's apartment, dad stayed at mom's. about to drive to put things in storage closet now, then drive to philadelphia, help zachary move things to new jersey, move the rest of my things back here tomorrow.

11:45am: I asked z for a razor to take care of 'lilith fair business' under my arms. Put razor in sink. Z came in bathroom and said 'oh I see you put the razor back.' I said 'oh razorbacks! That was the name of the bar in the storage plaza. Minimart. Er, strip mall. Where I worked.' then said 'storage plaza minimart strip mall' in riff raff's voice, laughing some. Could tell I was alone in room.

11:50am: z was pooping. I said 'I'm just going to start shaving you while you poop.' z said 'great.' I splashed water on his face. I said 'is that the sound of you pooping?' he said 'no, the shower is still on a little.' rubbed dr. Bronner's soap on his face. I said 'sometimes my poops sound like that.' and imitated the sound. He said 'me too. Never for this long though.' I said 'sometimes mine are this long.' he wiped and made a funny face and

128

flushed. He said 'I never sit while I flush. I'm afraid it's going to like, suck me in.' I smiled and said something and he stood and washed his hands.

11:52am: z turned on 'wait wait don't tell me' and resumed his seat on the toilet so I could continue shaving his face. He doesn't like to waste water. I left the sink on and said 'yes Zachary, sometimes we must use one of the earth's endless resources' and he smiled. thought I heard the radio say something. I said 'unlike triangles, squares have an additional fourth side. Is that what they said?' z said 'they were talking about granola bars. A company made triangular ones but they had to recall them because you can poke yourself with a triangle. Squares, though. They have four sides but are less sharp. But really a circle has endless points, so.' I said 'yeah, remember Tao's poem where he talks about the sphere of knives or something?' Zachary smiled thoughtfully and said 'no.' I said 'it was funny.'

12:01pm: left apartment. Face feels tight. Want lotion.

12:36pm: following z. Hell tarp.

1:31pm: did not take long to stow things in storage unit. Wearing a pink sweater from high school and gave zachary a blue one. He peed in a 'neuro passion' bottle while I chugged water from another bottle. He said 'get it ready' and I put it under his pee stream. He said 'man i got a wide stream.' It was like, directly on his penis head. Looked really funny. The stream was wide.

1:33pm: a lot of these times are arbitrary, like now it's actually 2:39 but I just remembered something that happened after the thing you just read, before the thing you're about to read. Here is the thing: I found the all-white breo watch broken on my car floor. I showed Zachary. He said 'well. You know. They're cheap, yeah. They break. Hm.' I said 'it broke' with inappropriate unintentional cheerfulness in my voice. The inappropriate cheerfulness was punctuated by me then jogging to my car.

1:34pm: Zachary is following me out of the storage unit to 95. He's going to Philadelphia. I'm going to mom's to deposit a check then dropping things off at Dad's then going to Philadelphia. Think adderall shipment will be at mom's.

1:57pm: talked with mom. Feeling unexpectedly sad. Told her that. Having things seems 'evil' or something. Things make you have memories. I don't know. Seeing all the things from our old house in the storage unit. All the things we're forgetting every day. Why are we saving a computer desk chair with wheels from 1996. Where is anyone ever going to put that. Stomach is doing weird shit.

2:09pm: Ran to the alley where I used to park. Wanted to see the back of the building and my kitchen window and fire escape (fourth floor leftmost window). Barely remembered what it felt like to park in my spot. Like as I'm writing this liveblog, there are instances where I think 'I want to include this, I want to remember this' and when I start typing I only remember the idea of wanting to remember something and maybe something about the scenery or context of whatever it was I wanted to remember. That's how I felt in the alley, taking the picture of the back of my old building. Like I was in a moment of almost remembering something. I knew in the future I'd remember this moment because I had a picture, but the feeling as I was taking the picture was like 'I can almost remember.' I think what I'm saying is all sort of understood as 'a thing of life,' maybe to the point that it's a cliché, but thinking that doesn't stop me from feeling what I'm feeling.

2:10pm: heard a feminine coughing above me. I am parked across from my old building. Looked up to the left and saw the coughing woman on her balcony. I didn't have a balcony. Her shirt was really green. Other than her, it feelss eerily, scarily quiet. The air.

2:19pm: turned key in ignition. Hope there is adderall shipment at mom's. But also like. Doesn't matter. What good is anything going to do me. That sounds dramatic but it doesn't feel dramatic.

2:20pm: arrived at mom's. Asked if she'd seen storage unit. She said no and 'what's he got in there.' told her about the wheely desk chair. She said 'oh, jeez.' talked about keeping things, memories, whether memories are good or not. She had found letters from our ancestors in Oregon and read one aloud from February 4, 1879, containing these phrases:

> 'I suppose you have heard of the death of our dear mother Johnson.'

> 'She fell asleep and gave us no warning of her departure.'

> 'Jesus took her home'

> 'I presume you have heard of the death of brother George'

> 'Please let me hear from you occasionally'

Received shipment of bulk 'noopept' powder with a 'microscooper' device and 30 30mg adderalls. Ate 20mg noopept. Seems interesting, definitely caused some kind of feeling. Mom asked how it made me feel and I said 'brighter. Not like, intelligent-brighter, just brighter.' she said 'well if you don't die maybe I'll try it.'

2:45PM: told mom i was never going to stop the liveblog, like, just keep doing it forever, writing everything down forever. she seemed confused. i said 'like, until i die, this is going to be my sole output, i'm not going to do anything else. like, with writing.' she still seemed confused. i said 'the liveblog thingy, remember?' she said 'oh, right. is what you're saying…are you saying you're still writing in it?' i said 'yeah, yeah. yeah. people have been contacting me and stuff and it feels really good. i feel really focused on it, i'm happy when i'm writing it. i'm just going to do it forever, write down what i do forever, and that will be what i will have done. when i die. like. it'll be my output. the only thing i ever write again. do you get it?' she paused and made a face and said 'oh my. has anyone done that yet?' i said i didn't think so. she said 'oh my' again and seemed excited and supportive.

3:15pm: I like how short this shrunken sweater from high school is. Really gets to the point of the shirt. Takes out all the bullshit. Sweater: removes the bullshit.

3:36pm: exiting mom's. She said 'don't worry, it'll all be over soon and you'll have everything to look forward to,' regarding moving, I think. Used a robot voice to say 'interesting double meaning.'

3:40pm: ate a b-vitamin and 30mg adderall 'for the hell of it.'

3:44pm: Zachary called for Philadelphia arrival time update. He said 'so like, around seven?' Low-level conversation.

3:50pm: a Camry with 'help save the next girl 241' in some kind of neon window paint on all its windows passed in front of me into the left lane. Thought 'interesting. Literary. Er. Something.' yes I thought 'er,' I wouldn't lie about thinking 'er.'

4:07pm: about to pull into bank parking lot. I am about to deposit a check and my shirt says 'retarded faggot.'

4:08pm: nevermind, bank closes at 2pm on Saturdays. Pulling into road again. Window is down. The weird eerie scary hollow quiet thing is happening with the air again.

4:11pm: I never want…like…when I'm on adderall I never want to be feeling anything else ever again. How come you can't feel that normally. Do people with degrees and houses and jobs and happy relationships with people they see regularly feel this all the time? Did I mess up my brain somehow, with drugs? Like if I had never taken them.

The first amphetamine I took was vyvanse, in 2009. I wrote all of 'clams' in like a few hours at the university of Baltimore computer lab. The vyvanse was bright blue and pretty. Now I'm going the wrong way on highway again, shit, got distracted.

5:15PM: i can smell my feet big time. i'm sitting cross-legged on a chair by a table facing a wall at dad's house. the table and chair are from the house i grew up in, surprised they 'made it out alive' from storage closet. seems like my dad would just not think to look in storage closet for things and just buy a new thing. sweating. poured another 10mg 'microscooper' of noopept under my tongue. feeling noopept and adderall effects, i think.

TO IMPROVE MICROSOFT WORD, IF ANY MICROSOFT WORD C.E.O.S ARE READING: instead of doing 'change back to [uncapitalized version of word]' and 'Stop Automatically Correcting [word],' maybe just have an option under 'Format' that's like 'don't do any auto-correcting, ever.' that also would be good for numbered lists.

slept on air mattress in closet-sized room last night with zachary. it was comfortable. i'd like to live in a house with like, a kichen, bathroom, two regular-sized rooms, and 15-20 little rooms. all of the little rooms could have themes. they could all be painted different colors. it would be funny to take people to the 'sex room.' the sex room would have padded walls and floors. yeah. or. no, need to think about this. would like to have a 'fish room,' like at pet stores when you go to the fish area and it's just like, walls of fish. need to have a butler to feed the fish for me.

5:40PM: my dad has one of those freezers that has a 'water dispenser' and 'ice maker' on its door. you can choose 'cubed' or 'crushed' ice. seems great. i love these things. filled a glass with crushed ice, then pressed a button and water came out of the ice-hole. remembered holding the bottle up to zachary's pee stream.

6:20PM: deleted tweet reply where i said i had not blown 3-5 writers yet. considered deleting the 1:02AM update about this from last night, then considered adding another meta-edit thing to it, then thought 'you're getting carried away, you haven't even written about yesterday, you're getting carried away with meta element, you are getting lost in a meta loop, this is probably only interesting to you.' imagined adding 'EDIT: please scan down to 6:20PM for more information about this update' and laughed forcefully out my nose. getting carried away. this entire time i've been typing about yesterday i've been feeling like 'get this done fast so you can respond to tao's comment about involving him in liveblog, to further liveblog.' there should be a thing for this. when you start thinking things like this you should have to get 'slimed,' like on nickelodeon. originally i pictured getting body-slammed by a human-sized black letter 'X' or '/,' like what happens to numbers when you cancel them out with your pen or whatever. sliming seems better. like no matter where you are, when you start thinking meta things, ten gallons of green liquid gets dumped on you. the 'X' would vanish but the slime would stick around and make you think about how you let yourself get carried away with meta things.

6:35PM: i'm further letting the meta thing get in the way of writing about yesterday. it still seems interesting to me that i haven't written it yet but you've already read it. trying to think of ways to further the meta thing. seems like it would just involve me being there the moment you were born, saying 'you will read this someday. i want you to know that i haven't fleshed out the section on march 29, 2013 yet.' i'd need to type about going back in time to the hospital, to do that, in the liveblog.

8:20PM: zachary called to see where i was. have been writing about yesterday and feeling bored but committed to writing boring things. i said 'i'm still writing.' he said 'we're gonna go to the bbq barbeque burrito bar.' the reception was bad. i said 'you're going to what?' he said 'barbeque burrito bar. we're going.' the 'we' meant him and travis, i think. i said 'okay, sounds good.' he said 'alright' or something. we kept interrupting each other without saying words. he said 'so i'll see you later' and i said 'want me to call when i leave?' but he had already hung up.

9:44PM: finished writing yesterday. left out a lot. at some point dad entered apartment with cat food and said things about how he knew it wasn't 'the right kind' but he got it anyway. he doesn't like animals, and i think feels guilty about not liking them. he's always interacted with our animals really weirdly. like. competitive, almost. resentful and competitive and aware that they have some kind of upper hand, which he pretends they don't by like, being overly nice to them. putting on displays of niceness. he doesn't seem to mind them overall, and mom has strong feelings about avoiding situations where things could get knocked over, so that's why i'm staying here with the cats in april. dad said he was going over to mom's to order pizza and watch 'homeland' and spend the night, i think. unsure if it makes sense for me to go to philadelphia. seems like a 'waste' to not go, but also no reason to go. feel like, connected to something, doing this. this seems like the only thing i've got going for me.

9:55PM: smelled something and thought 'have been enjoying the multi-faceted crotch stylings of my crotch.' limited crotch stylings. crotch edition. i just like 'crotch stylings,' i think. like. sounds like an action movie star. my dad has christmas decorations everywhere, still. think christmas decorations have been up year-round in every place he's lived since 2008.

that's just his style: christmas style. he just really likes christmas. jesus. that is very not true. sad.

11:14PM: walked outside to the front of apartment building with computer and cigarettes and keys. since locking my keys inside last night i've very key-conscious when i leave, like, i check for keys three-to-five times instead of zero-to-two. a buick-looking car with red and blue flashing cop lights was parked outside. it idled for the duration of my cigarette, then a few moments after i finished. i thought 'i want to go inside' as it simultaneously turned off. thought 'no, that means. they're going to get you if you go inside, they heard you think 'i want to go inside.'' went inside anyway.

11:21PM: called zachary back. he was understandably upset, that i didn't call at all tonight to say i'd be late. it was always him calling. he asked what i was going to do. i said 'i don't know, there's no TV there. or internet.' he said 'yeah.' i said 'or books.' he said 'what?' i said 'or books. just us.' could tell i was being annoying and indecisive. apologized for not calling. he said it was okay. asked what i should do. he said 'you're not going to want to come tomorrow either so you might as well just come tonight.' i said 'you're right,' unsure if he was right. i said 'are you upset? i don't want to come if you're upset with me.' he said 'i'm always happy to see you.' he has said this when i've doubted if he's wanted me around. rarely feels reassuring.

11:51PM: alvie has been meowing a lot, but also not eating and acting like he doesn't know me when i pet him. walked to bedroom and he trotted behind me, then kneaded my arm hard, seemingly angrily. feeling drained from typing. will be busy and internetless in philadelphia tomorrow and want to milk the internet at dad's. milking the internet to update thing i'm currently tired of updating. good one, me. big dick boyle over here. alvie left bed abruptly to drink out of the toilet. now he looks asleep on a bathmat.

MARCH 31, 2013

12:01AM: saw something on kitchen table and thought 'dad seems to be doing a lot of seminars.' charging computer now. alvie followed me to kitchen. constant meowing. want to be able to satisfy him.

12:08AM: realistically imagined tomorrow being 'the end of it all' and felt a sinking thing.

12:11AM: peeing and leaving. no updates until tomorrow evening, probably. no plans to stop updating this.

12:23am: Zachary left voicemail saying if I hadn't left already to bring toothpaste, but if I had left, not to worry about bringing. I was in car but hadn't started it. Debated not going in for more toothpaste so it would seem like I had already left. This was really a tough one. I'd have to drive extra fast to increase realism of 'I had already left when you called.' remember some movie...jesus, seems like it's a movie I've seen a lot but I don't remember anything about it...someone is like 'why hasn't anyone ever told me about this?' and a cop-like person says 'two words: plausible deniability.' went back for toothpaste, making myself sound more reliable than I am didn't seem worth it to deny both of us toothpaste. Still lied a little on phone though. I said I had already left but 'just barely,' which is sort of true, I was in the car when I got the voicemail.

12:33am: thought 'right on red, motherfucker' and 'every day is a school day' while making a right turn on a red light near a sign that said something about school days.

12:39am: the 'plausible deniability' movie is 'independence day.' the president is asking about why no one told him about Area 51.

12:45am: passed 'not-obviously cop car' cop car who had pulled a person over. Thought 'do cops ever do bad stuff...should I be a cop now...would it be funny if I was a cop...[picture of ICP in cop uniforms]...it would suck to get pulled over and the cop happened to be a k9 cop...they should just train people to smell drugs instead, create more jobs...'

12:50am: for a long time I didn't know why people would say 'it's not a tumor' in Arnold Schwarzenegger voice and I'd say it too.

12:51am: sometimes I'm like 'thought '[thing]' and sometimes I just say the thought.

1:24am: reading this from the beginning, trying to see if I like it as a thing. Lit second cigarette of drive. Pictured map of rt. 95 between Baltimore and Philadelphia with little red circles indicating all the places the matches I've thrown out the window have landed. There would be tracking devices in the matches and it'd be a 300-year map showing where the matches went after I threw them and how they've disintegrated.

2:32am: passed familiar street sign that says 'marlborough,' where last year (exactly one year ago, I think, or one year tomorrow) Zachary and I made a wrong turn. I was driving a u-haul containing the things now arranged in storage closet. Have a feeling I'm going be feeling very stereotypical 'endings' things, like as my dominant emotion for next two days. Read beginning half of this on the drive here. Seems impossible to imagine the time before I started writing. Like, meeting Colin at Dunkin donuts in the beginning of march. Jesus. The reading. Jesus. All of the things. Seems crazy that people are allowed to live this long. It would be funny if they do a new kind of autopsy of me in 300 years and figure out I was supposed to have ended up in the body of a cricket instead of a 'Megan Boyle.'

2:44am: got lost a little. Ate 1mg Xanax and used a 'say yes to cucumbers'-brand face towel Tao and I used in Spain, that I bought again recently and every time I use makes me feel like Spain.

2:45–3:15AM: opened apartment door. the lights were off but i could sense that things weren't in their normal places. the air felt different, a little confused. i dropped my keys and made a noise. zachary said 'hey peg' from the living room. i said 'hello' and something else. i turned on the hall lights and walked to the kitchen. in the room before the kitchen, a line of stacked boxes and garbage bags looked like a firing squad to the formerly room-dominating picnic table, which had been made into more portable pieces. opened the fridge and saw condiments and sauerkraut and two cans of schaeffer's or schlitz, i forget. the cans were side-by-side and leaning in ways that wouldn't be supported without the help of plastic six-pack rings. didn't know what i expected looking in the fridge would do.

zachary had put a sheet on the couch like it was a bed. he was under our three 'watching TV in the living room' blankets. the only other thing in the room, that i remember, was the lamp that used to be on a nightstand by his side of the bed but was now beside him, on the floor. i think some of my bags were also in the room but i can't remember where or what they were. oh, and a water bottle. zachary motioned for me to lay by him and i did, with my head below his chin. felt conscious of the size of his body and mine, the warmness and the comfortable distances between what we were touching and our bones. he had sweat through his t-shirt. i could hear the nuances of our breathing in a way that made me unexplainably uncomfortable. shifted my head and he made a sound like he wanted me to leave my head where it was. a few moments later he picked up a water bottle.

i tried to ask things about his day in a normal tone but i could hear my thoughts in my voice and think he could too. he responded minimally. i said 'i'm sorry i was stupid today. i should've been here, i could've been here with you on the last day, helping you. i was stupid.' he said 'yup.' i said 'i want to make it up to you somehow. you did all the rest of my packing.' he said 'well, i had to do something.' i said 'i want to make it up to you.' he said something about brushing teeth and going to sleep and i agreed and followed him to the bathroom. he said 'i'm still asleep' in the bathroom. brushed my teeth, then put toothpaste on his toothbrush and handed it to him. he left first, said 'can you turn off the lights on your way back' from the living room. i didn't want to be asleep yet. thought about the beer in the fridge. hesitated mid-room in the direction of the kitchen, rapidly switched where i was walking a few times, then 'succumbed' and got a beer. somehow turned off lights in reverse-order, so i was walking to the living room mostly in the dark. bumped into things and made struggling/laughing sounds. zachary said 'make sure you turn them off in the right order' as i reached for living room light. i said 'okay i will.'

sat on couch where zachary's lap would be if he was sitting. started drinking the beer. knew the beer was to put off sleep, to talk more with zachary, something seemed unfinished. i wanted him to say something. don't know what. asked if he remembered getting lost on marlborough street and he said he did. stopped myself from continuing to ask 'do you remember [things about our first night at this apartment].' we said all we had to say and i finished my beer and turned off the light and we fell asleep at different times holding each other.

10:54am: was getting tired laying on my side of couch. asked to switch sides. Shirley was laying between zachary's and my calves. Zachary said 'or we could just get up, it's eleven.' I said 'can we just lay here a little more' and he said yeah. My head was on his chest and my nose was too stuffed to breathe and z turned away. Thought my breath probably smelled. Told a long dream. Left out parts involving sex with attractive men. Zachary said 'hm.' I said 'you dream?' he said 'nah.' continued to lay quietly. I said 'rabbit rabbit.' he said 'huh?' I said 'that thing you say on the first of the month for good luck, remember, 'rabbit rabbit?'' he paused, said 'think about March.' I said 'oh shit it's March thirty-first.' he said 'April fools it's March thirty-first.'

11:02am: asked for water. Zachary had an elastic in his hand. He said 'Shirley loves this thing.' I spilled a little water on Zachary and he said 'hm.' he said 'Shirley, are you the mustard man?'

3:57pm: all Zac's things moved out

Would jump down from pickup and picture landing on my legs, leg snapping completely off, z finding me saying 'oh shit'

Very hard packing the truck but also felt focused

Moved like a fast machine this time. Yes, it was the faster times this time. Thought of that while looking at a lamp in the front Seat that I knew would need to be rearranged.

Standing in kitchen now. There are things we forgot under the sink. What do you do with these things. You take them with you? Zachary is struggling with the tarp. It started raining as soon as we started moving boxes. He said 'maybe just go upstairs and chill for a little bit. I'll just do the rope by myself, I need to think and putz and I'm going to be unpleasant to be around.' I said I wanted to help still, knowing there wasn't anything left for me to do, my muscles are weak and I have, if anything, been slowing us down today. Zachary said 'yeah it doesn't make sense for you to stay. Shirley's upstairs. You should just go home, let me do this part.' I said something about following him to new jersey to ensure things didn't fall out of the truck, an idea I knew he'd reject, and he did. I said 'I'm just going to chill upstairs for a bit.' he said 'okay, whatever is fine.'

I don't think we were looking at each other much. I said 'hey, can we hang out this week?' he looked at me a little confusedly and said 'sure, we'll see, fine, whatever.' I said 'or sometime, ever?' he said 'sure yeah' and hugged me weakly. I said 'okay.' I brought his last box of books down to the truck and readjusted the lamp in the front seat so the box could fit. Now I am upstairs in the apartment, mostly empty except for these things that seem impossible to want to bring with me. To someday unpack someplace else. There is this cylinder of sea salt I bought right before we moved in together. The salt became damp early-on. It has always been hard to use, it is the object we have probably used the most and vocally resented using the most. Zachary urged me to keep it and I said I didn't want it and he said 'well I'm not going to be the one to throw it out.' I don't mind throwing them away. Salt is first to go.

3:58-11:59PM: drove to NJ. did not update.

APRIL 1, 2013

12AM–5PM: unmemorable mostly.

5:18pm: using zachary's ipad to update this. last night shortly after updating we argued more. he was like 'will this get better eventually, can we still go somewhere tonight' or something and i said 'yeah just let's watch another king of the hill then i'll feel fine.' then had totally amazing smart oh wow idea to record a video of us summarizing the argument, like talking about what happened, which is sort of what the argument was about anyway, and i spilled chicken noodle soup on computer. i was more drunk than him, i think. we sat in my car in his parents' driveway, trying to unscrew back of computer so its insides could dry. it took a long time. i ripped off the back panel with a screwdriver before all the screws were unscrewed. everything seemed fine. then i ripped out the battery in a similar way and the battery broke. the computer still turns on but the screen is fucked. felt.

i drove us around. bars were closed. zachary held computer up to the air vent, the entire drive. nice of him.

realize now that i have had minor liquid spills on computers and removing the back or any of that was probably unnecessary.

when we came inside from the drive i realized i had left my iphone and keys in my locked car. i could see the iphone and figured the keys were near it, under the seat, but i could not see the keys.

argued again before bed about drugs and spiritual experiences from drugs and some other dumb unnecessary shit. i slept in another bed in the room and tried to lure shirley onto my bed so zachary would see that she liked me more. (last night after arguing i said 'are you going to say you're sorry? if you say that i'll feel fine.' he said he wasn't going to apologize. i said 'fine then i'll take [2 or 3mg] xanax, i won't be able to sleep otherwise.' i took 4mg, i think.)

today zachary's dad's friend tried to get the door unlocked. then zachary and i went on a boat ride, to turn off his dad's houseboat. (on boat remember saying 'remember when I talked about how I remembered easter egg hunts were fun to your mom,' zac saying 'yeah something like that, it was bad'). when we came back a AAA truck was parked in the driveway and a man was doing things to my car.

the man got my car open and an alarm started honking. my keys were not in the car.

the keys were peeking out of a couch cushion.

now i am going to take zachary out to a steak dinner in atlantic city. this will probably be only update until very late tonight when i'm in baltimore and can use dad's computer.

6:00pm: Z: 'Meg's being annoying so she's driving,' he says to parents as we leave.

Driving:

> me: 'What's your favorite hip hop noise thingy?'
>
> Z: [pause] 'The kind of question you ask because you just want to say what your answer would be.'
>
> me: 'is that why you ask questions like that?'
>
> Z: 'yeah, mostly I ask to be polite.'
>
> me: 'interesting. Yeah, sometimes I ask knowing I won't be interested in the answer.'
>
> Z: 'you could do that as an article, like, add something quirky after, like 'kinds of questions not to ask in a graveyard."

Signs for 'lucy the elephant: a national monument.'

> Z: 'this is a national monument, we're about to see a national monument.'

Walk quietly to fence, make matter-of-fact anticlimactic declarations like 'Lucy,' walk quietly to car.

> Z: 'I'm always thinking of questions for yahoo answers like 'is lancaster nice?"

Merging onto highway:

> Z: 'how close is the nearest dildo to us, do you think?'

6:30-8:30pm: Seated at Knife and Fork fancy restaurant. Ordered $14 manhattans, lobster thermadore.

> Z: 'Did you feel douchey going to places like this with Tao'

me: 'No, we were both just weird, it didn't matter.'

Z: 'I'm weird but I feel like a douche here.'

me: 'I don't know it was fine.'

Z: 'Yeah haha you guys were on drugs all the time.'

me: 'I don't know, maybe,' restraining saying 'just Xanax, usually, if we went out to eat.'

8:38pm: me: 'Are you supposed to give your kids what they want, or do you buy them things you think will be good, or what? How do you know what to give them?'

Z: 'Just, TV does it.'

me: 'Oh, yeah.'

Z: 'TV raising our kids is sick.'

me: 'But no, maybe it's like that thing, 'it takes a village to raise a…''

Z: 'Interesting.'

8:53pm: Entering Bally's casino. 'Lust for life' playing and I bounce around like a maniac having the time of my life on a Royal Carribean cruise commercial.

me: [Iggy Pop voice] 'drive a G.T.O.'

Z: 'You got a real lust for life.'

me: 'He goes, he's like, 'drive a GEE TEE OH.''

Z: 'Yes that's right.'

me: 'Gotta walk on this walkway I got a lust for life'

10:18pm: bartender not letting him have two beers then I came out of bathroom and he said 'wait'll bartender sees you're real'

Gonna stay at this bar

'Gimme a shot' Z says

10:21pm: Z: 'I'm old as shit'

me: 'Compared to some kids these days'

Z: 'I miss those days'

me: 'All young women here seem like paralegals'

10:58pm: Z: 'I accept things, like Instagram,' sarcastically says more things about it.

me: 'The next girl you get pregnant you'll have to marry.' Later I say 'it's fucked up that you expect me to feel better, I tried that earlier on drive here, nothing works.'

He makes fun of the word 'matter.'

In convo about what I'm doing w/liveblog, what does he want to write/ does he wants to write again, I say 'Melville house.' Making eye contact he says 'I got it cause Tao knew them.' I kept stressing if you find something that interests you great, I don't get why he feels pleasure at disapproving of me. Asked him for help remembering a few things. He said what I'm doing w/liveblog seems great, as if 'multitude of idiots think you're great, I know what real greatness is.' I called him out somehow. He said 'you're right' a few times and seemed to want to be happy, like, touch me, be silly. On escalator he said something about how his parents wouldn't have believed I was getting ready earlier because I looked so bad.

11:06pm: Woman a few toilets down is confidently improvising 'when do we know I don't know' + other new lyrics to 'bring me a higher love' song playing on speakers. She is soloing hard over toilet flushing next to me.

11:07–11:59PM: did not update.

APRIL 2, 2013

12-1:03am: argument in car. 'There's no way to make you feel how I feel.' Back at his house I write two pieces of paper analyzing argument, feel dumb, can hear Jeopardy in living room.

Nothing left to say

'I'll get Shirley'

He's watching jeopardy

I said 'snow white' as response from the kitchen.

'I feel fine wish you didn't want to be a bitch'

'I'm not a bitch'

'We are different'

Did I leave charger

Go back to house

Saw him

'Oh that's right people don't lock things here'

Thought about calling but no

2:16am: Set cruise control. Saw shooting star.

2:27am: Swerving everywhere. Ate 30mg addy, noopept. Listening to Cocteau twins.

4:59am: Shirley sleeping. Drove around beltway again. Sober now. Intensity of argument feels foreign

Have been singing along to things

When I'm procrastinating I like to drive around the beltway in a circle, singing intensely

I know before I talked about how weird it is how people feel compelled to sing

I sing 'under pressure' a lot

I sing some taking back sunday songs

Imagining people watching

Feels good

Used to wear headphones and stare out the window imagining I was all the people in the band, usually the singer or drummer

5:08am: Saw another shooting star

5:21am: Dreading returning to dad's big time. Wherever I drive I'm just getting closer. The security guard will be there and he will write something on a clipboard and say 'have a good night.' seems terrible, what this will be now. He will be smiling and his teeth will be…he has fake teeth, they are the only young-looking thing about him. When I started liveblog I felt this thing I'm feeling now only I knew I always had two places to stay, and a person I liked to talk to.

Mouth is dry, maybe from adderall alcohol combo.

Interesting thing: I have been receiving more contact from strangers and less from friends.

5:44am: I don't remember the past two days as two separate days

Shirley awake now

Listening to 'into the shadows of my embrace' by why?

Displaced or misplaced

Driving on unfamiliar road

5:58am: Pulled into parking spot at dad's. Don't want to be in the same time unit as what I have been for past however many hours. Sleep. When I wake: take the rest of my things to storage unit, drop computer off at macmedics to repair, respond to emails.

6:03am: Can hear birds. Still in car. Sky looks bluer. Feel something inde-scribable right now. Like I don't know…what's…I don't know. Looking at dad's apartment building.

6:39am: Fed cats. Wrote dad a note asking to borrow his computer. Don't know where my toothbrush or pajamas are, know there are things in boxes in storage unit but I forget what they are or if they're important. Sitting on floor in Dad's apartment. Alvie seems unquietable. Wish I knew what to do. Ate 2mg Xanax. Alvie is annoyingly unquietable right now. I pet him and call him over and he keeps scratching inside his litter box and howling, kind of. Don't know what to do. Tomorrow I'm going to wake at some time but it will still be today. Zachary will be doing things. So will everyone. Need to find visitor parking thing for my car.

7:00am: woke dad to see where visitor parking slips were. They're strict about towing cars without slips. Gated community. I've been towed. Ate 2mg Xanax.

7:33am: ate 1mg Xanax.

2:03pm: Woke feeling like I had slept forever and not at all. Room was dark. Thought '6pm? No might even be like, 11am.' Shirley was on my leg, turning to find a place to sit/purr. Shirley: the only calming presence in my life who wants to be touched as much as I do.

2:15pm: saw notes from dad and his computer on kitchen table. Ate the last chocolate chip cookie in a bag, then the last 'petit ecolier' cookie in another bag, half-awake. Remembered Henry Rollins diet and ate odwalla bar. Going to get metrx bars today. And cans of tuna. Soup. Oranges. I want to eat more fruit than Rollins. Heated coffee in microwave.

2:32pm: it's crazy that I would re-heat the coffee. I don't like hot drinks. Why would I heat the coffee?

plans for today: go to macmedics, deposit check, retrieve hair dye and maybe masha package from mom's.

I AM NOT FUCKING WITH UNLOADING THE CONTENTS OF MY CAR INTO STORAGE UNIT TODAY. THE BACKSEAT AND TRUNK ARE FULL. IS ANYONE INTERESTED IN BUYING/TAK-ING MY 'ESTATE' (dresser, schoolwork from high school and college, stuffed animals, desk, three night stands, drawings, collages/art things, lamp—maybe a few lamps—clothes, shoes, I think a bed frame, I don't know there's way more, I don't want to think about any of this shit, feel physically heavy, like since I've started writing what things I have it has felt like water is pouring into me from every body hole)

if anyone wants to come to the storage closet with me and take whatever they want that would be nice. tired of moving things around to places where no one cares about them. tired of seeing/touching them inducing sadness. i want my things to belong to someone who wants them, like me when i first got them.

2:39pm: maybe I should move to Florida. I lost a ring mom gave me. When I wear it I feel like an impostor, but I don't know what I'm pretending to be.

2:41pm: drinking coffee: step one of getting more out of bed.

2:45pm: I'm a shitfuck.

5:50pm: sitting in car, parked outside dad's. Ate 50mg noopept. Put on eye makeup. Skin looks older. Need gas fuck I forgot. Here we go. Here comes the day. Good old 5:53pm. People say 'nowhere to go but up' but you can always go down or another direction or just stay in the same place forever. I don't know. Feeling bad. Absence of Philadelphia apartment. I still have keys, Zachary left his keys. Another year. Great.

5:58pm: macmedics is closed. So is bank. I am stupid. Going to get…er… jesus this is an embarrassing female cliché: I want to wear something that's not my old clothes. Ceremonious dress buying is about to go down. Get ready. Look the fuck out forever 21 I'm coming for you.

6:52pm: in mall parking lot. Answered phone call w/Los Angeles number. Woman said something about health insurance and put me on hold before I could respond. Man said 'is this Megan Boyle,' enunciating almost sarcastically. I said 'yeah can you guys please take my name off the list.' He hung up.

7:24pm: huge sinking sadness at seeing nice clothes on mannequins at nordstrom. Aware of my insane outfit. Feel so far away from everything, like I might be in a space station controlling 'Megan Boyle entering Nordstrom' with a joystick. The space station would be in another galaxy—maybe a long-forgotten first draft of a better space station, got caught in a wormhole or something, is now so far from everything that it's become the thing that's been making people think the universe has an end.

7:28pm: passed a man in a suit leaning on railing as he said 'I couldn't even walk today.' there is not much fabric separating my naked body from any of this.

8:47pm: watched reflection as I tried to do sexy thing the tarp was doing with its ass. The thing where the ass bumps up and down independently of the body. I can kind of do it. Thought 'I am presenting, for the males. This is presenting for the males.'

9:03pm: took picture of an area in the mall where you can sit. You can sit and do anything here. You can read James Joyce if you feel like it. You can stare. Whatever. It is here, in the middle of the mall: an area for you to enjoy. This area is here to enrich your mall experience. Now you can check 'sitting on a black leather sofa near potted plants' off your list of activities to do at a mall. As I stood here taking the picture I felt my heart expanding, like, wanting to grow into something parachute-sized that could launch out of my chest and envelop me.

9:10pm: leaving mall. Bought a lot of cheap ass shit from forever 21 (to improve attractiveness? I guess?)

9:51pm: driving to mom's to find & email or make new crying video for Rion Harmon music video solicitation, garner hair dye, books to mail. Have been searching for songs with words that make me cry and trying to sing along and cry. Cried a little while singing 'a better son/daughter' by rilo kiley.

9:54pm: on the phone, dad said 'well, around 3am you might see a man with white hair get an ice cream sandwich from the freezer. I don't know who the man is but, so,' laughing. I laughed too.

9:57pm: pulled into mom's driveway.

10–11:59PM: ordered coconut oil for mom and me. did other online things. jesus. barely remember. received package from masha containing adderall, vyvanse, fish stickers. one of the fish had a caption above his head that said 'dando.'

APRIL 3, 2013

2:58am: taking the long way home through Baltimore. On 50mg vyvanse, got distracted by twitter conversation as I sat in my room and then my mom's floor as she watched 'the graduate.' heard emotional/weepy noises coming from bed, where I thought mom had fallen asleep. Watched last scene together and felt affected. Last scene reminds me of last scene in 'mumblecore' when Tao and I are in the car after getting married. Earlier tonight Tao emailed that he wanted to get a divorce when he had more money via things being complicated with taxes and explaining marital status to people. I replied 'sweet, sounds good.' smells like Mrs. Meyers lemon hand soap in my car. Soap is near the air vent and the heat is on high. I forget when I bought it but the bottle is a little less than half-used. Zachary and I had it in our bathroom. It never fit on the sink very well.

6:51am: ate another 50mg vyvannse when I arrived at Dad's. Unpacked and hung 'temporary clothes for the few weeks I'll be here.' Responded late to an email from Jordan. Have been sitting at kitchen table, reformatting liveblog, pressing 'enter' key and dreading seeing spinning rainbow circle since maybe a little after 4am. Now sitting in car for a cigarette break. Thought, in a combination of David Bowie and Donovan's voice, like, this was sung jauntily: 'when mailman calls then the mail is due for the muppet boys at the muppet zoo.' Chewed 15mg adderall with front teeth.

7:01am: car is getting warmer. Lighting second cigarette. Keep mentally replaying mailman David Bowie song thing. Alvie has been loudly running around and meowing at a rate probably five meows every two minutes. Insatiable. The Insatiable Alvie and his traveling shitshow of terrible fiendish delights. Worried dad is going to wake and use his computer and see liveblog. An older Asian woman in shiny matching hot pink pants and jacket seems to be dragging two almost identical small dogs into dad's building.

Things to do today:

- drop off computer at macmedics
- write and mail gyno letter
- emails, as many as you can

7:25am: Alvie howling. Pet him on kitchen floor then Shirley came over and I picked them up at the same time. Shirley is drinking water out of my glass and now Alvie has joined her. No, he gave up. Alvie has given up on the water glass. Did he give up? Yes, he has officially jumped to the floor, hit the floor with a loud thump, but he is unscathed, perhaps even happy about the thumping—yes, he seems to be thumping deliberately, furthering his kitchen shitshow of tragic sounds. Trying to get more bass for the shitshow. He needs more bass, that's all it is. Once he has the bass he'll be happy. Alvie and the thump squad (a.k.a. his feet) hot on the trail for more bass. Got a craigslist tip about the sickest subwoofer, it's on top of the fridge. You don't even have to install it anywhere, it's included. All you need to do is climb to the top of the fridge and jump off. That's it. All the bass in the world. The sickest bass. Any hour, any time, really any time, all yours: just climb to the top of the fridge and jump. It's about how you hit the floor. BOOM. Thumpmaster Alvie and the thump squad will not settle for anything less than the highest gravity fridge-top bass. What I'm saying is he seems to be jumping off the fridge a lot.

7:31am: Shirley walked backwards to sit on a folder, is now staring at a lamp, bumping nose on lid of dad's computer. She has been fiending for the space between my arms and the keyboard all night. Offered water glass to Alvie, which he smelled, looked concerned at, and walked away. Oh my god. Way more meows than five every two minutes. Over ten times a minute.

7:46am: rubbed the shit out of Alvie. Gave him the nicest longest petting. He didn't purr but he looked very pleased and squinty-eyed. Seems to have quieted him. Jesus. Need to pet him and let him hump and knead on me more.

7:55AM: coffee maker started automatically a few minutes ago. can hear dad doing alvie-like thumping in bathroom. searching for bass, at this hour...jesus...nothing can stop the search...

11:39AM: emptied trash on dad's computer. forgot about volume and 'empty trash' sound startled me, mostly in genitals. a genital startling, via 'empty trash' sound. jumped alvie-style. heart still normalizing. it was like, a protective startling.

11:41AM: on some level i am always fantasizing about being on an endless cruise ship and there is no money and it's full of people i like. i think i believe that can happen, on some level, somehow. i have an automatic tendency to 'hitch a ride' on the closest things resembling the cruise ship (a.k.a. 'lack of responsibility') until i can get to the real cruise ship. seems like a really easy metaphor i just did even though it occurred in my head as original. i'm listening to the 'e.t.' theme song. the flying part. 'flying theme.'

11:52AM: it stopped playing. would constantly playing john williams movie score music at a mental ward improve things for anyone? i feel so much better listening to this. are there any people who are into really obscure movie soundtracks, like, obsessively?

12:20PM: two more people 'liked' my facebook activity on 'books.' i don't like reading things where the person is like 'this sucks' about what they're doing. but i do that. wait…i don't like it when it seems really obvious that they're enjoying writing about how much they think they suck. i'm not enjoying or not enjoying this, at this moment. this gives me an opportunity to talk about something that i don't think people have talked about but annoys me:

there is this thing…

it's impossible to talk about it without shittalking, so i will shittalk. i don't like it when people seem to fetishize depression to the point that it's like. it just seems really obvious, to me at least, if a person is saying 'i'm so sad' but they're not. it's funny to say 'i'm so sad'-like things when i'm sad sometimes, but when i feel really sad, like, can't-do-anything-but-lie-there-hoping-for-tears sad, i'm not going to tweet 'i'm so depressed i just so hate myself so much hehe.' i'm probably not going to tweet or write or do anything can't believe i'm typing this. i'm getting it out. okay. these are things i've been thinking. constipating my brain. shittin' em out rah nah.

here's the thing about my thing:

why does that bother me? because i think i'm the only person who experiences sadness/depression 'correctly?' i don't think that. okay, so problem solved. i don't think that anymore, maybe those people really do feel as sad as they seem to want to be perceived to be. they probably do, because they've been alive long enough to know how to type. they're just different. i don't know. people can bond over anything. seems like a lot of people are just looking for friends. i'm not shittalking that, i want that too. going to try to do this logically, as an 'i'm so sad lol' person, assuming their 'starting mood' is neutral/not sad, really going to try to some brain surgery on this one:

- things are going on around me, like the things in the room. i'm looking at things in a room.

- i don't feel anything (but person would not be conscious of not feeling anything, i think).

- i'm being quiet now. some people act loud and make jokes and are seen around more people, and some people are quiet and seen around less people.

- what type of person do i want to be? do i have to be one or the other?

- i'm at an age where i'm deciding things like this, where i think there are only two major personalities i can have, maybe.

- i would rather have friends than not have friends.

- it seems harder/requires more effort to be talkative and make jokes.

- i am alone, looking at things in my room, looking at the internet.

- i feel more bad than good, because i think people are having more fun than me. i consider these people my 'sources of my misery.'

- since i'm starting to think of things in terms of opposites/'sources of misery,' it means there might be a real enemy out there, my enemy is my opposite.

- my enemy, the loud person, is what made me notice my quietness, by defaultedly being louder than me and creating the position of 'less-loud person,' which feels limiting.

- i want to seek vengeance on my enemy for showing me how i'm not like them, and for having more fun than me.

- i'm going to 'take back' my enemy, i'm going to get them at their own game.

- the internet allows me to be loud without saying anything.

- what would my enemy not say: my enemy seems happy, so i must be sad.

- i'm going to 'shove it in the enemy's face' by saying 'i'm so sad.'

i have no idea.

pretty sure i can only write something like that because there was a time when i felt/thought those things. i remember deciding 'when i get to college i'm going to show the world just how likable i can be, i'm going to be friendly as shit, that'll give the world a taste of its own medicine, nothing like being affable and pleasant to really rub in the medicine.'

you could probably argue that i'm doing the same thing right now, with writing this whole thing. it certainly is a whole lot of myself i'm rubbing into something. i don't know. i seemed really different around 17-19, also. i'm like...defending myself...against myself...because i'm afraid i secretly do things for the same reasons i imagine 'i'm so sad' people doing...and i don't like that...? 'too close to home...?' oh fiddlesticks. i can't even tell if that's accurate. i don't even know if know enough about why i do things that i could admit to doing the thing i don't like. i just know how to identify/describe the thing i don't like. i don't know that about me. my instinct is to say 'no, i don't do this thing i don't like,' or 'i have done but now rarely do this thing i don't like.'

i already solved the problem when i said i don't think i'm the only person capable of experiencing sadness/depression, i don't think there's a 'correct' way to do it, and i can never know how another person really feels. so. rationally i'm set. it's still annoying to imagine someone saying 'i'm so sad' or 'everyone hates me' but without...like...so let's just say they feel okay and people like them. then like, what are you trying to do?

heard somewhere that it's easier to make people cry than make people laugh. i agree with that. laughing requires surprise. crying requires less surprise. like. hm. jesus, i actually don't know about this. because if i make myself think the same phrase over and over i'll probably start laughing. but the source of the laughing would be that like...i'm surprised at the absurdity of hearing something repeated and how easily i can make myself do it. but in 'good will hunting' robin williams kept making him repeat 'it's not your fault' and he cried. or did something like crying. i don't know let's just everyone be chill, i'm sorry for not being chill.

2:29PM: matthew donahoo emailed me an interesting question. here is what he said:

> 'Felt really interested in what you said about decrease in correspondence w friends and increased correspondence w strangers via liveblog
>
> why do you think that is happening?'

2:45PM: looked at 20-30 facebook pictures of someone i sort of dated in 2008 to see if he was still attractive. he was. not as attracted to him as i remember, but still good. not 30+ pictures good, ho ho ho. oh yuck at me.

3:58PM: emailed matthew donahoo my response. looked for video of myself crying, for rion's video thing. couldn't find. guess i'll make a new one.

4:05PM: i've been sitting in this chair for longer than some of you have been planting corn. some of you just started planting corn a few minutes ago. i'm an old pro. i'm a bass pro outdoor fishing outlet store. there is a mall in maryland where you get off an exit called 'coca cola drive' and enter the mall on something called 'bass pro drive.'

4:14PM: you can say 'several' or 'many' or 'mostly' or 'always' but probably…you can also say 'probably'…you want to avoid 'always' and 'never' because someone can probably always correct you. i learned that in law school.

4:16PM: look, another day where i didn't do what i said i would do. gotta try going to macmedics before they close at 5pm.

4:22pm: dressed in jeans, blue button-down, black cardigan. That sentence was to inform you of what I'm wearing. Laughed a little, 'on purpose,' thinking 'I hate you' mostly at myself.

4:27pm: exited apartment while making eye contact with Shirley, thinking 'I got rats on my head but don't call me the rat king' like how the Andy milionakis theme song is 'got bees on my head but don't call me a bee head.' contemplated each versions of theme song walking to my car. Remembered David Bowie song thing from this morning as I entered car.

4:31pm: just thought I heard Shirley meow to my right. Have heard 'her' meow three times since previous sentence.

4:39pm: unrolled window so 'Shirley' could have fresh air while I smoked. It's just…that…bookbag is arranged in such a way that it looks like her cat carrier on the seat the other night.

4:47pm: no way I'll make it to macmedics by 5pm. Still want to drive. Bumper sticker on Prius says 'hybrid cars: so many miles, so little gas.' Shithead. Haven't eaten since jelly beans. Food is hard. The least they could've done was made it so there was only one thing people could eat.

4:54pm: when I looked at not-as-attractive-as-I-remember person's facebook pictures I thought 'yeah but look at how much better he's doing than you. Also look at how you look, man.' pictured him reading this, grimacing and sucking air through the sides of his mouth, yanking collar for comic effect.

5:22pm: traffic. responded to emails in rapidfire manner. Matthew donahoo response got me emotional. Worried I didn't respond to Jordan in time for him to see, or maybe he just doesn't want. I don't know. Feeling heavy today. Feeling like everything hurts and dense invisible gas is infiltrating all my pores and there is no way to escape, ever. Unsure what I mean, where would I escape to? Pictured myself on bed in mom's apartment and on bed at Dad's apartment. I need to be put in a storage closet and forgotten. I'm driving to a place that closed a half an hour ago. I'm lost near d.c. Going back. What is there for me…I don't know what I want but I know it's not this…is that a country song…I felt okay leaving apartment. What happened. There is no one to talk to, really. I'm talking to this because there's no one to talk to.

5:32pm: I will be in my car again but I will never be driving home to my apartment in Philadelphia again. Okay. Don't get lost in heavy emotional thing, you are losing awareness. Why does the sun always look so bright when I feel like this. Cloudy or less bright wouldn't be better, it's just why is it always this bright when I feel this. Maybe have light sensitivity disease.

6:17pm: listened to Why? songs and let crying happen. Passed a gray-haired man with a green shirt and a tire jack on the shoulder fixing a flat during 'this blackest purse.' This was the climax of crying, seeing him caused sobbing climax, thought 'how do you do this for so long, how is he doing this, his family, all of these people around me facing forward in our cars helping us get somewhere, the same way they put blinders on horses pulling carriages in cities, it's because without blinders they can see everything around them and they panic and run, I told that to Zachary, oh my god Zachary: an old man someday, or not, how can this go on like this, remember mom said 'you're mourning, you're just in mourning' in 2011 and you didn't know what she meant died, even all the people who have ever held you and meant it and wanted you to be closer to them so they could touch more of you, remember those people, even in 2006, they couldn't hold you tight enough to make you somewhere else right now, to save you from right now, or tomorrow, going home again oh my god endless goings home, it's like they forgot to tell you they had to amputate something, phantom limb of some happy future that could've been if only not for you, all of the people around you in cars, too many, how will you ever talk to one of them again, imagine being held again knowing all this, all the good nothing will do you, you were on a comforter with flowers after everyone's parents had picked them up from your birthday party, where is the comforter now, where is the video of this, how many of your cells are always dying and flaking off to unknown places, you're always in mourning for something, little endings of you everywhere, if you saw a picture of this when you were little would you believe it, this is how you end up, they should've warned you before you started'

154

6:56pm: I'm technically wearing pieces of Philadelphia apartment/my dried sweat particles. Haven't showered in MD yet.

7:34pm: Ate 30mg adderall. It will improve. Picturing mom watching TV right now and her hair looks so pretty and bouncy and she has the green bathrobe. Maybe I should make crying video for Rion now. I look bad but I can't write and definitely seem quick to cry. Okay will try. Might be better that I look bad. His video will have insider liveblog coverage now. No don't say 'insider liveblog coverage' don't get in a good mood.

7:35-10:30PM: mostly concentrated on finding things to make me cry, fix computer/camera problems. face is big and swol from crying. had a vague memory that the last scene of 'midnight cowboy' made me like, lose my shit big time, sob for 20 minutes or something in high school, so i found it and filmed me watching it and it was pretty much like that. continued to cry after the movie. then dad's computer…camera on photobooth…damn. yeah. so. it didn't work. cried a lot to make up for it. feel good about the quality of crying i will be providing for the music video.

splashed water on face and reapplied mascara. skin looks old. cried at the final scene of 'glory,' final scene in 'one flew over the cuckoo's nest,' and listening to 'this blackest purse' and thinking a little harder about shitty things. shirley kept walking in front of me during 'glory.' picked her up and used her as kleenex. very cute-looking, her face when i do this.

10:30-11:59PM: dad came home at some point. offered me lemon bundt cake several times. i kept saying 'thank you, but not right now' and he kept asking me how i was, like, 'how are you,' thoughtfully stressing 'are,' and i'd say 'i'm really tired really don't feel social right now, would like to talk later.' i seemed to be upsetting him by not answering but didn't feel capable of answering. he said 'how's that computer working?' and i said 'slow' without thinking about what his reaction would be and he started a line of questioning like 'what should i do, should i take it to macmedics, have them clean it out?' i said 'i don't know, it seems really old, you could probably just get a new one.' he said 'you don't think macmedics could clean it out, you know, really fire it back up?' i said 'i don't know, i don't know what to do with computers, why did you ask me, can we please not talk right now, i'm sorry, i'll talk later.' he seemed upset.

forget if i've talked about this:

there are like 600 pictures of me on this computer from a few years ago. guess i used this computer for a while. many of the pictures are me being 'sexy,' like, using strategic camera angles to show off body parts in underwear, going about this in totally obvious/indulgent ways i see other girls do as if no one thinks 'this girl is being totally obvious/indulgent with her strategic camera angles.' most of the pictures were taken via request of boyfriend at the time, though i've taken similar ones alone, with no intentions to share.

have no idea if dad has seen these. at some point i started thinking about 'person seeing all the parts half their genes contributed to' sounds better than 'dad saw my sexy pics.' it was difficult to make eye contact tonight.

12:23AM: alvie howling/meowing from last night has been replaced by dad seemingly going out of his way to make noises with every part of his body. mom has noticed this also. very loud man, that dad. forgot about the loudness. he can't hear well.

12:57am: dad brushed teeth standing across the hall, in bathroom where I shaved Zachary's face a few days ago. Teeth brushing seemed to take a long time. I was in my room, putting on shoes. Apologized for acting rude and mostly unsolicitedly pointing out that the noises dad was making were my reason for leaving. Said i hadn't slept and dad reminded me of the Xanax he gave me and said 'two milligrams per night is good for me' and I said 'I don't want it now, you just gave me another pack yesterday' and remembered the thing about how I childishly refuse coffee offers from parents. Dad said 'oh I gave you more? Do you need more?' I said 'no I just said you gave me more, I don't want it right now, I don't want to sleep' and something about feeling obsessed with this. Shirley perched near me and is now purring on my leg. I turned off my light and laid on the mattress with my feet hanging off. Dad came out of bathroom but I didn't open eyes. Dad said 'just so you know rent is eleven-hundred dollars a month, twelve-hundred if you use the lights.' I sort of laughed and said 'just hire someone to murder me for that amount.' he said 'oh, no,' in a tone like he was saying 'oh, no, I had considered that.' he said 'im glad you're here.' I said 'boy am I not,' meaning less his apartment and more 'alive.' he got it, I was surprised that he got it and didn't want to say defensive things about the apartment.

1:05am: he is being loud with weed things. Drawers. Stinky weed. He like, threw money at my head, two $50s, it was weird. This was before the weed though. He said 'would you be opposed to having two fifty dollar bills?'. I said 'no that's extremely nice, you're doing the thing where you ask my permission, you don't have to do that ever, remember,' as he threw them at me. He said 'oh is that what I'm doing' stressing the 'that,' walking away in an upset way. I said I was sorry again and thanked him for the money but pretty sure I sounded irritated.

1:07am: it sounds like a long, heavy, beaded, wooden rope is rolling down wood stairs.

1:14am: said 'when are the noises going to stop?' dad appeared in doorway, said something defensive, I said 'but you said the noises would stop a while ago.' he said he was putting on a quiet guided mediation cd, that he should maybe play loud enough so I could hear. I said 'I gotta go. Your pot stinks.' it really is very stinky weed. I apologized for acting rude, not trying to cover up not being in a bad mood.

1:22am: unsure where I'm driving. Very hungry. Headache. Itchy eyes from crying and allergies to something, I think, maybe. Allergic to me. If a cop pulls me over they might smell Dad's weed, see my red cry-eyes, search me and find 'worse' drugs. Damn, where am I going?

1:24am: here are my jeopardy categories:

> Where is Megan Boyle driving
> Food amounts not 'mg'
> Days it could be
> People you have disappointed
> Tree homophones
> Famous 18th century adult children

The daily double would be its own category which is 'do you feel shittier now than ever.' I'd write like, '[crossed out] no.' Alex would say 'no, 'trout' is the answer we were looking for. Trout: that's the fish.'

There really was a 'tree homophones' category the other night.

1:50am: keep reaching for things in my jacket, thinking it's another jacket, forgetting what I was reaching for.

1:54am: pictured Joaquin Phoenix/Yoni Wolf hybrid in 19th century oil tycoon suit preaching in a sparsely furnished brown room where I'm the only other person, kneeling in the center, thinking 'will this end in sex...I hope this ends in sex...'

1:57am: button fell off my shirt. All my major jackets have lost at least one button at some point. Buttons got the right idea: stay away from me.

2:04am: what kind of food could I possibly buy and eat now. Want a Wawa BLT. Headache Jesus oof. Uff. The Rick Ross watermelon went 'uff,' remember?

2:06am: going to do words I think of as I think of them thing again: suburban banshee, banya, baobab tree, homophones, Bose, licking a grilled cheese, January, hair pattern bald spilling looseage, three ring binder, zooming canopy monkey, tres little blind mice, condominium, mortgage, a fleece seat, debbiderra, Derrida, debbie Harry, three blind mice again, horticulture, speed lasso, Tasmanian devil, bronco sleeves, a tourist attraction, blind mice (not three), twelve step dildo introduction, big ship mathematics, snorlax, bison, person saying 'it smells like…a bra' after smelling my bra, I'll never forget that I don't think, it was the person whose pictures I'm not as attracted to anymore but wish I we were in his basement sniffing my bra right now, just like in the olden days

2:14am: I want to get rammed really hard. Sexually rammed, not dodge rammed. That would help somehow. I am a self-diagnosed borderline personality disorder person. The only nice thing I have touched in days is this hot pink rubber thing on the back of my phone. It is supposed to help the phone not break. Or something. Help me help myself not break my phone when I drop it. And you better believe I will drop it.

2:20am: I shouldn't tell dad his pot stinks.

2:23am: an ambulance is behind me with its lights going and no sirens. Would be funny if an ambulance just…always followed me…reverse 'ambulance chaser'…do any billionaires hire ambulances to follow them 24/7?

2:26am: in my memory there was a period of today where I was unconscious. Or. I guess I was just barely functioning, sitting on mattress. Sheesh, right? Sheesh? Did anyone else ever say 'sheesh' like it means 'throwing in the towel, man?' Is that a Kermit the frog thing?

2:29am: impersonations I have been told I do well: Kermit the frog, Tao Lin, Zachary, a Russian person, an Indian person, Kenny. Mom and I used to do Anna Nicole smith. Both my dead grandmas. See Megan it's not so bad. Everyone thinks they can do Bob Dylan. And Bill Cosby. The nerve. The gaul. The gaul of some people. The Charles deGaul. Gaulle? It's an airport in France I think. I'm in parking spot at Dad's.

2:42AM: i feel undeserving of the colorful packaging of a 'berries go mega' odwalla 'food bar.' but. what is there to do.

3-4:40AM: ate 2mg xanax, odwalla 'berries go mega' bar, dipped potato chips in sabra 'classic hummus.' think there were some fucking cadburry mini-eggs. often fantasize about being able to relocate weight to other places on body. like, reshape my legs and 'take 'em down a few' and put them on my boobs and ass. take in waist a little, move to boobs and ass. reshape upper arms, and as usual, send that excess over to boobs and ass. face. um. i liked how pointy my face looked when i weighed 120-125lbs. that's the least i've weighed as an adult. seems like a lot for girls to weigh or something, i have some idea that most 'pretty girls' weigh 100-115. i weigh 140-145 now, probably. actually probably 135 now. highest weight was 167, in 2004. my thighs man. hehe. i think the french word for 'ham' is 'jambon.' in 2004 my thighs looked 'jambon.' bigger than ham. jambon. stereotypical female body rambling, how groundbreaking, jesus, where's my applause…waiting on that encore…i'm an insatiable george clooney, waiting backstage for my well-deserved encore…

2:00PM: woke to emails. jordan is sick and having car problems, can't come to baltimore today. felt sort of relieved via i seem to not be in a very good place, mentally, right now. also sad to not see him and sam. unsure if sam is still coming, assuming he's not. jordan expressed understanding losing contact things that i had apologized for in my email, and i sympathized with his plight to do 'can't make it to the reading' emails to people while feeling shitty today. have yet to respond.

2:15PM: poured cup of cold coffee. texted with colin. he used the phrase 'i'll create a sense of urgency' re talking to the apartment committee people, who are slow to look at tenant applications. 'create a sense of urgency.' so funny, coming from colin. i would say that. ate around ten mini chocolate cadbury eggs and read note from dad that said 'you are entitled to feel cranky' and 'i understand,' re my note from last night where i apologized for acting cranky and rude, that when i don't sleep i become sensitive to light and noise, and that my irritations were my fault, not his.

3:23PM: on bed, next to shirley. little puffy shirley. i'm sad about wandering howling alvie thumping around nervously, like he's experiencing trauma all of the time. last night he kept looking at me like 'i've lost my passport, please may i still board the plane?' i am giving him extra long pets and saying 'you special boy, you're my very special alvie' in gentle voice.

4:30PM: ate 60mg noopept, chewed a 30mg adderall with front teeth.

5:08PM: re-watched crying videos, emailed rion.

6:53PM: have been doing minimal computer things. think i need glasses. normal 'looking at words' face now involves squinting. typed 'screaming' instead of 'squinting' unconsciously. emailing jordan. headache has returned. ate another 30mg adderall. tolerance is shitty now. still haven't showered. still unmotivated to do another B.D.O. thing. interested in full-body muscle atrophy, becoming some kind of cephalopod.

7:09PM: endeared by a youtube video for a chief keef song with 25 million views not having an ad.

8:03PM: finished third email response to jordan. feels really good to be talking to jordan again.

TIMES I HAVE LEFT AIR MATTRESS TODAY:

- to get coffee

- to get coffee refill and eat noopept

i saw myself in the mirror once, on the return-walk to air mattress room. reflection looked like 'me: age 8,' 'me: age 40, heavily beaten,' and 'me: ageless me-looking ghost desperately trying to leave this body.' wearing a pink hooded sweatshirt and shiny red pajama shorts.

9:28PM: called dad back. amicable phone call. he offered to bring home food again. neither of us ever know what to eat. he said he was considering arby's because they seemed healthiest, among fast food choices, then described some of their sandwiches. he said 'sliced turkey.'

9:48PM: treated myself to a nice tall glass of water with crushed ice from the ice-maker/dispenser fridge console. using glass from old apartment. fed cats. alvie is usually the most vocal about being fed and eats the least. he follows me closely while i open cans and i trip on him sometimes in a way that feels like 'my feet get caught in alvie.'

9:52PM: in tao's email he said he wanted to get divorced for taxes before april 15, but then i'm like. 'does he just want to involve himself in the liveblog, he commented that thing about wanting to directly influence liveblog.' i know that's not it. i think. i think he's being honest about taxes. but that would be funny. i would love it, i think, would delight in including it all the more, if he did it to directly influence/place situation in liveblog.

10:47PM: chewed maybe 17mg adderall with front teeth. ate 60mg noopept. i hate how pills/drugs taste at first but then i like it. cats heard noopept bag and ran to me, thinking it was their bag of 'greenies' treats, no doubt. i gave them treats. now we are all partying. bathroom light is no longer doing a strobe light effect, though. had to fix it. couldn't take it anymore. out-partied by yet another bathroom light: the megan boyle story.

thought some version of this as i sealed noopept bag and distributed 'greenies:' for my next update i'll need to say i looked at sam pink's blog to see if he came to baltimore without jordan, saw no information about that, typed 'yo is you in baltimore' in a comment box, deleted, thought 'no just email it,' then 'no, maybe…no…since you've already debated what to do it will take you forever to type in a way you don't hate, plus you smell strongly like all the things that smell on you, plus you were afraid to buy food last night because it would've meant talking to another person, so maybe you are not exactly DJ funbags right now,' then thought 'if i type any of this on the liveblog it's going to seem indirect or manipulative, but i'm not aware of wanting to manipulate anything. this would be indirect of me to include if contacting him was my goal, but i gave up on that temporarily, and talked about giving it up, so i'm not being indirect.'

feels weird to know that he could be reading this, or that anyone could, and the possibility of it influencing anything. but also good, like. why not? this is the closest thing to telepathy i can think of. i kind of wish the world functioned on telepathy. this is as much of me i can transport into a document at the speed of typing. i am limited to how fast i can type (and the availability of typing-reading situations). i think much faster than i type.

'thinking speed' ratio to 'typing speed' ratio: jesus. didn't factor in autonomous body shit things like breathing, which. jesus.

SOME THINKING RATIOS:

- existential speed to thought speed: 100,000 : 1

- thinking speed to typing speed: 16.6 : 1

- thinking speed to talking speed: 60 : 1

- thoughts that seem interesting enough to become language vs. other thoughts: 3 : 500

- thoughts that seem interesting enough to become language vs. thoughts that become liveblog: 5 : 1

- thoughts that seem interesting enough to become language vs. thoughts that become talking: 15 : 1

- thoughts i'm aware of vs. autonomous/unconscious thoughts: 100 : [no idea]

WHAT DO I MEAN BY 'EXISTENTIAL SPEED:'

including autonomous/unconscious things, i feel like my thoughts move at probably around 800-1000mph, except when i'm sleeping. i type maybe 60 words per minute (unsure of this, 60 seems easy for this example), so that's 3600 words per hour, 60 miles per hour. wait, like one of my tiny motions between key presses is moving at 60mph? that seems high. i don't know. it also feels really fast. i just tensed my arm muscles and thought 'go as fast as you can go' and like, vibrated. it was definitely faster than how fast i type.

60mph feels like nothing in a car, but if i'm standing on the side of the road, a car passing at 60mph would look fast. consider that cars usually only move 60mph in one direction (forwards). imagine a car going forwards 6" at 60mph then immediately reversing 6" at 60mph. okay, now think about your fingers when you type. 6" is a generous estimate for the distance they travel between keys. that's, like, if you're a really bad typer. this seems wrong though. seems possible that my fingers type something comparable to 60mph, scaled-down. 800-1000mph is how fast thinking feels in my head—no way to measure for sure, just 'suspend disbelief' for this one. so:

- 1000mph (maximum thinking speed) / 60mph (maximum typing speed) = 16.6

- 16.6 thoughts per 1 second

- light travels 186,282 miles per second

- 60 seconds in 1 minute * 186,282 miles travelled in 1 second = 11,176,920 miles traveled per minute

- 11,176,920 miles per minute * 60 minutes in 1 hour = 670,615,200 miles per hour

- damn, so is the speed of light…um. why is shit always '60.' this is hard. this is hard. this is hard. this is hard. i'm laughing.

- light travels at 670,615,200 miles per hour (in a vacuum)

- 16.6 thoughts per second * 60 seconds per minute = 996 thoughts per minute * 60 minutes in an hour = 59,760 thoughts per hour

- 670,615,200 (miles traveled by light per hour) / 59,760 (thoughts per hour) = 11,221.8 (rounding that shit up)

- 11,222 : 1

what does that…

i think that would be the ratio of how many miles per hour a unit of light travels versus how many miles per hour one of my thoughts travels

so the light surrounding me in this room is actually moving. it's moving at a rate of 11,222 (whatever) times as fast as the speed of one of my thoughts

light slows down when it travels through transparent objects (glass, air, water)

you can't see through people because light stops being able to pass through them they should invent a thing...oh, x-rays, haha. i guess that's what's going on, with x-rays

forgot where i was going with this, feel like i'm getting there though

11:42PM: dad appeared in doorway, wielding a paper bag containing a sandwich and chips, or so i am told. we will see later. the sandwich was made by nuns who...i guess my dad rents an office to a priest who...somehow the nuns assemble sandwiches and other things into paper bags and sometimes my dad receives a bag. o! a sandwich has been bestowed onto me this blessed night, and for this i thank ye lord. for real though i am happy about this. friendly interactions with dad. he tripped on a fan in the hallway and there was a big crash. then from somewhere in the living room he said 'is it 'sherry' or 'shirley?'' i said 'shirley.' he said 'what?' i said 'shirley, like certainly.' he said 'is this shirley?' i said 'yeah, that's shirley. shirley, like surely, like 'surely that's the cat.'' thought 'trout: that's the fish.' i missed jeopardy tonight.

APRIL 5, 2013

1:24AM: ate 20mg adderall. dad helped with ratio math. alvie seems particularly insatiable tonight. he doesn't seem to want to knead me or be pet. he's been walking hesitantly and meowing with big eyes, sometimes with with his tail up like he's happy. he is batting at my slipper and acting startled. now he is trying other shoes. smelling, not touching. now the carpet. smelling and very light batting, more like 'pawing.' earlier he looked at me and meowed. when i stood he started trotting confidently, like he had wanted me to follow him. he led me to the middle of the kitchen, where he sat and looked me in the eye and meowed. what could it mean. pictured woody allen going on an alvie rant, finishing with 'and that's just like how it was with [woman]. women: [something about women]. i never figured it out.' which is funny, i forgot i named alvie after woody allen's character in 'annie hall.'

now alvie is sniffing between the air mattress and the corner. he is trying to go between them, head-first. jesus. really getting to the bottom of it. investigative journalism. alvie's after the nitty gritty mattress details.

now it's a little later, he got stuck and struggled. pulled him out.

1:53AM: mattress seemed to be reducing in height. felt corner where alvie got stuck doing his investigative journalism. felt/heard air leaking from a few holes too small to see. i did a duct tape treatment on the holes. say what you will about alvie's crazed, fearful disposition—he knows how to expose an air mattress for what it really is. he will spare no expense. relentless, insatiable, hard-hitting: alvie. recipient of the 2014 pulitzer prize for investigative journalism.

2:00AM: i'm always writing '2:00AM,' i feel. always. paranoid mattress is deflating again. moving this shit to the kitchen. or living room, why not? haven't tried that one yet. alvie and me bringing you the highest quality investigative journalism from the frontline of dad's apartment. the freshest sources. the timeliest updates.

2:04AM: debated moving piles of things on a desk and setting up 'workstation' there but couldn't find an outlet. just going to sit on couch until battery dies. then i'll move somewhere else. 'dad's apartment: the place you only thought you hadn't left since sometime last night. more at 11.' 'dad's apartment: a rapidly developing hot-spot for barely moving, but to what expense? more at 11.'

5:05AM: i've been typing the 'existential speed' part of the math thing. refilled water glass once and ate 15mg adderall. you are getting behind the scenes shit with this info. i feel like weird al. like weird al's voice is making me continue typing the math thing, pushing me onward, 'baying.' weird al baying at me in a voice faster than i can understand. tried to picture weird al and pictured matthew broderick on his horse at the end of 'glory.' forever picturing that one scene in 'glory:' the megan boyle story.

5:31AM: starting to hear birds.

5:45AM: staring…

6:09AM: would be crazy to read this as a 16th century italian farmer.

6:12AM: noticed i haven't been making myself laugh as much as i was in the beginning.

6:28AM: plugged in computer charger in bedroom. tried to discern source of air loss in mattress. felt around for leaks and duct taped most of a corner. as i was doing it i thought about writing about it in a more detailed way, like, going into a lydia davis thing. like the story about the hurricane that's actually about her writing the story about the hurricane but sometimes it's hard to tell. wish it had been easier to tell. felt averse to doing the lydia davis thing, and kind of averse to all fiction.

6:37AM: responded to zachary gchat from 10PM. dad is making a wide variety of loud snoring sounds. the variety is astounding. he just went 'phew, shhhhphew!' alvie meowing again. frightfest.

6:42AM: one of alvie's traveling bouts of sorrow ended in bedroom door-way. coaxed him onto mattress, where he seems tentatively/shamefully obsessed with smelling the corner where his head got stuck. pictured alvie watching my back re-tape the mattress a few minutes ago. seems lynchian, from his perspective.

6:44AM: alvie is kneading blankets close to my side.

6:46AM: alvie stopped kneading abruptly to smell the corner-area, paw at an area on the mattress which startled him, then jump off the bed.

6:52AM: dreaded sounds of a waking dad. i don't like talking to recent-ly-awake people unless i'm one of them.

6:54AM: dad walked to bathroom, said 'you're still awake, how's it going,' i said 'good,' he said 'you like what you're doing,' i said 'yup,' he used bathroom, he went to kitchen, passed my room, waved, said 'see you in a while,' i waved and said 'see you in a while.'

7:04AM: dad has elaborated on his waking sounds. at least he elaborated. also he didn't ever say he was going to elaborate, he just did it. smells like coffee. he stood in doorway and said there were some guys coming at 8 to fix a leaky pipe. i asked if he would be here and he said yes. i said 'oh that's fine, i don't care, i mean. whoever, you know, i don't care.' looked up from screen, to his face displaying an expression of 'ancient, grim, deeply-felt concern.'

7:10AM: keep thinking 'i need glasses.' also i don't like that this is called 'liveblog' and that i keep having to say 'liveblog.' i want to call it 'thing.' or 'something.' or 'thing i feel equally pressured to refer to as 'thing' and 'liveblog' and to a lesser degree, 'something." or 'jebadoh.' or 'jebadoh's complaint.' does anyone remember 'jebadoh?' mom's asswiper thing? those were the days. anyone still reading? embarrassed, a little. gotta keep going though. keeping going forever. i will not be able to do this forever. maybe. maybe calling it 'i will not be able to do this forever' would reverse-motivate me to do it forever. oh my god. the amount of times i think/try things like this. the 'what neurotic thing can i do to motivate myself' things. didn't realize it happened so often. seems like so often.

7:35AM: pasted liveblog text into a google document so now there can be this one and another one and i can put their faces up to each other and make them go 'kiss kiss kiss.'

7:43AM: today i have to shower. if nothing else. i have to eat and sleep also. maybe do some light exercise and chill the fuck out.

7:53AM: brushed teeth and washed face.

'the girl who could never get it together despite her relatively consistent commitment to hygiene.'

'the girl who sat on the air mattress at 8AM and almost graduated college'

'the girl who was asked some version of 'do you have a CVS card' exactly 76 times: a cautionary tale'

a trilogy, by stieg larsson

8:16AM: opened safari browser to dad's default homepage, aol.com. watched video called 'stranded sea lion won't leave man's car.' a man saw a sea lion on the side of the road and when pulled over to investigate, the sea lion jumped in his car. the man's voice said something about a 20-minute wait at sea world, over shots of the sea lion in a white net, kind of wagging its tail. the anchor sounded wryly cheerful as she said this has been happening a lot lately—sea lion puppies ending up in weird places, 'due to their mothers leaving too early, but no one knows for sure.'

9:55AM: ate 30mg adderall, 60mg noopept, banana. poured coffee. colin texted that my application was received and they want me to send a copy. i don't have a copy. if they have the original, wouldn't it be easier if they made a copy? colin said if i didn't have a copy, he'd 'have to email me one.'

11:33AM: 'it was scarily almost noon.' that's probably somewhere in 'ulysses' right? a good thing to do for a book like that would be to insert one sentence everyone will glaze over and forget. it has to be the same sentence for everyone, all must forget this sentence. when someone glazes over it means you can hack into their brains to find their passwords or whatever. even when you're dead. that's why you wanted to do this, see.

11:39AM: can't write a sentence without deleting some of it. including that sentence. i made a space between 'in' and 'cluding' which i deleted in previous sentence, this one was okay until i typed and deleted 'btu' after comma. bad bad bad. is jim croce the same thing as…is he associated with new orleans…creole…is he a crawdad..is leroy brown black…is jim croce black…is anyone alvie…alvie caught in the sick rapture of remembering his traumas…staring at me sitting on hind legs right now…less than a foot from my face…is he the one…is he a crawdad…

11:57AM: 16th century italian farmer on the top of a hill, holding live-blog, calling to his friend, saying 'what is 'formspring" in italian, staring at 'formspring' like the answer will come with staring, saying 'foh-rums… preenk…'

12:00PM: exit music from 'one flew over the cuckoo's nest' and 'glory' have been alternating in my head since making the video last night. so. not much to report here. good job. you're still doing good.

12:03PM: the truth is i'm stalling because i'm nervous about posting this update because i'm not in the habit of doing it anymore and i feel like i went a little overboard with some things that are maybe embarrassing. man this is stupid. i just want to do normal shit. this feels fucked up to me now. this is a documentation of a time period where i barely talked or moved or slept. also, like. fuck. let me set the scene for you:

you are late for something you said you'd do every day

nobody cares as much as you, probably

you have an outstanding balance in a bank no one cares about as much as you

and that bank is capital one

capital one: the bank for today, for tomorrow, for you, for life. check out our low financing rates online at our website capitalonebank.com.

not trying to be whatever but i never noticed the way 'alone' is situated in 'capital one'

here's a writing exercise, try to make this the last sentence of your romance novel:

'it would take her 27 years to notice the hidden word in 'capital one;' until then, there was nothing to do but wait.'

12:34PM: scrolling down the endless scroll of facebook, not looking at anything long enough to fully understand, thinking 'oh my godddddddd...' and 'how is it real' (not condescendingly, more like overwhelmed with... something...that doesn't involve the things i'm barely looking at...)

12:38PM: here's another example of something that gives me that feeling: my dad has a 'people' magazine and a 'rolling stone' magazine and some kind of hand-held game called 'pass the pigs' and three remotes and his folded pajamas and and three books and two cats and me on his bed.

12:41PM: maybe my dad thinks he's going to die soon and has, like. started asking god for repentance, not telling anyone because he agreed with god to keep this secret, if it meant he could get into heaven. that's the kind of thing i'm going to do someday, i bet. that's what the things on the bed are about. feel like i'm the only person who will fully understand the 'things on the bed' thing. this might help you understand more, i left it out at first because it feels sad and innocent and tragic and endearing but people might see it as 'making a character out of my dad,' but i'm not doing that: there is a sweatshirt that says 'number one dad' folded at the end of the bed and my dad wears it to sleep. it's like he doesn't believe it. there's nothing i can do to make him believe it.

12:52PM: vision is doing weird depth perception/enlargening/'swelling' of areas and can see neon shadow-like inverse images of things when i move my eyes. they like, follow my eyes. hm. i stink to high hell.

i know i'm the ideal candidate for something. i have always felt like 'you are the ideal candidate for something, you're going to find out what it is someday.' it's probably like, 'the ideal candidate for research about baking soda that will be cancelled before it starts.' or 'the ideal candidate for going to jail for missing jury duty due to receiving the jury duty notice months later.' i'm halfway to one of those things already happening. maybe there's still hope for me yet.

1:07PM: dark feeling very very dark dark dark maybe time to stop writing it's making dark more apparent...how could you have written this much today dark dark dark dark...done this...that's all...you...dark...jesus look at you, you're not doing anything about it...you...need to do something... make another to-do list...shit that would make it worse...all those lists... there is something else you need...the thing you need is out there...it's looking for you and it wants to help...the thing you need

4:23PM: that seemed like a good place to stop forever. missed opportunity to make that the 'stopping forever' point. could still do it but then i'd have to delete this, which feels dishonest now. sitting outside on a black wicker table, smoking cigarette i wanted at 6AM. it is sunny and warm and i'm wearing a jacket. what would i be doing if i wasn't doing this. seems like i might be dead. not dead now, dead if. you know. have been sitting in bed reading most of what i've written since atlantic city. seems hellish, repetitive. hellish document. what is there to do.

4:35PM: walked inside and locked sliding glass door, thinking "walked inside and locked sliding glass door' would be a good point to stop forever.'

7:50PM: now treating my ass with not looking at liveblog. nursing a sparkling water. why am i treating myself for...? today was the day with like. big time. big time nothing today. i am still unshowered. fingers feel strong, hands are like gollum hands again. i feel resentful nostalgia for march 17. everything that's happened. not happy there is a record of it right now but i'm not being realistic. i'm just resentful of 'better times.' what's with this thinking there's always a 'better time?'

think it's because of that staggered reinforcement thing. giving a rat a treat at staggered intervals makes them most interested and obsessed with the treat. you never know when you're going to stumble on a 'better time.' sometimes you don't even know. you're probably in one right now, soak it up. i am too maybe. no really seems like i'm in hell...i'm like...needing to punish myself or something, i don't know.

other thoughts re 'better times:' over time the people who could have ideas/ feelings about their futures survived over people who didn't, also people who could think about potentially moving their houses/potential predators survived more than others, so now there is something kind of encoded in

170

our brains, via years of evolving, that makes us think 'no don't settle for that, if you settle you get comfortable, keep looking.'

8:01PM: animal-like digging and something like gregorian chanting noises are coming from upstairs (in that order, both gone now).

REAL TALK BREAK:

- laughing re me re REAL TALK BREAK rRERER RRERERER

- 'gregorian chant' word count for total document: 2

- i don't think i've lied about anything in this that i haven't later corrected. if you know i am lying get at me. there are probably like, 12% various things i choose not to include every day, which would involve names. excluding shit like this is helpful, i don't like the amount i think about people and what people are thinking.

- why do i shiver so much. seems like i'm always shivering.

- hands look a little more 'holocaust' than 'gollum' from little cuts from moving. extra transparent bone hands. love my stupid tiny hands.

- when can REAL TALK BREAK be over, just, it's always the real talk break. that's why i laughed. also right after i typed REAL TALK BREAK it looked like a poster for dairy or something, from my elementary school cafeteria maybe.

8:18PM: i forget why i haven't been updating this to blogger, lol. that's right, have said 'gregorian chant' twice but this is the first 'lol.' damn, nevermind, there are a lot. really felt this one though. people reading this are going to react differently to what it was before, maybe. seems really dark and obsessive and desperate now. i don't feel obsessed with myself when i do this, i feel the opposite, like i'm thinking about how to say…hm. i'm imagining there is a person there and it's someone who i like but maybe i don't know them. it's definitely not me. sometimes it's people i've interacted with but most of the time it's just this idea of a person. or maybe not even a person. maybe just this. i don't know. maybe this is enough.

8:33PM: i want to watch an eight-hour holocaust movie.

9:20PM: this is day two of barely talking. also this is day two of crushed ice. things to consider. important. life. life: consider it done.

APRIL 6, 2013

9:21PM[yesterday]–12:53AM: have been fixing picture things in blogger and hitting the 'return' key a lot again. feels horrible, today. i think two days this week i've been awake for 36 or so hours, doing very similar things.

got to the update about brad and thought 'what's going to happen to brad,' started crying as i looked at pictures of him

then peed

all night the end theme song of 'one flew over the cuckoo's nest' has been looping with end theme to 'glory' and fucking me up. also the shirley song from earlier. have been reading through march 17 - now. seems so different now. i stopped taking pictures. maybe i didn't want to elaborate on moving out and atlantic city because i don't want to remember because it feels bad to remember some things. it's like a pulling sensation, like the rubber bands around your heart and stomach and face get so tight. your blood feels different. that's exactly what it's like. i keep crying, reading the earlier parts of this. looking at all the pictures on my phone. it wasn't that long ago. i'm sorry for…i don't know.

there is something so sad about dad's apartment. the christmas decorations. i'm here with the cats. alvie is unhappy.

dad returned around 11:30 from dinner with his friend. he said 'i've had one too many beers' maybe four times and kept offering me help. i didn't know what to say, i'd say 'no thank you' or 'i know you're here to help, thank you dad.' he kept coming back into the living room to say a new thing to help me or that i should take xanax or 'i hope you can take a break' and i'd say something like 'it's not exactly hard work, it's okay. i'll watch some TV.' in the kitchen he said 'you know how they say 'this too shall pass…?'' like it was the first time but he's been telling me that since i was little. felt far away. i said 'i know, that's good. you seem more worried than me dad, it's really okay.' think it started with him asking me how my night was. i had said 'not feeling great' and not much about why, but he didn't seem curious about why, he just went into 'things will get better, this too shall pass, take a break, i'm here to help' mode, maybe because of drinking.

i asked him about the TV. he showed me how to use all the remotes and said 'one of these doesn't work, so i don't know if you want to try one of them, or both, so, just so you know: it's one of these remotes. uh. it's one the comcast cable remotes we have here, here on the table, see—and here's another one for the TV. that one works pretty well. so it's not that one, it's one or the other of these two comcast remotes, here on the table, one of them doesn't—i don't know what's wrong with it—but one remote here, doesn't work.' i said 'thank you for letting me know, i'm sure i'll figure it out.' he said 'i'm sure you will, you're so smart,' saying 'you're so smart' in a way that sounded like 'you're so smart and i'm so stupid,' like he had started thinking things like this a long time ago, that his saying 'you're so smart' to me had nothing to do with me, outside of my saying something that reminded him of things other people have said that have caused him to think he's stupid.

a little after the remotes on one of his last help-offering trips i thought i wasn't going to be able to act okay and say 'thank you, no' anymore. i was thinking 'how am i still saying this' and the event of still-saying it was upsetting me, like the 'it's not my fault' part in 'good will hunting.' dad left after i said 'thank you, no.' my voice cracked when i said 'goodnight, sleep tight,' sounded blanche dubois-style, like, tremory and fragile, about to fall apart, but it was an accident. dad said 'what?'

heard teeth-brushing sounds end, then tensed at approaching footsteps. dad looked like he had a new thing to say. he said he hoped whatever it was would get better and wanted me to know that i could wake him to talk or whatever and that 'this too shall pass,' again, seeming to know in his face that i'd say 'thank you, but no' to all of these things, disappointing him somehow, making the rubber band thing happen in me. i said 'dad, remember when we talked, that talk a couple weeks ago? you're doing the thing you don't have to do, really the most helpful thing would be if you stopped offering to help me.' something seemed temporarily understood. now he is asleep. keep thinking 'there is nothing i can do' about dad and me and here and the cats and zachary and mom and all of you and everything.

i remembered something from the pre-help-offering, around the 'one too many beers' time:

dad was telling a story about his friend's wife, kind of like how i imagined the friend told it, like dad was playing back a hologram of the friend. i listened, looking mostly at my computer. the friend's wife ate a bag of popcorn and needed surgery because of an old appendectomy. dad started describing the surgery, then something about her appendix, which was gone. i said 'so now they're going in to get the other one? the one they left behind?' he laughed. i don't think he thought i was paying attention. it felt good when he laughed.

i feel a little better after writing all of this. now it's been another time unit.

before dad was here i smoked more cigarettes on the black wicker table and put a new visitor parking pass on my windshield.

2:22AM: texted masha back. can smell dad's jacket from chair-leaning position to type. he's never going to get that he's okay and that i love him and think he is a good man who is doing the best he can. his TV is made by a brand called 'life's good' with a little happy face emoticon that loads before the stations. when we were talking about the remotes, dad said he had only watched TV four or five times since moving here. i think it's been over a year. he calls it the 'entertainment center.' the thing i feel about that is so big. it's sort of like 'touched' but bigger. like the end theme song of 'glory.' he is trying the best he can. he is like alvie and afraid of everything and defending himself, i understand.

2:23–3:30AM: ate 1mg xanax. watched 'minority report' and 'project runway.' ate wheat thins, cheese-flavored potato chips dipped in hummus, chocolate snack cake in a box labeled 'great value.' cats have been oddly quiet.

watched commercials feeling like 'this is my duty, i will watch them and consider what they're saying, they were made to show me about a product, the people who made it like the product, someone wants us to know.' fell asleep on couch.

7:00AM: woke enough to see dad place comforter-style blanket on me, touch my head, leave. he left two canteloupes in pots on the stove, and wrote 'hi megan' on the bathroom mirror. both seem accidental. maybe this is a new slow-cooked melon recipe, though.

12:00PM: woke feeling unsure of where i was. remembered and thought 'oh no it's still like this.' there was a movie on TV with a woman who looked like sally field. at first i thought it was the one where she has multiple personality disorder. then i realized it wasn't sally field. the woman was on the phone. a scary little girl voice from the phone said, 'starlight star bright [something] help me it's so dark in here.' i was like 'fuck this shit.' changed the channel to something like 'the cat whisperer.' it was called 'help me with my hell cat' or 'my cat from hell.' the cat whisperer man looked like he played with smash mouth before they got big and left because he was 'on a rockabilly kick' and later got into metal and became a P.A. for the guy fieri cooking show. he was great. he whispered to cats. he had a 'clicker.' he demonstrated the 'clicker.' the couple with the hell cat looked like models for k-mart brand sleepwear. nice, ageless, inoffensive faces, dirty blonde hair, plain fitted t-shirts and jeans. the cat whisperer told them to sit on the floor and they did. he said it was good to tell their cat affirmations as the camera showed a close-up of the couple's hands touching each other's knees. then there was a shot of the cat's face with the woman behind it, petting its head, giving it an affirmation. the cat whisperer said 'marvelous.'

i turned the channel back to the not-sally field movie. the woman saw 'starbright' on a map and went there in her car, then the camera vibrated as if to show 'mental something,' then she had a bloody nose. a scary man appeared at the passenger window and yelled. thought 'they could've made it more scary, like he could've appeared near her or the car without her knowing, you'd still get to see how scary he was.' it was on lifetime, it was called 'sweet [i forget].' debated waking. put on a cooking show.

2:53PM: woke with a weight on my chest. the weight was shirley. i sat up a little and she dismounted. alvie was on a nearby ottoman, also just waking. college basketball was on TV. i walked to kitchen thinking 'liveblogblove-blogblobrloolorglr shitshithsithsishtiishit shit the internet doesn't care it's okay, nobody cares about your life as much as you, don't worry, it's okay, you're not doing it for…[trailed off as i picked up cat bowls and filled them].' washed grapes and ate a handful. poured coffee. sat at kitchen table.

4:16PM: motivated to keep doing this until forever again. the two or three barely moving/talking days are a time period that is over. thank you if you are still reading. feel less like i'm talking to myself/audience i'm inventing, more conscious of real people reading this, think that's how i felt in the beginning.

probably felt so bad yesterday and last night due to coming down from over 100mg adderall, and even being on that much feels bad after a certain point. i didn't write it down but i kept eating more, thinking 'now it'll work, now you'll complete things,' but my brain was probably like. fitzing. distracted by body aching/shivering.

5:09PM: typed 'blogger.com' as my username signing into gmail. alvie has been okay all night and all today, not meowing. think he is afraid of the air mattress.

7:28PM: smoking cigarette outside. opened photobooth, the little green light flashed on. my image on the screen looks mental ward-style, can't get my face to not look like that. face doesn't reflect how i feel, which is 'neutral/okay.' hair accurately represents unshowered-ness. the photobooth icon is red curtains over black and white tile, like the black lodge in 'twin peaks.' seems appropriate somehow.

8:43PM: last night before emotional dad update, while i was fixing layout of this/smoking/hanging new visitor parking pass on rearview mirror, i was thinking of things i wanted to include in an update of this and getting anxious that i wasn't updating/including, then thought 'no it's okay, you can say them later if you remember' and it felt nice to take a break from thinking i had to include everything.

other stuff i remember about last night:

- listened to funny voicemails from drunk masha last night. laughed in second one when she said 'rock and roll is all we have'

- ate 60mg noopept

- talked with dad on the phone, he is staying at mom's tonight

- think it is officially one week since i've showered

- fed cats

- looked for blender to make 'the least you can do' smoothie, couldn't find it, ate a banana

- now it's dark outside

- colin texted that i'll probably be able to move by the end of the month

- i miss talking to zachary; others

THINGS I WANT TO DO TONIGHT:

- re-dye hair

- shower

- email copy of application to colin

- 'take a break' from liveblog for tonight. seems necessary, if i want to keep going forever. like if i don't take little breaks i'll lose interest in updating, obscure my 'order of operations' priorities and become neurotically focused on non-helpful things

THINGS I WANT TO DO IN THE NEXT FEW DAYS:

- mail packages

- go to yoga/start exercising again in some way

- respond to more emails

- get 'continuous water flow' water thing for alvie

- take broken computer to macmedics

- no adderall until monday but if i don't want it monday then just keep going with not eating it

- deposit check i keep trying to deposit but bank is closed

- go to sleep by 2AM tonight

- wake before noon tomorrow so things won't be closed when i wake

- write and mail letter to gyno so she will refill my birth control

- take more pictures, listen to more music. felt good when i was doing those things more

TWO THOUGHTS:

- 'adderrall' looks like kind of what it makes your eyes do, feel like they removed second 'r' to evilly sway people

- i forget the second thought

10:34PM: halved one of dad's slow-cooked melons and lost interest a few bites in. catapulted a seed at the wall with my spoon. it was good. i told that seed. so much for 'taking a break from this.' no fuck that if i want a break i'm taking that break. i'm going to watch TV with my melon and you can't come.

10:37PM: pictured myself spinning a globe and going 'deedledoodoodoo-doodoodeee' and wherever my finger lands to make the globe stop, that's the place where i send the next person i kidnap, using all my money. like, i'd pick someone, buy a ticket in their name, and somehow force them onto the airplane. imagine if i had kidnapped a person or had hostages with me this whole time, or like, i'm a sick serial killer, none of you know. i'm so good at hiding it. this would be the perfect way to continue hiding it, saying something like this.

REASONS PEOPLE KIDNAP PEOPLE:

- seeking vengeance against person or person's family

- ransom/hostage thing, for money

- strange sick obsession, like to 'hoard' the person or have sex with them

- to kill them for fun

- accidental (?)

i would just want to kidnap for fun. it would be more fun to be kidnapped by someone you like. maybe. or more interesting. like if we're friends...you know that time when it's like 'this was nice, i'll see you later?' that wouldn't be allowed. i would be forcing you to continue. it would be good if that's why some people were married: one of them just kidnapped the other one for fun, then forced them to marry them. seems hard to think about how this would work or what would happen. seems like what my parents did. i'm not sure what i mean. let's say i kidnap jordan. i'm laughing.

WHAT WOULD HAPPEN IF I KIDNAPPED JORDAN CASTRO:

- he would be confused about how 'kidnapping' works if he wants to hang out/be there

- i would say 'i'm just kidnapping you, this is now a kidnapping situation, when you want to leave you won't be able to' (i'll have a gun or something)

- he would think it was funny and go along with it and be like 'oh my god, where'd you get the gun'

- we would tweet about it maybe

- at some point he'd say 'i'll just let you kill me when i want to leave' and that would become a thing we repeat to each other as a joke kind of, both probably wondering 'will it really happen'

- when it was the 'someone wants to leave' time one of us would address how it's a kidnapping situation (would be interesting if i was the one who wanted to leave, i would be kidnapping myself too then i guess, maybe/technically)

- damn what would i do...i don't think i could kill jordan...

- realistically i would probably just abandon the idea if 'am i going to kill you' or 'i really want to leave' things became too tense

- would be interesting if he developed stockholm syndrome and just liked being kidnapped by me and continued to be my (kidnapee? hostage?) forever

- would be interesting if that happened and one day we both decided to kill each other at the same time, like 30 years later

- would be interesting...30 years later...i'm assuming i'll have a job again. he would need to come with me to work every day for it to still be kidnapping

- pictured leading him on a leash and saying 'bad jordan'

- feels a little like i'm kidnapping already, by saying this, getting the gears in motion

- would be ideal if i was a high-powered criminal with a private plane and like…the stakes kept getting higher…jordan on a leash…flying to brazil to pick up the thing i'm a criminal about, like maybe more hostages or guns or drugs…would be good if i was simply a 'high-powered melon criminal'…i just always knew where the ripe melons were…that is my power over people…the police are afraid of me also, somehow… because i'm not in jail yet…but i should be…everyone knows i should be…i commit sick twisted saddam hussein style melon-seeking crimes involving a lot of technology…

11:27PM: big spider approaching. appears to be strictly floor-based spider. interesting. does the person who thought of the 'a spider walks across your sleeping face an average of eight times in your lifetime' statistic get money, from inventing that?

11:54PM: still unable to update, am still trying to fix blogger/tumblr layout things. i need to chill and maybe just stop looking at computer tonight. feel isolated, extreme minimal contact with others, extreme looking at same surroundings, extreme looking at a computer.

APRIL 7, 2013

12:38AM: have spent an inordinate time finagling with blogger.com and doing stupid computer things to try updating one big update with all my previous days of updates which i haven't been updating due to problems i've been having with updating (which were originally stalled due to moving out of an apartment and spilling soup on the faster computer i had been using).

3:54AM: sudden urge to watch 'titanic,' or just like. pictured leonardo dicaprio in a tuxedo like in that one scene. he's happy to see kate winslet on the boat, they're about to go to a fancy dinner. imagined him with that 'beaming boo boo boy' face, james cameron makes a director's cut with that shot of his face for two minutes, the rest of the movie. laughing in chair now. that would've given more attention to 'titanic.' i wanted to call it 'taiwan' just now. debated smoking dad's pot earlier. ate 1mg xanax. still haven't taken a break from computer.

4:02AM: eating 'hint of lime' tostitos and cooking pasta. eating another 1mg xanax before pasta.

4:13AM: entertainment tonight is on TV. they are showing something about the mary tyler moore show reunion. have recently been watching mary tyler moore DVDs with mom and feeling comforted by them and glad they happened. the woman who played rhoda said 'it's what life is really about,' about how much she loved mary and betty white. saw myself standing by the couch, turning up the volume to hear this, waiting for pasta to cook and felt something complex.

3:11PM: woke to some kind of 'interviews with artists' show on public television. someone had interviewed camille paglia, who looks like a shirley maclaine joan didion hybrid. listened with closed eyes while waking. camille paglia said george lucas was the greatest artist ever, because of 'return of the sith.' she talked about qualities of art made in other centuries. she observed those qualities in 'return of the sith.' she talked about 'the longest recorded scene of physical combat over a lava pit' at the end for a long time. i didn't believe her about anything.

3:41PM: i'm sitting at the kitchen table. made coffee fed cats. ate unknown quantity of cadburry 'mini eggs,' sometimes tasted them. ate 60mg noopept. plan to do tao's suggestion for re-organizing liveblog. seems monumental and annoying. every task seems monumental and annoying. shat and thought about how my external hard drive is missing. doesn't seem to matter. there have been other periods in my life like this, i'm pretty sure. maybe most of my life. it's been a week i think, since i've been at dad's. seems funny to me now. joke that takes one week to tell, unknown punchline. smell seems to have normalized, or i've normalized to it. hair looked oilier the second or third day in, now it's just hanging there. 'hanging in limp resignation.' sounds like a garfield…something…caption on 365-page garfield calender…

3:56PM: someone should insist that everything they write be published in one of those hard-to-read cursive fonts like 'lucida handwriting.' cursive is stupid. they're just teaching you 'in the future when you write printed letters, you will do it faster than you do now. some areas between letters may become connected by your pen lines. cursive will prepare you for this. don't you worry. don't lose sleep over this, little one. as long as you practice and do your homework you will be fine.'

4:42PM: seems impossible to imagine what i could be doing one week from today. no one to talk to but this thing. me and the cats in the hell room. the last time i said words was around 12AM last night when mom called.

4:54PM: 'the things i've been wearing for at least four days in a row' by tim o'brien. it's like if i do something to change right now, then. something. no one to talk to. no voice in my head telling me not to do exactly what i'm doing. usually there's a voice there, think it took the hint and is now taking a break from yelling at me.

5:05PM: there should be a charity 'life donation' thing. if my immediate death would stop the suffering of 100 people, i would donate the shit out of me. the charity organization has to make it so no one is sad about you dying, also. like, make sure no one remembers you. i guess that's what happens anyway, eventually.

5:17PM: it's sunny and 66 degrees. i'm sitting on the black wicker thing, smoking. cats are staring out the window like they're missing something. college guys are playing some kind of sport maybe 100 feet away at my '11 o'clock.'

5:20PM: something that's not my computer is making a noise like the 'volume +/-' function on macbooks. a bird maybe. or. a dog usually barks after it happens.

5:23PM: it happened again. the noise twice, then the dog four times.

5:25–11:02PM: walked inside. saw that my experimental 'last try to update' blogger update actually worked and decided to run with that. tweeted that i had moved liveblog to blogger as temporary solution until i reorganize on tumblr tonight. sam cooke and ethan ashley favorited tweet. thought 'wait for the goods to roll in, sit back and wait for those tasty retweets, you motherfucker' and felt pathetic but excited.

- showered. washed hair twice and used skin brush on my body.

- dressed in navy blue skirt, black tights, light blue button-down, black cardigan, thinking something vaguely about 'don't wear lazy/easy clothes.'

- fed cats, cleaned cat box, administered treats.

- checked internet for 'goods that have rolled in.' scant goods.

- moved 'new car'-scented tree-shaped air freshener from table to book-bag.

- walked to car. it felt distinctly 'sunday,' like this 'sunday' feeling i remember days having since i was little, some kind of impending doom.

- unwrapped 'new car' air freshener. it smelled like the smell i've been smelling for past few bad days, like it is maybe the lead singer of the band of that smell. hung it from rear-view window.

- somewhere around 7PM while driving, felt like 'it will be too soon before i'm at mom's' (mom made corned beef and cabbage for herself and dad, invited me over last night during 12AM phone call), called mom to say i'm going to whole foods first and they should eat without me.

- called zachary, not knowing why exactly. left voicemail where i said 'corned beef' but think it sounded more like 'help me.'

- didn't drive directly to whole foods. listened to xiu xiu. periodically checked phone for 'goods that have rolled in' and watched screens close automatically.

- zachary called as i made left turn into whole foods. parked far from the store. talked for maybe 15 minutes. felt a shaky/maybe mutual back-ground awareness of 'there is no more apartment between us, megan is the one who called.' think my voice sounded like 'there is a scorpion on my neck and i must remain calm' for most of the phone call. his voice sounded weak and distant, like it was getting blown away or something.

reminded me of phone calls near the time our relationship officially ended. he said he's been eating healthy foods and running every day, making things out of wood, thinking about taking a vacation, asked me what i've been eating. i said 'not much, hahaha! ohhhhh nooooo. well, there was the melon...bananas...took care of the hummus...half a sandwich? er. oh and pasta, last night i made pasta.' he said 'oh, pasta.' sky was darkening to a blue shade. watched a shadowy triangle resembling a lightless landing airplane descend into distant trees. remembered watching the end of 'signs' this morning. earlier i had asked if he wanted to hang out soon and one of us changed the subject. i asked him again and he said 'maybe...maybe next weekend.' i said 'next weekend like, how today is sunday, not this coming sunday? the one after that?' he said 'yeee-ah, the weekend after this sunday.' i said 'yeah. yeah, that would be good. we could go to atlantic city. or i could come help you make stuff with wood and ask your dad questions, so he likes me.' he said 'well, i don't know about that.' i kind of laughed and said 'yeah, yeah definitely not that.' he paused and said 'i don't know, maybe not.' i don't remember what i said. i knew it would be a 'maybe not.' a little later he said 'well, so long.' i said 'so long' and waited for the sound of him hanging up.

- saw 8:38 on my phone's clock. brought both knees to my chest in my seat and checked phone for goods, seeing none. thought about how this would be a good scene in a shitty movie.

- entered whole foods. walked quickly past someone who looked like boyfriend of former co-worker whom i nearly dodged a threesome with on a night in 2010, in the produce section.

- whole foods cashier said 'clear barcode, never works' about a water bottle that failed to scan. i said 'it's clear?' he turned the bottle in his hands then moved it closer to me, pointing at the code. it felt like one seamless motion. we didn't make eye contact, we just looked at the bottle together and he knew exactly when to take it away. i said 'oh shit, i see.' i liked him. we continued to not look at each other as he entered the code. he said 'i mean it's good for the bottle, like, it makes it look good and all, but man.' i said 'yeah, but like. man. jeez.' he just went through the motions, noticing and not-noticing me. felt so good. i wanted to continue. swiped my credit card and it didn't work. swiped it again. he said 'it says 'no card read?'' i said 'yeah, no...card' he said 'here, try it backwards,' miming how i'd do it, and i did. he tried it on his machine. he said 'it's been like this all day man, 'no card read' all day.' i said 'damn, whoa.' i couldn't figure out how to say 'first the barcode and now this, right? two things.' he handed me the bag without looking. i said 'have a good night,' sounding fake, meaning it. i looked at him but there was another customer.

- entered car and swallowed 15mg adderall. didn't want to be at mom's yet.

- names of where i drove until a little before 11PM, in order: 83N, 695 towards pikesville, 140 towards mom's apartment [called mom to say i'd be later], 695E, 70W, exit for marriottsville road, 70E, 95S, 395 into baltimore city, 83S, 695W, 795 towards reisterstown, 140 towards reisterstown, back roads to mom's.

- greeted 'homeland'-watching parents. ate 15mg adderall. have been listening to 'building nothing out of something' album by modest mouse on repeat. also in the car i sang 'me and bobby mcgee' a few times. i like going 'na na na nanana nanana nanana' and 'lawdy lawdy lawdy lawdy lawdy lawdy lawdy lord.'

11:02PM: made a text document of how i'd organize the days of liveblog in groups of four. heard kitchen sink running and parents talking in kitchen. dad said 'a six karat nugget of gold, isn't that great?' mom said 'oh no.' continued to hear talking but not words. heard dad say 'you can tell it's gold by the sound, yeah.'

APRIL 8, 2013

1:33AM: got water from kitchen in preparation for thing i'm about to do. thought 'this is better than dad's apartment because you have more memories here, it's been 22 days since you started liveblog which is the last time you remember feeling good but when you started liveblog the last time you remembered feeling good was only 10-11 days prior; how are you still living this way, how is anyone still…'

1:42AM: ate a sniggly niblet of adderall, maybe 7.5mg.

10:23AM: wrapped blanket around shoulders as socially appropriate alternative to wearing hot pink jacket indoors. have been inside, organizing pictures. parents woke a while ago. thought i would be sneaky and pre-emptively garner coffee to avoid being asked if i want coffee. it worked. ate remaining 75% of former 'snigley niblet' of adderall. mom saw me with blanket around my shoulders and said 'oh no are you frozen?' i said 'i'm fine, thank you' but felt the same coffee thing.

11:01AM: heard mom say 'in the fifties, you know, she had what they call a nervous breakdown' and a little later, 'she started selling oranges from her estate, you know, her orchard, from her estate in florida.' dad is clearing his throat and saying 'mm-hmm' with extra subwoofer bass in his voice.

11:04AM: mom is still saying the same story…laughing…just heard 'anyway, i thought it was interesting, she died at eighty-one.' they said things about aging for a while, think my mom wanted to squeeze out the drippings of the story. dad said 'oh boy time for me to get that rock salt out of the trunk.'

11:10AM: overhead mom tell a story about an old man who volunteered at the aquarium with her a few years ago. the old man volunteer was very old and frail. he smiled a lot and didn't say much. sometimes he and mom would say 'hi' to each other at the beginnings or endings of their shifts. sometimes mom would watch him answer people's questions. sometimes mom would see him sitting on a bench, staring at the fish tanks or some distance beyond them. she said 'he wanted to be left alone, i'd just as soon be left alone, i didn't want to talk to anyone either.'

i like imagining them in a giant open room, staring at fish tanks at different times, or seeing each other through a fish tank and not knowing they saw each other. the man was in a concentration camp. not sure how mom knows this.

11:52AM: in a quavering voice, mom said 'she said 'don't forget your name' to the little girls, every night before they fell asleep, she said 'be sure to say your name so you don't forget it." dad paused and said 'hm,' matter-of-factly.

12:13PM: dad approached my bedroom, opened hall closet door, walked away. a few minutes later he asked mom where the WD-40 was. mom said something about the hall closet. a few minutes later the front door opened. mom walked into the hallway and said 'mike?' she went into the bathroom. i said 'i think he's outside.' she said 'what?' i said 'i heard the door open, i think he's outside.' she made a noise like 'jesus christ' and said 'yeah, he's just. looking for something.' a little later it sounded like something small and made of metal had been tossed up the stairs. dad said 'i hope that fixed it, that oughta do it.'

1:57PM: drinking coffee. some inane shit is happening that i don't want to take time to write about more than to say 'shit is inane.' getting ready to do something B.D.O. style but this time it's baby's day out: no big whoop. would be a bigger whoop if my phone wasn't [inane shit omitted]. seems like the solution for something should be 'pour a gallon of milk on your head.' or 'pour a gallon of milk on the head of the first farmer you see.' like one or both of those are probably 'troubleshooting' answers in the manual for one of the first cell phones. instruction manual for the internet, made by the department of defense in the 70's or 80's: it's just one page that says 'pour a gallon of milk on the head of the first farmer you see.'

4:36pm: Driving to macmedics now. 77 degrees and sunny outside. Seems bad, though. Surreal 'why is it always too bright sometimes' thing combined with 'too hot, can i still breathe if it's hot?'

5:04pm: dropped off computer at macmedics. The same man who's helped me before helped me again but I don't think he recognized me. He brought his friend out from the back. They had similar reactions to computer damage. The friend took out the battery and said 'that's a fire hazard, that's a fire hazard' and they repeated that and 'not good' to each other a few times. Told them I had spilled soup on computer and got scared and drunk friend had a screwdriver, which is all true except I was the one who ripped off the back and did most of the unscrewing. The friend said 'is your friend an 800 pound gorilla?' I said 'admittedly my judgment was not the clearest at the moment,' feeling like a pro-conversationalist. The man I knew said 'it's okay, it happens to all of us. Pictured him and the friend, both in their mid-40's I think and wearing wedding rings, getting drunk in a basement LAN party with computer guys I knew in high school. Seemed hard to picture when they would've been doing that. computer seems probably okay, needs new parts, they took it overnight. I signed an iPad saying I understood things as the man I knew described. When it was time to go the man looked at my hand like we might shake hands. He gave me his card. It seemed like we might shake hands again.

5:17pm: on the way to dad's office to drop off storage unit keys. Have slammed foot on brakes to avoid collision twice so far. Liveblog seems isolating now. Passing 'coca cola drive' exit. Going 15 mph. Only person in the world.

5:24pm: earlier on the phone after it had been established several times that we were ending conversation, like had said 'okay see you soon' a few times, dad interjected to excitedly say things about getting a box spring and mattress to replace deflated air mattress in my room. He said 'it's just good for if when Jeff or Joe wants to stay over, it's good to have that for' and I interrupted him to say 'I understand.' seems shitty of me.

5:33pm: favorited tweets by Mira where she said things about spring feeling apocalyptic and worse than it was before. Feels now more than ever like 'this shouldn't be happening.'

5:36pm: am I doing something differently than in beginning of liveblog or did people just lose interest via inconsistent updates…troubled by this to annoying degree…like feel like I should stop and hide in a hole for a long time to redeem myself, big time overexposure…interested in people's thoughts re this

5:43pm: dad pulled out of office as I pulled in. Following him now to the bank. Have bloody nose in left nostril.

5:48pm: used 'say yes! to cucumbers' wet face towel on my face and looked up savings account number online. Remembered being in Spain re smell of face towel, then remembered smell of using towel the last night at the philadelphia apartment. Have less money in savings account than I thought. Wanted to deposit vice check from January. Bank was closed. Filling car with gas now. Nosebleed gone.

5:56pm: I started this thinking there was an end somehow. Like I'd figure something out and my life would improve. Maybe shitty people just stay shitty.

5:59pm: thought 'what is a sinkhole.' pictured road/oncoming traffic lowering six feet but otherwise staying the same and the six-feet-lowering movement would make a sound of 'person opening can of soda and going 'ah!''

6:27pm: conversation with dad. Did not go well. He showed me around an office building. Seems like all I want to type about this.

6:42pm: no energy to try to take photo of escalade in front of me with 'QDILLAC' license plate. This happened maybe ten minutes ago, now I have a little more energy. Now at another stoplight. Woman pulled into empty left lane, slowed car almost to a stop maybe three cars behind me, honked.

6:49pm: this thing has gotten me into some kind of…like a rhythm of something making it hard to think non-negative things about everything I see. Feel that updating this is the cause of this, also that it doesn't matter what the cause of this is, can't write anything but shit like this right now. It's like when you get comfortable enough in a relationship that you don't think about the other person and argue, but 'other person' in this situation is me. I'm repeating myself I'm repeating myself I'm repeating myself I'm repeating myself some people just chill on porches all day and drink mountain dew. People don't like shit like this for the same reasons I don't like shit like this. Need to take baby steps to get out of this.

7:56pm: does anyone call American spirit menthol lights 'punishers?'

7:57-8:17PM: while driving to mom's re-read dreams from the other day and felt i also experienced them a little, like the back corner of your brain that remembers dreams can be activated by text.

why do people hate listening to dreams?

i used to hate it too. at some point i started thinking 'it's not any less real than being awake, you're 'hating' for irrational reasons.'

8:18-8:30PM: talked with colin on phone. i will make a copy of my application and send tomorrow. seems strange to do this, like. hm. you probably get why it's strange.

8:31-11:15PM: talked with mom.

MOM CONVERSATION HIGHLIGHTS:

*   telling me she referred to a period of her life where she was mostly miserable and the only hope was that it would end by dying 'the abyss.' she said 'i thought i was in hell and my dad was the devil, i really believed that was happening.' she thought this every day but never told anyone. i said 'i feel like i'm in hell right now but dad's okay.'

- hopalong cassidy (cowboy TV star of the 50's) picked her out of a crowd and kissed her on the cheek when she was 6. when she was in her twenties, she was transcribing the memoirs of a guy who was friends with gene autry (another TV cowboy). she said 'i never asked for this, i never wanted cowboys.' seemed so funny, she looked confused. i said 'the world gave you cowboys.' we laughed a lot.

- when she said 'i just never felt like i belonged anywhere...out there... but anyway,' can picture her posture on the couch saying this, the way she said 'out there.'

- the end when we were laughing at the thing she asked me to omit, when i was picking at corned beef leftovers, she said 'you think you have it bad? come look at this.' on TV, saw a black and white room of 40-50 gaunt, terribly drained and broken-looking faces (she'd been watching a holocaust documentary). the faces looked like they'd been watching me 'this entire time' in a way that seemed shocking and hilarious and i immediately lost it. remembered a part a woody allen movie where he talks about watching holocaust movies to put himself in perspective (actually can't remember if he ever said that), then imagined mom... mom and woody allen...side-by-side with concerned faces watching an eight-hour holocaust documentary...didn't actually imagine that, that's the picture that represents the connection i thought was funny. mom was laughing and said 'this is terrible.' i said 'i'm not laughing at that, i'm laughing about you...your situation...' she said 'this is like chuckles the clown, from mary tyler moore.'

- hearing about the ticker tape room she worked in. she said 'it made a sound like...' i said 'i think i know.' she said 'it's not like a type-writer exactly.' i said 'i think i know it, the sound.' her job was to read everything on the ticker tape and cut out things that had to do with broadcasting. i said 'you were just being the internet' and she said 'that's what it was, that's exactly what. i'm so old with the ticker tape.' i said 'when i'm your age i'll be like [crotchety old woman voice] where's my gmail, how do you get the gmail, tweet tweet' and she laughed and i felt good.

- time she cried a little and said 'you'll be happy you had those experi-ences someday, very happy and very sad.'

- story about how she walked out on a job without telling anyone and she never went back

- story about how she 'made it snow' by thinking

189

- story about how she covered a consumer reports thing about technology in las vegas and interviewed the guy who made one of the first VCRs. no one knew about them yet. she was taking notes really fast, then said 'i don't know what i'm taking notes about.' the VCR man said 'do you want me to write your article for you?' she said 'i wanted to say 'yes! yes, and i'll pay you!'' but she wrote it. i said 'and you did it all without adderall.' she said 'nope, and i did it, all me no adderall.'

ate baba ganoush and three rice cakes.

11:24PM: thinking about computers…singularity…can't remember if mom and i talked about the singularity…

11:55PM: want to update really fast so i can party with mom more. hearing holocaust violins from her bedroom. going to make her turn on mary tyler moore or something. when you have a B.D.O. that's no big whoop you get to treat yourself by partying with mom.

APRIL 9, 2013

12:30AM: have been partying with tao's mushrooms liveblog, holding my pee despite abdominal laughing motion, holding pee still to write this, briefly unsure if i meant 'i have to pee' or 'i'm on mushrooms' and 'what is the difference between having to pee and being on mushrooms.'

12:31-7:59AM: partied all night long. have been partying since 3PM april 7, i think. no sleep party invitations go to only me and mom, only if she'll party hard. watched three episodes of 'homeland' with mom. she fell asleep and i watched four more in bed.

i want the red-headed slut from 'homeland' to pound me, the marine p.o.w.

can't think of his name, feel like it's 'bobby sox'

brody

brody the red-headed slut marine

what an interesting face

he's probably one of those 'secretly british' people, like christian bale

identified with claire danes when she was obsessively watching his spy cameras of the red-headed slut, feel like i do that but use the internet so i don't get the actual 'goods'

a yawn is circular-feeling, spherical

wanted all of 'homeland' to be the part at the cabin where they're making pasta, or any times they get to hang out, or knowing more about the torture parts

can barely understand what mandy patinkin is saying, he sounds like he's talking backwards most of the time

sun is up

this was nice.

8:21AM: could easily go into another 'just not going to sleep for forever' thing again right now.

4:27PM: woke a little before 4PM. calls from macmedics and colin. have a headache. read and liked heiko julien's beyonce story. i feel a little like nardwuar when i type what i've read by people i know online, like if i'd look someone in the eyes and say their name in person.

SO FAR TODAY:

- before opening eyes, thought something like "kicking the bucket.' why? it's from fishing, there would be a bucket of fish. when the fish were cooked you could kick the empty bucket. that's good. that caught on. try to make up something like 'kicking the bucket:' two syllables, one syllable, two syllables. it can also be one syllable for all three. it has to also mean dying? it's like, a situation, a bucket getting kicked? too hard.'

- ate two sugar-free sprouted cookies

- poured coffee

- printed apartment application copy

- listened to voicemail/checked email/text messages

- held one b-vitamin and looked for headache medicine. shook excedrin migrane bottle. held two capsules. peed. i've been hoping i would someday catch one of these things in action, caught it, here is what happened:

saw an almost-empty water bottle about 20' away, in the next room. thought 'complete this after flushing the toilet, before it starts refilling: swallow all three pills with the remaining water in the living room. you must be sure there is enough water before you start. is there? [seems hard to tell, will say 'yes' to up the stakes]. if there is not enough water to swallow the pills you have to swallow them with nothing or with hot coffee, so you'd better be sure there is enough water in that bottle. [doesn't look like there is enough water]. don't give me this last minute backing-down shit. i don't want to see another baghdad disaster. you let us down big time boyle. this is your chance to redeem yourself. REMEMBER: AFTER FLUSHING BUT BEFORE IT STARTS REFILLING. ONE SECOND LATE AND YOU'RE GONE. GO GO GO GO.'

i did it. i swallowed all three. there was water to spare. sitting back and waiting for the goods to roll in.

5:02PM: my ten-year high school reunion is in a few days. i think i permanently removed myself from the facebook group somehow, but now i wish i hadn't. would be a funny event to 'cover.' i could show up on a motorcycle with a chainsaw, like 'meatloaf' from 'rocky horror picture show.' like, a diamond-encrusted chainsaw. i'm not mad about high school. i don't want to hurt anyone or use a chainsaw on anything. hm, no. too 'loaded.' too much potential to be misread.

someone should bring a 'baja style' entourage to a high school reunion. like, 200 people in sexy outfits, and a DJ. like that club in level two of 'max payne 3.' brazilian, not baja. baja would be funny though, what is baja? it would be good to call your brazilian entourage 'baja style.' people would be like 'what've you been up to for the last ten years' and your eyes would roll back and become money signs and you would yell 'BAJA STYLE!!!!!!!!! !!!!!!!!!!!!!!!!!!!!!!!!!!!!!!!!!' and your entourage would lift you and carry you away.

ten-year high school reunion crashers. owen wilson and vince vaughn pretending they've only been out of high school for ten years.

'ten-year high school reunion crashers:' a sobering, cautionary tale. directed by p.t. anderson. coming to a theater near you this fall.

5:18PM: still in bedroom, finishing coffee. motivated to do something unexpected for liveblog, add variety to life. thought 'what could i do after my errands' and pictured myself with an open mouth, standing under a rock with water flowing off it, in the woods. other people would be there too. i think that's a real place i've been, a fresh water spring in maryland somewhere, there has to be…

seems impossible to not to do this now:…

STUFF I WANT TO DO BEFORE I TRY TO FIND THE ROCK WATER PLACE:

• scan application/lease, get dad's signature, scan, email to colin

• call macmedics back

• feed cats (can do after if it's getting dark)

STUFF I WANT TO DO AFTER I FIND ROCK WATER PLACE:

• go back home, send emails, get packages ready for tomorrow

• exercise in mom's gym tonight. shit i need shoes. shit my dad thinks i'm staying at his hell vortex again and will be sad that i don't want to and look disappointed. that's no reason to stay at the hell vortex, to please a person. you're not really pleasing them if you're doing something you don't want to do, for their benefit. it makes you resent them long-term.

5:35-7:00pm: downloaded, printed and signed lease. Walked to kitchen to eat something while filling out copy of apartment application. Mom was reading on the couch. She said the water spring was real, it's near our old house, she drove me there once, Vietnamese people were filling water jugs. I was little, I remember now. I pulled the skin around my eyes and said 'me rike water, hong kong.' mom laughed really hard, did not expect that.

Microwaved a pizza slice. There was a knock at the door that neither of us wanted to get. A little later mom went downstairs and returned, holding a big cardboard box. I said 'oh it's my drugs, my drug shipment.' she said 'no no no!' and swatted at me. I said 'no i bet it's our coconut oil' and unpacked the box. I said 'it is, it's the coconut oil. Why is the box so big?' mom said 'I don't know, I've noticed that recently...they're using big boxes now, everywhere...everyone.'

7:03pm: called dad to see if I could get his signature, left voicemail, started driving to his office. Listening to less than jake. Can tell I will associate this album with this time period in the future. Had previously associated it with senior year of high school.

7:33pm: dad's office lights were on but his car wasn't there. Knocked on office door. Read email from Matthew donahoo.

7:45pm: dad called, was getting a haircut when I arrived.

8:07pm: made wrong turn. Have been listening to less than jake, singing along. Minimal thoughts.

8:12pm: fake teeth security guard saluted me.

8:32pm: gave each cat a nice hard petting. Fed them and cleaned box. Humped Alvie. Placed Shirley on top of Alvie. Brushed teeth, peed, ate eyedroppers of zeolite supplement. Just kidding. I didn't hump Alvie. You thought I humped Alvie...you sick fuck...

8:34pm: rubbed Alvie's belly hard and said 'feewf...feewf...you're my wet boy.' Shirley swatted his head and ran away. Now petting Shirley one-handed. These cats like to be rubbed so hard. You can swing them around on the floor and lift them by their tails. They seem to love it. Can't believe they're real.

8:47pm: older woman with dog talked to fake teeth security guard at the gate. He gave me a pointer-finger salute. He was busy petting the dog. If you are petting a dog it's more appropriate to salute with a few fingers. Save the whole-hand salute for when you're alone and can fully focus on the salute.

9:30pm: waited for dad outside his office. Did not bring phone. Walked to back room, where he was doing something on a computer. Told him I'm staying at mom's tonight, to watch more 'homeland' and go to the gym. He said there is a gym in his condo/neighborhood too. I said things about yoga while walking to the door. Hugged him and said 'goodbye' and he said 'love yourself.' I said 'oh okay, you too, see you tomorrow' or something. Yesterday when I left I said 'this won't be the last time we ever talk, I don't know why I always think you want me to assure you of that.' he said 'I know it won't be the last time,' unconvincingly.

10:01pm: taking the long way home to listen to less than jake and sing 'me and bobby McGee' more.

10:15pm: it's harder to think 'i before e except after c' than remember how words are spelled.

10:17pm: pictured music video montage of my life (moments: sitting in car after Zachary phone call, my dad smoking weed alone last night, matthew donahoo's face in front of email to me, me and Sam pink looking for my car in new york, me in car now) during emotional part of 'the brightest bulb has burned out' by less than jake, felt moved, didn't realize this was a cliché-type image/situation until I typed.

10:25pm: the most emotional part of the song is the bass. snickered typing that.

10:28pm: the most emotional parts of the song are from 2:10-2:31 and 2:57-3:17. Emotional mostly because of lyrics…and bass…snickering… the bass isn't totally synced or something…I can't think about bass without thinking 'dad's basso voice' or 'thumpmaster Alvie's high-gravity subwoofer.'

10:38pm: smells so good outside, memory-encoded smells, the smell is making me emotional now also. spring smells like dying, like 'you had your chance.'

10:41pm: if I only wear bras without underwire will my boobs be saggier when I'm old?

10:43pm: going to punish myself so hard at gym tonight…even if I barely move it'll punish me…

10:45pm: what if spring smelled like ass

10:52pm: parked outside mom's. Unintentionally skipped then did it on purpose and laughed a little then stopped to type this.

11:02pm: stood on balcony with mom and talked about how spring smells. She said 'look at that, is that a star? It's not the bright one, it's the lower thing.' It was blinking. Remembered reading part in tao's book where I asked him if a star was moving and we talked about aliens, then remembered moment he wrote about. Told mom about dark airplane shape I saw fly over the trees at whole foods during zachary phone call. She said 'that sounds like a drone.' I said 'but it wasn't making any noise.' She said 'that's how they're making them, I heard something today. They want to make them so they can shoot a missile to north Korea from here. The missile would go all the way to there, from here.' I was staring at the star she had pointed out, trying to see if it was moving. I said 'it's an airplane I think, see? It's going. Moving.' she said 'where? Oh I see, it's an airplane.' told her about seeing two shooting stars on the way from new jersey to dad's apartment. She said 'I don't think I've ever seen one. I've seen a double rainbow.' we walked inside. I said 'do you remember hale-bopp?' she said 'yeah…was that when we were living on Brentwood?' I said 'yeah like nineteen ninety-seven.' she said 'I remember it happening but I don't remember seeing it, I don't think.' I said 'you must've, it was like, for a few days. Or like a week maybe. It was a comet, so, you know. I remember I took pictures with my camera, I remember taking pictures' and stopped myself from rambling thing I didn't see having an end. She said 'well I must've seen it.'

11:25PM: scanner isn't working. eating an orange to quell carb cravings. stomach has been hurting from pizza this entire time. updating this then going to kinkos to scan lease/application copy for colin.

APRIL 10, 2013

12:30am: arrived at FedEx. Had left driver's license and credit card at home. Drove back. Arrived at FedEx. Had left paper with signatures at home. Jogged to car and felt for driver's license. Not there. Searched FedEx and car. It was in my pocket, I didn't feel it.

12:34am: slammed brakes at red light.

12:36am: this is a little number I like to call 'the 24-hour FedEx shithead shuffle.'

12:43am: stuffed shrimp jumbo lump crabmeat 24-hour FedEx shithead shuffle relay just outside the taco bell that's right the taco bell on reisterstown road can't miss it.

12:45am: followed cab into shopping plaza containing 24-hour FedEx. A Safeway employee got out and stared at the Safeway door. Now they're gone.

1:05am: watching man with big glasses, long dreds in loose ponytail and graceful flowing sweatpants enter FedEx. He looks 'long-haired' the way long-haired cats do, from top to bottom he is long and flowy. The shithead shuffle relay is complete. When you see the long-haired man, you know the shithead shuffle is complete.

1:11am: I completed all the things I wanted to do before I find the fresh water spring and stand with my mouth under it. Mom said the water might not be flowing off a rock. It might just be a pipe. Gonna check that shit out now. Get the scoop. Scoop that shit up.

1:18am: I feel really good right now. Invincible and stupid. Wonder when I'm going to have sex again. Feels like I'm having sex right now, kind of. Invincible and stupid.

1:27am: spooky out here.

1:41am: scoop on fresh water spring: have driven up and down road mom said it was on, I see nothing, turning back.

2:15am: parked outside mom's. Sleepy. If I sleep now I can wake at a more normal time. Will be motivated to continue completing tasks at a consistent pace. Will exercise and do emails tomorrow. 'I earned it.' -J. Lo.

THINGS I AM EXCLUDING:

- romantic daydreaming, that if I included more of, might effect its likelihood to happen

- don't always say when I've peed/shat/brushed teeth/eaten noopept or vitamins

- don't talk about every text message/email exchange

- not much said about nervous habit of picking at skin on my back/neck/ears

- not deliberately excluding masturbating, whenever I talked about masturbating is the last time I did it (march 29?)

3:17AM: made corned beef + sauerkraut sandwich and felt full after a few bites. thought 'mom would think i was on drugs if she saw 'new item: sandwich, feat. bites' in fridge,' sliced off bitten parts. ate two oreos, 1mg xanax, and went to bedroom. set alarm for 11:30.

2:57PM: hit snooze. dreamed zachary bought six cans of male birth control. it like, seals up your penis hole. drinking coffee. colin says i should be able to have a meeting with the apartment people next week and i need to fill out and scan a new lease.

it's 88 degrees outside.

THINGS I WANT TO DO TODAY:

- exercise

- emails

- fill out/scan new lease

- assemble packages

- eat something not meat or carb-based

- mail letter to gyno

mouth watered when i typed 'meat or carb-based'

must do at least one thing that's not 24-hour fedex or eat vegetable-based thing if i fail to do at least one thing outside of those things: something bad will happen to five people i think about the most (they can blame it on me too, i'm already saying it will be my fault)

3:30–5:13PM: zachary called. played tic tac toe over the phone. nice time. i ate the other half of the sandwich and caramel corn.

5:50PM: drinking coffee. mom is asleep on couch. crippling indecision about what to do right now. no interesting thoughts.

POSSIBILITIES:

* dye hair (probably one hour total), buy envelopes, go to yoga class at 8 or 8:30

damn nevermind guess that was easy

6:35PM: drinking a 'the least you can do' (spinach/banana) smoothie. hair dye sinking into roots. catching up on masha's liveblog. can't believe she's still doing it, happy she is. haven't read a hand-held book for a while

6:53PM: sitting on balcony. a helicopter is circling so close in the sky that it looks the same size as a lighter on the table in front of me. dye sinking into hair. it's hot outside. in the beginning of the phone conversation, zachary said something and i said 'what?' and he said 'nevermind.' i said 'tell me.' he asked if it was okay to put a stick in a bottle of water or whiskey, because he really wanted to put a stick in his bottle. i said it was probably okay but you might end up eating some pieces of stick. he seemed happy to eat the stick pieces. confirmed with him that the stick would not go up into the neck of the bottle, it was a short stick. stick in a bottle.

8:25PM: showered and dressed and dried hair. seemed like there wouldn't be enough time to make it to yoga. wrote consent letter to gyno so she will refill my birth control. felt irritated writing it, think irritation shows in the word 'another.' the worst thing that could happen to me is i have cancer/will die sooner and if i cared about that, my consequence for not getting shit done today wouldn't have been 'something bad will happen to the five people i think about most,' it would've been 'i have cancer and will die sooner.' i'm like. re-reading 'colposcopy' things on the internet and feeling cancer in me, or just…it feels….i can't even read it all the way, like, 'forceps'…shit…i don't even know what that is…feel like a guy watching a movie where the main character's balls get kicked. i feel torture chamber-like dread about getting this shit done again. cancer would be better than torture. okay. good. confident in my decision. now i can continue regulating my…goddamnit, i don't even think birth control is a good idea.

can't imagine what would've happened if…i would have an almost five-month old baby right now…no way to provide for it…life seems…is this actually hell…

8:57PM: buying envelopes for packages now. then feed cats/get dad to sign lease. 24-hour fedex again. assembling packages. exercise. eating shitty food today. i just ate pringles dipped in baba ganoush then two little cookie things. ultimate shit eating. if i take adderall now will i need to take more, because of food? goddamnit. have really letting myself eat the worst shit the past few days. smoothie was a small improvement. okay. eating 7.5mg adderall.

9:33pm: smelled like a day in North Carolina in November 2010 when I stepped outside. Smelled hopeful. Feel instantly better being in car listening to music, reminds me of good mood yesterday. Additional tactic for feeling better: wearing dresses or skirts and showering. It makes everything an 'occasion.' 'occasionally' vs. 'occasion' in context I just used seems interesting. Ate 10mg adderall.

9:45pm: dyed hair reddish. Matthew donahoo video from email yesterday is a scene from a movie where the guy draws a diagram of what negative thinking is like. He lays down some real shit. Highly recommended. Avoid that triangle. Considering making ten triangles of my greatest hits of negative thinking image things. Seems hard at the moment.

10:09pm: bought envelopes, exercise shoes, mint green dress without trying on, gum that said 'buying this gum will feed a hungry family somewhere.' felt woman behind me in line, looking at me, standing too close to me. Thought 'feed your own goddamned family' at her, not knowing what I meant. Thought it really hard though.

10:31pm: this is my last pack of cigarettes from the carton. After this I'm buying an electronic cigarette. Caving in. Will probably 'accidentally' throw out window.

10:59pm: things went well at dad's. When I walked inside he was talking to Janice, a therapist I think, who I used to like talking to when I worked at his office doing secretary stuff in summers home from college and one high school summer (2003-2006 I think). She said 'I haven't seen you since…' and my dad made his hand child-height and I said 'two-thousand three?' Highly pleasant person, that Janice. She is 'salty,' I think. I asked how she was and she said something like 'how good can you be? I think I'm evening out after a period where things have sucked.' I said I was moving to rockaway park and wanted to be a nursing aid. She said 'that's good to hear, you're making a change, I sit and listen to these people all day and it's like 'oh my god, it's the same thing,' for years.' I said 'yeah it like, doesn't even matter what the change is to me, it's just been too much of the same thing for too long.'

11:13pm: it's raining big fat droppies hell yeah. Hell yeah rain smell. On the way to feed cats.

CLARIFICATION TO UNIVERSE:

When I said 'if I fail to complete at least one thing besides 'FedEx lease' and 'eat something non-meat/carb based' today something bad will happen to the five people I think about most' I meant 'today' like 'from now until I sleep' not 'today' like 'from now until 11:59pm.' I think the universe understood that but people reading this might not have, and they are part of the universe, so maybe could effect universe maybe.

11:18pm: I'm on 83S. Ambulance with lights on but no sirens is behind me again, on the same road/in same lane I noticed the same thing a few nights ago.

11:29pm: I'm using liveblog as surrogate boyfriend or something. There is this thing, 'Harlowe's monkeys.' they let hungry baby monkeys pick between a food dispenser and a foodless wire monkey resembling a monkey mom. They always picked the wire mom.

11:33pm: arrived at dad's. Fake teeth security guard yelled something friendly and incoherent.

11:52pm: slammed hard enough on brakes to make skidding sound before red light.

APRIL 11, 2013

12:23am: walked from FedEx to car. Man in taco bell drive thru was cackling.

12:31am: didn't want to be home yet. Driving to 24-hour grocery store to garner kale and energy drinks for 'flushing greens through my body' drink.

12:46am: pulled into parking spot at 24-hour grocery store.

12:54am: bought bunch of kale and four-pack of sugar-free red bull. This was written over a picture of Kim kardashian on cover of 'star' magazine: 'Kim ignores dire health warnings; Getting paid to binge on junk food; She demands a c-section.' Lady with white hair and 'leah' nametag rang me up. There was a card read error. Thought about whole foods cashier from the other day. Leah said 'you're not doing it fast enough.' I went fast and it worked. She said 'very good.'

1:39am: have just been driving around, listening/singing along to music. Lost focus of goals. I only feel good when I'm driving. That's false.

3:03AM: ate 10mg adderall and noopept in preparation for beasting out emails/assembling packages to mail tomorrow/exercising.

6:31am: it's 63 degrees. Sky looks pretty. I'm sitting in my car, smoking. Mom was awake when I went outside. Ate 10mg adderall. One week ago at this time I had just arrived at dad's apartment from helping zachary move to new jersey. Two weeks ago at this time I was alone in Philadelphia apartment and had probably just fallen asleep after putting all knives/sharp objects/keys/phone under my pillow and would wake in the afternoon and it would be baby's day out. Three weeks ago at this time I was smoking two cigarettes on mom's balcony re-reading things I had written earlier that night on heroin and said 'FFFF' to scare away a noise I heard from the woods. Four weeks ago at this time I don't remember at all. Even though those things aren't the best memories of my life I'm glad I wrote them down because I wouldn't remember otherwise. I don't know why that feels good. Guess it's just like 'hey, I was there, it happened, it's not that different than now, it's not something to idealize.' but I still idealize it. Smoking second cigarette. Woman with backpack is approaching and I'm typing this to avoid eye contact.

7:27AM: made kale/cantaloupe smoothie and drank fast. told mom it had been three weeks since we watched 'the master.' she had curlers in her hair and the balcony door was open. she said she wished she had been writing down things about her sophomore year of college, when she lived in a dorm with six girls who were 'always laughing,' and so could remember more now. the only thing she remembered, she said, was making fake poop out of peanut butter and bird seed to put on a toilet and leaving 'an artful trail out the bathroom door.' she laughed as she told the story and sometimes said 'it's not even funny.' i said it was funny.

9:29AM: sitting on balcony. obsessively checking all online things. writing this to stop feeling obsessive. ate maybe 20mg adderall maybe 20 minutes ago. have yet to feel effects. things i've searched on youtube: 'learning how to speak english conversation,' 'how to speak english,' 'how to be less depressed.' watched a tim and eric thing about going to the 'shrek 3' premiere. funny.

THINGS I REMEMBER HEARING ON TV, AS I REMEMBER HEARING THEM:

- this is a story about how seven strangers lived together in a house where they stop being polite and start getting real

- because you hear it [DJ record scratching] first

- the touch, the feel, of cotton: the fabric of our lives [sung in a certain way]

- pow pow power wheels

- crossfire you get caught up in the crossfire you get caught up in the crossfire you get caught up in the

- just…keep…i'm just hearing the 'where they stop being polite and start getting real' thing over and over…think that's all i really wanted to say, everything else on this list is irrelevant

THINGS THAT MADE ME CRY WHEN I WAS LITTLE:

- the part in 'goodnight moon' where it says 'goodnight mush'

- an alphabet VHS tape made by toys 'r' us where each letter was an animal, for 'n' it was 'newt.' the last line of the song was "'n' is for newt and i think he's cute, i'm sorry he plays all alone'

- big football player in 'free to be you and me' who sang a song like 'it's alright to cry, crying gets the sa-ad out' when zachary and i were taking trips from our apartment to move things into travis' basement, i saw an empty plastic container that looked like it came from one of those 25-to-50-cent toy vending machines. it was on the lid of the washing machine. for some reason i kept looking at it, probably every time we dropped off a load of stuff, and thinking "n' is for newt and i think he's cute, i'm sorry he plays all alone.'

think i just wanted to say that. all of this, everything you've read until now, everything since march 17, 2013 was all to say:

1. where people stop being polite and start getting real

2. the plastic container on the washing machine reminded me of the newt

10:08AM: that would be a good place to stop forever.

7:55pm: in parked car, thought 'doing this is making you feel worse, no you just aren't regularly talking to anyone but parents anymore, that's what was going on before you started this, you weren't really happier then, you were just enjoying writing funny things and hadn't used up all your insight/ examples, like the beginning of a relationship, everything always just planes out maybe, no don't say that you can still make it exciting'

8:20pm: entering Walmart. Figured out I could store credit card and driver's license between iPhone and hot pink rubbery phone-sleeve thing and envisioned this being the first of many times I do that, it will be the way I avoid carrying a bag/purse this summer. I'm here in Walmart to look for a continuous water flow device for Alvie.

8:23pm: when I wrote all that shit, like, big amounts of text from April 2-5, part of me was thinking 'if you write all there is to write you can fast forward to the future where you don't have any more to say.'

8:26pm: do not see continuous water flow devices. Nary a continuous water flow device to be seen at ye walmart, young goodman brown.

8:30pm: sensed something in my peripheral vision watch me walk up and down the aisles at target. Then I was closer to the 'something,' a pudgy little girl. She twisted her ankle shyly and smiled. I smiled back. She said 'I like you dress.' I smiled bigger, said 'thank y-oouuu. It's from target' sort of unconsciously and walked away, feeling like a commercial.

8:32pm: the idea of decorating dad's apartment as a birthday surprise: is it sad? Sadder than if there'd be nothing, he'd come home to nothing? Something vs. nothing. No win on this one. This one is what you'd call a 'draw.'

8:35pm: something would be better

8:47pm: waiting in long line w/small basket. Have been thinking of a rap:

> yeah I wear a target dress when I go to target
>
> and you know it's my dress cause I got it at target
>
> my shoes an my dress got em both at target
>
> and if you tryna mess we goin outside target
>
> all target eythang all target eythang (4X)
>
> a birthday dad is a birthday occasion
>
> step in line to the checkout least ragin
>
> scanner shut down but dads stay agin
>
> barcode price check hurts when they page em
>
> red shirt uniforms all upstagin
>
> Fred Durst rearrange em
>
> all target eythang paid freemason

8:52pm: the beat for that is so real in my head. When it goes 'all target eythang' people make background noises like 'tawget' and 'oh pawty' and 'guhhh' and there's this...sneaker skid? A whistle. There is a whistle. Sounds like the beastie boys.

8:58pm: driving back to dad's. Listened to a YouTube video called 'how to pronounce 'Julian Assange'' (like it rhymes with 'carte blanche,' yes that's really the first thing I thought, no I don't know what it means, I also don't know what Julian Assange did or why people are mad at him).

9:25-11:00PM: taped crepe and shiny paper decorations to ceiling. ate 20mg adderall. i liked thinking about where the next strip of paper should be taped. i preferred doing that to taping. if this was a job i'd start out as a taper and work my way up to 'telling tapers where to tape.'

11:01-11:45PM: dad didn't notice the ceiling when he walked in, which was both surprising and not. hugged him, said 'happy birthday' and 'seventy-one, look out, whoa, big time.' he said 'oh, thanks' absently. he seemed very tired, stressed about the construction of a new office. thought he'd go to bed right away but we sat and talked for a long time. he said something about how scientists think the observable universe is only fifteen percent of the universe. i said 'what happens…so if there's a fifteen percent that means there's a one-hundred percent, so what happens after the one-hundred percent?' he shifted a little in the chair and said 'you know? i don't know.'

at some point he handed me a book called 'dialectical behavioral therapy for teens' and said 'we're all teenagers when it comes to emotions, really.' book contained sentences like 'emily has problems with eating.' looked funny. dad said 'dialectical behavioral therapy is really the best, it's all they're doing now for borderlines. but i don't really think you're a borderline.' i said 'i don't think it'd be bad if…i mean i fit like, ninety-nine percent of the criteria. wait nevermind it doesn't mean anything.' it was quiet. he said 'i told my therapist you said you thought you had borderline personality disorder and she said 'borderlines are fine, they go through life fine." he looked concerned. i said 'i didn't think i wasn't going to, either way.' he said 'i think you'll be fine.' his face didn't change. i said 'i know, there's nothing…everybody's just fine, no matter what.'

11:53PM: listened to dad get ready for bed and walk around living room area. forgot he was there. he stopped by my room and said 'it's really something, you went up there like a monkey on the ceiling, taping that up there. that's going to be up there for a while, it's something to be celebrated.' i said 'it's for you, for your birthday. you get celebrated, not it.' he said 'well, it's very neat.'

APRIL 12, 2013

12:34AM: smells big time like big smoky weed. smell hit me like 'WOOF.' a guided meditation CD is playing.

1:13AM: dad seems to be chuckling in his sleep.

1:43AM: thought 'tuna forest' and pictured scary, endless gray cat hairs that go up and down forever against a white background, getting lost in them.

1:51AM: twinkly music stopped.

2:16AM: ate maybe 10mg adderall for. i don't know. i like being awake. 36 hours awake currently. thought of a good new extreme sport: it's basketball but everyone has been awake for a minimum 48 hours. the winning team gets to sleep and the losers have to stay awake until they win or they fall asleep.

3:07AM: staying awake for days in a row while having not-urgent tasks to complete means i could lie and say i fell asleep and just do nothing-type shit like what i did from 1:45-7 today, not telling anyone anything. maybe i should start posting screenshots of web history.

WHY IT'S GOOD TO SLEEP: so body can rest (?) for the next day; because other people sleep; to feel more 'part' of something; [something about success, sleeping for success]; you are more coherent (i.e. just deleted 'over time things become harder' from this part what did i mean).

WHY IT'S FUN NOT TO SLEEP: everything is funnier; you can use this time to do the fun stuff you kept forbidding yourself to do earlier; body/brain feel dynamic and shifting around a lot; being extreme feels good; everything is quiet; you know what to expect from artificial light; don't know why my body wants me to do it/seems sneaky of body.

3:30AM: pictured kramer sliding through jerry's door going 'i got a case-a the rapes, man! hacheecheecha!' and a few moments later jullian assange is wheeled into the room from his wheelchair which is more like a 'sitting sled' pulled by expensive exotic cats.

3:33AM: the last time i smoked weed i was on cocaine and very little sleep also, i think. remember feeling like everything was a game show. i kept interrupting conversations to say what would happen on the game show next.

6:20AM: answered ask.fm questions. ate maybe 15mg adderall. in bed-room at dad's. just thought 'wonder when i'll go inside the mall, i've been in this parking lot for a while.'

7:55AM: ate an amount of noopept. miss the goddamned mini-scooper. micro-scooper. briefly started writing dad's birthday card as if i was thank-ing myself for being alive for 27 years.

8:09AM: throw a little time in there why not. there are people who. jesus. tried to form thought from images of 'screaming nu-metal man against firey background' and 'pick-up truck in driveway' and 'gravestone' and 'people actually try to do this after they die.'

9:53AM: made coffee. gave dad birthday card. thought something like 'they'll find the liveblog, someone 1000 years from now will find it some-how,' then 'it doesn't matter that i'm me, that i ended up in me, body is just the spaceship i get to drive around until it's dead.'

10:00AM: people will laugh really hard at a picture of a face sometimes. candid facial expressions. that's all it takes sometimes.

10:08PM: laying on back on bed.

10:09AM: there are some faces i see for the first time and it feels like i've seen them like 500 times but for the first time, every time.

10:11AM: it would be good if you were here so i could sing this part of a pearl jam song and you could tell me what it's called. it sounds like, middle-eastern. 'nr-nr-nrr-nr-nrr-nr.'

to my eyes right now this looks like a cartoon: 'nr-nr-nrr-nr-nrr-nr.'

eddie vedder's face is like the charmander to DFW's charizard

imagine how annoying all the women who've had one night stands with DFW are

they're like 'yeah, but you know what? all of that aside, it really was perfect that it happened that way'

10:23AM: losing…something…grip on something…you can only achieve this level of consciousness by staying awake and letting time move through you. there is no short-cut to no-sleep consciousness except maybe an equally large dose of LSD and xanax.

10:25AM: THIS IS THE HOUSE WHERE SEVEN STRANGERS STOP BEING POLITE AND START GETTING REAL:

- procure continuous water flow device for alvie

- interesting: can see 'rips'/dots or something, kind of hot red-colored. they seem to be on the same layer of my eyes that the neon orange and icy blue overlays were. focusing eyes on the rips or on any of the shapes makes me feel dizzying/not-unpleasant vertigo thing, like when my lips felt pins and needles-y on top of each other. have not been thinking since the word 'vertigo.' i like, told another part of me 'write about the lip thing' and stepped away for a moment

- mail the goddamned packages

- was going to say 'exercise' but man i don't know

11:27PM: isn't it a little odd that i know what noise music is but [everything else about my life]…think zachary said something like that first as well.

11:54AM: dad left. sad when he left all of a sudden. he seemed happy today, it was nice to see him like that. he said he wouldn't have cared about his birthday but he liked my card and decorations. 'emily has problems with eating.'

11:57AM: immediate plans, big time punisher plans—not the healthiest, i am aware this is not the healthiest plan—yes i have been informed of the risks and i give my consent not to have a colposcopy—

IMMEDIATE PLANS:

- eat 30mg adderall

- beast out emails

- beast out packages

- mail that shit

- obtain continuous water flow device

- exercise?!?!?!?!?!?!?!!?!?!?!!?!!!?!?!

12:20PM: drinking coffee. heart pounding. holding off on adderall, coffee is doing the trick. just like how it does with normal people. craving the feeling of being on more adderall. think i can see inverse image of rear view window in upper half of peripheral vision, mostly right side, there is a light up there and movement. why does adderall fuck up your eyes. jaggedy. shit this shit isn't healthy. next week will be for being healthy, this week was focused on 'do tasks you said you would do.' WHICH YOU HAVE YET TO DO. you are allowed one pack of cigarettes before switching to e-cigarette. you don't need to know why i am allowing you this. i am allowing it because i make the rules and you do as i say.

12:31PM: do people know when i'm not being serious? that's why i can say stuff like that…making fun of my horrendously slow plight to do things that used to feel regular to me. 2:57PM marks 48-hour awake period, now i'm ready to play basketball. i'm a real sherman shanty. i'm shoe city. a real, how you say, 'lender's bagels.' your textbook h&r block, that's me. they make an h&r block drive thru, i think i've seen that. majesty. pray for your baby at 2:57PM, baby better be knocking em off that immediate tasks list by then.

12:32-4:19PM: sat in backyard and smoked two cigarettes. thought of something: someone should say 'THERE ARE ONLY FOUR LEFT OF [whatever it is] IN THE WORLD' and sell [whatever it is] to four people, along with a letter that says 'i lied. there are infinite [whatever it is]. only the five of us know the secret. now it will be valued more.'

is that what oil is…are they doing that with oil…

i thought of something else interesting but i didn't write it down.

wanted to be sure to include that i heard a squirrel or small animal chewing during cigarette break but now that seems stupid but maybe now it's okay, since now you know i thought this was stupid.

last night i thought i'd be going back to mom's and left the envelopes i need to put the packages in there. will not make it to post office today anyway. starting to feel disadvantaged by not sleeping, i think.

NEW PLAN OF ACTION:

- return call from macmedics

- procure continuous water flow device for alvie

- get envelopes from mom's and pack things [NOTE: I FORGET IF THE POST OFFICE RUNS ON SATURDAY. IF IT DOESN'T I HAVE TO FEDEX EVERYTHING AS PUNISHMENT FOR BEING LATE].

- make smoothie/eat something, think kale/cantaloupe smoothie yesterday morning is last thing i ate

- do emails if you feel coherent

have been stalling via email stress (not anything about people i'll be emailing, just keep picturing sounding incoherent or like i'm not giving full attention to emailing). writing this down is a step towards pushing through it. i have pushed through 'stopping rambling things.' maybe 'write emails faster' is next. got on an email kick another time during liveblog. perhaps that reign of peace and glory shall again inherit my inbox.

want to concentrate on driving and not look at phone so i will be updating minimally. feeling good about this shit again.

5:49PM: thought i was in philadelphia and couldn't deposit check. L.O.L. this is crazy should i just keep not sleeping as a social experiment

6:22PM: texting with colin. progress is happening. going to new york next week for a meeting. also 'alt citizen' wants to interview me and have a photo shoot. new york luxury treatment. thought i could go to the walgreens on reisterstown road to buy cigarettes. remembered i'm not near that road.

7:16PM: ate unknown amount noopept and saw 'blinky things.' then that stopped. i've been sitting in the same spot. feel like i'm on a debilitating hallucinogen but mostly only physically/thoughts are mostly normal. i'm taking the night off after i get alvie's water source. thought 'the chrysalis. the 2014 toyota chrysalis: hybrid car that will fly after six weeks in the garage.'

thought 'going to smoke a coffee and be right back'

going to:

- alvie water source.

- mom's? forget why but it seems good there is food.

get it together boyle man up

i'm just being lazy with typing, i feel fine, i'm better typing this is improving something

why is shirley licking the bed, you ask?

because shirley knows how to party

7:25PM: feeling more alert, engaged in act of typing, i was just needing to engage myself in something. colin just emailed me lease signed by landlord and says i should hear from them soon. okay. 'leaving here' act [unknown] scene [unknown], take two.

wait before you go, you need to mention that as you were typing all of that you thought 'this would be an interesting place for this to end, like if i died in car crash and couldn't update again.' so. by saying this right now i'm undoing that thing. though now it would be interesting, this new element. if i died after writing any of this. hm. just have a feeling, very strong feeling i'm not going to die. damn, but now…that thought is in this vortex, it's gained some kind of intelligence, like in 'contagion' where the virus keeps mutating and beating everything. hold on i think i'm beating it. in my head. not typing this part. my face just…i like, made 'a person is watching as you are suddenly attentive to something' face but no one is here. okay i beat it, i beat the dying thought. shit. shit…there are so many thoughts i'm not including now, about how i just needed to restart process, am now re-beating/outsmarting it, because that's part of the process. this is fun. i've done this before, i think. shit need to restart. shit. hold on.

i figured out a system to beat the afraid i'll die thing. it's a pick-up system. i can't update right now because anything i type will seem like 'perfect last words.'

9:12PM: it's raining. does not bode well. got in car and said 'you can't look at your phone if you want to get out of this' aloud and the mothership-like seriousness stopped. drove to petsmart. raining hard at petsmart.

9:20pm: have been sitting in car looking at instagram since 9:13pm. Scrolled to the bottom of my feed and something happened. looked like pictures were coming out of my phone. Red-orange lights on the edges of peripheral vision are twinkling mildly. Sometimes there is a blue light. Realized this via thinking 'is it a cop moving towards me.' Why is this happening, this didn't happen the night I was up for this long in march, is this from adderall

9:40PM: mom is making eggs for me. hrrrl yarll.

10:12PM: watching judd apatow movie about being 40. feel better after eating. in the beginning paul rudd was talking about his penis and i was eating sausage. said 'well i can't eat this right now' comedian-style and mom laughed. paul rudd's peepee. now he's trying to wake his daughter by saying '[whisper noises] i actually hate youuuuu.'

10:17-11:59PM: ate toast, banana, chocolate ass milk. i liked the movie. it turns out paul rudd was 40, also. surprise ending. started eighth episode of 'homeland.' shittalked mandy patinkin's backwards-talking a lot, to mom's delight, it seemed.

APRIL 13, 2013

12:01-2:21AM: finished seventh episode of 'homeland.' mom brought in pringles and the baba ganoush. tricked her into giving me most of the chips, by making her think she had taken too much…seemed devious, what i did…at some point i said 'i haven't eaten in three days,' out of guilt, wanting to justify eating. mom said 'and i have, ho ho ho!'

2:22AM: woke near the end of a 'homeland' episode. mom said 'i'm too sleepy.' i said 'me too i'm going to sleep.'

2:25-2:45AM: peed. picked at face in mirror. thought 'you look so old, your skin. eating so poorly.' got in a trance. skin picking trance. washed and applied tea tree oil to face, coconut oil to body. put on pajamas. didn't feel tired anymore.

2:45-4:00AM: ate 1mg xanax. tweeted that i've been awake since 2:57PM april 10. felt dehydrated bladder irritation things and drank water. set up camp on toilet for a long time, waiting for water effects to 'kick in.'

watched aol.com newsreel, 'morning rush.' mostly entertainment-based news. they interviewed hugh hefner's new wife, who is 26 and looks older than me. in the newsreel i remember…oh, it was about a kidney donation. strange to me, their coverage of a stranger donating a kidney to an old man. the stranger was a woman on a couch with her girlfriend. thought 'they're doing this for political reasons but [lost interest].'

peed finally (a lot of pee) and went back to bed. covered head with blankets and fell asleep to an ASMR video.

1:26PM: got a glass of milk and two oreos from kitchen. mom was reading on the couch. i said something about cookies. thought 'sweet, i'll sleep for another hour.'

6:46PM: woke. made four small pieces of toast. toast was fucking good. sat at dining room table, between kitchen and mom on the couch. mom asked if i dreamed and i told her my dream. i was driving to D.C., to meet with a therapist in adam's morgan, at her apartment. she asked if i wanted to have a sleepover and turned off the lights. i couldn't sleep. there were sick dogs outside.

mom said something about how she thinks brody's wife on 'homeland' is a terrorist. she used examples, one of which was that mandy patinkin's wife is indian. i said 'there aren't indian terrorists.' mom said 'well, i know, i know, but remember he calls his wife 'brown?' i said 'people just call…that's normal.' felt endearingly, half-seriously irritated at her, like 'come on mom, you really thought people lived on the moon?'

mom said, about bread, 'it's not even the whole foods kind, it's from wegmans!' i said 'i bet it actually has been the wegmans kind all along, they're doing that on purpose. because look: look at the bags. the bags look so similar.' she said 'you! i'm gonna punch you in the face' and walked over to me with the remaining baba ganoush dip and sort of…put the dip up to my face. it was funny.

8:09PM: sitting on balcony. the sun was setting when i came out here but it's mostly down. considered making today 'extremely short day,' where i mostly sleep. i don't feel like doing anything. just want to watch TV or read or passively absorb the internet.

8:14PM: dad came over. i'm still on the balcony. feel really good for some reason. like, 'the first night of a calm vacation in a log cabin with someone i've been in a relationship with for three months, but we still lovingly debate over when it officially started.' that feeling is influenced by how it smells like someone is lighting a fire, like, burning leaves or something. smells really good. traffic sounds and spring peepers, also. hm.

8:42PM: mom opened balcony door and said dinner (lemon chicken over pasta, with these sick as hell rolls called 'popovers') would be ready in '[blinks fingers on the palm of her hand] five minutes.' feel happy right now. why do i feel so happy.

balcony door opened, mom asked if i wanted her to make a plate for me and bring it outside. i said 'no, no, no thank you. i'll get it.' she said 'it's just the pasta, it's taking a little while to not be al dente,' pronouncing 'al dente' with a self-conscious italian accent. i said 'that's okay, i'll just get it in a few minutes. thank you.' she said 'dad and me actually figured out he's seen all the 'homelands' but two, to where we're up to from last night. so, he's only two behind.' i said 'oh good good.' felt overwhelmed with 'goodness to everything' urge. i said 'i would even like to watch the entire episode, from the beginning, from last night. that we fell asleep during.' she said 'oh good, me too, me too.'

8:53PM: ate 1mg xanax to maximize taste for impending chicken dinner. hrrrrlllll yarrrrllll. ('hrrll yarll' is what you say when your teeth are too clenched and excited for 'hell yeah'). on a maybe related note, i've lost 10lbs since beginning of march.

11:30PM: answered backlog of ask.fm questions. dad is bringing home ice cream. going to watch the shit out of some 'homeland' with parents. partying hard tonight, need to stay hydrated. might eat another xanax to make the ice cream party harder on my tongue. fucking…fuck ass…live from new york it's saturday night!!!!

11:34PM: repeated 'I WANTED THE PINT ALL TO MYSELF BUT YOU CAN HAVE A SCOOP BUT TAKE A SMALL ONE' to parents… a lot…goddamnit…have church hymn stuck in my head that goes 'glory to god on the highest / and peace, to his people on earth.'

APRIL 14, 2013

2:10AM: ate 1mg xanax, brushed teeth, washed face, peed.

4AM: woke. ate 1mg xanax, wafer-like cookie thing.

12:40PM: woke.

12:41-[unknown time]PM: answered questions on ask.fm. some idiot thinks i'm liveblogging to be ironic. i don't care about being nice or detached or whatever anymore if i think someone is saying something truly idiotic, thinking they know what i'm doing more than i know. i wish bad things upon this person, even if it's someone i like. i wish for this person to burn.

[unknown]PM: woke and read nice/funny emails from tao.

7:22PM: going to dad's to give alvie his continuous water flow device and feed cats. then back to here. jesus. tomorrow will be 'get stuff done again' day. want to forget today.

7:43pm: Listening to smashing pumpkins. Ate 1mg Xanax. On the way to do kitty business at dad's. I only have 'mayonnaise' and '1979' on iPhone. Responded to nice things moon temple + others were saying on Facebook re my liveblog, felt warm.

8:14pm: bought monster 'absolute zero' energy drink, pack of american spirit menthol lights, gas from gas station. Unknown number texted to see if I'd still do the shower noise. Responding 'yes will do it to the best of my memory then hang up.'

8:19pm: the person called. I made the noise and hung up. They texted 'thx that was great,' I texted ';) thanks I'm grinning'

8:46pm: set up continuous water flow device. Made/drank cucumber lettuce juice. Dreading carraba's take-out. I want to be healthy for the rest of the day. This could be 'transitional day into being healthy.'

9:23PM: arrived home. ate 1mg xanax. eating unhealthy things today as motivation for being healthy tomorrow. 'one last hurrah, one bleak goodbye to unhealthy eating, the green juice you had was your '[healthy dinner they give to people pardoned from death row, maybe]'

9:51PM: looking at a spread of fiendish delights i will be eating, arranged on dinner tray. fiendish italian chain restaurant to-go carby shitfuck nummmynum xanax benefits shithead delights. we're watching 'les miserables' instead of 'homeland.' fiendish fiendy fiendish...should i eat another xanax…might eat another one…shit…going 'all in,' going all in, alert: i am going 'all in' eating third 1mg xanax of the evening, basking in the delights, treating myself to a star spangled shitfest.

9:52-11:59PM: ate less than i thought i would've. fell asleep during 'les miserables,' i think.

12:00-2[something]AM: slept at the end of the bed, parents put on 'homeland.' think i was administering xanax to myself…during waking parts…during this time…i think. have very little memory of how i ended up in my bed.

6:41AM: woke and ate 1mg xanax, ate some kind of wafer cookie, went to sleep.

11:30AM: woke and ate 1mg xanax, ate some kind of wafer cookie, went to sleep.

2:26PM: woke and parents were getting ready to leave for things. feel confused and far away from the obligations that seemed important for me to complete. i think mailing packages was one of those obligations. might take a vyvanse from tao and just…beast that out…want to be healthy today, also. colin also asked me to scan and sign 'house rules' for him. i feel like a xanax zombie on my third cup of coffee and it's just making me want to sleep more.

PLAN: shower/'dress for the occasion,' eat vyvanse on the drive to whole foods, get materials for 'least you can do' smoothie, packages.

every time i see 'PLAN' or something in here it seems so futile. like, my unfinished plans from earlier, how it all keeps being a very similar 'plan'… when is this shit going to end…

i do tend to get more things done when i dress for the occasion. ODDLY.

pictured myself sitting at a table on 'the lido deck' of a cruise ship, a fat woman in a hat approaching me, saying 'ODDLY! the LIDO deck of ALL PLACES! i see you've DRESSED FOR THE OCCASION! ho ho ho!'

3:47PM: listened to a song i like by the ohioans. sounds like it'd be on the 'clueless' soundtrack, or like, playing in the background of an aerial shot of a high school that follows the main character into the school and you see how all the people in the hall react to the main character and the credits are playing.

i'm still sitting on my bed, drinking third or fourth cup of coffee. feeling less groggy. going to start stop being a shithead.

4:42PM: experiencing memory loss re 'things i'm preparing to do,' via xanax. extreme amounts of xanax the last two days, i think. unsure if i typed the total amount i ate (unsure of total amount).

THINGS I THOUGHT IN THE SHOWER:

- 'congo.' tim curry was the main actor in 'congo.' was it their plan to make him a hot sexy superstar? brandon scott gorrell said something about 'congo' and it was funny, i can't remember. tim curry was in 'home alone 2' and 'rocky horror.' he is gay.

- shave all the pubes. what good did pubes ever do you. they're just there, pubey. maybe shave for sex, you feel more sensation without pubes, plus someone…why do men have such strong opinions about pubes? men are stupid. shave pubes to 'dress for the occasion.' today's occasion: the things you'll do today. oh, the places you'll go. pubeless.

- walter mackey steak bites

- you are supposed to mail things but the post office will be closed again you dipshit. you dipshit. oh well, just actually like, just do them now.

- do i feel vyvannse? seems like…no…0.025% vyvanse effects. eat a little more adderall after the shower? but why, what are you even supposed to be doing?

4:49PM: found the underpants i was wearing moments before a penis entered my vagina for the first time, february 29, 2004.

4:51PM: i want to walk around a mall on a lot of drugs and document everything i see, like. hm. just be on a lot of molly, at a mall. this might be a shitty idea. shit. i want to do something like the 'PRESS KIT' movie tao and i made in taiwan. 'made in taiwan:' a phrase i have seen on many objects since childhood.

5:00PM: assembling packages. might…fucking. goddamn my stupid life. someone surprise me already.

5:17PM: ate 20mg adderall, 60mg vyvanse. starting to feel big time. making packages like a….frrrrrujjsjdkjksdfjkfdhdsf…macmedics employee called to inform me there is $800+ damage from my '800lbs gorilla-like' drunken machinery dismantling event of the century. he is nice. at the end i said 'what's your name again?' he said 'brendan.'

8:09PM: beasted out book packages and answered emails. going to brooklyn wednesday, april 17, for interview with alt citizen magazine.

11:59PM: finished three packages. addressed envelopes. wrote 'behind the scenes' commentary in books. doing a good job on the drawings, i think. got carried away looking through old family photos to include with books.

APRIL 15, 2013

12:00-1:43AM: mostly looked at old photos. emailed matthew donahoo a photo collage involving my mom, me, and difficulties with a horse. i like vyvanse better than adderall. forgot about liveblog/internet. enjoying assembling packages. wish these weren't my last books to mail because i like annotating/personalizing them. feel like an idiot for not doing it sooner, sorry to all who haven't received their copies yet.

2:21AM: i don't know how it got to be so late. troubling loss of time today. i don't remember showering or before showering. seems like i lost a day, or more maybe. xanax. bad news.

8:23AM: mom stood in my room's doorway and said 'you're still up?' and i said 'i'm still up.' she said 'do you want coffee?' i said i did. this is a first, i think. i don't know why i said 'yes' because i wanted to be neurotic and say 'no thank you, i'll get it when i'm ready.' i don't even really want coffee right now, though.

8:27AM: now i have coffee.

1:26PM: mom left, said she'll be back around 4. have been wanting to avoid typing in this. have reached level of 'talking to myself/listening to my thoughts' where it seems impossible to surprise/amuse myself.

need a swat team...

'opposite of self-help' swat team...

just want...i don't know...

should i get chic-fil-a...

i'm goddamned shivering a-goddamned-gain when am i going to sleep i'm supposed to be in new york tomorrow at 11AM.

4:29pm: bank teller's name was donata. 'Crying of lot 49' style name, like 'de nada' and 'donate.' Asked her to look up my savings account number. She said 'did you used to live in Philadelphia?' I said 'yup, yup Philadelphia, fifteen-oh-four north fourth street, that's me. I might be Margaret, or Megan, I'm not sure what I said.' she typed things for a while. she said 'did those hurt' about my tattoos. I said 'you know? Only when they were getting done.' she said 'hurts just looking at 'em.' Put arms behind me and said 'I'll hide I'll hide,' so she wouldn't have to look. Man with white ponytail and woman approached and donata said 'can I help you?' ponytail man said 'I need to see the manager. The manager of the bank.' donata continued typing my savings account thing and said 'one moment just a sec.' ponytail man's woman said 'we have a problem for the manager.'

4:41pm: professional-looking woman being helped by post office person was saying 'how do I know someone's not going to read my mail? That's my whole point in doing this, otherwise I'd save myself the trip' and looked back to everyone in line for sympathy, it seemed. People were paying attention to other things.

4:46pm: mailed everything media mail. Post office lady said 'you need to re-sign that card, I can't see a signature' and handed me a red sharpie. She looked back and forth between my name on my license and my card a few times but didn't say anything about one of the names being 'Margaret.'

4:55pm: turned key in ignition and tied hair in ponytail. Neck tension built or released. Felt good.

**IF ANYONE IN A 50 MILE RADIUS OF BALTIMORE IS READING THIS: I AM INTERESTED IN BEING PET, LIKE HOW YOU WOULD PET [ANIMAL OF YOUR CHOICE], FOR AS LONG AS YOU FEEL LIKE IT. NOT A SEXUAL THING, STRICTLY SPECIES ON SPECIES RUBBING, WEARING CLOTHES. OFFER LONG-STANDING BUT TONIGHT WOULD BE ESPECIALLY NICE.

5:01pm: I'm going out on a limb to say this. 'A limb.' Haha. Going out on all my limbs and my torso and head to say this, this thing I thought in line at the post office: I have reached a point of no return of sorts. I can't imagine functioning the way I used to before I was so involved in the internet. I don't know how much good any of this is actually doing me. Some interesting things have happened to me and I've met interesting people but I feel like in order for me to live a life where I'm mostly happy I should not continue to do this, like, write the liveblog but also probably not write or show anyone. I also can't imagine not doing either of these things. I feel like I'm in some kind of hellish limbo area where no alternative seems easier to commit to, to cause long-term satisfaction. It doesn't work for me to go this long without experiencing some kind of meaningful interaction. It feels good to know people read this but I miss the thing of seeing a face and feeling the face see me or whatever. Also I don't know…who I could ever potentially have a relationship with…seems like I've…there is a limit I've reached that other people could exceed but I feel unable to, if that makes sense. Not just about relationships, about all of this.

People throw around 'I don't know what to do, what do I want from life' but I really don't know…like has anyone who has said that felt these things I'm talking about? Don't most people at least have, like, an idea of what they could contribute to the world? Aren't most people, like, considering a few internships, if not day jobs? Night jobs? Any jobs? Anyone? Bueller? Bueller? Bueller?

6:10pm: in parking lot outside FedEx. Too bright. Re-read email I sent Tao in February then re-read his reply from earlier today. Picked at shoulder then pulled back sleeve to see if there was anything to watch pop out of me. Popped small blackhead I thought 'my savior' about. Disappointing results. Thing I was not going to include: dark red car with license plate that said 'CLOSURE' passed on a speed bump to my left. Universe fake as hell man. This has gotta be some kinda Ashton Kutcher prank. Blew bloody nose scab thing into hand but nothing else came out so I got a napkin and tried harder. Success. Checked other shoulder for things to pick at, no results. Wonder of I'll ever be nostalgic for now. Seems like all times are preferable to now but I doubt I'll think that tomorrow about now. I'll be like 'ah, the parking lot, the bloody booger: how young I was.'

7:02pm: someone asked four ask.fm questions in a row with answers I don't automatically know/sense. Interested in who this person is…they can lead me to an 'elsewhere' lol…picturing them as Tom cruise in 'lord of the rings' (know he wasn't in that, am just picturing a shrunken mischievous tom cruise in hobbit clothes who is also a 'mysterious old sage.')

Saw email from Austin about spacedads reading and panicked a little. Completely forgot I agreed to do this. People will be watching my head talk 'live' soon. Mom will be at apartment, I don't want her to hear.

I SOLVED IT I WILL JUST GO TO DAD'S AND BE ALONE GREAT I CAN FEED AND PET CATS ALSO

Jesus in-person interview photo shoot thing is tomorrow morning in Brooklyn I haven't been considering this sitting in FedEx parking lot looking at phone not sleeping shoooooit sheeters shiddly poo come on auto-correct let me curse the way I want to, with peepee head misspellings

7:20PM: responded to austin's email. said 'mom there's too many things and no sleep i did it again and noooooo' or something while bending over to hug mom on couch. she asked about what was going on and said 'i bet you'll feel better after a shower.' i said 'oh no, am i…sorry,' re how i smell, and she said 'no, no no no, i didn't smell anything' (aware of probably smelling like cigarettes, but it hasn't been long enough since the last time i

221

showered for 'worse smells'). i said 'i mean no, it's fine, i know it'll feel better, thank you.' she said 'i really didn't smell anything bad on you.' checked skin in mirror. not as clear as i thought. i repeat: skin IS NOT as clear as i thought. had unconsciously picked at my chin in the car, i think. this feels like a musical comedy. musical comedy of fiendish errors full of sound and fury and in the end signifying nothing.

7:56pm: on the way out the door I said 'I'll be back later tonight. Then new York tomorrow.' mom said 'oh be careful up there. You know, the Boston marathon.' I said 'maybe they just bombed because they wanted them to run faster,' laughing. Mom laughed and said 'no no no! It was when they were already at the finish line!' I put an orange in my bag and said 'well I'll be sure to use all the back roads on my way up, as usual.' mom laughed and said 'yes yes.' I said "ey! I'm walkin' here' like Dustin Hoffman in midnight cowboy. Mom laughed really hard, surprising me. I remembered the walking/marathon connection and laughed. Mom said 'this is terrible, think of all those children without parents!' I said 'and how lucky those parents must be.' mom said "surround you with a bubble of light,' she doesn't mean it, I swear!' I said 'it knows I don't mean it.' mom said 'I know they know you don't mean it.' I was at the bottom of the stairs and said goodbye and locked the door. Before school my mom would say 'surround you with a bubble of light, keep you safe from harm' and wave her hand around me in a circle. The 'it' and the 'they' we were referencing is/are the universe, or god.

8:38pm: made a few turns to continue scanning liveblog for interesting things to read while smoking two cigarettes

8:42pm: fake teeth security guard saluted me and I saluted back. He said 'have a good night hon.' I said 'thanks, you too' and meant it.

8:51PM: fed cats. walked around apartment, like someone watching would think 'she's busy.' ate 60mg vyvanse before leaving mom's. texted rachel back. matthew donahoo emailed that there was a jeopardy question about 'homeland.' going to shower, promote reading on social media, practice speaking part of liveblog i'll be reading. feel like i'm about to audition for acting school.

9:22PM: this is an introduction to my reading tonight. i will be reading an excerpt from a liveblog (which i am currently typing this sentence into) documenting my daily thoughts and activities, which i began on march 17. i started the liveblog because i was feeling unhappy and like i've been unwittingly allowing myself to act in ways that further my unhappiness, so seeing these things written down might help me be more aware, and if nothing else, get me in the habit of writing again because writing used to feel good.

the sentence you just heard has been said aloud maybe seven times in less-organized forms as i was showering about twenty minutes ago.

APRIL 17, 2013

9:21PM[yesterday]–3:44AM: insane circular argument with dad. allowed myself to continue arguing mostly via thinking the amount of times i was repeating myself would become ridiculous, like dad would definitely notice, which he didn't, even when i started accompanying repetitions with 'i'm repeating myself again.' dad is big into 'cause and effect, family history, explaining things' and i am big into 'if you ask for permission to interrupt me you're already interrupting, just do it or don't do it, it doesn't matter, you're doing it to be polite but it actually feels impolite, it doesn't seem fair to expect me not to act annoyed when you said you didn't want to ask permission anymore but you keep doing it.' felt like i was 'channelling tao' and dad was 'channelling me.'

at the end he said 'it's just an innocuous movement' about a...jesus. i noticed he was turning out the lights and asked him why, because we were still talking. he said 'this? this is just an innocuous movement' in a 'neener neener neener' voice. followed him to the bathroom and sarcastically said 'me too, look at how 'innocuous' i am when i follow you.' he brushed his teeth slowly and said 'i see.' i said 'why not brush your teeth again.' he said 'i don't know what that means' like he knew exactly what it meant but it was 'beneath him' to acknowledge this (i didn't know what i meant by 'why not brush your teeth again' but felt like a class-A-bitch-to-high-hell as i said it). walked outside with backpack, to drive to new york for interview. looked for my car.

3:45am: looks like my car has been towed. Dad drives a dodge challenger, which suits his arguing style. Sat on stoop and smoked cigarette. Man with dog said 'good morning.' Thought I saw a giant full moon rising from ground but it was just a window.

5:17AM: twinkly music i heard on dad's birthday is coming from his bedroom. the guided meditation CD. seems 'hard to take.' it was sad the other night, but tonight...jesus. one of the cats peed on my bed. car towing place isn't answering phone. dad and i hugged and apologized three times but seems like we each sadly and silently agree that the other is impossible.

5:28AM: it feels good to be laying down. wearing 'clothes for 11AM interview/photo shoot.' no car. no busses to NYC until 8:45AM. comically bad timing. rescheduled interview for next week, april 22.

quotes i remember from argument:

'well is there anything you want?'

'no i tried everything i don't want to be awake i don't want to be asleep i don't want a person i don't want alone i don't know what to do i don't want to be here i don't want to live anywhere i don't want to be awake or asleep or awake' (me, crying)

'you're staying here and going to therapy for six months'

'that doesn't work, i know you don't mean it, you're just trying to take initiative and do parenting instead of letting me, which is nice but i don't think ultimatums work'

'it would really do you some good, do you the trick, this lady i found'

'i don't think i would make it for six months here'

'well, you know what i think'

'wait this is actually helpful because now i know what i don't want, so this is good, i know something i don't want now, that's sort of like wanting'

(this was a good part, before hugging and it being over for a little while)

'it's a real head trip [forget what followed this, was surprised i spontaneously said 'head trip']'

'so what you're saying is your view of me from your perspective is the only view there is?' (dad, multiple times, this one really gets the circle going)

'you seem so angry to me, in general'

'i don't believe in anger, anger is bullshit'

'it's just an emotion'

'yes but it is a secondary emotion. anger: the emotion secondary to pain and fear.'

'well then you seem very in pain and afraid to me, in general.'

[seems like he agreed, facially]

"tired' is not an emotion, it's a physical sensation.' (he said this a lot)

225

'to me it feels like both. it doesn't even matter, we know what 'tired' means.'

'it is absolutely based on your physical state.'

i sound rational in this description but think argument was mostly me talking in an uncontrollably emotional voice. dad sometimes sounded intentionally calm/machine-like, which provoked me or something, like he was 'showing off' his calmness and suppressing calling me on my bullshit. at one point i said that. but no bullshit was called. at another point i said i was continuing to argue only so we would remember the argument as insanely long and un-repeatable, because we had learned. dad seemed briefly interested in this and we like, shared a moment of 'should we?'

6:06AM: eating an apple. roof of mouth is hot/itchy, maybe swollen. turned fan to 'white noise' but can still hear dad snoring. headache. no sleep for close to 36 hours again. alvie is howling and being insatiable. worried he's going to pee on me.

6:11AM: goddamned me and arguing and car shit and not replacing the visitor pass and thinking i'd just be at dad's for a few hours. 'told by an idiot full of sound and fury in the end signifying nothing' is good to mentally repeat, instantly calming. when i came inside from the cigarette after discovering car was towed dad opened the door before i did, think we both looked the same way, like 'drained of shit.' was surprised to see him at the door but unsure of why.

6:38AM: trudged through itchy mouth apple. eating 1mg xanax. 'master of the house' playing in head. yuck.

12–2:30pm: dad woke me and had made coffee. Paul McCartney live concert video he likes to play in the morning was playing. We were acting careful around each other. Felt heavy, still do. Apologized for letting argument be so long. He did too. I said 'I don't want to do that again, it doesn't seem to help, we just feel bad and say things we've said before and we won't remember.' he said something like he's okay with talking that way and not remembering and doesn't want to avoid in the future. I said 'I'm just not going to let it happen again, I could've prevented it.' he said something like he didn't want to prevent it. Felt like 'fuck…'

2:42pm: have car again. Woman drove beside me asked if she could get in front of me. Seemed nice. Had epiphany that 'I'm the one deciding my life feels bad, I could just as easily think it's fine, yeah it's just fine, there's just always good and bad parts, the main thing I feel bad about is aging/things

I thought I'd be doing now, might as well accept things how they are.' Not the first time I've thought this but seemed helpful.

2:53pm: in whole foods parking lot. Watching teenage-looking boy sit on a ledge with his back to me, doing some kind of 'sharpening chopsticks' whittling maneuver. Thought 'Walter Davis, I wish.' Still feel heavy from argument. Parents are at the beach until Monday, invited me to come.

3:01pm: whole foods was out of the green juice I like. Mostly wanted to go there to 'do a lap, check if it's still there,' didn't really want anything. Chopsticks boy was still there when I arrived at car. Going to 'take it easy' on me today, no pressure to do shit, I'll feel less heavy and more able to do things if I don't pressure myself for a little bit.

3:06pm: one thing I want to say before break: a Kia SUV was behind me at red light. Remembered getting trained at the book store with two people: Nate, who would become my friend, and a girl named Kia, who didn't make it through training. She called out twice due to car problems. I forget if Nate or me started saying 'Kia dead.' It became a thing we'd say.

One more thing: one time in the back room Nate and I were on the schedule to do 'book buyback' orders and we found a Santa Claus costume, which we took turns wearing. We put on Christmas music and took people's orders with the Santa outfit. This was in May or June, I think.

3:15pm: car ahead of me honked again. Girl on sidewalk said 'hey! Where you going?' driver said 'to study hall, what about you?' she said 'I'm going to donnelling.' they were quiet and looked at each other and waved when the light changed.

3:41PM: feels like 'doom.' does anyone else reading this feel 'doom?' solitary confinement christmas basement doom. want to do something fluffy today, like frolic around in nature, escape the doom. unsure of where to go in nature where i won't feel doom. i'm in nature. shit. i'm going to drive to… western maryland…see mountains…do i want to nap…shit…just want to frolic about…want to take alvie and shirley on a walk with leashes… picturing me in a meadow and '20 tubes of colored liquids appearing in the sky, slowly targeting and 'tunneling' down to me on earth, pouring onto my head/into my mouth, completely engulfing my body but i don't get wet.' is that so much to want from life…lol…

3:42-9:50PM: looked at internet passively. answered questions. i forget most of what i did. decided to see 'the place beyond the pines' at 10:35PM and order take-out. strong urge to masturbate before i left apartment.

9:54pm: driving to 'asian taste,' to pick up sushi. No longer hungry after masturbating. What would happen if I did nothing, like less than this, for as long as possible. Wearing sheer black shirt with a galaxy print over a sheer beige bra. If you look carefully you can see my nipple. Two nipple asteroids hidden beneath galaxy.

10:07pm: 'Asian taste' called to ask if I was coming. Picked it up. Going to eat in car now before movie.

10:44-11:59PM: bought ticket from a guy in a suit with long dreds. he said 'for how many?' i said 'just one.' impulsively livetweeted movie from unedited twitter account as placeholder for liveblogging.

APRIL 18, 2013

1–1:30AM: Eating seaweed salad leftovers w/chopsticks in car. Man who sold me ticket and janitor just walked out of theater. We are the only people I can see in the parking lot. Heard car start behind me and 'make em say unh' playing, then car driving away, fading out, and now nothing.

I want to keep partying all night in a 24-hour movie theater. I want to work an overnight shift doing whatever in a huge strip mall place with huge empty parking lot.

3:46AM: parked far from dad's apartment door. imagined person mugging me, giving them everything i have on me, then if they wanted to rape me i'd say 'i have AIDs' but somehow that wouldn't stop them from raping me, they'd just kill me after the rape. arrived at apartment door. imagined me sprawled out in front of apartment with blood coming from two big gashes on the backs my thighs that went down to my knees and me staring up at the sky like ryan gosling when he died in movie. gosling-style. there was also blood around my head.

3:50–6:00AM: ate a cadbury mini-egg, 1mg xanax. tried to fall asleep to ASMR videos about food, then thought 'you haven't eaten much lately, treat yourself.' decided to smoke some of my dad's pot eat the rest of the cadburry mini-eggs. then i put peanut butter on three fig 'triple berry' newtons. then i ate half of the bag of fig newtons without peanut butter, just raw-dogging it.

6–7:00AM: smoked more pot. wanted to watch people eating chocolate as i was eating it to 'intensify the sensory experience.' looked at nigella lawson video, then porn.

7:40am: wonder who the first person to order pet meds to get high will be. probably me, re alvie's anxiety. i'll get him pet meds for me. how do some people just know how to cook, they know enough to have shows about how they do it, we want to see that, this is what people want to see

everything looks/feels like porn right now

friends = comets that orbit every few years

3:35PM: woke feeling good. ate two fig 'triple berry' newtons, wanted more. ate under ten quaker 'cheddar cheese rice quakes.' ate under ten cashews.

4-6:58PM: fed cats. made coffee. watched youtube videos about life in prison. jogged to move car in ridiculous outfit. smoked cigarette in backyard. have been feeling plagued by not knowing what drugs/food i want.

7:12PM: gave cats treats. drinking a canned 'amelia earhart' brand of sparkling water with 'essence of raspberry.' seems insane that my dad bought this...like aol.com morning rush playlist thing...eating smallish stack of cheddar cheese pringles. read ingredients and felt solidarity with inmates from prison food documentary.

8:02PM: going to yoga at 8:30. cheddar cheese pringle-eating has stabilized, half the can remains untouched, no longer interested. want to eat sushi and seaweed salad again. last night i ordered a shrimp tempura roll, salmon/avocado roll, and spicy scallop roll from 'asian taste.' so good. asian taste. i want to see another movie again but it'll be too late after yoga. feel like i'm on vacation.

9:47pm: looked for parking spots near yoga for about ten minutes and gave up. Drove to mom's to check mail and get books to mail tomorrow. Feel shitty. Ate an orange. Talked with mom on the phone and felt looming thing, she asked me how I was and I told her I'm not doing anything, seems like life is going to continue being nothing, so hard to want to do anything right now. Like even talking to people I like who I feel happy around seems hard. The world is happy and functional without me in it. I'm barely in it now and it seems to be thriving, aol.com has news to report, people have things to say and other people are interested in hearing them. It would be fine without me here. People would adapt and continue to thrive and say interesting things to each other.

9:56PM: mom called as i was parking at dad's. she said something like 'i just wanted to say that i know you're going through a hard time and i don't want to minimize the fight you had with dad, i want you to know i've felt the way i think you feel before, and that it'll get better, and no matter what i'm always less than five minutes away on the phone, if you're ever feeling hopeless and alone and like there's no one.' it felt like she meant it. thought 'she might actually really get it, people might actually really understand what it's like for you, that's a possibility, start considering that possibility more, you don't believe people enough.'

10-10:30PM: milled around apartment, changing clothes and petting cats. put on a little black eyeshadow. ate 20mg adderall. emailed with rachel white about when we'd start skype-ing (she's writing a profile of tao for the village voice and wanted to talk to me about him)

10:24PM–11:59PM: talked with rachel on skype. felt really good to talk to another person who is alone with a computer and their writing all day. highly enjoyable conversation. felt like i was not being very clear about some things/was rusty with conversational skills. it's 5:16AM right now and i'm tired/ate 1mg xanax and drank a beer, leaving out details from this conversation but might elaborate later.

APRIL 19, 2013

12-1:25AM: still talking with rachel, internet cut out twice and the last time it was when i was starting to talk about something interesting/sex, exchanged emails a little).

1:26-2:45AM: masha texted and i saw another text from her from 4/13 about doing DMT. read and related to her DMT account. texted her a long thing but it kept failing to send.

2:45-3:41AM: picked at everything on my skin that looked like it could contain something that would pop out of me. i looked at my back in the bathroom mirror. have two painful ingrown hairs or...somethings...i don't know what they are, they're in my right armpit. picked at them until they were big and red and it felt hard to put my arm flat against me. kept thinking 'why are you doing this, you know you don't want to be doing this, this will make you feel bad tomorrow, what drug do you want [not adderall anymore, xanax? no, just drinking? maybe. molly? molly would change your thoughts but you'd feel depleted tomorrow. you mostly just want your thoughts to be changed. pot would make you feel even more dissociated or something, than this, don't do the pot, you're doing devious skin-destruction things, the pot will make you paranoid. drink more green juice so your skin is better and you're not afraid of cancer, the gyno is going to find cancer in you tomorrow maybe, maybe if you squeeze stuff out... something...there is the perfect thing that if you watched pop out of you it would make you never want to do it again, that's the drug for you, keep looking for that].' then used a skin brush on my skin and rubbed all of me with raw coconut oil.

3:42-5:29AM: emailed masha and sara long emails. ate 1mg xanax and drank another beer. ate leftover spaghetti, put 'prego' sauce on it. gyno appointment is at 2:40 tomorrow.

1:36PM: hit snooze several times.

1:37-2:07PM: email-confirmed board meeting with apartment committee people: april 25 at 7PM. ate 20mg adderall, drank coffee from yesterday, showered, ate zeolite eyedropper supplement, b-vitamin, 60mg noopept, showered, dressed.

2:29PM: my car got towed again. it was parked where it was night before last. my visitor parking pass is not good 20' from the building. more than 20' requires a different color. $340. i'm not telling dad, he paid the last time it was towed ($280). using money from the check i deposited a few days ago, so as to seem less like a fuck-up.

called gyno to reschedule.

funny how often my cars get towed and how often i drive. i'm going to take a nice walk to buy cigarettes and get money from an ATM and then take the muhfuggin bus. i should work for a tow truck company, i can drive tow trucks and i have a lot of experience being towed.

3:46PM: considering eating a molly before i walk to buy cigarettes. or smoking weed. or more adderall, i don't fucking...jesus. i don't know.

3:47-7:17PM: answered backlog of questions. emailed colin that i confirmed april 25th meeting with the apartment committee. he responded with something nice about being neighbors. mom called at some point, i told her about the car getting towed and she told dad. ate a snigly niblet of adderall. looked at bus schedules to impound lot. seems easier and faster and not that much more money to take a cab.

7:18PM: raining lightly. on the phone, mom was giving mom-like recommendations about something i forget, like listing things with a worried voice. passed security guard with fake teeth. he saluted me and said 'where's your umbrella?' interrupted mom to say 'forgot it!' mom said 'oh, forget it, i know.'

7:24pm: walking to Royal Farms with ATM, cigarettes, maybe cabs. Enjoying this. There is a little lightning and thunder and it's warm and the rain is not hard.

7:39pm: bought 12oz sugar-free red bull and cigarettes at royal farms. Standing outside under an awning by a trash can, smoking cigarette and drinking red bull.

7:51pm: rain is harder now, I'm wet and dripping but it feels nice. Inside I asked a farmer-looking guy next to a young boy if he was in line to use the ATM. He said something I didn't understand but I thought meant 'no.' He moved over to the lotto machine next to me and said 'but thank you for asking.'

Debit card didn't read at the ATM but it worked when I paid for stuff. Old royal farms employee said 'what is that, menthol?' Employee ringing me up said 'American spirit menthol light.' I smiled and 'yup.' Receipt printed but I still asked 'do you guys do...debit?' Employee said a long sincere thing about how...seems boring to type. The older one was watching me and smiling. I was smiling and looking at both of them. I said 'okay, thank you.'

7:54pm: typed above thing standing under royal farms awning, where I am still standing. Car parked in front of me just turned on and I jumped, like, raised my hands holding phone maybe eight inches in the air.

7:56pm: raining hard now. People running from cars into the store. Lotto machine farmer man and little boy walked out of royal farms. Farmer man said 'shit [something I didn't understand] really coming down.' I said 'hell yeah' and raised eyebrows and nodded. He said 'you're still here.' I said 'yeah I'm not walking in that.' He said 'shit when it [something I didn't understand] it ain't [something]' and made a noise. I smiled, looking down at phone, then he and the boy were gone.

8:03pm: imagining asking one of these people entering and exiting royal farms for a ride to gas station/next area where there will be an ATM, a little less than a mile away. We could become best friends, maybe. Maybe they would kill me. Rape me and slice open the backs of my thighs and leave me in a Ryan gosling-style pool of blood in the back of royal farms. Even if I told them I had AIDs first. Raining extremely hard. Smoking another cigarette to wait for conditions to be more walkable.

8:15pm: female royal farms employee approached, kind of close to my body and reached behind me and said 'excuse me.' I said 'sure.' she said 'mind if I smoke in your face?' I said 'no that's fine, I'm smoking too' and took out another cigarette. I didn't really want it but knew if I was going to continue standing there while she smoked I should have a reason. We looked at our phones. She said 'what is that, Marlboro?' I said 'American Spirit menthol light. What is that, it smells like pipe tobacco.' She said 'Black and Mild. You ever smoke one?' I said 'yeah, but like, not with the tobacco that it comes with.' She laughed and said 'I love you, you're awesome.' I smiled and thought 'that's good, that'll be it.' We looked at our phones. She said 'you know, I only started smoking these cause I thought they didn't have nicotine, but like, this thing has a hundred fifty milligrams and a regular cigarette only has like nineteen.' I said 'damn, nineteen.' She said 'yeah, eight or nineteen I heard.' Her facial expressions were animated and she had three face piercings and cornrows. She seemed easy to make eye contact with and talk to. I said 'yeah that's kinda why I switched to these, there's like, no additives.' She said something about electronic cigarettes. I said 'I was gonna do that, I'm not supposed to be smoking this, my other pack before this was supposed to be my last one.' She laughed and said 'yeah right, last one, yeah right.' I said 'they're not even that much better for you, the e-cigarettes, I think.' She said 'yeah like, and you ever go to one a them hookah—' a person exited the door to Royal Farms and we looked. I said 'yeah, they're like, hookah-style feeling, to smoke.' She said 'right? You breathe it in and it ain't even like nothing.' I said 'plus like, they never go out, but with this thing you get a unit of time. Like I know this is going to be seven minutes, I have seven minutes.' She said 'right?' I said 'did you always smoke Black & Milds?' She said 'no I never even smoked, I didn't like cigarettes ever. My friend gave me one of her Marlboro, I think reds? Marlboro reds, a little while ago, and I didn't like it at all. But then my other friend had a Black & Mild in his car one time and I was like 'alright.' They make you nauseous and all, if you do it too long.' I said 'you're not supposed to inhale them, right?' She said 'yeah, but I'm like, why you smoke anything you're not gonna inhale, right?' I smiled and said 'yeah, that's why you do it.' She said 'you sposed to breathe em in and breath em out, right? That's what you do?' I said 'yeah, yeah, breathing it in and out. Why else, you know?' She said 'and just one of these? It last like twenny hours, that's how long it takes. You said like seven minutes?' I said 'yeah, like seven to ten, depending.' She said 'see, I do this all day long. I just put it out and start it back up.' I said 'really? Cause sometimes I put one out to save for later, but I hate how it smells.' She said 'right? That's why I just leave it out here, leave it outside and come back to it, cause when you grind it out and keep it with you it's so nasty, that smell and that way it taste, so I just put it out here.' I remembered her reaching behind me. I said 'you don't put it out and it doesn't burn away?' She made a big surprised face and said 'naw! It goes out all by itself!' I said 'damn, all by itself' and smiled really big. We looked at our phones again. She called someone and said 'how is the event,' then 'HOW is the EVENT' and hung up shortly after. I typed '8:55pm: female rf employee.' She said 'well, that was a short conversation.' I made a noise/gesture like 'I know how that goes.' The employee who rang me up opened the door and had a phone to his ear. He said something to the Black & Mild employee and she said 'okay okay' and he shut the door. She said 'shit man they're tellin me I gotta be in here at like five tomorrow, and I got class at eight and I'm like, shit.' I said 'five in the morning? Are you guys twenty-four hours?' She made a compassionate face and said 'no, no, but we do open at five.' I said 'damn, so early. I would just stay up all night.' She made a face and said 'really? I can't do that. I mean the earliest I ever woke up was like, three-thirdy, but then I just went right back to sleep.' I said 'so you have class at eight a.m. but you have to be here at five a.m.?' She said 'well yeah like—what's tomorrow, Saturday?' I said 'yeah' but wasn't sure. She continued 'so I got class at eight in the morning usually during the week, but then tomorrow they got me in here at five, and I'll probly even stay till five!' I said 'jeez, long day, long ass day.' She said 'right? And I don't even get a break!' I said 'what? That's not allowed I think, they have to give you a break.' she said 'well it works like, so if you got a full shift you get one, but if you only work like a, like a five-to-ten, you just gotta eat standing up.' I remembered that's how it was at jobs I've had. I said 'jeez. Five in the morning, so early.' She said 'I know. I know. I told them I'm only doin this shit once, only tomorrow. I mean it's enough to get my ass outta bed for my eight class, not even five.' She exhaled and I watched her cloud of smoke move towards the light slower than my smoke. She batted at the smoke a little. She said 'man it was raining like this before?' I said 'no, it's better now, I can like, walk in this now. Because my car got towed. So that's why I'm walking.' She paused and said 'you got towed? How'd that happen?' Her Black & Mild was almost gone. I said 'well, it's stupid, I'm at my dad's and he lives in this weird gated community thing where they like, tow you a lot if you don't have the right pass on your car.' She said 'what? How they even know what to tow, they just like, sit and wait all night? How do they even do that?' I said 'they just creep around, watching.' She shook her head and went 'pshhh.' I said 'did you ever get towed?' She said 'no, no I mean. I do a little bad stuff, like if I park in a handicap it's only like seventy dollars or whatever but.' She flicked her Black & Mild into the parking lot and said 'so you gonna get your car?' I said 'yeah, I'm just walking to' and was interrupted by a big metal noise at the other end of the store. We jumped, looked at the door, then at each other with big eyes and grinned. I said 'shit.' She looked like she suddenly remembered something and said 'oh no, well it didn't get towed, but the other day I parked on York road where it was like [gestured like 'not much space'] near a sign, and I was just getting out real fast to get my friend at like seven-thirdy, so I left the car on, but I locked it with the keys inside. And it was on!' I said 'oh no, how'd you get back in?' she said 'I had to call my insurance and just wait. Yeah I waited and it was like seven-fifty and I was sposed to meet my friend at eight so I had to call and be like 'hey, I'm gonna be late.'' I said 'oh my god, jeez, at least you got back in' as she walked to the door. She said something, smiling really big. I said 'good luck tomorrow, for your five a.m.' She said 'right? Don't know if I can make it' as she opened the door and, for the first time in the conversation, looked like she wasn't sure of what she was supposed to be saying or doing. I waved and watched her walk inside, extinguished my cigarette on the trash can, tossed it in, and started walking. I felt dizzy and swerved a little. My right leg was tingly and numb. Think I had been rigidly putting all my weight on my leg and my back against the brick wall, to appear laid-back and approachable, for the entire conversation.

8:36pm: walked into pizza restaurant, no ATM. Walked into Alonso's bar and ATM was off.

8:40pm: colder now. Buttoned cardigan.

236

8:45pm: withdrew $340 from Wells Fargo ATM. Surprised card worked. Now it's the cab part.

8:48pm: saw cab. Female cab driver. Neither of us are familiar with address or the towing place, it seems. I told her both addresses they told me. She said 'I'm gonna use my GPS.' I said 'oh good good.' I said 'the North avenue address is the only one that shows up, I think. Or.' A few moments passed. She said 'is that east North ave or west?' I said 'west North, thirteen-seventy west North.' She said 'mmkay.' Didn't see a credit card thing in cab. I took my money out and put it on my lap. She said 'what's the address?' I said 'thirteen-seventy west North ave.' I'm wet all over but wearing mostly black. Some kind of sexy moody slow pop or r&b song started playing on radio.

8:53pm: it's the song that's like 'beautiful girls around the world I could chase them [something] but try got nothin on you girl nothin on you.'

8:58pm: driver stopped at red light and turned to face me. She said 'you know what kinda place this is?' I said 'uh, a towing place? Like a towing… they have my car.' She said 'oh, I know it now. You almost there.'

9:18pm: how do you tow an RV, is that legal? Wouldn't that violate some kind of property law, like a house law? Why would you tow an RV? Is it because you're jealous? You want an RV? You can't just take an RV because you want it. That's not how it works. I'm pretty sure that's not how it works.

9:30pm: mom called for update. She and dad have been watching coverage of the Boston massacre terrorists. She said 'and actually everyone had to stay inside all day today, and it sounds so boring to talk about but it's actually very uh, dramatic, to see on tv.' She said she had ordered room service, and hoped I was going to do something nice for myself tonight. I said 'I am, yeah, I'm going to Wegman's now to get some juice stuff.' She said 'well good, that's a good thing to do, it's just so shitty that you had to do this today, I'm so sorry.' I said 'It was all okay, it was just like. Something to do today. Everyone was really nice.' She said 'they were nice?' I said 'yeah, everyone was really nice.' She said 'well honey I'm glad, and I want you to know that everything is alright, dad is just on the toilet, we love you very much and don't want you to worry.' I said 'I'm not worried. It's all okay, just another thing to do. I love you guys too.' She said 'I just don't want you to worry.' I said 'I'm not, I'm not, I'm actually a little lost so I should focus on driving.' she said 'okay, okay honey. Here's a hug.'

10:01-10:23pm: sat in car parked at Wegman's. commented on around eight instagram pictures in mischevious, belligerent, rapidfire 'not caring what anyone could think, just want to say things' way.

10:29pm: sitting on toilet in wegman's bathroom stall. It has been at least two minutes since pee left body. Clothes and hair are totally wet. Shivering a little.

10:56pm: bought kale, cucumber, cilantro, celery, lettuce, two coconuts, deodorant, kombucha, and a leave-in conditioner. Tense moments in deodorant aisle when faced with absence of Dove scent option I usually buy and presence of 'aluminum free' options. Unsure if aluminum is 'evil.'

Deciding factor: too many non-aluminum-free options, aluminum-free thing smelled good.

Tense moments in the hair aisle reading ingredients of things to decipher what chemicals seemed less 'evil.' What I bought seems 'evil.' It's called 'moroccan oil intense [something].'

Deciding factor: prettiest packaging, thinking 'moroccan terrorist overlord,' instructions seemed like they were written by a person.

11:20pm: received email from dad with subject line: 'not to worry...'

11:40pm: fake teeth security guard saluted me.

11:41pm: closest available parking spot is in a zone where I think they can justify towing. Severe parking/towing anxiety. No other available spots. Cars are stupid. Might stay at mom's after I make juice and feed cats.

11:42-11:59PM: sat in parked car, typed most of the royal farms employee conversation.

APRIL 20, 2013

1:36AM: made cucumber/lettuce/celery/cilantro coconut water juice. fed cats and cleaned box. alvie has been hiding under dad's bed and peeing in the shower, i think. continuous water flow device is making little chug-chug noises, to which the insatiable alvie is responding with opera-like meowing. like a little eunuch opera break-out star. the first opera singer to be famous for sounding simultaneously confused and full of conviction. he is singing the 'waiting for godot' opera. gotta take his fine ass to the vet like i know he hates. ate 20mg adderall to aid in updating this, emailing maybe, finishing book packages.

2:05AM: car is visible from bedroom window. have gotten up to check if moving vehicle sounds are a tow truck maybe four times since i sat down ten or so minutes ago.

2:13AM: heard car drive away and ran outside to confirm that my car was still there. it is still there.

2:37AM: saw movement in peripheral vision. walked to window. a man was handling something behind my car. watched until i saw he was helping a girl lift something out of her trunk.

2:56AM: stood on bed to watch truck pass slowly by my car.

2:58AM: whenever i've ran to look out the window alvie has jumped and ran off the bed. this time he stayed in his spot, kneading the blanket.

3:01AM: jogged in bare feet to investigate idling noise. opened building's main door. stared incredulously at pick-up truck with its hazard lights on, parallel to my car.

3:02AM: back in bedroom. pick-up truck left. taking this shitshow to mom's house. can't take this shitshow car anxiety. thought 'two tows in one week makes lil mami one hot cross bunny.'

3:10AM: first egregiously early morning bird has been heard. something flashed in peripheral vision. stood on bed to check window, didn't see anything suspicious.

4:07AM: couldn't remember how gollum talked, looked at wikipedia, was moved by this:

'*Gollum*: They cursed us. Murderer they called us. They cursed us, and drove us away. And we wept, Precious, we wept to be so alone. And we only wish to catch fish so juicy sweet. And we forgot the taste of bread… the sound of trees… the softness of the wind. We even forgot our own name. My Precious.'

my liveblog is my precious, kind of.

3:01PM: on twitter, saw mira's and tao's MOMA reading, which i had loose plans to attend, started at 3PM. pictured muted trumpet going 'wah wah wahhhhh' and tomatoes pelted at a shrugging me.

3:03PM: now would be a good time for things to start happening that launch my life into a 'pineapple express'-like coming-of-age buddy comedy where i have huge ragers at both dad's AND mom's apartments tonight (a.k.a. the last night i have two hot single-lady pads all to myself, a.k.a. the last night before my parents come home, a.k.a. 'THE LAST NIGHT:' DIRECTED BY JUDD APATOW).

the black & mild royal farms employee would be the only person who'd show up to the ragers. she would rage at dad's apartment and i'd rage at mom's. it'd be a summer hit, we'd come of age together. she'd call me and would be like 'hey, you come of age yet?' and i'd be like 'come of what?' and she'd be like 'right?' we would cover our phone-free ears to better hear over the noise of the ragers. it would be quiet though, in our rooms.

there would be some kind of high stakes mistaken identity caper, for mass appeal. i would end up at her rager, pretending to be her to 'party guests' that haven't arrived yet, while on the phone with her. then i'd hear the door unlock and open and i'd hide and narrowly escape. she would've been pretending to be me, at my rager.

4:20pm: I can just call Judd apatow on the phone, right? He has a phone?

4:22pm: something I have found shocking:

In the month I've been doing this, no one has called me out on how self-absorbed/obsessed I am, how I'm not intelligent or cultured, how I'm not contributing anything to society, how it's weird that my lifestyle is to rarely sleep and talk almost exclusively to my parents, who I also live with, how irresponsible I am about my physical and mental health and how drugs are bad and I'm addicted, how I contradict myself (can't think of examples but I'm sure I do it), how my 'voice' is just the combination of like five clearer stronger 'voices' I like

I don't know whether to say 'thank you' or

People just like it when I'm funny or insightful

No one really cares

Imagine a gang leader in a maximum security prison saying any of this

Take a moment, really imagine who that person leading that gang would be

Imagine that dead guy.

4:38pm: now it's sunny. I was here yesterday but it was waining.

4:43pm: motivation has plateaued because I tried to motivate myself to do all those things I thought would motivate me and look at where it's gotten me.

4:46pm: here, I'll do it for you: MEGAN YOU ARE NOT HAPPY LIVING THIS WAY YOU USED TO FEEL BETTER YOU ARE NOT MAKING THIS UP OR ROMANTICIZING THE PAST YOU IDIOT YOU ARE NOT GOING TO BE ALIVE MUCH LONGER IF YOU CONTINUE ON LIKE THIS SO FIGURE OUT WHAT YOU WANT ALREADY DO YOU WANT TO BE ALIVE OR NOT THERE MUST BE THINGS FOR YOU OUT THERE REMEMBER YOU USED TO BUY RECORDS AND BIKE AND DRAW AND READ AND THERE WERE PARTIES AND LONG UNINHIBITED TALKS AND INSIDE JOKES AND COWORKERS AND THEN YOU MADE THE MISTAKE OF WRITING ON THE INTERNET AND USING DRUGS REGULARLY AND SOMETIMES IN EXCESS SO NOW YOUR BRAIN IS MAYBE REWIRED TO EXPECT SIGNIFICANT REWARDS OR PUNISHMENTS AND NOT MUCH IN BETWEEN BECAUSE YOUR BRAIN PROBABLY NATURALLY PRODUCES LESS SERATONIN AND DOPAMINE PLUS YOU ARE OLDER AND VIEWING YOUR EARLY TWENTIES FROM THE PERSPECTIVE OF THEM BEING OVER YOU HAD YOUR CHANCE AND YOU MISSED IT AND ALL THOSE ROAD TRIPS AND VISITS TO FRIENDS IN OTHER CITIES NOW SEEM GRANTED TO YOU IN SOME SICK ACT OF MERCY BY THE UNIVERSE: A COMPLICATED, SYMPATHETIC, REGRETFUL NAZI, WHO ALWAYS LIKED YOU: THE SPIRITED LITTLE BOY WHO ASKED QUESTIONS AND MADE JOKES, WHO THE NAZI HAS BEEN ORDERED TO KILL TOMORROW MORNING AND HE DOESN'T WANT TO BUT HE'LL GET KILLED IF HE DOESN'T, HE ALREADY KILLED YOUR PARENTS BUT YOU DON'T KNOW THAT, YOU'VE ACTUALLY GROWN TO LOVE HIM AS IF HE'S YOUR PARENTS, HE HAS INVITED YOU TO HIS BUNKER TONIGHT AND HE IS GIVING YOU ALL

OF THIS CANDY AND ACTING SO EXCITED TO BE PLAYING WITH YOU ALL NIGHT LONG, BUT YOU DON'T KNOW HE'S DOING IT BECAUSE HE'S SO SAD AND GUILTY ABOUT KNOWING HE'S GOING TO SHOOT YOU IN THE HEAD TOMORROW MORNING, HE IS JUST LETTING YOU HAVE YOUR FUN YOU POOR STUPID LITTLE IDIOT YOU DON'T KNOW WHATS IN STORE FOR YOU BUT HOW COULD YOU, YOU ARE JUST A CHILD WHO THINKS YOUR PARENTS DIED HONORABLY AND YOU LOVE YOUR NAZI FRIEND WHO IS NICER TO YOU THAN ANYONE SO WHY WOULD HE HURT YOU, HE COULD ONLY HURT YOU IF HE DIED OR LEFT IN SOME OTHER WAY AND YOU WOULDN'T GET TO TALK TO HIM EVER AGAIN, OR IF YOU KNEW THE TRUTH ABOUT HIM, IF YOU KNEW HE KILLED YOUR PARENTS IN DERANGED WAYS AND WILL KILL YOU IN THE MORNING BUT HE WILL KILL YOU PAINLESSLY AND HONORABLY BECAUSE WHEN HIS SON WAS YOUR AGE HE DIED IN A HORRIBLE ACCIDENT AND THE ACCIDENT HAD SOMETHING TO DO WITH JEWS SO IN A WEAK GRIEF STRICKEN MENTALITY THE NICE MAN WHO RECENTLY LOST HIS SON BECAME THE NAZI WHO KILLED YOUR PARENTS SO HORRIFICALLY—HE RAPED THEM BOTH EVEN AFTER THEY SAID THEY HAD AIDS AND THEN HE SLICED THE BACKS OF THEIR LEGS FROM THIGHS TO KNEES AND LEFT THEM IN POOLS OF THEIR OWN BLOOD—AND WHO WILL KILL YOU TOO, IN CASE YOU ARE LISTENING, BUT YOU AREN'T BECAUSE YOU ARE A LITTLE BOY WHO WAS BORN IN THIS CONCENTRATION CAMP AND YOU HAVE ALREADY ENDURED MORE SORROW AND PAIN IN YOUR SHORT LIFE THAN MOST ADULTS, WHO DON'T KNOW WHAT YOU KNOW: THAT THE ONLY WAY TO NOT FEEL PARALYZED WITH SADNESS IS TO ACCEPT WHAT HAS BEEN DONE AND TRY TO LAUGH AND CHERISH EVERY SMALL KINDNESS BESTOWED UPON YOUR POOR STUPID LITTLE HEAD THAT DOESN'T KNOW IT'S GOING TO HAVE BULLET IN IT TOMORROW MORNING DELIVERED TO YOU BY YOUR BEST FRIEND IN THE WHOLE WIDE WORLD WHO HAS BEEN PLAYING WITH YOU AND GIVING YOU CANDY ALL NIGHT, TONIGHT, THE BEST AND LAST NIGHT OF YOUR LIFE

SO THAT'S HOW IT FEELS TO LOOK AT PICTURES AND HAVE MEMORIES BUT THAT'S ALL I'VE GOT SO PLEASE CAN I PLEASE JUST GET A BREAK OR A PARDON FOR ALL MY SHITTY BEHAVIOR NO NO NO I DONT WANT THAT I DON'T WANT TO

ACT SHITTY ANYMORE EITHER IM SORRY IM SORRY I DONT KNOW WHAT ELSE TO DO CAN SOMEONE JUST HOLD ME FOR A FEW MINUTES NO PLEASE A FEW MINUTES LONGER NO PLEASE PLEASE JUST FIVE MORE MINUTES PLEASE

5:40pm: the gas pump said 'please remove nozzle and select grade.' it didn't even ask for my zip code. it said 'please.'

5:41-8:15pm: drove around. Ended at petsmart. Woman confidently said her phone number in response to 'do you have a petperks card?' she looked 50-70lbs overweight. Both of us looked up when a young girl's voice said 'skinny.' Petsmart employee asked if I had petperks card. I said 'I have a phone number' and the screen prompted me to type it on the console. Pressed button to donate $2 to Petsmart charities. Employee said 'thank you for your donation have a good night.' I looked at him and said a hybrid 'thank you,' 'you too,' and 'have a good night,' which sounded kind of like 'yghyeahh too, thanks.'

8:16pm: flicked lighter. Pictured spark catching on my hair and this car scene suddenly turning really 'metal.'

8:32pm: after I feed the cats I'm going to mom's to take a bath or watch a movie or something. Treating myself to a shithead special tonight.

8:38pm: no fake teeth security guard. Was presented with 'googly-eyed window-leaner' instead. Leaving computer in car to discourage dilly-dallying.

8:55pm: walked to car twisting bag of kale and one of dad's slow-cooked melons, which i thought 'my only friends' about, then 'we'll get through it. Wait—if we'll get through it, I have make it to the sidewalk before the door closes.' Jogged a little and made it.

8:59pm: turned key in engine and plugged in phone. Thought 'my only friends' mostly about hot pink phone case.

9:04pm: 75% of music on phone reminds me of Zachary, 15% reminds me of Tao, 9.7% is stuff i'm tired of hearing, and 0.3% is the promise ring

9:14pm: baby's nasty night of treating is not counter-productive. A night of treating will increase 'life enjoyment' and incentive to complete more tasks, because I'll want to be alive more.

9:16pm: think I've lost weight. Weighing my ass and posting that shit on here straight up no tweaking increase uninhibited behavior up that life incentive.

9:24pm: I would be so happy if 'make me a chevy' by the promise ring was about me. If a song like that had been written with me in mind. It's short and simple and sounds so sad and good. Wouldn't you be happy if someone wrote 'not as good as the interstates are I just can't take you that far away, so stay' about you.

9:38PM: i weigh 135lbs. weighed a little over 140lbs when i began live-blog. not trying to gain or lose weight, just wanted to record this, notice things. or something.

9:42PM: turned on TV to beginning of mixed marital arts fight 'henderson vs. melendez.' henderson is 155lbs and melendez is 154lbs and both are 5'9", so i think, to scale…factoring in 10lbs per inch…so i'm 5'7" and 135lbs…so it's sort of like…i'm…see where i'm going with this? someone is holding a sign that says 'THROW DEM TANGS.' people are booing the shit out of henderson. would be funny if someone had a sign that said 'THANK YOU.'

9:51PM: assumed '15 minutes could save you 15% on your car insurance' was a statistic about one of the fighters.

9:54PM: baby's big nasty incentive #1: pizza party.

10:01PM: papa john's store #3052 is 'Taking Orders now' and 'Now Accepting Online Orders.' that is what i like to hear.

10:04PM: i wonder if melendez is mad that his name isn't menendez…i would be, i think…a little mad…

10:07PM: i believe some people use their papa john's 'papa rewards' account as their primary social network. also i believe that they switched to domino's 'pizza profile' recently, expecting something. they haven't checked their papa rewards account for maybe two weeks and now refer to it as 'the graveyard.' also is 'domino's'—so it belongs to domino? it's his? domino's pizza? people know who papa john is, we don't know who domino is. domino seems…i like him more. domino would know how to get me 'in' places. domino is a back door man. he has mafia connections maybe. his enemies flick his forehead and go 'plink! and there goes the dominos.' i'm ordering domino's instead now…heh heh heh…baby's big nasty…

10:13PM: papa john and domino would make so much money if they fought each other live on HBO. they could put their kids through college.

10:25PM: henderson won. he proposed to his girlfriend and she said 'yes.' people were booing him big time. he said 'we all know melendez is tough' and they booed more. he looked happy. good for him. he should've been like 'we all know menendez is tough.' ordered eight hot wings with bleu cheese and a medium 'pacific veggie' pizza.

10:31PM: presidential candidates should have to fight each other physically in the final debate.

10:36PM: how is the domino's pizza tracker at 'bake' already. it switched right after i rated my online ordering experience five stars. holding off on rating other categories until they happen, maybe.

10:39PM: now the news is on. does every head-on collision get reported? the news is like aol.com morning rush but less nice…more 'hungry'…aol.com is like 'why are we here? how is this what we end up doing?'

10:45PM: pizza tracker says 'delivering.' so prompt. they must not be live-blogging. tracker says 'jeffrey has left the store with your order at 10:42PM.' i will liveblog jeffrey for jeffrey.

10:49PM: jeffrey has my pizza. inappropriately coy-sounding news anchor said 'is syria the next afghanistan…?' what if jeffrey could write a song like 'make me a chevy' about me.

10:52PM: jeffrey called. it sounds like they beat him, at domino's. or he's an efficiency robot. he said 'i'll be there in one minute.' jeffrey. jeffrey dahmer overdrive. jeffrey domino's overdrive. they must really wring him out, the way he requested i have my credit card prepared, so he could make 'an imprint.' papa john's commercial on TV.

10:56PM: tipping jeffrey $5. i think he's a good man.

11:02PM: jumped at doorbell. jeffrey was maybe a few years older than me. i liked him. he said 'you ordered of, hot wings?' i said 'yup.' a pen dropped and he said 'butterfingers.' watched him struggle with boxes in the pizza carrier and thought 'i could just take mine. i don't know which ones are mine yet.' he asked to use the door to make the card imprint. i said 'that's why it's there.' he said 'this is a very precise, uh.' i said 'it's a science.'

11:12PM: rated everything five stars, commented 'Great, thank you!'

11:13PM: thought 'because it is bitter, and because it is my heart' at spread of food in boxes, sprawling across mom's bed. drinking one of dad's beers and watching 'the office.' michael scott just said 'i had a great time at prom, and you know what? no one said 'yes' to that either.'

11:20PM: i used to say 'i'm the female michael scott' around zachary. wanted that to become 'a thing' and it didn't. that's like something that would happen to michael scott.

11:37PM: reading reviews of 'pacific veggie' pizza on dominos.com and feeling good-willed and big-hearted about reviewers. that they would. one review ends with 'thanks, bernardo.' unclear whether reviewer's name is bernardo, is thanking bernardo, or is named bernardo and thanking some-one named bernardo–maybe thanking himself.

11:48PM: watching the end of 'pretty woman.' forgot there was shit like this. her life is so good in this. he pays her to have sex and hang out and fly on his private jet. doesn't seem like he'd be generous with oral sex though. he pays her not to care. thanks, bernardo.

APRIL 21, 2013

8:23PM: product on TV claims to 'take any punishment your family can dish out.' product is called the 'side socket.' it does look like it can take a lot.

things i did since sleeping last night:

- ate 1mg xanax

- watched 'big rich atlanta,' then something called 'the kandi factory,' about a woman who thinks she can make people famous

- ate 1mg xanax, ate wafer cookie thing

- debated deleting entire liveblog via thinking about my life without it and reading something that made me think 'shit…,' decided i'd probably feel something different tomorrow/why not keep going

- woke around 11AM and TV was on, didn't want to be awake, ate 1mg xanax

- woke around 3:30PM and TV was on, 'top chef' marathon

- ate two pieces pizza, nestle 'drumstick' ice cream bar, dove ice cream bar, two hot wings, orange, water

- masturbated three times orgasming fast, not picturing anything arousing, thinking 'keep doing the thing that makes you orgasm'

- fell asleep around 6:30PM

- woke around 7:30PM and people had shaved their heads on 'top chef' and someone had been punched

- responded to emails

- called mom and left voicemail

- mom called back and said she'd be back in an hour

8:35PM: after a comedic pause, 'top chef' contestant said 'my plate isn't beautiful.'

8:45PM: ate remaining hot wings, handful jelly beans, three bites pizza.

8:52PM: have noticed i've been leaving room when shows come back on, instead of during commercial breaks.

9:40PM: helped arguing parents carry things inside. infomercial on TV for the "dap x-hose:' the world's first expanding hose.' it is said to make all other hoses obsolete.

10:08PM: soft-voiced parental arguing. forgot about interview in NYC tomorrow. i don't like those black-screened '[adult swim]' promo things. feel like some people have criterion collection DVDs of just those things, just the black-screened promo things. they love them.

10:44PM: dad left. mom is unpacking now. watching 'planet earth.' ate last piece pizza and two pieces of toast with butter and jam, chocolate milk. an elephant got lost and was following the footsteps of the other elephants. the narrator said 'sadly, in the wrong direction.' the camera panned out to show the elephant alone in the desert for about seven seconds and then there was a commercial.

11:04PM: mom told me about their trip and asked what i had been doing. she sat on the bed next to me. told her about a woman in a prison documentary using three stacks of cards to walk back and forth in her cell because 'that's how i know i walked a mile, it's so i know i'm not just going nowhere.' mom laughed and said 'oh no, do you know how depressing that sounds?' i said 'no it's good, it's really good, the documentary show. it's on MSNBC. it's not depressing at all, everyone is really nice.' mom said 'please tell me this isn't something you're considering for your life' in a joke-warning voice. i said 'i wouldn't be happy doing that. it doesn't seem that bad though.' she said 'i know, you're right.' i said 'you're like. just, real life is like prison, kind of.' she said 'yeah, well. yeah, you're right.' we were quiet for a few moments. mom said 'you'd have to be someone's bitch.' i said 'no, i don't think so, they haven't talked about stuff like that on the show.' she asked what the show was called and i said "locked up,' on MSNBC.' she said 'i'll have to look for it, it sounds good.'

11:12PM: watching 'heroin: chasing the dragon' with mom. got up to pee at a long commercial for 'MyPurMist.' mom said 'now i know you said you've done it, and that you say it's not true that you get addicted the first time you do it, but do you really still think that?' i said 'yeah, yeah, no. i don't even like it that much, i get nauseated and throw up sometimes.' she said 'well then why have you done it, why would you keep doing that?' i said 'just, it's been around. i've just had it. i don't know, it's interesting. it's sort of like being that stage of drunk where you're like 'uhhh' but your thoughts don't change.' i could tell i had to poop. started pooping. i said 'it's just your body feeling different, not your thoughts that much.' she said 'that doesn't sound like fun.' i said 'i like it sometimes. don't worry though, i like, i've never liked it enough to do it a lot, i've never gotten why so many people seem addicted.' the 'MyPurMist' commercial was still on. i said 'you know when you don't think you have to poop but then you do?' she said 'yes, it's perfectly natural, i can't see you at all don't worry' (the bathroom is attached to the bedroom). i said 'no i mean the smell, just in case it smells, i'm sorry.' mom said 'i love these commercials they don't show on the normal channels.' i said 'yeah, there was one earlier, for 'dap x-hose.' she said 'oh the extendable hose!' i said 'yeah but it's called 'dap.'' she laughed and said 'the 'dap hose.'"

11:40PM: there is some kind of hallucinogen they use to treat drug addiction called ibogaine. they talked about it at the end of the documentary.

APRIL 22, 2013

12-1:45am: sudden intense abdominal cramping like I'd get in high school that'd sometimes make me faint and I'd go to the hospital. Also felt urinary tract infection-like pee pain. Took computer to bathroom to 'wait it out.' felt more comfortable to be on toilet. Answered ask.fm questions and drank two liters water. When water would hit stomach it would hurt more. Pills eaten: two azo standards, two gas x's, two stool softeners, two laxatives.

1:46-2:00am: went back to mom's room. She seemed concerned and was watching 'mad men.' I said medicine was taking longer to work because my stomach was busy digesting shitty food. She said 'this very thing happened to your dad on vacation, it happens a lot, he'll say his stomach feels like a boulder.' I said 'it's because he eats such shitty food.' she said 'yeah he really does eat like a shark, he'll just eat nothing for a long time and then have a big meal.' I said 'I do that too, I think that's why this happened tonight.' she said 'my poor girl, she doesn't eat' and hugged/patted me. I said 'it'll get better. Let's watch something together, do you want to do that?' she said 'yes, let's do something funny. Or 'homeland,' or did you lose interest already?' I said I didn't remember the last one and she said 'yeah, you had fallen asleep' and started re-telling the plot of episode ten and I felt guilty because it was my big Xanax night, the night of carrabba's take out and 'les miserables.' I started looking up 'homeland' on the ondemand menu and said 'let's just watch Mary, do you want that?' she said 'Mary Tyler Moore? Yes I always love Mary.' she asked questions and I'd respond 'I don't know, I have no preference, you know it better than me, I like them all you decide.' she said 'so we could watch an early season, like season one, or the last season? What do you want?' I said 'I want…to not answer questions, you decide. I'll like anything.'

Ate eight chewable tums. Walked to kitchen chewing them to maybe un-covertly get 1mg Xanax from bookbag, thinking it would help calm stomach. Mom had a black clay face mask on, was trying to figure out DVD. She said something in a making-fun-of-minstrel-shows voice, like 'massa don't let me use the DVD,' looking closely at the remote. I laughed and said 'it's okay, I understand your struggle, you already have it hard, being born.' she said 'oh no we shouldn't joke like this,' laughing.

2:10-2:26am: watched the first episode of the second season. The opening credits came on, showing Mary smiling in her car over the part of the song that goes 'who can turn the world on with her smile.' I said 'I thought 'fuck you, Mary'' and snickered. Mom said 'oh no, no 'fuck Mary'' and laughed a little. I said 'fuck you Mary' and we laughed quietly. Mom left to rinse off face mask. Mary and Rhoda were in Mary's apartment. I checked email on phone. Mom said 'what did I miss, what's going on?' I said 'I don't know, I was paying attention to my phone instead.' Mom said 'I'll just figure it out. Oh you don't know either? Let's just rewind' and used the wrong remote to rewind. I said 'no, no, that's the wrong remote, let's just watch and figure it out.' mom said 'oh let's just figure it out then.'

2:27am: mom said 'oh no I'm falling asleep, you keep watching.' I said 'okay, do you want me to say goodbye when I leave in the morning?' she said 'yes, and don't worry about waking me up, I'll just wake up and say goodbye, so don't worry about waking me.' I said 'I won't worry, I figured you might have to be awake to say goodbye.' mom laughed sleepily and said 'yes, yes I guess I'll have to be awake for that.'

2:28–2:50am: set alarm for 5AM. Played third episode. Rolled to lay on my side and closed eyes, thought 'maybe don't do this, maybe be an adult instead, or just stay awake.' It was the episode where Lou gets promoted and has a big office with a wet bar and a desk with no drawers. He asks his new secretary for a trash can so he can use it to store his scotch. The next day he's back in his old office and Mary is happy. She says she missed him and he says he missed her, and that all he was expected to do at his new job was sit there and smile and it didn't feel right to him. Mary says 'that doesn't sound like you at all.' Lou says 'I didn't mind taking the money, but the smiling, oof.' I love them. I want to work there, where Lou is my boss. Brought red quilt to the living room and fell asleep on couch.

5:10am: hit snooze.

5:40am: woke for real and showered, dressed. ate noopept, 60mg adderall. Masha texted about the dap x-hose. Got computer from mom's room. Mom said 'can you get coffee?' I said 'yeah, I have plenty of time, interview's not until 11.'

6:16am: driving to dad's to change clothes. Map says it'll only take three hours 19 minutes to get to NYC.

7:15am: dried hair. Applied new outfit, high heels, makeup. Fed cats and cleaned box. Left dad a note on coffee machine.

7:18am: bought two 16oz sugar-free red bulls and cigarettes from royal farms. Black & Mild's employee friend was there. She had taken out her cornrows. She didn't ring me up. Seems so nice to work there, everyone is so happy there. Like 'king of the hill' happy with their lives happy. Starting to feel vyvanse.

9:14am: have to pee badly. Pulling into j. Fennimore copper rest stop.

9:19am: 'rio' by Duran Duran is playing. I'm peeing. Pee no longer hurts. Walked in bathroom thinking 'looking professional as hell. Professional ass interviewee bitch c.e.o.' People are speaking Spanish and flushing toilets. I like this song. So emotional and empty-sounding. Patrick Bateman murder playlist style.

9:24pm: still on toilet. Feeling vyvanse things of having a lot to say. 'I want you to want me' is playing. Smells really clean, familiar cleaning agent smell, like my dorm at DePaul. Now 'blue velvet' is playing. I like singing 'blue velvet' and 'in dreams' in the car and pretending I'm being watched by Kyle maclaughlin in 'blue velvet.' For 'in dreams' I imagine singing at karaoke and people who like 'blue velvet' getting excited. When I sublet Tao's apartment in February I got really drunk and stayed up all night made embarrassing videos of myself singing.

9:37am: going 81mph, interview is one hour 43 mins away, I can make it faster though, I dilly-dallied thinking I had more time than I did shit

9:44am: behind pick-up truck with 'masters of disaster' bumper sticker.

9:58am: now gmaps says I'll arrive in 56 minutes hell fucking hell yeah. I want to smoke something that's not a cigarette and I don't want to smoke it, I don't want to feel a drug thing, just want a cigarette alternative.

10:00am: traffic has rapidly slowed. Going 12mph what the shit hell hotdog ohhhhhhhhhhhbbnbn nooopoolkooo

10:12am: smells strongly of cinnamon all of a sudden, gmaps says 43 minutes now, cutting this shit close, TO THE UNIVERSE: I WILL SACRIFICE ONE FUTURE HAPPY MEMORABLE EXPERIENCE IF YOU MAKE IT SO THERE IS NO MORE SLOW TRAFFIC AND A PARKING SPACE NEAR 988 ATLANTIC AVE BROOKLYN NY THANK YOU IN ADVANCE.

10:30am: 25 minutes away looking good.

10:31am: I spoke too soon major traffic shit shit shit on me.

10:50am: ate 20mg adderall. Traffic still bad, I'm at exit 21 need to be at exit 27. Going 0-2mph.

10:56am: texted interviewer that I'd be late. She's running late also, meeting at 11:30 instead hell yeah.

11:07am: ate a snigly niblet of adderall approaching exit 27

11:33am: got pulled over for using cell phone while driving. Gave cop expired registration and insurance then found current registration. Signed ticket. Said 'I'm sorry, I gave you the wrong things.' Cop said 'mmhmm. This is a ticket you drive safe.' I said 'okay, I'm sorry.' She looked at me like 'mmhmm.'

11:44am: jogged to 988 atlantic. Man said 'you have a nice day' and I turned head to say 'thanks you too,' making clippy-clop shoe noises. Called Nasa (interviewer), told her about cop and quickly changed subject. Nasa said she's getting iced coffee, asked if I liked iced coffee, I said 'yeah a lot,' she said 'with milk and sugar?' I said 'no just black is great, thank you.' she said 'no problem see you soon.' felt effortless.

11:47am: bald man in van head-checked me and said 'hey.' I head-checked back. 'Person with hair reciprocates lesser-haired person's head-check, does not vocalize 'hey:' next up on aol.com's morning news rush.

12:56pm: exiting interview place. It was a mostly empty apartment with two desks in the front and a photo-taking area in the back with a white background and lighting equipment. Nasa was easy to talk to, calming presence, I didn't feel uncomfortable or inhibited answering questions. Felt like we could be friends. She and a guy took pictures of me holding an American flag blowing in the air of a fan, holding copy of 'the fountainhead,' holding the ticket I just received. She said they usually transcribe interviews word for word then something like 'but that can be vulnerable, don't worry we won't do that for you,' and I got excited and said I'd like it if they transcribed it word for word and told her about the mdmafilms screening/interview I transcribed word for word, including like, [I said 'like, 'dot dot dot,' 'uh,' all those things like that people usually leave out, I'm interested in reading stuff like that']. Said I'd write something for their website. Think when article comes out I'm going to tweet responses to comments/tweets from their twitter account. Excited for this. Nasa said 'the weirder the better' re what I could write about for their website. When the guy was taking my picture nasa and I were talking and something came up about feminism and she said 'oh! Are you the one who said you're not a feminist?' I said 'yeah' and she said 'oh I almost forgot to ask about that' and got her iPhone and started recording me again. There were professional lighting white umbrella things around me and the guy was still taking my picture and nasa held the phone near my face and said 'so why don't you call yourself a feminist' and I said 'oh god, there's all these lights around me' and we kind of laughed and I said things about how it's better to just act as if men and women are equal than to create content about women not being equal and felt my legs and voice get shaky and heart beat faster. I think a radiohead song was playing.

That was the only uncomfortable part. I asked nasa what she thought about feminism and she said she understood what I was saying but appreciates feminist efforts, and talked about a women's music festival she organized. I said 'oh you did the Lilith fair?' she laughed a little and said her thing was called 'tinderbox' and something about coco rosie playing, also something about the Lilith fair. I said 'I went to the Lilith fair when I was like, twelve.' she smiled and said 'oh really?' and continued taking pictures. I asked her if she knew twin sister and she said she liked them a lot and I said…Jesus… something like 'I thought 'tinderbox: that's a thing like twin sister.' she said 'they're the ones that do that eighties video where they're like' and danced a little. I said 'yeah!' and did the dance a little and tried to do the twin sister voice to sing 'all around and away we go.' she said she had tweeted at them about how she thought they were great. I said 'you seem to have a knack for social things' and she said 'I really don't, like I'm okay with something like this where it's people coming to me that I've asked, but put me in another thing and I'm like [made 'no way' face and shook head 'no'].' I said 'me too, me too' smiling, liking her a lot. She reminded me of Chelsea in looks/personality/ambition/intelligence/self-awareness. Gushing over interview parked on some little street. Unstoppably gushing. In interview I talked about the silk road. Nasa asked if I really thought the world was going to end soon and I said I really thought it would in December, and that I still feel like 'where else could this possibly go, how is this still happening,' and that the internet needs to change into something else soon. Nasa and the photographer sitting at nearby desk said things about the (cessna?) act that means it's okay for the government to look at everyone's private browsing now. I said 'they must be so bored.' laughs. Fun goodtime interview. Feels like I just got out of a matinee. That feeling when you walk out of a movie and it's still daylight. The last time I remember doing that was with 'source code.' I feel like that. Like I've been dropped from a 90-minute airplane ride but the airplane was only 5'7" in the air the whole time.

2:24pm: driving to library on 5th ave to work on things until Mira and Sam Cooke are free to hang out. Ahead of me an old man in flimsy orange 'grubhub' vest biking past three men 'pampering'/washing a school bus.

2:53pm: truck with sign: 'just in case you don't have time to [picture of back of blonde female head in tropical setting] SHRIMPING IN PATA-GONIA'

3:04pm: ominous/depressing lighting since crossing into Manhattan, which I initially attributed to tall buildings. Shadows look flatter and deeper (hollow?) somehow. Paranormally bleak sky. Paranormal dizziness, like sky saw its reflection and got vertigo. Sky is experiencing vertigo. The sky i'm seeing is the reflection of the sky being shown an image of itself kind of resembling an exciting pre-storm, all I'm seeing right now is a slide in an infinite series of images reacting to each other, that nobody's supposed to see. Sunglasses made it worse. No parking spots scared of getting towed considering going back to library in Brooklyn. Freakishly depressing lighting. Looks like some day 1 wanted to stay home from school but wasn't allowed. Forebodingly familiar and hard to place.

3:18pm: parked in garage on 44th st near 3rd ave, did not want to risk getting towed. Guy said 'how long?' I smiled and looked to the left and said 'uh' like I had been asked 'you have 15 wishes to be granted, what will the first one be?' guy said 'you can put it in park' and I did. I said 'uh… until like…like…eight…eight-thirty?' he smiled like 'when is this child going to finish their story.' I said 'eight-thirty. eight-thirty.' he said 'good, great.' Removed things from bookbag, turned off car, started walking. He said 'the key?' thought I had left it in the car but it was in my hand. I kind of laughed and gave it to him and said 'oh the key of course, here, thank you' and walked a few feet ahead to a space where I could put on jacket and bookbag. Put the wrong arm in jacket twice, somehow. Said 'thank you' to another parking attendant who continued staring ahead.

3:34pm: walking to deli to garner sugar-free red bull. Have to pee badly. Also feel impending big time laxative results.

3:36pm: depressing lighting.

3:43pm: behind deli counter was a two-tiered shelf containing eight rows of condoms, four small Vaseline containers, one axe body gel. Swallowed 30mg adderall with 12oz sugar-free red bull on the street. Re-entered deli, threw away can, asked of they sold headphones, then 'earphones, earbuds' and employee smiled and said 'no' like a little elf. Short man in tank top walked close to me on street and whispered 'sexy.' A few seconds after passing I wished I had said 'BOO' and done something scary with arms.

3:50pm: peeing. Heart beating fast and I'm breathing hard and sweating a little, from climbing stairs, I think. Or from the exciting release of pee. 3:50pm red carpet event celebrating the long-awaited spring blockbuster: peeing for the second time today. Will there be a surprise v.i.p. appearance of shitting out all that domino's? Only time will tell.

4:00pm: surprise appearance unlikely, despite rumored 3:34pm sighting. Surprise v.i.p. guest is notoriously late and unpredictable, is truly the Robert Downey Jr. of bodily functions.

4:14PM: shoes echoing in reading room at library. mild coconut oil outbreak in bookbag has rendered bottom of computer oily, sexy, ready for penetration.

4:30PM: wearing earphones, not playing music, to feel 'plugged in.'

4:38PM: man behind me is periodically laughing like leonardo dicaprio in 'what's eating gilbert grape.' girl sitting diagonal to me has been 'setting up her station' for over two minutes, i think. she said 'i can hear you' to the gilbert grape man.

4:51PM: gilbert grape laughing situation has escalated. four outbursts in one minute, garnered three head-turns. laughing man has 'dirtlip' mustache. he looks so happy.

4:52PM: cop said 'what's that noise comin' from. who makin' that noise over there.' girl diagonal to me said 'right there.' i turned and smiled at gilbert grape and cop.

4:53PM: two giggles since cop: first one was a little muted and second one was back to normal. glad he's back to normal. loud 'heh heh' just now. people are just annoyed with him because they're jealous, i think.

4:58PM: wonder how many people in library right now have killed someone. there has been a time when this library has contained 'highest amount of people who have killed other people.' it's the most okay to kill someone if you're in the army or navy or marines or air force or [think there's a few other ones]. probably most acceptable in the marines. otherwise: less okay.

- army: mostly on the ground. the one that lets everyone in (i think).

- navy: mostly on boats/submarines. the one my dad was in.

- marines: mostly...i think it's harder to get in the marines.

- air force: mostly in the air.

5:56pm: sat outside on marble ledge to smoke. Squinty-eyed 'has five-year-old okcupid profile and m.f.a.'-type man asked me for a cigarette. Warned 'they're menthol.' he said 'that's okay.' asked if he needed a light. he said 'yes that would be great.' tried to disguise thinking the Sean Paul song that goes 'just gimme the light and [...].' man thanked me. I was instructed to have a good night. Watched him walk away. Thought 'another conversation successfully averted: ding!'

6:27PM: 'good library' closed, moved to table in 'institutional-looking distinctive-smelling library' across the street. think i've smelled this on airplanes. smells like an old friend. forget why i ate adderall.

6:28-9:10PM: answered ask.fm question about college. responded to one email. seems 'crazy' of me to have done this, especially because there are still errors/unclear things in the answer to my question, but i like feeling so obsessed with writing that i can't tell time has passed. texted with mira, in all caps, about where to meet. texts took on a christmas motif near the end.

9:11pm: pooped in library. Ate 1mg Xanax. Walking to parking garage to get car, then pick up Mira and Sam Cooke at dumpling place. Man stared and whistled as he passed. Want to start whistling and whispering 'sexy' to men. What would they do.

9:12-11:59PM: on the phone, mira said she and sam had finished eating and i should call when close. they'd get in the car so i wouldn't have to find parking. moved stuff to the back seat, still full of things from philadelphia apartment. seat was still very close to dashboard. drove maybe 20 blocks south to the dumpling place. called mira twice but no answer. left a voicemail saying 'poo poo dumpling.' circled block and parked outside dumpling place. made a 'lobotomy/tongue-sticking-out' face at a person obstructed by a sign, who i thought was sam. texted mira that i was outside. saw sam and mira sitting inside.

sam maneuvered around garbage bags i didn't realize i had parked near, then opened passenger-side door. i drove in reverse, at first to move away from the garbage bags/make entering car easier, but kept doing it to be funny. the door made a scraping noise against the curb and everyone said 'shit' and 'oh my god' excited things and i stopped the car. mira sat on sam's lap, think a pulling motion was involved in getting her into the car, multiple door-shutting attempts. i started driving before door was closed and it scraped against the curb. mira said 'no, you have to, ahhh [something about the curb].' then the curb thing was over and i felt something shift. i said 'hi sam hi mira' and they said 'hi.' they talked about the new places their bodies were being forcibly positioned, sounding more like they were making amused observations than complaints.

i said 'so you guys just want to drive around all night, right, and not go anywhere, just be in the car?' think mira said 'yeah let's just drive like this all night' and sam made a noise. then it was quiet. seemed clear that my joke would not lead to a 'where are we going/what are we doing' conversation.

in my memory mira was laughing the most but all of us were kind of, at the cramped situation. it was quiet for a moment then sam said 'how are you megan' in a robot voice and i said 'i am fine sam how are you' and he said 'i am fine' and i said 'how are you mira' and she said 'i am fine.' i think it was the robot voice this whole time. i said 'what are we doing, where am i driving us, does anyone know?' mira and sam said distracted 'i don't know' things, sam was trying to push mira out the window (had been doing this since getting into the car, i think). mira said something about how we should be careful of cops, laughing. i said 'for real though, where am i driving us?' someone suggested mira's apartment and i asked the address and mira said it, then something happened and i was distracted, asked her to say it again. she said 'brooklyn, en-why' at the end. she was in a position where she could only face the passenger-side window. seemed extremely uncomfortable. i felt 'rusty,' conversationally, like i could feel my voice having an uncontrollable quality of 'has not talked to friends in a long time,' sounding extra-aware of words and less expressive.

mira said something about having a big empty box in her room. seemed hard for her to say it, via sam trying to push her out the window. felt like i wasn't understanding something about the box. i said 'you have a box?' sam said 'your box.' mira said 'yeah, i have a big empty box, it's in my room.' sam said something i didn't understand and mira responded kind of quietly and fast, about their positions in the car, i think. i said 'so what's this i hear about a box?' mira said something involving comparing her position in the car to the size of the box. a little later she said 'this is like when i was in child's pose, at [name of coffee shop], when i was doing child's pose.' sam made a noise like he understood, then something about yoga in a coffee shop. i said 'you were doing child's pose? in a…coffee shop?' mira said 'yeah when i was at [name of coffee shop] i wanted to just be really, really small, really small, so i went into child's pose.' could tell she was smiling. i said 'sometimes it's nice to feel small.' she said 'yeah it feels good to feel small, i like feeling small a lot.'

a lot of things were being half-seriously said about the lack of space in the front seat and resulting uncomfortable position for mira and sam. sam seemed focused on pushing mira out the window. the 'no seatbelt' alert beeped. i said 'you guys are going to get ejected now.' stopped at a traffic light. sam held mira's shoe out the window and mira said 'my shoe!' inched my car over to the accordian-style bus next to us and said 'here, you guys can just take the bus, i'll pull up close so you can get on.' sam continued to push mira out the window. mira said 'no he's doing the egg thing!' i said 'is he trying to have sex with you?' sam said 'i'm already doing it' and mira said 'no, the egg thing, oh no,' laughing a lot. i said 'oh is it the [made a fist and trickled fingers down her back, a thing my mom used to do to me when i was little and say 'oops, here comes the egg,' which i had forgotten i'd shown mira and sam] thing?' mira said 'yes, the egg thing, oh no!'

seemed hard to concentrate on gps during car ride. i kept missing things and recalibrating. conflicting desires to talk and to pay attention to gps. i asked how the dumpling place was. mira said 'i got this thing, it was just like, pork. pork in a pancake.' sounded like she was grinning big. i said 'a… pancake?' she said 'yeah it was like this sesame…pancake thing.' i said 'i can smell the dumplings on you' and snickered. some time passed. sam said 'oh, that's the IKEA ferry.' i remembered in maybe february, driving mira to her apartment and talking about how we should get drunk on the IKEA ferry. excitedly said 'let's go drink on it now, is it open?' people said things about it not being open, probably.

i said 'this was my sadistic plan all along, to get you both in my car, so i can make you sit uncomfortably forever.' mira something about veal, how i was trying to use veal methods on her, to tenderize her. i said 'yeah like, atrophy…i'm doing a compression…something, to you.' mira said she was going to get thrown out of the window and die, laughing kind of. sam said he wouldn't die. i said he would die worse, because his weight would propel mira out the window and he would be behind her, in a worse position. then it seemed agreed-upon, how it would happen, people stopped saying things about it. i said 'live bad, die worse.' sam said 'we should all get that tattooed on us.' i said 'we should get it on…as a knuckle tattoo.' mira laughed and said 'that definitely would not fit on knuckles, [more words i can't remember, suggesting how to fit 'live bad die worse' on all knuckles].' i said 'we should just get it on one finger,' then a little later, turning onto a highway thing, 'you guys know how they can write your name on a grain of rice? we should get it that size.' sam said 'they always want to make them bigger.' i turned sharply, a driving/car thing took attention away, mira gasped i think. then i was on a highway thing. i said 'they always want to make them bigger?' sam said 'yeah, like, whenever i've gotten tattoos, they're always wanting to convince me to get them bigger, like convince me to have them do it bigger.' i remembered that being true for me also. i said 'oh yeah, so they can get more…space on you…' sam said 'more money' i said 'to leave more space on you, for their legacy.'

sam spit out the window maybe three times. think mira said something about it the first time, there was a conversation about not knowing how to spit properly the second time, and the third time i said 'get the fuck out of my car right now, you are disgusting' in a 'stereotypically easily offended bitch' voice.

sam said 'chinese citibank.' i saw the sign he was talking about and said 'how do you know that's in chinese?' sam said 'what else could it be?' i said 'japanese, korean, vietnamese, any of those [squinty-eyed racist face].' they laughed. i said 'they don't even know what they're writing, it's just… nobody knows, they're fooling us.' mira said 'are we in chinatown?'

traffic slowed on brooklyn bridge. i said 'i asked everyone to go slow, just for you guys.' sam pushed mira's head into the window and she said something like 'what are you putting me, how am i going to do this,' laughing. i said 'you just have to do it, now is the time to make your brother proud (mira's brother is a contortionist).' mira said 'yes, sam is my brother.' after a moment i said 'are you guys on poppers?' mira said 'yes, we've become poppers addicts since we saw you last.' sam said 'that's why i'm trying to push you out the window' (i think). i said 'that's the thing, that's why, this whole time…you guys didn't come out of the dumpling place right away because you were talking about whether you'd tell me you were addicted to poppers or not. sam didn't want you to tell me, that's why he wants to push you out the window, that's why…' mira said 'we just didn't want you to know because we want all the poppers for ourselves, where are my poppers?' pictured a bottle of poppers as she was saying this, felt distracted by image of being instructed to close an opened poppers bottle.

we talked about mira's moma reading on the 20th. mira said it took all four readers a collective ten minutes to read, but it was supposed to last an hour. she said tao had attempted to read his entire poetry book, reading the words very fast, but it was hard to hear and after a few minutes he said 'i can't do this anymore.' some time after this i remember looking at the blue and white lights of a tall building in the distance and regretting saying 'they took my picture holding an american flag today, at the interview' before we were on the brooklyn bridge. i said 'what if this entire time i was just talking to you guys incessantly about my interview today, like, incessantly describing, non-stop.' mira said 'oh my god.'

i pointed to a billboard that said 'march to help babies.' sam and mira said things about how mira was a baby who needed help. sam said 'bam' about a sign mira couldn't see and fake-chided her for not being able to see 'the bam.' at some point someone said 'smartdog.' there was a vaguely-worded billboard about cell phones or networking or a business…something. we started saying things like 'rethink dog: smartdog' and 'man's best friend, nation's best coverage: smartdog' and 'jumpstart your start-up with smartdog.' wish i could remember more of the smartdog things. that became a thing, seemed to overtake conversation, we were laughing a lot, saying 'smartdog.' at some point it seemed agreed upon that no one knew what 'smartdog' was, exactly.

arrived at the other side of the bridge and cars moved faster. mira said 'home stretch, home land' or something. sam said 'bam, you're missing the bam again' as we passed the 'bam' building. mira said 'oh no, i can't see the bam.' i said 'what should we do now?' sam suggested smoking crack in a staples parking lot and for a while we talked excitedly about how good that would be. drove past a pathmark grocery store. mira suggested the pathmark parking lot for crack. sam said it wasn't as depressing or funny as staples, and it didn't have a parking lot. i pointed to a gated area under a bridge and said 'there would be good.' someone said it would be humorlessly depressing to do it there, because people already probably do it there. sam said 'this is actually all really depressing, this idea.' i said 'i was just thinking about writing like, 'the bleakest places i've done crack,' and us doing that, but that actually seems bad.' we talked about how it's off-putting when people write journalistic things like 'guess i'll try to be homeless hehe,' which seem exploitative of 'real pain.'

as i parked mira said 'we have to blow up the air mattress thing with our mouths. there's like, a device, but we couldn't get it to work. we did it all with our mouths before and it worked, though.' the walk from car to mira's apartment was mostly 'smartdog,' a little about her roommates. mira said 'we could get beer, i only have like, one twenty-four ounce can.'

followed mira up the stairs to her apartment. felt sam do something to my bookbag and collapsed, pretending like whatever he had done had killed me. mira said 'oh no, you're dead.' they tried to pick me up a few times, each time joke felt less funny. stood.

something seemed different or less exciting when we put our bookbags and jackets down in mira's room but i didn't think anyone would say anything. mira and sam said 'shit' and 'oh no' and 'now it's bad' and 'oh no it feels bad.' i said 'now what are we going to do?' sam meekly said 'smartdog.' mira said 'smartdog…' i said 'smartdog is all we have.' felt like we were silently chuckling. i said 'i really love what you've done with the place, mira' using a poorly executed joke voice. she said 'yeah, i haven't changed anything like, at all, since you've been here.' i said 'oh, there's your empty box you were talking about, we could tear up mira's box.' mira walked to another room and sam and i broke the box into flat pieces of cardboard and put them under mira's bed. there were little styrofoam thingies everywhere. i held up a white convex piece of styrofoam and said 'rice bowl?' sam made the styrofoam thingies 'snow.' mira re-entered and said 'the box is gone.' sam said 'the box was for the lamp?' mira turned the floor lamp on, said 'yeah,' turned off florescent overhead lighting. i said 'that's so much better.' she said 'yeah, it's really so much better,' and something about brad listi seeing a picture of her room and either suggesting she buy a less depressing light or he ordered this one for her.

removed shoes. sat on mira's bed with sitcom-like synchronicity, as if directed to sit 'not exactly at the same time,' which is what we would've done. mira and sam looked at their phones. thought 'if i get my phone from my purse they'll know that's why i moved.' i said 'i have molly, xanax, adderall, does anyone want any of that?' there was an interesting silence. mira said 'i'll take a xanax,' sam said 'me too.' distributed xanax. there was another interesting silence. someone said 'how much is this?' i said 'one milligram.' sam said 'let's drink your beer.' mira stood and walked to the kitchen. i said 'we'll have eight-ounce servings. it's like we're drinking craft beer.' sam said 'is that how they do it?' i said 'i think so, small glasses.' mira re-entered with the beer and she and sam passed it between them to swallow the xanax. it was passed to me. mira said 'are you chewing the xanax?' i said 'yeah…i like to…chew it' and grinned and stopped chewing and sipped the beer. mira said 'isn't it bitter? do you like it?' i looked at her and sam, both looking at me. i said 'i like it, to do it. i like to do it.' we were sitting in a line on the bed, mira in the corner, mostly facing sam and me, then sam facing the wall, then me facing the wall but turned a little to sam and mira. i said 'how many fonts do you guys think are on this can?' they guessed five or six, then someone took the can and counted eleven. sam said 'someone searching 'how many fonts are on this can' in google.' i said 'help, how many fonts' in a stunted lummox voice.

somehow we all ended up googling 'tap out' and showing each other pictures of boxing shorts. there was some debate about if boxer shorts were boxing shorts. i said 'i like the really tight ones, search 'ufc shorts'' and showed them pictures of tight ones. we pointed out ones we liked. i said 'do you guys know 'no fear?'' someone said 'is that the thing with the guy with the white head?' i said 'i don't think so' and showed them 'no fear' pictures. they didn't know. sam said 'it's like an aggressive white head' and mira said 'yeah, the white head guy.' i said 'like, calv—' too quietly to hear, i think. i said 'i want to get a tattoo of, like you know how there's those stickers on cars where calvin is peeing on 'ford?'' someone said something funny about the pictures of shorts being endless. someone said 'we should all buy these and wear them around.' i excitedly said 'yeah i want to do that,' knowing we probably wouldn't do it. someone said 'are we really doing this, we're on our phones searching for pictures of tight shorts' and i chuckled a little, still looking at 'no fear' pictures.

mira said 'i tweeted 'any parties' but no one's said anything yet.' i said 'should i tweet that…'any parties'…'' seemed like we were all looking at our phones again. mira said 'isn't 'smartdog' like, an actual kind of vegetarian hotdog?' i said 'yeah, yeah. tofu dogs.' sam said 'rethink dog.' forget how this turned into a thing where we were all excitedly saying 'smartdog' slogans again. someone said 'it all comes back to 'smartdog.' i said 'we've devolved into 'smartdog'-only,' grinning. mira said 'no one's responding to my 'any parties.'' i searched 'smartdog' on my phone and the first result was for a website called 'oracle support & upgrades | smartdog services.' i said 'oh my god' and mira said 'are you looking up 'smartdog' too?'

read this aloud, from the oracle services website:

> 'SmartDog Services is the leading provider of Oracle EBS and Core Technology consulting services and recognized as The Oracle Customer's Best Friend. An Oracle Platinum Partner, four-time SMB TOLA Partner of the Year, and Oracle Titan Award Winner, our consultants are US-based, full-time employees and offer an average of more than ten years of Oracle experience.'

sam and mira read things aloud from other parts of the website. the website was so hilarious and perfect. we couldn't find an area on the website that described exactly what 'smartdog services' was or what service they're providing, but there was so much information about how they provided it. sam said 'this is exactly it, this is what smartdog is, this website is exactly the joke about smartdog.' i was laughing really hard, reading the things, the 'awards and accolades' section. found a section called 'partners' with pictures of people. zoomed in on a man's face and showed it to mira and sam, laughing so hard i was crying a little and they laughed too. took a screenshot of the zoomed-in face of the 'smartdog partner' (wasn't laughing mean-spiritedly or condescendingly, just 'couldn't believe' the website was real, it was so perfect, the way it was aligning with my formerly non-actualized idea about how the world sounds like it's running on business jargon, continuously surprising me with perfect examples of this).

tweeted 'any partners? i'm looking to invest. rethink dog,' 'i'm looking to invest : rethink smartdog #smartdog,' then 'any roof bombings?' i said 'this is…i'm destroying my twitter account.'

mira said 'wait stop, listen to that noise.' heard something squishy, slow-moving, and maybe close to the window. i said 'what the hell is that.' mira said 'i don't know, i have no idea, it just sounds like this sometimes.' sam said 'if there actually was a smartdog it would be the size of your phone, oh my god, and it would be pink and have that face too, and its legs would be boneless and they'd make the squishy sound.' felt momentarily frozen/ awestruck by the unexpectedly complex creativity of the image. decided to go to sam's apartment and smoke crack. i said 'i don't want to wear my jacket, can i wear one of yours?' mira said 'yeah, of course. we should all wear my jackets.' picked a black one with a furry hood. sam looked at the jackets and mira picked one for him.

drove to 7-11 for gas and beer. there were maybe five cop cars in the parking lot. mira said 'there's always a lot of cops here, getting stuff, i don't know why.' watched mira and sam buy beers while i filled car with gas, then drove suspiciously around a parked cop car to an open parking spot, which turned out to be blocked by a hidden car-leaning cop. drove suspiciously to less-favorable parking spot between two cop cars. brought two 'crazy stallion' 24oz beers to cash register that could only give $10 cash back. walked to ATM to withdraw $40 for crack. waved to mira and sam. the little circle cartoon guy with arms and legs did somersaults on the ATM screen. i said 'i love that guy.' sam said 'me too.' took money and walked out and everyone got in the car again.

mira had bought 'sour straws' (sour gummy candy strings, forget what they're really called, don't think it's 'sour straws'). she said something about this 7-11 only being good for having this brand of 'sour straws' and gave me one. tasted strongly of something. i said 'it tastes like the moment you discover you're gay.' i said something about how we were eating candy on the way to smoking crack, that this was...something. earlier sam had texted his dealer, who lives next to him. the dealer texted back something about prices and '~WORLD FAMOUS~'

APRIL 23, 2013

12–3:00AM: seems to be taking forever to type all of this. it's 6:46AM april 24, typing this now. also this is where i start to remember less. rapidfire list of everything i remember happening in this time frame in the order i remember it:

- sitting at sam's kitchen table and waiting for response from crack dealer, either sam or mira was on the bed

- mira saying 'i keep having to pee, i'm peeing so much tonight' and me bending over to touch my feet and saying 'that's what happens when you drink water, you pee. classic cause and effect. classic.'

- leaving apartment to meet dealer and sam saying something dad-like, referring to an earlier joke about how it would be good to try to act like a dad. sam said fatherly things and made faces like 'stern guidance, kindly acceptance, soon you will know the way, my son' as we walked out the door. he said 'does anyone have to pee? i don't want to go back because someone had to pee, so make sure you pee now.' i made an urgent child-like 'oh no, i have to pee, i'm in trouble' face. he said 'you better do it now' in a threatening voice. i continued the 'in trouble' thing, started to walk to the door, then went 'back to normal' and we walked down the stairs.

- smoked five pinkie-nail-sized bags of crack using aluminum foil/dollar bill method that had been 'honed' by mira and sam, since the last time i did it with them.

- listening to lightning bolt, mira saying something about liking light-ning bolt or knowing them, me saying a misguided story about how i almost saw them play in an alley once, but i didn't, but it was raining so…'lightning bolt'…bad story.

- mira said she wanted to listen to rap. i said to put on chief keef. think the only song sam had was 'that's that shit i don't like.'

- something about biggie smalls…actually becoming smaller…shit, this actually happened in the car on the way there but i don't feel like going back to type it there. someone said something about there not being space for their legs, then something about biggie, then that it would be good if biggie had surgically reassigned his limbs to different 'outposts' on his torso. i said 'would he have gotten gastric bypass, to be smaller,

265

if he was still alive, so he could be both big and small?' then there was an interesting silence.

- talking and giving examples about how people can be 'endearingly depraved' or 'annoyingly depraved' (this was in the car on the way to sam's, and the word wasn't 'depraved,' can't believe i'm not remembering this, we were saying 'ED' and 'AD' or 'UD'). the 'depraved' quality was another way to describe 'itchiness' (term sam and his friend ralph invented to describe people who act eager to garner attention for 'being themselves' and seem equally unaware of saying things to indicate wanting attention, which often draws the opposite kind of reaction/ attention desired...like, people who would abruptly change the subject of a conversation to an unrelated thing about themselves, then kind of squint or stare at their 'audience' like they must be either 'considering this very important thing that has just been brought to their attention' or 'not there at all.' that sounds funny. it's more annoying than funny when it happens in real life).

- pretty much solely concentrating on/talking about the process of smoking the crack as we were doing it, saying like, sports-commentary things. everyone would watch 'the smoker' or the crack very closely. remember saying 'teamwork' and 'what i'm doing right now is fiending, actually fiending, i can't think about anything else but wanting more,' and mira saying 'yeah it's the only thing that makes you want instantly more, even more than cocaine.'

- looking at each other after the five baggies were smoked and sensing we all wanted more. sam or mira said 'i want more' and i said 'let's just get more' and sam texted dealer

- dealer texting with regular frequency all night, then turning off his phone as soon as we got to sam's. sam said 'this is what he does.' dealer texted something vague which i think meant 'don't ask me how much it is, say how much you want.' remember thinking mira and sam understood text or felt more interested/amused about it than me.

- after inhaling sam and mira made the same faces. seemed hilarious, how consistently exaggerated their faces would look, and how they'd 'maintain face' as we'd silently exchange matter-of-fact 'masculine' nods every time. i said 'let me take a picture, you have to see' and got sam's face but at not the funniest angle/maybe slightly post-face.

- walking fast to pizza place where there was an ATM, walking slightly behind mira and sam due to high heels

- the first time the dealer wanted to make exchange inside sam's building and mira and i waited outside, the second time it was just going to be sam but then mira and i wanted to come, dealer said 'let them inside,' i said 'yeah be a gentleman' quietly, mira and i exchanging looks as sam let us inside, dealer didn't have change for $20 and sam gave me $6, i said 'what's his name,' surprised when sam didn't know

- saying 'world famous' a lot

- all of us saying 'i'm just drinking from all the beers on the table' and 'it's okay, we're all doing that' at some point

- mira excitedly saying 'do you know how to do a headstand?' and following her onto the bed, to use as a headrest and prop feet on wall, picking a spot by the window and falling over/somersaulting into large gap between bed and window, switching to a wall space and mira switching to floor, sam taking pictures then doing a solo handstand and mira taking a picture

- something about belly-buttons

- sam and mira calling the first hit 'greens,' saying 'who wants greens' or 'let's give megan greens' a lot, i said 'should we call them 'whites,'' sam said 'greens' seemed funnier because of pot, group agreed 'greens' seemed funnier

- re-entering apartment with second round, sam saying 'i don't know what to listen to,' me finding/playing 'schism' by tool on youtube, mira saying 'you guys never went through a 'tool' phase,' me repeating 'i just like their videos' maybe three times, feeling a little out of control

- standing near the table before we left for ATM and doing a short spontaneous freestyle rap, hearing someone say 'you're good at it'

- having same extreme focus on last three baggies, talking about 'where does he get baggies so small,' feeling like i was fiending big time, like i wasn't getting any smoke and…like, very unseemly greediness…sensed mira wanting to 'give me greens' more because i paid for it, maybe, which made me want to deny greedy impulses and give everyone things equally, but definitely felt extreme greed

- talking about how it felt similar to cocaine but more calm and euphoric and like the effects lasted significantly shorter, i said something like 'i don't even know why i want to feel it again right away, not sure what it's doing exactly'

- unanimously/effortlessly deciding to sleep after last baggie

- distributing 1mg xanax, going to bathroom to change into pajamas, emerging from bathroom and asking if anyone wanted another xanax because i was going to eat another one, seeing mira and sam sitting on the bed slowly saying things like 'what time is it' and 'how many milligrams,' then deciding they each only wanted half, saying 'are you sure' and felt willing to give more, half-thinking it would be 'making up for crack greediness'

- mira using the bathroom and sam and me sitting on the bed, sam taking out a piece of gum with 'startling comic unexpectedness' and saying 'i want a piece of gum, this gum is shitty,' me saying 'i want one too, give me the whole thing,' getting entire mostly-full package shoved in mouth, laughing, trying to chew it, eventually it became chewable, mira coming out of the bathroom, showing her 'the wad,' seeing two pictures she took of me chewing 'the wad' and saying 'oh gross' (about me more than 'the wad')

- using bathroom again to brush teeth, hearing mira say 'do you want the middle or the end' a few times. asking where toothpaste was and, while brushing, thinking 'cool, someone else's toothpaste,' sam saying he had work in the morning but mira and i could sleep

- falling asleep easily, spooning mira in 'oddly un-awkward way i tend to spoon mira, but that might be awkward for mira, should maybe check about this with mira, feel similar to alvie kneading on my arm when i have done this, this is the first time this is being acknowledged publicly, i'm laughing a little'

4:10pm: woke to sounds of Mira moving around, making coffee I think. Mira emerged from bathroom and we sat at the kitchen table. Sam had left for work much earlier, I think. Mira said 'I made coffee, I put it in the fridge,' and took out two white mugs of coffee. Was happy/interested that she had put them in the fridge, I like putting ice in hot coffee. Remembered being at her apartment in march the morning after we made a 'how to figure out people' chart and ordered thai food and putting ice cubes in my coffee, feeling moved that she had maybe noticed this.

Things we talked about at table: crack and Xanax being a good combination/ not regretting saying things the next morning like how cocaine can make you regret, confusion about a reading Scott mcclannahan is organizing, how we're both bad at responding to emails, how I'm moving there soon/ going to look for jobs at nursing homes, liking old people, relationship

things a little. I'm leaving NYC to mail books from Baltimore and returning Thursday for the interview with the apartment committee people. Mira
said I could stay with her again/anytime and I said something like 'thank
you' and 'I don't want to be like [person who overstays their welcome]' and
she said I wouldn't be and I believed her.

5:20pm: driving back to Baltimore. Wearing Mira's big black coat (left
mine at her apartment last night). Man in car said 'hey baby' and I stared
at/'ogled' him back with an intensely neutral, slightly-deranged-in-its-dis-
play-of-zero-reaction face. Continued staring as I drove away, then turned
head to continue aggressively neutrally staring.

6:50pm: passing Delaware. Sky is starting to be sunny again. Feel encroach-
ing emptiness, imagining arriving at one of my parents' apartments. Mira
is at work. I'm not sure where Sam is. Seems daunting to fill in details of
hanging out with them last night. It was good to see them and be reminded
that soon I'll have a place to live, a life. Sky looks simultaneously oppres-
sive and indifferent. Keep having memories and wondering what I should
do. Read Sam pink's captions on a photo of Mira reading at the MOMA,
thought 'shrimp' and 'perceptive ass person.' A little worried about not
having my period yet.

7:09pm: skimmed march 21-25 to see if I had gotten period. I am still
'safe.' listening to 'ruins' by aloha to see if I still felt moved by it like how I
did in march, and I do, big time, the lyrics—hoo, big time. Goosebumps.
Cried tearlessly, more like a 'what the fuck' helpless laugh/shuddering
thing. Want to type lyrics. Resisted typing them before, you know how to
skip shit, skip it if you want:

The cupboard is bare

I've been watering the fields

That I should be harvesting

Treatments come, I never turn the page

Months are a mistake, it's like 29 days

Keep my daybook clean

I'm never ready to leave

Keep my calendar clear

I'm not going anywhere

(One moment goes by)

I walk in the stagnant sun

A chemical reaction if there ever was one

(One moment goes by)

I fought the tyrannical sun

I try to forget but your memory won

(One moment goes by, by, by, by)

I walk among the ruins

I tried to forget but I couldn't do it

The cupboards are bare

I've been hunting things

When I should be gathering

Weekends are a waste, I never leave the grounds

The weekend can break me, it's like 24 hours

Keep my good days free

Keep my eyes closed, please

To everything, everything

I've been seeing the signs of my surrender

I've got it backed up and nobody can send it

I've been seeing the end

I've been seeing the signs of resurrection

Got it backed up and nobody can send it

I've been seeing the end, seeing the end

We were giants on a plywood stage

In evenings I was your household name

And for a little while, I knew all the words you'd say

Cut me from the movie

Pull me from the credits

I was just beyond camera

Right outside the frame

Waiting for a getaway car that never came

At the end of the story I was just beyond camera

Right outside the frame

Waiting for a getaway car that never came

Waiting for a getaway car that never came

Waiting for a getaway car that never came

7:36pm: experimenting with sunglasses to see what makes sky look less depressing. It's starting to look prettier now.

8:10pm: have been listening to 'ruins' on repeat, reading lyrics to add 'sight' to sensory experience of song...seeing + hearing song...now...

8:14pm: undecided about eating adderall. Tolerance is higher, I don't want to stay up all night again, have seven left and one vyvanse. I bought it so I could eat it, why conserve it all of a sudden? Feeling drained. Nothing I want to do right now and no matter what I'll be doing something. Getting on exit for mom's house. Humorless dread, no funny ideas, unable to readjust mentality to be like 'you're fine, consider how much worse other people have it, better things are on the way probably.' was just passed by screaming ambulance. 'ambulance' is a pretty word, sounds like it would mean 'inspirational lighting, similar to the lighting of Oprah's colon.'

9:08PM: talked with mom. said i had fun in new york and expressed similar things as above few updates. she said 'i think it's spring fever, it's so hard to make myself do anything right now.' thought 'mom understands, i think.' she said dad called a psychic last night who said it was 'a bad year for libras.' mom said 'it's something about your saturn, uranus, i don't know. i don't know about these things, they're interesting to hear though.' i said 'yeah they're interesting to hear.'

washed kale, halved cantaloupe, combined in blender while mom said vague consoling things about how it didn't seem 'right' that i was feeling this bad for this long, and that she also had been feeling directionless. finished blending and asked what she was reading. she said 'i don't even know, it's some crappy mystery, i couldn't even tell you the title or who it's by. sometimes those things are just good.' i said 'yeah, crappy stuff is good sometimes, i like it.' she walked to the kitchen and moved plates in the sink as i drank my blended thing. the corned beef from a few weeks ago was in the sink, in a plastic container. i said 'how about that bad boy.' mom made a face and said 'oh i know, it's really, you know. don't open that lid.' i smiled. she said 'oh i'll take care of all this later, you're using the kitchen, i'll get out of your way.' i said 'you're not in my way at all, i'm just drinking this.' she said 'well, i'll just wait' and hesitated. she said 'i'm starting up that sensa powder diet thing again, which seems fruitless.' i said 'well, not unless you put it on fruit.' she said 'haha, fruit, get it?'

9:17PM: ate an amount of noopept, 30mg adderall. i have eight and a half left, not seven. feel more justified eating 30mg now. it will probably take this much to have significant effects on me and it will cause me to feel a little better physically, at least. going to focus on updating this thing and drawing. will feel better to do small productive things like this instead of laying on my bed looking at things in the room or the computer or trying to sleep.

11:25PM: sensed dad before he said said 'knock knock?' walked into my room and i hugged him. we had been emailing back and forth a little and he seemed happy. he said they're starting to build his new offices, which he didn't think would happen. i said 'oh man, i'm happy for you, that's so cool.' sort of stood to hug him and he leaned over to hug me and said 'it's cool! you're cool! i'm cool! you bet your sweet bippy i'm cool!' during the hug. a 'sweet bippy' from dad. he said mom had probably already 'hit all the headlines.' happy and surprised to see dad so happy. he was holding a paper bag.

APRIL 24, 2013

12-2:15AM: responded to emails and text messages. texted mira and sam picture from last night.

2:16AM: mom walked to my room and said she was going to sleep, probably no movie tonight. asked if it was okay if i smoked on the balcony. i don't usually ask, it's like, an unspoken thing. she said 'well yeah, it's okay, i just wish you wouldn't, for you.'

2:17-3:21AM: continued writing update about the car ride and mira's apartment. remembered i also wanted to be writing about what i'm doing now. i've been sitting on mom's balcony. have smoked two cigarettes. ate remaining 15mg of an adderall a while ago. fingers cold, numb-feeling.

3:51AM: felt too cold, went inside to bedroom again. looked at email and responded to one fast. read response from gabby gabby which included essay she wrote about liveblog, didn't expect a response so fast. felt very interested reading her essay and [hard to describe something] about her wanting to write it, funny to be typing this after reading essay, now knowing she feels less interested in the content of liveblog than the time it spans/other things (i'm not saying 'feels funny to be typing this' to showcase an ego bruise or something, like 'she doesn't like my content as much wahhh'—i'm similarly interested in liveblog for 'time span' more than 'content' reasons—just a funny awareness of the moment where i'm typing the specific content of something which seems more interesting as a sum/method of relating its contents than its specific content). rachel white asked to gchat as a follow-up thing for her tao article, going to do that now. unsure if i want to continue elaborating details of last night to the degree of car ride/mira's apartment specificity. i like remembering that stuff though.

4:22AM: rachel white was no longer 'available,' emailed that i'd look for her tomorrow. stared at pill container. adderalls. it's probably already working, i'm just used to the effects so i don't notice them as much and think i want more. still, it would help to have a little more. i think. there are seven. unsure if dealer wants to sell to me anymore. maybe. this is 'that time of the month.' savings account depleted. i should get a prescription. i should email masha to trade xanax again. if i eat half of one now...just bit maybe 15mg off, then maybe 5mg more. removed hot pink puffy coat and looked at myself in bathroom mirror. i'm wearing a gray hoodie sweatshirt and blue 'yoga pants.' lifted sweatshirt to see if stomach looked okay (not really). fluffed hair to see if it would improve face (not really).

4:29AM: considering eating entire adderall so instead of prolonging/barely noticing the effects, it will feel like something. shit. hate this shit. soon it will be gone and i'll have to adapt. okay. if i eat the whole thing, i am decreasing the time between now and the future where i'll have to adapt.

thing i haven't mentioned: for some time (since i've started liveblog definitely, but also maybe before then) have been noticing an area on left side of chest that feels tight and sometimes aches, especially if i breathe deeply, or if i'm out of breath/can feel pulse, like yesterday when i climbed stairs. when i notice these things i think 'something to worry about, maybe.' not saying this to get you to worry about me. i…

WHENEVER I TALK ABOUT SOMETHING THAT FEELS SHITTY TO ME, ABOUT ME, LIKE A SHITTY PHYSICAL OR EMOTIONAL THING I'M EXPERIENCING, I'M NOT WRITING ABOUT IT AS A WAY TO SOLICIT ATTENTION OR SYMPATHY. WHEN I TYPE ABOUT SOMETHING THAT FEELS SHITTY TO ME I FREQUENTLY HAVE THE URGE TO WRITE A DISCLAIMER LIKE THIS, WHICH IS STUPID I THINK, NOT ONLY BECAUSE THERE IS ALREADY A DISCLAIMER AT THE TOP OF THIS PAGE, BUT LIKE…WHY THE FUCK WHY, BOYLE?!?!

SO BY WRITING THIS ALL-CAPS DISCLAIMER RIGHT NOW— I'M DECIDING THIS IS THE FINAL DISCLAIMER. PEOPLE EITHER PAY ATTENTION TO THE FIRST DISCLAIMER AND DON'T THINK I'M LOOKING FOR SYMPATHY, DON'T PAY ATTENTION AND THINK I'M LOOKING FOR SYMPATHY, PAY ATTENTION AND THINK I'M LOOKING FOR SYMPATHY, SKIP OVER THIS/DON'T CARE AT ALL, OR [UNKNOWABLE AMOUNT OF OTHER THINGS PEOPLE MIGHT THINK].

I FEEL GUILTY ABOUT COMPLAINING, ALWAYS, I THINK. FEELING GUILTY ABOUT COMPLAINING IS A GREAT WAY TO CREATE MORE SITUATIONS WHERE I FEEL LIKE COMPLAINING. LIKE RIGHT NOW. THIS IS SECOND-LEVEL COMPLAINING, I'M COMPLAINING ABOUT THE COMPLAINING, AND THIRD-LEVEL/BACK AROUND TO FIRST-LEVEL, BECAUSE I'M WRITING THIS OUT OF A DESIRE TO NOT RECEIVE OR BE PERCEIVED AS WANTING TO RECEIVE SYMPATHY CAUSED BY MY COMPLAINING.

I THINK IF I MAKE THIS MY FINAL DISCLAIMER, I WILL BE 'FORCED' TO PAY LESS ATTENTION TO THINGS LIKE THIS,

WHICH WILL MAYBE EVENTUALLY LEAD TO ME ACTUALLY BELIEVING THAT PEOPLE BELIEVE ME.

5:03AM: first fucking morning bird fuck that shit. fuck that shit. i want to live somewhere birdless. also sunless, maybe. without sunrises. i just never want to know when it's about to be morning again. like how some married people are like 'i don't care if they cheat, i just don't want to know about it.' that's how i feel about the sky 'becoming morning' on me, like it's my unfaithful spouse and i've said 'please i don't care if you do it, just don't let me know about it,' but it doesn't pay attention and continues on with the morning birds and the sun and the whole gang and there's no way for me to divorce it. actually i could divorce it by dying. pictured it saying, 'i'm never going to be silent about becoming morning, it's nothing to be ashamed of and i want you to stay informed, but if you can't deal with it, why not just leave me already,' then me dying quietly in the night without telling it, then a few days later it finds out and thinks 'that's exactly what i thought she'd do, i knew she was no good,' then eventually it forgets me and happily continues its shameless displays of becoming morning after night forever.

6:16AM: ate 15mg adderall. thought 'damniny shniggets, like the evil jiminy crickets. no wait, they did that, lemony snicket.' thought 'much to the favorites of none, [something about twitter]' and turned off hall light. didn't think anything but 'damniny shniggets' that i'm aware of from hallway to balcony, where i'm currently smoking again.

8:02AM: have been typing crack summary, not looking at anything else. sun up, bright.

8:07AM: bright light, 48 degrees, can hear a lawnmower. feel like i'm writing myself into…not understanding words…starting to feel embarrassed about all of this, myself, etc., but significantly less so than i have in the past.

10:37PM: got my period. seconds ago. period descended into underpants. alert the presses. it does seem a little interesting that i opened the window i'm typing in before i got my period. 'seconds ago' was real-time liveblogged. i'm in my bedroom. outside people are yelling like they're playing sports. postponing finishing/mailing book packages in favor of finding remaining 'mumblecore' DVDs to mail to people who want to screen it in spain.

10:47AM: something so indescribably…jesus…it's this sinking feeling about the internet, looking at all of this stuff at, now, 10:48AM…all the tweets and the facebooks and the websites and the emails and then this liveblog shit…me in relation to all this and me sitting here…not removing myself…this feeling will be gone soon.

10:48AM–2:17PM: same extremely slow pace different tasks.

2:18pm: masha texted 'Feel physical chest tightening aversion to taking adderall today even though I'm more fucked without it.'

7:50pm: droplet of water fell on back. parked in front of dad's. Touched ceiling to check for leaks.

8:19pm: fed cats, cleaned box, found storage unit key, searched all boxes and bags in car for DVDs, found none. Driving to storage unit despite darkness, they close at 9pm I think, thought 'what day is today, it's Saturday?'

8:22pm: it makes more sense to go back to mom's. No I shouldn't be rewarded with 'easier better alternative' in this case, I didn't do something I felt was important to do today. I had all day. Forget today. I wrote notes on every page of one book and finished packaging mostly. Nervous about being seen, looking the way I do. When mom woke I asked her for a hug and said 'could you honestly tell me how I look, like am I haggard and tired and like, old.' she looked concerned and said no, I looked young and pretty, but that my eyes looked big and tired and worried. I said 'are you sure? The hair?' she said 'well, if you just brush it a little. No, you just look worried, you look young.' I said 'you would tell me if I didn't, right?' she said 'I would, I would.' I said 'okay, okay I'm less worried now, I believe you, thank you' and walked down the hallway to bedroom. She sort of followed me and stopped where the hallway meets the kitchen. I turned and said 'can I just try something where I tell you this is my last pack of cigarettes and if I buy another one it means something really bad, like, you'll be extremely angry?' mom looked puzzled, said 'yes, well yeah I guess so, but you know you can always comfort yourself, you can allow yourself cigarettes, I mean I don't want you to but.' felt frustrated and tried not to show. I said 'it's okay, it was just a thing I thought I'd try, sometimes it works on the liveblog if I give myself a fake consequence, thought saying it aloud this time…think it won't work.' long hallway conversation followed. At some point mom said 'I know we didn't raise you with any rules or, well you know basic 'right or wrong' things, we didn't want to discipline you the way our parents did, so. You have your own set of drawbacks, you have to do it yourself, but you know that.' I said 'I know…' mom said 'but me saying that doesn't help.' I said 'yeah…it's okay though.' mom said things about how I need to sleep or I won't be able to function, that not sleeping is probably what's making it hard for me to focus 'like this conversation has no focus, it's just how [she] thinks combined with how she wants to but doesn't know how to help.'

8:33pm: sky looks grimly, velvet-y, purple-y black, 'like my lungs maybe.'

8:50pm: made it to storage unit before they closed hell yeah.

8:52pm: rondo caddy shitshow

9:12pm: thought 'I did it all for the [pile of ten damaged pastel-colored DVDs].' repacked boxes, 'rescued' four stuffed animals from fate of certain forgotten death, welcoming to new loving foster home at mom's. going to fucking FedEx now better believe bitch gonna live up to her word and mail this shit tonight.

Wanna thank the universe for giving me this opportunity to push my shit ass to the limit today, I saw some lows man not gonna deny it looked like I wouldn't come out with a win today, but I slid in at the end and turned the shit around man, it's like when you already gave up and you get the chance to come back you're gonna come back fierce, tonight I'm sleeping like a blessed woman knowing I put those ten DVDs in their place, thank you universe, thank you Elliott city storage facility, thank mom, thank you dad, and thank you all my unborn babies, remember this day when mama showed Spain how it's done!!!!

9:36pm: parked at FedEx. Haven't eaten since domino's.

9:52pm: cheapest shipping option was $116. Oof. That means $84 profit though, which is $84 less than if I hadn't done this. DVDs will be in Madrid by May 6 guaranteed. Spain is thirsting for these broke ass-looking beat-up cover forgotten last copies ever of these films DVDs.

10:18pm: worried mom went through bookbag and found drugs, re asking 'what are you addicted to' re quote in gabby's article where saying I was shocked that people didn't confront me about being addicted to drugs (I said I didn't feel addicted to anything but that whenever drugs are mentioned people think 'addiction,' was just surprised no one had wanted to tell me I was addicted to things, then said 'are you looking at me?' mom said 'yeah, yeah, it's just my glasses' and took them off in a little demonstration. I said 'don't worry, I'm fine' and changed the subject fast).

11:05PM: have deduced that it's wednesday. did not believe it was wednesday. i go to new york again for apartment interview tomorrow. seems…how am i going to…tonight i want to eat and sleep. no more trying for anything else tonight.

11:06pm: mom made me eggs and toast. Stood with her in kitchen, kept pausing and snickering before I talked. Mom acted eager and a little nervous, maybe careful around me. I paused and snickered and said 'I'm worried you think I'm on drugs right now, I'm not, I'm not on anything.'

she said 'I don't think that, wait, why, am I acting weird?' I said 'you seem anxious around me a little, but I could be imagining it.'

11:10–11:59pm: emailed apartment committee per request of Colin, to inform them Colin had asked me to ask them to call me and I didn't know why (annoyed to be doing this). Mom said eggs were ready. Ate 1mg Xanax. Took eggs to mom's room to eat while we watched Mary Tyler Moore. When the theme song said 'who can turn the world on with her smile? Who can take a nothing day and make it seem worthwhile?' I said 'Mary actually doesn't know the answers to those questions, she's actually wondering those very things.' Mom laughed and said 'she's gonna make it after all. You're going to make it after all, honey.' felt a little weird. The episode seemed 'slow,' felt aware of my chewing noises and fork motions/toast handling. A lot of pepper came at once and I tried to blend it by rubbing eggs with my finger. Mom was laughing weakly along with the laugh track but knew she probably didn't think it was funny. I said 'how do you feel?' she said 'I'm a little worried the food doesn't taste good.' surprised. I said 'no its great, it's perfect, thank you for making it.' Agreed the episode wasn't funny or interesting. Switched to an episode of Homeland.

APRIL 25, 2013

12:00-1:[unknown]am: mom asked about what episode I wanted to watch, if I wanted to put in another Mary Tyler Moore instead, what I remember about where we left off with Homeland, what my preferences were. I said 'I don't know, I have no preferences, my preference is to not answer questions,' grinning a little. She said 'okay okay, I know, you don't want questions. Let's just pick up where we left off, I know you fell asleep, [described plot of episode I fell asleep during], I'll put on the next one.'

Brody suspiciously clutched a laptop-sized package. I said 'yes, now I have my fish all to myself' in Brody's voice and mom laughed hard. I said 'no one can know about my delicious fish dish' as Brody unwrapped the package, a bomb, and strapped it to his body, enjoying making mom laugh and laughing too.

6:03am: woke to strange breathing noise. Thought it was me. Opened eyes and saw I was in mom's bed and she was sleeping to my left. Remembered falling asleep here. Walked to kitchen and ate small piece of whole foods cherry pie, a graham cracker/chocolate 'digestive biscuit' cookie, and drank a glass of milk. Went to my room and got under covers. Set alarm for 10:00am. Feeling 'cozy' and peaceful.

10:00am-12:49pm: hit snooze every ten minutes but would fall sometimes deeply (I think) asleep every time, or hit 'snooze' without waking. Dreamed something about Zachary and me, watching him have sex with a muslim woman who seemed angry at me and said 'he can have sex with whoever he want.' felt mad/hurt by him. We were trying living together again, but only because we were going to live with everyone on the 'real pain: future dead friends' tour. It was our job to find the apartment for all of us, we had found a small one-bedroom apartment attached to a pizza place on a road technically in NYC but far away from Manhattan. We signed the lease and were excitedly planning for people to arrive. When everyone got there they seemed unhappy, and I realized what a huge mistake/oversight Zachary and I had made, there were only two rooms in the apartment, not nearly enough space for everyone. Zachary would also transform into a sandworm from 'dune' once a month and eat people, I was worried about living with him again because of this. Then the dream switched to he and I in my mom's new condo, which was above a sears and a grocery store. I was rubbing pink cream on my legs that was supposed to make it look like I was wearing tights. Mom had a new haircut, it was very short and shiny. She tousled her hair in front of her face and said 'I just hate it, it's so Ella

Fitzgerald.' Then I was looking at candy in the grocery store and the Mary Tyler Moore theme song was playing and I thought 'huh. It really is a song, not just a theme song.' then Zachary and mom and I were driving out of the condo at night in three cars. Zachary and mom were not allowed to leave the condo and were stopped by the police for 'thinking about food.' I could still leave. Then it was morning and 'Zachary' was suddenly in the passenger seat next to me, but it wasn't him, it was a relaxed, jovial-seeming man who looked like a young Don Cheadle. He was telling me how to get to NYC for my meeting with the apartment committee people. He took my phone and said 'nah, how do they [other 'real' Zachary and my mom] got you going this way?' he told me a faster way, which seemed slower, but I believed him.

1:00–3:14pm: apartment committee person called, said 'so what did you want to talk about?' I said 'oh, I don't know, the real estate agent…Colin told me to ask you to call me. I thought you wanted to talk about something.' apartment person sounded like he was smiling and said 'nope, you're coming tonight right?' I said 'yeah, should I bring anything?' he said 'no, they just want to meet you in person. It'll be in the laundry room of the building so, you know, just wait there in the hall and someone will get you.'

Responded to a ghat from Zachary from a few days ago, where he had said his ex-girlfriend would be at the Fishkind show (Fishkind is the band he was listening to nostalgically while drinking a few days before we moved out of Philadelphia apartment, guess they reunited, are playing a show I'm planning to go to at NYU on Friday). Zachary said his ex-girlfriend (who I had friendly interactions with when I met in 2009, when they lived together with Tao in Brooklyn, then un-friended me on facebook and expressed negative thoughts about me to Zachary when she learned I married Tao in 2010) said she would act cold towards me if she saw me at the show. Zachary said still wanted me to go, so he could have sex with me in the bathroom. I told him a little about my dream and said "see you in the bathroom, like that one strokes song, "see you in the bathroom,' deliberately misquoting the title, to sound cute/'carefree.'

Showered and packed. Aware of not responding to Mira's email yet and saying I would. Aware of not getting new computer, which dad had asked me to do yesterday so he could have his back. Aware of not mailing books yesterday. Rubbed coconut oil on body. Changed outfit twice. Ate 350mg tramadol, b-vitamin, niacin, noopept.

3:15–7:05pm: drove to rockaway park. I'm here early. Colin texted around 5:30 asking if I was coming, what time I'd be here. I said I'd be there in an hour or so but the meeting was at 7:30 so I'd be there then, and had already confirmed this with apartment people via email and phone. I don't think he'll be at the meeting, unsure why he texted. 'Can't believe' I'm early. Was so sure there would be bad traffic and I hadn't allowed for enough time. Feel like this bodes well for the meeting.

7:09pm: sitting in parked car near apartment building. Fixed hair and applied concealer to zit between nose and upper lip. Excited and nervous. Feel like they're going to 'find me out' or will say 'we've been reading your liveblog all along, we know you're a no-good slumlord.' I'm picturing myself living here, the things I'm seeing now eventually becoming normal. Ate noopept covertly even though it's legal, pictured saying 'it's a smart drug, no not like a drug though, it's a health supplement, a nootropic, it's for improving cognitive functions' to troubled judgmental faces of apartment committee people.

7:18pm: palms are sweaty and stomach is making noises. Googled 'rock-away park newspaper' because in my cover letter I said I was interested in becoming involved in it because Colin told me it would be good if I said that. In a window of a house to my left, four dogs have been staring at points in the distance, mostly motionlessly this entire time. One just walked away. Took a picture with my phone.

7:21pm: walking to building now. Heart beating fast.

7:27pm: woman said 'are you Megan?' and led me to the laundry room. She said 'I'm actually just getting here so I'm going to use the bathroom.' She said a woman with long blonde hair named Jennifer might come into room. She said 'sit here and make yourself at home' and walked away. Heard Colin's voice say 'are you meeting Megan?' from building entrance.

8:59pm: after meeting Colin told me I got the apartment. Texted mira to see if she still wants to hang out. Feeling tramadol things big time I think, like very spacey, forget how I act normally or what kind of things I say. At one point in interview Julie was telling a long story about how she ended up with a Christmas tree this year and I was looking at her and nodding and for a moment felt like I was on LSD, like 'I have no idea what this means, how is this happening, I'm going to freak out and not be able to talk the next time I have to say something.' Julie and Jennifer seemed to think I was from north Carolina. Surprised not to be 'grilled' about how I'll be able to pay for apartment, or that they didn't ask me more questions about my job. Jennifer said 'I think that's so cool that you're a writer, what do you write?' I said 'I do humor things, humor things and personal essays.' Surprised I thought of 'personal essays' on the spot.' Jennifer said 'oh-hhhh' and smiled and looked unsure of what to say. There was a lot of talking about hurricane Sandy during interview. Interviewers and Colin seemed to know everyone who walked in to the laundry room. When a conversation about my cats finished I said 'so it's okay if I just let them walk around in the hallway and on the beach, right?' Julie paused and said 'well I'm not sure if—' I interrupted, 'I'm kidding, I'm kidding.' People nodded and went 'haha' without laughing. Julie said 'would they do that, your cats? They go outside and they know how to get back?' I said 'no, definitely not, they're inside cats, definitely, I wouldn't do that.' Jennifer said 'they could go outside on the fire escape, to sit in the sun?' I said 'I mean…probably not.' Colin said 'yeah, I like cats.'

Colin walked me outside and said it was okay to smoke pot and cigarettes in apartment. Julie walked out at the same time as us. She and Colin knew each other but had forgotten each other's names. He said 'Colin, like Colin Farrell.' she said 'I'll remember because of 'love actually.'' he said 'yeah, Colin Farrell.' she said 'no there's a character, 'Colin.' and you're…?' I said 'Megan.' she said 'I'll remember that.' Colin said 'Megan Fox.' I said 'oh yeah.' he said 'Colin Farrell Megan Fox' and I followed him out the building.

9:17pm: sitting in car. I'm going to be moving everything Monday. Hard to imagine. The logistics…

9:27pm: texted Mira that it was okay if she is feeling antisocial and reconsidering hanging out.

9:48pm: have seen '9:48 PM' on phone clock maybe six times. Now it's 9:49. Still sitting in parked car. 9:50. Worried Mira thinks it's not okay to tell me she doesn't want me to stay over tonight, unsure if I should've texted to confirm earlier.

9:59pm: going to text this to Mira: 'Shit just realized not texting you to confirm letting me stay over earlier was 'faux pas'/could lead to inconveniencing you or you not being sure of what you're doing tonight and making other plans, I should've texted dog, I'm sorry. Think I'm gonna head back to md, feel anxiety about not doing all the stuff I was supposed to do yesterday + starting to plan/pack/figure out how to move. Sorry again for no contact oof, big dog faux pas.'

10:02pm: I texted it. Feel unable to discern…anything, I think, about situation…like if I did a faux pas or if Mira doesn't like me as much anymore or if her phone is broken…those are the only reasons I can think of but none of them feel like the reason. Unsure if it's more socially acceptable to tell Mira I'm going home, or if I should find something to do in NYC until

I hear from her. Imagining Mira never talking to me again, like this would be a logical point, the most likely point in our friendship to 'abandon ship,' would be funny if that happened.

10:19pm: missing Zachary for some reason.

10:27pm: read Mira's twitters. She lost her wallet and had an upsetting phone conversation with dad, has mentioned crying in public and ordering a side of bacon and a side of bread from somewhere. If those things were happening to me I wouldn't want to respond to text messages either. Hope my last text/me going home reduces stress for her.

10:34pm: interesting that I've never gotten lost or made a wrong turn in rockaway park but I get lost like, driving to dad's apartment, or other places I've driven many times.

10:36pm: hunger pangs.

11:25pm: Mira texted that she had forgotten about me coming today, described hellish circumstances of life like I had read on twitter, that she thought I was easy/fun to be around and I didn't do a faux pas and she was down to go to fishkind tomorrow or hang out any time. Texted this:

> 'Jesus re wallet and arguing and 10 texts bro, read this and your twitters, seems like you are in hell big time. Side of bread side of bacon Jesus. I understand 100%, I also forgot about coming today/thought yesterday was Tuesday until some time last night. Relieved to read your texts, you are easy/fun for me to chill with also. I'm down to go to Fishkind tomorrow. Your hellish circumstances…Jesus..I'm sorry all that shit is going on. Stay strong mami, boost boost. I will sprinkle you with Xanax tomorrow.'

11:35pm: big time drowsy nauseated itchy body lazy eyes. Forgot tramadol lasts so long.

11:40pm: parked at Richard Stockton rest stop to buy sugar-free red bull and maybe a food unit.

11:50pm: burger king was open but didn't want to do that. Tried credit card in red bull machine but it didn't work. Walked to Sunoco snack shop. Bought 16oz sf red bull, neuro sonic, and white chocolate macadamia clif bar. Lady who rang me up had bright red hair. I said I liked it. She said the salon had left the bleach on her head for too long and she hated it so she got her hair for free, and is going back in a few days to get it darkened. I said 'you don't like it?' she said 'naw, don't you think I look like a stop sign?' I said 'no, it looks great. I mean I used to do blue and all that.' she said 'select credit or debit.' I did 'credit' and picked up the plastic pen to sign the machine. She 'no, you have to sign on the paper.' I signed and picked up my things. She said 'you don't want a bag?' I shook my head and said 'no, and well, good luck when you get it re-done in a few, whenever, you look great.' she said 'thank you, you have a nice night' and we were smiling at each other.

APRIL 26, 2013

12:53am: they would make a lot of money from a snack food called 'carbs.' still driving home.

12:56am: names of rest stops on 95, between Baltimore and NYC (not in order):

- Chesapeake house

- Maryland house

- Clara Barton

- Richard Stockton

- J. Fennimore Cooper

- Walt Whitman

1:28-1:43am: pictured something and got aroused and tried to masturbate. Came close to orgasm a few times, kept getting distracted.

1:44-3:00AM: drove, minimal thoughts/feelings, listened to ipod on 'shuffle.' there was construction and i took a wrong turn, ended up taking the long way back to mom's through baltimore city.

3:01-4:07AM: picked at face/back/chest skin in mirror, washed/disinfected, texted with mira, applied coconut oil to hair, applied pajamas. out of tampons so i wrapped long strip of toilet paper around 'blood zone' in underpants. have never heard a rapper compare their 'flow' to a menstrual flow...seems like, really good...hard to rhyme 'menstrual' with stuff though. or they could say they do something once a month, like laundry or something, like 'my laundry got menstrual flow.'

4:50pm: driving to NYC for Fishkind show. This is a bad idea. Committed to doing bad idea. Woke around 1:30pm, fell asleep around 6am. Vaguely antagonistic internet communications with Zachary. Showered and dressed. Measured myself: chest 34", waist 26", hips 36".

5:20pm: merging onto 95n. Traffic slow. Passed sign with chic-fil-a and panera bread logos. Almost out of gas. Why am I doing anything...

5:49pm: stopped at a wawa. Bought 20oz and 8oz sf red bulls, clif bar. Wanted to throw in the towel and buy blt and go home and go wah wah wah. Radio dj keeps saying 'funky Friday.' Ate 1mg Xanax to...I don't know…should I just stop at the next thing, the next service center, start a new life there…I could work at the z-market or travel mart…it would be fine.

5:57pm: dj said 'we have a request here for 'funky Nassau,' next up on funky Friday.' he sounded unsure of himself but I think he was making up the request, I don't believe someone requested this. I don't believe anyone requests songs anymore. When I was little I wanted to hear 'eternal flame' by the bangles because I had never heard the whole thing, just a few seconds of it on an infomercial for one of those Time Life mix-CDs. I requested it on lite 101.9 WLIF. The dj asked me who I wanted to dedicate it to and I wasn't prepared so I said 'Allie, Jamie, and Ashley.' little girl on the radio pressured to dedicate a love song she'd never heard to three girl friends. Cute.

6:33pm: ate .5mg Xanax and clif bar. 8884272643 is the suicide hotline number in this area, somewhere in Delaware. The suicide hotline thing came on after end of 'goodbye stranger' by supertramp. That song. The way it sounds. Makes me feel stuff. I have to pee damnit. Now on nj turnpike.

6:41pm: radio dj said 'hear what we've done, what we did, and what we're doing n-ooooo-w' in a sexy confident voice.

6:45pm: starting to feel good from Xanax, the loving Xanax brain hold… thought 'stussy'

7:06pm: finna get some chicken lickens from this nast burger baby king and let this pee outta me. J fennimore cooper rest stop worldwide.

7:10pm: huge ass bathroom line huge ass burger king line fuck it man I'm

7:16pm: chicken lickens hell. I want chicken lickens. Woman behind me in tie dye shirt has 'grazed' me with her titties twice. Abandoning ship.

7:51pm: 44mins away gonna try Joyce Kilmer rest stop gotta get my chicken lickens. Woodrow Wilson was the stop I forgot

8:02pm: chicken lickens

8:23pm: 30mins away. I feel shitty from the chicken lickens.

8:58pm: ate another .5 Xanax, used face towel, looking for hair brush.

9-11:59pm: walked in late to Fishkind, it was almost over. Sat by Mira. Traded her two Xanax for three vicodin. Some kind of argument between Zachary and Jamie (name of his ex-gf who has 'hated me' since 2010, just learned he's tentatively moved back in with her in their old apartment) which I didn't think was serious. Tao was there, surprised.

Hi to z and he seemed cold Jamie stepped over me to use bathroom a lot

Z was wearing my dads blue sweater that I gave him on the storage unit day

Mosh pit thing, saw Tao watching me maybe

Talked with Travis and Kat about bike accident, they were going to stay at Jamie's but Zachary (something about how he and Jamie argued, him not picking up his phone), Andrew Colville driving them back tonight instead

Gave atcolv a Vicodin for a Xanax and I ate it

Atcolv and cass moving here to hunter college, relationship problems

Walking to sly fox bar

Talked with Tao and Zachery Wood on the way to sly fox, Zachery offered to trade mushrooms for adderall, I said 'yes' at first then 'maybe' Tao said 'but you already said' or something, felt residual relationship anxiety re if it would be better for me to trade or not trade, both Tao and Zachery were smiling/good-natured seeming, think it was quiet for a while then Tao left before we got to party

Adam and Lauren going to Mexico

Someone said something re me and liveblog remembered I want to be updating this

Several people have asked what I've been up to and I've said 'nothing' grinning, they ask 'no really what've you been doing,' I say 'nothing, living at my dad's, doing the liveblog'

Miles gave me beer

Miles said funny things, smiling a lot, about a wilderness preserve near where I'll live in rockaway

Sam said cocaine and my eyes lit up

Texted Tao whered u go from bathroom he said he went home

$1 pizza with Sam Mira Zachery wood

I'm contributing $97 to coke

Goog to andrew worthington's apt

David and atcolv want coke

Stood outside and smoked with atcolv zachery wood

Said 'you guys are like my solace' to Sam Mira on steps

Went back in, drank water

Sam pink doing Baltimore reading

Sam pink had tips about crack to Mira Sam

Mira sam wanted to read part of liveblog aloud where i talked about when we hung out

People keep asking what im doing I'm saying I'm moving Monday

Texted David 'I dunno where dealer is'

David belligerently wanting coke, saying things like I came here to see his band, I should give him coke, I owe him, funny

Talked w Dierks about thought catalog

Maggie convo re coke, asking if they were getting a cab, zachery says 'you don't want us around'

Me saying I feel Xanax things big, shoe discomfort, will I be ok to drive

In bathroom 11:58 seems hard to talk to people David texted 'you make me sick'

Said goodbye to people, sorry re not bringing david and atcolv line of coke, we're going to andrew's to do coke, walking to car parked near nyu kimmell center to meet Mira and Sam

Drive to Andrew's talked about David, I said 'sometimes he acts like Zachary, I've called him out on it but he doesn't seem to notice,' people agreed he acts like Zachary sometimes

Mira and Sam sat in similar positions on front seat due to cramped car, read crack parts of liveblog aloud

APRIL 27, 2013

12-7:[something]am: split eightball between all of us [will elaborate on this + disjointed notes later] **EDIT: as of 3:15AM, may 1, 2013 i have no plans to elaborate

7:[something]-6:30pm: drove Mira and Sam to Sam's. ate 1-2mg Xanax and gave some to Mira and Sam, all slept in Sam's bed.

6:31pm: jossled awake by a pokey hand of Sam. Mira had left for work at 4 and Sam was getting ready to leave for somewhere. He was sitting at the kitchen table wearing headphones. Asked what he was doing and he said 'movie stuff' in 'I don't like talking about creative stuff as I'm doing it' voice I understand and use. Said 'oh my god' and 'xanax, I still feel xanax' and sam kind of laughed and there were crusty boogers around one of my nostrils. Washed face, blew nose, used mouth wash, dressed. Asked about Mira. Sam said they had argued, kind of, about Sam spending time with his girlfriend. I don't know details, but on a broad level felt I understood and had been in each of their places/sides of the argument, in past relationships.

7:16pm: driving home. Vincent Lombard rest stop, I had forgotten. Thomas Edison also.

8:20pm: ate bk tender crisp chicken sandwich with mustard, salad, fries, large diet coke. Called z in response to things from last night, asked if he still wanted to help me move Monday (he offered).

9:15pm: pulled into Molly pitcher travel stop to rest. Debating vomiting fast food.

9:30pm: Zachary called. Sounded business-like, a way I've heard him talk to Jamie on the phone when he hasn't wanted to talk. I said something about how he'd be in NYC for three weeks and he said it wouldn't be that long, he had just taken a job 'being nice to Jamie, moving things around for her art gallery a few times a week.' He said something about me getting the rockaway apartment, asked about meeting with apartment people, sounding vaguely condescending or like he was making fun of me. In a better mood, I would've riffed or something, also made fun of myself. I said 'it sounds like you don't want to talk, it'd be nice to see you sometime.' he said 'ok gotta go' and I hung up. Continued resting my head on passenger seat in a half-nap.

9:40pm: texted Zachary 'sorry won't bug you anymore. Have a nice time with everything. Will think about you in good ways.' Drove out of travel plaza. Remembered last year at this time, didn't know I was pregnant yet. Remembered being in Florida with Zachary and Adam, who was filming a documentary about Zachary, and my friend Alec, who'd invited Zachary and me to read and hang out at his college in Sarasota. Called mom to say I was coming home. 'one hit wonder' by everclear played on shuffle. Have been listening on repeat.

10:01pm: received this text from unknown number: 'just zachary, texting from his ipad. feel free to reply to this number, which goes to my ipad, somehow. but yeah sorry if that's how late interactions have made you feel, you don't need to stop bugging me, you haven't been bugging me. glad new place thing is working out, that seems like a good place, would like to say hi sometime. okay!!!'

10:37pm: pulled onto shoulder. Made myself vomit into burger king bag paper bag inside of a plastic bag. It leaked. Put everything into another plastic bag and vomited until nothing came out. Tied bag in a knot. Heavier than I thought it'd be. Threw it into woods.

10:39pm: cleaned face, fingers, areas of the car with cucumber face towels that smell like being in Spain with Tao and, now, the last night in Philadelphia apartment, sleeping on couch. Un-paused 'one hit wonder' by everclear and it played where it had left off.

11:22pm: swallowed Vicodin from Mira. Texted response to zachery wood and texted atcolv that I hoped he got home safe.

APRIL 28, 2013

12:06am: feeling optimistic things from Vicodin. Nearing mom's.

12:59AM: have eaten three pieces of toast with butter/jam, another vicodin, glass of 'fake milk' (half & half mixed with water and chocolate milk powder). ate b-vitamin, niacin, omega-3 oil thing that makes burps taste lemony. both parents are here. stupidly interpreted remarks about my 'stuffy nose' defensively.

6:25PM: fell asleep watching ASMR videos. ate 2mg xanax. think i ate maybe five small pieces of toast with butter and jam.

earlier mom brought me a ham and cheese sandwich and hugged me really hard. she said 'you're not really going away, i know you're not.' it sounded like she was crying. i hugged her really hard back and, aware of a double-meaning i preferred not to acknowledge aloud, said 'i'm not going anywhere, mom.'

earlier i asked dad for xanax and he gave me 60mg in 'blister packs' and made his face look fake-concerned and said 'i needed to steal these from a priest' (he was just giving me what he usually gives his friend, who is a priest, he likes to say…exaggerate things…with a look on his face, things like this, like 'i'm going against the rules' sometimes).

tomorrow i'm getting a computer at macmedics while dad and two 'mover friends' load my storage closet things into a u-haul.

then we're driving to new york.

then all my stuff will be in once place.

me and the cats and the stuff.

then everyone will be gone but me and the cats and the stuff.

7:16PM: laying in bed. sky is very gray and almost night again. woke around 3PM after falling asleep around 2AM. called superintendent of new building to see if i could move in tomorrow. pooped. mom is saying unprompted things about how it'll be okay, people from ikea know how to put together furniture. i said 'i know how to do it, or zachary can help.' she said 'oh i thought you weren't on good terms with zachary.' i said 'no we're fine, it's. he would help, it doesn't matter, don't listen to me, everything is fine.'

8:27PM: A FEW HOURS AGO:

mom: [sits on piano bench] i want to visit you on friday, we can go to ikea. i don't want you to think i don't want to visit, i just need to be asked to visit.

me: i want you to visit. will you visit?

mom: yes. i'll visit friday.

A FEW HOURS AFTER THAT:

me: [entering kitchen, mom on couch] there's an ikea ferry, when you visit we can take the ferry.

mom: i want to take the ikea ferry! where does it go?

me: just to ikea, i don't think other places.

mom: of course, where else would it go, haha. we'll get you things at ikea.

me: great. i think i only need a bed frame, it would be fun to go to ikea with you though.

mom: what about your old bed frame?

me: that was zachary's. the mattress didn't quite fit it anyway.

mom: what about the white one from dad's house?

me: my mattress is too small for it, i think. then the one from my baltimore apartment is broken, then the other one from brooklyn broke too. i can just sleep on a mattress.

mom: don't sleep on just a mattress! you and dad can use the u-haul.

me: good idea.

A FEW HOURS AFTER THAT:

dad: i heard your mattress might be too small for the frame, from mom, so maybe we should use the u-haul tomorrow morning to—

me: oh yeah, the u-haul. we can go to ikea tomorrow.

dad: well ikea is far away, so i thought mattress discounters would be good.

me: i don't care. i have no preferences. mom said ikea.

dad: it's just that ikea is, i don't know where it is in relation to the storage closet, but we have mattress discounters right here by—

me: yeah, yeah. i don't know. i don't care at all, about where. any of this.

dad: well okay sweetie, i'll see you soon.

8:4[something]-9:16PM: slept. mom woke me to ask if i wanted food, said 'oh i guess you don't, you're asleep.'

10:32PM: dad brought home bar-be-que. there was an extra pork sandwich, in case i got hungry. stood by dad and picked at food. he said 'do you want me to wake you with coffee, like in the old days?' i said 'yeah, yeah, at seven-thirty, that would be good.' he asked how far i had gotten into 'homeland' and i said 'somewhere near the last episode.' he said watching it before bed made him tense. i said 'i don't want to watch it tonight either.' dad said 'me neither.' he was preparing coffee, said 'oops, this one isn't ground,' about a bag. i concentrated on eating. mom talked about 'mad men.' dad said 'i might watch.' i said 'does it matter what's happening on it? would i get it?' mom said 'well it's, er. nineteen sixty-three, i think, it's right after martin luther king was assassinated. no, it can't be that early. mike?' dad said 'yes, it was nineteen sixty-three, no, i remember very well, i was sitting on my lawn saying the rosary, the day martin luther king died.' he paused, said 'no! that was john f. kennedy. it was nineteen sixty-six.' mom said 'nineteen sixty-six, yes. because of the music.' dad said 'people were swinging to the music.' he said 'oh look, this bag is already ground.' i said 'oh good, a grounded bag.' i knew if i stood by him, picking at food, it would take him long time to finish the coffee. i wanted to be quiet. i got a cold water bottle from the fridge and said 'will you leave everything out, just like that?' dad said 'the food? just like this?' i said 'yeah, just like that. i'll finish it,' and felt a little sad.

11:41PM: surprise appearance from mom. she said she had a good feeling about rockway park, that good things would happen. i said 'thank you for saying that. i'm not excited but i'm not worried either, i don't feel anything yet.' she said 'you're just afraid to be excited because you think you'll be disappointed.' looked at wall and thought 'maybe.'

imagined reciting paragraph about standing by dad making coffee, when i took a water bottle to my room so we wouldn't have to be talking anymore, at dad's funeral. i would be saying 'how could i have taken the water bottle like that?' the extra sandwich, just in case. when i woke, there it was. he would do that, for me. i said 'roast pork?' he said 'with tiger sauce.' i said 'i love tiger sauce.'

293

APRIL 29, 2013

12–2:56AM: read interview with richard yates…keep thinking about his life…description of the last apartment he lived…iowa, i think…boxes of recorded things…mildew…filth…one suit in closet…brown…

it will be hard to hide in new york because colin will live across the hall

think i am doing this on purpose…i think…

no, it's always easy to hide

i want to walk around a financial district at night and feel that gutted-out lit-up feeling i get from being around tall buildings in a big city

i'll be able to hear the ocean

i'll be able to go smoke a cigarette in my front yard, which is the ocean

too many boxes to unpack

richard yates' family going through his things after he dies

my parents and me with little silent 'end dates' floating over our heads, filling boxes with things we think we'll eventually find places for

then there will be boxes for the ones who stay alive

three chances to get all the boxes

three people: mom, dad, me

someone will have the most boxes at the end

4:42AM: chewed 2mg xanax with teeth. sweating a little. turned out all lights. just broke earphones in attempt free from head. thinking about tomorrow.

thought 'my life is an objective failure, if you looked at graphs, other people my age, research students would easily identify me at 4:40AM blowing my stuffed-up nose from drugs, body full of food i wasn't hungry for, inbox full of nothing, getting ready to sleep so i can be rested for moving in to an apartment in an area of new york about 40 minutes from people i like by train, which is only one hour 20 minutes closer than i am to them now, five colleges eight years zero degrees, 27, last time she had sex she was too drunk to remember but was apparently 'begging for it,' it is documented somewhere, at the end of march, 2013.' i'm not saying this to be cute or to have an internet personality or some bullshit. this is someone's life, it's shitty, and what's shittier is that it probably looks good to people, it is definitely better than some people's lives, so on top of it already feeling shitty, i feel shitty because it's not the shittiest i can get, other people have it worse.

i feel like the guilt for not having it as shitty as you imagine some people to have it takes you one level down from 'feeling bad' on the 'global barometer of feeling bad.' like you do have it a teensy bit worse than someone who isn't aware that they could feel worse. i feel a little better writing that, in a sick way.

9:28am: raining and cold. meeting dad's moving friends (Leo, Debbie, Naiem) at his office, getting gas, picking up cats from dad's. considering taking adderall. Feel shitty Xanax things from last night, fell asleep around 5am watching asmr videos and ate a Dove bar. Relieved it won't be Zachary and me today, lifting stuff. Listening to 'one hit wonder' by everclear on repeat.

9:49am: followed dad's car to office. No one else was there. Gave him directions to rockaway park. He gave me sudafed and nose spray, said he would just guess what I'd want from storage unit, to save time. Confirmed plan. Ate 20mg adderall, noopept, licked cocaine baggie.

9:56am: bought gas, 16oz sf red bull

10:31am: dad called with a question about a wooden thing. I said 'just don't bring the dresser' and described it. We exchanged descriptions of the wooden thing…I don't know what he was talking about. Seemed like there would be extra time. Garnered two blueprint green juices and an energy shot from whole foods. Same checkout station as a few weeks ago, when I was rung up by the man I liked, who showed me the clear barcode.

11:27am: cats are in car. Got the impression dad is leaving most things I asked to bring and bringing things I don't want or aren't mine. Picturing Zachary and Jamie acting cozy/domestic in the video I saw last night. She doesn't like his long hair or glasses. His hair was pulled back in the video and he wasn't wearing glasses. I'm weak. Stupid. Cats are howling. Raining. They are confused about how fast the car is moving and all of the noises, I think.

11:52am: dad and Debbie passed on the left, smiling and waving.

12:00pm: kitties in kitty hell aka kitty carriers on front seat of car. Texted/responded to a lot of low-priority emails fast. Have to pee.

12:24pm: peeing in rest stop. Wearing pre-9/11 panties I've had since high school. They're white with a lavender graphic of the NYC skyline, featuring the World Trade Center. Didn't realize thematic appropriateness as I was dressing for success this morning. Two toilet seat liners have been blowing into, through, and past stall, tumbleweed-like, during this pee session.

1:10pm: have been thinking things like 'how did I decide to do this, how is this happening, this is a mistake, what else could I be doing, what the fuck am I doing.' Have to pee again.

2:38pm: nearing NYC. Anxious re amount of stuff I've accumulated, finding places for it, throwing it away. Liveblog. I wanted to write or something, is that what all of this is about? Unable to 'place' what I'm doing right now, like, compare it to other events, this doesn't feel real, the only person I'm romantically interested in lives far away and we haven't talked in a long time and what does that say, I don't know what I want to have happen to me, where will I find internet, I don't want to be out of control with drugs, what will happen to mom and dad, where will I pee, the pee needs to happen soon.

2:54pm: figured out how to situate 32oz burger king cup under crotch. It might come to this. Going 5mph Jesus okay speeding up now you got this Boyle you got this.

2:56pm: oh god these bumps in the road are killer, lighting cigarette as distraction, fuck you red bull, whole lot of good you did, way to get me here, christ, 'at least i'm awake (!?!?!?)' is that the moral of you, red bull????

3:02pm: six exits away you got this Boyle

3:04pm: omg it's stop and go again this is hell pee hell four exits away ok 35mph

3:07pm: positioned cup, removed seat belt, unzipped pants. Can't do it, pee urge lessened when I tried. Two exits away, Jesus am I gonna have to re-title and register my car, bumps in the road are AXTUALKY KILLING ME MY LUFE IS LESSENING WHEN I GO PCER BUMPSDSSSDSSSSDSSSSSS THE BLADDER OH NY SWEET BLADDY BAG NOOPOOO THE BUMPS OK 54mph again exit ahead 1.75 miles 'let the river run' is a lyric in song playing now lol

3:19pm: 11 blocks oh my fucking shittttytyy

3:37pm: superintendent, Mark, led me to his first floor apartment, where the keys to my apartment 'had to be, somewhere.' Felt like I was on drugs, the intensity I was holding in pee. Moment of comedic horror when Mark put his fingers through holes in Shirley's carrier and said 'can I let it out?' I said 'sure sure' without thinking, wanting to say whatever was required to speed up to get to the part where I could ask to pee. The burger king cup wouldn't have held it all. Such release. Oof. Shirley had hidden under a heater-like appliance in a room crowded with tall, disparate, barely-keep-able objects and no lights. Mark said 'she'll come when you call her, I know how cats are,' smiling the generous smile of someone who does not know how cats are, 'I'm going to make copies of your keys, you want anything from Dunkin Donuts?' I said 'thank you, no thanks.' Walking to the door, he said 'oh! you got another one too, this one's a little bigger,' stunning me with his egregiously late discovery of Alvie. I believed him too, this really did seem like the first time he noticed a second cat. Superindenent seems nice and easy to talk to. So hard to spell, though.

5:13pm: here is car, the building, a little of the ocean. Moved everything in. Cats ran away or are hiding. Looked on all floors, stairwells. Walked Dad outside, where Debbie and Naiem had been waiting. Leo had left in the u-haul without telling anyone. My car battery had died. Dad's face looked worried in a new way once he accepted battery was dead. Naiem and I pointed at things under dad's hood, looking for 'negative charge' area of battery. Dad said 'no, you know, you'd think to look under there, but it's just computer chips under there.' Removed the casing to the thing and he was right. He said 'the negative charge can be on anything metal,' but he continued to look for an 'official negative charge' area, saying distracted/directionless things about how my battery could've died, how it usually works with cars. His worried face. The way it looked when he said 'if it doesn't start tomorrow, well. Someone will have a jumper. You really should take it to a place soon, a mechanic. New batteries aren't supposed to die out this fast.' Felt aware of double-meaning. Then Debbie and Naiem walking to us from some place I didn't see them go, talking excitedly about the ocean.

Alone ass…car needs to run for an hour to charge battery. Going to drive to ikea.

5:43pm: someone left eight beers in a line under the sink. Drank still-cold green juice from this morning. Sitting in car with engine idling. Remember searching apartment for an extension cord and the cats. Dad said 'I found one' and held up a cord. I thought it would be a cat. I said things I didn't believe about the cats like 'they're here, I know it.' he said 'I know they're here' and 'they couldn't just run away, someone would've seen' a few times. Debbie and Naiem and Leo were already downstairs, there was tension, knew dad was about to leave. I said 'I wish you could stay for dinner.' He said 'here, why don't I get rid of this tape,' and walked to the rolled-up mattress. I said 'yeah, yeah, let's move it to the corner. It'll be a corner bed.' dad said 'I lived in a place about this size with Galen' as we held opposite ends of the mattress. Dad cut the tape with his pocket knife and we unrolled the mattress. There was a quiet moment. I opened a bag containing the mattress pad I've used since 2008. Dad bought it for me when I found a king-sized mattress and box-spring on the street and was moving into a house with two friends. He seemed giddy when he surprised me with the pad, I think because taking a king-sized bed from the street would be something he would do, 'much to the disapproval of the stupid world,' and he liked that I would do something like that too. Instead of getting a new pad I cut the king-sized one to fit my next mattress, slightly bigger than the one I use now.

Positioned mattress pad on bed, said 'here it goes, it goes right on top.' It smelled like the Philadelphia apartment, Zachary's and my bed. Thought 'I didn't bring sheets or pillows.' Dad paused and said 'maybe you should just get a new everything, a new bed, new mattress.' I said 'oh, well, this one is fine I think. I don't know, maybe, I'll see. Thank you.' The thing I was feeling in the car of 'what am I doing' seemed amplified, thinking about how alone I would be when dad left, that this was my last moment of 'at least I'm not completely alone.' Hugged dad hard. His face was wet from sweating or the rain and he was wearing a blue windbreaker with a 'Holland America Line' emblem embroidered on it, from one of the cruises we went on when I was little. I hugged him and said 'thank you for helping me with this, it means a lot' and my voice broke. I was hugging him tight. He said 'oh, I'm happy to help' and it was quiet. He said 'I think this time it's really going to work out, it really is, just you wait and see.'

5:53pm: impulsively texted Zachary to see if he knew where to buy cat food, am now picking him up from Adam's.

6:10pm: need to get electric switched over to my name, change address, feel hollow and scared and alone, driving, picking up Zachary, what will we do, what're we doing here, what the shit hell…young family song came on shuffle…the fuck am I doing…

6:14pm: mint green nail polish has almost chipped off, I painted nails the morning I had been up all night and went to whole foods and Zachary went to nj before our apartment was all packed up, March

6:17pm: mom called said I'll talk later parked on Zachary's street ate 1mg Xanax shit fuck me.

6:18–11:59PM: zachary came out of adam's apartment wearing nice clothes and with his hair tied back, holding a hand-rolled cigarette.

here is what i remember:

- drive seemed tense, something felt different, sad, like more time had passed than i had known. asked about the jamie video and about why he seemed upset at the fishkind show. felt like i was talking to someone i had only met a few times. think this made it easier to transition into making jokes/reading signs/pointing out stuff on the street. talked more about the show and felt my stomach pulling, re-enacting the 'sting of obviousness' i felt that night watching him interact with jamie in a way that reminded me 'these people are neither friends nor strangers,' remembering how when the show was over he passed me and said 'oh hey' without looking up, leaving with a man i'd never seen, then not showing up at the bar due to rumored arguing with jamie, all the moments of him 'not at the bar' stacking up, helping me form a familiar-feeling epiphany that someone's life was better without me in it and there was nothing i could do, except try to replace that feeling with excitement about the cocaine that would help me ignore two phone calls from him a few hours later. in the car he said the man i saw him walk away with had confronted him immediately after the show to give him a hard time about how he says 'faggot,' and zachary had been crying from other things about the show and talked with the offended man for a long time, explaining how he doesn't want to hurt anyone. vestigial shame about my reaction to him that night, he was having a shitty time, and what did i want anyway.

- started kissing when we walked in my apartment. don't want to type details. felt aware of the thing that happens if i'm doing anything sexual, where there's a part of me watching me or afraid or saying 'react' or something but that wasn't there at all. seems notable to me, actually… we didn't…because i'm not on birth control, but i feel like this…i can't remember ever feeling as 'emotionally integrated' (not the right words, maybe 'not anticipating anything' or 'uninhibited' or 'not thinking there was a chance the other person could hurt me, so i could feel things spontaneously, didn't know i could feel so many things while doing something like this'—know all of that is big time female cliché bullshit but guess that's what i am) during anything sexual with anyone to the degree i felt it yesterday. not like now, now i'm thinking 'he's going to read this and think i'm icky or that i 'cheapened' it and oh no it's even worse now because i wanted to put quotes around 'cheapened' great. he would like it if i hadn't said any of this but now that i've said it he would like it if i didn't think i was stupid for saying it too, he would rather i didn't express uncertainty about saying the things i think he thinks and i'm not sure i think are stupid. so here i am, great.'

- zachary assembled a shelf he had dissembled and set up the TV/ antenna. a nets/bulls game was on, i think. froze the beers before sexy stuff so now they were cold and we drank them. i unpacked things in a 'bee pollenating' manner, not spending much time on any one box/ bag, getting distracted. felt like it was okay to be quiet. sometimes one of us would repeat something on the radio or TV and the other would respond minimally, but kindly, more like exhaustedly. sometimes i'd say something about what could've happened to the cats.

- colin 'popped in' to collect checks for rent/broker's fee and give me a copy of the local newspaper. zachary's shirt was off. beer. sitting on curtains serving as sheets on a mattress pad on a mattress on a floor. my unwashed wet hair and leggings. saying my cats were missing. seemed…funny. 'look what you got yourself into, big shot.'

- no pizza places seemed open. we walked to the 'where stuff is kind of' area, about two blocks from me. passed a basketball hoop and a black plastic bag had been wrapped around the net. zachary said 'yeah, because no one wants to play with net that hasn't been wrapped.'

- the 24-hour deli by me is called 'pickles & pies' and there was a sign with an old-looking corona bottle (like just old enough for you to be like 'huh,' like '1999-2002 old') and a product called 'pepsi twist' that was almost covered up. also a man working on a grill, could see him from the outside.

- saw a grocery store in the not-far distance. sign said 'wa[something] mbd's.' tried to sound it out. zachary said 'do you want to just make food instead?' and i said 'yeah.' we had to walk over some kind of generator-run ATM area/parking lot/police station. figured out the sign said 'waldbaum's fresh.' approached store. repeated 'waldbaum's fresh' a few times, chuckling and using a variety of curious-sounding inflections/pitches, like beavis and butthead. when they do that thing.

- a few minutes after we walked in there was a storewide 'ten minutes to close' loudspeaker announcement. zachary seemed joyless and busi-nesslike, looking at food. i felt the thing of 'how long have i known this person' again. remembered being in 'fresh grocer' with him the night we gave up and threw the rotten watermelon into the water at penn treaty park, but i didn't remember the watermelon part until now. in waldbaum's i just remembered walking around the grocery store and commiserating in our indecisiveness about food and agitation at each other/the situation, and how even though that was bad, something seemed better than now.

- bought kale, cucumber, yellow pepper, two strip steaks, avocado, banana, spinach. zachary said 'beer...' and i said 'oh beer.' he said 'sometimes in grocery stores in new york they'll sell beer,' which i knew. i said 'o-hhh.' we saw beer. i said 'look at schaeffer's, i want schaeffer's.' zachary chuckled and said 'okay' like how ferris bueller would say 'okay' to a leprechaun at his door with surprise room service. compared with other things this felt extra good. still felt the 'something has changed, am i just meeting this person' thing but not as much.

APRIL 30, 2013

12–1:30AM: (things i remember, continued:)

- talked about warheads/candy on the walk back to apartment. i said something bad. it was…i asked if zachary ever ate very gross things, at lunch, as a child. he said 'no.' the bad thing i said sounded probably like this: 'because like, i like, we would like, for all of lunch in fourth or fifth grade, like it would be things like tuna mixed with jell-o, like that, we would like, just dare each other to see who could eat the worst thing, for the whole time.' the point of the story, i thought zachary was thinking, was so he could see how i did unexpected interesting stuff as a little girl (the kind of 'usual tricks' i do in the beginnings of relationships, which he seems tired of hearing and i wasn't sure i was saying/doing intentionally), which resulted in me saying 'like' a lot, because i knew if i said 'nevermind' and stopped talking that would mean things were unsalvageable, not worth trying for. my 'likes' were an attempt at stalling i think, like (haha), to see if i could think of something better instead of the bad story i was unstoppably telling.

- stove gas did not turn on. i said 'i guess we'll just eat salad.' zachary asked to see my phone and looked up how to cook a steak in a toaster oven. he read something excitedly, a person talking about the benefits of cooking steak in a toaster oven. the person really had it figured out. it was funny.

- felt cluttered in the kitchen, thinking about what i would do to help cook. i said 'do you want me to help around here? i've got plenty of other stuff to do.' zachary said he didn't need help and i felt good not helping, continuing to unpack. we listened to an urban outfitters sampler, i think, from the early 2000's. sometimes i'd say 'what is this, i remember this' and zachary would sometimes say what it was and if he remembered it.

- at some point the thing i had hung all my dresses on became unattached from closet and it made a loud noise and i made a noise just as loud at the same time. zachary came over and we were shrugging/grinning. asked him what to do, sort of thinking he would know because of his carpentry stuff, and he said 'i don't know, probably call the super,' looking at the fallen clothes.

- zachary said he figured out what happened to the cats. i walked to the kitchen. he leaned the stove/oven forward. the cats were huddled together behind the stove/oven in an impossibly tight space. alvie jumped out immediately and shirley tried to squeeze under the oven and her hind legs flattened, then she either got stuck or gave up half-way. zachary said 'you thought i was going to say a bad thing, like i found out they were dead?' i couldn't remember. i said 'y-eah. that they had died.'

- watched 'the office.' toaster steak was fine. zachary had expressed concern about its wetness and color as it was cooking. he said 'not bad, right?' i said it was good. felt happy.

- they played in a band on 'the office'…they're in a band…andy isn't good, but he thinks he is, but he knows the band isn't working…then at the end he's okay because darryl thinks of the words…andy says 'how are you thinking of that, you just thought of that?!'…they keep going…andy says something about how they're no longer 'on the clock' but they keep going. i like how much everyone appreciates each other on 'the office.' i like how much they want friends. michael scott and andy the most. they seem so sweet and alone and full of this desire to love and be loved, like the best people on earth, but they're not even real. just think of how happy michael scott would be to hear how much people laugh at his jokes. sending a soundbite of everyone who has ever laughed at a michael scott joke to 'parallel universe michael scott' who is a real person not played by steve carrell. hearing that would solve 'the problem' of michael scott. like he would…lose his personality…or no, he would just talk about how much he loved how much everyone loved him.

- 'king of the hill' came on. then there was going to be another one. the TV was situated in the room a way that…you know sometimes something is only in a certain way because it makes sense in the moment, but it's just a temporary thing? like covering your head with a newspaper in the rain? doing your best to manage a temporary thing? using the curtains as sheets also contributed to the feeling. it felt really good. i said something like 'it's so good, i'm getting more!' about salad i didn't end up finishing. zachary ate the rest of my steak. then we laid down. it felt good to be near his armpit and to smell him and to feel him breathing and moving in smaller ways and getting to know he was that close.

- peggy wrote a paper for bobby in 'king of the hill.' there was some kind of rivalry with the english teacher. did sexy things with the volume off

303

for most of it. i think at the end…at some point in the night i started putting dishes in the sink and beer cans/bottles in the trash. started to fall asleep. zachary said 'no peg you gotta brush your teeth.' remember feeling interested in if/how his glasses were changing something about his eyes. thought 'shit, now i won't be able to sleep, especially if water touches my face right now.' something about this seemed nice. he let me go first. i washed my face. when it was his turn i ate 2mg xanax. think he suspected something.

10:36am: woke to zachary dressing. asked if he was leaving and he said he was. he leaned down to kiss me, i think. i said something about how i was glad he stayed over, it would've been bad if he hadn't have been there. if i didn't say this in the morning i said it before going to bed. remember him reacting to me saying it like i didn't mean it. tried going back to sleep but knew it wouldn't work. thought about zachary walking to the bus. thought 'if i was better i would offer to drive him back to adam's.'

10:40AM–7:46PM: had planned to go to ikea/thrift store/pet store/library but got obsessed with unpacking.

7:48pm: have eaten maybe 30mg adderall since waking. Unpacked everything and hung pictures. Looks good. Called mom. Smoking cigarette on window ledge. Have gyno appointment tomorrow 3:40pm, going back to md now to garner internet all night, write & send overdue story. Feeling good to be here. Haven't thought about being alone since Zachary left, if I had done the other not-unpacking stuff like I had planned and came back to see still-packed boxes I would feel shitty I think.

8:35pm: showered without shower curtain. Wetness. Alvie has been hiding under the sink. Think gas hasn't been turned on yet, water was cold. Don't want to leave apartment, feel like this is my safe ass hobby hole. Feel at least a little better being here than at mom's or dad's. Thought 'And Now: A Life (To Be Continued).'

8:40pm: looming sense of dread re potential car towing. The sign by where I parked said it would be safe until Friday. 'Just in case' I'm taking the paranoid measure of not bringing the box dad mistakenly packed. The box is full of slides. Because details like 'the box was full of slides?' That's what matters! Oof.

9:26pm: car was there. Mom called and said 'did you get gas?' I said 'no, maybe I will on the way home.' she said 'oh no I meant in your apartment.' she was looking for motels for when she visits, had called to see if I knew my zip code.

9:36pm: drove back to building. Saw Colin standing at his window, I think, while I loaded boxes in car. First time I've been lost here. Want to be on a lot of drugs. Drug dealer texted there were 'specials' tonight and dad gave me $200 cash yesterday. Considering…seems too hard to pick a place in manhattan to meet…he is the one with heroin and Molly and coke…not worth it, considering it would delay me being in md and writing the story/ updating this, also guilt at spending money in that way. Passed accident on side of road. Details. Not just thoughts, details also. Wheeeeee.

When I get to Maryland I 'have to' do story first, will post shitty update of liveblog then eat 60mg vyvanse and do story. If I stay up all night I can get a new computer tomorrow before gyno at 3:40pm. I'm saying this as like… it's a warning to myself, if I don't do these things I'll feel bad. Always forget 'in the future you'll feel bad if you don't _____.'

9:49pm: something feels more manageable, looking inside of apartment, even though I don't know what I want to do. Wonder if vice 'will still have me.' Passed animated highway sign that said 'slow down' then 'give us a break.'

MAY 1, 2013

12:05am: bought gas, neuro sonic drink, four-pack 8oz sf red bull from rest stop. Mom called as I was pulling out. Nose has been progressively stuffier on drive, have headache. Mom said 'oh you've got a stuffy nose too, the pollen is everywhere, it's these fucking flowering trees, someone needs to cut them down.' I said 'on a species thing, it's like they're doing harm to us, they want to overcome us and take our place.' mom said 'they're actually an alien species, this is an alien plot' and chuckled. My nose has recovered from cocaine the other night, had felt worried about it getting hard to breathe again, allergies thing makes sense though. I'm in delaware. Mom said something about a funnyordie.com thing she wants to show me when it seemed clear that I wanted to drive and she wanted to sleep. I said 'you'll have to show it to me tomorrow.' she said she would, heard a smile in her voice and 'awareness of earlier silent agreement we had that conversation was over.' she said 'well you drive safe.' I said 'I will. You sleep good.' she said 'oh there are just these things we have to say to each other.' I could picture her face and I liked it. I said 'yeah, now we're saying these things we say at the end of the phone call.' She said 'I know it's all whatever, you know, but I really love you and I'm happy you're coming home.' I said 'me too, I love you too, big.'

1:16am: almost at mom's. Forgot about broken earphones, driving to 24-hour rite aid. Have been extra swervy, answering ask.fm questions while driving, have seen over ten cop cars. Tonight: a hot night for inattentive cops. Pigs looking elsewhere tonight. Hot sizzly inattentive bacon. Little hot bacon oil spurts doing all kinds of repelling off my swervy ass Honda. Bypassing the bacon bigtime.

1:30am: an m83 song I initially felt averse to played on shuffle. It's excited/inspiring-sounding music playing behind a little girl talking about a frog you can touch and then it 'changes your vision, it makes blue look red, and your mom looks like your dad, and everything looks like a big cupcake and you're just laughing and laughing, and then you become a frog too,' or something like that, then something about how 'everyone would be friends, it would be the biggest group of friends ever.' Have been listening to it on repeat, think I'm buying earphones mostly to prolong car ride listening to this, then to continue listening when I get home. Seems kind of embarrassing, like something people would call 'twee' in a negative way, but fuck that I think people just say that shit because they're jealous they didn't think of it first. Like they're pissed because they initially like it, then they're like, 'that's so obvious but it's so unusual at the same time, how come I didn't think of it?' I think. That's what I've felt anyway. I think. I can't remember. Actually I did just…I remember 'hating' this song when I first heard it, but I don't remember the reason behind the hating, I just skipped over it.

1:47am: heard something like a motorcycle entering rite-aid and stopping near the back of the store. Thought 'that's how they do deliveries now.' There was a problem with ringing up my earphones and I started walking away. The cashier said 'it's almost ready' and I said 'no, I forgot something, sorry.' Walked to the cold medicine aisle and quietly said 'ex-cuuuu-se me' to female cop as I passed her to kneel and look at nasal congestion sprays. Thought 'she thinks I'm buying cough syrup to get high. No, she just knows I'm buying nose spray so I can funnel more drugs into my stuffed-up nose' (knowing I am not planning to do that). The cashier continued to have problems ringing up the earphones. I said 'sorry' and 'oh no' as she walked to find a scannable/non-defective package of the same earphones. The motorcycle noise was coming from a man pushing a floor polisher. Thought 'I want to do that.' Cashier said 'your total comes to twenty-two seventy-eight,' I think, but I heard 'it all comes to seventy-seven.' Thought 'it all comes to seventy-seven, that's what it all comes down to' and something about the demeanor of the cashier, who had one earphone in her ear and one hanging on her sweatshirt, and didn't seem to be wearing a name tag or anything indicating she worked at rite aid. Checked the card reader scanning device thing and saw '$22.78,' not '.77.' Continued thinking 'it all comes down to seventy-seven,' like, dazedly obsessed with 'it all comes down to…,' while she bagged my things and told me to have a nice night.

2:06am: typed above thing sitting in parking space. Left nostril is so clogged I don't know how the spray could've gotten in. It's running down my nose a little, I am tilting head typing this trying to reverse gravity and funnel spray liquid up there. Man is loading something into a white van. I think he is the floor polishing man. Van is driving away.

2:09am: gravity working, nose less obstructed. Reversed car just in time to inconvenience white van, now directly behind me.

2:13am: prolonging car ride to finish cigarette/avoid productivity. I'm only allowed this one cigarette. Drive your diddly ass around all you want Boyle, you're just getting this one cigarette, and you know you have to pee, so. Enjoy this. Enjoy this dilly-dallying you diddly peehead. Oh look, the moon. Soak up that moon, you diddly. Yeah that's right you know how to auto-correct whatever I typed to 'diddly,' you sexy telepathic iPhone, sensing my desire to type 'diddly' somehow, but oh no you remain mysterious, why did you want to auto-correct 'sensing' to 'sending,' I didn't even misspell it, you irresistible minx, keeping me guessing the way you do, will we ever understand each other?

2:22am: pulled into mom's. Would be interesting if I forgot vyvanse.

2:40am: peed, ate two Tylenol for headache, saw package from Austin (payment for doing spacedads spreecast reading) on my bed. Package was expertly packed, like the most intricate packaging I've ever unpackaged.

Also was expecting just one or two pills, he sent me 16, wide variety. What to do.

2:53AM: ate 60mg vyvanse. i'm not going to do the thing where i type what i remember of yesterday here, i'm either going to fill in with as much detail in order, or leave things blank.

10:37AM: pretty convincing fake 2:53AM update, huh? as you can see i was trying to cover my tracks in a way that…would lead to…i don't know. i was setting a scene for you. trying to make that one easy for you. it's probably true, i was thinking things like 2:53AM all night. i got in a vyvanse hole bigtime.

a little earlier the gyno office called to see if i could come in early, at 12:20PM. thought 'i don't want to go earlier but if i agree to then maybe she won't find cancer in me.' i told laura i could come in at 12:20. doorbell rang a few minutes later. it was a package from UPS. watched the truck drive away. something mom had ordered from HSN. walked up stairs and thought 'mom will be the saddest if i have cancer, sadder than me, 'don't have cancer' just for mom, i don't want to have it either, the thing the gyno wanted to re-do to me is a scam, it planted the idea in my head and cancer grows from ideas maybe, i don't want health to be bad i just got other stuff a little good shit shit shit.'

10:48AM: i'm on the balcony. it's very sunny and 58 degrees but i'm wearing hot pink winter coat anyway. mom's downstairs neighbor (old man who i can sometimes hear singing operatically) stood on the sidewalk maybe 30' from me and mumbled something, staring in the same direction i'm facing. he walked on the sidewalk until he was under me, then walked to the edge of the woods, staring upwards. heard him say 'schtoopy' but no other words. he seemed to be directly addressing a tree. nodded/acknowledged each other at different times as he walked in the direction he came.

12:00pm: removed necklaces to look 'less likely to have cancer.' brushed teeth and hair and washed face. Swapped hot pink coat for Mira's black coat. A 'no less unseasonable, but much less unsavory coat.' Took pill box for 'just in case it's bad news.' feel that bringing the pills is 'dooming me.' mom pulled into driveway as I walked to my car. She stopped and rolled down window and I said 'I'm off to see Abrams, she wants me early.' mom made scrunchy nosed face and said 'oh no, it'll be fine,' then did Abrams voice (we both see her) to say 'jasht remember to cuff.' I said 'jasht a teensy cuff, and then you vill feel a little peench.' waved goodbye.

12:10pm: did risky ponytail-tying hands-free driving maneuver going 74mph. Imagined accident. Thought 'no, that would be too predictably 'like me' to do, so it won't happen, I'm safe.'

12:12pm: imagined quiet intense Freddie mercury voice singing 'when the gyno sees it in your eyes-ah / that you've been up all night-ah' right before the song 'really starts rockin'

12:17pm: it's going to be really stupid after the appointment when she tells me I have cancer and I will have been listening to this innocent inspiring m83 song on repeat this entire time. There's no way to stop it now. Oh well. What if I'm pregnant again, it's not even possible but who knows. It's anyone's game right now. Who knows. Oh well.

12:24pm: what if she gives me an orgasm. Anyone's game.

12:31pm: in waiting room, there is a new section on the medical update form at the bottom that says 'date of last colposcopy' why is it a routine now

1:06pm: interesting dynamic. Laura took my blood pressure and I said it would be higher because I had been smoking. I like Laura and dr. Abrams, for the record. Feel like I disappoint them. Laura said 'oh no, it is a little higher' and didn't scold me for smoking but I said 'I gotta stop.' I said 'also I'm a little nervous.' Laura smiled and said 'oh why, you know it's just us.' I said 'I know, I don't know though, you never know.' she said 'I always get nervous before I sit up there too.' wondered if dr. Abrams is her doctor. She said 'okay meg, everything off, gown open in the front, I'll leave you to get dressed' and kind of winked at me. Thought 'Laura…no…my friend.'

Dr. Abrams knocked and entered and without saying hi (I like that about her) started saying a thing about how there was no sense 'putting me through misery' with another pap smear since it wasn't likely that my body would've changed much in six months, but 'let me tell you why I still want to do it—so we can have a complete record.' thought she would be pushing the colposcopy on me big time, like last time. She said she hoped my body had taken care of it and that I should take 1mg folic acid every day. We talked about juicing and smoothies. She recommended blending, not juicing, which Tao also recommended. She said she makes an almond milk, Greek yogurt, kale, raspberry drink that is 'supposed to energize, but I don't know,' while feeling my breasts. She motioned for me to lie back with my hands behind my head and I did. She handled my right arm and I remembered upside-down cross tattoo on my side that she maybe somehow didn't know about and her envisioning me as 'the devil.' she said 'now are these real, or are they the ones you peel off?' I said they were real. Thought she was maybe indirectly alluding to my aversion to colposcopy pain/refusal to endure pain she probably views as minor. She said 'what happens when you know, you don't want to see it there anymore? When you want to take one off?' I said 'you know, I don't like how some of them look anymore but it's still nice to see them and be like, 'I was there in that moment." she made a face like she understood and told me to scoot down and put my feet in the stirrups. She said she was friends with a girl who was in the Olympics and had an Olympics tattoo on her back that 'actually looked very nice.' I asked her if the girl placed. She said she did, she would've gotten a bronze medal but since the girl from China ahead of her lied about her age she was disqualified and she got the silver medal instead. Thought 'there is no way...no wait doctors are the same level as people in the Olympics, they could know each other somehow.' Felt conscious of my potential crotch smell and watched her looking at my crotch and saying things about the Olympics, trying to discern if her face meant I smelled or looked bad. She inserted speculum and I felt something widen and my knees reflexively draw together but I remembered to keep them far apart. I asked about the Chinese girl who was disqualified. She said 'and you know how they found out? Facebook.' felt afraid, like she knew about my Facebook and was maybe inventing this entire thing as some kind of obscure warning-parable about how I shouldn't talk about this on the internet. She inserted two q-tip swab things and I felt 'the tickle' and squirmed a little while trying to look 'normal'/attentive about a tangential story about how that year they figured out they had mis-measured the uneven bars, and the bronze girl's coach was so upset he walked out before the Olympics were over. I said 'whoa, he just walked out.' She made a face and said 'yah. At the Olympics, he walked out.' one of her hands had two fingers in my vagina and the other hand was gently feeling around my lower abdomen. I said 'well, that's the Olympics.' She nodded and said 'now I'm going to do your rectal,' and tried to insert a finger, then made a face looking down like 'technical difficulties' and said 'oop.' Then it went in. I said 'that's a funny moment, 'that's the Olympics." she smiled like 'I'm maybe not supposed to smile' and I wanted to 'egg her on.' Remembered my first visit when I was 18 when I said 'I bet you feel like you're doing muppets all day, like, you're Jim Henson and I'm Kermit' and she reacted similarly.

She told me to sit up and get dressed and meet her in her office. She said something about how she figured I was out of my birth control and needed a refill, without mentioning how she wouldn't authorize a refill without me sending the letter I wrote authorizing her to not perform the colposcopy. No mention. Seemed 'suspect' or…like a family secret, no one mentions that one uncle's drinking problem, they just let him do it and pretend it's not happening. Felt shitty about me, being the drunk uncle, doing things people want to pretend I'm not doing. Refusing…erroneous…painful medical procedures…but still. I don't know.

In the office she said 'now Laura got your pee and you're negative,' I said 'for everything?' she said 'that's a good question. Now that's a good question, let me answer, I just have to click some things to update you in the computer.' I waited. She took a breath and said 'now—I'm just sending this as a pap smear, but usually we stop recommending the other tests to women older than twenty-six and that's! Because. Women tend to become involved in monogamous relationships. You come in and you've been with Eddie for three years and we say 'no reason to do this, now we stop.' But then! Say you're with Eddie for a year and then, who knows, maybe Ted—no wait they're the same thing,' I didn't get it right away, 'so maybe then you're with, John? So we say it's good to send a check for everything once a year, if you're an unmarried woman, no children, you want to do what you want.' I was nodding the entire time and wanting to hurry it along. I said 'yes, yeah that would be good to check' maybe too eagerly. She said 'okay well we're going to check you this time, but since I've put it in as a pap smear it takes a little longer, so you're going to have to give me two weeks.' Her face was like 'we're so glad you came uncle Ted, please be careful on those stairs.'

Something printed out and she said 'oh! I thought I had sent your refill to the pharmacy but it printed instead.' I said 'that's okay, I can just give them the paper.' she signed it without hesitation and said 'yes you'll just have to give them this.'

We talked a little about what I was doing. She remembered truck driving. I told her about New York. Felt like drunk uncle Ted big time. Had labored conversation about hurricane Sandy and megabus. Labored for me, only seemed to belabor her in that I think she was re-adjusting to act around a belabored person. Remembered my last visit when she asked me if there were complications in my abortion in a medical conversational protocol way, and I described fainting and the blood loss and she asked why I didn't go to the hospital and I started crying unexpectedly and had to stop talking for a moment, then said 'oh god I'm so sorry I don't know why I'm like this.' She seemed befuddled and refused my apology in a kind goal-oriented way. Her face listening to me talk about New York looked similar to how it looked then. She asked me if I was taking the bus to New York and I said I drove. Her face lit up a little. She said 'have you tried megabus?' I lied and said 'bolt...bus. Megabus just drops you off in white marsh, right?' she told me about how she and her family saved money booking in advance on the megabus. Felt comforted to hear this, for some reason, I kept asking her questions. I've taken the megabus probably over 50 times. It felt good to hear her talk about what the bus was like and how it surpassed her expectations. She said she didn't care about luxury, she just wanted to be comfortable. I thought 'how long can we keep this up, I want to know more about her riding the bus, where she was going,' but then it seemed like I was asking too many bus questions and she was aware of talking a lot. Somehow the conversation wound down. Have an image of my face looking like it's about to say something it's thought about, then the conversation taking an abrupt 'winding down' turn. She started to say goodbye. I said, 'oh, wait, so before I go, can you say how does it look? Compared to last time?' She closed her eyes and did a single nod and said 'to me, from what I saw today, from this medical examination, you are completely normal. There are no lesions, you look perfect. But we will have to see in a year.' She wished me a good year. I said 'you too, dr. Abrams,' feeling weird about hearing myself say her name in that context, then doing something loud to the door as I closed it.

Laura was smiling big at me, like Christmas style, a little sad, and said 'bye bye Meg.' I felt 'caught' by her smile like I felt 'caught' about the megabus, wanted to prolong. I said something about my co-pay. Laura said 'we'll just run it through the insurance company like normal,' still smiling, seeming 'onto me,' my swindling her into a co-pay response to prolong her smiling at me. My awareness of the 'swindling' as I was doing it seemed limited to a vague feeling that I was doing something automatically. Now seems obvious, what I was doing and why.

2:50pm: have been sitting in parked car in macmedics parking lot typing into phone. Kids came out of somewhere for a minute, like a day care thing.

3:00pm: I am being serviced by the macmedics employee who I have always wanted to be serviced by. Ever since I saw that mom lady talking to him about his tattoos. Really chatting him into a corner, grilling him about 'healing times.' He kind of seemed to like it, in an 'I enjoy sharing perfunctory information to those who ask it from me, I am happy to help' way. I'm making that up, he probably liked hot interrogator mom attention for normal reasons. Still tried to exude 'don't you worry baby, I would never ask you to tell me what your sleeve means, plus I know how to treat you nice' at him.

He is in the back room checking the trade-in value of busted computer.

He is checking prices in the back.

How else can I say this…

When will he return, it has been minutes since I have known how tall he is

Maybe he doesn't really have the little face mole/freckle cluster thingy I thought I saw, I hope it's still there when he comes back

3:17pm: froze while trying to charm him with a story of how…oh no. So, he said it would be better money-wise if they just replaced the busted parts instead of selling me a refurbished used computer. He said 'machine.' I like it when computer people call computers 'machines' instead. Got a little turned on writing that, imagining the mind of a computer person, feeling insecure that computers aren't as 'machine-y' as other machines like cars but they're technically still machines. Seems sexy, frail. Frail and knowable. I would say 'I'd like to see the machine' when I pick up repaired computer, then he'd retrieve it from the back (I'd let him retrieve it to increase waiting time so there could be a bigger-feeling reward, because I too am looking out for his best value) then I'd take it from him and set it aside without breaking eye contact and say, 'I'd like to see the other machine, the one in the back,' moving closer and just…Jesus lol…grabbing his button-down where it meets the pants. Pulling it out. Right on the button line. I would be pulling from the button line, because it's like a little handle. Zoom in for a close inspection of the freckle/mole face area. Check to see if that shit needs refurbishing. Refurbish the shit out of that face mole cluster thingy. I think it's near his eye. Give him a nice hot quote on that mole cluster, try to get him a good deal, I'll check online to make sure my deal is the best. Then I'll call him on Monday, the full refurbishments will have to wait until Monday, because I want to make sure I have ordered and stocked the very best parts. The waiting will increase the reward, also.

Forgot I was trying to describe how I froze up around him. It was because of thinking something like that while he was in the back room, expecting he would return 'less attractive.' That face mole thingy though. Hoo. Some real Achilles' heel type shit, me and face moles. IT'S LIKE HOW DO THEY EVEN GET THERE ON THE FACE, HOW COULD A FACE PRODUCE SUCH A MARVEL, HOW COULD IT KNOW TO GEN-ERATE SUCH A PERFECTLY SHAPED USELESS THING IN THE MIDST OF THE HIGHEST CONCENTRATION OF SENSORY

ORGANS ON THE BODY, HOW COULD IT LET THAT SLIP BY, SO OBVIOUS, JUST SITTING THERE LORDING IT UP DOING NOTHING BUT LOOKING SEXY AROUND ITS BITCH ASS OVERWORKED EYES AND NOSE AND MOUTH. I PROBABLY THINK MOLES ARE SEXY BECAUSE ON AN EVOLUTIONARY LEVEL IF I BREED WITH A FACE MOLE PRODUCING PERSON OUR OFFSPRING WILL HAVE MORE GENETIC VARIETY AND CERTAIN TRAITS OF MY DNA WILL LIVE ON FOREVER, I'M JUST THE PRODUCT OF MY ANCESTORS' GENETIC SURVIVAL MACHINE, I'M TRYNA GET THIS MACHINE SERVICED WHICH IS FUNNY BECAUSE I'M ON MY WAY TO PICK UP MY BIRTH CONTROL REFILL RIGHT NOW ALSO DAMN HOPE MACMED-ICS HOTTIE DOESN'T GOOGLE ME HEHEHEEHEHE

OR WAIT, I HOPE…

JUST DON'T TAKE ANY OF THIS TOO SERIOUSLY ED, IF YOU'RE READING. OR NO, TAKE IT HOWEVER YOU WANT. IF THIS CREEPS YOU OUT MAYBE THIS SHIT AIN'T MEANT TO BE. MOSTLY JUST, REALTALK: IF NOTHING ELSE JUST KNOW IT WAS NICE SHAKING YOUR HAND AND I AM NOT KID-DING ABOUT WANTING TO DO STUFF TO YOU IN THE BACK ROOM, P.S. SPEAKING OF BACK ROOMS, IF YOU PERUSE MY HARD DRIVE, THAT PORN IS ALL MY EX-BOYFRIEND'S BUT I'M OPEN TO WHATEVER BUT PROBABLY NOT THE FIRST TIME, BUT JUST SO YOU KNOW, JUST WANT TO GIVE YOU AN ACCURATE GAUGE OF MY FREAKINESS, HARD DRIVE DOES NOT ACCURATELY REPRESENT MY RELATIVELY PASSIVE AND BROAD AND ACTUALLY KIND OF BORINGLY STRAIGHTFOR-WARD INTEREST IN SEX

NOW NO MATTER WHAT IT WILL CERTAINLY BE MORE INTERESTING TO PICK UP MY MACHINE ON MONDAY OR WHENEVER ONE OF YOU FINE TECHNICIANS CALL ME

I'M A NICE PERSON SORRY IF YOU FEEL OBJECTIFIED

I HAVE BEEN CONSISTENTLY SATISFIED WITH THE QUALITY OF SERVICE PROVIDED TO ME AT MACMEDICS

FOR THE RECORD

4:44pm: sitting in waiting area of rite aid pharmacy. It's going to be a half an hour.

4:46pm: is it okay to just consume any product sold in rite aid, while you wait in the store? You stay there for like eight hours. You gotta pay at the end, no getting around that bullshit. Can't you do that?

4:48pm: person chewing gum near me is giving me ASMR head tingles with her gum chewing noises. A little worried to look and find out we know each other. Then the magic tingles would be gone. Never works with someone you know. 'raspberry beret' by prince is playing.

4:53pm: pharmacist asked me my last name, then asked gum chewing friend, her name was the 'correct' last name, I don't think I know her but went out of my way to avoid eye contact just in case.

5:15pm: sitting in fucking parking lot. Man in 'OBEY' brand tank top walked by. 'OBEY' did a good job because when you wear it you're also doing exactly what they tell you to do.

5:28pm: navy blue toyota corolla passed me as I thought 'Asians are misrepresented'

5:34pm: it makes more sense to call any time the sun is out 'a.m.' I'm tired of this m83 twee ass bullshit song.

6:49PM: have been ranting with mom about 'the gaul' of doctors and dentists 'presuming to act like they know something.' talked about 'like life,' lorrie moore short story. ate a concerta 36mg in preparation for first installment of a video interview to be done in installments over course of liveblog that will be on electric literature 'the outlet' blog. blogblogblog. said 'isn't it weird that your teeth stop growing' mid-rant to mom and she said 'yes! yes that is extremely weird!' like it was an additional injustice… or something…lol…

7-8:40PM: talked with juliet escoria on skype. we had met before, at the KGB reading. she reminds me a lot of someone else though, i sort of remembered meeting her there but mostly remembered her from having one of those 'eerily familiar faces' i can never quite place (in an interesting way). didn't tell her this. felt myself holding back re some things…drug things…damn, i'm doing it now too…she asked me a question about if i really said everything on the liveblog/didn't withhold anything, like i said i would, and i've been thinking i should stop withholding. have been milling this shit over.

the official interview part was short/business-like but then we talked about other things, covered a lot of things. boogers…seemed to get on a good thing with boogers: we've tried them and don't like them, one time a broccoli head came out my nose when i vomited, she has a friend who vomits so loud it sounds like a scream, i said she should rap while screaming through vomit, juliet vomits once every two weeks due to medication and coffee and is filming vomit…feeling giddy remembering the 'nasty parts' of talk… bad little boy parts…boogers…she talked about blue and orange boogers and said you can't snort addy balls, then a few minutes later i interrupted an unrelated topic to say 'someone just snorts the adderall xr, the whole pill, and then after that they snort everything, all food.' she said something about how that wouldn't work, then something that made me picture raw beef in a tube. she has a friend who farts a lot and they might move in together. one time juliet ordered a pizza alone at a bar but the bar sold pizza, i thought she meant she ordered domino's. she and the fart friend made up 'folo' which is like 'yolo' but it means 'forever alone.'

favorite moment: finding out that when she walks down stairs she imagines falling and something violent happening to her teeth. i imagine falling and my shins going up through my knees. also liked talking about how beavers and horses seem fucked up and a lot of things seem fucked up.

my 'big fumble:' juliet expressed worry about her pen name. i said she should make a new pen name called 'megan boyle,' then rammed this thing home big time about…how she should not post the video interview we were doing at all, instead post an oprah episode as 'megan boyle inter-viewing megan boyle.' think she understood but repeated 'AN ACTUAL OPRAH EPISODE' as i indulged in my cute idea more than listened to her understanding the idea and maybe wanting to move on. big fumble.

8:90PM: i was going to write '8:90'…i went through with it, as you can see…

10:25PM: after the interview i went to mom's room. she was watching a documentary about a special kind of horse. i said 'am i interrupting?' mom seemed oddly eager to have me watch. i said 'juliet said horses look fucked up, they have googly eyes.' mom said 'their eyes are like that because they're preyed on, by wolves, they are preyed on.' i did a 'leg noogie' to her and said 'what? they do look weird.' she said 'well it's just that they're only my favorite animal of all time. and these, these are the littinger stallions, they start out gray like this but then they get big and white—this one is four years old, so he's still gray, there's a process—oh i think you'll hate it but will you just watch?' i leaned against the bedpost. i said 'they look like that one actor, with dark stuff in the front of his face. who is he?' mom said 'javier bardem?' i said 'no he's more of a character actor. i think he's italian.' the horses were made to perform…they do this…it's called 'dressage,' i knew about it before this also but i don't remember seeing it. mom said 'there are only seventy horses in the world like this. they were all picked. and now they're in austria, performing, will you just stay and watch for a minute with me, it's so beautiful.' there were hardly any people in the horse arena. it looked old, people were wearing old time-y clothes. the horses had been specially trained to walk funny and kick 'battle style,' where all of their hooves leave the ground at once. the camera showed this happening in slow motion, the battle style kick. the voice said '[name of horse] has worked up enough rage' and there was white foam coming out of its mouth. mom said 'it's how they would fight, in wars, when the horses were also weapons. they treat them very well, they really do, i wouldn't like it if they didn't treat the horses well.' then there was a shot of a person in old time-y clothes approaching a stable. the voiceover said something about how the mare in the stable was about to give birth. the belly was so big. i said 'i can't watch anymore, i don't want to see horse eggs.' mom laughed and said 'horse eggs, oh no' as i walked back to bedroom.

there was this part where it's just a close-up of undulating horse feet…was laughing so hard there were tears…

looked at videos on a person's youtube channel i was brought to by another person's baboon invasion video. the first invasion is a lot calmer than the other one.

11:00PM: watching 'tweaking on meth in walmart' videos on youtube. i wanted them to keep going. seems like a beckett play. beckett's lost magnum opus. he figured out time travel and he took two actors with him and they filmed this time travel piece together. then they invented meth, the three of them, and planted it somewhere for us to find in the future. that's how we have meth. 'tweaking on meth in walmart' videos were recommended to me because of things about dressage horses and other drug things, i think. youtube thinks i want to watch stuff move differently.

11:18PM: i feel significantly stupider than when i woke. actually wait, i woke in new york last. i forget. people like to watch 'tweaking on meth in walmart' videos to make fun of the meth people or walmart culture or something. seems stupid, i would spit in the face of someone who watches to laugh at the people. pictured spitting into a comment and it hitting the person and my scalp got tingly with ire. tingly dressage horse ire, working up my rage.

11:21PM: GOING TO EAT SOMETHING NOW AND THEN SLEEP FOR THE NIGHT SO I CAN HAVE ENERGY TO GET BOXES OF CLOTHES/BOOKS FROM STORAGE UNIT, DRIVE BACK TO NYC,

GET KITTY LITTER AND FOOD, WORK ON STORY, RESPOND
TO THINGS. ALL BY TOMORROW NIGHT. OR ELSE.

11:54PM: for the past hour there have been cashew chunks lodged between
my nose and somewhere in the back of my throat. 'somewhere in the back
of my throat' = first draft title of 'somewhere i have never travelled, gladly
beyond' by e.e. cummings.

i only know about that poem because of 'hannah and her sisters,' which is
semi-famous for being responsible for letting people know about 'the easter
parade,' but i think i just found 'the easter parade' online and didn't notice
it in the movie.

it's crazy how much shit there is like that floating around in my head and a
lot of that shit will never have words.

here is another example of one of those things, this one almost vanished
into the ether: have noticed mom has hung most of her framed pictures
low. i like mine to be high. it feels safer when things are above me.

MAY 2, 2013

2:36PM: slept 2AM-5AM, 7AM-2PM. ate 5mg xanax, two macaroons, three 'pecan meltaways,' glass of 'right from the cow' milk. drinking coffee. last night i ate an everything bagel with cream cheese, half a pit of hagen daz coffee ice cream, bites of other carby shit, cookies. watched youtube things about the universe and ASMR videos. currently sitting cross-legged in bed, texting with colin. there is a problem or something. he gave me the wrong name of the owner and i called the owner but his nephew picked up but said the name is fine.

4:50PM: assembled package for matthew donahoo. 5mg opana feels similar to heroin but feel more awake and euphoric/optimistic.

started reading old livejournal, notdownwithopp.livejournal.com. sweet as hell. memories. big time. forgot being so happy subletting then living with two friends for a few months in 2008. i just made everything public without looking.

STUFF I WILL DO NOW:

- buying e-cigarette from walgreens

- getting key to storage unit from dad

- putting boxes from storage unit into car

- buying kitty litter kitty food

- returning to NYC

5:20pm: Judd apatow guy next to me at stop light is listening to death cab for cutie-like song with lyrics 'when there's a burning in your heart and you feel like it'll fall apart.' His windows are down. I don't know why I'm mad at him. He has a bike rack and a plaid shirt and is driving an oddly new Volvo.

5:22pm: opana feels like that feeling when you first get to the pool and you're looking for where to put your towel and there are all of these people sitting in plastic chairs under umbrellas. Like 'why not here?'

5:40pm: bought shitshow from Walgreens: neuro sonic, neuro passion, white monster zero drunk, sparkling water, e-cigarette. There was trouble with my card and a big line formed. I said 'oh great right when there's a lot of people, right?' and 'sorry about this,' cashier seemed appreciative.

6:27pm: e-cigarette smoke tastes good, doesn't hurt throat. Seems futuristic. Opana wore off fast, want more. Showed dad e-cigarette and he showed me his new offices. In good mood. Dad and I bowed to each other when I left.

7:31pm: loaded things from storage closet to car. Found old 'tv shows' I made when I was little, other VHS movies, emotional t-shirts. Bringing all that shit. Excited for VHS player. Eating another opana to treat my ass. Trying cherry flavor e-cigarette. Listening to less than jake. Thought 'I'm a shimby shooshoo. Shoofly, hm!'

7:50pm: I could be a spokeswoman for e-cigarettes, feel so positive about them. Favorite new toy.

8:28pm: petsmart employee 'Regina' helped me pick out cat food. Her phone alarm went off when she was selling me on this walnut-based kitty litter, saying 'I love my job so much I need to set an alarm for when I leave. I mean I wouldn't leave mid conversation with you, I just love helping people with pets.' she had a dog and two cats but no kids. I liked talking to her a lot. She asked me to keep her posted. The people who rang me up were also good. Man near the bag area asked me a few times if I wanted a cart. I said no. He wasn't wearing a petsmart uniform. The woman non-committally asked about my tattoos and said she doesn't like needles. I said 'it's different than needles, kind of' and the man said 'he really doesn't like getting his nails clipped.' I looked where he was looking, at two dogs on tables behind a glass wall.

8:35pm: thinking about Regina. My car battery definitely seems…there is a problem

9:04pm: feel like treating myself to Chicfila for no reason. Reason-free treating. Shit hell yeah just saw a sign.

9:14pm: in chicfila drive thru. Chicfila is located in white marsh, in an industrial park/'chain store wasteland.' Think every chain store is represented here. Staring at menu now. Almost went to panera but worried about parking w/weird battery thing going on. I'm…yes, I have decided I am going 'grilled' tonight. Grilled chicken club meal. Mouth watering

9:18pm: drive thru said 'will that complete your order' and I forgot if I had said a diet coke, then if I had ordered at all. Speaker said 'Elena will help you at the window.' Thought 'okay I'm rolling with this, I'm rolling with this'

9:20pm: Elena asked if I wanted sauce. She said 'we're just waiting on your sandwich.' I said 'okie doke.' she said 'hey what new salad dressing is the best?' Male voice said 'I like ranch.' she said 'really? I don't like ranch.' Jealous of people's jobs at petsmart and chicfila tonight. Driving now.

9:47pm: hard to manage dipping sauces while driving. I was short-shafted on fries. Sandwich was 'misty,' like how they spray vegetables with that automatic mist thing at grocery stores. Misty chargrilled chicken club deluxe. Medium-dark green lettuce. When it was gone I wanted more.

9:53pm: had 30-60 second-long thought process thing about the interview with Juliet last night that concluded 'don't share right now.'

10:33pm: imagined creating 'beach blanket bingo death party' Facebook event, inviting everyone I like to my new apartment for a pre-death funeral celebration, like on the event page it says I plan to overdose and die that night. Nice way to go out.

11:45pm: car brightened from highbeams behind me. It was a Chiquita banana truck.

11:53pm: intense craving for unidentifiable food.

11:59pm: want a Cinnabon. Orange sign by Grover Cleveland service center says 'fuel only no fuel services.'

MAY 3, 2013

12:03am: while feeling around for birth control I touched cat food and thought 'should I eat this.'

12:05am: dealt with 'modest—all things considered—sparkling water spill.' blew nose into hand even though I have napkins.

12:11am: 'hotcha girls' by ugly Casanova is playing. Love this song. Long-time big love. 'don't you know that old folks homes smell so much like my own.'

12:13am: damn almost out of gas. Juliet emailed that it felt weird to read about our conversation from my perspective. OH NO TAKE THIS JULIET, NOW IM WRITING ABOUT YOUR EMAIL OH NO, IM MAKING YOU TAKE YOUR MEDICINE, I AM JACK IN THE SHINING AND YOU ARE DANNY NOW COME OUT HERE BOY AND TAKE YOUR GODDAMNED MEDICINE

12:15am: a cover of 'tripped' by Neva dinova with Jordan on backup vocals/guitar, Tao on drums, me singing is playing. We made it in September 2010. nostalgic.

12:32am: I read 'Goethals' as 'goebbel' or whoever that third reich guy is almost every time.

2:23am: laying in bed leisurely smoking e-cigarette, Shirley purring and kneading on me. Feels so nice.

6:24am: laying again. Unpacked more. Earlier I walked on the beach bare-foot. I was the only one there. Stood with my feet in the water. Two beers one banana 2mg knlonopin 1mg Xanax. It will be sad to leave this place, to pack these things. I feel good for life here.

6:34am: took afrin, zeolite, magnesium. Also I had a memory about this time last year and magnesium and Zacky and me. Was trying to replace xanax with magnesium. The memory was the bottle on our bedroom dresser. My hands taking the bottle from the dresser. No, then taking the bottle to bed, eating some, telling Zac I was doing this and why I was doing this. He was in another room. Not sure which. He had recently left the bedroom, for the other room. Maybe. That's all I got. That's all that's left. That's all folks.

12:16pm: woke saw clock went back to sleep

1:16pm: woke saw clock went back to sleep

2:48pm: woke next to chocolate bar and cats. Ate bite of chocolate. Nose is very stuffy. I dreamed a lot.

2:52pm: there was chocolate on my face in the mirror. Also little pieces on the 'sheets' (curtains) and pillow. Today I want to get sheets and a duvet cover and pillowcases.

4:03pm: called insurance agency to clear up things about my car, called Verizon to set up internet. They're coming Friday. Leisurely smoking e-cigarette and sweeping little crumbs into piles. No dustpan yet. I want to do dishes, shower, then call the superintendent to fix closet, give me mail key, see about gas/stove. Listening to a stereolab record. I forgot I had so many records and how nice it feels to listen to them wee wee wee wee wee in the potty weewee!

4:12pm: set text message and voicemail alert sounds to a noise called 'suspense.' sounds '2001 a space odyssey' style. My phone rings to a theremin-like thing called 'sci-fi' now. Everyone uses the same iPhone sounds, I feel. These ones are so unpleasant and ridiculous sounding...so good to imagine them startling people in social situations...

6:27pm: washed dishes using soap and hands because you know this motherfucker is spongeless. Made spinach banana smoothie. Showered. Dressed in 'secretary from the 1960's who is also a dominatrix and sort of falling apart' outfit.

Nervous about car. Sleepy. Mira texted about a party tonight, think I'll feel unsocial, I don't know. Want to lay in bed all goldang day. Huff my (thought 'internet cheebah') e-cigarette.

6:38pm: Alvie is enjoying his continuous water flow device. Shirley is sleeping near me. Happy. Yeah I am a little happy.

6:52pm: I got excited thinking about eating 30mg instead of 15mg adderall, I think that'll help me go to ikea a little. Okay doing it.

8:20pm: Ikea was closing when I arrived, hurriedly selected things, forgot maybe 30% of things

Huge lines, people still browsing after second 'we are closed' announcement.

Couple in front of me: 30's, severe looking man in almost transparent blue (lol) plaid button-down, girl in all black, black leather sneakers designed for zero laces but with 'laces spaces,' thought they were from another country but no, she is on her iPhone a lot, he is explaining something to her, like he is convincing her about the value of the chocolate bars, they buy six or eight. They have the same trash can as me but different price tag. I took the display one by accident.

Couple adjacent to that couple: 40's, look sponsored by j crew, man is wearing button-down sweater vest under a 'Nantucket' or something cardigan/blazer, he keeps leaving the line looking lost and returning with nothing, wife is wearing hot pink Capri pants. They are buying patio furniture stuff. What if I had bought all outdoor furniture for my room. Insisted on that. They probably own a brownstone, this couple.

Line confusion, I had brought two display items (trash can and dish rack). People behind me commented on how full my bag was and that I'd need to buy a blue ikea bag. I said 'yeah I know how to fill a bag. I'm buying that blue bag too, yeah.' smiles all around, somehow.

Cashier said 'is this your first time here?' re my two display items then seeing that I had cash and it was a credit/debit only line. I pulled out 'quick recovery' visa and said 'no I'm just stupid about the display things, I'm sorry about that.' I started putting things in my bag and she said 'no hurry, here, there's paper for the glasses, you can wrap them.'

9:31pm: little girl behind me said 'mommy lets go on the alligator' as I entered elevator. Woman entered behind a man in all denim who said 'Ladies first.'

The 'ladies first' woman said, to a man with cart, 'everything goes so fast here, it's so narrow. I like to drive on open highways.' More people entered. Someone said 'yeah they [carts] don't go in one direction.' Maybe six people with carts on elevator now. Denim man said 'That'll work that'll work.' Thought something about disaster movies, getting stuck with them in elevator.

Elevator door closed and it seemed to move. Few seconds later it opened to the same floor we entered.

Someone said 'how did this happen, we're all particularly educated people'

Someone said 'Twilight zone'

I mumbled 'It's just two buttons, also'

People said other things and someone pushed the 'parking garage' button.

I said 'Watch, it'll open up to the same thing.'

The woman who said 'we're all particularly educated' looked at me fake-threateningly. The door opened to the parking garage. She looked at me and said 'A-ha!'

9:40-10:15pm: looked for 24-hour wifi in ikea parking lot, seems impossible

10:21pm: took the wrong tunnel to 24-hour starbucks, going to manhattan one

10:16pm: somehow it says 10:16 now.

10:20pm: Hugh Carey tunnel is $7.50 Jesus, that's the one I took by accident, gotta go back through. Think I've been largely operating under the misconception that ezpass on my car means 'free.'

10:39pm: how did I get so lost I'm not even looking at the internet. Definitely third tunnel of tonight. Hugh? Perhaps! PERHAPS THIS IS MY THIRD HUGH THRU!

10:44pm: here is the plan. If I divert from the plan it means I have aids, they will discover aids in me somehow, I will have had it since 2005.

10:47pm: hold up a minute now I'm on the wrong bridge how in the hell

10:53pm: I've definitely been lost here before. Hylan drive. I went over the verrazano bridge, it's like I'm coming from Baltimore again. Getting on belt pkwy I know where I'm at now okay. Told Mira I was not partying tonight.

10:56pm: the order of things which I am not to divert from otherwise it means I have had aids since 2005:

- get energy drinks and green smoothie materials from waldbaum's

- see if you can garner internet from parked car on 116th st or by the McDonald's on Beach 90something st., update liveblog quick without elaborations on Ikea stuff

11:28pm: nixing 'look for internet' plan. Will take too much time. Sitting in waldbaum's parking lot now.

11:36pm: wish I had goddamned internet at my house. Goddamnit.

11:55pm: trouble checking out. Neither ice cube tray had barcode. Man named 'Candy' went to look for them. He was real 'New York style.' like ratso rizzo with a happy family instead of poverty and gimp leg style. He asked me where I found them and I didn't know. Had planned to ask him when I walked in, where the ice cube trays would be, then I found them somehow. I scanned things. Candy returned with four trays. He said 'it's a two-pack, see?' I said 'oh no it must've gotten…' he scanned the two-pack for me, said 'three-nineteen for a two-pack,' handed mine back. I said 'thank you, that must be annoying.' he said 'nah no problem. three-nineteen' as he walked behind an area customers aren't allowed to go.

Waldbaum's looks so similar to the super fresh Zachary and I would go to in Philly. I miss that. At this time last year I had no idea. No idea this is how it would end up. I usually think 'where will I be in a year' whenever it is but I don't remember at all, what I thought then. The first two months in Philadelphia were the happiest. April and may. One time in line at a thrift store Zachary said something about how we were being annoying and laughing and that it was good we didn't have friends, because they would be annoyed by how in love we were. That was the day we bought the matching gigantic t-shirts, floor-length pink 'hers' and blue 'his' t-shirts, that we rarely wore, that he was wearing the night in late march this year, the night before the week we spent together before moving things to storage units and parents' houses and new places and eventually it started becoming now.

MAY 4, 2013

12:31PM: colin knocked on my door. i had been recording an audio file of me reading old things i've written for a website that solicited me for an audio submission of some kind. worried colin could hear me talking, i don't think he can. covered up 'old things,' spread all over the bed, took a few extra seconds to get to door. colin gave me a newspaper and we talked about an irish music festival and my cats and school a little and he left. i stood in front of the mirror. pupils look huge from adderall/concerta, wonder if they're noticeably huge. studied them in the mirror.

heard another knock i thought i could be imagining. stood still in front of mirror. a few seconds later i heard colin's voice say 'megan?' i went to the door. he asked if i wanted a lamp. i said 'i don't not want a lamp, if there's a lamp. i mean, yeah i'll take a lamp.' he went to get it. looked at my stuffed animals on the bed and my…just…it doesn't quite look like 'adult' decorations. thought 'oh no, he…knows…he knows i'm a big baby.'

the lamp is cool. he didn't remember where he got it. he said 'the bottom lights up, like for a night-light' a few times. he reminds me of someone in a samuel beckett play. he asked me if i knew about a restaurant and said 'i gotta invite, i mean introduce you to some of the people on the floor, we'll all go' and looked down the hall. followed his eyes and thought 'invite vs. introduce.' i said i was doing a thing, helping my friend film a video tonight. he said 'take it easy.'

here is what happened after waldbaum's last night/this morning:

- unpacked items from ikea and waldbaum's, sort of broke shower curtain rod i think. the curtain i bought requires rings so i made rings out of wire. i have pliers and wire for some reason. the wire is of 'paper-clip-thickness.'

- cleaned floor, scrubbed toilet, did dishes, cleaned cat box, looked for AA batteries for swiffer in 'technology drawer,' thought 'look in 'memories drawer' for content for the 'gabby gabby lucy shaw self yelp story'

- responded to gabby gabby email with links to mdmafilms passwords and told her i was working on the story from now until it's done

- read through things i've written saved by my parents from 1991-1996, then journals from 1999-2009…felt….personal hell…it's all the same shit, same shit as this one journal is funny and from 2007 and seems to be exclusively thoughts/ drawings i made while high, like every day almost. thoughts seem similar to things i've thought on mushrooms and DMT but less comprehensible/ less funny/people would 'understand' less, i think

in that journal i had a lease for an apartment in chicago with a co-worker/ friend but then we went…the friend…something happened, he wasn't pre-pared for me knowing people there already, we fought about stupid stuff…i broke my end of the lease, think we're still friends

i had forgotten i had done this thing where i filled up five notebooks in an effort to 'get me out of depression'

like each notebook would be a step forward

the colors went from darkest (black) to lightest (light green)

they devolve into driving directions at the end, some are not all the way full

1:26PM: keep hearing this whining, half-door half-human sound coming from the hallway.

have plans to eat mushrooms and help film a funny video with zachery wood today. feel incapable of interaction and like mental state would not currently be good for mushrooms. kept wanting to 'go home' last night, to 'home' i don't know, like neither of my parents' and not here, very real/ intense urges to be in 'home i don't know.'

e-cigarette smoking is giving me a dry cough. have been smoking consis-tently, since i bought it day before yesterday. but other than cough body feels fine and it doesn't smell. can discern when it tastes/smells 'electric-y,' like a hot outlet or something. thought i was losing interest in them but then put in a new cartridge and 'boop boop ba doodoo.'

i have 30mg adderall left, feel like since i'm not smoking real cigarettes i'm being a little healthier, i could allow myself the adderall if it meant i would really do things.

this seems like hell

there is no escaping the hell of yourself

all of those journals…

there are 15-20 journals, most are completely or almost completely full, some big in size, from 2004-2009

all the same shit

same shit as now

i'm saying all of the same things

same things slightly different words/circumstances

what is there to do

should i start doing things that are extremely unlike me now, just for…variety…i don't know

i don't know if i want to be not-me

just seems hellish, a hellish amount of records, plus consider the liveblog, plus my gmail account, plus four hard drives full of video files and other things

how is this all still going on

i used to 'wax existential' or whatever, the thing i did in my book, like, i'd enjoy kind of marveling at 'how much further could i take this thought, do i really think this'

now i feel a new level of 'i can't believe it's still like this' almost horror

not being…'cute'…not trying to be anything except clear about what this feeling is

seems like buddha-like people, like, enlightened people feel the same thing i'm feeling but they get joy out of it

it feels horrible to me

horrible and exactly equal horrible consequence of it not being there

here is a moment documenting me being as close to the 50/50 'want to live/ want to die' line while still being alive

<1% is keeping me on 'want to live,' the 1% is just me defaulting to this/ not wanting to exert effort into dying

thought 'if i had more adderall i'd probably feel motivated to die' as a surprise joke (i don't mean that)

wish there was a pause button for when you want to be dead for just a little bit

wait that's what sleep is

maybe

maybe i just need to sleep

i don't sleep…really…much…in 2013 i have definitely slept the least out of any year

wish i had been measuring exactly, this entire time

it is 1:37PM now

1:55PM: texted zachery wood i was flaking on mushrooms hangout tomorrow. mountain of…just wanting to run away from everything, i am a child, i need to grow up. how is every single network password-protected, there is always something.

1:57PM: put phone face-down to avert zachery's 'reaction to disappointing text' text ooooof ooof oof oof oof oof

1:58PM: phone went buzz buzz zachery w fast response, sympathetic, good he can do tomorrow phew. motivation for today: get it all done today so it can be fun tomorrow

3:40PM: why do the cats want me around. i get why i want them but why do they like me. that's so nice. it might just be for food. they don't have a choice.

6:48PM: i did it, i did something i liked. for the website that solicited me. the vocal thing. recorded myself talking non-stop for three minutes. as i was talking i decided to just keep going, like how i'm keeping going with liveblog for as long as i can. just talked non-stop for as long as i could.

decided to do an extended 'personal keepsake' version. talked for a little over an hour. i cry for the last 30 minutes or so, maintaining constant/non-stop talking. think i took a few accidental two-to-five second breaks from talking via sobbing. uploaded file to meganassboyle soundcloud account.

7PM: shittalked sam cooke's movie on twitter (which he'd asked people to do), crying a little less, suckling e-cigarette.

8:43PM: room darkening. switched from 'java jolt' to 'menthol' flavor e-cigarette.

9:12PM: peed. put on jeans from 2005, blue & white striped dolman-sleeved shirt that tao said was 'nylon magazine-like' in an airport in 2010. washed face. have plans to go to dunkin donuts…update this…don't care enough, so far…

laid face-down on bed and shirley laid on my back

then shirley laid on my legs when i turned on my side

shirley purring the whole time

9:53PM: made spinach/banana smoothie. tweeted a little. smoothie was so cold and good.

10:50–11:59PM: tweeted, sort of talked with mira/mira's mom via twitter, thought 'joey buzz 'got' what i was saying in tweet mira also 'got' that i thought 'only a specific kind of person would 'get' this because it's written so unclearly due to the thing it's about,' watched TV, ate 2mg xanax and leftover kale salad from the night zachary was here, half a chocolate bar, drank two beers, changed into pajamas.

MAY 5, 2013

12–1:[something]AM: did the same things as above, i wasn't watching the clock. knew i fell asleep after 1AM because i set my alarm for 10AM thinking 'yeah, nine hours, that's enough, plus then you can have a 'morning."

[middle of the night sometime]: woke craving food, ate an orange

10AM: alarm went off, hit snooze a lot

1PM: woke, thinking about the dream. remembered the orange from last night. it's good that i've only bought fruits and vegetables, when you only buy healthy things you're forced to just eat them. text from joey buzz about BBQ today at 3PM. texts from zachery w asking if i felt okay to hang out today.

1:11–1:38PM: made spinach/banana/orange smoothie, cleaned cat box, swept floor, did dishes, made makeshift obstruction thing in front of the door alvie likes to bang so he can hide in…the door under the sink…the banging is so loud. started to write 'things to do this week' in dad's 'action day 2013' calendar he bought for me, then thought it would be better to write in this. feel sick, facially sick. like throat/nose sick.

1:46PM: filling in 'gaps' of this from last night until now. drinking smoothie. it's good with the orange in it.

2:00PM: shirley purring and laying a few inches from my head. experiencing facial sickness. smoothie will help, i feel. have been taking an extra lot of vitamins/zeolite/noopept past few days. coaxed alvie and shirley onto bed with me.

2:11PM: looking at the rockaway newspaper colin gave me, 'the wave.' the good-natured efforts of 'the wave.' what they write about. someone quoted the ramones. remembered something about a punk house being on rockaway beach somewhere. thought 'yeah…80's punks, they did it here, they…somehow i can do this, if people who felt…maybe they didn't feel as bad as me though.' thought 'people don't believe i feel bad because i laugh and make jokes,' then 'joey buzz feels as bad as me maybe,' then 'i'm just thinking that because of joey ramone and the other interactions with joey buzz.' wonder how his ketamine study thing went.

on the second page i saw something called 'Boyleing Points' by kevin boyle. the first sentence is 'I've got nothing to say.' seems…damn. then he says

'Unlike most weeks, I'm not wasting 500 words saying nothing. Nobody swerved a car at me (so it's your fault).'

2:17PM: shit i missed a 'beach clean-up' event yesterday. i would've liked that, helped someone. done that instead of what i did.

2:44PM: a $12.50/hour secretary position is available. ad says 'visit your new company at callahead.com.' it's a port-a-potty company. you bet your ass i am applying.

2:55–4:47PM: looked at internet on phone, re-scheduled plans w/zachery to film video and do mushrooms thing today, showered, dressed, debated taking xanax, ate 15mg adderall while walking to dunkin donuts and huffing on e-cigarette. felt 'better than' people who i thought looked heavier than me (like i was beating them in a game or something, not like, morally/otherwise 'better,' i don't like thoughts like this but i still have them).

4:57PM: heard/peripherally saw a figure behind me say 'dodomeedledododo' really fast and i jumped. i said 'i'm sorry, you startled me' and looked, thinking it would be zachery, but it was a short grinning man holding open a bookbag, offering me CDs.

5:12PM: at dunkin donuts, waiting for zachery. table of three high school-aged girls in front of me at dunkin donuts. one said 'so we were in…the bronx.' they are eating rainbow sherbet. (this is also a baskin robbins).

5:30PM: surprised all of this updating/uploading of things is going so smoothly and zachery w isn't here yet (he said something reassuring in his last text about how he would prepare for if i wasn't ready when he arrived/would bring a 'get-out-of-hell-free card' and look at things, still would rather not inconvenience). usually if i flake on things people seem upset or feign 'being mad' or are actually a little mad/disappointed. filed/neutrally processed zachery w as 'favorable: does not express disappointment at flaking, seems understanding of 'personal hell' things' yesterday, which i think made me more likely to follow through with hanging out today.

5:49PM: zachery w texted 'will you bring me a donut.'

7:28pm: ate/halved mushrooms, saw mayonnaise thing out the window, said 'I'm going to take notes in iPhone' on walk to tree, asked zachery when the halving of mushrooms happened he said '7:30, no 7:28'

7:39pm: walking to riis tree, using cr instead, mushroms

7:59: mushrooms bigtime, watching z on tree, seems extreme meh misguided

8:12: how is he not feeling them at all

I feel like notw

11:20pm: looked at phone for first time

here is what i remember:

decided to chop zachery's mushroom chocolate thing in crumbles to divide it more equally, then walk around outside to find a tree to fall out of

trees seemed hard to find, we saw my car, i said 'let's go to jacob riis park' and drove us there

i started to feel effected by mushrooms while driving, like, being confused about where to park and, like, saying free-associating things and mostly 'i feel mushrooms'

i parked on a residential street near a marshy-like area with trees that seemed insane to me...there was a sign that said 'we know how to do it' or something that we passed, walking to the trees

i said 'i feel more concentrated on finding trees for you to fall out of than you' and kept telling zachery to try to fall out of non-tree things like grass, bushes, sticks, etc. and thought it would be really funny. i said 'it feels like the trees you could jump out of are almost in vision but they keep running away.'

there were airplanes flying near JFK and i remember saying...something... about the planes, like i didn't understand how they were flying like that. zachery said a kind of long sentence about how he thought i was going to say something else about the airplanes, like the depth of the airplanes in the sky. i felt 'dread' like 'oh no, i'm going to have to explain things.' think we were both saying 'i feel mushrooms.'

filmed zachery falling out of maybe two trees. with each fall he said he felt mushrooms effects less, the fall was throwing mushrooms out of his head.

i tried falling out of a tree to see if this would lessen the effects of mushrooms. it did. uploaded video of this to vimeo account.

zachery said he didn't feel things anymore and i was starting to feel like things were harder to put into language, like it was suddenly coming on very strong to me. we stood by a marshy area by the planes. i said 'look it's the sign again, it feels different this time,' pointing at the 'we know how to do it' sign.' a flock of birds passed really low and i thought something dumb like 'birds. huh-huh.' zachery said 'i wish they'd do it again.' we were saying things about how the birds were police, i think. i asked if zachery could drive us to my apartment.

when we got to the car i said 'i just felt an extreme bleakness that we wouldn't be able to talk about anything but [something i now forget, it was a normal/'non-mushrooms' thing, about locating the car].'

in the car zachery said 'how are you going to write all of this down?' i typed the 8:12 update on my phone and felt suddenly struck by 'when i type i am addressing a different kind of audience, there are other people out there who read things, it's a different 'me' who types than the 'me' sort of talking in the car right now' and like, afraid of that 'me,' the 'typing me,' like it was my enemy or something, or just something i had no idea how to interact with and didn't expect. then i felt afraid of the 'me talking' me, and the apartment we were going to, and that i had no idea what we were going to do for the next however many hours, and that this person wasn't feeling the same things i was.

zachery asked me to try to explain why it felt weird to type. i think i was saying things like 'i can't explain it' or 'it's just...i can't...there's no way to say it right now' and 'i think i need to lie down.' zachery said things like 'i'm disappointed i'm not feeling it as much as you' and i didn't know how to respond. he asked why i wanted to lie down. i felt unable to talk, and like there was maybe something socially inappropriate about my desire to lie down. as we walked to my apartment i said 'how the hell did i end up here, i was just at my mom's house, that was earlier, now i'm here' and felt nonspecific terror about what i was walking into. zachery kind of chuckled i think, and repeated what i said in a way i interpreted as 'friendly,' but i felt very 'alien.' zachery said things about how he liked it when we were walking towards the trees and how he wished he had eaten more mushrooms. i said 'you should eat more mushrooms.'

in memory there is a maybe inaccurately exaggerated extended period of zachery asking what i was feeling and me trying to articulate 'i forgot how to type, writing feels scary,' combined with all of the other background factors adding to the strangeness i felt about my current predicament (like 'what is my life, is this my apartment, what is an apartment for, what is the goal of writing, how can i make sense of any of this, is anything i think related to anything i do, how can i increase the relevance, where am i in general, where was i before this moment, was anything before this, do i have a choice about any of this'), and like there was nothing i could say but that, but zachery seemed to want me to say more. i felt afraid i would be stuck in this feeling of not being able to communicate myself around someone who wanted to know what was going on with me, and that this would continue for hours, maybe indefinitely.

when we entered my apartment all my lights were off. the sun was almost gone. my room looked how it normally looks, but i was seeing this neon 3-D visual overlay of tiny, colorless, perfectly-sized, uniformly-oriented 'grid dots' (a little smaller than the dots on an intercom speaker, both stationary and synchronized with my vision in a way that produced a not-unpleasant, silently/languagelessly 'giggly' effect of feeling 'trapped' in my visual field) behind everything. have experienced this once before on mushrooms, in 2011, for maybe only a few seconds or minutes. felt momentarily distracted from 'pressure to explain how i was feeling' by the extreme visuals. i think i said 'i'm experiencing visual things, i don't usually experience visual things.' i tried to explain the visual thing and zachery said 'i just see shadowy shapes' or something (later i think i said, maybe insensitively, 'you were just seeing normal stuff').

felt better after turning on a light. i felt extremely disoriented and like my fixation on the pattern might be boring at best, or a marker of the start of my permanent future lifelong descent into insanity at worst. i said 'i need to lie down,' and laid on my bed, wearing my coat. felt afraid to take off my coat. sometimes opened my eyes to see zachery cutting up more mushrooms on the cutting board.

when my eyes were closed i saw an intricate, bright geometric DMT-like pattern of mostly neon pink, defined shapes that seemed to be 'intelligently swirling.' when i opened my eyes the pillows around me looked just as 'unreal' as the thing behind my eyes. i said 'i think i want it to be over.' think no one said anything for a while, then zachery said something about how he hesitated eating the mushrooms he had just cut. i felt suddenly aware of zachery again, aware of my foreign ability to comprehend the phenomenon of 'zachery,' and bizarrely aware of how there weren't many places to sit in my apartment. felt like i had no...there was no 'me' to... this seems hard to describe. i just felt extremely dissociated from everything i was telling myself i should be experiencing in a normal social context. i said 'i'm not being a good host' or something. zachery said 'do you think if you could just stop thinking 'i'm not being a good host' and enjoy what you're feeling it would be okay.' i reacted with irritation, then felt irritated at myself for being irritated. i said 'yes of course, yeah, i'm enjoying it,' because he couldn't know the thing going on with me that was...it was an autopilot thing i didn't even feel when i said it. this seemed to 'equalize' our levels, or something, to me, and i began to enjoy myself and enjoy zachery's presence.

after that the experience was much funnier and lighthearted, but i'm tired of typing, for now. we tried to do a yoga dvd and invented an elaborate origin story about the universe, using an analogy of the dvd, objects surrounding where we stood in my apartment, and what we could see of the rooms behind windows of the building next door.

MAY 6, 2013

2:12am: looked at phone again, 2mg Xanax for sleep

7am: woke peed ate 1mg Xanax for sleep

1–2:00pm: woke and wanted to continue sleeping. zachery couldn't find wallet, asked if I wanted to go to dunkin donuts, said I wanted to sleep and offered him red bull, ate 'sugar donut' from yesterday in bed, he fed me spoon thing of kratom (have tried once/am curious, he eats daily), he found wallet, walked to dunkin donuts, large coffee, talked about tryoto-phobia and funny things, made plans to film him falling out of more trees in central park tomorrow.

3:09pm: at post office, cop behind me in line excitedly described seeing a man in women's clothes to an unclear audience. held door for him as we exited. i told him about a man in a clown outfit laying on the ground in union square. he said 'that's what life is today, there's nothing else to do.'

3:47pm: walking to head shop that sells kratom, I think. Stopped to pet a cat almost identical to Brad the cat for some time. Fatter than brad and less sick-looking eyes.

3:55pm: queens smoke shop employee asked what kratom was and I said 'an herbal…thing.' he said 'like medicine?' I said 'like, um. An herbal thing.'

4:03pm: driving to other head shop thing on long beach…seems…mis-take, to be doing this maybe, but I'm already committed. 26mins away.

4:21pm: at bridge toll I went in the…it didn't say 'all passes,' thought that would include ezpass but no. Backed out of lane, no honks, people seemed understanding. Said 'I thought it included ezpass' and toll booth lady seemed understanding. Gave her $2. She told me to have a good day.

4:33pm: Zachery texted that he got hit by a car but it didn't hurt. I'm in long beach, searching for kratom. Feeling a crushing empty thing, re the choices presented to me, endless possibilities for what I could be doing right now and it's this. Listening to young family. Skimmed Zachary's (ex-boyfriend, not mushrooms friend Zachery) interview with Jamie. Saw no gchats from him.

4:59pm: kratom place doesn't seem there, like, the building is not there. Talked with dad on phone. I am pulled over on some residential street next to a house where a boy is shooting baskets alone.

5:05pm: called macmedics. my computer will be ready tomorrow. tried to take a picture of boy playing basketball.

5:11pm: went to 'jack's pizza' place, then deli. both no restrooms. felt 'looked at.' now peeing at 'mar di tierra' restaurant. feel like vincent gallo in 'buffalo 66' when he couldn't pee.

5:14pm: fighting urge to treat myself with pizza slice from 'jack's [seemingly restroom-less] pizza.' Will feel worse if I eat it. Going to…Jesus… everywhere where there's internet seems so far away. Feel far away from everything in general, things I felt yesterday. Keep thinking 'I want to go home, I've made a mistake' but I don't know what 'home' I want.

5:19pm: surprised 'Hollywood nights' by Bon Seger is on my phone. Skipped seven songs that all sounded too painful to hear, via memories of listening. Stopped at a train track. Long beach or wherever I am looks like town in Ohio where Tao and I got tattoos in 2010.

5:23pm: damn I like the words to 'hollywood nights,' haha. I like how…it sounds parodic of itself but…I believe it, the intention before the parody, or…it was made to sound like this er…nevermind.

6:11pm: dreading the image of me in a library on ritalin (zachery gave me) and adderall, trying to remember details of mushrooms hangout to retroactively update with whatever you've just read. Confident I'll remember 'the good parts.' Can already feel myself getting into a 'writing hold,' like it wants to take over me right now and have me write all the details, but I want to chill out, lay down, eat pizza, watch TV. Chill out so I can feel better in the future. Recharge things. Okay. It's okay.

6:48PM: parked outside dunkin donuts to milk their internet from my car. zachery texted. ordered 'grandma pizza' and a caesar salad from a place called 'plum tomatoes' to celebrate not thinking about this anymore.

6:58PM: zachery texted he is interested in helping me not flake on 'filming falling out of trees not on mushrooms' hangout tomorrow. motivated to not flake.

6:59-11:59PM: did not update.

MAY 7, 2013

9:54am: meeting zachery in greenpoint at 11am. Have been hitting snooze. Think I ate 4-6mg Xanax, pint of hagen daz 'white raspberry truffle,' five valerian root capsules last night.

Drank 8.4oz sf red bull and a spinach/frozen banana/orange smoothie. Took b-vitamin, zeolite, 'brain/memory' tonic, zeolite, magnesium. Fed Alvie and Shirley. Now Alvie is snuggling in my 'space left by fetal position,' Shirley is snuggling at shins.

10:58am: on traffic on bridge. Still tired. Confusion with owner/landlord, meeting him tonight. Whatever I wish sam pink was next to me that's all no homo I still whatever whatever yeah think about that homo a lot as if it's not obvious oh well. Yet another passing desire!

11:33pm: depressed. Xanax carb sleep aid beer overload. Ate 20mg Ritalin. Traffic terrible.

11:38am: want to write 'everything I remember about the KGB reading'

12:00pm: parked on kent st and manhattan.

12:02pm: feel like I'm walking alone in Spain, the day I wore the blue shorts and white top and Tao was promoting 'Taipei' and I think was upset with me. It was after we had decided we'd eat whatever we wanted for the rest of the trip. Resigned. I was on Xanax in a park, doing pushups on concrete fixtures.

12:49pm: zachery gave me kratom coffee mixture and kratom in bag. We gonna take the train to central park. He is filling water bottle. He works in a young person Brooklyn motivated people studio space thing. One step towards Lena Dunham land.

2:17pm: have been filming zachery falling out of low-to-the-ground trees.

2:30pm: zachery fixed my phone, it can take pictures again. Sitting on rock.

2:31-5:20pm: walked around central park, recorded videos, talked re relationships, went to whole foods, vague/confusing/funny conversation about identity, took crowded e then g trains to zachery's office, peed, stood in office door. Alluded to omelette joke from mushrooms night, that I have been secretly resenting him for wanting to order an omelette, me covering up my omelette rage is responsible for every minor miscommunication we've had. Joke seemed to take on a new quality of 'I'm not sure what the thing metaphorically in place of the omelette is, is lack of metaphor the new 'omelette,' that there is no thing?' Asked if I could buy Ritalin, seemed hard to work out details. Zachery asked to kiss me. Felt my face immediately react. Said something like 'oh, oh no, I don't think so, I'm not, like, anything right now.' maybe apologized. I think I apologized. I said 'I like you' and felt aware of this having maybe the opposite effect, as it's understood that we like each other/have had fun together, saying 'I like you' in this context seemed to point out a new imbalance or something. Zachery reminded me of Niles Krane, Niles Krane reaction kind of. When it was quiet I said 'I'll have Verizon on Friday, then I'll be around more, to hang out more, I'll be more available' not knowing if any of that would be true... why...uncontrollably. Walked out of building feeling a small sinking.

5:37pm: scooped four plastic lids of kratom into mouth and 'with great futile purpose' organized things in car while listening to dancehall station, taking a long time to plan route home and make sure everything is 'in order,' buildings around me are tall

6:04pm: zachery texted that he was curious about how he misinterpreted me/could think I wanted to kiss too, texted this to zachery:

> 'Re social animal misinterpreting: I felt aware the other night that maybe you wanted to kiss me and I didn't, thought maybe you had interest, so I was thinking things today like 'I wonder if he thinks this is more than platonic,' so maybe you picked up on that/weren't 'wrong' in identifying some kind of subtext. Also I see how it could be confusing because I like talking with you and maybe [something about how I don't hang out with people much but the last person I hung out with a lot was my ex-boyfriend, unsure about this 'brackets' part]. Seems 'full of myself'/presumptuous or maybe insensitive or something, to say this, I'm just wanting to resolve confusion. Also if you don't want this part to be on liveblog I understand 100%/let me know what you feel comfortable with me including. I like hanging out with you a lot and had fun today, sorry if I sent mixed signals, hope this doesn't negatively affect how you feel about future interactions'

6:46pm: arrived home, unpacked whole foods things, peed, cleaned cat box. Texted Danny (owns my apartment) I was here and he said he'd be over in 30 minutes

7:15pm: zachery seems okay/accepting of text. Heated two pizza pieces in toaster oven to allow for more storage space in fridge, knew if I heated pizza I wouldn't want to put effort into liveblog, would want to 'fail' again tonight and drink beer and watch TV or read or do nothing. Opened beer. Took out trash. Lost interest in pizza when I was inside again but there the pizza was.

7:25pm: wrote date on a new check for Danny (landlord, not owner, actually, or something). Chewed gum so he won't smell beer breath. Waited outside by the ocean for a while, smoking e-cigarette. Woman held the door for me and I walked inside. Sat on steps and filled in the rest of the check except for Danny's last name. Went to hold the door for a woman with a stroller and she said 'it's really not necessary' more times than I think normal people would've responded to. Sat on steps and watched her walk inside.

7:51pm: resigned to Danny not coming.

7:56pm: mark came, fixed oven. Will be back tomorrow around 10am-12pm to fix the closet. He talks to me like he knows me. I like him. We talk easily about cats. Guillermo is his cat, who looks like Shirley with less hair, who is an outdoor cat.

8:16pm: Danny came. His name is Durim. He said he likes to collect rent in-person, so he can look at the ocean. Thick accent, big smile.

8:48pm: too relaxed on bed to get second beer. I want to apply to callahead tomorrow.

8:55pm: here is how it went, exactly, I really liked how this one went. I searched 'wine' on the maps part of my phone. Then I touched a phone number. Then here is how it went:

> Woman: harbor wine?
>
> Me: what time do you guys close tonight?
>
> Woman: ten.
>
> Me: thank you.

That's it. That's all. No hello or goodbye. I liked it so much. No bullshit. This is motivating me to give them business tonight. After I drink another beer. I want to sleep so long. Cradled...want to be cradled by a yacht. Not a yacht, something with the magnitude of a yacht. What it must feel like to be on a yacht. Want that to cradle me.

9:48pm: tweeted things at Mira, sent tao $45 in exchange for $50 tomorrow. Wanted to watch some/any David lynch movie. Looked on old hard drive. There are all of these movies of late 2011. Watching movie I made of Zachary and me on 11/27/11, 12 days after we had started hanging out. We were in Vermont. Jesus. So sad so sad so sad. We went to Vermont for fun. Neither of us had jobs. This shitty motel in Vermont for no reason. It was so good. I've had three beers but. Remember Zachary saying 'I like your character in the film' and me lying about filming us at the end. We look so young, somehow. We're not that much younger. I just said 'I really really very much like kissing you' and a little later Zachary said something about waking me up with a kiss, like 'I'd wake you up with a kiss,' but the music (an atlas sound song I had forgotten until now and associate strongly with this moment) obscured our words.

10:10pm: drunk and watching stuff on old hard drives, beginning pts of two relationships recorded, drunker & drunker, drinking feels 'kinder' than drugs.

11:13pm: heating pizza square in toaster oven. I'm doing one at a time. I feel 'at home' tonight. Drinking whiskey. Reading 'every hour of every day sept 2011' first version of liveblog. Newscaster said 'special needs' just now. I am heating one pizza piece at a time so as to discourage overeating but know I already have and will do more tonight. That feels good. I feel good being drunk. For the first time here I feel not confused about whether I belong here, maybe, first time I remember anyway.

11:52pm: watching jimmy kimmel, he looks skinny, called Zacky, hanging out tomorrow I think, wish he was here right now.

MAY 8, 2013

12:24am: ate 1mg xanax, thought negative yelp review i was reading was for actor coming onstage for kimmell show

Unsure of when I went to sleep, I ate the other pizza half

7:[something]am: woke, ate 1mg Xanax and bit frozen banana then ate orange instead

10:45am: mark came, fixed closet thing, funny talk. Have been putting away clothes, listening to records, drinking kratom-heavy smoothie. Tentative plans to hang w/Zachary tonight. Feel like he'll cancel.

3:23pm: Donna (insurance lady) sounds increasingly disheartened with me on the phone.

Plan: shower, print resume at library, apply to callahead, go back to library and use internet to update liveblog.

4:58pm: Zachary cancelled, is making mackerel ('a two or three syllabled fish,' we discussed) with Jamie tonight. Going to library now. Wish it were Friday night and I hadn't gone to ikea yet and felt different.

5:51pm: queens peninsula library was a 'portable,' the other one was still under construction. Man who gave me laptop to borrow said something about his leg cramps. I said 'like a Charlie horse?' and he said 'yeah' and I said 'I just stomp them out.'

5:52pm: uninterested in updating this. Going to push through. Uninterested in my life right now. Oddly felt more interested at mom's apartment, the week or so ago when I was on a lot of adderall, transcribing the crack night with Mira and Sam, know I felt really bad that night (not the crack night, the transcribing night) but I like it more than now.

5:57pm: memory of being in the Toronto airport eating/choking on an apple in line to a flight to Spain I think.

7:22pm: man in deli said 'ladies first.' sitting in car now. Treating my ass to a hot nasty Reuben, salt & vinegar chips, 1mg Xanax, coconut water. 'waiting on the world to change' by John Mayer played annoyingly symbolically.

7:46pm: read Sam pink things while eating the hot nasty and thinking 'when comes the part where he's been in my backseat the whole time and knifes me like in 'goodfellas" before he got to a similar part. Sandwich stopped tasting as good after a while. I'm driving to ikea again.

7:51pm: ran over a tree, seems okay

9:35pm: bought things from ikea. Biting frozen treats in car. Parked next to car far from store to call wine stores to see if they'd be open. Realized I have whiskey at home. I want to be drunk. I'm eating an orange chocolate thing, very thirsty.

9:39pm: no desire to update this, the <1% of 'want to update' putting me slightly over the 50/50 apathy line. Have thought 'fuck the liveblog' and 'huh liveblog huh' today a few times.

9:40-11:59PM: did not update.

MAY 9, 2013

12–2:45AM: have been watching TV in bed.

2:46am: confusion at pickles & pies with man who seems to dislike customers. Back at apt. Afrin before I left.

3:21AM: watching 'hanging up' on 'cozitv.' drank and ate four tortilla hummuses trhee high life's (lives?!!>?) 2" mm whiskey 1mg xanny

9:20AM: looked at clock fell back asleep

11:30AM: woke to jackhammer noises.

12:19AM: made kale cantaloupe kratom smoothie gonna nail three pictures to wall then pick up my 'machine' from macmedics in maryland.

1:33pm: told off gynecologist. hung up on her. Shaking. I said 'you can't just go around telling people they might have cancer and then that they seem perfect then that they might have cancer again if you really dont know. You can't just throw people around like that.'

1:36pm: there is a possibility my car has been towed Jesus I can't see it I know I parked it all the way at the end of this road. Taking off sunglasses because that might do something

1:39pm: car was there Jesus thank you

1:48pm: behind a school bus. It says 'drivers wanted.' I could do that.

1:53pm: insult I should've dissed gynecologist with: 'did you decide to become a gynecologist because when you're born a cunt, you get to skip medical school?'

Er

'Did you even need to go to school to study vaginas'

'Did they let you bypass gynecology school because you're already a cunt?'

Or just…well. Simply, 'cunt'

3:17pm: pulled over at Walt Whitman travel stop for peeing and red bull and gas. This is where I pulled over on October 26 or whenever it was before hurricane sandy, I left new York because I heard about the hurricane and I had a flight to Argentina coming out of Baltimore and thought I would get stuck in new York. Then…it seemed clear that I had missed the flight, somehow, but I went back to NYC after the hurricane to hang out at Gian's with Jordan and Mallory and Tao and Katie on Halloween. Yeah, then I was driving back to Baltimore after that, and I pulled over here, and called Zachary and asked if he wanted to get lunch because I was passing through Philadelphia. Then I just started living there again. Then I stopped responding to emails from Jordan and Sam. So here is where I made the mistake on October 26: somewhere near the stall I'm currently peeing in. I lied I've been done peeing for a while.

3:21pm: exited stall holding keys by biting, for 'bridle-like' variety.

3:25pm: in line to buy water red bull and a new jersey shirt. I like the color. It's only $12. Seems funny to have a souvenir of this moment. 'The moment I remembered something I now regret not-doing or doing oct. 26, 2012.' Standing near a book that says 'have you felt like giving up lately?'

3:32pm: reciept flew out of van ahead of me in the gas line. The gas-filler man chased it, smiling. Beaming. He signaled for me to move my car to where the van had been, continuing to beam. Asked him how he was doing and he said 'really well today, thank you,' in a way that suggested he…I don't know if he's always doing this well, or like, if he thinks he needs to act a certain way for customers, but either way I believed him when he said he was doing well, and I believed his gratitude when he said 'thanks,' and I wished I had more to offer him.

3:39pm: eating 10mg opana for the hell of it. I am an hour 45 minutes from macmedics. They close at 5pm. Farting nasty egg smell farts. Trying to chew the opana with front teeth but it's 'gummy' and a little slimy and 'highly solid,' also tasteless.

3:47pm: the opanas are still dissolving, coaxing with teeth still, flavorless and gummy as ever. What a. Huh. What a thing.

3:50pm: they have a chia seed effect. Gelatinous membrane. They started smaller and pale orange.

3:53pm: swallowed opanas. Macmedics opens at 8:30, I could…Jesus, I would be risking missing Verizon if I got the computer tomorrow morning instead…if gynecologist hadn't called goddamnit.

3:56pm: now there is an accident.

3:57pm: 'pictures of success' played on iPod shuffle, feels comforting.

4:03pm: voicemail message began 'it's nicolle, from callahead? the port-a-potty place where you applied to work yesterday,' as if this was something i could've forgotten. They want to interview me tomorrow at 5pm. I have plans to meet with Jaime (Zachery's friend/roommate, not Zachary's ex-girlfriend/roommate of the same name) about being in 'point break live' around 4pm. Maybe Verizon will come early. Maybe I will make it to macmedics in time today.

4:22pm: called dad to see if he could go to macmedics for me, no. Called mom, who was eager/excited to help in way that made my chest big. Big and beaming towards mom, like the gas-filler man possessed my heart. Running on a little treadmill inside my heart, wearing his light blue gloves, beaming and saluting me. Mom and the gas man.

4:27pm: can't believe Callahead wants to interview me. Fortune.

4:53pm: Mom said the macmedics guy said he'd stay late for her. What if he's the face mole macmedics hottie and my mom seduces him

5:12pm: mom made it to macmedics. I am also on the macmedics road. Tried to sing earlier but voice seems 'shot' from e-cigarettes maybe. Have been smoking probably 75-80% of the day, every day, 'burning through' cartridges. Don't feel shitty body things or chest tightness like with normal cigarettes.

5:16pm: mom called to say it worked, the guy was there, can't believe it worked and they stayed open. Now my drive down here wasn't 'misguided shithead' style hooray. She is calling again

5:24pm: entered macmedics area at the same time mom was exiting, pulled over in an office center thingy and mom gave me computer. Mom wants to get some kind of cream from Lord & Taylor and we talked about eating together at the mall near here. I said 'what about Clyde's [restaurant on the lake where we used to go when I was little, have a strong memory of going there July 4, 2007 with mom and telling her how depressed I felt, like 'why am I here' things, had started feeling those things strongly that summer, then crying in the car and later going to a 4th of July party in college park md and stopping on the way there to watch fireworks on the road, had never seen that. The next day mom and dad and me went on a ten-day cruise to Alaska]?' she thought a moment and said something about money. I said 'maybe we shouldn't.' she said 'no, no, yeah let's go to Clyde's' making a face like 'it makes more sense to rob this bank,' like 'it makes more sense to conspiratorially do the evil thing'

Craving hummus tortilla bad but also envisioning salmon on a plate, getting excited

5:50pm: on the same road I was on the day in April I passed coca cola drive. Practicing what I'll say at interview tomorrow.

6:00pm: mom called with Lord & Taylor face cream/time update. We are going to eat outside. Feel almost boringly 'sane'/normal, typing this and everything today.

6:08pm: arrived early. I used to try to swim in this fountain when I was little. Also feed ducks, we would feed ducks here. My phone wants to change things to 'dicks' and 'sucks' and 'fucks.'

6:13pm: went back to car, used face towel, got jacket. Nervous about getting table for some reason.

6:23pm: difficult to maneuver ice cube into mouth, needed straw to help.

6:28pm: table next to me said things about it starting to rain and a few moments later a waiter said something about water dripping from an air conditioner.

6:33pm: ordered glass of chianti. Mom has been referred to as 'my guest.'

8:22pm: wish I had been recording the whole thing. Mom is so funny. We were throwing down a lot of Lorrie Moore style puns. There was a sad thing behind all of it also. At the end she said I had always reminded her of Diane Keaton (who she reminds me of). She watched a Woody Allen documentary where Diane Keaton said she met Woody and thought 'I want to make him fall in love with me' but she never thought he loved her. I asked mom if he was in love with her. She said 'it didn't seem like it, really.' I asked why. She described a behind-the-scenes cut from 'sleeper' where Diane Keaton is talking with a Yiddish accent and Woody Allen can't stop laughing, then said 'he said 'she was the funniest woman I ever met.''

8:29pm: picked nose with thumb while eyes locked on distant staring point. rolled down windows and thought 'you stopped typing about moments like this.'

9:06pm: did the 'no you go first' dance with older lady behind me in line at roots natural food market (bought shampoo).

10-11:59pm: watched billy eichner 'billy on the street' with mom. Laughed a lot.

MAY 10, 2013

12–1:30am: still watching billy on the street.

1:31–4am: sat in room and transferred files from dad's computer to mine. Mom stood in doorway and said 'i just have to know if you've opened your packages on your bed.' she had bought me my perfume I've been out of for a long time, Marc Jacobs. I wear it because she gave her bottle to me a couple years ago, not liking how it smelled on her. Sometimes she buys it for me. That's what was doing at Lord & Taylor. Hugged her big.

Opened matthew donahoo package. Sweet ass package. Wrote him an email. Got caught up in looking at folders/pictures I'd forgotten from 2009-2011.

4:07am: ate 15mg addy noopept driving back now swervy gonna concentrate

6:33am: peed at Joyce Kilmer travel plaza. Have been speaking into voice memo thing that didn't record but am glad it didn't. Man resembling Victor Vasquez is sleeping in van next to me. Under his passenger-side door is a Chinese food soup container full of what looks like milk.

6:38am: man is now studying his phone. Re-entering plaza to buy red bull.

6:41am: travel mart was selling more sizes of the 'new jersey' t-shirt I bought yesterday. Thought 'it's because I'm driving in the opposite direction now, this isn't the same rest stop as yesterday.' woman ringing me up was smiling coyly to herself.

7:59am: parked on Newport avenue. Have to pee again. Return of empty dread feeling. Return of 'the day ahead.' Humorless. Miss last night, hanging out with mom.

8–9:12AM: talked with mom on phone. positioned body to prolong cats' rare simultaneous nearness to my head and stomach.

11:15AM: woke to door-buzzer. jogged to buzzer and pressed all three buttons frantically, thinking one would let verizon man in. ran downstairs and saw verizon van with no people inside. sun was bright and heard the ocean and there was sand around the van. post-apocalyptic. looked at phone. mom had called at 11am but i had slept through.

saw man walking in the hallway confidently carrying a coffee cup. hallway smelled like coffee. the man was saying something to an older woman, seeming to 'strut.' beaming. felt unsure if he was a person who lived on my floor who if i stopped to meet, would make me more late for the verizon man, or if he was the verizon man. he was beaming bigtime. there was a little confusion about our names. he said 'i'm fronz.'

he pointed at picture on my wall of asian men sitting in 'personal hot tub devices' in some kind of monorail. he said 'the japanese, they don't think like us,' beaming. i said 'isn't that great, i found it in a book, i used to work at a book store and people would use things as bookmarks, that's what the stuff on my wall is.' franz beamed. he said 'oh? they don't think like us at all, the japanese, always they are thinking one step ahead.' i said 'yeah, definitely. definitely.'

franz said something about how it would take a while. i said that was okay. he asked if i had a step-stool or ladder and i said no. he left.

swept around where the cord would be installed. ate 15-20mg adderall.

door buzzer made noise. noticed 'talk' and 'listen' buttons. held 'door open' button for a longer-than-normal time, then held 'listen' button. eavesdropped on franz talking to a woman as they waited for the elevator. woman said 'verizon guys are here today?'

12:10PM: franz said 'you're not going to see me for a while so. i'll be in the stairwell, running wires.'

12:16PM: ate 20mg adderall c/o matthew donahoo.

12:24PM: heard door buzzer and walked to it with 'spacious awareness' replacing 'anxiety about not knowing what the buttons do.' pressed 'door open' button extra-long, but less long than other times. interested in this 'listen' feature.

franz said 'who's this, einstein?' about a small framed picture of kurt vonnegut. i said 'i could see that.' he said 'he look like the white al sharpton,' beaming. i said 'yeah! yeah he's got the hair, too, kind of. you can't see though.' he said something i listened to with delight about not being able to see the hair, einstein, al sharpton. i said 'yeah, totally. he's even got the hair.'

12:27PM: i said 'i've never lived in a building with one of those that works,' gesturing to the door buzzer. franz said 'oh, cable box?' i said 'no, one of those things, the buzzer things.' traded beams and 'heh heh heh's' with franz. the 'heh heh heh's' tapered down. he said 'ya. it dahzwork. fanally. that one.' beaming between the periods.

12:33PM: insane noise from franz. he said 'i love it, don't get me wrong, [noise like uhhhhrrerrerreoohreh-huh], i love the money,' holding a drill.

12:34–12:39PM: something i asked lead to hearing about how fios works, details about cables/wires.

12:40PM: franz is on the phone. i said 'take your time, i only have a job interview today at four thirty.' he thought a moment, looking ahead at a point on kitchen counter, and said 'yes. four thirty we'll be done.'

12:43PM: door buzzer rang. i pushed 'door open' then 'listen.' heard clamoring, two mumbled voices. unconsciously pressed 'door open' again fast for an 'added signature noise burst.' pictured the already-let-in-by-the-long-first-buzz people standing calmly by the elevator, jumping at second buzz and making startled kramer-like noises.

12:45PM: can hear drill on other side of the door. franz is improving my life big time, i feel. it is fun to write about him and soon i'll have internet. mostly i like franz. i like hanging with franz. beaming franz. his beaming thing, his smile, it's so…it's like when you see the .gifs of the person's face that never changes? he has a big perfect beam every time. it's really really good.

12:47PM: franz whispered 'thissis weird' to himself, to the wall. facing the wall. franz: the wall whisperer. taming the insides of walls. he just barked what sounded like 'EYALOPH' into the phone. the process. do not question the process of the wall whisperer.

1:11PM: al has entered building. confusion about al. confusion. al maybe didn't need to come, i think, has come anyway.

1:16PM: franz said 'garth called me back,' he is telling al about garth, garth…garth…i thought garth was al, originally. that was the confusion. standard 'al/garth' confusion, common with verizon. we talked about my name, repeated 'mar-gar-et' a lot, the three of us. margaret and megan. 'maurice,' once. name bonanza. al is on the phone with garth, i can hear garth. the warped voice of garth. garth vader.

1:18PM: chimed in to al/garth conversation with 'wishing for no work? it's usually the other way around.' franz said 'what?' and i repeated. repeated that shit a little louder. al beamed. we're all beaming buddies. beaming with fios.

1:19PM: listening to story i doubt verizon would want customers to hear. involves water. franz said 'this is what verizon wants' and 'once you close that wall' and 'gon be my way or no way.'

1:42PM: i gave them each my book, somehow. they wanted me to sign it. oh man. they left saying things about taking out garbage and 'what is that chicken place? boston market?' have worried one of them will see video i've been recording, sort of hiding computer from them if/when they approach.

1:47PM: stopped recording video and saw video of what i think is a drunk argument between zachary and me at his parents' house in march. footage of what we were saying before i spilled chicken soup on this computer and opened the back and it was getting repaired 'indefinitely, seemingly' at macmedics. i feel good from the adderall. adderall made me a chatty cathy with franz and al. reverend al franz-gar-et chatting it up. uploaded video of this to vimeo account.

1:51PM: just realized since i gave franz and al my book there is an increased chance of them googling me and reading this. hi you guys, if you are reading. my morning/afternoon would've felt extremely bleak if not for you guys.

2:11PM: worried they are reading my book right now and saying 'her apartment is so clean because her head is so dirty' and chuckling and… also…franz being afraid, maybe, to get the things he left. have concluded that they went to boston market. i don't know where there's a boston market here.

2:19PM: door buzz again. going to hide this just in case.

4:13PM: HAVE INTERVIEW WITH CALLAHEAD AT 5PM, GOTTA GET FAST NOW

4:42pm: surprised it is not later. Jogged half a block. Wearing outfit that my bun (via unwashed hair) makes look more hasidicly Jewish.

4:44pm: pug dog in window barked what sounded like 'a-buhbuhbuhbuh. Moof.'

4:48pm: why won't nose stop running also pupils look huge worried I am sweating and they will oh no, what if what I practiced saying in the shower comes out…just eased anxiety via thinking of this line of thinking re job interviews as 'ridiculously common, cliché' and myself as 'funnily unaware of being seduced by the cliché.'

Ate giant scoop noopept. OD-ing.

4:52pm: deja vu

4:53pm: listening to 'Hollywood nights.' callahead is so close to apartment. So is airport. If I don't win today I'll just work at airport.

4:54pm: this gum tastes like the smell of cat pee.

5:16pm: seems like I fucked up big maybe. Charlie. Charlie the boss. He is like Lou grant yeah, from the mary tyler moore show, Mary's boss. Oh no. Best thing about me seemed to be my car, from his reactions. Oof. My interviewee persona (maximum grin, wide eyes, occasional spasms from uncontrollably spasming body) seems like Ren from 'Ren & Stimpy.' Charlie said 'I'm interviewing twenty girls after you, how do you stick out?' I said 'how...' and he said 'how.' I made 'jazz hands' and he sighed.

8:12pm: the rainbow light in my room creates a similar light as right now. If sun was a little brighter it would look like mulholland drive dumpster man. Old woman I've seen before approached me in opposite direction, shielding her eyes from the sand. I was squinting. Looked up from phone and made neutral eye contact with her. She is wearing turquoise jacket and me turquoise shoes. I'm on the way to meet Jaime for pre-tomorrow-morning-audition for 'point break live.'

8:30pm: got the 'listening to 'Hollywood nights' with volume barely loud enough to hear because I don't want to be hearing anything but it's stuck in my head and I have a headache and noise sensitivity from adderall and no sleep and I don't know what I'm doing but am glad or no just neutral and maybe a little nervous about the idea of not just doing theater again but an intense physical improv kind of theater no it'll be fun plus she will also probably not pick me for the role but hey it's all practice anyway my breath stinks and face feels oily and I keep anxiously picking at scabs on my back who is going to see me naked next yikes hope it's no one damn driving by a pretty bridge why do all these insurance companies keep calling me almost out of gas I miss feeling physically near to a person no this highway is just brutal and bumpy to drive on and its wnnoying to fix typos am I upsetting anyone do I need to apologize when will I sleep shut up you sound dramatic and I don't remember exactly but I know you're diibg or have recently done sonwthibg mbarrassing' blues

9:02pm: sitting in maybe same space I parked the first/last time I was here, after central park. Interpreted license plate to mean 'it's letting me know it's a 'GAR:' the correct spelling of 'car."

9:05pm: seems like...I am unemployable...even as...no one wants me, I am squeezing out 'do you want me' with continuing to liveblog, squeezing vice grip on the balls of nothing.

At least when someone wants you and you want them it's like. At least you have that. Boahbapahwbwkqaihwheh how many moist face towels does it take to get to the center of a nervous breakdown

'actually having a nervous breakdown' is the new 'what is a 'nervous breakdown,' has anyone actually had one'

Headache

Complainy

Who wants it…

Just me and the e-cigarette suckling on each other until whatever

Imagine suckling a life-sized life-like portable 36C breast

Would smoke or milk be the more appropriate thing to suckle

Or like one on either side of your head like one of those beer helmets

I feel okay again

And that's how the cookie crumbles

The world famous crumbling manner of the cookie

A 'crimble' would be cute

It'd be the word for an exquisite kind of tininess, like the tininess of a mouse nose

9:23pm: walking to studio. Texted Jaime that I'm outside already. Am being presented with an 'utter slew'—a legion, really—of attractive people slightly younger than me, stinking up the street with how much they belong here. Can smell brick oven pizza and some kind of cooked meat.

MAY 11, 2013

1:29AM: leaving studio. have been talking with jaime and zachery. good talk. drank beers and a kratom thing. my face felt 'ren & stimpy'-like again. wasn't sure it was an audition at first...hard to write about conversation right now, all the topics. laughed hard about something at some point, an idea to start a band called 'practice' which is always...you just are always watching them practice, if you go to their shows. they don't know how to play. oh shit there was other funny stuff. i said 'so you guys were born in what, nineteen seventy-six?' they said 'nineteen seventy-seven' and i said 'you're punk as fuck' and jaime laughed and i thought 'good comment.' talked about...hard to type...an albino man with three sets of teeth, parenting, stuff we used to do, stuff we do, accents, cheese skin people, zachery said something funny about leaving, a man named vlad...

3:03AM: raining. credit card doesn't work. almost out of gas. filled tank with maybe $4 cash in pocket. sang along to 'possum kingdom' by toadies and a desaparacidos song and felt afraid of cops on drive back. obsessed with this light thingy in my room. it changes rainbow colors. ate 1mg xanax. need to be back at studio 10:30AM for for-real audition where i will be the stand-in keanu but in the for real play i will be the cue card person who bosses keanu around, maybe...if they will have me...'point break live:' sweet as hell.

3:44AM: haven't eaten since clyde's with mom oh shit.

4:09AM: forgetting to judge things as 'embarrassing,' they're all blending together, all the thoughts. it doesn't matter, just. at all. if i'm thinking whatever it's equally fine to say whatever. i think. hungry. hummus tortilla madness.

9:11-9:45AM: woke to radio and phone alarms. high level of in-bed annoyance re feeling of sand or cat litter or crumbs, hotness/smell of me, smell of nearby cat food, cats jumping and meowing. thought 'they're being loud because they're annoyed too.'

11:06am: on manhattan ave not as late as I thought I would be, burping hummus taste, have been accepting lateness/doing the best I can and not feeling needless anxiety about things I no longer have control over (like what time I left), calmly accepting fate as 'will be disappointing and/or inconveniencing people I like with my lateness.' ate 20mg adderall noopept 16.8oz sf red bull.

11:12am: I spoke too soon now I am ashamed to show my late face.

12:48pm: Zachery met me at studio door, said there have been technology/phone/internet problems all morning. Gave him adderall he seemed to have forgotten I owed him for mushrooms. He offered Ritalin I regretted refusing, thought 'why would you turn it down, it's like when mom asks if you want coffee you automatically say 'no' even if you want it stupid.' Two actors showed up at the same time but one was late. I read line prompts for the not-late guy auditioning to be bodhi. Nauseated from earl gray kratom tea. Sometimes I vomit from black tea if I haven't eaten that day, hope I don't now, the toilet I've used doesn't work, Zachery and Jaime are on their computers, shit no good this is distracting me

12:55pm: aly from the internet is here

12:56-2:45pm: ran lines, grocery, teeth thing, 'no. 7 sub shop,' person in line, no coffee $, cue card napkin, aly viral 'is thatvtaggig,' found and took silver-wrapped bottle of chartreuse in the park, wendingo, feels weird today/surreal, thought it was just me, swag a fish, I can't hang out

3:18pm: left people in park, walking back to car. Need gas. Worried card no longer works.

3:41pm: filled gas at Hess. Amahd. Amahd's $20. Had thought 'maybe I'm wrong and card will work, I can fill up after the audition thingy.' card didn't work at a sandwich place, then at two ATMs. Looked for spare change on the ground but didn't see any. Looked for spare change on the floor of my car. Found 20 cents. I was composing email to zachery asking for gas money and considering calling zachAry and leaning on a fixture outside a building across from where my car was parked. Two men approached and leaned on the fixture. They had weed. One of the men said 'hey sweetie' to me and smiled. They smoked. The smiling man left. I said 'is this your house, do you live here?' the other man said 'no i wish it was my house.' I said 'is it okay for me to be leaning?' he said it was. The smiling man came back and asked me how I was. I said I was okay, then actually not really okay, I was out of gas money and lived in rockaway park. He ran away, in the direction a nearby cafe. Thought 'fuck' and 'that's funny, he's high and scared to talk. Or hungry.' felt uncomfortable standing by the other man, like he knew I would want to beg him for money, so I just continued looking at my phone. The smiling man came back holding a $20 bill. He hugged me extremely hard and kissed my cheek and said 'honey you get your ass home.' I said 'oh my god I could cry,' starting to cry. Laughing and crying, like on reality TV shows. He said 'don't cry.' I hugged him back extremely hard and said 'you are my savior.'

Surprised it didn't feel weird to be doing any of this and that 'you are my savior' was the most natural thing for me to say. I felt it though. He was. His name is Amahd. He said he had helped clean up rockaway park, from the hurricane. I said I had just moved there. He works at the coffee shop/restaurant he had ran into to get the $20 and said I could come in any time. I hugged him again and he kissed my cheek and I kissed his cheek. So big and smily. Amahd.

3:58pm: stomach achy and hollow. Drank water. Zachery and Masha texted, can't respond yet, still reeling from Amahd's kindness. Mentally replaying him. Have been holding e-cigarette in fist, listening to 'pictures of success' on repeat. Crying a little. Unexpectedly moved the same way I never thought I'd have strong feelings about having a baby in me or aborting it, I thought I'd be practical and detached. Seems like I would feel obligated to feel gratitude, in a 'stranger helping me' scenario. Felt so lost looking for change, trying the ATMs, drafting the email to Zachery while planning for him to not have cash so then I'd call ex-bf Zachary, dreading asking for money, dreading it at first when Amahd and his friend leaned next to me on the cement thing.

4:49-5:21pm: mom called before I wanted to leave parked car. Told her about the interview and audition thing last night and today and Amahd and my credit card and other things. Felt hard to talk the same way it sometimes felt hard to talk with everyone today, only a little more stressful, more like when the times I felt 'Ren & Stimpy'-like talking last night and on job interview. Like I wanted to race to the end of certain sentences before they started. Talking is hard. Hard when it's not always Amahd. Imagined Amahd giving birth standing up in a hospital gown but…like I felt sympathy pains for him, or like it was kind of happening to me too.

Stared at two raindrops during the conversation, thinking 'if i can mentally will them to join together it means something good will happen to me.'

There is a point where anything becomes exhausting or redundant. Think something is missing from my brain. I'm stupid kind of, like actually stupider than most people in some way. Has something to do with the long amount of time it takes me to translate thoughts into language, combined with not storing…phrases…something…I rely on things like 'things' or 'something' or inflection or gesturing or facial expressions, conversationally. Like. I trust that that's what's getting me understood, mostly. The overall look/sound, not just words.

Brain feels caught between 'awareness of intricate interpersonal things/sensitivity to environment/background less-immediate-feeling abstract worldview' and 'slow to process those things into language/bad short-term memory/forgetting what I'm saying if I'm saying words to another person for more than maybe 20 seconds non-stop.' it's okay when I'm alone. Short-term memory gets affected when other people are around, it's like too much data...my RAM is not good.

7:02–7:36PM: mom called. talked more extensively about job interview at callahead.

8:51PM: phone keeps vibrating. irritating. noise sensitivity marathon.

9:51PM: I'm still typing about today, probably not going to elaborate on 12:56-2:45pm.

9:52–11:59PM: did not update.

MAY 12, 2013

12–2:00AM: looked at internet and felt ashamed of myself. chalky eyes. bad bad headache and no pain helper pill. cats asleep on bed. colin texted about a 'welcome to the building dinner' at his apartment later today. wearing a white, men's size-large, old navy t-shirt that says 'MONDAY NIGHT BEER RUN' under a vague-looking football graphic. i found it on the ground near travis' apartment after zachary and i finished moving the couch there. we were looking for a neon green tool bag. zachary was worried about losing the tools because they weren't his. think i was responsible for the tool loss. i was in a good mood and not paying attention. then i saw the shirt.

STATISTICS:

- # hours slept since may 9: close to five

- # mg adderall eaten since may 9: close to 100

2AM–4:39PM: made and uploaded two videos of myself talking to youtube. want to…do…something else…shit. i don't know.

6:43PM: colin texted that food wouldn't be ready for 25 minutes. fed kitties. looked in freezer, at two pie-like ikea desserts i had bought (and apparently bitten twice) on xanax. i could bring him chocolate bar or half a cucumber or a miller lite. there are other people there, oof.

7–11PM: i was the fourth to arrive at colin's 'welcome to the building dinner.' a freshman finance student and an ex-MTA worker in a wheelchair were the two other guests, both from the fourth floor. the freshman finance student had made the dinner, lemon chicken, in his apartment, and brought it downstairs. his self-proclaimed 'fancy food interest' was unconsciously snobby, but his unselfconsciously socially anxious affect made his interest in 'fancy food' seem not snobby at all. like, he clearly didn't think he was better than anyone—we were causing him anxiety. the MTA man had brought a large bottle of wine. he said he and colin used to sit together on the boardwalk, before the hurricane. i said 'the MTA is a union thing, right?' he said it was. a few years ago on the job, he had experienced some kind of neuromuscular paralysis. he thought he had gotten it from driving the trains—something about the motion from the trains—he later discovered it wasn't from that. the MTA man and colin smoked marlboros and used a clam shell ashtray. i said 'have you guys seen the fishermen on the highway,' and a long conversation about fish followed. the 'fancy food' student talked about ordering eel from somewhere overseas. he kept saying 'they overnight it.' people didn't seem interested. i felt bad i wasn't interested. colin and the MTA man knew about fish from growing up fishing. at some point i was talking about making smoothies in the morning. the MTA man said 'i need to be healthier, my sister says i need to stop smoking.' i said i would make him smoothies. at the end i got his phone number and apartment number. i like him. he said he just turned 50. i figured out my sister is almost 50. at one point he said something that sounded like 'black flag' and i said 'black flag? like the punk band?' the MTA man said 'no' and smiled like he knew what i was talking about. colin and 'fancy food' student were having a separate conversation. veterans. the government paid for their college. they said being in the army showed them 'the worst case scenario.' like when you think things are really bad, the army showed them 'it can always get worse.' we joked about that a little. i remember saying 'now you know for sure that it can get worse' and grinning and thinking i was being insensitive.

MAY 13, 2013

12AM–10:16PM: did not update.

10:17PM: watching thunder vs. grizzlies. i have a lot of local programming channels, like over 15 i think. local access. spanish. watched something called 'new york originals,' where they talk to store owners in new york. this episode featured emlee umbrella company and a hobby shop. nice people. nice things. the owner of emlee umbrella company stressed that their umbrellas were 'made for shade from the sun.' that was good because i wasn't sure at first, maybe they made rain ones, rain ones seem to have the market. his grandfather started the company in 1933 and he is an old man.

pictured myself applying for a job at the factory...saying to the owner, something like 'i saw your factory on 'new york originals' and i must say i fell in love, the mission behind...your years of service...quality product, [lie about being a seamstress via the umbrellas are the big beach umbrellas and made by hand], i want to make sunshade umbrellas.' most of the jobs i'm thinking about doing are like that, like 'i'm a person just like anyone, i can do stuff, i don't need to show you a degree to show you i can do stuff just like any person. doing stuff with my hands.' i would like a job like that. i feel underqualified for things like that and underqualified for 'data entry' or other things. definitely can't be a teacher. do not recommend 'taught by me.' also no degree. no experience. experience laying down. if i don't have something else by the end of the month i'll apply for food service. also feel underqualified for that.

11:45PM: i should learn spanish. i've wanted to learn spanish since 2006.

MAY 14, 2013

12:06AM: men's wearhouse commercials still feature the 'you're gonna like the way you look, i guarantee it' guy. memory of the men's wearhouse at towson town center, trying to see who worked at men's wearhouse, to see if i thought i could work there.

12:10AM: drinking second beer. almost done. miller high life. finished mug of whiskey that had been on windowsill by bed, making it smell like whiskey since 'apartment building dinner' night.

12:43AM: matthew donahoo tweeted he felt less lonely during the playoffs. @-ed back and forth during overtime.

12:57AM: memory of driving on york rd. to apartment in baltimore, july 2009, after work then buying a red backpack at towson town center, texting with brandon gorrell. stopped at discount liquor store outlet.

1:02AM: they should hire the oldest living NBA player to announce games. or just some 102 year-old man, almost incoherent, saying sometimes poignant nonsequiturs.

9:26AM: woke maybe ten minutes ago to alvie. watching 'repo games.' the guy repossesses your car. last night i ate three bleaksedillas and fell asleep watching something i forget. spilled beer on mattress. feeling bad and like it's too hard to do anything to feel better. the bad feeling is for no reason maybe. writing helps a little. no i'm annoyed. i don't know. want to be asleep again.

9:35AM: the man on 'repo games' just said 'there is another superhero on an invisible plane and a lasso of truth so deductively it must be wonder woman.' he said he had a 180 IQ. it's his ex-wife's car. teenage boys with no shirts came out of their house first. they live with…the ex-wife has a boyfriend and the ex-husband has a fiancee and they all live together. he said he reads a lot of sci-fi books.

12:44PM: woke from nap. 'repo games' still on. dreamed i was yelling 'it's just harder for me to do some things' at colin. he had found out i had lied about something on my apartment application. he was also upset that i wasn't a christian.

12:51PM: looked at phone even though computer was a few feet away. funny voicemail from rachel bell from last night. another number has been calling me every day saying 'call us for your estimate on the roof remodeling.' they always say to call a different number than the one that left the message.

1:01PM: the 'repo games' premise rules. i'd be so happy if every time before something shitty happened to me i had the chance to be asked five unrelated trivia questions and if i got three out of five right the shitty thing wouldn't happen. wonder whose idea this was. i like the repo men in the show. they got to take a cop's car. they talk and look like pro-wrestlers. the people are always yelling and confused when the repo men show up.

1:05PM: the repo man is flirting with a girl. she said 'can you give me a ride to work?' he said 'what time does hooters open?'

that reminds me, i dreamed a misogynistic joke the other night, keep forgetting to type it:

i saw a table where two women were watching another woman read a jonathan franzen book aloud. i said 'that's the only way women know how to read.'

1:10PM: IDEAS FOR THINGS TO DO TODAY:

- take the ferry to wall street, go to library, look for jobs
- see if mira wants to hang out
- read on the beach
- stay inside
- laundry
- eat adderall or xanax or vicodin or opana to motivate me do any of these things (even staying inside option…seems…like it requires something)
- shower
- respond to emails or write something that isn't this

3:03PM: answered ask.fm questions. life seems so stupid…my life… haha…the repo man needs to bust through my door right now

oh my god if the repo man busted through with a camera crew

'your life is about to be repossessed, you have not been making payments'

'oh no, has it really been that long?'

'yes m'am, but i am giving you the opportunity to reclaim it: just answer three out of five of these trivia questions correctly'

at this point it always seems like a person walks out of the house to help the person getting questioned

my cats would like, try to run out the door, at this point in my show

do my cats think i'm also a cat

5:15PM: watched maria's 'draw my life' video. paypaled her $20. maria is the first ASMR person whose videos i watched. ASMR people have been uploading 'draw my life' videos. getting to watch a memoir comic/graphic novel. and they're narrated and written by people i know, kind of. people i subscribe to on youtube. maybe this is the thing people feel when they say something about how i'm doing this. like 'oh cool i get to know a person more.' maybe. not saying this well.

sun is coming out. made spinach/cucumber/banana/avocado/coconut water smoothie.

7:47PM: laid with closed eyes. i didn't do anything on the list of things i could do. oh shit no, i did, i did 'stay inside, doing nothing.' gave cats treats. turned on lights. watching knicks vs pacers. want to eat pizza or do something 'bad' to motivate myself to be 'better' tomorrow. wonder if credit card works yet.

7:50PM: i did do something: looked at pictures of people i was friends with at depaul. i was friends with a lot of people in the acting school my first year, kind of accidentally/coincidentally i think, because i had auditioned for the acting school but didn't get in. they all still seem to be friends. shit.

8:41PM: answered ask.fm questions. swept floor. knicks losing. i like stoudemire. they did a voiceover about his eye surgery and about how his first game in months is in the second quarter of the playoffs and how he has to be playing really hard, showing him sitting between (guy he was talking to) and shumpert (staring into court, who they'd earlier said 'there's no physical reason for him to be sitting out right now, maybe his knee started acting up')

8:45PM: called pizza place. they close 10PM. going to try my card at an ATM, then if it works, order something. eating 1mg xanax before leaving apartment.

8:49pm: walking to ATM. I've been inside since Friday. Forgot to eat Xanax.

8:55pm: man watched me swipe. Didn't see car where I thought I'd left it. Walking to 'potential car area' now, to get the scoop. Canvas the scene. That would really take the cake.

8:57pm: I see it. Okay.

9:02pm: trying to discern something boring about parking. Pizza will will arrive in 40 minutes. Maybe I will get beer. Okay.

9:04pm: THINGS I HAVE PASSED:

1. Small Rottweiler style dog and fluffy white dog 'kissing' each other in a yard.

2. Older gender-neutral couple who I first thought had developmental disabilities when I saw them clutching each other after I got money from the ATM but now I just think that's how they do things. Strong new York accents, both maybe 5'4", short hair.

3. Vanilla-scented girl I ignored due to her 'extreme seeming to look at me.'

4. Old woman with walking device.

5. Old man sitting on the curb, smoking cigarette and sniffling. i was also sniffling, smoking e-cigarette. thought 'solidarity' at him vaguely/ meekly/in the tone i've been thinking 'go knicks.'

9:25PM: bought 12-pack budweiser, sabra 'supremely spicy' hummus, vitacoco 'decieves many into thinking it's healthy' coconut water. cashier with voluminous black hair in a hairnet said 'you younger than you look' and 'don't drink too much' twice. it was like a big ass outer brain of hair. it looked 'fly.'

girl was entering the elevator as i was entering building. she made a face like 'should i hold this' and i jogged and she said 'take your time.' she asked me what floor and i said 'two, please.' she made a face like she thought something. i said 'i know it's just two floors and all, i'm just, [noise] tonight.' she said 'i'm on the second floor too.' i asked her for how long. 'a few months.' i said i'd just moved in. her name is crystal. HERE IS THE BIG RESULT, THE ULTIMATE...OF EVERYTHING, OF CRYSTAL AND ME: we like the apartment building. we consider it 'nice.'

9:33PM: knicks lost. people on TV are milling around in desultory post-game haze. stoudemire sitting alone on a bench, holding a towel. something twinkled in left side of my peripheral vision. gchatted zachary. door buzzed.

9:45PM: pizza ass. pizza man asked if i wanted change and i said no. $13 tip. i don't know. they never come all the way up to your door.

MAY 15, 2013

1:15AM: fell asleep around 11PM. put on 'the office' and ate pieces of chocolate bar.

4:42AM: woke again. now the news is on. cats fought and i stared at alvie like the crying indian in those commercials and said 'noooo.' ate 1mg xanax. missing zachary and philadelphia apartment. pictured waking there 4:40AM instead. we would've ordered shittier pizza and there wouldn't be leftovers. maybe he'd be snoring and i'd go to the other room and turn on TV. in the morning i'd be on the couch and the wheelchair man with no legs at the corner store would be yelling 'i'm on a highway to hell.'

4:45–6AM: downloaded 'secretary' and fell asleep watching. rewound to where i had fallen asleep and fell asleep again. shitty 'it's morning again. the morning is gray' feeling.

1:12PM: woke around 30 minutes ago. answered ask.fm questions. someone said they thought drugs have been affecting my moods. annoyed at this person, not on drugs. ate 1mg xanax. enjoying leftover pizza slice 'as much as i can,' knowing it will feel shitty when it's over. wish i had coffee. they should make an energy drink you can brew at home. dreamed something 'high stakes' like there were landmines or something everywhere.

A PLAN YOU AT LEAST NEED TO DO PART OF TODAY:

- go to petsmart for carpeted 'kitty tower' structure, cat food

- maybe look for a table at goodwill

- maybe go to the library or somewhere in NYC other than your beach ass island

1:23PM: should i vomit the pizza and xanax and start over with adderall. hm. considering. answering two emails before anything.

2:30PM: ate b-vitamin, zeolite, 'brain/memory' herbal tonic. smoked e-cigarette. not going to vomit. might go to hot yoga. the pizza feels bad. yearning for someone i don't know. listening to song on sam pink's blog on repeat, reminds me of some feeling i don't know how to articulate, like something from childhood i can almost remember.

2:56PM: drinking kale/cantaloupe smoothie.

3:09PM: sitting on kitchen counter. wrote this for a long time the night of may 11:

WAYS I KNOW HOW TO TALK TO PEOPLE: EASIEST/LEAST STRESSFUL (FAVORITE) TO HARDEST/MOST STRESSFUL (LEAST FAVORITE)

- saying immediate thoughts/feelings, passive observations about surroundings

- reviewing 'what happened last time I saw you'

- making jokes, riffing, 'what if…' scenarios

- [if I talked to more kids maybe 'talking to kids' would go here]

- talking about relationships

- gossiping/shittalking/drugs

- reviewing 'what happened other times I've seen you' (just as easy as 'what happened last time I saw you' but feels a little worse so it's lower on the list)

- curiously trading ideas about 'what is the universe/why is this shit here/why am I here/what is life/what's going to happen'

- talking about sex

- encouraging people to do anything to make whatever we're doing more interesting

- analyzing interpersonal things slowed-down Woody Allen style (must be slowed-down to be enjoyable)

- social scripts/customer service/formal/impersonal/'knowing each other's roles' things (this feels like the mid-point, it starts becoming harder after this)

- listening/learning/following instructions

- consoling (would be higher but don't feel like I can really help ever)

- exuding calmness during cop-like/high-stakes situations I don't care about

- exuding anxiety during lower-stakes things like 'saying 'hi''

- apologizing

- talking about internet/books/current events/art/movies/stuff that feels like school

- 'quietly enduring'/'politely restraining'

- shooting the shit with parents of boyfriends

- aggressively reassuring someone that I think they're okay

- repeating conversations/reminding/getting reminded

- begging forgiveness at the last minute so I don't fail a class or get my license suspended or car repossessed or things like that

- expressing irritation/sadness/disappointment about a person to that person (seems really easy if I'm close to the person, is low on the list via how unpleasant it feels to do and depressing it is that I will probably always do it)

- arguing 'theoretically'/intellectually

- arguing bitterly

- yelling uncontrollably

4:04PM: did 300 crunches, 50 push-ups, 50 squats. ate 10mg adderall. fuck it i'm eating the other 10mg. going to shower, go to petsmart, deliver kitty things to kitties, go somewhere else. a library. something.

4:52PM: ate noopept. mom called about visiting tuesday. feel empty thing. big empty. big empty. wanted to keep repeating 'big empty' for indefinitely. no one to realistically fantasize about and it's all my fault. cool. liveblog mad less interesting now. okay. what can i do. i don't feel like doing anything. i'll do these things i said i'd do, then i'll come home, then what. i should try to be more social. it takes so long to get from where i live to where anyone else lives. losing pleasure in social things. i don't know. therapy. they would put me on a pill to make me feel less. it would probably make me feel big empty style. liveblog is boring now because i'm not interesting. okay. there is nothing else to do but do the things you said you'd do today.

6:20PM: starting to feel adderall. feeling better. started writing account of 'mushrooms night' that was too big to answer for someone's ask.fm question, going to finish it after going to petsmart, then post it on may 7 or 8....you've already read it if you're reading this and didn't skip that part.

7:15pm: showered, dressed, dried hair, applied coconut oil to body, perfume, put water in plastic bag to not disturb electronic devices I'm not sure why I'm bringing. Wandering aimlessly around apartment. Leaving. Adderall wearing off maybe, vague pangs of '[indescribable].' feel better than yesterday.

Stuff I want to write: 'self yelp' thing, most emotional t-shirts, livetweet of something on MDMA…moma on MDMA lol…ask if thought catalog is interested, alt citizen article I said I'd write to go along w/interview

Tomorrow I will return attorney phone call and get my car inspected

Also email Brad Listi egregiously late email also Mira egregiously late email also Jordan not egregiously late email

Friday I have an update interview with Juliet

7:20pm: teenage blond boy was 'perched' on railing outside my building.

7:23pm: entered car. Had epiphany-like feeling of 'I'm far in distance to wherever I was when I was mostly at my mom's, I'm not sure how to do this [live].'

7:29pm: fishermen. They always seem to be there. I like them. Listening to 'goodbye stranger' by supertramp. Song gets me emotional in weird stabby molesty perfect in its hopelessness way. Like there is a lost montage of my life to this song that they couldn't find a place for in 'boogie nights.'

8:10pm: non-anxiously shot the shit with guy ahead of me in line at petsmart. He said he wanted his dog to eat food to 'remain masculine.' he thought he was going to receive three free tennis balls. Guy ringing me up said he had two dogs, two bearded lizards, a fish. I said 'bearded lizards are friendly, right?' The petsmart man said they're some of the more friendlier lizards, definitely. But his aged at different times. The female was bigger and she doesn't like the male. They had to be separated. At the end he made some comment like 'so you gotta trade in your lizards sometimes, it's alright.' he asked me if I needed help loading my 'kitty tower' into my truck. I said 'no thanks I got it, I got it, let me just get my bag maneuver' and put all the bags on one arm.

8:15pm: still sitting in parking lot. Not enough time to go to Ikea to look at tables. Which is good. I want a free ass Craigslist table. Mama just love smelling that Ikea smell fuck you I like smelling it and lookin in all them fake ass rooms they made look all nice

8:29pm: passed cop car and remembered I was supposed to handle ticket for using cell phone weeks ago. Also have maybe seven parking tickets since this winter. I am in trouble. Handling this when I get home.

8:54pm: just noticed mysterious gazebo outside of Duane reade on 116th st. Bought e-cigarette refills, swiffer batteries, two sf red bull four-packs on sale.

9:00PM: parked two blocks north from apartment bulding. carried 'kitty tower' thingy with me. passed a woman sitting on steps in a fenced-in yard who said 'he's just jealous' about her dog. it was a pug dog. it started barking after i passed. i said 'hey woof woof.' the woman said 'here, [dog's name], you want some cheese?'

9:01-10:36PM: unpacked kitty tower and put catnip on it to try to get them interested. put batteries in swiffer and swiffed the floor. put down cat grass. cats seem uninterested in cat tower, especially alvie, who i bought it for mostly (he likes to sit ontop of the kitchen cabinets like ten feet in the air). shirley seems a little interested. threw away trash. texted (am still in the process of texting) back and forth with jessie from canada who made me the mix and who wants me to edit a story and zachery. sitting on bed. ate 20mg adderall to 'help me do the thing i forget.'

THINGS I WANTED TO DO:

- elaborate on funny parts of mushrooms night with zachery

- send emails

- write alt citizen article

i'm doing all of that after i finish editing the story.

10:37-11:59PM: sat on my bed and drank 16oz sf red bull. edited jesse's richard brautigan style story. edited the shit out of that shit. if anyone ever wants me to edit things i like editing maybe more than writing, i'm happy to edit things.

MAY 16, 2013

12–2:11AM: edited and sent jesse's story. listened to 'bamboo cactus' by i, cactus on repeat. didn't look at other things on the internet at all, i think. i took a pee pee break. focused big time on editing. listening to 'goodbye stranger' by supertramp now. archived may 12-15.

3:22AM: how is it now 3:22AM. thought of myself as 'fluffily hurtling towards death' instead of 'placing red bull on windowsill.' considering re-reading parts of this to see 'how it came to this.'

3:30AM: i don't know what i did from 2:12-3:21am. going to look at my internet history and fucking…i'll upload a screenshot to flickr…seems like it's going to be embarrassing.

3:40AM: i must've been doing other things. i don't know. want to be held by something. should i drive to maryland now…for just…sad…i don't know. what the hell am i doing. have been liveblogging for two months, tomorrow.

3:44AM: seems like i lost focus of something but i don't know what. i would pay someone to read this and tell me where i lost focus, and of what.

6:31AM: typed 3k-word summary of every day i've liveblogged in msword document. e-cigarette definitely broken. want to drive to maryland. feels so hard to do this. i'm not even doing anything. look at all of that shit, all of that summary shit. i'm not even doing anything. i don't know what i want. how has all of this time has passed. i don't feel like i'm here right now, at the apartment. i don't feel like 'yesterday,' i can't remember yesterday. going to petsmart. i can't do this anymore. i don't know what i can't do anymore. i know this isn't making sense. this is how my brain sounds. i feel horrible. i don't care about sounding. just, whatever. i don't care about whoever's reading. nobody cares about me. how do people look at this. people say stuff to me. my parents like me but why. people keep looking at this and asking me questions. nobody really wants this. i'm not saying this to…just, whatever. i don't have an agenda. if you're reading this and you think i have an agenda i think you're an idiot and there is no hope for you. there less hope for you than there is for me. that is sad. there are people like that, with less hope than me. i know that. there's nothing i can do about it. i'm not condescending to whoever, it's just. goddamnit. i know something is different about how i'm typing. let me be dramatic. give me a goddamned break. i don't want to be funny. i don't want to say stuff to make anyone like me. the sun is rising. i don't feel happy about anything. the e-cigarette doesn't work. there's nothing i want. i get excited when i get to feel different, chemically. i feel hopeful when i'm driving because i'm not in the place where i'll end up. there's nothing i want. the thing i used to want is stupid. the thing of wanting another person. it's stupid. it's always going to be the same thing unless i want to force myself to be with someone forever and then i'll always be wondering 'why did i do this.' if i don't do that i'll always be wondering 'why am i doing this, why didn't i do the other thing.' i'm not happy and i'm not fun to be around right now. it takes me forever to respond to anything because i know i'm going to just end up feeling the same after anything. it's always this. no matter what everyone is going to leave at some point. i'll mess up and they won't like me or maybe they'll mess up and i won't like them. or we just won't talk. it's always me, alone. or me feeling obligated to all the people who don't realize whatever is happening between us is going to end in some way. nobody gets it. or no, they don't get it because that's not true for them, people just stay in their lives. my life is not somewhere people want to stay. statistically. you could figure it out. my life isn't even somewhere i want to stay but i don't want to die either but i can't think of anything i want from this. i don't know if i'm being dramatic or not. my life is stupid. it's the stupidest joke of a life. a psychologist would say i haven't gotten over relationships or the abortion. they would maybe be right. i don't know. it doesn't matter. i can't tell anything. all i know is the only thing i have to look forward to is some idea that it's not going to be 'now' someday. it's always going to be now though. a lifelong series of different 'now's. if anyone thinks anything bad about me the joke is on them because i think so much worse shit about me than anyone could ever know because nobody knows me as well as i do. i don't know how to change anything about me, that would make me not think things like this, but if i didn't think things like this i would be happy probably. i don't know if i'm exaggerating, i feel completely serious and rational, like rationally assessing my potential to feel better. i'm not looking for attention. the only thing attention does is make me feel obligated to say 'thank you' or comment in some other way and i feel so shitty when i do any of that. any kind of talking i feel bad doing. i'm sorry. i've been lying the whole time. if you think i'm nice or funny or a nice person or a good friend or something it's because i'm good at lying. i feel so bad when i talk to anyone. unless it's a certain kind of talking or a certain kind or person. or unless i'm on drugs or alcohol or something. i'm lying the whole time. i'm sorry. it feels bad in a different way when i'm not talking to anyone. there is more hope when there's another person around maybe. i get more distracted but i also think i'm stupider and i can't think as well. i am annoying and i try to make too many jokes. or else i feel paralyzed and like everyone hates me and i say stupid things i don't mean to help make something go by faster. it's not always like that, i'm not being realistic. i'm being dramatic. just please read this and think 'she's being dramatic' if you think anything. don't think anything. just keep doing whatever else you were doing. i'm jealous of whatever else you were doing or whoever you are. i don't want to be this anymore. i don't know what to do. what do people do. i already did therapy and it didn't work. do i just...i don't know...i just should try to not pay attention to thoughts like this and find something else to make me busy. i guess. it's always going to come back to this feeling though. for years i think, since...i don't know. actually this is recent i think, for it to be happening to this degree. i think it started last summer. wait. i don't know. the one before that. i don't remember. it wasn't always like this. i think i'm happy also. sometimes i'm also happy.

7:47AM: ate 2mg klonopin. considering driving to maryland. want to lay without thinking for a while and maybe sleep.

1:19PM: woke around 30 minutes ago.

1:36PM: did 300 crunches, 50 push-ups, 50 squats.

2:13PM: picked at skin.

2:44PM: did 50 squats, 50 push-ups, 100 crunches. e-cigarette works again.

3:10PM: received email coupon for 50% off rite aid brand products.

3:29PM: it's good when shirley is here.

3:37PM: colin texted about a 'business networking' event in manhattan tonight. have been texting funny/commiserating style with masha, arranged drug trade.

4:14PM: going to drive to maryland.

4:32PM: ate 10mg opana, 5mg vicodin.

4:47pm: have been carrying things Matthew donahoo mailed me, in my purse, 'for good luck.' Colin said 'hey Megan' when I left building. He was in the sand, seemed to be using a metal detector.

5:24pm: listening to 'parking lot music' by e*vax, a 'reminds me of an ex-boyfriend' album.

5:26pm: heavy traffic. That is okay. I'd rather be in traffic than anywhere else. Want to re-read 'slapstick.'

6:52pm: gas station attendant said 'hey howya doin man.' Listened to around 25% of a Schopenhauer audio book about pessimism and thought 'yeah I think this stuff anyway.' listened to around 25% of einstein's theory of relativity and thought 'I almost get it, would be better as a powerpoint.'

8:45pm: pulling into parking space at mom's. Thoughts in car were mostly 'what could I have done differently' and 'why am I doing this' and 'will someone be mad at me for doing this.' A little 'that looks interesting' and 'why isn't e-cigarette working' and 'I don't feel effects from the pills I ate' and 'am I hungry.' I am hungry.

9:08pm: mom was watching the second to last episode 'the office.' She hugged me hard and asked if I was sick. Knew I wasn't but felt my face look like 'maybe.' I said 'no I'm just feeling not so good.' she hugged me again and said 'you have to watch the farewell 'office." I sat beside her on the couch and said 'I didn't know it was the last one already.' she said something sweet and goofy and cheerful and sounded a little embarrassed.

When Jim said he hoped someday someone would be inspired by 'the office' mom made a crying noise. I ordered Thai food. Mom said 'is the pizza coming?' and laughed knowingly, said 'I mean are you going to the pizza place to pick up your Thai food.'

Ate handful cashews, bite of whole foods cookie, 1mg xanax.

9:16pm: 'the office' is on TV at the Thai place. No other customers.

9:24pm: warm and spring-smelling outside.

10:22pm: sleepy. I wish I was on 'the office.' I love mom. So sleepy.

10:32PM: watching 'the office' on demand with mom.

10:37PM: ate tom kha soup, pad thai chicken, piece of peach pie. great. trying to find old episodes of 'the office.' mom said 'well we have both agreed that we like to see the ones with jim and pam in love.'

11:02PM: started falling asleep saw mental image of hands over a sink and cans kept dumping different colors of paint to maybe wash the hands which kept pulling away.

MAY 17, 2013

[some time before 1AM]: fell asleep during 'the office' and 'grumbled' childishly to bed.

[some time in the night]: woke distracted by the blue light of e-cigarette, moved it to my bag.

11:50AM: woke from sex dream with the second guy i had sex with, one of the joaquin phoenix-looking brothers, who looked more attractive as he had aged. it felt really good. i was on top, we were both facing the ceiling. then i was outside tao's old apartment in brooklyn and i think we were having sex standing up near a small pole, like a toilet plunger. tao said 'i have new roommates' as we walked inside. there were three 40-50lbs overweight women and six bunk beds in the room where the kitchen was. i said 'where did your room go?' tao said 'it's still here, you just can't see it because of them.' he asked if i could stay two nights and i thought 'he wants me to stay two nights, sweet.' one of the women was 'lounging' in a top bunk bed. she said 'no not two nights.' tao got in the bottom bunk of a bed and the top was empty and he motioned for me to join him. there was room for two people. i realized we wouldn't have sex. the overweight women talking continuously and making food and tao and i were looking at each other and grinning and being like 'what the fuck is this shit.' woke next to half a glass of milk by bed.

12-1:08PM: ate an apricot and drank two cups of coffee while talking to mom about the army. i told her about colin and the fancy food student. mom got emotional and cried about the government putting agent orange on people in vietnam and 'the things they do to those boys, they don't even know it when they go into it.' she apologized for being emotional and i said 'it's okay, you don't have to apologize.'

i said 'maybe i'll join the navy, then they'll pay for my school and i can get a physics degree and then i can work for nasa and be an astronaut.' mom seemed supportive. i told her about chris hadfield (astronaut whose videos i was watching the other day). she knew about him. i said 'did you see his 'space oddity' song? the david bowie song?' she said 'i saw a clip but i want to see the whole thing.' i brought my computer in and sat next to her on the couch and we watched it.

mom cried and laughed a lot. i cried a little i think, feeling affected by her crying. she said 'he's just adorable, what a sweet man' at the end. i told mom about the female astronaut (suni williams) whose videos at the international space station i was also watching for a really long time the other day. she's logged the most 'spacewalk' hours of any woman. she was a jet pilot in the navy. mom said 'i knew your truck driving thing wasn't for nothing, and then the other day when you talked about being a flight attendant, oh meggie, i see this happening for you.' i read from the nasa website about 'basic requirements for an astronaut pilot:'

> 'Bachelor's degree from an accredited institution in engineering, biological science, physical science, or mathematics. An advanced degree is desirable. Quality of academic preparation is important.'

i said 'i'd probably need four more years of college, i'm not got at math.' mom said 'oh i bet it would be less than that.' i said 'no, i only took one astronomy course, and like, qualitative reasoning. that's my only math. but that's okay.' i walked to the bathroom and my room, looking for my e-cigarette. mom said excited things about how she thought i could be an astronaut. i said 'i'm good at physics but that's like, the only thing on that list. grad school also.' i found the e-cigarette. mom said 'can you hear me?' i said 'i think so, can you hear me?' she said 'i can hear you.'

i sat on the dining room chair and continued to read from the nasa website:

> 'In addition, the pilot may assist in the deployment and retrieval of satellites utilizing the remote manipulator system, in extravehicular activities.'

i said "extravehicular,' that means doing the spacewalk, getting to repair the ship in space.'

mom said 'i can see you doing that. all you have to do is try to do that.'

i read the rest of the pilot requirements in a scanning manner, saying like, "must have vision correctable to twenty-twenty' i got that, 'must be between sixty-two and seventy-five inches tall' i got that, blood pressure i think i got that.' mom said 'you have all those things.'

mom expressed anxiety about the e-cigarette making things smell, but also that she knew it didn't smell. she asked if nicotine was bad for you. i said 'i don't think so, it's just the other stuff in cigarettes that's bad, this is just like, water.' i said i'd go outside.

1:27PM: sitting on balcony. excited about the astronaut idea. i would go to more college and the government would pay. i would get to fly planes. sweet as hell. how can i not do this. writing is shitty compared to being an astronaut. i'm going to…look into being a navy pilot now…

i should've thought more about moving to new york. i could've just like, transferred to the naval academy in annapolis and lived at home. shit. what have i done…maybe i can…maybe there is a way…shit…goddamnit… why didn't i think of this earlier, i've always wanted to be an astronaut but i just thought 'you're bad at math, you can't do it' but if i really worked on it i could do it…goddamnit…thought 'want to blow all this shit to hell'

1:36PM: walked inside to get refill battery for e-cigarette. i said 'i'm calling the navy about enlisting' to mom. she made excited noises and said 'oh honey i'm so happy for you, this sounds so good.' i said 'i feel like i need that, it'll be good for me. i need someone to tell me to do things.' she said 'i just think it sounds so good.' walked to balcony.

1:48PM: called two naval recruitment offices in queens and 'garden city.' the first one didn't have an option to leave a message. the second one had a recording that said to call back during normal office hours, from 9AM-4PM (which i was calling in). the third one was on flatbush avenue and allowed me to leave a message. i said 'hi my name is margaret boyle, i'm interested in enlisting in the navy and pursuing a career in aviation. i don't have my full bachelor's, but i'm interested in asking you questions about that, and more questions in general [laugh laugh]. please give me a call back.' i sounded 'professional as hell,' i feel.

2:05PM: dad called to see about eating dinner together tonight. he said construction was moving fast and he'd be able to rent the offices by june 1, then said something like 'i want to set you up with an apartment building to rent out to people so you can have passive income, so you don't always have to be working.' i said 'that'd be cool and all,' then told him about my plan to join the navy and finish school and be an astronaut, that the places weren't picking up their phones, and that i was just going to go to a recruitment office in-person when i get back to NYC. he seemed really excited. i said 'they'll probably be happy because you were in the navy too, what did you do, were you an officer?' he said 'well in four years i went up to an e-six officer, a 'petty officer,' i don't like that name—but you can tell them your dad was a radar technician on the joseph p. kennedy, which is the ship that stopped the cuban blockade.' i forgot he did that. i was smiling a lot. dad told me things about ROTC and that there were tests to be an officer that he was 'sure i would pass' and then i could fly jets or 'nuclear submarines.' i said 'jets, i want to fly jets.' he laughed like 'ah-hahaha!' and said he was happy for me. i said 'plus since i have my CDL they'll know i can drive trucks so that must be good.' he said 'that's right, they'll see that you have your CDL.' i said 'even if i don't get to be an astronaut i could probably get a job at nasa.' dad said 'there'll be more opportunities for you to go to space, in your lifetime.' i told him about applying to callahead for the secretary position the other day and knowing i didn't get it, and how i've just been thinking about all the shitty jobs i could do, not really wanting to do any of them, then i just had this idea. dad said 'maybe you'll take me for a ride in your jet one day.' i said 'yeah, they'd probably let me, since you were in the navy.' he was laughing really happily and i was too. i said 'i figured it out i think.' we said things about meeting at 8PM for dinner and hung up.

2:38PM: mom has been filling a pitcher of water and taking it to the balcony to water plants. she said 'you could be like fred astaire and gene kelly: 'on the town.''

2:40PM: mom said 'you want a half a bagel?' i said 'no thank you.'

2:58PM: mom said 'you know what else? you might be going to mars in your lifetime.' i said 'y-eah' unfocusedly while typing 'yeah' in a tweet response. mom said 'or other cool places. as-yet-undefined.'

4:10PM: paid all my parking tickets. i had five. bad news. mom just said 'plus! you're so good with a gun! you could be a sniper,' laughing like 'just kidding.' tried to pay ticket online from april 22, for using cell phone while driving, but website isn't letting me, i think because the ticket looks like 'LAST NAME: Matlock FIRST NAME: Margaret MIDDLE INITIAL: Megan Boyle ['Boyle' is 'scrunched' above box that says 'LOCAL POLICE CODE 088'].

tried all combinations/variations of my name that i could think of. seems like they either didn't enter the ticket yet or she…i don't know what they could've thought my name was. my PA license says 'MARGARETMEGAN MATLOCK BOYLE' because there wasn't enough space to write 'MARGARET MEGAN.' i also tried 'MARGARETMEGAN.' i don't know why the cop wrote 'MATLOCK' for my last name. i simply. don't. know. can't believe my parents named me 'margaret megan.' that's like naming someone 'william bill' or 'richard dick.' but they always called me 'megan.'

here's a story about my name: somehow i didn't end up with a social security card until i was eight or nine years old. at that time i had been spelling my name 'meghan.' that's how my parents showed me it was spelled. my birth certificate says 'margaret megan matlock boyle,' though. i think i didn't like it that my middle name was 'matlock' and nobody was paying attention or…i don't know. they let me write 'margaret megan (no 'h' for some reason) boyle' on the social security card and i ended up with a social security number that didn't correspond with the name on my birth certificate. it was 1993 or 1994 so things like that mattered less, i guess. pre-9/11 style.

in 1997 my family went on a carribean cruise and i needed a passport. i went with my dad to a place where they took passport photos. i'm assuming he brought my birth certificate, and maybe there was some kind of conversation between the photographer and my dad about how 'margaret' and 'megan' are essentially the same name, so i ended up with a passport that said 'megan matlock boyle.'

when i got my driver's license in 2004, the maryland DMV required the name on the license to say the same thing as my social security card.

so the names on my forms of identification as of 2004 are:

- birth certificate: margaret megan matlock boyle

- baptismal certificate: margaret meghan matlock boyle (this one doesn't really matter but why the 'h')

- social security card: margaret megan boyle

- passport: megan matlock boyle

- driver's license: margaret megan boyle

i sublet a room in brooklyn from december 2011 to march 2012. as i was walking to the train one of the first days i was there, i saw a storefront covered in 'CDL license, driving school, truck driving lessons' and other words. i signed up for a CDL preparation class with a mostly polish-speaking man. i liked him. we met for one-on-one lessons for about two weeks. he said he would teach me how to pass the written CDL test, but before i could get behind the wheel of a truck for driving lessons, i would need to transfer my maryland driver's license to a new york driver's license.

i brought my maryland driver's license, social security card, birth certificate, and passport to the new york DMV. they wouldn't give me a new york state license because of a 'four-point system.' i needed one 'proof of date of birth' (birth certificate = zero points) and four points of 'proofs of name' (u.s. citizens usually use their social security card [two points] and passport [two points]). they all have to say the same name.

the first time i went to the NYC social security office i was drunk and had brought whiskey in a flask and saw a sign that said 'no liquids permitted' so i went home. the second time i was sober. i waited in a holding tank area, downstairs in a belted maze-like line at the front of which was a security gate, guarded by police. the police would periodically point to heads near the front of the line. these were the heads permitted to pass through the security device to another waiting area upstairs. when i reached the second waiting area i was instructed to get a number from piece of paper by a device. then i stood behind the person i had stood behind in the first line, in a similar but tenser-feeling belted maze-line. the room's perimeter was comprised of people sitting at desks behind bulletproof glass. the line-waiting mass stood in the center of the room, about twenty feet from the wall of desk stations.

when my number was called, i handed a tired-seeming woman my driver's license, social security card, baptismal certificate, and birth certificate. there was some kind of las vegas souvenir on her desk. i tried to exude apologetic 'i understand' mental waves to her. she looked at my papers and typed into a computer, making 'something is wrong' faces. she said 'you got a double name?' i said 'i don't know, what is that?' she said 'why they give you a double name?' i said 'i don't know, i'm just trying to get all my IDs to say the same thing as my birth certificate.' she continued making 'something is wrong' faces at the computer. she tore up my old social security card and said i would receive a new card in the mail in two weeks. i said 'will it say the name on my birth certificate?' she exhaled audibly and looked me in the eye and said 'no m'am. you have a double name. your social card is going to say the same name as your driver's license. if you want us to change the name on your social you need your driver's license to say the name you want us to change it to.' i said 'so wait, my new card will say the same name as my old card?' she said 'that's right' and something about how i had given her the right to tear up my old card, by applying for a new card.

the card that came in the mail said 'margaret megan boyle.' i drove to the maryland DMV where i got my license. the DMV is out in the country and i thought they'd maybe be more lenient than the new york people. the woman behind the desk looked at my IDs with her eyebrows close together. i explained i was trying to get my IDs to all say the same thing, and that the social security office had told me i needed my driver's license to be changed first. the woman said 'i don't know why they'd tell you that, we need your social first. we use whatever your social security card says.' i said 'what about my birth certificate, does that matter?' she said 'why does your social security card say a different name than your birth certificate?' i said 'i guess i got it with my dad, i don't know, a long time ago, i don't know why no one checked to see if they said the same thing.' she said 'now why does your passport say 'megan matlock boyle?'' i said 'i don't know, no one checked.' she said 'you at least need your passport. you need at least two things to say the same thing. but really, they all need to say the same thing.'

it had been over a month since i had stopped CDL lessons with the polish guy. near the end, we had started studying the license requirements list and 'conspiring' about how i could get a new york license without getting a new social security card or passport: i find my marriage certificate [worth 2 points, knew it said 'margaret megan matlock boyle'], high school diploma [worth two points, pretty sure it said 'megan margaret matlock boyle'], and 'something else, you figure it out, two more points.' he said the only new york DMV that issued immediate temporary licenses was in coney island. he would say 'so you go to coney island, hm? with your papers, hm? then they give you new license, then you say 'can i take CDL test' and they say yes, you get it the same day. coney island is the only place. you gotta wake up early.' i would say 'that's fine, i'll wake up early that day.' he would ask me when i thought i'd have everything straightened out and i would lie and he would nod and say 'good, you straighten it out' with a wary but not hopeless facial expression.

around the time i visited the maryland DMV the truck man left me a voicemail asking if i had gotten my name straightened out yet. i called him back and said not yet, it was taking forever, waiting for things to get mailed to me. zachary and i had started looking for apartments in philadelphia. we were hoping to move in together by april or may, i think. there would be no reason for me to have a new york driver's license (commercial or standard) anymore. didn't tell the truck man.

i looked online at passport things. i printed out an application for a new passport and wrote 'margaret megan matlock boyle' as my name. i checked a box that said 'name correction' and wrote 'it has never said the same thing as my birth certificate' next to it on a line. i got a new passport photo at a UPS store and mailed a package with the photos, the application, and my birth certificate to the passport offices. i knew i wouldn't be living in brooklyn much longer and i never 'officially' lived there in the first place so i listed my mom's apartment as my permanent address. it seemed likely that the passport offices would return my application with an 'INVALID' stamp, maybe an 'INVALID' stamp on my birth certificate if it hadn't already been 'confiscated.'

a few weeks later my mom called and said a package from the passport offices had arrived. i drove to maryland and opened the package containing my birth certificate, a 'leftover bonus keepsake photo,' and a new passport which said 'first name: 'margaret megan,' middle: 'matlock,' last name: 'boyle.'

felt like the happiest day of my life.

i went to a social security office in maryland with my passport and birth certificate. there was only one 'waiting area' in the maryland office. only a few people were there. the woman who helped me didn't notice the blank space under 'father's social security number.' she said 'so wait, is 'margaret megan' your first name?' i've never been sure if 'megan' is my first or middle name. i said 'yeah, it's my first name. double name.'

i forget what address my new social security card was mailed to, but it said 'margaret megan matlock boyle.' i went to the maryland DMV with my new social security card and passport. they changed my license so easily i don't remember what was said.

i think i had a maryand driver's license that said 'margaret megan matlock boyle' for less than a week.

this is when i did something i don't understand fully. i know i did it on march 28, 2012, when zachary and i had already signed the lease (effective april 1, 2012) for the philadelphia apartment.

i went to the coney island DMV and had them give me a temporary new york state driver's license. a permanent license, which i still have, would be mailed to me. i didn't ask to take the CDL test, i just left with a paper license that would expire in a few weeks. i took pictures of the coney island boardwalk. the sun was bright. only a few people were walking around. i had never been there. i think i was thinking i would live in philadelphia but occasionally drive to new york for truck driving lessons with the polish man.

some time in may or june 2012 i got my new york driver's license transferred to a pennsylvania driver's license. they had a new computer system and 'margaret megan' wouldn't fit under 'first name.' the DMV woman urged me to list 'megan' as my middle name, which i foresaw leading to future hells of confusedly explaining what my name is 'technically' to frustrated desk clerks behind bulletproof glass. i said "margaretmegan' is really fine, no space, it's really really okay, i just want to be sure it says the same thing everywhere, on everything.'

6:39PM: sitting at desk in my room at mom's. oh shit i forgot to mail masha's package. i will fedex that ass. i forgot i decided to enlist in the navy.

8:00pm: asked mom what movie she was going to watch tonight while fumbling around the kitchen and dining room table, gathering things. She said 'maybe the Abe lincoln vampire one, but I don't want to be scared.' I went 'ooooooh.' Walked to my room and picked up my phone and walked back to the main room. I said 'I can't believe I figured it out. I'll just do space.' mom said something positive about college and NASA. I walked to her bathroom and applied deodorant. Pictured something vague about 'the steps ahead of me' and felt a pang of fear and loss. Mom said 'driving trucks just didn't seem like you, I don't know, somehow.' I said 'y-eah, now I'll be driving spaceships. Flying jets and spaceships' and heard slightly forced childish enthusiasm in my voice. Mom said 'well or whatever.' I said 'I'll have something new to concentrate on.' mom said 'you should never stop writing though, but you don't have to, you can always come back to it.' I said 'I'll write in space. If I feel like it.' she said 'and who knows where you'll go. They'll be going to mars, in your lifetime. You could go to mars!' I put on my shoes. Mom said 'did you hear about Angelina Jolie? She's gotten her breasts and ovaries removed.' I said 'she did it on purpose? Without cancer?' mom said 'well, apparently her mother had this type of cancer.' I said 'talk about attention-seeking.' mom said 'I know, really' and laughed. I said 'I don't like her. She'll never make it in space. Especially without her boobs.' mom laughed and I smiled and walked downstairs and out to my car.

8:16pm: driving to dad's office for dinner. Not hungry yet

8:17-8:45PM: dad gave me a tour of his new offices. they built them really fast and he's rented out most of them. i've seen the tour before but i didn't want to mention it.

dad told a story about how he put $200 in the building contractor's hand when he shook it for the first time the other day. the contractor refused the money. dad said 'wait, but don't you have a friend?' the contractor said 'yeah.' my dad said 'this is for your friend, buy something for your friend.' i said 'oh man' and grinned. dad's nose scrunched up and he 'cackled' giddily, 'my dad-style,' in a way he does rarely.

dad showed me an area which he and mary (other landlord) are converting into a 'meditation/relaxation room.' it used to be an office. he said 'and i'm putting my elliptical machine in here, dr. oaken says 'forty-five minutes a day on that thing, if you wanna live until you die.''

i said 'i'm so happy for you' and things like that and asked questions which would normally sound 'fake' but i was sincere asking, and interested in his answers. i was happy to see dad acting so happy.

dad gave me a headset for talking on the phone while driving. i put it in my car and dad said 'are you driving?' i said 'oh i don't know, i was just putting the headset in. or. i'll drive, do you want me to drive?' he opened the passenger-side door and paused a moment, looking down, then said 'no, i think i'll drive.'

we walked to his car. there was a toolbox on my seat. dad said 'i got you tools, here are your tools!' i said 'oh boy, oh tools, thank you. tools in a toolbox. does it have a drill?' he said 'no, well. this one, this box doesn't have a drill. but you can borrow mine.' i said 'no no no, i'll just hammer the thing i was thinking of drilling, hammering is fine.' dad said 'i thought i bought you this toolbox a while ago!' i said 'i'm pretty sure you did. yeah i think you did, it looks familiar, from my old apartment.'

dad pulled into the parking lot of the seafood restaurant where we had planned to eat. a handful of agelessly old-looking, 'active lifestyle' people in silk shirts and jewelry were milling around outside. dad slowed as we passed them. i said 'what if there's a wait, looks like a wait.' dad said 'is there a wait?' the people looked 'bleakly unfamiliarly acquainted' to me. i said 'seems fancy.' dad said 'yeah, it might be.' i said 'let's do the double T instead. this seems too fancy.' dad said 'yeah, long wait, too fancy.'

i showed him the e-cigarette. he tried it, nodded, matter-of-factly said 'it hits you.' i said stuff about the batteries not working well and ordering new ones. he said 'where do they sell those things?' i said 'like CVS, rite aid.' he said 'wanna go to CVS and get a new one before we eat? so you're not thinking about it at dinner?' surprised he would think to ask/offer that. i said 'oh no, it's okay.' he said 'are you sure? it's right next to the double T.' i said 'okay.' i said anxious things about how it's not really smoking and dad would respond with a 'padding' comment, like a repetition or slightly different phrasing of whatever i had said. he pulled into a parking spot at CVS. i said 'thanks for offering to do this, i wouldn't have even thought to.' he said 'well now you won't be wondering about it all night. plus, i think they're a stress reliever, cigarettes can be stress relievers.' continued anxiously saying things, walking fast into CVS with dad behind me, increasingly aware that i was about to ask for an e-cigarette battery with my dad, and there was maybe something socially 'off' about this.

the man behind the counter said they didn't sell 'blu' or any brand of e-cigarettes. i said 'thank you' and started walking away. turned my head to see if dad was following. saw him gesturing vaguely and saying 'do you know where else they're sold' to the man behind the counter, whose head seemed like it could've been politely shaking 'no' from the moment we walked in CVS.

dad seemed ready to abandon dinner to hunt for an e-cigarette battery. i remember him doing stuff like this when i was little. one time at the beach we were in an arcade, taking turns maneuvering a joystick controlling a 'grabbing claw' in one of those impossible toy machines. we were aiming for a stuffed 'dino' dinosaur toy from the flintsones. there were two or three non-traditionally colored 'dinos' in the machine. the claw wasn't picking up anything. i wanted a 'dino' really bad. dad gave me quarters and told me to keep trying while he used the bathroom. a little later he returned to the machine with a man holding a set of keys. the man opened the machine and gave me three 'dinos.' i was so happy. i think even then i knew 'this doesn't happen to most people.' over the years my dad got really good at getting things from claw machines. it's like his 'thing.' he and my mom went to the movies every thursday and he would almost always bring home a stuffed toy for me. by the time he got really good at it i was in high school.

8:57pm: typed '8:57pm: diner' in phone while exiting dad's car outside the diner.

8:58-10:33PM: as we walked inside i continued a story i had started in the car about chris hadfield (astronaut in 'space oddity' video). he was answering a class of sixth grader's questions from the international space station. someone asked him why he wanted to be an astronaut. he said something like 'just after my tenth birthday they landed on the moon.' dad opened the door to the diner. i said 'how old were you when they landed on the moon? nineteen sixty-nine?' dad thought a minute and said 'i was…twenty-seven. whoa-ho-ho-ho! twenty-seven! you're picking up where i left off.'

a waiter approached our table and said his name was danny. my dad said 'dana?' the waiter and i said 'danny.' dad said 'oh, oh, i have a bad ear, i'm sorry. i'm mike' and shook danny's hand. it used to embarrass me that he'd introduce himself to waiters. i ordered a spinach salad and maryland crab soup. dad ordered some kind of chicken pasta dish and a salad and matzah ball soup.

mostly talked about the navy. i asked a lot of questions.

the most interesting things my dad had to say about when he was in the navy (1958-1962):

- when he got off the bus of enlisted guys the first thing they did was shave everyone's head. then they took them to a room where everyone got naked and their clothes and belongings were stored in bags. they were issued uniforms. on the ship, he shared a room with 50 guys. there was a table, a garbage bucket, and a radio in the middle of the room.

- he showed me how to salute. you put the tips of the fingers of your right hand to your temple and move it fast to chest-height. the marines make a more exaggerated chopping downwards motion. dad said the general rule was 'if it's moving: salute it. if it's not moving: paint it' (they did a lot of painting on the ship).

- dad worked his way up to be an officer in charge of 13 guys (i said 'you told them what to do? how did that work?' he made a face and said 'not very well'). he was a radar technician. he had a tiny office with a door sealed with ten latches. sometimes he would go to his office to nap, which wasn't allowed. if someone was about to catch him, by the time all the latches opened he would be awake enough to pretend he had been working the whole time.

- he described all the stripes and things that get added to your uniform the higher you rank, with 'tour guide'-like interest, miming stripes on his sleeve. he said 'and then when you're an e-six you get a chevron with an eagle coming out of it, you know, which is what i had, you've seen that picture of me.' i thought of the photo of him in uniform on the top of his bookcase by the plastic flowers, that would be there when he came home from dinner. he inhaled and held it a moment, then shook his head like he had surrendered something and said 'oh no, i don't know why i'm crying, why do i do this.' i said 'it's okay.' he said 'i don't even know why' and chuckled a little, crying less as he continued describing the stripes and chevrons.

- most of the time at sea was spent playing 'war games.' dad's ship would leave from rhode island and a submarine would leave from connecticut at the same time. dad's job was to use radar to track the submarine as if it was the enemy. if the submarine crew detected someone tracking them, they were supposed to turn off the submarine to appear invisible to the radar. if the ship crew 'caught' the submarine before the submarine crew knew about it, they'd send depth charges ('cap gun missiles that just made noise') down to it. the submarine would surface and they'd say 'hi, good job' to each other. one time the submarine went off the radar for a long time. dad's ship continued sending depth charges but it stayed dormant. they got worried and stopped. the submarine surfaced. it was russian. dad said 'and then they blinked their lights, you know, morse code, they said: 'hi how are you.' we said 'hi we are fine.' and it went along on its way. it was just there, in connecticut, a russian submarine!'

- john f. kennedy and jackie kennedy and walter cronkite were on dad's ship, the joseph p. kennedy ('john was on the ship because he wanted his brother's name to be historic'), during the blockade. there were a lot of ships and jets. the whole navy, maybe. sounded really exciting, i'm not describing it well. russian ships were moving towards cuba so they could attack the u.s. and the u.s. found out. all the russian ships retreated but one merchant ship. dad said four or five guys from his ship got on a small boat (he described as 'from here to the other side of the room' i said 'like one of the lifeboats on the cruise ship?' he said 'yeah, yeah, almost exactly like that, yeah. a little smaller') to make sure there were no missiles on the russian merchant ship. he said 'and then we told them to go back to russia, and they did. they didn't really do a thorough check of the ship, the guys. everyone was nervous.' he said something about khrushchev. jesus, wonder if i can describe… he 'acted' the conversation between JFK and khrushchev with a lot of attitude, like this: 'khrushchev said 'look at our ships, look at what we can do.' and we said 'oh yeah? well look at our ships, think about what we can do.' the merchant ship was just khrushchev saying 'don't forget, i'm not afraid to do this, too.' so we said 'oh we see that you can do that. you'd better not do any more though, because look at us.' he was giggling kind of, seemed really happy to tell this story.

- by the time the cuban missile crisis started, dad didn't need to be in the navy anymore, but they made everyone stay an extra six months. he really didn't want to be there. he started growing a beard. cleanliness was big. you were not supposed to grow beards. he told his friends he was growing the beard so when he got off the boat 'castro would be able to recognize whose side he was on.' the guy in charge of my dad noticed and called him into his office. he said 'boyle? get that goddamned thing off your face.'

- drill thing: after the missile crisis, they started doing this circle thing for practice. the u.s. owns an island in the carribean near the panama canal. they test bombs there. dad's ship was in a circular line with a lot of other ships. there were jets, too. just…it was everyone, moving in a circle around the island and the panama canal. whenever your ship or whatever reached the island you just 'gave it all you got.' you shot everything. some ships contained marines who would run onto the island while it was getting 'practice-shot' at, who would then shoot 'giving it all they got' at nothing (when i asked about this dad said 'they were marines, they just knew how to not get shot' which i don't…jesus, i don't know about this one). i said 'seems like a thing kurt vonnegut would put in a book, going around in a circle to take turns shooting at nothing.' dad did his 'dad-style' nose-scrunch cackle and said 'yes! yes that's exactly what it was like! a kurt vonnegut thing.' he looked happy. later he said 'it was really something, to do that. it was like all the fourth of julys, just going off, shooooom.'

NOT A NAVY THING BUT INTERESTING:

we had been excitedly talking about my 'realistic course of action' that would result in me becoming an astronaut. dad said 'did i ever tell you about the astronaut who put his thumb—' i smiled and nodded and made a 'squinched-out' thumb gesture. dad continued 'well, so i guess he became some kind of preacher after this. he has a following. after he figured out you can do that thing, blot out the earth with your thumb, it's just this tiny dot.'

a little later dad said 'this story is a little embarrassing but i'll tell it anyway. so, the astronaut who did the thumb thing, he apparently grew up in chicago in this poor neighborhood where the walls were paper-thin, and his bedroom—he lived next to the mcmanus family—his bedroom was right next to mr. and mrs. mcmanus' bedroom, so he heard everything. this might've been another astronaut, this might've been neil armstrong. anyway, so one night he hears mrs. mcmanus [looked away and sort of chuckled], mrs. mcmanus from the bedroom, she says 'i'll put that thing in my mouth the day they send a man to the moon!" dad laughed and i laughed a little less. i said 'oh noooooo. no way. you're making that up, that's not real.' dad was still laughing. he said 'no, it's really real—they asked him what he was thinking about when he landed on the moon, so that's what he [continued laughing].' i laughed a little more.

10:34pm: throughout dinner waiters added tables to a maybe seven-table 'spread' of high school-aged girls in the center of the room. a waiter added a table connecting the seven-table spread to the booth behind dad. the girls were loud. at some point after we had finished eating i was telling dad about how astronauts exercise in the international space station (which was built by people adding onto it, like how the waiters were adding tables, didn't realize this). dad said 'how do they do it without weights?' i explained something poorly about a video i watched, think i was gesturing a lot and saying things like 'they harnessed the vacuum, it's negative resistance, they use the space vacuum.' a waiter added another table and dad and i noticed and i took advantage of the moment to say 'these bitches are annoying, can we go? plus i have to pee.' dad made a face like he was also annoyed by the bitches and relieved to be relieved of them.

10:58pm: dad drove us back to his office. i forget what we talked about and what reminded me it was probably a year ago today when i found out i was pregnant. i said something like that. dad said something in a gentle voice. i said 'it's may seventeenth, right?' he said 'yup, may seventeenth, that's today.' i knew i didn't find out on may 17, i felt that not being true. i remembered 'may 16' as something important. dad made a right turn into his office. he said 'what was that like, finding that out?' i said 'i threw up, after i saw it. found out. threw up in the toilet. then i cried a lot. i didn't know what to do so i called mom. i was just crying a lot. then i called zachary, i think, or no, i waited for him to get home, he was at work.' dad parked and didn't turn off the engine. he said 'i remember we were parked in this very spot, or one like it, when you told me about how you had that done, the d&c. i was happy you told me but i was so sorry you had to go through all that.' i was embarrassed for having brought it up. i knew we both knew i didn't have a 'd&c,' and that he was maybe embarrassed too, which is why he'd want to call it that. i said 'i'm happy i told you too. i wasn't going to. i thought. something about nana, you'd get mad at me like nana got mad at you.' i stepped out of the car before he turned off the engine. he said 'oh no, no, no. i want you to feel like i'm,' (sensed him stepping out of the car and walking near me but i didn't want to look), 'you can say anything, have a seamless, open communication with me.' he hugged my arm a little. his other arm was holding the toolbox. i did something 'icky' that i do sometimes, in situations where the other person seems more emotional than me, i'm embarrassed to type this. i said 'i do, i feel that.'

dad said i should always feel free to call him or leave him voicemails or emails, he always wants to hear more from me. i said 'i know you like voice-mails and stuff like that. i think i've been feeling too ashamed of myself, to talk. like i know you want to hear from me but i'm ashamed to tell you about what my life is like because i'm not doing anything, i haven't been interested in anything. and it's always nice that you want to hear from me. it's just hard to imagine why, for me, like why would anyone be interested when to me it feels so, you know, so it's hard, yeah it's felt too shameful to talk about.' dad nodded a moment. he said 'you know, i think i get that. i didn't think about it like that.' i said 'but now i'm interested in something, so' and smiled and we hugged. i said 'now i'll get to tell you about space.' dad said 'that's right. oh i can just tell things are getting better now. there's nowhere to go but up,' broke the hug to point at the sky, said 'hey! mars, that's up, you'll go to mars, you're going up!'

11:55pm: remembered i had left a bag of clothes and my guitar at dad's apartment when i got to mom's. drove to dad's. the fake teeth security guard was there with a 'cop buddy.' i was on the phone with dad. the guard didn't remember me maybe, motioned for me to stop so he could write down my license plate number. the cop said 'you know, when you see a cop you have to at least pretend to not be on the phone.' i sort of hung up. made a face and said 'i know i know, i'm sorry.' the cop said 'he's writing down your plates so i can give you a ticket.' i said 'really?' he said 'no, just pretend better next time.' the security guard saluted me (for people just tuning in, he always salutes).

MAY 18, 2013

12:32am: dad helped me transfer clothes from the broken bag to two bags. we looked for a capo and a tuner. then we were standing by my car for a while. we seemed to be prolonging conversation intentionally, maybe. dad reminded me to get my oil checked.

dad always wants to show me how to check the oil. when i was little i liked watching him wipe the dipstick with the paper towel and put it back and take it out again and kind of turn it and say 'looks about right.' he also used to cut open vitamins. there would be a bunch of vitamins on a paper towel and he would dissect them with his pocket knife. he is always ready to help cut something open with the pocket knife.

i checked my oil and dad watched. i did it right. i put in a quart.

12:33am: fake teeth security guard saluted me and i saluted back. haven't felt confident that my 'salute' would not look like a 'heil hitler' until tonight. he said 'have a good night hon.' dad calls him 'captain [something].' now i know a captain is almost the highest you can get the navy. now he is a security guard. this and the previous thing and to some degree all the stuff i've written about dad sound corny. it didn't feel like it.

1:14AM: walked inside mom's a few minutes ago. she's been watching youtube videos of the international space station. she said 'there's gotta be long periods of nothing, i know there needs to be, before you feel like something makes sense, you know. before you feel like you fit somewhere. i know, it's happened to me a lot. there are just these periods.'

5:41AM: snorted 40mg adderall. thought it'd work better since stomach is full.

6:27AM: it would maybe be bad to enlist today since i didn't sleep and i have adderall eyes.

9:01AM: took a break from typing a few hours ago to figure out why i thought 'may 16' was important. found the number of an abortion clinic in gmail. looked at text messages. on may 16th i texted zachary 'it's the building attached to the bank's apothecary...suite 202'

he was parking the car. the place was hard to find. the next text from him is five days later, about work.

i'm not trying to make a big deal about this. i am thinking a lot of clichés. it's a cliché to get sentimental about 'anniversaries.' also hard to not think about this right now. reading old emails and chats and text messages, knowing how things turned out, the stuff we weren't paying attention to seems so obvious. all the parts where he was trying to pretend he wasn't getting more and more disappointed and i was trying to pretend everything was okay. getting drunk and arguing and apologizing the next day. i'm the worst. 'the one who took the ship down.' real sinker.

it's childish or uninformed to think 'one person is responsible for a relationship failing.' i know it's not just one person. blahballah.

10:15AM: TWO THINGS:

1. i hate it when the computer or the google says 'look, it's a new thing, this is how it works, click this box to make this window go away. i said click this box to make this go away. you need to click it. you can't do anything until you click it. i need to know that you understand that i am doing something new for you, i am showing you my new thing i made just so you have an easier time with me, HM, do you like that, do you...can you at least show me you NOTICED my EFFORTS by CLICKING this SIMPLE, EASY-TO-CLICK BOX, TELLING ME THAT YOU UNDERSTAND THAT I HAVE IMPROVED FOR YOU?!?!?!' I'M NOT ASKING FOR YOU TO FALL IN LOVE WITH ME AGAIN, JUST NOTICE SOMETHING I DID FOR YOU, OKAY?'

2. would think perfect geometric shapes would grow the same way as plants, like why is there no 'cube patch' where families take pictures of themselves picking 'cubes with cubic leaves'

(#2 is a little lofty)

10:47PM: mom has entered room twice this morning.

TWO MOM INTERCEPTIONS:

1. mom said 'can i ask you a science question that i don't think you'll know the answer to and that probably doesn't matter?' i said 'sure.' she said 'alright. well. so, with all of this sea salt, the sea salt has gone up in popularity. we're all buying sea salt. and i used to buy morton salt, you know, because they said it had iodine in it, which is supposed to be good i guess. but does that mean...? with all of this non-iodized salt now, that we're suddenly eating—or rather not eating—iodine. so what does that mean?'

2. mom said 'do you know of a movie that came out this year, that's about two people who just almost get to talk to each other? you see their lives, like how they would talk if they could? because they're in parallel universes? but i think they can see each other though.' i said 'is it that one, 'another earth?' they actually see another earth in the sky, and the girl killed the guy's family?' mom said 'no, no—no. but that's what got me thinking of this one. i think because we've been talking about space too and i don't know. well, so no, so in this one—i think it's recent, this year, two-thousand thirteen—so you can almost see how the guy and the girl will get to meet and they're so close to meeting, you get to see them—the guy is on this one end of the mountain and the girl is on the opposite end and their [motions] hands get to touch. does this sound familiar?' i said 'sort of.' looked up the list of 'parallel universe' movies. keep picturing a movie poster that's mostly blue, like swimming pool blue, surrounding a mermaid woman with blonde hair and outlines of 'different earth spheres' across her body and the movie is called like, 'eu' or something.

11:05AM: licked finger and inserted in nose, to probe for adderall crumbs. harvested 'sweet taste.' neurotic concern about 'wasting' close to 2mg that is now trapped in nose. i could bite close to 2mg from the last 20mg. 2/20ths of an adderall. to ease. to quell my stingy fiending mind. yuck.

TWO RESPONSES TO THINGS:

1. 'marie cattoway' posted a facebook status update saying: 'Do any women actually enjoy getting oral…seems made up by men'

I ENJOY GETTING ORAL!!!!

orgasms caused by another person doing something to me:

98% oral sex

1.9% finger sex

0.1% penis vagina sex (think i'd remember it, if it'd happened, allowing for 0.1% not-remembering error)

it's fun to say 'penis vagina sex.'

vaginal penis sex…vagina penis…(just trying that out, honestly doesn't matter which one comes first, both are equally funny to me) ('vaginal penis' is not funny to me but i haven't really thought about it) (penis vagina)

2. read article about how it's legal for women to be topless in public now, it's discrimination if…what normally happens happens

that's cool

imagine the person who ogles men's chests the way breasts will be ogled before they look 'normal'

you could make a case that it's less socially appropriate for men to be bare-chested because their nipples would've grown into breasts if they had remained 'XX' chromosomes, like they're freakishly underdeveloped

if you are a topless female ever i am going to ogle you hard because i bet you will look sexy and i like to look at boobs and sexy stuff!!!!!!

not kidding!!!!!!!!

11:52PM: refilled coffee. talked with mom about 'why do insurance agents keep leaving me voicemails to follow-up on my online inquiries,' 'has the attorney called you about the accident settlement yet,' 'horoscopes'

12:49PM: going to use this once-in-a-lifetime opportunity to tell the world i don't care about craft beer, but i also don't care about 'anti-craft beer,' like, 'reclaiming shitty beer as cool american heritage beer,' or any beer

also don't care about wine

also don't care about coffee

what are other things people care about…

i don't care about macs vs. pcs

i generally don't care about the quality of things

1:52PM: what else

2:01PM: i don't care about lateness

2:03PM: i don't care about being 'female,' that's a big one people care about

2:24PM: walked to kitchen to recharge e-cigarette battery, thinking something like "umbilical' and 'unbiblical' are similar. more could be said about this. 'unbiblical cord." the bagel mom offered me yesterday was still in the toaster. i said 'they call it 'smoke juice." mom laughed like a heiress having a 'marvelous time' at a gala, then said 'yeah.' i said 'smoke juice.' she said 'what are you saying?' i said 'the people—'johnson creek,' it's called, i think—that make this [gestured with e-cigarette], they call the insides 'smoke juice." mom said 'they call what?' i said 'the water, the liquid nicotine stuff. in here. i like it: 'smoke juice.' it sounds cool.' mom laughed the same way and said 'oh, that is cool.'

2:41PM: afraid to drive to NYC. want to keep partying with mom. planning to going to naval recruitment office monday.

5:12pm: heard movement in the kitchen after maybe ten minutes of silence, then mom's voice, sounding both distracted and consoling, say 'soon it'll seem like nothing.'

5:23pm: re-toasted bagel while mom put away groceries. Spread cream cheese and said 'I know you're embarrassed and anxious about me writing about you and you don't want to read it yet but I just want you to know you have nothing to be embarrassed about, you're my best friend.' mom said 'oh-ho-ho. Oh no. You're my best friend too Meggie, since you came into my life.' Felt heat behind my face and it was hard to stop looking at cream cheese. Gave mom big hug.

Mom took a box of toothpaste from a grocery bag and walked to me. She said 'now, do you know how long it took me to find this? I figured out it has to say the color, it has to say 'radiant white,' it has to say it's white. Because I bought this other kind and it was blue, there was all this blue gook everywhere, yuck. I know it doesn't matter but I just think that's not what whitening toothpaste is supposed to be! And then I made the mistake of buying this other kind that turned out to be 'psychedelic orange."

I said 'was it orange flavor too?'

She said 'yes, it was. It was really, really sick.'

She told dad about the astronaut video but she didn't think he'd like it. I said 'he definitely won't like it if both of us told him about it.'

5:42pm: wandered around 'looking for things,' stalling drive. I said 'I can't find my water bottle lid, it's black.'

Mom said 'I'll help you look for it, it's black? A black lid?'

I said 'yeah, definitely a black lid.'

Mom said 'black lid, definitely, definitely a black lid' in 'rain man' voice.

I said 'yeah because it's definitely a black lid.'

Searched different rooms at a similar pace, saying things in 'rain man' voice. She said 'do you want these? I found them in the car and they are [funny voice] so not me,' holding a pair of glasses that looked sort of like Zachary's. I said 'I'll take them, sure. Were they grandma's?' she said 'you know, they very well might've been. They very well might've been, because I don't know how they ended up here. Your grandma used to like to steal other people's glasses, at the end of her life.'

I said the black lid was probably at my apartment. Mom said something about a case of water bottles in the garage, then 'don't bring them up, I'll have dad bring them up.' Picked up case of 36 small water bottles and started walking up stairs. Mom said 'oh honey you didn't have to lift those things.' I said 'I know, it just seemed easier for me to do it.'

Mom said 'what would I do without you' in funny voice.

I said 'you would be okay, you would just be dehydrated.'

She said 'I wouldn't pee.'

5:45-9:25PM: drove.

9:30pm: emailed Juliet that I'd be online in 30mins for Skype interview. Parked ten blocks south of apartment.

10:30PM: i like the walk from 108th st to 118th st. a lot of open windows, unnamed stores, hurricane-damaged buildings that look easier to forget than repair. passed a tattooed woman leaning out a window, looking somewhere i wouldn't go, facing the same distance.

a crowd of kids were playing a running game on my street. i live at the end of a dead end street. funny. smiled at the kids and felt close to them in age. attempted eye contact. if they'd seen me they'd probably think 'creepy adult.'

fed cats and cleaned their box and heated pizza slice and drank a beer and downloaded skype. juilet said she was grading papers and would be available whenever. going to sign in to skype.

MAY 18, 2013

1:20AM: have been talking with juiliet. interview portion was short. wish i had typed jokes. she told me about 'cock docking' and showed me pictures, then we showed each other pictures of vestigial tails and ex-boyfriends. i felt happy imagining her life.

drank three beers. forget how we ended up talking about bill clinton. i said we should bet on how old he's going to be when he dies.

HOW OLD WILL BILL CLINTON BE WHEN HE DIES:

- megan: 92 (all-in).
- juliet: 87, 92, 93. definitely not 89, 90, 91, 98.

we didn't discuss money but he is currently 66.

1:48AM: looked at clock.

2:11AM: fiev beers two pizzasloices

2:57AM: brushed teeth turned off all but rainbow lights has been 40 or something hours since i slept

3:13AM: UTI feeling taped cabinet doors shut to stop alvie from trying to open.

12:00PM: woke, ate chocolate thing, gray sky, going back to sleep.

3:19PM: woke from what felt like three-day long dream. featured sex. bunk beds. race track/locker room. ate more of the chocolate thing. it's almost gone. shirley is kneading next to me, running her motor (purring) hard.

4:18PM: cleaned cats' water device.

4:46PM: ate bonsai dwarf pizza. typing comments on tao's flickr photostream via 'it's always nice to see someone has commented.'

5:00PM: do not foresee leaving apartment today.

7:03PM: commissioned tao to make a version of 'fucked tuna' art, did other internet things, fed cats, read 'slapstick.' thinking of today as 'getting ready' for navy tomorrow.

7:27PM: zachary texted 'Is you in ny and have a set of hump's keys with you' i texted 'Yeah/yeah.' don't want to drive or shower.

7:41PM: mom is visiting tuesday for two days. tomorrow i'll go to the navy and get car inspected. then it'll be tuesday and mom and i will go out on the town. good two days coming up.

9:24PM: ate an orange.

MAY 20, 2013

1:28AM: have been reading 'slapstick.'

1:37AM: zachary, then a number i didn't recognize called. called zachary back. he's at a ramada inn in queens with stephen. at some point i said 'you guys should just come here' and he said 'i wouldn't do that.' he put stephen on the phone. i said 'mo rocca inn' or 'ramada mo rocca.' stephen said they ate burger king and drank dom perignon with his parents. told him about finding the chartreuse on the street and he knew, zachary had forwarded him my email. i said i couldn't open the bottle. he said he could open it. zachary was on the phone again. he said 'so you got your macbook pro,' then an address, then 'that's how it's like in queens, it's like [number] dash [something].' typed addresses in google maps. he said 'if it's going to be more than twenty minutes i mean, don't do it.' directions loaded. i said 'google says thirty minutes,' 'and also my car is ten blocks away,' 'and also i'd like to shower before.' he said 'no you can shower after i do stuff to you.' looked in mirror. pulled elastic ponytail holder and watched greasy hair fall to shoulders. thought 'he likes it better 'down."

asked if he was drunk and he said 'am i drunk? are you talking to me?' he asked if i was on birth control and i said 'yes' and he said 'well definitely come over.' i said 'i don't want to do it with stephen in the room' and he said 'stephen needs to get ice.' i said i would come.

1:42AM: put hairbrush back on sink. stood. didn't know what i wanted to do. looked at things in bathroom. thought 'i should refill it with a new toilet paper roll, for in the morning. i'll want that.'

1:43AM: called zachary. asked if he'd had sex with anyone since the last time i saw him. he said he had, with two people. asked when. he said 'like, i don't know, six-to-twelve hours ago.' i said 'oh. okay, i don't think i can have sex with you then, i don't want to come over, i'm sorry.' he said something i forget. we hung up.

thought a lot and fast. examples of thoughts: 'does what i'm doing make sense,' 'what do i want,' 'earlier i was about to solicit person i don't know from the internet for sex so why would this stop me,' '[picture of zachary saying things to both girls he's had sex with before having sex with them, then his face and body having sex with them] and immediate ['repulsed' isn't the right word, it was more of like a general pang, like a stabby pang] feeling,' 'zachary hasn't been talking to me and has been posting videos of jamie's apartment and cats but he didn't have sex with her,' 'it would feel bad to write about how i had sex with him,' 'sam emailed me a few minutes ago,' 'i have a crush on sam still but he lives far away,' '[imagining myself from the perspective of anyone who could become interested in me, reading that i had had sex with zachary tonight in these circumstances, felt less interested in 'megan'],' 'i wouldn't have an orgasm because of all the things i've been thinking about,' 'my back looks bad from picking at it,' 'i haven't showered in a lot of days,' 'my car is ten blocks away and i've been drinking and i want to be productive tomorrow,' 'i want to do it,' 'this is what it's like this is sad,' 'i miss how it used to be,' 'why did everything go like this.'

1:47AM: 'pounded' 1mg xanax and got another beer.

1:48AM: zachary texted 'That's stupid.' i texted 'Naw it ain't nothin' and 'Just trying to be better.'

2:06AM: no response. seems like the last time we'll talk, maybe. i can picture him reading this and thinking i'm stupid and it's stupid that i didn't want to have sex with him and hating how i write and other things about me. fuck that. i can picture him before calling me, thinking 'megan has sex with anyone, i'll just call megan to have sex with her,' having had sex six-to-twelve hours before me.

2:24AM: i'm glad he told me. he could've not.

2:40AM: got another beer. relieved to see one more will be left, after this. have been texting with mira and sam cooke.

UPPING THE STAKES:

if i don't talk to the navy recruit tomorrow i have to eat a bowl of dry cat food.

if i have sex with anyone i don't want a relationship with i have to eat a bowl of dry cat food and half a can of wet food.

2:53AM-4:[something]AM: texted with mira and sam. they were on coke at sam's apartment and wanted to have a threesome with me. thought 'it'd be different than zachary maybe, we'd still be want to be friends, we've already had a threesome didn't affect the friendship.' showered. ate 2mg xanax. fell asleep composing an email to them about the porn i look at (they were 'analyzing sam's porn stash'). texted i was too tired and on xanax and drunk to drive.

1:45PM: woke. saw five missed calls from zachary around 7AM. ate ikea apple pie, noopept. called zachary and he sort of apologized. i said it was okay. made tentative plans to make dinner tonight.

2:16-2:36PM: meditated. you're supposed to do it for 20 minutes. surprised i was still 'trained' to do 20 minutes exactly, like, looked at the clock at 2:36. the lady who taught me said sometimes if you haven't done it in a while you feel fatigued afterwards and it was okay to sleep. curled up in a ball surrounding a purring shirley.

4:16PM: woke. drank red bull and made a hummus tortilla thing. emailed mira and sam cooke and sam pink and someone named adriano who showed me this article of a fucked guy who has apparently made 13,000 edits to wikipedia pages of writers he doesn't like.

4:58PM: navy recruitment office closes at 5pm. shit. going to eat a bowl of dry cat food now i guess. i will film it. seems 'deserved.' i failed at something today.

5:40PM: i ate the cat food. maybe half a cup. kept burping 'fish meal' taste and vomited. the only bad part was the 'fish meal' taste. a little tangy and bland and vitamin-y. uploaded video of this to youtube.

5:46PM: drank a shot of whiskey thinking 'the hair of the dog that bit me.' post-cat food recovery. the whiskey will burn the remaining 'life source food bits' from stomach maybe. what i ate today is a Real Man's Meal. served my task-incompleting ass up a Real Man's Meal.

7:04pm: walking to car to drive to Zachary's. Going to eat salad. Drank two or three more shots before leaving and straightened my hair and tried on a lot of outfits. A tall old Asian man wearing an adidas track suit smoking passed on my right. Would rather hang out with him than anyone.

7:07pm: called mom, no answer. Still burping fish meal.

7:10pm: A woman with a similar facial expression/gait as me is walking slightly behind me. Smells like marijuana and 'the beach.'

7:23pm: driving to Zachary's. Smells like beach big time. Feel nothing.

7:24pm: I lied. I feel 'sitting here now and always with incommunicable memories of the past few days' and 'horrible emptiness caused by listening to 'goodbye stranger' by supertramp.'

7:30pm: Want to abandon plans and eat alone at the empire buffet and yeah I know that sounds funny or like I'm exaggerating but no it's not meant to be funny I am serious. Excitedly imagining getting into a little squabble and 'abandoning ship' to come back here and buffet it hard.

7:33pm: giant Lufthansa airplane flew over car. So huge and loud. It's going to JFK. Jealous of everyone on it.

7:34pm: smells like cheap ass Chinese food fried noodles and I love it

7:39pm: THING TO REMEMBER: HOW SICL AND DISGUSTING IT FEELS TO IMAGINE ZACHARY FUCKING THE TWO GIRLS AND LIVING AT JAMIE'S AND NOT TALKING TO YOU

FUCK WHY AM I DOING THIS

ITS NOT LIKE HE LIKES YOU HE ACTUALLY HATES A LOT OF THINGS ABOUT YOU AND SEEMS JEALOUS AND DISCOURAGING PF YOU YOU GAPING ANALLY FUCKED ASSHOLE

HE GAVE HIMSELF A FAKE FACEBOOK NAME WHILE YOU GUYS LIVED TOGETHER BECAUSE HE WAS EMBARRASSED ABOUT HIS IMAGE HE DIDNT WANT TO BE ASSOCIATED WITH YLU AND THINKS YOU ARE NASTY

WHY AM I DOING THIS

7:50pm: ate 1mg Xanax after practicing potential 'flaking out' phone call. Stop emotions.

8:04pm: parked near adam's (where Zachary is house sitting). Texted mira and talked to mom on phone. Feel something strange.

8:05-9:[something]pm: sat 'airplane style' with me on Zachary's legs and arms kind of. Seemed happy to see each other. A baseball game was on, said things about how baseball is boring. Asked him details about having sex with Vic and Candace and sat further away from him. The lights were off. Asked if he liked anyone and he said he was seriously interested in a girl Jamie introduced him to, Beth.

9:57pm: kissing

10-11:59pm: I don't remember. We've been drinking chartreuse, I are more Xanax. We went to a deli and got sandwiches. I got a tuna thing and he got a roast beef thing and orange juice and sea salt chips.

MAY 21, 2013

12:00-[unknown]am: had sex. Towards the end he asked why I was crying and I said 'I miss you.' He said 'I miss you too.' I don't cry during sex ever, usually, except kind of once when he wanted me to, I wasn't thinking about that then

Had sex again and didn't cry but asked to stop because it hurt for some reason. I don't remember when this happened

[unknown]am: woke to penis in mouth, gave blowjob

Sat on fire escape and held each other. Zachary smoked real cigarette and I smoked e-cigarette. Listened to 'odelay' by Beck and talked about songs. Said 'hi' to guy smoking weed on fire escape below us to the right. Girl in American flag bikini emerged from fire excape with a flamingo on it above us to the left but she didn't stay long enough to say 'hi'

Zachary drank charetreuse all morning. I drank coffee. At one point he said 'just drink this don't ask questions' and poured clear liquid from unmarked bottle. I said 'it's just vinegar' and 'is it everclear?' He said 'I'm not telling you, just drink it.' Tasted motor oily. Zachary said it was mezcal Adam bought on a street in Mexico. I said something about 'the master'

At some point I drank another shot which Zachary tried to 'chill' by doing an ice/knife trick and spilled most of

Zachary took the sheets off the bed for laundry (he does laundry whenever he housesits for Adam)

Tried on Adam's and Lauren's clothes they put in 'donation bags,' felt care-free

Laid together on bed. I did something 'raucous' I think, like, bounced around. Zachary said 'I just want us to be friends forever.' The radio was on

At some point Zachary said he came in my mouth twice while I was sleeping, unsure if he was serious

Zachary filled pillowcases full of towels and sheets of Adam's laundry and we walked to the laundromat

At some point it was directly or indirectly addressed that I wouldn't be going to the navy

At some point we were sitting on the couch or bed and Zachary asked me how I felt about him wanting to date Beth and I said 'as long as I don't think about it I don't care'

At some point I asked about the discrepancies between him being so upset that I had sex with Jordan when we weren't officially together and him having sex with three girls while pursuing Beth. He said something like 'I was drunk most of the time then' and that if it got serious with Beth he would stop having sex with other girls

Walked to check on laundry. Felt bad and like I wanted to be more drunk but not drunk at all but I didn't know what else I wanted to be doing. Zachary had his arm around me a lot and said things like 'hi puppy' and 'it's so nice outside' and I'd say 'hi' and 'yeah it's really nice out.' he said 'it's crazy nice out'

Zachary brought chartreuse in to laundry. I said 'you can't do that' and he said 'yes I can' or something, I was grinning

Remember saying 'I want a bagel' repeatedly

Ordered Mexican food from place next to laundromat. I said 'could I get three ahi tuna tacos, chips and guacamole, a bedford avenue burrito.' Zachary was acting belligerent, was embarrassed to be ordering with him. Walked to condiment station and filled around ten small containers with sauces. Zachary helped fill some, made mess. Wiped area with napkins before we left

Walked back to apartment

Zachary took some cash I had and went down to the beer store and bought us beer. I set up plates and silverware, lined up the sauces and got napkins

Ate on couch watching something

At some point I asked Zachary why he liked Beth/preferred her to me. He said she was quieter and more aloof and they had less in common/less immediate connection he felt with me, got sad/quiet, he said 'oh no now you're mad at me' I said 'not mad at all, just sad, not even about you, all of this feels sad'

At some point he said 'you know it wouldn't have worked out with us' and I knew and I know and I said that too

I said 'I don't want to do these dishes' as I did them and he put clean sheets on bed. Stopped doing dishes and sat on couch. Didn't know what to do. Restarted dishes, crying some

At some point he said he wanted to 'do good by Beth' and not hit her like he hit Jamie and me. At some point he said he thought it'd be good that he wasn't 'immediately in love' with Beth and that she was quieter, that she did printmaking. At some point it was addressed that a problem he and I had was that I didn't like it that he thought my writing was stupid and only stupid people liked it, and it was a problem that I cared what he thought about my writing. He said Beth did printmaking and he felt indifferent about it and like he thought she wouldn't care what he thought about it. She is currently visiting friends. He described their interactions. They haven't had sex yet. Asked if she was pretty. He smiled and said 'I don't know, she looks like Rick. She has a round face. I don't know' and something about how I was pretty

I was collecting my things and Zachary was finishing packing. He said 'don't be dramatic, just wait.' Thought about how I'd be dropping him off at Jamie's and thought about Beth and me and him talking to beth and him having sex with me and Candace and Beth and everyone and felt shitty vomit thing in stomach. I said 'why should I wait.' He said 'just, watch me, for moral support.' Waited and walked slightly faster out the door and down the stairs. Left my beer and taco and mostly undrank beer in fridge

6:23pm: waiting for him to get something from inside

Ate 2mg Xanax. When Zachary got to car I said 'do you want to go to my apartment.' He said 'yes.' Rested hands on each other's legs on the drive. It was hot. Zachary put on chief keef and daft punk then the music stopped. Saw his head 'nodding off'

7:20pm: entered apartment. he said 'we'll make it for final jeopardy.' Watched a little. I think it was college jeopardy. Had sex. Orgasmed twice with finger up my ass 'reverse cowgirl style,' fingering myself

Zachary said 'I like your back.' I said 'even with all the marks on it?' He said something about liking the shape. I said something about wanting a fatter ass.

MAY 22, 2013

1:10am: woke ate 1mg Xanax apple pie thing

12am: woke ate more Xanax think I said 'I want to get a sandwich.' Zachary said 'we're not getting a sandwich.' Toasted bread and made salad with cucumber, pepper, chickpeas, avocado. Watched 'the office' and 'king of the hill.'

4am: woke again ate 2mg xanax

9am: woke confused. I said something like 'are you my boyfriend,' unsure/foggy. Zachary seemed upset I asked

At some point in my apartment, maybe the night before, I said I was still doing the liveblog and he said 'oh, so this'll be in it'

At some point he said something about how I wasn't writing for vice anymore and made a noise like 'that's what I thought' when I said I hadn't officially said I was stopping, I wasn't sure I wanted to stop, I had nothing more to write

Got ready assembled Masha package

Went to Duane reade

Got gas

1:18pm: dropped him off at Jamie's and his place. He said Jamie's e-cigarettes were better and they sold them at a deli near her. Parked. Bought e-cigarette Jamie uses, 'logic' brand. Said 'see you soon' to Zachary's body, mostly half-out the car. He said 'yeah I'll see you around kid.'

1:19pm: ate 20mg adderall going to navy place in manhattan

2:06pm: parked on church and Barclay in a parking lot. Street parking seemed impossible. Don't want another ticket. Told parking man I would be a couple hours. Chugged 16oz red bull. Hid e-cigarette in birth control packet.

2:25pm: walked out of navy office. disheartening things were said about my age. Disheartening. Talked mostly to man in uniform who said 'call me 'rice,'' then a lot of things I didn't understand about enlisting. I asked if he did active duty in other countries and he said he went to Germany and his kids got to come and it was great. I asked what he did now and he said something about working at the desk I was facing. He said he liked it a lot. I said 'I have my CDL, for truck driving, would that help?' he made a face like I had said 'I'm batman.' he said 'yeah that's good, I mean there's tons of jobs in aviation for driving, but the guy behind me knows more.' I said 'could you explain some more to me about college, if I could finish college then, I don't know.' he said something I didn't understand. I said 'ROTC' at one point and he said 'I think you're too old for that, but maybe not.' He said 'so you wanna be a pilot?' I said 'I want to be a pilot, planes, I wanna work for NASA someday' and nodded vigorously. He smiled. He said 'I wasn't ever on a ship.' I said 'my dad was on a ship, the Joseph p Kennedy, the Cuban missile crisis.' he looked interested, asked me how much longer I have for college. I said 'maybe two semesters, but I think I'd need to change my major to physics, I was psychology.' he said things I didn't understand but I didn't know how to ask him to clarify. He said the man behind him was his supervisor and might know more about if I could be a pilot. The supervisor man got off the phone. He seemed younger than me but older than 'rice.' He asked if I was a us citizen. Rice said 'she's twenty-seven, she got some college.' Superior guy said 'what's your major?' I said 'psychology mostly.' he said 'that might work, but twenty-seven, I don't know, twenty-eight.' I said 'I heard there were age waivers.' they nodded. The superior guy said I could do other aviation navigation jobs until I was 32. Rice gave me the number of a lieutenant who knows more. I said 'should I just go talk to him now?' Rice said he was usually just walking around but it was better to make an appointment. I thanked them and left. Rice said 'good luck.'

Walking to FedEx to print resume then am going to walk to organic avenue and apply. Have to pee badly.

2:33pm: keep walking the wrong way. In line for bathroom at library. I want lieutenant whoever to call. Goddamnit. He's not going to call. Will maybe just print out resume here why not oh god oh god.

2:37pm: three people ahead of me in line. Woman said 'I don't see how they have one bathroom for men and women.' man said 'in a new York public library.' I said 'maybe because there's so many of us.' we all looked at each other. Man who took a long time exited. Man ahead of the three of us entered and exited quickly. Woman said 'don't worry I'll be fast.' she was fast. Man is in there now. Woman exited, tapped my shoulder and said something about being in queens this morning. She knocked really hard on the door, she said 'what're you doing, taking a shower in there?' I smiled and shrugged and said 'I don't know man, just hanging out.' she said something else, laughing a little, tapped my shoulder again and said good luck. Man exited. Now I'm peeing. Now I'm done peeing.

2:48pm: at UPS, getting three resumes printed on 'ivory' resume paper. Woman behind counter said 'the phone keep ringing man.' I said 'y-eah. Yeah. Nice ivory paper. For it to stand out.'

2:53pm: cheerful UPS woman wished me good luck.

3:03pm: standing at corner of church st and reade st in manhattan. The organic avenue website said to email a resume and cover letter. Should I go to the library and write a cover letter then get them to print it out… so fucked, all options. Shit. I just want to fly planes shit I forgot mom is coming okay I'll go back home goddamnitdkakajsjjajj

4:42pm: have been texting/tweeting/using phone irresponsibly during ride home. Construction worker wagged his finger disapprovingly and said 'no no.' Someone named Kristie from baltimore who I have texted with re liveblog responded to my tweet request for adderall and has come to my rescue and is on a megabus to NYC now. She's not coming just to give me adderall.

5:33pm: cleaned cat box and fed them and swept and swiffered fast, mom is lost in rush hour and said it would make sense for me to drive to brooklyn do adderall/book + xanax exchange, 'eternally thankful' to Kristie (lied to mom in that i said i was only giving kristie a book/not exchanging drugs)

6:28pm: met and did addy/Xanax exchange with nice ass Kristie twitter person who apologized for being drunk and didn't seem drunk. She is visiting her boyfriend in a pretty part of Brooklyn.

6:46pm: in traffic. No new emails.

6:59pm: mom called with address. Have been typing Zachary, feels like 'bankruptcy.' Filing for emotional bankruptcy.

7:14pm: I'm glad mom is here. I'm going to see mom.

7:32pm: this area looks bleak. Looking forward to rescuing mom.

7:36pm: parked in motel parking lot, by picnic table in front of a mass of Verizon trucks.

7:52pm: in mom's hotel room, talked about her trip sitting on her bed. She said she gave a guy a tip for helping with her bags, then later the hotel manager helped with something and she tried to tip her and she said 'are you the lady who gave bill a tip?' mom said she was. The lady said 'that made his night, no one tips here.' Mom said something about stopping for directions at a rite aid with an employee 'you would just fall in love with,

I know it.' A garbage truck stopped to help her in traffic and she fell in love with him too. I said she had a harem. she said 'i like to call them my 'swains" in a British accent. Figured out dinner plans. We're going to sel de mer. She said 'is it okay of I wear glasses?' I said 'of course mom.' She said 'the other night I asked that to dad, if he thought it was okay if I wore glasses,' laughing like 'oh boy this is silly of me.'

8:03pm: mom walked into hotel bedroom from bathroom, saying 'I could just go like this, goddamnit,' laughing.

10:07pm: drove to williamsburg. Showed mom Tao's apartment I sublet in November 2011. Showed her where Zachary lived with Tao when I met them in 2009. Discreetly ate 1mg Xanax while exiting car, aware of being near apartment Zachary is probably inside now. Told mom Tao and I would buy kombucha and sometimes chipotle powder from a deli near sel de mer and the head waitress said something once about how we brought kombucha and didn't order alcohol, like she 'knew' us as 'people who order lobster and don't talk and bring in their own spices and drinks.' Mom said 'why would you always get lobster?' I said 'it was just good...really good... it was like eighteen dollars.' Mom said 'the green apple deli, now I know 'the green apple deli." I said 'the sign looks new, I don't think it used to have a name.' Waiter at sel de mer seated us at table close to door. Mom got up to use the bathroom. Waiter said 'and just so you know, we're out of [hard to understand] tonight.' I said 'you're out of what?' he repeated it. I nodded and said 'oh okay, thank you.' He walked away.

10:18pm: mom walked back from bathroom, smiling embarrassedly and rolling her eyes. I said 'was there a line?' She sat and said 'well, you know, I don't know. There was something going on with the door, so maybe some-one was inside? I think I'll just try again later.'

I said 'I couldn't hear what the waiter said they were out of—he said they were out of something. I think they're out of lobster, maybe.' Mom said 'oh no, I'll ask him to say it again when he comes back.' I said 'no no no, no, I think they're just all out, I think there's just no lobster maybe. It's fine, I'll get another thing.' Mom said 'maybe he'll say it again and we won't have to ask.' I said 'we can dream.' Mom said 'they can't stop us from dreaming.'

Waiter returned, told mom they're out of the thing. Mom said 'what was that?' he repeated. Mom looked at me action movie-style, like 'should I proceed,' I shook head 'no,' mom smiled at waiter and said 'thank you.' He said he'd come back in a few minutes. I said 'it seems like there's no lobster.' Mom squinted and said 'it would seem that way, wouldn't it,' nodding conspiratorily. Mom said 'oh honey, it's just so nice to be here with you, I'm so happy we're here.'

Mom said 'I think I'll have a glass of the sove-in-yon blonck.'

Ordered kale salad, clam chowder, scallops. Mom ordered beet salad and trout. She said 'is the trout especially good' after ordering. Told her Tao and I would usually sit at the bar and she said 'he was usually heavily on something right?' I said 'no, we'd just both be on Xanax.' she said 'I thought there was a time he was really misbehaving, being on something and telling you what to do, right?' I said 'I don't think so.' Thought she was referring to a time he was vomiting on heroin, and I was insisting he drink water and we argued and I came home early.

10:21pm: they brought us bread. Remembered how Tao and I would refuse bread. Didn't say anything.

10:22-11:[something]PM:

- mom liked the food a lot and said things about how cheap it was for what it was

- told mom the last time i was here was when tao and i had 'let's tell people we're separated, officially' conversation. she said 'oh dear.' i wanted to reassure her it was fine, i was just noticing something i had forgotten, but i was unable to put it to words other than 'it was really okay' or 'we were sitting at the bar'

- drank two glasses of wine each, remember mom pouring remainder of her first glass into second glass and thinking 'mom knows how to do it'

- mom said something about liking the music and asked me if i liked it. think i said it was okay but too loud. she told the waiter she liked the music but thought he was probably tired of it. he said the music changed every night and it was okay

- remember mom's face smiling a lot and both of us saying stuff about the food

- remember asking what was going to happen with her and dad

- started to feel pressure to…something…like at some point it seemed like mom was happier than me and i had to 'keep up' with saying cheerful things. i told her that and she said she didn't want me to feel pressure at all, she was just happy to be there, she thought she understood the thing i was feeling. i could picture 'happier 'me:' across from mom in five to ten minutes,' but for some reason the possibility of that was shrinking with each thing said. mom said 'do you feel like you have to be fake right now?' i said 'a little, i feel like i'm not being good company and like i wish i was better to be around.' she said something about how she didn't want me to feel pressured to act cheerful, something about how she remembered how before her brother died it started to feel like every time they saw each other they were each being 'fake' and she didn't want me to feel that. i knew/remembered the thing about her brother. i apologized and said i didn't want to be acting fake-cheerful and would act normal. mom said something compassionately about how there was no need for me to apologize for anything. i didn't know what to say. felt guilty and embarrassed for turning dinner conversation into 'this,' a situation where it was hard to know what to say, or that what i wanted to say was 'i'm sorry for apologizing.' remember a period shortly after this where i felt completely blank, like i didn't know what to say or if i was even sad or happy or anything, and that i wished i hadn't eaten xanax

- waiter said it was okay we were staying late and they close at midnight

- mom ordered coffee and lemon meringue pie that we ate with spoons while talking about the waiter's sexuality and hard-to-understand voice and not many people were there and it felt good

- mom said things about how nice sel de mer was and that the bathroom was decorated and that she appreciates things like this more as she's gotten older and that someday i would feel happier and maybe like i appreciated things like that too, then 'but you don't have to, i know you'll find something though'

11:[something]–11:59PM: drove mom back to the motel. she said things about how it seems hard to drive or know where you're going in NYC and i agreed. think i continued apologizing for not being 'better company' and reassuring i would be tomorrow. hugged mom and thanked her for dinner. didn't want to leave or drive home.

MAY 23, 2013

12:26am: driving to apartment.

6:57am: didn't sleep, have been responding to ask.fm questions.

11:00am: woke. Called mom. Said I'd sleep but responded to more questions. Put goodies in Masha package. Ate Ritalin drank red bull.

2:20pm: Bleak puppy store by costco

4:55pm: peeing at ikea mom asked to take in cart, tense ride re he I o exote nd I felt bad

Maggie I'll meet you outside a woman was cleaning at the same time now I'm waiting

7:17pm: gramma leg thing by bed

Tennesee Williams glass leg megagerie

Pile of dirt make a wish

I realize that (toothpick)

It was cuter (shirt said 'help me')

Denzel (I can't look you in the eye)

7:25pm: 'already ate ribs but I have them' Horsemeat (I didn't like it as much the n) (they didn't use good enough horse) 'I'll be outside mom I'll be outside thinking about what I've done'

11:03pm: its the quilt I have to bear (about gray quilt)

MAY 24, 2013

12:04AM: called mom and talked while walking to apartment. passed dumpster with 'LATIN AMERICAN' sign. a car slowed and stopped about halfway, then reversed and parked on sidewalk.

2:05AM: ate 1mg xanax. read 'taipei' and looked at internet.

4:04AM: i was watching a video of a man with shoulder-length hair whispering to a younger man. they were in my apartment, near the door. the video looked filmed maybe from the kitchen counter, with my mattress and sleeping body mostly outside the frame. i wasn't supposed to be seeing this. i knew i could only see because i wasn't awake. that was the problem the men had paused filming to discuss. i wasn't supposed to be awake. the men were the evil behind ASMR. they had embedded themselves inside some kind of subliminal code that tracks brains that respond to it with ASMR tingles. when you feel tingles it's the men inside your head, filming themselves doing whatever they were about to do to me. i knew they knew i was watching because they started talking in code. remembered an unfilmed portion of the video, where they had been closer to my head. woke scared, to earphones in ears and ASMR video playing on youtube.

ate 1mg xanax and heated tortilla on stove and ate while heating a second tortilla, 'without thinking.'

looked out window at fire escape. anyone could get in through the fire escape. selected 'sharpest knife' from drawer. restrained from taking all knives, thinking 'it will be better in the morning, to see i didn't need all the knives.' held 'sharpest knife' on guard, while walking to retrieve keys from hook by the door where the men had been. checked locks.

placed 'sharpest knife,' keys, and phone under pillow. internet/computer seemed unsafe. but i also knew if someone had been watching and waiting for a good time to kill me all night and had maybe nodded off, closing the computer would cause the light to change, and if something changed in the killer's peripheral vision, their attention would be drawn to the light source, and if they saw me closing a computer at 4AM it probably meant i would soon be asleep and more available to kill.

thought 'you're already in trouble if they saw the light change, but they've probably been watching everything, they saw you put the knife under your pillow.'

looked at internet, thinking 'they know you're putting on a show. they know you know their plan.' looked with increasing difficulty, thinking 'it's okay to sleep, that's why you ate xanax. if the killer wants to do it they just will, you can't stop them.'

10:55AM: i was wearing baggy gray jail clothes, walking near my old apartment in baltimore. this was my day off from jail. the sun was bright. people on the street were stopping to squint at the sky and i did too. letters were appearing as clouds that eventually spelled 'CHELSEA I LOVE YOU' and an inside joke. the clouds fell gracefully, retaining their shapes until they hit the tops of buildings. when the last cloud fell it was quiet, like everyone thought they were they only person thinking 'was that really the last one,' then started cheering and hugging. it felt like this would be considered 'a national event' someday. then i was in a diner sitting next to chelsea's boyfriend. we were surprised to see each other and joked a little. i asked if he saw the chelsea sky messages. he said he had organized it and talked excitedly about the skywriting service and chelsea. i said 'i love her too' and felt a dense sadness, like one molecule had been added to all my cells. he asked why i was wearing jail clothes. i had forgotten. neither of us knew what to say. i said 'tell chelsea i love her. i love you too. i love that you did the airplane thing.' walked to a garage/yard not far from the diner. stood in line with other people in jail clothes, waiting for our turns to go inside a trailer. i knew i would have to have sex with whoever was inside. woke crying/'choking.'

11:13AM: woke to alarm. called mom. made plans to get pizza before she leaves today. had idea for 'taipei' facebook photo album. put 'taipei' on my face and took picture. held 'taipei' upside-down and took picture. took pictures of cats with 'taipei,' picture of 'taipei' hanging out of VCR with asian newscaster on TV. fed cats.

11:59AM: mom called to cancel pizza due to driving anxiety. i said 'that's okay, i want to be productive today and pizza would slow me down.' pajama shorts slid down legs and i let them hit the floor when i got to my closet.

12:16PM: mom called to say she's outside apartment building. brushed teeth.

8:03PM: updates from today got deleted. there isn't enough time but then there is all this time. i've just been sitting here and it still feels like not enough time.

8:33PM: fed cats. discovered biting technique for hands-free e-cigarette smoking.

8:41PM: all it's going to be for the rest of my life is a series of 'right nows.'

8:44PM: alvie vomited wet food in bowl. he did this yesterday too. in the bowl, both times.

9:00PM: scanned email from dad containing 'I hope this makes sense…'

9:43PM: i was optimistic in maryland. i was going to join the navy. then NASA. not so long ago. jesus. how. what else could i do. so much time.

10:27PM: slipped and spilled most of 'monster' energy drink on leg, bed, trackpad/keyboard. cursor isn't responding to fingers.

11:03PM: stood in bathroom and blew cold air from hairdryer on trackpad. felt like part of the montage in 'gattaca' where it shows vacuuming cells from his keyboard so no one would know he wasn't genetically qualified to be an astronaut.

11:41PM: mom calling.

MAY 25, 2013

2:55AM: first it was okay then there was an argument and then other arguments based on the arguments and so bad of me and stupid and crying and hating me and i can't talk about it well and couldn't on phone either except i think at the end it was okay, i don't want or am unable to say more now, i think it's okay to not type details, it would feel bad right now no matter what i say or type or even if i talk to mom, i love mom, i'm crying now again only alone now

4:45AM: have been answering antagonistic ask.fm questions antagonistically.

6:41AM: ate 3mg xanax, hummus/avocado tortillas.

12:07PM: woke. felt dread. laid and sometimes opened eyes. searched 'beth' in zachary's facebook friend list. one 'beth.' looked at pictures. there will be a ticket on my car, probably. i forgot to move again. plan of action: eat as much xanax and food as you want today, just be absent today.

1:26PM: mom called. good to hear her laugh and be mom again. she said 'just promise to do one thing for me, will you? just seventeen seconds long, one thing that makes you happy, will you? just think about something good for seventeen seconds?' remembered talking about her ex-husband at dinner the other night, who she married when she was 20 or 21 and pregnant with my sister. pictured her in my apartment.

she asked about reading the liveblog and i said 'the only reason i felt apprehensive about you reading it earlier is that i talked about doing heroin and i thought you'd be worried.' she said 'oh no, oh honey i am worried, i don't want you to do that, i don't want to think about you doing things that make you feel worse.' i said 'i don't shoot it' and 'people are prescribed opiates' and 'i don't like it that much, it's just all the guy had that night' and other, in hindsight, boldly untrue things. she said 'i don't want you to end up being a bag lady on the streets of new york city.' i said 'me neither, i won't, i don't even have many bags.'

she and dad are shopping for furniture. she said she was in gastric distress from something we ate this weekend. i said it was probably the ikea ribs. she said 'that's right, they could've been 'horse.'' i said 'miniature pony ribs. they take them from little miniature ponies, i heard.' she said 'well it could've been ikea, but i think it's that what i did on the way home—i went to the first rest stop on the new jersey turnpike, which you probably know, it's so huge and you can buy all of this stuff there, even perfume and, oh, i don't know, sunglasses [laughlaugh]. well i made the mistake of seeing this nathan's, and they had this special where you could buy two hotdogs wrapped in pretzels, and it was next to a cinnabon, and then these giant auntie anne's pretzels, and oh…you know at the mall? when you buy them at the mall they taste good? well it was like they extracted it from that, it tasted so fake. not even real food. it didn't even taste like real food.' i said 'food like that shouldn't count towards weight gain because it's not even like food. it's like, a remote. if you ate a remote. or like, a lighter.' she said 'i know!'

2:16PM: mom called to say she was worried about potential employers googling me and seeing i've written about doing drugs, reporting me to police. i said 'i've taken that into consideration.' she said 'i know when you're feeling depressed it feels like nothing you do matters, but please just think—just remember that someday something is going to matter? i think?' i said 'okay. i know. thank you for saying that, i think i know. i might delete it. i go by 'margaret' on applications anyway so. also it's like that thing, when women get raped but there's no evidence, they can't prosecute the guy? i could just say all of this is fiction.' she said 'yes, yes! can't you say something—you could preface your liveblog with 'this is the fictional crazy account of, i don't know, a demonstration, of a fictional…' i laughed a little. i said 'i might say that.'

4:29PM: a number i don't recognize texted 'Hey meggie ive been thinkn bout u a lot and Jus want u 2 know how much i lov u and miss u. Crissy'

it's my sister

cried like when amahd gave me the $20

wind is so hard outside

4:34PM: fed cats. ate b-vitamin, zeolite, 'brain and memory herbal health tonic.'

i want to live in a mansion cruise ship where everyone is happy forever and no one has to do anything they don't want ever, ever, ever forever

i just want the whole world to live there, i want anyone who has ever been in pain ever to live there, it's where everything will be okay again

i want brad the cat and all the other homeless everyones

5:22PM: did two shots of whiskey. going to go all the way drunk.

5:44PM: do people talk about how it's hard to do shots of whiskey?

ORDER OF EASINESS OF SHOTS
(EASIEST FIRST HARDEST LAST):

- 'lemon drop' or 'red-headed slut' or sugary mixed dealies

- whiskey

- vodka

- gin

- cognac?

- moonshine-like things

- tequila

- scotch

yuck, scotch

why would you do that

why have i ever done that

9:06PM: thought about moving my car. but. also i need to eat? MAT-THEW DONAHOO AND NICHOLAS I SAW THAT YOU GUYS CALLED I'M GOING TO CALL AFTER I DECIDE WHAT FOOD TO PUT INTO ME AND GO GET IT AND [OH SHIT] MOVE MY CAR WAIT SHOULD I NOT MOVE MY CAR MAYBE I JUST WON'T MOVE IT UNTIL TOMORROW SINCE I KNOW IT HAS A TICKET I..ER..ER…ER……ERRRRRRR. kind of scared to listen to nicholas' message like 'oh no what if he hates me now oh no oh no.' oh doh. i am a defectie anus. seamless nor grubhub doth delivereth to mine ass-eth. i am drunk as a dkink. sunk. skunk. let me readjust. isn't there a rap song like 'let me readjust…wait (one, two, three…) let me readjust.' i forget. ikea delivering my bed and table tomorrow. so.

why do i have to worry about what to eat or 'am i tired enough to sleep?' can't those decisions…i wish someone had made those decisions like how someone decided 'it will start 10/15/1985, the body will be female' or somehing.

REAL TALK PART TRES:

even when it's like 'shit my faculties are shutting down' from tiredness i am thinking 'DON'T DO THAT, WHEN YOU WAKE UP IT'LL BE LIKE YOU WILL HAVE DIED A LITTLE BIT'

because

um

nicholas is my old co-worker and he is an accountant now and i feel a big huge thing in my heart about him

it would be good to talk

i want to not be so isolated anrmore

do i want pizza or thia?

thai?

thai food? or pizza?

what is the thing i want?

9:15PM: fuck everyone who is every have been dumb to me or not treated me nice

you know who you is

closed pop-up ad for a nonspecific item with the text 'your opinion counts' over a stock image of a highway

SO NOW IT'S A PICTURE OF A HIGHWAY?

WITH?

'YOUR OPINION COUNTS?'

ALL OF A SUDDEN!??!

ON THIS HARD-TO-VERIFY-IF-MENU-IS-REAL WEBSITE?!?!

OH

DO YOU KNOW…

THE WORLD NEEDS TO CHEKC UP ON ITSELF FOR A MINUTE BECAUSE…HOW IS THIS REALL..

HOW DID JEBADOH APATOW GET SO FAT

I MEAN JUDD APA...JESUS

THE SUPERBAD MAN

YOU KNOW

HE IS NOT FAT IN A NEGATIVE WAY

I'D ROLL ALL UP IN THAT

I'M JUST WONDERING WHAT HAPPENED

JESS? JESS BRIDGES? JEFF APABRIGE?

JUDD HENLEY

LAUGHING REALLY HARD

GOING TO KEEP GOING UNTIL I FIGURE IT OUT

HONESLTY NO CLUE WHAT THIS PERSON'S NAME IS ISTILL

JUDD APATOW: I KNOW THAT FOR CERTAIN. IT IS NOT HIM.

SETH ROGEN: SAME

JEFF BRIDGES: I KNOW IT IS NOT HIM

BEAU BRIDGES: THE BROTHER OF JEFF

MICHELLE PHEIFFER: IN A MOVIE WITH TOSE BROSE ABOUT PIANOS

'BROSE' LOL

LOOKS MORE CORRECT THAN 'BROS'

OKAY

SETH ROGEN: NOT THE NAME

JUDD APATOW: NO

SETH MEYERS: ?!?!! HOW DID I JUST THINK THAT

SETH: IS IT SOMEONE NAMED 'SETH?'

SETH BRIDHGES?

JOHN MCKINLEY?

THIS IS ACTUALLY SEEMING IMPOSSIBLE, TO FIGURE OUT THIS PERSON'S NAME, AND I KNOW YOU PROBABLY KNOW WHO IT IS

JEBADOH

SOMETHING LIKE 'JEBADOH BRIDGES-MEYERS'

I'M LAUGHING REALLY HARD

SETH ROGEN

FUKCKCKXJKLKJHFKDFJKHDFHJKDFKJHD

FUUUUUUUUCCCKKKKKKKK

'FUCK' IN 72PT FONT

SETH BRIDGES

JEFF APATOW

HELP

WHO IS THIS MAN

9:39PM: I GAVE UP I LOOKED IT UP, IT'S JONAH HILL

LDIES AND GENTLEMENT, IT HAS BEEN HIM THE WHOLE TIME

WITHOUT FURTHER INTRODUCTION:

JONAH HILL

LOOK AT THAT MOTHERFUCKER

I WANT TO TAKE HIM TO IN-N-OUT BURGER

I WILL BE LIKE 'BABY I REALIZE THIS MIGHT NOT BE A GOOD TIME IN YOUR LIFE FOR ANOTHER CHIN BUT BTU DO YOU WANT ANOTHER ONE? I COULD BE THAT FOR YOU, I WILL WRAP MYSELF AROUND YOUR NECK AND NEVER LEAVE'

HE SEEMS LIKEA GOOD PERSON

LOOK AT THAT FACE

REMEMBER HOW HE WAS A BOY ONCE? SO EASY TO REMEMBER, NOT EVEN KNOWING HE WAS, LOOKING AT THAT FACE

LOVE HIM

JONAH

IS HE…FROM…'SQUID AND THE QHALE'

NICKI MINAJ SHOULD DO AN ALBUM CALLED 'DA SQUID N DA WHALE'

NO ONE WOULD SEE IT COMING

LENA DUNHAM/NICKI MINAJ DUET CALLED 'NOAH BAUM-BACH'

LIKE

EVERYONE WOULD LOVE IT IF THAT HAPPENED, RIGHT?

I WANT TO BE JONAH HILL'S MINK STOLE

MINK STOLE

THAT'S RIGHT

I GOTTA…

THINGS WOULD NOT BE VERY DIFFERENT IF I HAD BEEN BORN WITH A PENIS

10:19PM: it went something like this:

>me: hi, can i place an order for pick-up?

>thai rock: oh yes, please hold on for one minute

>me: okay, thank you

>thai rock: what may i get for you?

>me: um, can i get a tom kha soup? with chicken?

>thai rock: tom kha soup, hem, tom yum?

>me: oh no, kha? the tom kha soup?

>thai rock: well, actually, maybe i interest you in tom yum? because i think we are light on coconut today.

>me: oh! oh oh, yes, yeah, tom yum soup then. that's fine.

>thai rock: so the tom yum soup, two orders?

me: oh no just one, with the. and

thai rock: you want veggies tofu or chicken? shrimp?

me: the...uh. veggies and tofu.

thai rock: am i understanding two orders, or one?

me: oh just one, just one order please, and

thai rock: and anything else?

me: yes please. may i have the pork dumplings?

thai rock: pork dumplings...

me: yes please. and pad thai? with

thai rock: pad thai with chicken, or tofu veggie, or shrimp, duck?

me: the. just tofu veggie also. pad thai tofu veggie.

thai rock: i see.

me: when should i come pick it up?

thai rock: oh, well, wait one second because actually i should've been writing this down, wait one second.

me: oh oh okay, okay, thank you.

thai rock: [shuffling] o-kay. so: let me start. what is your name?

me: megan?

thai rock: megan

me: m-e-g-a-n, yeah

thai rock: megan

me: that's the one

thai rock: okay megan, now you are having the tom yum veggie...the pad thai veggie...

me: yes (felt myself like, quivering, like puppy heart quivering with joy)

thai rock: and what was the other thing?

me: a pork dumpling.

thai rock: ah yes, the pork dumpling.

me: yes. yes. and that'll be it.

thai rock: will that be all?

me: yes, that's all, thank you.

thai rock: well megan, i think…i think this'll be ready in fifteen minutes. okay?

me: fifteen minutes. wonderful, yes. i'll come pick it up.

thai rock: thank you megan.

me: thank you, see you soon.

when i pick it up he's going to be santa claus.

heard a knock on door during phone call. hung up and saw texts from
colin, asking if i could show an apartment to a couple tomorrow. applied
jeans, perfume, and 'technically slippers, but is anyone really paying attention?' no longer felt drunk.

neared door with slowed and lightened steps, to be indistinguishable from
background noise. didn't want colin to hear me. turned key softly, feeling
for the weight of the latches.

walked to car, delighting in hearing 'nicholas voice' on voicemail. at one
point he said he knew i was in new york and 'i guess you're ignoring me'
like maybe he thought i wouldn't be listening. he said 'i don't know what
happened' and there were a few seconds and he hung up. there were two
tickets on my car. i called back said something a little embarrassing like
'things are floating into the ethers,' then 'i want to hang out any time, i
don't do anything, i want to see you.'

drove to thai rock listening to 'bamboo cactus' by i, cactus on repeat, aware
of hearing the same sounds the first time i heard the song. if i could remove
the emotional context i would have more in common with myself the first
time i heard it, and could maybe re-experience that moment from a new
dual perspective. tao played it the car and i said 'i like this' and the lights
looked magical. for a long time i was doing 'serious bureaucratic intern
detective work,' trying to figure out the song's name. this fall i figured it
out. at a party at tao's in december people were passing around a computer,
selecting songs for a group playlist. i put on 'bamboo cactus' and said some-

thing about not knowing what it was for a long time. tao said 'you could've just asked me,' or something.

thai rock looked permanently closed but i could hear restaurant noises. a guy was smoking on a porch. i said 'h-iii, do you know where i go for pick-up?' he gestured like 'hold on' and opened the door. a woman holding a plastic bag said 'hello, $28.' and i handed her my credit card. she said 'oh no we take cash only.' i said 'oh no, i'll go to an ATM, i'm sorry.' she said 'no you come back tomorrow.' i said 'are you serious?' my face felt big. she said 'yeah, you come back tomorrow.' i shook her hand and said 'i will, i give you my word.' she and the smoking man looked at me. we were all smiling a little.

parked on 115th st. mom called. i had to walk backwards so she could hear me over the wind. she said 'oh honey, that's so great, how are all these strangers giving you money?' i said 'i don't know, i'm gonna get it someday.' she said 'what?' i said 'i'll probably get it, i'll get what's coming to me.' mom said 'what?' i said 'nothing nothing, can i call you when i get home?' she said 'i can't hear you, i think it's too windy, why don't you give me a call later?' i yelled 'okay i'll call you later, i love you.' she said 'i love you too.'

a hulking gender-neutral presence in embroidered jeans stood with its back turned to me at the ATM. withdrew $60. the deli entrance was blocked by a man who seemed bored and totally capable of doing something with wet concrete that usually requires a team. the man behind the counter said 'watch your step' as i stepped over the concrete-fixer man, who didn't look up. the counter man said 'how are you' unconvincingly and i mumbled 'yeah.' brought six-pack of blue moon to cash register.

the counter man said 'you smell nice.' i was like 'wiggitywiggity' but tried not to show it. i said 'oh jeez, i'm surprised you can smell anything, it's so windy.' he said 'i know, it's real windy out.' i said 'have a nice night' and he handed me change and said 'you too.' stepped over the concrete-fixer man and said 'thank you' meekly, as a placeholder phrase for 'when you step over someone.' he didn't look up.

11:36PM: called mom when i got inside. she told me things about crissy. i was happy she called. part of the argument…the other night…i had said 'it seems like you're not interested because you don't call.' she said 'i want to call, i think you don't want me to.' i said 'i always say i want you to and you never call, you never believe me.'

MAY 26, 2013

1:37AM: called masha to re-enact dialogue from g.i. joe public service announcement. recorded video of us talking for a long time.

9:03AM: woke worried about sleeping through calls. missing social event of the century.

11:16AM: woke to phone. louis from ikea was downstairs, furniture wasn't. he'll be back around 1PM. he has a soft voice.

1:43PM: woke to phone, 'kevin.' he and and 'mrs. kevin' are going to get pizza before i show them the apartment upstairs. dressed in sloppy encore of last night's outfit and put hair in bun.

2:03PM: kevin called from downstairs. jogged to catch open door from person exiting ahead, where i tripped and stopped fall by doing a dance move that ended with my limbs splayed starfish-like, propping open door.

shook hands with kevin. he said 'this is my wife, tacokia' as we walked inside. i said 'oh taco what?' and looked behind me. she said 'tacokia' with an accent. kevin said 'just call her 'taco.'' i said 'okay, taco, good, good.' we stood and waited for the elevator. i asked how the pizza was. kevin said 'we actually got a quesadilla, from that 'chinese food/mexican food' place, you know it?' i said 'i know it. quesadilla. nice.'

led them down hall, to apartment 6H, and followed them inside. i said 'i almost moved into this one, this is the one i almost moved into.' watched them walked around, opening doors. in the fridge were a six-pack of various beers, two king cobras, and a four loko. remembered the variety pack of beers in the cabinet, when i moved. anonymous beer gifter.

taco made an excited noise in the bathroom. kevin said 'look at that, what is that, do your apartment come with this too?' they were looking at a metal box with four sticks coming out the top. i said 'whoa. no. i don't have that.' they were raving over the thing. i said 'maybe you could use it as an ironing board.' walked away to give them private bathroom time with the thing.

kevin asked taco if she liked the apartment. she said 'so much space.' i said things about the view. kevin kept asking taco what she thought and she kept saying 'oh.' i said 'new kitchen.' at some point they asked if i was a real estate agent like colin. i said 'oh no, no. i'm just here today.'

i said 'i could show you mine, mine's a little smaller.' they didn't react. i wanted them to find a box with sticks coming out the top.

4:25PM: read 'slapstick' and 'frowns need friends too.' mom called and we talked a little. mom asked about the furniture arriving. she said 'oh boy, it's sooner than i thought it'd be! are you excited?' i said 'yeah, i don't know, i'm looking forward to stepping out of a bed instead of rolling.'

a little after we hung up the furniture delivery person called to say he was downstairs. 'knew 'neither of them are louis, i know this isn't louis' and gave angry-seeming man $20. i said 'memorial day, i'm surprised you guys are working now.' the happier man said 'yeah i wanna be at a party.' they brought boxes upstairs. the angry man asked me to initial a paper. resentfully. big time. i asked where he lived. he said 'around beach thirtieth, little further down than you.' i said 'is this the last thing you have to do, then you guys can, like, have fun?' he said 'yeah.' the happier man brought up the last of the boxes. he said 'you know you gotta call ikea to get them to see when the assembly guy is coming, right?' we looked at each other like 'we know things were supposed to happen another way.' i said 'oh sure, yes, i'll call, thank you guys.'

4:43PM: louis called. interesting dynamic, these phone calls with louis. we sound slow and happy and surprised to hear each other's voices. let him in. assembled table and chairs while he assembled bed. NPR was on and i felt sometimes…like i wanted to say 'the opinions on this radio do not reflect the other person in this room.'

6:37PM: took cardboard down to trash room. took smaller trash to trash compactor room. an old lady was exiting the apartment next to the trash compactor room. it went like this:

lady: hello, are you just moving in?

me: oh no, i moved about a month ago. i'm just doing furniture things now. i'm megan [shakes hand in atypically cavalier motion she didn't seem to notice/just 'accepted' my hand into hers. she had soft warm small hands]

lady: well i can't believe i haven't seen you, you must be very quiet!

me: oh yeah. it's just me, me and my cats

lady: oh you have cats? i have to show you this, then! [opens door to a small mostly shaven white dog sitting on a carpet. it didn't move but it looked at us] me: oh my god, what kind is it?

lady: shitzu. i had to give her a haircut, you know

me: sure, summertime

me: you have a really pretty apartment

lady: why thank you! i'm barbara, by the way

me: barbara. it's nice to meet you

barbara: [points to cartoon of old lady in superwoman costume] look, it's me, my grandson made it. does it look like me?

me: [squints] well, maybe the 'superwoman' part

barbara: oh-ho-ho [walks down hall] well, it was very nice to meet you

me: you too barbara

barbara

wonder if she'll ever let me sit on her rug…motionlessly…

maybe we can work towards this

walked back to apartment. door was open to pleasantly domestic scene of louis, from ikea, assembling bed. asked if i could help. he said 'nah, this, i mean it's all complicated so i got it.'

6:54PM: this is going fast on the radio now, it's a woman and a man going back and forth like this, typing everything i can discern:

'excuse me the oxygen is failing' 'is there somebody else' 'i don't care to talk about it' 'dr. harris' 'i need time to think i've told you that before' 'because you badger me' 'please don't tell me over and over' 'alright i'm sorry' 'hand me a needle' 'needle' 'thread' 'thread' 'i don't even know what i'm doing' 'i have this joke for you' 'knock knock' 'knock knock' 'who's there' 'catgut' 'cat gut who?' 'stop trying to cheer me up' 'this is absolute blackmail' 'dr. harris you're a doctor, a doctor' 'the oxygen is failing again'

stopped typing to laugh. 'what the hell is this.' louis said 'what?' i said 'i wasn't even paying attention and the radio just started being this.' he said 'oh no yeah, i know, it's weird.' i said 'yeah, what is this?' he said 'i don't know, it's weird.' now he is using a drill.

7:17PM: louis said 'just so you know, this is a two-man job.' i said 'oh shit, i can help.' he said 'no no, that's just why it's taking so long, usually two guys.' i said 'so, the other guy...you usually...' he said 'yeah i usually got a helper.' i said 'but he just didn't show up?' he said 'yeah he didn't show up today.' i said 'shit.' it was quiet. looked at bed frame and said 'when i saw that thing in the store, it looked so complicated—i thought it'd come already put-together.' he said 'nah, i gotta put this together. it's annoying.' i said 'your helper friend is, like, at a fun memorial day party.' he said 'yeah, and i'm here.' i said 'he sucks.' he said 'i know.'

have periodically...when i first saw louis i thought 'i wonder if we're going to have sex.' he has kind eyes. kind intelligent 'i'm not just cruising somewhere behind these' eyes.

7:25PM: stepped over skeletal bed frame to get red bull and said 'are you sure i can't help, this seems annoying.' louis said 'nah.' i said 'so how does it work, how do they pay you?' he said 'well you pay for the assembly and furniture together, right?' i said 'yeah, at the store. er. i think so. there were two lines.' picked up the receipt. he said 'you see that seventy-nine dollars?' i said 'yeah.' he said 'well i get half of that,' chuckling a little, like, mournfully. his voice is soft. i said 'that's all?' he said 'y-eah' and looked at me slowly. i said 'well at least you don't have to split it with another guy.' he said 'what?' i said 'like, your helper. guy. at least you don't have to split it again.' he said 'oh, y-eah.' i said 'they pay you by the hour though also, though, right?' he said 'nah.' i said 'what' and made a face. he said 'nah nothing by the hour.' i said 'i feel like that's...not allowed, somehow.' he made fists and said his fingers hurt from stretching rubber on the skeletal thing. i said 'do you want like, a beer?' he said 'oh, no, thank you.' i said 'i have like, beer, a beer, hummus, and. cat food. i wish i could offer you something.' he said 'no, that's fine.'

7:35PM: steve martin banjo music has been playing on radio. i said 'do you want to listen to something else?' louis said 'nah i don't care.' i said 'me neither.'

7:37PM: i said 'this shit is killing me, i can't take it,' walking to radio. louis said 'what?' i turned off the radio. i said 'the banjos.' louis grinned and shook his head, making a noise like 'tssssssh.' like 'there goes my silly girl again, turning off the banjos.'

he asked for a glass of water. i said 'you want ice?' he said 'okay.' heard fabric rustling and thought 'oh shit, will there be another shirt or just.' it was another shirt. louis said 'sorry i had to take my shirt off, it was too hot.' i said 'you do what you gotta do.'

7:43PM: some things have been established: louis has been at ikea for two months, has lived in the bronx 20 years. we agree that there is crime in philly.

8:15PM: imagining saying something like 'wanna help me break in the bed,' leading to sex. realistically imagining sex. nudity. a new person. it would feel bad, i think.

8:32PM: louis is in rubber fastening hell. wonder if i'm going to say something about his white sox hat.

10:09PM: helped louis put the frame on bed. i said 'that seemed hellish.' he said 'what?' and looked at me with his soft slow smart louis eyes. i said 'putting it all together, seemed hellish for you. i appreciate it.' he said 'nah.' he said 'i'll help you put the mattress on?' i said 'that would be great, thank you.' we did it. there was a moment of us looking at it like 'we did it.' he said 'you wanna jump on the bed or something now?' and smiled a little. i thought 'this is your moment. this is when your 24-year-old self would've flirtatiously asked him to jump on the bed with you.' i got on the bed doggie style and hopped and said 'hooooo-hoohoo. it works!' tried not to look at louis. then i did. he was smiling. i'm smiling. he asked to use the bathroom.

HERE COMES THE LOUIS BATHROOM FACT:

EXTREMELY OF INTEREST TO ME:

louis did not close the door all the way. he left the water on. i heard him peeing. thought 'man and wife. it's true, it really is true, what i've been thinking the whole time. he thinks it too. bathroom door open.'

when he came out he seemed sleepier. i said 'do you have to do this tomorrow too?' he thought a minute and said 'hm. y-eah, tomorrow too.' i said 'early?' he said 'mm-hm. like eight a.m.,' smiling a little. i initialed a paper. how can i describe louis better? his demeanor. the slow louis demeanor. 'the louis way.' slow-cooked louis. his face was so interesting. like, barely expressive but…expressing…i don't know, he had scars i think, he was… who does he look like…so handsome. shit. kind of like lil b + wes bentley. wish he left his sweaty ass t-shirt here.

i tend to date skinny guys but i like me a big hulking hulk of a big man. like. oof. muscles. oof. louis could destroy me. love me a man big enough to destroy me. oof. oof.

louis said 'you want me to take that cardboard?' i said 'no, i'll put it in the basement.' followed him to the door and said 'here, i want to give you this' and handed him $29. thought i had more. his face brightened.

the light in my lamp went out as i put the table in front of it. then i did dishes and cleaned countertops and fed cats.

then mom called. 'jolly' conversation. i told her about louis and jumping on the bed and she said 'oh no!' i said 'no, he didn't mean it like that, like jumping in bed with me. it was me. who thought that. my mind was in the gutter.' she said 'bad megan.'

she and dad decorated his new office today. there was an issue with carpeting, a woman tripped and fell near a lamp. mom and dad were trying to figure out where to put the lamp. mom said 'don't be afraid of the lamp, mike.' she described dad straightening his back and looking at her curiously and saying 'i'm not afraid of the lamp.' she said 'it was a 'male' thing, this fear of the lamp, i think.' we talked for maybe 25 minutes. i said 'i'm happy you're calling me a lot, i'll call you more too.' she said 'honey i really think—when i say something like 'you should buy flowers for your table,' don't take that seriously. i think you can do whatever you want.' felt flummoxed. i said 'i know, it's okay, i don't think…i forgot you said that, i think it's nice that you said that. i was thinking about buying a plant.' she said 'i think that's a great idea, aren't there plants cats like to eat?' i said 'yeah, yeah, there are, i didn't even think to do that. i just threw away cat grass that got old but i could grow it, for shirley. shirley likes cat grass.' mom said 'oh, shirley. i like picturing you with the kitties. will you send me pictures on the computer? i can't do it on my phone for some reason.' i said 'i'll send you pictures. the apartment looks like somewhere someone who 'has it together' would live now. it's weird. i feel better now, having a bed. it's stupid, but thank you a lot.' mom said 'no, i think that's absolutely true. sleeping in a bed helps, it's a wonder what sleeping in a bed does, i think." she was going home to eat burger king she and dad bought, and watch a thing on HBO where michael douglas plays liberace and matt damon plays his 'young male lover.'

drinking a beer on the bed currently.

MAY 27, 2013

12:37–3:[something]AM: talked with juliet on skype. there were technical difficulties at first, video-related. she asked 'are you the most depressed you've ever felt' and i said 'yeah' and laughed. eventually couldn't see her at all, due to video issues on my end. she said 'i'll just be like this ghost' and i said i'd probably feel more able/comfortable answering things like that. she said 'if you're uncomfortable talking about some things we can just keep it light, i don't want you to feel uncomfortable.' i said something about how i felt my face blushing but that i thought it was interesting to feel uncomfortable and i wanted to be asked uncomfortable questions. ate 1mg xanax. it's easy/fun to riff with juliet. interested in her life and look forward to video interview time. i told her 'you're one of the only people i talk to' and she said 'why?' and i said 'because…you asked me, and…it's easy,' grinning like an idiot. she said 'why don't you talk to other people?' she mentioned wanting to experiment with liveblogging for three days for the interview. encouraged her to do it right now and didn't think she would, but she has been all night.

3:20AM: standing in pickles & pies. Unanticipated 'after bar crowd' is in a loud college-looking grouping in line in front of me. That poppy bluegrass-y song that goes 'I will wait I will wait for you' is playing. Girl in jean skirt is 'jamming' to it, performing her jamming to tall uninterested friend beside her. She said 'you know how hard he's playing right now?'

3:22AM: cashier with majestic orb of hairnetted black hair, who said 'you younger than you look' and 'don't drink too much' twice to me the other day, is behind the sandwich counter.

Exchanged glances that felt like they meant 'you're not one of the bar people, good, I will help you soon' and 'I understand, take your time.' Compassionate ass glances with majestic hair orb. Love the hair orb man. Watched him carry a large bag of frozen fries and dump them into a fryer, then get a pad of paper and walk to me without looking. Felt intimate. Understanding 'now it is time to tell me your sandwich.' Ordered 'reuben on a roll with thousand island and mustard. And that's all.' he didn't look up from paper.

Put cherries, mangoes, lime, 'sugar-free ruggelah-like date product,' apricots, six-pack amber woodchuck cider into metal carrier and stood by the sandwich counter. Watched 'jean jacket jamming girl' maybe argue with 'tall uninterested friend' in peripheral vision and tried to listen but it was too quiet and fast.

Paid for things. Cashier who I had previously identified as 'does not like customers or anyone or working but likes showing everyone he hates everything' seemed happy to see me. He is older. He said 'you. Hi.' I smiled and said 'he-lloo' sounding unintentionally child-like. He read the prices aloud as he entered them in the cash register machine. He picked up the 'sugar-free ruggelah-like date product' and said 'eeh-uh. Hm.' I said 'I think it's five dollars, five ninety-nine?' he looked at me and continued handling the box. I said 'I'll get another one.' he said 'you get another one.' brought one with an orange price sticker back. He said 'ah, five ninety-nine' and looked at me like 'blackjack dealer who knows the person won that shit.' Other people were approaching me on both sides and he was kind of 'dealing' with them as he rung me up. Octopus-like ability to wrangle three registers. As he was 'dealing' with someone I bagged my things. He had taken out another bag then saw that I did and made a face like 'I've had enough of this. You are part of the 'this' that I have had enough of, but thank you.' We told each other to have a good night.

4:15AM: made chia mixture (chia seeds mixed with water and raw honey in jar) for tomorrow. if you soak chia seeds they develop little jelly-like membranes. have some idea that this is good for me. ate 1mg xanax, drank two woodchucks, put chips on reuben and ate sitting at the table. watched an episode of 'the office.' brushed teeth and put on silky black and white short nightgown, thinking 'you have a bed, now you can wear the nightgown.' bought it when i moved in to first apartment in baltimore, thinking 'you have an apartment, you should have a nightgown now.'

9:[something]AM: woke feeling UTI pain. ate two apricots.

11:11AM: woke from dream, the only image of which i remember is being in my apartment and seeing a 18"x10"x16" off-white shiny loaf of bread with 1mg xanax and a note taped to it, from my dad, that said 'you could've asked.'

sitting on the toilet, to wait for water and azo standard to relieve UTI pain. started reading juliet's liveblog. happy that ass is liveblogging.

read about amanda bynes throwing a bong out her window and wearing a wig and two fake nails and sweatpants to court. she is on violation of probation for driving with a suspended license. remembered a few days ago the DMV emailed me about my 'using cell phone while driving' ticket that said i needed to contact them because the officer entered my name wrong, and that…as a consequence, could be my license could be suspended. it has been suspended once before, in july 2010, for not paying a parking ticket.

left toilet and looked for azo standard. i am walking outside. i hate buying it. it says 'FOR URINARY PAIN RELIEF' on the front. the store brand also says this. one time at CVS the cashier ringing me up said 'i hate that, i gotta drink more water.' i said 'oh shit, it happens to you too?' though at the time i knew UTI pain was from sex, not dehydration. it happens with both. all my life. really bad in fourth grade. peed my pants. one time it went into my kidneys and i got sick. okay great yumyumyum UTI stuff.

pounded three large glasses of water. currently sitting in bed.

11:56AM: listening to 'folky' spotify playlist juliet linked to. i like it.

SHIT I MUST ACCOMPLISH TODAY:

* repay thai rock

* answer backlog of ask.fm questions

* call lieutenant re navy

* call NYC traffic violations re ticket

* make 'taipei' facebook photo album

* see if they mail shit on holidays and mail masha's shit

* dye hair

* buy fruit and coffee and salad related groceries

* hang out with nicholas at 10PM

12:42PM: no longer in UTI pain. i was just dehydrated. fucking. hell yeah.

12:47PM: luxuriating in bed smoking e-cigarette. i'm going to answer questions now and luxuriate a little more before completing to-do list.

3:48PM: drinking a woodchuck, to feel full without eating. nicholas and i are going to eat at wild ginger, then see prinzhorn dance school. i didn't know prinzhorn dance school, listening to them now. near the end of phone call, nicholas said 'could you not write about everything we say and do,' laughing in 'nicholas way.' i said 'oh no, i won't, should i take down what i've written already?' he said what was up already was fine but it would be distracting/anxiety provoking for him to be thinking i was going to write about tonight as it was happening. i said 'no no no, i won't think about

434

writing it down, like the past few times i've had fun i've thought 'have fun, you don't have to liveblog.' i'll just think of us as having fun tonight.' nicholas said 'okay good.' grinning thinking 'nicholas' now. excited for nicholas. thai ass food. kind of i wish i could liveblog tonight. nicholas is one of the most interesting people i've talked to, ever, like, highly distinguishable voice and manner. oh no. feel i am writing too much already and he is reading this. IT'S OKAY NICHOLAS DON'T WORRY IT WILL BE OKAY I PROMISE, I THINK YOU ARE GREAT!!!!!!

5:34PM: took photobooth picture of myself at 5:30pm, when i was 'wailing on my abs.' i have since ceased wailing on abs. listened to 'nookie' by limp bizkit and thought 'i actually really like this, i think…like if i had been a teenager when it came out i would've liked it…wait, i was a teenager when it came out.' shirley is on my lap. she burped and it smelled so nasty and good. she is currently wailing her paws/'making biscuits' on my thighs. do you guys know about 'making biscuits?' that that's what you call it when a cat kneads their paws? drinking another woodchuck.

5:40PM: fred durst says 'she put my tender heart in a blender but still i surrendered.' in 'nookie.' i think that's a reference to the eve 6 song that's like 'wanna put my tender heart in a blender watch it spin round to a beautiful oblivion.' how has no one said this out loud yet? we all know it, right?

5:43PM: i like the lyrics to 'nookie.' i'm laughing. i like the lyrics. haha. i've heard it so many times but i haven't paid attention to words until now. should i get into numetal now? who likes numetal…stage crew…drama club…hm.

5:50PM: the shower is maybe four feet away. i'm still sitting here like a chump (hey) like a chump (hey) like a chump (hey) like a chump (hey)

7:03pm: walked to 115th st. white sulfur-smelling liquid was frothing around sewer drains. people were in the street. almost every porch had a person on it. my car wasn't there. passed more white liquid and a group of boys. a boy said 'that smells like butt.' passed man sorting through trash. car was not on 114th st either, less people on porches. it was on 113th st.

7:05pm: nicholas texted something about still feeling apprehensive about me liveblogging tonight. i texted 'off the record.'

7:46pm: parked on metropolitan ave, near bedford ave.

8-11:38PM: ate at wild ginger with nicholas. ordered summer rolls and red curry. not going to elaborate via nicholas' request. walked to 'cameo' and bought ticket. there were giant iridescent 'chandelier/stalagtite-like'

LED rainbow lights in a formation descending from the ceiling. no one was onstage and nicholas and i went out into the other bar-like room and talked. then we went back in the room. a man in a baseball hat who seemed to enjoy the sound of his own voice sang onstage next to a girl standing by a macbook who i thought of as 'his slave.' nicholas and i went to the other bar-like part and sat and talked again. then we went inside again and prinzhorn dance academy was on. i liked them. the guy left the stage and i said 'they broke up' to nicholas. the guy came back holding a bottle. nicholas said 'and only over a beer.' couple in front of nicholas and me. the guy was jonah hill-like and the girl was 'looks like she's in the supremes'-like. jonah hill was drumming on the speaker with a drumstick.

11:39PM: after the show nicholas and i wanted to use the bathroom. there were three guys and one girl in line. i said 'usually it's the other way around right, more girls? more of a line for 'girls?'' no one said anything. the jonah hill/supremes lady couple stood in line. supremes lady was holding the drumstick. i said 'is that from the band?' jonah hill said 'yeah.' i said 'are you keeping it?' supremes lady said 'hell yeah, this is mine now.' i thought 'jonah hill thinks i think it's bad to keep the stick, how do i let him know i think it's okay.'

jonah hill and supremes lady were still in line when i exited bathroom. didn't see nicholas. i said 'if only you had gotten the wishbone, not the drumstick, you know,' and continued to a not-seeming-to-'get-it' jonah hill, 'not the drumstick, the wishbone, so you could have a wish!'

11:42pm: waited for nicholas on a wooden table by the bathroom. i told him the 'wishbone' thing while we walked to my car and he thought it was funny. we passed a couch and a shelf with a lot of appliances on it. i said 'oh great, a blender! i need a new blender.' nicholas said 'i'll take the frying pan for you.' i picked up the blender. it was sticky. nicholas said 'it seems a little sticky.' all the appliances were sticky. i said 'yeah no, don't worry about the frying pan, just leave that there.' i drove him to his apartment and parked. we hugged. i said i wanted to have him over sometime this summer for a beach party. watched him walk into his building. thought 'nicholas.'

11:45-11:59pm: downloaded 'all these things that i have done' by the killers. sang along to it and 'born to run' and got really into it and a little lost.

MAY 28, 2013

2:36am: back at apartment. texted with mira. wished her happy birthday. ate 1mg xanax and drank the last woodchuck and felt catatonic. ate handful salt & vinegar chips and two 'sugar-free date products.' brushed teeth. applied nightgown. ate two tylenol and drank water. watched the beginning of an ASMR video.

9:08AM: woke from dream where i was peeing to me peeing. i was peeing. peeing in the bed. i peed myself in the bed. it happened. i just cleaned it. oh god. there was only a little pee, like a fist-sized amount. ate 1mg xanax.

1:13PM: woke. the pee was gone. cats were on the bed. read seven new emails. thought 'i am responding to three of these emails today.' read 'frowns need friends too.' ate remaining 'sugar-free date products' and felt heavy and lethargic, like gravity had become stronger in my apartment. feet are 'extra-attached' to floor and body is 'extra-attached' to bed.

1:29PM: mom called. she said attorney's office called her with an accident settlement offer. i told her i peed the bed and she said 'i hate it when that happens.'

1:51PM: called attorney. soon i will have $3901.42 because a drunk driver rear-ended mom's car with me in it in 2011. so much money. i could get 39 $100 bills and give them to people on the street. 39 temporarily happier people.

2:14PM: danny the landlord called. last month's check bounced, this month's rent is due. meeting him tonight with non-bouncy checks.

2:59PM: dad called. talked about navy and job things. i said i'd visit soon, to see the new offices and say 'hi.'

3:20PM: sitting in bed. i didn't repay thai rock or make 'taipei' photo album yesterday. wrote a to-do list in notebook. here is a more organized version:

TO-DO 'CREATIVE:'

- stories for 'self yelp' and 'readwave'

- 'taipei' photo album

- article for alt citizen

- review 'you private person' for richard chiem

- decide if i want to try to get liveblog published as a book or continue updating
- articles for thought catalog and vice

TO-DO 'SOCIAL:'

- respond to emails
- call chelsea to see if she's still living here and wants to hang out
- hang out with nicholas and mira and sam cooke more
- wednesday 6/5: tao reading/book release at powerhouse
- thursday 5/30: marie calloway reading/book release at st. mark's
- thursday 6/6: my/mira/scott mcclanahan reading in baltimore

TO-DO 'SHIT OF LIFE:'

- call lieutenant
- apply to organic avenue, book stores, libraries, more
- go to DMV to sort out 'officer wrote the wrong name' ticket, pay parking tickets
- get car inspected
- mail masha package
- find new gynecologist to give me birth control
- hang up clothes/laundry
- groceries
- buy lightbulb
- get $200 'move-in fee' refund
- find out when garbage people pick up large items, throw out moldy ass mattress
- repay thai rock
- repay amahd
- exercise

i'm afraid to call the lieutenant until 'using cell phone while driving' ticket and parking tickets are paid.

5:28PM: post office closed, going to fedex. still feeling strong gravity in apartment. hard to move. giving thai rock 'extra large tip' via two day delay. fed cats. walked in and out of the bathroom several times, looking in the mirror and thinking 'you forgot something' every time. rubbed coconut oil on legs. applied 'stop looking so tired' beige stuff under eyes.

5:44pm: heard 'heard it through the grapevine' playing loudly as I walked downstairs. It was coming from mark, working on his old apartment I think, on the first floor. Checked mail. Thought 'now is the time to ask mark about getting your check back and throwing away the mattress.'

5:54pm: young-looking cashier named Hamid, who I have sort of flirted with/'accepted the flirting of because he seems nice' rang me up for a 'monster zero' and 16oz sugar-free red bull. I put them in my bag. Hamid said something. I said 'oh, no bag.' he gestured to the straws. I smiled and said 'oh, straws, I see, no, no straws either' and left. Man smoking outside 'concrete fixer-man deli' was still there when I left pickles & pies. Felt him looking at me and avoided eye contact as I passed. Approached man sitting on street and smiled. He said 'fitty cent?' I said 'what do I got, I got a dollar.' he took it, said 'thank you' and stood, like I had just passed a relay stick to him and now it was his turn to walk.

6:03pm: have been hearing a signal-like whistle sound periodically since leaving apartment. Sitting in car now. It is raining. Driving to Thai rock, then FedEx.

6:23pm: wandered around thai rock area and 'bungalow backyard bar.' All doors were closed. Thai rock restaurant/seating area seems totally closed, it just runs from the person's upstairs apartment. Walked upstairs and knocked on door. The smoking man from the other night appeared. I said 'hi, it's me from the other night, I wanted to pay you guys back.' I gave him $41. He said 'oh, you?' and looked confused. I said 'yeah, I didn't have cash.' he said 'oh you! You look different I din reconize you!' I said 'yeah I look different' and made 'I understand' face, felt myself blushing. I said 'thank you guys.' he said 'thank you.' walked to car.

The mcdonalds next to Thai rock is boarded up. Someone had graffitied 'Nothing here 2 take u r 2 late :)' + 'Trust me save your Energy!!' + 'Someone beat u here already' on the restaurant and 'we were already hit! Don't bother! U R 2 Late ;)' on the playplace.

6:34pm: Danny texted 'Hey i like to meet u tomorrow i work late tonite'

So…

7:08pm: circled around looking for free parking. Got that shit on lock-down. Dropped e-cigarette. In line at FedEx now. There has been some confusion about what line I'm supposed to be in, some confusion about a 'purple white form.' Now things are on the up and up. Definitely less confused about where I'm supposed to stand. Filled out the form. Everything's coming up Megan. Asian man wearing bright mint green shirt, khakis, and skate shoes that appear to say 'rmax' (Carmax? No the label has been revealed they are not skate shoes they say 'airmax') is looking at his phone. Can hear mother and child behind me oh I have been summoned

7:19pm: FedEx man said I checked the wrong box. Okay it went like this:

FedEx man: you want it there by tomorrow morning?

Me: yes please, if possible

FedEx man: you supposed to check 'FedEx priority then'

Me: oh, oh no, sorry

FedEx man: [puts my box into another box labeled 'small box']

Me: busy time-a day huh?

FedEx man: yeah we actually just getting ready to close

Me: [looks at desk] oh doh. Sahwee (this…Jesus…can't believe it came out like that)

FedEx man: [types stuff]

Me: can I get this too [holds up package labeled 'help i'm tired' caffeine pills]

FedEx man: oh nah, he's gonna have to ring you up for that

Time: [passes]

FedEx man: so that'll be [amount]

Me: oooh-kay [hands card]

FedEx man: [does stuff with card, hands my card to another FedEx man]

FedEx man 2: [looks at me with deadpan expression, then other FedEx man] what'm I sposed to do with this

440

FedEx man: oh shit, I thought I was giving you the box, she gotta get rung up for that [points to 'help i'm tired' box in my hand, gives me credit card back]

Me: [big idiot grin]

FedEx man 2: [maintains deadpan expression and eye contact] I thought I just got some free money, I was about to go shopping

Me: nope, not today

FedEx man 2: [walks to register and starts to ring up 'help i'm tired'] we'll go shopping after this

Me: okay, after this

FedEx man: [gives me receipt] here is your FedEx receipt

Me: thank you [walks to other register]

FedEx man 2: 'help i'm tired' huh. You tired?

Me: [uncontrollable 'ren and stimpy' 'public encounters with people vibrating grin face'] yee-up [hands him $10 bill]

FedEx man 2: I need like four of these

Me: me too

FedEx man 2: well it comes with eight, you wanna split it?

Me: [grinning] uh, no, I can't afford to after that package

FedEx man 2: you're not tired, you like, wired

Me: no I'm just good at covering it up

FedEx man 2: you're good

Me: thank you, I've had a lot of practice

FedEx man 2: how many years of college you got?

Me: uh, like seven. And you?

FedEx man 2: [deader-than-deadpan expression] three [hands me change]

Me: [takes 'help i'm tired' and change, starts to walk away] well, good luck

FedEx man 2: you too

Me: [turns to wave and smile while walking out the door]

7:48pm: still in parking space. Took hot pic of 'help i'm tired' pills. They are 200mg caffeine. I just bought them for the packaging, I've seen these thingies and thought 'whoever buys that is a sucker for packaging.' Chewed one pill with front teeth and swallowed it with water. Still feeling 'strong gravity' heaviness. Going to grocery store now. Okay. Then laundry. You got this baby. Big baby Megan doing weal peepool fings aw day wong, whudda good baby Megan! Good baby! Wook attda good baby smoking her play-toy in her parky-warky-poo-poo spot! Dawwww. Oh honey, take a picture! Look honey she's gonna suckle her play-toy again, quick, get it! Get it!

8:45pm: have been looking at instagram and other things on phone in waldbaum's parking lot for unknown amount of time. Sky has darkened. No idea what groceries to buy. What could I want to eat.

8:49pm: 'forcing' myself to get green juice materials. Okay. Entering the shit outta this waldbaum's.

9:34pm: exiting. Sitting in car now. There were issues with the self-ringing-up-thingy kiosk. Candy (waldbaum's employee I sort of remember from around the time I moved in, a night I didn't go to a party...he had left waldbaum's after midnight and I was sitting in my car, typing something and watching him enter a van playing traditional Mexican-sounding music). I scanned the celery and it said 'please place on scanner to weigh your item.' I did. Nothing happened. I did it again and nothing happened. Tried again and was approached by an older woman with a clipboard. Candy had plastic gloves. He said 'lemme do it, I got it.' he tried the same things I did, then walked rapidly between me and the 'overseer of self-checkout register/kiosk station' in the middle of the self-checkout aisle. Candy looked at me and said 'it's a quantity issue.' Then he walked back over. The celery scanned. He started scanning my groceries. A man in a waldbaum's apron entered, riding one of those motorized wheelchair things grocery stores have. The clipboard woman said 'where you think you're going with that thing?' Candy was scanning my things with the intensity I imagine arguments about 'magic the gathering' can reach during games. He said 'we need a pineapple code, someone get me a pineapple code.' The clipboard woman didn't seem to hear. She stood close enough to me that we might be considered 'interacting' to passersby. I said 'sorry, mine seems difficult.' She said 'it's just that they keep freezing. We don't want it to get frozen, because then it's really bad.' Candy picked up a garlic bulb, which

I had selected after an embarrassingly long period of indecision resulting meekly with 'I might want this for the future where I'm more interested in cooking food with garlic in it,' and exhaled sharply through his nose and looked at the ceiling as if the PLU code for garlic was somewhere in the ceiling. The man with the mechanical wheelchair was clowning around in the background this whole time, garnering infrequent attention from the clipboard woman. Candy bagged my things as he scanned. Scanning and bagging me. I thought 'I know Candy is no one's dad. Maybe, though. I don't think Candy wants to be anyone's dad. I don't think he's ever even thought about being anyone's dad.' that sounds negative but I wasn't thinking it negatively. He said 'how you wanna pay?' I said 'card, uh. Credit.' He pushed buttons and disappeared and I 'took over machine duty.' He reappeared with a shopping cart and said 'here, this makes it go faster, put it in here.' I said 'oh no, it's really okay, my car is just right there. Thank you, though.' he didn't protest and the woman with the clipboard didn't seem to notice any of it but remained in her 'close enough to be considered interacting with me/Candy' position. Walked towards exit. Heard the mechanical wheelchair employee say 'that's the way you roll out.'

9:57pm: another song I like to sing is 'all these things that I have done' by the killers. Seems like people would be surprised to hear I listen to Bruce springsteen and the killers. NOW YOU KNOW. HO HO HO. OOLIE-CACA HAN SOLO HO HO HO. Estimate <2% of people reading will get that that's a 'star wars' reference for reasons besides 'han solo.' it's not even a full 'star wars' reference because I forget what jabba the hut says. It's a Matt reference. My friend Matt used to say 'OOLIE CACA, HAN SOLO. HO. HO. HOOOO.' I am sitting in another parking spot now. It is the parking spot where my car will be all tonight while I am sitting in my room. Thought 'how am I going to survive tonight.' how am I going to get out of this car. That is step one: leaving the car. Next I just have to put away groceries and maybe make green juice or…I don't know. I have to do things until I fall asleep. That is the one thing I can count on. I will be doing things until I fall asleep. Maybe I will wet the bed again tonight. Hot nights. Hot rockaway park nights. Star bet-wetting 27-year-old motherfucker lobotomy princess of queens, new york. The wettest beds, the hottest cats, the most unwanted groceries, the least deserving of this meager lonely existence: all right here. I'm not being whatever. I'm not being cute. No I am, I'm being cute about something I don't feel cute about.

10:06pm: liveblogging opening my door. I already did it. It's opened a little, propped by my knee.

Put e-cigarette and keys in pocket

Had to stop to rewrite that one because at first I had only put the keys in

Door is a little more ajar

Car is approaching behind me gonna wait

Okay unlocked door

Leg is out but not on ground

Foot is on ground

I can hear another car or movement

Looked at road behind me and slid ahead in seat a little but stopped putting other leg forward to write this

A person is walking to my right now they have passed

Airplane has almost fully passed

Two more cars

Still one leg out

Now the airplane sounds closer

I live by JFK, the airplane is probably doing one of those circle things before it lands

Can almost not hear it

Still hear a little

Mostly hear light rain

Uh oh another person to my right

I looked, there was a man in a red t-shirt and a bike

Now a bus, I hear a bus moving in the same direction as the airplane

More cars

Another airplane, 'high pitched' noise coming with this one, sounds 'landing'

Lights of a car approaching

The car is backing into a garage 30' from me

Still one leg out

Here comes the other one

Right leg and foot both on the ground, seat made a 'ticky ticky' noise as I moved leg

Hiccuped

Hair is tickling my nose

Both feet on floor, door is ajar

Another airplane

Thought 'Did I mention I live by JFK' and pictured myself onstage looking around an audience for laughs

Scratched nose and moved hair behind right ear self-consciously, knowing I'd be typing

Scratched itch on forehead

Before I wrote 'self-consciously' I non-self-consciously scratched an itch on right leg

Looked again at street behind me, hearing cars to the right, scratched leg again

Another airplane

Okay here goes: you won't hear from me for a while because I am going to 'ornament' my arms with bags of groceries

I am going to walk to the passenger side of the car and open that door to do this

Then I am going to lock the door

Liveblogging this in advance because my hands will be full on the walk to my building

Pictured me buying beer at pickles & pies and thought 'mercy'

Another airplane

I can smell celery from my grocery bag, 'beckoning' me

Fuck

Another set of headlights approaching

Pulled door closer to me so car could pass but the pulling was unnecessary

Also scratched my head

Again, and my inner right knee

Am I really this itchy? Seems uncommon

Heart is beating faster

Enough clowning around Boyle go to the passenger side door, now is your chance to get away, ggogogogoogogo

10:22PM: thought 'i'm not going to make it' humorlessly several times while walking to building. did 'shoulder shrugs' with groceries on arms, endorphin rush was quickly replaced with 'this is horrible, i'm not going to make it.' about half a block from my building i lowered grocery bags to get better fist grips.

saw a person standing by the entrance as i neared. thought 'shit, i'm going to have to interact maybe, maybe i'll take long enough for them to comfortably pretend like they didn't see me or conclude 'it's too long for me to hold a door for someone." it didn't work. i recognized the person, it was crystal, i forgot when we met but i know it was in the elevator. she lives on the second floor too. she was wearing hospital scrubs and had a small dog tonight. i said 'thank you, have i met you before?' saw her eyes. she said 'i think so maybe.' i said 'you're crystal.' she said 'yeah, yeah i'm crystal.' i said 'crystal, yeah, hi, i'm megan' as we walked to the elevator and comfortably entered 'agreement that we would both be using the elevator and crystal would hold the elevator door for me' dynamic. i said 'and who is this?' she said 'oh this is hershey.' i said 'hershey' and smiled. we were in the elevator. i looked her in the eyes and said 'it seems like a lot of people have small pets in this building,' aware of intentionally acting like patrick bateman. slipping into patrick bateman style. think i was able to do patrick bateman style because of 'fleeting hopelessness' on the walk to the car. like. i can do patrick bateman style if i get to the level of hopelessness where i'm thinking 'there is nothing left to expect, nothing can surprise me, so why not do whatever.' just remembered the part in 'american psycho' where he's at the beach with his girlfriend and he can't sleep and he stands alone on the beach, feeling…i can't remember, something about this part was poignant. then he went inside and pictured smashing his girlfriend's head in with a statue/bust, was most tempted to do it that night.

back to crystal: i'm not going to write everything about crystal. i remember
not writing everything about crystal last time too. at the end, as we were
walking to our apartments (hers is diagonal to mine, next to colin's), i said
something about having two cats and thought 'evilly maneuvering this
entire conversation to get cat inventory off my chest.' crystal smiled and
kind of laughed and said 'you have a good night megan.' i said 'you too,
crystal' and unlocked my door. crystal would be an easy patrick bateman
victim. like you would know 'red flag: crystal will be killed,' if this were a
novel about how i killed people.

11:16PM: turned on red light by door. put groceries on table. impulsively
bought a push-button night light that's supposed to make stars and the
moon appear on the ceiling when you turn it on.

replaced old lightbulb in lamp. when i remove or replace a lightbulb i picture it exploding and slicing me open somewhere. this time i thought 'the
shade is placed in such a way that it would be my right wrist. gashing open.
blood pouring out. would i call mom? i would call mom to see if i should
go to the hospital but i wouldn't feel like going and she would tell me to
call an ambulance. would i do it? i would...what would i use to stop the
bleeding [memory of when i slipped and sliced open finger cutting open a
coconut in iowa with tao and it was bleeding a lot and i used a towel and
went to the front desk and they called an ambulance, then the ambulance
guy said the hospital was close enough to drive to and the ambulance would
cost more, then like, 'but it's your decision though, ambulance or not'].'

the light didn't turn on. tried the outlet above it. still didn't turn on.
removed poster covering the fuse box and turned on and off all the fuses,
remembering the part in 'jurassic park' where laura dern does that and
electrocutes the boy and then the velociraptor attacks her friend and there
is a close-up of her screaming. pressed button that said 'test' and heard door
buzzer go off as the lights of my 'main light area' by my bed went off. tried
it again. no dice. tried all the fuses again, thinking 'laura dern, it's going
to happen, the velociraptor, or no, just i'll be electrocuted, okay.' think
lamp is just broken. plugged computer into other outlet. thought 'buying
lightbulbs and throwing away old lightbulb when it was the lamp the whole
time, and now i have less light in my apartment than when i started, no
wait, that's better, i don't even like it when there's a lot of lights, [memory of
zachary liking overhead lighting and me 'dealing with his preference' most
times we used the living room, using lamps when he wasn't there].'

did dishes. thought about soliciting brandon scott gorrell for 'how did you
get out of depression, are you out all the way, for some reason i think
you're doing okay' advice. imagined his response being something like

'make yourself do things you think you want, make yourself be social, you will meet people you like, if what you're doing is making you unhappy think about why you keep doing it, maybe see a therapist.' thought 'that's the most anyone can ever say. the most that can ever be recommended. your choices are always this: stay unhappy, kill yourself, see a therapist.' felt hopeless...thing...of 'i can't imagine putting away the groceries, can't they just stay there on the table.' smelled the celery. the beckoning ass celery. washed the glass component and scrubbed sticky stuff off the motor component of the blender i found with nicholas last night. it took a long time. the sticky stuff was greenish brownish. thought 'maybe the sticky stuff is pesticide, all of the appliances on the street seemed sticky, maybe they fumigated their apartment and that's why they were getting rid of things, maybe the blender will work and small bits of pesticide will stay inside it and 'mercifully' poison me over time and they'll find out from looking at my hair, the poison will show in my hair, napoleon-style.'

put away groceries. took picture. thought 'it looks like...such...a nice-looking fridge, doesn't it,' like the rock man in 'the neverending story' when he says 'they look like such big...strong...hands, don't they.'

MAY 29, 2013

1:30PM: shirley is sleeping next to me. she yawned and arched her back to fill my hand. now she seems asleep again. there is no way to know really, if a cat that appears asleep is. or if anyone is, i guess. there is no way to know if a person is really asleep, everyone could be pretending. funny to imagine cats…the amount they sleep and how much 'pretending' would be involved.

3:58AM: listening to mitch hedberg youtube videos. he's one of the only stand-up comedians to make me laugh this hard. 'rice is good for when you're hungry and you want two-thousand of something'…jesus…think about how good his book/twitter/anything would've been…

4:44AM: ate 2mg xanax. i don't want to be awake right now. shit. i don't want to be asleep either. alvie is acting insane, howling again. he is afraid of beds, maybe. what is going on with that guy. would it have been better if i had named him 'kevin.' why don't i have a period yet. why is he howling in the bathroom.

now shirley trying to fight him off the bed. he wants to be on the bed, i think that's the problem. that's a nice-sounding problem for a person to have but what a hell for alvie. running around and howling and unable to communicate what he wants to 'large non-cat thing that feeds him, that is now repeating his name and gesturing to the bed, where a cat that looks almost exactly like him [though don't think he knows that] is trying to fight him.'

5:18AM: sun is coming out. sky is doing blue morning thing. i don't feel xanax working yet, or it is maybe just having a minimal effect. door to staircase has opened and closed twice. there is a 'rolling' sound right now, coming from the hallway. it stopped.

saw that tao 'liked' that i was going to 'taipei' release. scanned the list of other people going and considered belligerently 'liking' only the people i like's 'going to event' status. should i eat another 1mg xanax…how am i going to…do things…today…it…shit. two placebo birth control pills left for this month. usually get period a little before now. i feel like if i say this it will mean i'll get my period. why would i not get it. there is no reason for me not to get it unless i messed up with timing, but i don't think i did when that would've mattered. earlier i pictured going to an abortion clinic alone. they would ask me if i've had one before and i'd start crying. i wouldn't tell zachary. i would require mental hospital things if that happened, the depression that would follow, i think, i don't know if i could live with myself or feel motivated or try relationships with people if i did that again. the most humane thing would be if i killed both of us, if it happens. i'm not being dramatic please don't read into this. i'm just thinking. it's not going to happen. everything is going to be fine. i can feel 'period-y thing' in my lower half. like cramping kind of. i'll probably wake tomorrow and will have 'wet the bed' with blood instead tonight. zachary if you are reading fuck you if you think i'm doing this for sympathy i'm writing what i'm thinking. how many times do i have to say something for a person to understand it. it's impossible to make someone understand you if they don't want to, if they think you are just their thoughts about you. so many people are like that. i am like that maybe. i can't think of ways i'm like that but i'm not denying the possibility that i could be like that about some people. zachary reading the previous sentence and squinting and saying 'huh,' making a display of 'huh.' like making a display of 'i am reading words on a page that were not necessarily written by a person, these are simply words for me to understand, that are poorly written and so harder to understand.' then me looking at him and saying 'what do you think?' and him not looking at me, still squinting at the words and making a face like half-interestedly trying to figure out a math problem, then saying 'well, there's some content in there.' it is going to take a while to get 'disapproving zachary' voice out of my head. also zachary if you read that and think i wrote it for sympathy fuck you big time worse than the last 'fuck you.' also zachary if you are reading stop reading already, you said this wasn't 'worth your time,' go spend your time in better ways.

5:36AM: still no xanax effects. eating another 1mg. i've been eating 2-4mg and combining with alcohol recently, that's why i don't feel much.

5:57AM: considering eating another 1mg if i'm not sleepy by 6:15AM.

6:01AM: re-watching MDMAfilms movies. sweet/funny/nostalgic. seems like such a long time ago. there must be like 500 hours of footage of tao and me on external hard drives, floating around.

7:00AM: ate another 1mg. sam cooke tweeted 'xanax is a palindrome' recently. thought 'eyes wide shut' or something, re: that, something vague.

7:17AM: ate four hummus/avocado/salt/lime tortillas. i want curtains that block out all light. it feels so bad to see the sun do its sneaky thing on you. i would be safe in a black room with dim oscilating rainbow lights. memory foam carpet. loft bed as big as the room with security cameras that show what's under the bed. memory foam carpet would be a drag, realistically.

like for daily life. want carpet with wide textural sampling, like little squares of 'memory foam' and 'trampoline' and 'quicksand.' the squares could scatter randomly or dominate the whole floor sometimes, you could set the floor to 'oscillate' along with rainbow lights.

there was this thing at the adler planctarium, 'the space walk.' outer space simulation. i did it twice. i probably did it once, though. this is probably a case of 'memory so nice it must've been 'twice.'' you walk in a line moving in the direction of where 'the space walk' ends. behind the first door is a hallway where it's so dark your eyelids feel irrelevant, that leads to the the door 'the space walk' is behind. a room that doesn't look like a room because there are no floors or ceilings or walls, just blackness 'punctured' by star-like lights. it was some kind of mirror trick. that could be my room.

11:14AM: i was visiting juliet and tao—roommates in the midst of a bromance that had taken them both by surprise, whose mutual fascination seemed to have been taking place over one long dazzling conversation that was hard, as an outsider, to get in on. they were curious and distantly welcoming of me, though more preoccupied with referencing their 'lesbian relationship,' ignoring my questions about if it was a joke, or if it wasn't, how that worked. i was running out of ways to appear busy and stood by a sliding glass door. the mountains were volcanoes.

woke with UTI pain. no period yet. eating cherries and pounding water. sleepy.

2:04PM: woke almost peeing. no bed wetting today!!!!!!! sleepy xanax overload. 4mg. too much. i am not allowed xanax today. UTI pain gone. i just need to remember to drink more water. imagined joaquin phoenix at the DMV spelling both his names and heart skipped a little.

2:29PM: pictured myself looking 'calmly dead' in bed, getting found by mark probably, after transferring all my paypal money (~$350) to my savings account (~$100), spending it all on heroin to combine with all the xanax i have (~20mg) and a bottle of wine. mark would say 'ah jeez. that's too bad' and call whoever you call. that's if i find out i'm pregnant. i would make sure my cats had enough food for a few days before i did it. i don't know if i'd leave a note. my note would be an asterisk and my last liveblog update would be '*: see above.'

2:55PM: chewed caffeine pill with teeth and swallowed. ate noopept. the DMV is 26 minutes away. i think i got this. i can do this today. decided 'lacking interest in food' depression is better than the alternative, for health.

eating only fruits and vegetables makes me feel good, physically. maybe will cause other things to improve.

3:33pm: Danny texted 'hi'

Danny called less than a minute later

He said he wants cash instead of a check

Annoying

Meeting him at 6pm

3:45pm: seems like I'm not going to make it to the DMV. They'll also be annoyed with me for being late and will probably be less forgiving. I'll get my car inspected instead. That is actually the more annoying of the tasks. Okay. Going to call bp station by me to see about this.

4:35pm: went to the wrong gas station. Called the right one. The man said 'no we're a Mobil gas station now.' parked by a 'self-car wash' machine and wandered around service area and tried to open a door. No dice. Wandered to repair shop area and saw a probably female person working on an elevated car with a 24-pack box of sam adams in the open trunk. I said 'hi I called earlier about a photo inspection?' She smiled and said 'oh just hang out and wait.' walked to the edge of the service area and waited a little. She cheerfully said 'oh naw, you can bring it over closer, bring your car over and hang out.' I did it. I am hanging out. She said 'you got your insurance card?' I said 'yeah' and felt like I had won a 'price is right' thing, I haven't known where the card is for a long time and found it while moving a couple weeks ago. Took out insurance card. Afraid there will be an issue.

Woman pulled up to my left, wanting an inspection too. Mechanic lady said 'hold on, I have one ahead of you.' now the inspection-hungry woman is parked behind me. Have to pee badly. Their bathroom is out of order.

7:07PM: have been laying in bed feeling depressed. i am wearing a bikini. why did i do that. i don't know, but 'here it is.' smells like chlorine. i don't remember wearing it. i know 'laundry' is something i wanted to do.

7:25PM: dad called. i don't feel like typing details of anything right now. nothing has been bad or…i don't know. nice talk with dad. danny showed up at 5:31PM. told him i was looking for publishing jobs in manhattan to sound 'responsible.' dad said 'you can 'punch out' for the night.' couldn't make myself sound okay. dad said 'i don't know about you, but i think if i lived by the beach, i don't know, i'd like to take a nice walk on the beach sometimes. have you done that?' i said i haven't done it much and that maybe i would do that now. heard my voice sounding 'far away.'

tomorrow i'm going to do the other things i said i'd do today. i don't want to do laundry or hang up clothes. i want to be sleeping but i don't want to sleep and then wake and have it be another time. should i buy wine or something. i don't feel enough effort to do…just…it would involve… anything is going to involve my effort right now. should i just watch TV. there is nothing i want to look at. i don't even feel 'i want to be held by someone' right now. i don't know what's responsible for mood shift. mood has plummeted since returning from car inspection. i could make green juice. my face feels different. i'm sorry to everyone i haven't responded to yet, who has said something nice to me. i get in this place sometimes of feeling that i'm being 'sucked out.' not by people or…i don't know, not by anything. the feeling is like i have one IV needle spaced out every two or three inches on my body. like the 'hellraiser' needle-head guy but everywhere, and the needles are hooked up to tubes but they're not sucking out my blood, it's something else. i don't know what it's sucking out. it feels like breathing requires mental effort, or just like, laying here. i'm 'paying' the needle sucking things just by laying on my bed, like, if i let them do it for a while maybe i'll get left alone and i can start doing things again. when i feel like this it's like there's no question of 'what do i want.' like 'what do i want to eat' or 'who do i want to talk to' or 'how do i want my life to go.' i just don't have a choice for a while, i just have to let the thing suck whatever it wants out of me. then i can go. like today, i started to be able to 'go' again today, by going outside. if i drink i'm going to…i know what 'drunk' feels like. i know what 'xanax' feels like. i know what other drugs feel like. i know what 'soberly waiting for time to pass' feels like. i know what everything feels like. pictured myself in a transparent box at the coney island freak show behind a belted gate in front of which is a plaque that says 'UNABLE TO BE SURPRISED BY ANYTHING.'

7:58PM: meekly thought 'no one from mexico is reading anymore,' looking at statcounter

meekly

it's always 'meekly' these days

big bad boyle and the no-good meeklies

felt a little better writing this

looking at the lack of africa and asia

i am failing africa and asia

there used to be someone from alaska, i am failing them now too

it smells like someone is baking pillsbury crescent rolls near me

9:59PM: i've been re-reading shutupmom.diaryland.com. it starts with her in her mid-20's i think, she works at a nursing home and types in all caps and makes funny/poignant observations and gets drunk and stays at home and goes out and watches cartoons and eats cereal and has a dog and friends and there are guys sometimes…she called isaac brock once somehow…she reminds me of 'female isaac brock'…i've enjoyed re-reading her blog the same way i've enjoyed re-reading my favorite books, hope she never takes it down.

11:59PM: have been planning to leave apartment to buy alcohol since around 8PM when i made the bed and put on shoes, now i am wearing shoes in bed. considered going up to 6H, where the anonymous beer move-in gifts are maybe still in fridge, to see if the door was still unlocked.

saw that mira was tweeting at the same time as me and thought 'we could be hanging out right now. we're kind of hanging out.'

MAY 30, 2013

1:21AM: have been sitting in bed, typing captions to 'taipei' photo album. just posted to facebook.

2:02AM: worried people will think it's…somehow what i'm doing is negative…but i'm intending to just…do something funny/promotional/ supportive…or that they wouldn't think that but now me saying that will cause them to think that…worried about worrying, next level worrying. i wouldn't think anyone would think it was negative if i did this in like 2009/ before dating tao, i would be doing it for the same reasons then as now i think. though hard to say because a lot of the book is 'about' me and it's one of my favorite things i've read, so it's like, doubly impacting, which probably has something to do with me not doing this with other books. added links to tao's blog post about it and the book's page on amazon. why do people think about things differently if it's related to a romantic thing. i do it too, i don't know why. worried tao will think i'm doing it to solicit 'good job pat pat' or something, i don't care about that. think i'm just experiencing vestigial worry related to dynamic in relationship/not related to 'now.' felt good to be able to type funny captions the way i did in album.

2:10AM: ate 2mg xanax and birth control.

2:17AM: pretty sure i'm always going to be thinking something like 'how is it [whatever time it is].'

2:19AM: phone call from number that texted 'Heard your looking to buy some adderall, call back if interested' 2:56AM may 28. thought 'this is probably a cop.' left them a voicemail the next afternoon saying i was interested. saw matthew donahoo had texted a picture and 'Feel u re not wanting/being bored by seemingly everything' earlier tonight. texted 'Hell yeah' and a picture. feel like a robot right now, averting photo album anxiety by reporting…phone shit…

2:23AM: called number back. no answer. texted 'Bro…' not going to pay attention to this person anymore, they are either a cop or too difficult to communicate with.

2:26AM: texted the person 'I'm not interested'

2:33AM: have been listening to 'hotcha girls' on repeat since maybe 10PM

2:49AM: have been experimenting with inhaling e-cigarette through nose

3:12AM: feel xanax things more maybe due to eating only cherries today this morning. going to…actively avert interest…watch a netflix something

3:16AM: often think of the last bits of pee that drip out as 'tassles'

5:23AM: all i remember is eating another 1mg xanax, hummus tortilla, remaining bag of salt and vinegar chips and watching the beginning of 'manhattan' in bed.

11:17AM: woke. shirley was on my chest. an ASMR video was playing. listened and half-slept half-dreamed.

1:30PM: woke. looked at internet. people like the 'taipei' facebook album. drinking sugar-free red bull. feeling okay so far. okay-feeling day. presented with interesting things when waking. good.

1:46PM: felt something fall out of my vagina and thought 'please be blood.' checked shorts. it was blood. definitely one of the top ten happiest times i've seen blood come out of me. inserted tampon and there was blood dripping down my finger and when i washed it off some of it splattered in the sink. thought it looked cool. thought 'this looks too graphic maybe but fuck it i've been watching blood fall out of the part of me men want to stick their other part into since i was 12.' that sounds confusing. i got my period when i was 12, had sex when i was 18. when i was 12 i knew they want to insert their penis back and forth into this thing until stuff comes out of them, though. what's wrong with you guys.

2:31PM: DMV is open until 6PM today HAHAHAHAHAHHAHAAA. EVERYTHING'S COMING UP MEGAN. DO PEOPLE KNOW ABOUT 'EVERYTHING'S COMING UP MILLHOUSE?'

AND FURTHERMORE, 'EVERYTHING'S COMING UP ROSES,' WHICH THAT JOKE IS REFERENCING I THINK?

3:02PM: made chard/cucumber/coconut water juice, chia mixture for later. did dishes. nauseous from chlorophyll overload. sometimes this happens. surprised it happened with chard, 'a lesser green.' tried juicing mustard greens once and it made me vomit. okay. hot vegetable talk is over.

masha texted if i had gotten her package yet. i'm going to shower and get ready for DMV and check for package.

3:45PM: i was pooping and peeing at the same time when i wrote this sentence teehehehehehehee.

4:34PM: have been fucking around/pushing 'last minute' for DMV. mom is calling.

5:15PM: got off the phone with mom. when i asked how she was she said 'your mother is currently dealing with a fly, that is the one thing going on with me!' i said 'like a fly fly, a bug fly?' she said 'yes! it's been in my apartment for two days now, two days. and yesterday i said to it, i gave it the option—i went to the balcony and opened the door and i gave it the option: you can either fly out now, or i'll kill you. and it didn't fly out! so i've been after this…thing! it's just insane, it's flying into mirrors and pictures and just…bumping into everything. it woke me up this morning on my face, i must've had some really bad breath.' i said 'it woke you up, oh no.' she said 'i know! so i've been getting rid of just everything i think it could be eating, i found an opened sesame oil container—from the sauce i make for the dumplings, you know—and i threw away my toothbrush. i'm thinking it could be living off the things in my toothbrush or, oh it's so bad. i'm thinking it's thinking my apartment is an ikea eatery, everything in my apartment! your mother and the fly, it's the only thing i've got going [laughlaugh]!' she said something about finding crumbs behind the toaster. we talked more about other things and i emptied all the old cat litter into a bag and started washing it in the shower. mom said 'hold on a minute, i'm at the bank' and i heard an automated voice. mom said something about burger king. i took the empty cat box to the shower to wash it and said 'remember when we found the maggots? in the jeep?' she said 'oh no. oh no, what was that?' i said 'at…i think it was at brentwood drive, in the garage. the car smelled funny and we opened up the backseat and there were all the maggots and the mcdonald's fries, oh no.' the water from the faucet was kind of loud. i forget how we started talking about the next thing. mom said 'what is that thing, miss canada? it's not miss america, it's…' i said 'miss universe?' she said 'yeah, miss universe canada? well, i don't know, it was the new miss universe canada last night, and she won. but they found out today this other girl was actually the winner, and she was handling it very well, you know, philosophically, she was saying 'at least i got to know what it felt like for a day.'' i said 'well. at least she got to know what it felt like for a day, though.' mom said 'yeah, i guess so.'

mom talked about how she's decorating dad's new offices from an outlet store the sells old hotel furniture across from 'the worst trailer park in the world, with graffiti like in new york.' i said i watched part of 'manhattan' last night. she said 'i think that's why i cried on the verrazano bridge, the opening scene of that, and something about brooklyn too, and knowing you had all the memories and then all the things about woody allen, that's why i got emotional. i'm sorry i get a little silly when i'm emotional.' i said 'you don't need to apologize for that at all.' she said 'you could just fall asleep to that music, george gershwin every night.' i said 'i don't think i could fall asleep to that' and she went 'hohoho, no, that's right.'

earlier i had told her i was thinking about going to marie calloway's reading and she asked if i was going. i said 'you know? maybe. maybe i'll go. because why not. because the other night i found a blender, did i tell you about that?' she said 'no, when was that?' i said 'with nicholas the other night, there were all all these. well it was really sticky, all these appliances. i was going to take a frying pan too but it was too sticky [mom was laughing at 'sticky,' whenever i'd say 'sticky,' remember 'milking her for 'sticky' laughs' by further describing how it was 'greenish brownish'], but this blender! i mean it's a pretty basic blender, it's simple, like maybe from the 90's maybe, but i like that, so. the other night i scrubbed it and i let soap and water soak in the glass part overnight and then this morning—well, i think the thing is really that i just can't let it get too full. it works. i just can't let it get too full or it leaks. but it's a blender again, i have a blender again! it's cuisinart. so i guess all of this that i'm trying to say is that, i did that this morning and so i got off to a good start. it felt like a good start, like i made green juice also [mom went 'aw,' like 'honey i'm proud of you but i do not like green juice at all and i could easily go into a thing about how i think i should like green juice but i don't right now'], like, i could do things. but now i think, around when you called i'm getting to this place of 'it seems like i'm not going to do anything' again.' felt aware of talking for a long time. mom laughed and said 'i know the feeling.' i said 'well, so i guess i decided since i didn't do the laundry yesterday i at least have to do that today, since i think i'm not going to…there's no way i'll make it to the DMV but really i think i really just don't want to.' mom said 'there is really this thing meggie, that i believe, that if something doesn't feel right in the moment, there's a reason behind that feeling and you shouldn't do it.' i said 'yeah. yeah. i think i believe that too mostly. it's just i think…it's not that the things don't feel right, i'm just not interested enough in the the things.' she laughed and said 'well, yes, there's that too, there's always that too.' she said something about not wanting to take her car for an emissions inspection but she had to do it by june 7th. i was kneeling on the kitchen floor. i forget why. i said 'we just have to keep doing stuff. there keeps being stuff we have to do.' she said 'yes, yes.'

5:57PM: ate a caffeine pill. okay great. i don't know what to do.

6:08PM: i made a poll about what i should do tonight, encourage people to write in answers for 'Other.' i'll do whatever gets the most votes. voting period will end at 7PM.

6:28PM: going to shower now and prepare in case 'go to reading' wins.

7:02PM: here are the results of the poll:

- go to the reading (it starts at 7PM and it's 6:04PM now, i haven't showered and live 30+ mins away but am okay with showing up late, just information to consider) [RESULT: 17 VOTES]

- do laundry [RESULT: 8 VOTES]

- get drunk [RESULT: 8 VOTES]

- read/watch movie/look at internet/watch TV [RESULT: 3 VOTES]

- 'knuckle down' and write story/article for something i said i'd do [RESULT: 9 VOTES]

- Look up chords for "Butterfly" by Weezer and then play it on guitar post video [SOMEONE ELSE WROTE THIS, RESULT: 3 VOTES]

- 7pm is jeopardy [SOMEONE ELSE WROTE THIS, RESULT: 2 VOTES]

- live tweet good/bad sex [SOMEONE ELSE WROTE THIS, RESULT: 2 VOTES]

- Other [RESULT: 4 VOTES]

MAY 31, 2013

[DEPENDING ON WHAT PEOPLE VOTE ON THIS MIGHT BE LEFT BLANK]

JUNE 1, 2013

[DEPENDING ON WHAT PEOPLE VOTE ON THIS MIGHT BE LEFT BLANK]

JUNE 2, 2013

[DEPENDING ON WHAT PEOPLE VOTE ON THIS MIGHT BE
LEFT BLANK]

JUNE 3, 2013

8:43am: said 'listen: this doesn't work anymore. I don't eat solid foods. We're fucked.' in 'main character gives up' voice to attentive-looking cats. Have been up all night and want to sleep. Was not planning to write this. Caught some 'talking to cats on Sunday morning' hit action. Caught that shit to serve it up fresh to you like, eight hours from now, probably. I'm eating a xanax and going back to sleep. Stalling my update of the past three days.

8:52am: Alvie being 'insufferable' with loudly thumping off of high surfaces and scratching in litter box. Sleep not happening.

9:03am: cleaned Alvie poop after yelling 'Alvie.' sprayed 'auracacia lavender harvest calming aromatherapy mist' walking perimeter of room holding bottle with above-head/forward-thrusting arm. Cats looked confused and maybe hurt or afraid. Did bump of heroin.

9:07am: it smells like generic soap from someone else's shower. It's nice. Jumped at text message noise and watched 'Hey Meghan! I'm in a pinch...' appear. It is from Jaime, probably about the play. Imagined myself typing 'Wonder if I'm going to read it' and smirked.

9:24am: do the cats think MacBook is a cat also? It is silver and like them sort of.

9:29am: opened window. Feels better in here. Like, perfect temperature outside. Shirley found a place to sit on the floor, went 'MAAAAAA...?' and now seems to be 'ruminating.' Person who hasn't responded to my text probably thinks of me as having a 'novelty factor.' If they read this it means I have a little less 'novelty factor' to them than I thought, I am more 'a person' to them, but in this case I don't know if I want them to think I'm a person, seems a little scary in this case. Feels comforting to be Christmas decoration-like to someone sometimes. Like 'that looks nice, I'm in the holiday spirit now' but for the rest of the year I'm in a box in the basement.

9:39am: snorted remaining heroin I had left in baggie.

10:19am: pictured camera showing Zachary's gravestone: 'this man had impeccable taste' (his life as...that's all he wants people to know, that's the only thing he wants to hear...what he's aiming for...), zooming out to show the city, state, country, earth, solar system, galaxy, universe, billions of years of space.

10:51am: inserted 'broken english' dvd after concluding movie download would 'take forever.' felt interested in all three automatically playing previews and dreaded watching movie when main menu loop began to play. Pressed 'play.' snorted more heroin during opening scene—parker posey getting ready for a party alone in an expensive-seeming one-bedroom Brooklyn apartment (which, at the time I first saw the movie, some time in 2008, I identified as 'affordable,' 'modest,' 'like a place I could someday live')—and remembered finishing the second half of it with Tao, seeing it for the first time, on one of our MacBooks on my bed in my Baltimore apartment in 2011. I asked him what he thought about it and he paused and looked to the side and said 'her despair seemed believable.' abandoned movie to do 'thing I forgot I wanted to do before I re-watched movie.' have been re-reading 'Taipei.'

11:18AM: vomited. brushed teeth and started typing above update, which seems 'obviously influenced' by style of 'taipei.'

12:10PM: vomited again. have been alternating between making a 'HOW SHOULD I UPDATE THIS' poll, typing in this document, emails to jordan and tao. texted matthew donahoo pictures.

12:16PM: feel extremely nauseated and droopy, like can't believe i'm able to type at this speed. heart feels faster and slower at the same time. like, louder. eyes are crossing. effort to keep eyes un-crossed currently. skin is itchy. also feels smooth. unsure if white noise thing i'm hearing from outside is the air conditioners in the building next to me or the ocean.

1:02PM: here is the poll (and its results):

HOW SHOULD I TYPE ABOUT MAY 31–JUNE 2:

- largely unedited update of everything typed on my iphone; elaborate on details later [RESULT: 3 VOTES]

- update from the perspective of 'now (sunday afternoon): remembering what happened from thursday night until now (sunday afternoon)' [RESULT: 6 VOTES]

- largely unedited update of everything typed on my iphone; leave 'as is'/ no elaborations [RESULT: 5 VOTES]

- 'forget' the time period from thursday night (stopped updating) until 8:11AM today (resumed updating w/a frequency i want to continue) [RESULT: 3 VOTES]

- wait to update until i've elaborated on things so they look like i was updating chronologically the whole time [RESULT: 2 VOTES]

- Give detailed explanation of feelings and events that caused you not to update [SOMEONE ELSE WROTE THIS, RESULT: 1 VOTE]

- Other [RESULT: 1 VOTE]

12:24PM: starting to worry about overdosing, accidental overdose. got a sugar-free red bull from fridge via 'seems good to stay awake and wait this out, just stay awake as long as you can.' marathon staying awake. feels very hard. shit. started to typ.e 'if i start reading or watching the movie again i'll definitely fall as[i know i'll just fall asleep for a little bit]

12:31PM: heard ice cream truck playing the song zachary and i would sing at each other while making insane 'ren and stimpy'/'cartoon of a person going insane' faces. thought this ice cream truck song was only in philadelphia and i had 'escaped' it.

a lot of fast-moving mental picture things. seems foreign. they're all drawn in the same style, like 8-bit digital...sort of...like a .jpeg photo of...it's like when the edges of 8-bit things become softer in .jpegs

mental picture of black halloween cat, like, saw that when i closed my eyes

mental picture of...it was like it was painted on steel? aluminum? it was all in red: a man with red beard and...like it was drawn by the same person who drew the cat. the same style. it's a recognizable drawing style, people use it on napkins i feel...stationary...birthday parties? sesame street

mental picture of the same style of drawing but it was nutrition facts, a close-up/cropped picture of canned something

mental picture of a jeep (the SUV kind/not the 'off road' kind) in burger king drive thru line. ordering at the speaker part. other cars in line also. i think it's the burger king in eldersburg, across from the walmart.

i thought it was a cop but i don't know what it is: it's like a dog. kind of. it sounds like a video game cop/dog going 'bo bo bo bo bo bo.' it's definitely a dog for real, it's louder now, how i did i think that was a cop

mental picture of the window drops of rain on my window the day amahd gave me the $20 and i was in the car talking to mom

i can hear lifeguard whistles, people are at the beach

sometimes feel aroused imagining porno tao and i made in spain

1:04PM: i'm mainly seeing a series of vivid mental pictures that then causes 'the thing' to happen…'the thing' is a tryptophobia-like grid of tiny periods. tiny dots. they actually seem to be exactly the size of this: '.'

some are a little bigger and some are a little smaller. i try to look at them like, 'look one of them in the eye,' then i realize it's not a dot, it's a spinning thing. it's part of a very defined spinning checkerboard-like thing. similar to DMT. if i press on my eyes really hard normally i see this also, i remember pressing hard when i was little and seeing it. the spinning component when i was little was more of….well it was dark brown and light brown. it was like multiple sets of the same tiny hose/spiral. remember calling it 'the earthworms' in my head. now the version of it i'm seeing is like a warped dark neon purple/pink checkerboard…like that's underneath 'the earthworms.' the '.'/periods/grid turn into the checkerboard thing and 'the earthworms'

1:12PM: heard 'to get in-to this website' in neutral male voice and 'too drunk to get over here' in mom's voice. no longer worried about accidental overdose, seems like i'll be fine.

1:18PM: person i texted last night texted me back. text either 'bodes well' or 'bodes neutral/confirms 'novelty factor' suspicions.'

1:58PM: made photo of five things stacked ontop of each other for tao's 'tao day' at thought catalog and responded to emails. got glass of water. stood too fast or laid down too fast and feel like i might vomit again. alvie seems afraid of mattress pad, both cats curious about opened window.

2:05PM: eyes have been closed. seems strange that you can't see 'sparkly' things when you close your eyes. like it should be 'sparkly.' had 'premonition' that dad is going to die in 2007.

2:13PM: vomited. at the end it was just dry heaving. very…like, jesus. can't remember the word. it feels like 'spicy.' burning. acidic, that's the word. that's the fish. thought i had figured out how to 'hold off'/'dam' the flow of vomit to not go through my nose at all but got 'carried away' maybe and lost awareness and it came out my nose at the end. while vomiting felt motivated to write as much as i could about…like, filling in updates, doing 'self yelp' and 'tao day' article today. i can do the 'tao day' one easily.

4:05PM: talked intensely with mom on the phone for a little over two hours. saw lightning but no rain out the window a few times. ate and apple and heated two torillas on the stove and put olive oil, garlic, salt, vinegar on them while on the phone. conversation ended with me saying something like 'it'll be better if we just get off the phone, please trust me, i know we'll feel better if we just stop' and mom not really wanting to stop.

after we got off the phone i watched a youtube video of a man talking about 'the plasticity of the brain' and how it's possible to re-wire your neurons if you modify your behavior. started falling asleep. the man's face wasn't in the video. it was called 'ASMR motivational tips for anxiety/depression/derealization/depersonalization' or something. felt 'casually, not-interested-enough-to-disturb-falling-asleep process' afraid of the man. the way he was stressing he wasn't a medical professional in the beginning seemed scary. remember thinking things like 'it's possible he's included some kind of coding in the video that my brain understands but i don't and he's re-wiring my brain for his benefit somehow' and 'my window is open' and '[picture of something watching me from the perspective of outside my window, then a face like the 'mulholland drive' dumpster man showing up next to my bed].'

mom called again. short conversation, mostly like, consoling each other about previous conversation, like we were both saying 'it'll be okay.' ate 1mg xanax after we got off the phone, set alarms for 7:31AM and 7:47AM and 8:47AM, and fell asleep watching a youtube documentary about borderline personality disorder. will update with 'what i remember from thursday from the perspective of [used to be 'sunday afternoon'/will now just be 'whenever i finish thought catalog things']' (option that won votes) when i have time.

turned off alarms. ate noopept, caffeine pill, sugar-free red bull. thought i only had until 2PM to finish the tweet thing. finished most of one of the tweet things and was going to turn it in looking shitty. re-read email and saw deadline was june 4 at 2PM, not today. re-read email from last night deadline for chris killen transcription had been pushed up to june 4 at 6PM. i wasn't thinking things like 'time' yesterday.

2:01PM: threw away cans and paper recycleable things. talked twice with mom on phone. masha's package was outside door. sometimes a package will be sitting outside my door. haven't thrown out old mattress yet. seems 'annoyingly symbolic.'

ceiling fan stopped working yesterday but the windows have been open and cats are acting insane, i think because old cat pee on the curtains was activated by opened-window moisture. moisture-activated insanity curtains. need to do laundry today. wash curtains. "cats are out of wet food but they seem happy with dry,' she typed to make herself feel better.'

lit candle. swept/mopped floor and cleaned cat box. i did those things multiple times yesterday too. feel like the woman in 'woman in the dunes,' via cat litter granules being sort of like sand and...just...never-ending. i'm always sweeping things, it seems. have felt very preoccupied with having a clean floor and no 'crumbies' in bed since living here. not interested in why but am pretty sure there are annoyingly symbolic reasons for all of this too.

masha sent phenylpiracetam and aniracetam 'extra goodies' with vyvanse/adderall shipment. texted her something about her packaging skills and thank you and i was thinking about buying phenylpiraetam or another 'nootropic' thing last night. thought something like 'nice men and women in their 20's helping each other by mailing cutely wrapped and thoughtfully assembled packages of drugs and drawings and miscellaneous things' while opening her package and remembering my package to her and matthew's recent package. ate one of the...i'm not sure which one i ate. ate 50mg vyvanse.

downloaded 'camtasia' to keep track of the time i transcribe. am getting paid to do this. will wait on typing may 31-june 2 update until i finish.

3:33PM: transcribed about three minutes/one page of chris killen's 37-minute monologue about knut hamsun. ate 20mg adderall.

3:34PM: paused 'camtasia' recording to make celery/cucumber/coconut water juice and call mom back. only one and a half hours and three minutes of recording had gone by. i was doing the transcription the whole time except i looked at chrome to see how to spell 'edvard munch' once. 'camtasia' takes a video of your screen...seems funny to have a video recording of me doing the transcription...talked to mom in 'chris voice.' chris talks like british woody allen kind of. kind of. at one point he says something really funny and i was laughing transcribing. felt my brain being in 'mining for where punctuation would occur in a voice'-mode talking to mom. on the phone, washed vegetables. mom is going to a furniture store. seems like we are both currently 'worried about getting things done and potentially disappointing people/ourselves.' apologized to her about letting conversation get intense last night and she apologized too. she said 'what does the sky look like there?' i said 'it's like...blue. i mean. gray, white. it's white. white-gray. it's really bad, what about you?' she said 'oh it's just the same, just the same. isn't it so awful?'

4:49PM: going to focus less on getting down chris' 'microscopic if there could be microscopes for ears/voices' vocal tics and more on typing.

HUMORLESS ASS DAY.

LAUNDRY TODAY.

NEEDS TO HAPPEN.

THEN I CAN CALL MARK AND GET THE FAN FIXED AND THROW AWAY THE MATTRESS AND CALL BACK THE NAVY AND APPLY FOR JOBS…WHAT THE HELL…THINGS GOT OUT OF CONTROL SOMEHOW…LOSING FOCUS…ONE MONTH LEFT…NEED TO START…GIOSDIDSOFHDSOIFHD

SEEMS FUNNY ACTUALLY, ALL OF THIS, NOT HUMORLESS

A LOT OF THE TIME I THINK 'LOOK AT WHAT YOU'RE TYP-ING, THIS IS WHAT FEELS BEST TO COME OUT OF YOU' AND KIND OF LAUGH AND WANT TO APOLOGIZE TO YOU

WHOEVER YOU ARE

ALSO ONE LAST THING: THE WAY I OBSESS ABOUT SMALL CLEANLINESS-RELATED THINGS IN MY APARTMENT BUT HAVE BEEN NEGLECTING 'FIXING LARGE THINGS' AND NOT EATING PROPERLY REMINDS ME OF THE—DOES ANYONE REMEMBER IN 'THE END OF THE STORY' WHERE IT'S LIKE A LONG THING ABOUT…THAT, KIND OF? HOW SHE'S SUC-CUMBING TO DOING THINGS LIKE THAT…IT'S BEFORE SHE SHOWS UP ON HIS DECK/PORCH, I THINK…ONLY I'M NOT AS…LIKE I DON'T HAVE REASONS FOR FEELING DEPRESSED OR LIKE I'M 'SURVIVING' OR ANYONE'S DECK/PORCH I WANT TO SHOW UP ON, THAT'S JUST HOW I'M FEELING

ALSO DID THE GUY IN THAT HAVE RED HAIR

THINK I HAVE ALWAYS PICTURED HIM WITH RED HAIR AND HAVE FELT AVERSION

ALSO PAUL AUSTER'S AND LYDIA DAVIS' RELATIONSHIP SEEMS EQUALLY LIKE 'HUH' AND 'YES I UNDERSTAND, MAKES PER-FECT SENSE' TO ME

ALSO WHEN I THINK 'PAUL AUSTER' I THINK 'MOTHERLESS BROOKLYN…NO' AND '[PICTURE OF A CGI BLACK DOG WITH WET EYES]' AND '[PICTURE OF A SCRIPT]' AND 'TAPDANCING DETECTIVE' AND 'THAT GUY FROM 'AMERICAN BEAUTY' WHO PLAYS THE REAL ESTATE KING'

WHEN I THINK 'LYDIA DAVIS' I THINK 'SALTINE CRACKERS' AND '[PICTURE I ALWAYS SEE OF HER FACE ON GOOGLE IMAGES, LOOKING OLDER THAN HOW I THINK SHE IS]' AND '[PICTURE OF HER SITTING AT HER DESK IN THE ROOM FROM 'SECRET ROOM' OR SOMETHING MOVIE WITH JOHNNY DEPP BUT HER HEAD IS CUT OFF AT THE NECK AND THERE ARE A LOT OF PAPERS AND AN OPENED THING OF SALTINE CRACKERS NEAR HER TYPEWRITER WHICH SHE FEELS WEIRD ABOUT USING BUT ALSO LIKE SHE 'HAS TO' USE OR LIKE 'NOT ENOUGH MOTIVATION TO START USING SOMETHING ELSE YET BUT AWARE OF THE POSSIBILITY']

9:01PM: transcribed chris killen thing marathon style. a little under 4700 words. great job shitty shoo.

10:44PM: it's 10:44PM now. just so you. know. i'm addressing that the beginning of the ending of this break ends at '10:44PM:' so that probably means right now it is 10:44PM, i think you know that, addressing it now though. officially. going to resume transcribing chris' thing 11:05PM.

everything i remember doing from 9:02-10:44PM:

- went to pickles & pies to get more energy drinks/groceries/cat food. talked to myself in 'chris voice' while dressing. emailed tao to see if i was taking too long on transcription/if there were money issues.

- recorded video of me talking like chris but seems unseemly.

- drank remaining liquid in sugar-free red bull can.

- saw matthew donahoo text from 7:28PM, picture captioned with 'My roommate is making grunting sounds while I look at him from the couch'

- started typing response to mira's text from earlier thinking 'this will not garner a response but i want to respond more.'

- approached colin and 'fancy food friend' on the way to pickles & pies. seemed like we might not talk but then i said 'hi.' he asked where i was going. i said 'oh just pickles & pies.' he said 'word.' we had already passed each other, i was standing and had turned around to face colin and friend as they continued walking to apartment building. colin said i missed something on saturday, the irish music festival thing. he said 'my texts.' i was holding my phone. i said 'i dropped my phone' or something. embarrassed. he said 'feel free to stop by on your way back, we're just hanging out.' there was a moment. i said 'have a good night.'

seemed…obvious…that something has changed. not responding to texts has changed something. he understands something now.

- resumed typing mira text response.

- veered 'course of walk' trajectory into street to avoid potentially acknowledging person approaching on sidewalk. the person was wiry, puffily haired, wearing earphones and white t-shirt with greenish graphic. looked cartoonishly uninterested in everything going on, including themselves walking.

- passed man sitting in a wheelchair outside library. he was looking at me like 'i saw the whole thing, i saw you walk into the street to avoid the person who wasn't even paying attention.'

- texted mira about that.

- walked into pickles & pies.

- eventually used a basket to carry: four-pack of sugar-free red bull, two monster zeroes, sabra classic hummus, three-pack canned tuna, celery, parsley, lettuce head, two lemons.

- asked cashier for 'logic' e-cigarette refills. he asked if i smoke more now and i said yes, but it feels better. he said 'no like, no [gestures to chest and makes a face].' i said 'no, none of that.' at one point i said 'yeah i don't know, because like in twenty years maybe they'll figure out these things are worse for you.' he seemed to say a long thing about the mafia. i said 'what?' he said 'mafia, the mafia.' he said something i didn't understand fully about how much money is 'floating around' and 'you can't do it alone' and 'think about it,' then something like 'presidents? kings? you don't even know widdem.' i said 'you never know.' it was a good one. good conversation. can't remember. a man was walking around our 'area' the whole time. at one point he said 'fours? sevens? 'scuse me, y'all don't do the lotto anymore, do you?'

- matthew texted 'Looks beautiful.'

- tao emailed what i sent of transcription looks okay and to keep going, no money/time issues. started re-reading transcription and laughed through nose while walking inside. i like reading things like this a lot, like, word-for-word extremely detailed transcriptions of things that don't exclude 'uh' or 'um' things and treat punctuation like the same thing as words, kind of.

- pressed 'up' on elevator and debated saying 'hi' to colin and his friend, distractedly smoking e-cigarette. thought 'say 'hi' after you put away

471

groceries. what are you going to say. is he the one who brought up the package? thank him, that was nice, what if it wasn't him…'

- another light has gone out. the red light. the outlet above it seems to work.

- put away groceries and fed cats. cats officially enjoy fancy feast more than tuna.

- changed from jeans to pajama shorts but did not take off 'get out of the apartment' shirt, thinking 'maybe i will say hi to colin and friend. it's not too late. just say 'hi,' be a neighbor, a normal person.' looked at face/pupils in mirror. pupils big. pictured myself saying 'hi guys, i'm working on this thing all day and night, transcribing this thing' and eventually saying the word 'gig' and pee running down legs.

- ate an amount of vyvanse, think it's 25mg. it's the one masha drew something on, i think, to indicate it contained less. texted masha a response thinking 'this will not garner a response but i want to respond to people more.'

- willis texted if i'd be home/at rockaway tomorrow and…i thought today was tuesday and tao's reading was tomorrow and mira's/scott's/my baltimore reading was the next day. relieved. i said i might be sleeping during the day probably.

11:15PM: drinking monster drink. don't like typing 'monster' ever. ever. EVER. now, especially. shirley on the bed. both windows open. they don't let you do laundry in my building after 10PM. it's okay. it's okay. when i started typing this i felt insane…abberant…very not-normal lifestyle, very alone, very 'what am i pretending i know how to do, will it help to call mom?' lit candles. have been texting with matthew a little and feeling better. back muscles tense. whole back of body. stomach muscles also, like i've been exercising. can tell elbows/arms are tensed when i type. headache. chest tightness stuff. okay. chewing trident gum. it is a spearmint flavored. i'm leaving it typed like that, that's what it sounded like in my head. NO BUTTS ABOUT IT. no butts. resuming transcribing at 12:05AM. maybe if i liveblog long enough i'll eventually become consistent about saying 'AM/PM' all of the time or none of the time and figure out what i want 'number consistency: below 10 = spelled? not? when not?' and things like that. so. stay tuned for that. that's right, 'stay.' instructing you to 'stay' something, which means…assuming you are already something…'tuned,' in this case…instructing you to continue doing what you're doing, if what you're doing is what i think you're doing. okay. just so we're clear.

JUNE 4, 2013

12:26AM: have been continuing to luxuriate/lay/allow muscles to stretch in preparation for 'marathon transcribing to finish line.' peed. finished monster drink. perhaps will reward myself with headache medicine. backlog of 41 questions on ask.fm to answer. also emails. texts. overwhelming debts. i'm the one who decides the feeling is 'overwhelming' but knowing that doesn't change anything or comfort me. talked with mom about this last night, she said something about...she was nervous to go to dad's office and was physically shaking thinking about it. i said i felt that sometimes from just...laying ...passively laying and thinking about how many people are on the internet and not on the internet, like, 'waiting.' i said clichéd things about how the internet makes agoraphobia happen too. mom didn't act interested...or...felt surprised at her not immediately agreeing and not wanting to talk more about 'today's fast-paced culture and new parameters for social anxiety' or things like that. felt comforting, her not wanting to do that.

JUNE 5, 2013

did not update

JUNE 6, 2013

did not update

JUNE 7, 2013

11:12am: almost wrote 2011 just now. Sitting in petsmart parking lot. Liveblog has made me aware of how long it takes me to leave a parked or driving car. Will need to park far away today for the weekend, due to summer parking restrictions. Getting used to things like this.

11:43am: still in petsmart parking lot. Have been re-reading parts involving me/'Erin' in 'Taipei.' Imagined Tao writing the 'universe hugging itself' part, alone. Years later a journalist person who 'would be best for him, would actually be the person with whom a relationship could be sustained' would be reading the 'universe hugging itself' part. This would be far enough in the future so that he would be able to really do the thing where 'the dot of himself' shrinks past zero and ends up in a suburban neighborhood or city too big to know how big it is and starts living again, but by then he wouldn't want a relationship anymore. Not being clear. Shit. How do I say this. I pictured this person in the future reading the book and Tao would be 'technically dead by 2080' or something, but the component of him that lives forever past the singularity would be alive in a different way—not the way the person who he could be in a relationship with would. She would be alive during her version of 'tao 1983-2080' life. Tao would be alive during "source code'-like afterlife where…he might be in another dimension or something, concurrently existing with the relationship person but as a new kind of life form where he shrinks and ends up places, so it would be impossible to know the person reading the same way he would've in his '1983-2080 life,' but he wouldn't want that then anyway, maybe. It would be some kind of irony. Relatable to 'sirens of titan' somehow, the thing I'm trying to say. Hard to convey this. I don't know enough about the singularity to…like, would people still exist? At all? Would all people just be like 'tao post-1983-2080,' like there wouldn't even be a person reading experiencing life as 'someone born who is going to die,' we'd all just be integrated with computers? Jesus. Sounding stupid. Can't do it. Abandoning ship.

12:01pm: went inside petsmart. Tao wrote 'live blog' in my copy of 'taipei,' I didn't see until now. I'm in the car now. Didn't see many 'grilled' or 'sliced' options. Alvie and Shirley like those best. Walked to an area between aisles maybe three times. Every time I'd leave an aisle I'd see a cat looking at me. It was the only cat there. It was sitting in a metal cage inside an enclosed plastic-looking space behind which was some kind of endless-looking maze of metal things leading to a back room maybe. There were 6-8 empty cages in the 'cage complex,' which was under a large photo-printed decal (said something like 'PetSmart Adoption Charities,' 'Brooklyn [animal something, 'hospital' or 'rescue'], and a series of numbers strangely out of order ['4, 5, 1, 2, 8...'] just remembered something about how in lucid dreaming you're supposed to pay attention to if numbers make sense) that was big enough to give a pre-ceiling area the appearance of a billboard. The cat looked so small and so frozen in place every time. He was looking at me every time I'd walk out. Also not moving. Stomach and chest felt tight. Unsure if it would be nicer for me to look at him or walk over to him or leave him alone. Thought 'if you were my cat I wouldn't even be able to figure out what kind of food you like.'

12:11pm: leaving parking lot. Three pieces trident spearmint gum in mouth. Pictured myself driving around to find a dunkin donuts (not really that though, just like, vague image of 'the store containing all the carbs I could ever want') where I would buy no less than four but no more than ten menu items and take them out to my car, where loud rebellious teen anthem music would be playing, to 'party.' the windows of my car would be down...there were these kids who would hang out in grocery store parking lots when I was in high school. What I'd be doing with the dunkin donuts would be 'partying' harder than those kids could ever party. Like. More alone, drifting, hopeless than them. Significantly more. One time Zachary and I had a six-pack of high life and we were in some kind of strip mall parking lot and I drove slow past a group of high school kids 'partying'/ milling around and he handed one of them a high life out the passenger-side window. They didn't seem appreciative. I think this was Zachary and me. I forget. Remember laughing with whoever it was and saying things about 'how did they not want the beer.'

12:20pm: I'm in a dunkin donuts parking lot. Going to look at the menu online so I can know what I want before face-to-face confrontation with cashier person. Lovingly preparing myself for the transaction that's about to happen. Taking everything into account to ensure there will be no surprises, no unnecessary talking, the smoothest and quickest transaction possible.

12:42pm. Ordered bacon egg and cheese on multigrain bagel, coffee with cream and sugar. It was free donut day. Cashier said 'you pick a free donut' with his arm near the strawberry-frosted ones. I said 'oh wow, great, that's great, wow...um...' and felt pressured to pick a flavor. I said 'strawberry frosted.' he put it in the bag. He said 'you come in here before, you live...?' i said 'no this is my first time here. I live. In. Rockaway park, I think.' he said 'but this your first time in store, you never come in here?' i said 'I don't think so, I think this is my first time.' he looked familiar to me too. He said 'she fix your sandwich over there.' Walked to trash can. Saw man who had let me go in front of him so he could figure out what flavors of coffee the people ordering wanted. Man said 'now I know' to the cashier. Felt negative things about the man, waiting for my sandwich, like, 'how do you think you have so many choices…how do you not figure out what you want before you order…how do your friends make you pick up coffee for them without knowing what they want.' Looked at 'cherries jubilee' ice cream vat with one scoop removed. This is also a Baskin Robbins. There is some kind of 'special two-scoop day' promotion. Sad about donut day and two-scoop promotion. Seems like it's before my period, to be feeling things like this to the degree I am. Ate bagel in my car. Put ketchup on it. Thought about calling mom but I don't know what I'd say.

1:07pm: leaving parking lot. Turned head and experienced sudden barely graspable memory of dream, like turning my head released 'dream memory chemicals' maybe. Waited for man bouncing balloon on street to pass. In traffic now.

1:34pm: pulled into parking spot on my street. Thought 'what is today, it's winter' expected to see 'Jan 7' on iPhone when I checked date. Thought 'how do you say the thing about [omitted], without directly involving [omitted], but still involving [omitted]…but you don't want [omitted]… there is no way to write about it unless you do 'thought:' and don't say all you thought, like use vague language and say you're omitting things.'

1:35–11:[something]PM: put away cat food and fed cats. peed and felt UTI pain and sat on toilet to drink water and 'wait it out.' read more of 'taipei.' can only read small parts at a time without having memories and thinking stuff like 'what it's like now…what it seems to be like for tao and what it's like for me…no i'm being dramatic, this isn't that bad, i'm okay, good things are happening to him i think.' looked at pictures of courtney love and thought about her life to the extent that i could envision this period of time as a memory in the future.

courtney love should start doing something really unexpected, like getting really into live civil war re-enactments.

remember going to the bathroom a lot, bringing my bag with me every time, thinking 'drugs are in the bag, they are close, i can always just do one of the drugs,' then placing bag next to bed when i'd return from bathroom. didn't do drugs. sat in room. read internet and more of 'taipei.' mom called at one point. i said 'i don't feel talkative right now.' ordered pizza around 9PM. drank a lot of water. gave pizza delivery man $12 tip. he looked like 'lost present-day richard brautigan, unemployed, maybe just stumbled upon a pizza.' didn't want the pizza once i had it.

JUNE 8, 2013

9:30AM: woke. peed and refilled water glass. it was sunny and reminded me of a day in winter 2009. ate remaining pizza slice. looked at internet.

12:47PM: woke. drank leftover dunkin donuts coffee and ate maybe 5mg adderall. pooped. moved bed to look for missing e-cigarette in crack between bed and wall, where phone fell. didn't see. swept floor. read texts from last night. found e-cigarette. have been avoiding updating due to spending large portion of my time doing a thing i want to omit from live-blog, which i want to write about, but if people know about it there could be negative consequences for me or another person. have thought a lot about this. imagined consequences. the thing i'm omitting is making me happier. deliberately avoiding talking about why i want to omit this. new thing for liveblog, to exclude something to the degree i plan on excluding it. that's good, i think, in that it's new.

1:26PM: ate half a concerta, unsure mg. going to update this with 'everything i remember from may 31-june 2 from the perspective of [no longer 'sunday june 3 afternoon'] saturday june 8 afternoon (option that won the most votes on poll).' then i'm going to update 'everything i remember from june 4 (not written about)-now.'

goddamnit. wish 'disjointed iphone update' had gotten the most votes on 'how should i update this' poll. complaining stupidly. this is what i wanted, i wanted to do what people voted on so i wouldn't have to decide, and now i want to stick to what i'd decided, i shouldn't complain.

4:04PM: have been answering ask.fm questions. here goes:

EVERYTHING I REMEMBER FROM WHEN I STOPPED UPDATING MAY 30, 2013 – JUNE 2, 2013, FROM THE PERSPECTIVE OF SATURDAY AFTERNOON JUNE 8, 2013:

put on pink and white striped dress and dried hair. ate 3mg xanax on the way to marie calloway reading at st. mark's books. texted with mira, who would also be late. listened to less than jake in car. wrote mean response to a mean ask.fm question. parked on 6th ave and cooper square. kept walking the wrong way on the street to the reading. think i walked up and down 3rd ave maybe six times. tweeted things i was seeing. air felt hot/heavy and nice. withdrew $40 from 7-11 ATM to buy marie's book and drinks at the after-reading party. heard a woman on the street saying 'weed lolipops' or something, like she was selling them. saw a person giving her money. the woman was standing in front of a van that said 'high life' or 'high times.' walked to van. small couple ahead of me 'in line' were buying two lollipops. bought the last two for $10. the woman said 'i thought you all were together.' looked at the couple and didn't say anything. the man who bought the weed lollipops before the couple stopped them to talk, a little ahead of me.

st. mark's looked empty. asked employee if they had marie's book and he used a ladder to get it from a shelf. paid. mira texted that everyone at the reading was now at a bar closeby and gian was paying for everyone's drinks. walked to bar. seemed fancy, a fancy-people bar. gave bouncer my ID. walked upstairs to a bar-area where maybe 20 people i recognized from the internet or other events were standing. talked to stephanie georgopulos about her new job at gawker. remember asking about how the office was set up, like if there were cubicles or if it was open space. felt a little stupid. was also distracted by wanting a drink and seeing mira and sam cooke and ralph waving to me, aware of my waving back as maybe interruptive. saw brandon scott gorrell in a white t-shirt approach 'behind stephanie and me area.' thought 'it's okay to not say hi to brandon right now, he understands.' stood and talked with mira and sam. then ralph came back, i met ralph, i follow him on twitter and have heard stories about him from mira and sam. a container of limes/lemons/olives/onions/cherries was near where i stood. think i said 'i want to eat them' or 'i want to drink.' people were saying things about how ralph ate the drink condiments…he either ate them the other night at a bar, tonight, or he eats them at home. ordered a vodka club soda. mira and sam disappeared for a minute. seemed clear to me that people were drunk/had been drinking and had high energy and i needed to 'catch up,' but i was also worried about my car. seems like i completely forgot being on 3mg xanax, or the xanax had worn off. stephen dierks and spencer were nearby. saw 'tall head of willis, bobbling up and down.'

at some point mira, sam, stephen, spencer, willis and i stood in a circle. i said we should make it into a game where one person turns to face outside the circle, so one person is excluded from the conversation at all times, but no one tells them what they missed when they turn around. when they turned around another person had to immediately take their place as 'excluded person' and face outside the circle. this was fun. this deteriorated. spencer and willis each said things to me about coming to the beach the next day. i think willis said 'rockaway taco.' i said they should come. saw marie and rachel white walking out of 'VIP area.' saw tao talking to maybe two short girls near entrance of 'VIP area.' at some point mira and sam and stephen and me decided to walk inside 'VIP area.' it was loud. i think i hugged gian before this.

the 'VIP area' was mostly empty. remember it as 'red.' remember sitting in a group of maybe six people near the back, on a booth facing the room, behind a table, seeing the bar area where we were formerly standing. remember talking about the weed lollipops. mira said she thought tao had bought weed lollipops from the person on the street also. tao and a man in a suit approached table. the man in the suit seemed gregariously preoccupied with other things in the room. something about him reminded me of tom cruise. think i greeted tao by standing and hitting him or something, think we each hit each other playfully. tao said he was leaving because he wanted to do work. i said 'i bought weed lollipops' and took them out, i think, expecting to hear about how he bought them too. he said 'i bought weed from a person on the internet.' asked what was in his pill box and he said 'just...adderall.' the man in the suit seemed to pay more attention. tao introduced him but i didn't hear. the suit man asked if he could have a weed lollipop and i said 'if you have five dollars,' then felt like this wasn't appropriate, due to tao's face before he left. i said 'you can just have one, don't pay me' and gave him one.

other things in VIP room: stood away from group/table for a while. forget what incited this. i asked marie to sign my book and complimented her dress. rachel had an e-cigarette. i was smoking my e-cigarette inside. rachel said she did that so i thought it was okay. talked with suit man who i discerned was tao's editor. they had just come from another party. he asked me things about being a character in 'taipei.' felt unable to answer his questions. teeming with enthusiasm and gregarious preoccupation with other things. marie said 'can you hold this for rachel' and handed me rachel's e-cigarette. mira and sam and spencer and ralph passed and said they were going to 'java dog' and i said i'd meet them there soon. heard 'japanese hot dog' several times. gave rachel her cigarette and i think talked to her a little.

recognized my editor from vice. have not met in-person. we had 'the talk.' he asked why i had stopped sending things. i said i've been depressed and out of ideas and have been doing the liveblog but i want to start the column again. i said 'am i the flakiest contributor?' he said there were definitely worse but i was 'up there.' we did a shot of jameson in the main bar room. he said he had been there for a while but left for a little bit. something else was said. shit. something funny. i forget. felt good/fortuitous to see him. i said i wanted to go meet the hotdog people and he went to talk to gian.

left bar and searched 'java dog' on my phone. mira texted or called to say it was close to the bar, on 3rd ave i think. it was called 'japa dog' or something actually, though. when i arrived they had already eaten. remember feeling like 'i'm still not drunk enough' and that everyone had high energy and i was an 'out of context object' in their conversation (sounds negative, i didn't feel negative, just like, 'yeah'). put a red plastic hot dog container on mira's head and said…i forget. this was my attempt at 'high energy.' walked back to the bar in a group. spencer said goodbye. it was taking me a long time to find ID in purse to give to security guard. think i told people to go upstairs without me.

talked to gian and tao's editor by the bar. ordered another vodka club soda. remember seeing ryan o'connell at some point and hugging him and saying 'do you want to slow dance' and he said 'you know i do' or something and we danced a little, but we were both moving to other places. it was a seamless 'stop and dance transition to other places we were walking.' it was nice. thought 'i want to talk to ryan more but he'll probably leave.' remember having trouble discerning what editor was saying and some funny conversation that ended with me saying 'i bet ten bucks you can't remember exactly what you said.' thanked gian for paying for the open bar and talked a little about new orleans.

at some point it became clear that a drug dealer was coming. i said i wanted to buy heroin. have had difficulty swiping my card at ATMs. gian said the guy was coming soon and if i wanted things i should go to an ATM fast. walked downstairs, outside bar. saw marie and willis and rachel standing by the door. someone said 'are you leaving?' and i said 'no i'll be right back.' jogged to a deli. card didn't work. jogged to another deli, withdrew money from my savings account and i think it must've overdrafted or something, i don't know how i was able to withdraw $100 twice. jogged to bar. texted gian if they guy had coke, because i was able to take out more than i thought i had. took a long time to find my ID for security doorman again. downstairs bar still seemed very empty. gave gian my money and asked if he saw my text and he hadn't. i gave him all my money and said if the dealer had other things i'd like whatever he had, with the other $100.

a little after this the upstairs bar closed. tried to buy a drink from upstairs bar person. she said 'you can buy it downstairs.' tried to tip her but she refused. people moved downstairs.

sat at a table/booth between ryan o'connell and rachel white and talked about writing. further down the table were mira, sam, ralph, stephen, gian, one or two of gian's friends maybe.

sometimes i'd see mira/sam/ralph gesture to me in peripheral vision. saw stephen with his head in his hands at some point, maybe sleeping. distributed 1mg xanax to everyone at the table by…think i just said 'pass these down.' gian left and returned and gave me a baggie and $90. i said something like 'keep the ten bucks, you did open bar.' ryan asked what drugs i bought...i think...i said 'heroin'...remembered him saying disapproving things to mira about crack use and i think he said something disapproving or just 'i don't do that' about heroin. gian asked if i wanted to do a line. think i tried to get him to come to the bathroom with me to do it together but then it seemed like a bad idea. went to the bathroom alone and snorted large amount using pinkie-finger-length hot pink straw i keep in my purse. handed straw and baggie to gian.

i don't remember things for a while. have an image of myself...like, watching myself curl up in a ball on a booth. i was watching myself from a distance of maybe 20', like where the stairs were. then i was in the bathroom with mira. mira was reviving me with coke. remember feeling like denzel in 'flight,' like, actually very much 'coming to'/becoming aware of things the more coke john goodman administered to him. sam came into the bathroom. think i said things about how great they were and how much i liked them and was thanking them for reviving me. kissed mira on the cheek and lips, i think. it became may 31 at some point, during this night. omitting may 31 and june 1 until sometime in the afternoon when i picked up my car from parking spot on 6th ave. there was a group text message involving spencer, mira, stephen, willis, tao about going to the beach. tao said he didn't want to go and willis and mira flaked. spencer texted that he and his brother still wanted to go regardless of other people coming and asked for my address. didn't see this until it was too late. spencer sent another text saying they got restless and went to coney island. texted tao something like 'sorry to involve you in group message for this long' and he said he was joking by continuing to say 'sitting this one out.'

walked to my car. there was a ticket. it was sunny and warm. sat in car and read email from jordan asking for thoughts about him moving to NYC. someone asked if i was going to move my car so i did. snorted small amount of heroin driving on houston st. and felt happy. drove home. texted spencer that i wanted to shower and make juice/feed cats but i'd text when i was leaving for coney island.

walked to apartment, talking to mom on phone. in the apartment...jesus. i forget a lot. i made green juice. milled around for a long time. hung up clothes. the overhead light was on. around 6:30PM i texted stephen that people went to coney island instead and said i was leaving soon. texted spencer to see if he was still there and he said they had left already/figured i had flaked due to no word from me and me not showing up yet. he said there was a roof party in brooklyn. i was texting with mira about all of this also, she was at spencer's. they were going to the party together in a few minutes. i texted mira 'i told stephen to go to coney island' and knew he was probably there already. texted stephen sorry and that i messed up and would give him a ride to the other party. put on green dress and beige high heels and dried sweat from hairline. brought jar of chia mixture to eat in car, sugar-free red bull for stephen and for me, and macbook for [unsure].

walking to my car, made eye contact with older man. the man said 'excuse me, miss?' he said i shouldn't be walking alone. he had an irish accent, seemed drunk, moved slowly. he said 'one more thing' and 'why you doin' here' a few times. i said i lived here. i asked what he was doing here and he said 'surviving.'

driving to coney island, mira texted that she was leaving to pick up sam, would return with him, and the three of us would hang out after the party. picked up stephen outside of nathan's famous. he had gone to a biker bar. he was chill about the whole thing, also a little drunk. we talked a little about the after-reading party. i said i saw him sitting with his face in his hands, thinking maybe he'd say 'i felt alone then'/ talk about how he felt bad, but he said didn't remember that and was probably sleeping. he said something about how he doesn't like to leave right away, and how people are flaky and it's hard to get people together to do something. i agreed and said i was part of the flaking problem.

parked outside apartment building. stephen had to pee badly. the party was at michael seidlinger's house. everyone had left to get food. walked with stephen to find the party and pee place. saw spencer, his brother tyler, michael, and erik on the street. everyone was wearing white t-shirts. they were waiting for dumplings. i said i wanted a blt and was going to walk somewhere to get that, knowing...i think i didn't want one, but i didn't want dumplings and i didn't want to stand around. stephen was directed to a pee place. met michael who i knew from the internet already. met erik. remember shaking his hand and thinking 'i am being presented with an erik. eric?' shortly after this i think i said i was going to a deli. remember asking them if they planned the white t-shirt thing several times. asked it again as i was leaving. spencer said 'we're the plain white t's,' i said 'hey there delilah,' then he knew other words i didn't expect to hear as i walked away.

texted mira to see where she was. walked into maybe four delis, all of which had closed-seeming sandwich counters. typed about surroundings in iphone notes. a lot of people were on the street. got lost. typed 'what am i doing, why did i come here, what should i do' in iphone notes, standing in a deli listening to a woman in a green dress tell the deli man she wanted toilet paper and newport 100's and other things she wanted, in a funny way. exited deli. passed a man sitting on a stoop who said 'girl, you'd better be careful.' looked at him and said 'you too.' spencer called and i told him i was lost and couldn't find an open sandwich counter. he said things suggesting i was walking big time in the wrong way, and i must've missed the deli he was at…think it was on prospect heights something. prospect something. he ordered a blt for me while on the phone. felt good/reassured about entire thing. felt comically overdressed. green dress and high heels. walked maybe four blocks to blt deli. girls were petting tyler's dog. felt 'face definitely looks like it can't conceal lying about wanting a sandwich, all the delis, considering leaving, texting mira, feeling overdressed, deciding everything was okay and i want to be here.' paid for sandwich and bought a 40oz of ballantine.

entered another deli with michael and stephen to buy more beer. stood by a freezer. michael talked about working for melville house. stephen said something about wanting woodchuck but thinking people don't like hard cider. i said i liked it. opened freezer door and stepped inside and showed them my sweat-stained armpits. michael bought hoegarden, i think. gave someone $2.

sat on the roof in a chair formation and talked and drank beers. i don't remember everything. i liked this. went from 'shit…' to 'this is nice.' drank the 40oz and maybe four beers. everyone was joking and talking a lot. could see the skyline and it wasn't hot on the roof. at some point i said 'someone should name their dog 'june fifth, two-thousand-three.'' i drove stephen and erik home. erik lived in manhattan, kind of. we left mira a voicemail involving yelling something about fried chicken. sang along to things by myself on the car ride home and made a video. i hit a concrete fixture and the passenger-side mirror is fucked up now. got home around 4AM and went to sleep around 5AM. i remember how it looked in my apartment and what it felt like but it's hard to type.

woke a little before 9AM. felt bad. alvie was making noises. ceiling fan stopped working. felt stressed about [omitted] and how i would write about it. cut a mango and fed cats and…seems like i just continued typing into my phone until i decided i wanted to fall asleep watching 'broken english.' snorted amount of heroin i thought was small and didn't feel anything. read some of 'taipei.' waited for movie to download even though i have the DVD. snorted more heroin.

vomited. tao emailed asking me if i wanted to write '15 tweets by published poets that negatively reference hummus' and the chris killen transcription for june 4 (when he would guest-edit thought catalog). said i wanted to do that. vomited maybe six times and had mild hallucinations and felt worried about going to sleep and embarrassed for doing…just…not liking what i was doing, not looking forward to posting anything i had written that morning, aware that i hadn't been updating, worried about [omitted].

i think then i made the poll asking people how they wanted me to update.

6:41PM: peed and got water. ate 20mg adderall. answered ask.fm questions. it's hot in the apartment, fan still doesn't work. feel terrible, thinking about how i'm still in bed…doing this…yesterday…it was like this yesterday… all of the time that's gone by in june. i don't know what else i'd be doing. i'd be at mira's/spencer's reading. charging e-cigarette battery. i want to be in maryland. writing about all of this feels sad. i don't know why. shouldn't 'not knowing why you feel something' cancel out the feeling…like…you do a geometry proof and it results with 'there is no way to solve this' so you move on?

7:34PM: mira texted 'bb girl are you coming to this shit?' at 6:41PM.

7:47PM: texting with mira.

7:50PM: making short updates like this so people who scanned through long ass retroactive update will maybe see a new long ass retroactive update is about to begin but this is the 'present time' before that.

7:51PM: phone vibrated and i jumped.

7:52PM: considering eating last 20mg adderall for this shitass update, then using it to work on…goddamnit…article…need to restart column… things…shit…would take too long to describe this thing i'm feeing.

7:53PM: PEOPLE READING THIS: IT'S ABOUT TO BE ANOTHER LONG ASS RETROACTIVE UPDATE GET READY. MAYBE NOT NOW, MAYBE NOT TOMORROW, BUT SOMEDAY: YES. I WILL FINISH WHAT I STARTED.

7:54PM: my goal of this week is to get a job. if it doesn't seem like i'm going to get a job i have to do the navy thing. then school. goddamnit. there is nothing i want, really. i think. getting a job seems best. nicest. most considerate of me right now…consdering my state of…what i seem to be in…living here for a month after a year-long unstable living situation, preceding more unstable living situations…

7:55PM: it's getting darker and colder and smells like rain.

7:57PM: maybe i should shower and buy energy drinks and maybe alcohol for later. then call mom. jesus. e-cigarette cartridge refills.

7:58PM: texted mira i'd like to hang out later.

8:02PM: still don't know what i want to do regarding this update/what i'll do tonight/getting things from store/anything. shit. something i haven't written about: it smells like boat of heavy machinery exhaust outside. that's why i closed the window last night. to stifle the wafting.

8:13PM: cleaned cat box. stomach achy. wish juicer wasn't broken.

8:47PM: called mom and left voicemail. got in shower. heard phone noises.

9:06PM: i don't experience thoughts or feelings fully, i experience something else fully. it's pre-thought, pre-feeling. the text you're reading is maybe five steps down the line from what it started as. maybe. tried to discern how i was feeling in the shower but it felt hard to do things other than look at the wall and shower curtain and sometimes scanned down torso/legs. mom left a voicemail saying she wouldn't be available until tomorrow, but tomorrow would also be busy.

tomorrow i need to get my oil changed.

9:19PM: alvie shat. made plans to do something i'm omitting.

10:58pm: driving to IFC to do [omitted]. Drinking soaked chia mixture. Car is 3000 miles overdue for an oil change. A light has been coming on and a '-[miles] past oil life' flashes. I refilled the oil recently though. Ate noopept and antiracetam before leaving.

10:59-11:59PM: [omitted]

JUNE 9, 2013

PARTS I FEEL COMFORTABLE NOT OMITTING:

- walked around greenwich village after movie

- bought 12-pack corona beer at pickles & pies (around 2AM)

- heated pizza in unconventional frying pan way at my apartment

- went to sleep around 6AM

- woke around 5PM

- dressed in turquoise button-down shirt, navy blue skirt, high heels

- split order of french toast, bacon egg and cheese on english muffin, hash browns at 'last stop diner' on beach 116th st

- looked at A/S train next to the diner

- donned bathing suit, black and white striped dress, yellow cardigan

- laid on a towel on the beach in front of my apartment building from around 5:30-8PM napping and reading 'tracer' by frederick barthelme

- showered

- dressed in blue collared wrap dress, beige high heels

- watched spurs vs. heat in my apartment

- went to lenny's clam bar in howard beach

- watched second half of spurs vs. heat at lenny's clam bar

- [omitted] said 'i've noticed you do a lot of drugs when you're by yourself but not with me.' i said something like 'i think it's because i like to feel occupied...with something else. and don't take this the wrong way, but i think you're 'occupying' me.'

- bought toilet paper

- watched 'VHS' on netflix

- ate five valerian root pills

- scared to fall asleep due to images from 'VHS' playing on backs of eyelids

JUNE 10, 2013

10:00AM: woke. drove to Q train, then back to my apartment. almost out of gas, i have one bar. 'engine oil life' light is flashing '-89 miles.'

11:13AM: ate 1mg xanax to induce nap, heated pizza in toaster oven, think i made two hummus tortillas.

4:00PM: woke. drank corona with lime. read more of 'tracer.'

4:43PM: mom called but i didn't hear.

6:50PM: called mom back and talked. she is reading 'taipei.' she read this aloud to me and started crying at 'small and irreducible thing.' at some point she said 'are you still listening' and i said 'yes' and i remember tears on my face and trying to sound okay. forget when i started crying...i didn't expect to be crying but...something hard to describe...something:

> 'They sat facing hundreds of the same type of four-story building, the expanse of which, in most directions, darkened dramatically, creating an illusion that one could see the Earth's curvature, until blurring, in the distance, into a texture. Sometimes, looking at a city, especially a gray or brown one, at night, Paul would intuitively view it as a small and irreducible thing that arrived one summer and rapidly grew, showing patterns of color on its expanding surface, then was discolored by autumn and removed of its exterior and deadened by winter, in preparation for regrowth, in spring, but was unable, in its form, to enter the natural cycle, so continued growing, in a manner as if faceless and skinless, through summer, autumn, etc., less in belligerence or tyranny, or with some abstruse knowledge of its own rightness, than as a stranded thing, sightless and uninstructed with an objectless sort of yearning. Seeing the streets and bridges and sidewalks, while living inside a building, locked in a room, one could forget it was all a single, alien, seeking entity.'

after mom read this i think she said 'i'm sorry' and something like 'it sounds so much like you' and something about imagining me and tao as she was reading this and, 'i didn't know how alone you felt, i see it very clearly now, i had no idea.' we were both crying in a good way. read several parts aloud to each other. she said 'i just love this so much, this is so beautiful,' and tearfully read this aloud:

'...that the universe in its entirety was a message, to itself, to not feel bad—an ever-elaborating, languageless rhetoric against feeling bad—and he was troubled by this, suspecting that his thoughts and intentions, at some point, in April or May or years ago, in college or as a child, had been wrong, but he continued in that wrongness, and was now distanced from some correct beginning to a degree that the universe (and himself, as part of the universe) was articulately against him.'

at some point she said in a frantic/panicked/almost angry-sounding voice something like 'i had no idea how much drugs you were doing, i mean i think i knew sort of, i didn't want to pay attention to it—and i want to say things like 'don't do that, you're ruining your brain,' as your mother, but also then i read this and i thought it's fine, you're just...it's fine, the way he says it, i agree with this and i feel this and i don't think your relationship was about drugs or whatever, i agree with this,' then read this:

'...he felt, to convey (mostly by slowly saying variations of 'no' and 'I can't think right now') that there was no such thing as a 'drug problem' or even 'drugs'—unless anything anyone ever did or thought or felt was considered both a drug and a problem—in that each thought or feeling or object, seen as touched or absorbed or remembered, at whatever coordinate of space-time, would have a unique effect, which each person, at each moment of their life, could view as a problem, or not.'

she cried at 'space-time.' i was also crying. i don't know why. it's hard to read this sometimes. i feel lucky or something, to be sort of involved in this book, to be written about in this way, that tao found words to describe these things i remember feeling and thinking too, but haven't made into words. mom kept saying 'i had no idea.' she cried about the part where i'm in the fourth grade, putting glitter on my eyes and wearing the purple t-shirt every day so aliens would see and come take me away. she said 'i felt that too, as a kid. i didn't know that's why you did it.' i said 'he got it wrong, it was seventh grade, and only on fridays. do you remember herman? my herman necklace [ball and chain necklace with a glow in the dark alien charm on it]?' she said 'oh yeah. oh, herman.'

i said something about how tao was able to articulate things i didn't know how to, then i read this part, crying a little while reading:

'The unlighted space all around him—and outside the SUV, the trees, sky—seemed more visible, by being blacker, or a higher resolution of blackness, almost silvery with detail, than normal, instead of what he'd sometimes and increasingly sensed, the past two months, mostly in his room, since one night when, supine on his yoga mat, his eyes, while open, had felt closed, or farther back in his head, and his room had seemed 'literally darker,' he'd thought, as if the bulb attached to his non-working ceiling fan had been secretly replaced, or like he was deeper inside the cave of himself than he'd been before and he didn't know why.'

mom said things about 'jennika' and how she didn't know that was how our friendship ostensibly ended. she said she pictured tao as a little boy and remembered me in preschool hiding under tables and not talking to anyone and not knowing how to 'deal with' people, and how i'd cry before school a lot in middle school, not wanting to go in, and how she felt like 'why am i doing this to my child, why does she have to go to school where it's so horrible,' and that tao 'dealt with' what i was 'dealing with' by becoming quiet. she kept saying 'i had no idea.'

in a gmail draft, typed these things she said as she said them: 'it's about two essentially playful souls who connected but the real world got in the way,' 'when i was young i was this reactionary person, waiting for whatever meteor would come my way,' 'it's not about drugs, it's not about breaking the rules, it's about two people coming together in a moment that was beautiful and impossible to sustain.'

i said i wanted to come back to baltimore, was thinking about taking a bus tonight. mom said wednesday would be better.

7:44PM: drinking fourth corona. am supposed to figure out what's wrong with my credit card. if i just don't spend money for some amount of time it will be better. i have money in my paypal. going to find some way to transfer money from my paypal to my savings account, then to my checking, so i can pay for oil change and gas tomorrow.

7:47PM: zachary emailed that he was going to philadelphia, something about bringing my bike back from travis's apartment, then 'nevermind.'

7:58PM: mom called and i told her money plan. need job. more income. i haven't billed vice for my last four articles. getting paid for doing the transcription. will have ~$800 from those things. need to get a job. shit.

8:25PM: drinking another beer. is this bad. i don't know. can't tell. not interested. I AM GOING TO DO A YOGA DVD WHEEE!!!!! i live in rockaway beach/rockaway park someone come knock on my door already right now do it do it i'm here it's 129 beach 118th st queens ny.

10:44PM: smells like cigarettes in my room. listening to odd nosdam song…feels like an emotional map…like looking at a map of my emotions on earth from space.

10:56PM: person from facebook might sell me adderall or vyvanse. my idea of what my paypal looks like…jesus…

MY FUNDS, AS I KNOW THEM TO BE:

- paypal: <$200

- savings account: thought it'd be 0 by now but was able to withdraw $200 from it the other night to buy heroin. when i looked at it last night it said ~$500, seems like bank must've made an error allowing me to…something…also i have a CD that's maturing in july that's ~$1600, i thought that was my savings account that i was withdrawing/spending money from, i didn't know the ~$1600 still existed, think i'll be allowed to use it mid-july

- checking: it says i have $13.67 but it also says -$91, i can't use my card, i have no cash

MONEY OWED TO ME:

- vice: $400

- transcription: $325

- accident settlement: ~$3900

not as dire as i thought. dad agreed to give me money for groceries and things. he puts it into my checking account. guilty about this. seems shitty of me. i'm 27 years old. i'm sick.

THINGS RECENTLY WITHDRAWN WHICH SEEM TO BE ACCOUNTED FOR VIA MY DAD IS PAYING FOR ME TO EXIST FOR TWO MONTHS IN NYC WITHOUT GETTING A JOB:

- $750 – june rent

- $1500 – move-in fee + may rent

THINGS I OWE TO PEOPLE:

- $200 monthly truck school loan payment i'm two months behind on. they called and left a voicemail.

fucked

no i'm fine

11:43PM: pooped. unsure if this is a suicide. i took birth control. if i don't wake then i authorize everything i've written to be…everything i've done goes to tao lin, everything is his to decide what to do about. it's 11:44PM. my cats have enough food for a few days, please don't worry. i'm setting my alarm for 1AM so maybe i'll wake then and take this down. just not sure if i'll wake. it's okay if i don't, no harm or…it's not an 'ill will' thing, everyone has been nice to me, just not sure if i've got enough whatever to keep me going until tomorrow.

JUNE 11, 2013

12:45AM: made hummus/romaine/parsley/garlic/lemon juice/olive oil/salt/chipotle pepper tortilla filling.

12:55AM: the update before this seems extreme. i'm leaving it via...it's... what i wrote and did was stupid, there's no reason for me to cover up something i felt at the time. it was just a passing thing. i'm fine. ate another 1mg xanax. no more beer. i feel okay, like tomorrow i'll be able to do things at an okay pace. be a normal person. these are just thoughts.

4:57AM: woke, deleted 'extreme' update, drank gllass of water.

3:40PM: woke around 1PM i think, re-pasted 'extreme' update. hard to move. it was sunny and now it's cloudy. masha emailed. answered ask.fm questions. pooped twice. painted second coat of paint on nails. dad put $181 in checking account. the oil change place will be closed, maybe. think my license might be suspended already. okay. ate chia mixture. drank 8.4oz sugar-free red bull. tao paid me for the transcription. looked at zachary's twitter. it's funny. want to eat pineapple.

5:10PM: mom called. attorney's office called also, i'm picking up paper-work from them on thursday. money from paypal will take three-to-five business days to transfer to savings. left long rambling voicemail for dad. swept and did dishes. ate noopept and snorted remaining heroin. cut open the straw i've been using and licked it. licked container and baggie also. i feel good. made celery/romaine/parsley/lemon juice blender drink.

today i want to exercise and get a plastic bag for the mattress from the hardware store and take the mattress the fuck out to the dumpster. it has been in here too long. they won't pick it up if it's not in a bag. rachel white invited me to a thingy tonight. might go to that. okay. i feel better than i've felt since waking. unsure if it's due to heroin. i don't care why. if something makes you want to be more productive and improves your mood that's good, i think. 'defending drugs' boyle.

7:59PM: napped, remember also feeling conscious that i was a body on the bed. answered ask.fm questions. felt calm and good when i woke, like everything would be easy.

8:07pm: walked to hardware store for mattress bag. It was closed. Walked to sleepy's mattress something store. An employee was helping a man on a bike. The employee said 'why he-llo! How are you tonight?' I said 'I'm very

494

well, how are you?' he said 'outstanding. How may I help you?' asked him about mattresses. He said 'what size you have?' I said 'full?' he said 'full. I don't know about full. Let's see.' I said 'or queen? Queen, maybe?' and followed him to the back to an area of mattresses stacked on a wall. He said 'now these for a customer, they already bought, see? Sold.' I said 'oh.' he said 'they only send me twins, see? And it's wrapped like this, I can't, you know, I have to take it off!' he pulled at a mattress bag and laughed. I said 'oh no!' he went into a little room. I said 'I could just take two twins, and tape them together?' he said 'see but I can't take it off!' I said 'oh, well that's okay, thank you anyway.' he said 'I tell you what. You know kings plaza?' i said 'yeah, on Flatbush?' he gestured with his arms like a wingspan. He said 'yes, it's this big. And there two sleepy's, one on this side? And one on the other. You go there and you say 'I'm a sleepy's customer, dey sent me here for full-sized bag. And dey give to you for free!' I said 'oh great, thank you.' he said 'just ten minute drive? Up dere.' I said 'what train stop is it, do you know?' he paused and looked outside and said 'train? No, well it's just the q thirty-five bus! Q thirty-five, you get it right dere. Okay?' I said 'great, yes. Thank you' and left smiling.

8:15pm: stood by a bus area. Typed directions in iPhone notes. Bus sign said 'q53.' thought he maybe got it wrong. Asked teenage couple where the 35 was. The girl pointed to sleepy's and said 'over there.' walked to there. A woman in a green shirt with a cane was standing by the q35 bus sign. Went into deli next to the bus stop. The man said 'hello!' and smiled really big. Selected a thing of pineapple, sugar free red bull, water. Another man rung me up. The first man said 'you from rockaway? No.' I said 'I am, I just moved here, one hundred eighteenth street.' he said something about my tattoos while I looked for my credit card in my bag. I said 'and I left it at home, I left my card. I'll be right back.' he said 'okay take your time.' walked back home. Fed cats.

8:31pm: approaching deli with credit card. Four people are standing with two dogs, giving the dogs attention. A man said 'twenny-five dogs! That was my mission for my birthday: to pet twenny-five dogs. And I did it! That's what I did for my birthday.' bought the things I had selected. The deli looked empty. The man was talking in another language to someone I couldn't see. When I left he said 'you come back soon, right?' I smiled and said 'okay I will.'

8:38pm: bus approached. People disembarked. Walked onto bus and the driver said 'nine o'clock. That's the next bus.' a short older man made eye contact with me and said 'that's late!' I made 'commiserating face.' the bus driver walked out and said 'hi' to a man standing next to me, also leaning against a wall. The man said 'what's up man.'

8:45pm: waiting for the bus. The leaning man is singing. Seems like sleepy's will be closed. It's starting to rain.

8:48pm: they close at 9pm. Walking to waldbaum's to get green smoothie things. Deleted 'debating going to Manhattan to buy drugs,' jesus the second I typed that I got a text from drug dealer I'd buy from. 10% off. Shit. Going to buy wine from liquor store to use for something for dinner. Don't want to spend more money on drugs for now. Feel like I can do it. The only thing I need to do is to not buy drugs. Then I won't have them.

9:00pm: I want to make a nice ass dinner. Get a recipe from mom. The man in the liquor store asked to see my ID and I said 'that's kind of you.' he was acting suspicious of me the whole time. A man came in and asked for captain Morgan. They were playing 'dirty deeds done dirt cheap.' Zachary and I used to sing that in funny voices.

9:06pm: Walked to the opthomologist's office and torn-down papa John's to take a picture of the Manhattan skyline. Pretty. I don't think you can see the skyline in the picture. Feel really good.

9:34pm: sat on curb outside waldbaum's, talking to mom on phone. She told me to watch Amy Schumer on comedy central. She said 'she's turning into a feminist, surprisingly. I don't know if you'd like her personality, but some of the things she says are just really, really funny. She says women should exercise their vaginas so…they can use them, as weapons [laugh-laugh].' She apologized for crying last night and I said 'don't apologize, that was nice, I was crying too, I felt good talking to you about it.' walked by the plants, outside waldbaum's. Mom said 'oh honey you should do it, just buy a plant.' I said 'maybe tomorrow. I don't want the cats to eat it.' Asked her for a seafood recipe. I'm going to make this, typing before I forget:

Scallops

Butter

Garlic

Shallots

Mushrooms

Tomatoes

White wine

Lemon

Capers

Sauté the scallops in butter and garlic then set them aside. Using the same pan sauté the mushrooms, shallots, tomatoes, capers in more butter and lemon. Then you make it really hot and add the white wine and when it cooks down you put the scallops back in.

Hell yeah. Mom said she figured out the recipe from a restaurant whose t-shirt I have, it says 'chez Ferdinand.' Restaurant has since changed their name to Tersiguel's, I don't think I ever went to it when it was called 'chez Ferdinand.'

10:34pm: walking home from waldbaum's. Very windy. Followed a group of four college-aged girls in basketball shorts and team sports t-shirts and flip flops around the store. One of them said 'yeah but we can take the shuttle, we'll take the S and no one will see the liquor and we can take shots' and the rest of them laughed. They were leaving a check-out lane. Wanted to be hanging out with them.

11:07PM: called mom to confirm some things about the recipe. She said to call her when it was done, if I felt like it.

11:53pm: dad called. I chopped garlic, shallots, tomato, mushrooms while we talked. He talked about how he likes working with mom on the new offices, they're like 'partners.' he said 'it just makes my heart sing.' he said he was happy to see mom outside of work because usually they don't talk. He kept saying 'I'm so happy to have a partner.' mom is 'office manager,' he gave her that title. Dad said 'it's just so good to hear your voice, to talk a little bit with you.' I said it was good to hear his voice too. Made plans for dinner on Thursday. He seems very excited about the new offices. Felt complex things…it was easy to talk to him, it's not usually easy. I told him I was feeling better overall. Told him things about doing the transcription for Tao and the transcriptions I'll do for Zachery. Felt good to be talking with him comfortably/non-awkwardly. Hung up and made food. Texted Matthew donahoo a few pictures.

JUNE 12, 2013

12:45AM: finished eating. tasted so good. called mom at 12:45 to tell her how it turned out. drank two glasses of white wine with club soda. told her i wanted to go to yoga in the morning, then do car things, then i'd be in maryland. 'chopped' has been playing on TV since i got home. also i took out the trash. great.

1:43AM: typed most of this and imported pictures onto computer. texted [omitted] picture of food. watching 'tattoo nightmares' on TV. i feel okay. okay.

2:52AM: felt really nauseated. vomited. embarrassed to write that for some reason. want to say 'i didn't make myself vomit.' maybe there was as scallop issue. i think i also just ate too much, it was really good.

4:11AM: woke to an infomercial. ate some hagen daaz green tea ice cream. stomach felt better. put on spurs vs. heat.

7:23AM: woke to basketball stuff on TV.

11:30AM: woke. basketball stuff was still on. have been laying in bed petting cats and reading internet. detailed dream i can almost remember.

12:26PM: drinking sugar-free red bull. haven't mentioned this but i think i broke my right middle finger a few days ago. a door slammed on it accidentally a few days ago. it's okay. also haven't mentioned that the other night i spilled glitter everywhere and now my bed is sparkly. looks better this way.

1:41PM: answered ask.fm questions. got rid of the backlog of questions. okay. just deleted a long thing of me shittalking questions. i'm happy to receive questions still. some of the recent questions i liked. it's probably obvious, the kinds of questions i don't like. grea.t baearieakhjaekrhekjfhdksjhbfdskjhfbdskjfhbdskj. going to initiate 'preparing to leave apartment phase one: shower' now.

3:42PM: phase four (take out trash/feed cats/pack bag/make bed/look at american apparel 'sale' bathing suits and start an order you don't intend to finish) completed. preparing for departure of apartment. official departure sequence activating in 5, 4, 3, 2…

4:06pm: filled gas. Asked attendant inside of they do oil changes. He said 'nuh. Uh. But' and gestured to the back and shook his head no. I said 'are they open?' he said 'no. They close' and sighed heftily. I said 'oh okay, thank you' and started to leave. I said 'do you know who's open?' he gestured down the road and said 'euh. Mobil?' I said 'oh Mobil, thank you.' I liked him.

4:10pm: pulled into Mobil. Saw two sets of legs hanging out the front seat of a white conversion van. One of the sets of legs looked like they were attached to a female ass. 'bang a gong' by t-Rex was playing. Got out of the car and said 'hi, scuse me.' a set of man-legs attached to a man-body slid out the door. The woman's legs remained where they were. The woman turned around. I recognized her, she's kindra, she took pictures of my car for a photo inspection so I could get insurance. She said 'how'm I help you?' I said 'oh hi! Do you guys do oil changes?' she said 'yeah, you come back tomorrow?' I said 'oh no, I need it today I think, but…' she said 'you come back tomorrow, right now I tryna finish up dis one.' I said 'that's okay, thank you though.' she was smiling really big the whole time, leaning out of the van. When I left the man scooted back into the front seat. They were looking at the floor.

4:22pm: I'm in a waiting area at the gulf station across from the first gas station. Being helped by an attractive man named Chris. He is servicing my car. I think 'servicing' is really funny. I'm being serviced by Chris. It will be about 20 minutes. I smell a little like the scallop stuff from last night, I'm bringing leftovers for mom to try. A drake ringtone just went off. A man's voice answered the phone. He said 'ey ma.' he is talking in Spanish to a woman's Spanish-speaking phone voice.

4:25pm: man with a shaved head wandered into waiting area. Just felt excited about 'getting to do this,' like liveblog is my version of a living in Sims-like video game. Holding my phone like I'd hold my DS. Where the hell is my DS. It was a DS lite. It was pink. What happened…

4:27pm: insane email from dentist. this isn't the first time I've received an email like this from this dentist.

4:36pm: I have finished being serviced. Transaction complete. Going to start saying 'transaction complete' after sex. Maybe 'service me'…maybe… no I don't like it too 'Sarah Silverman.' Pulling in to Duane reade parking lot.

4:50pm: bought this pink silicone sea urchin toy for mom. Got 'snack happy' in Duane reade. Treating my snack happy ass to some stuff that's barely…I don't see how you can gain weight by eating 'white cheddar 'pirate's booty' puffs' and red licorice. It's barely there. The cashier smiled when I said 'this too' about the pink sea urchin. There was a problem with my card. I said 'I could go to the ATM...' she said 'sign here' and I did. She said 'your card is damaged.' she had gold lipstick and a Jamaican accent. Felt like she was my fairy godmother. I said 'oh yeah, it's been acting weird, I'll get it fixed tomorrow.' fairy godmother daycare person letting me have all the nothing snacks and the pink thing, lovingly tolerating my childish ways.

4:58pm: thought 'it's summertime baby and I'm your snack daddy' in Austin powers' voice.

5:02pm: so I'm going to poop this out eventually? That's how this is going to work? It's going to give me cancer? That's how stuff is done? These days? Nowadays? Hm.

5:05pm: these things are like what I imagine you'd need to eat as 'fuel supplements' before time traveling. Like how in 'the abyss' they breathed in this pink fluid so they could breathe underwater. Mmhmm. So these things are like that. Hypothetically. See? You feel me?

8:09pm: pulling off on an exit where there was a chic-fil-a sign. Have to pee bad, also very hungry. Sang along to nico in car, I made a video. I can impersonate nico kind of. Pretty embarrassing video. Uploaded to You-Tube. Responded to email from person from rolling stone who's profiling Tao and wants to ask me some things.

8:34pm: woman in handicapped spot next to me is talking to a man on my other side. She yelled 'shh baby. You know what that means?' now she is following a man in a truck, honked horn at him six times in a row.

8:58pm: listening to the new pornographers. Got caught up in a missing Zachary thing. He liked this band but the missing thing happened before I was listening to music. So. You could say I'm listening to this because of missing him. That is one thing you could say. Emailed rolling stone person. Can picture Zachary going 'they want to talk to an idiot like you? Huh.' I miss him a lot right now.

9:26pm: gave mom pink sea urchin. Dropped it on the way in, it makes neon rainbows. Mom liked it. She put it in her dress and said 'or it could just be, you know, like this, if you ever wanna va-va-voom.' I said 'yeah, for the club, for that extra boost you need sometimes. One boob only night.' An old SNL was on TV. I said 'oh, samurai...' mom said 'I know.' I said 'I have to talk to rolling stone now, hahaha.' mom said 'I kn-oo-ow! Want me to turn the TV down?' I said 'no it's just fine. I am going to shut my door though.' she said 'okay honey.' Messaged the rolling stone person on

Skype. Air is fizzing out of my sparkling water bottle. Ate noopept. Put a new cartridge in e-cigarette.

9:31pm: rolling stone person said he'd call on Skype in five minutes.

11:00PM: the rolling stone person was female. haha me. ambiguous name. worried i said 'too much' about tao, also don't think there's 'too much' i could say about anything.

11:59PM: watching steve martin host SNL. dad came in at some point and i left.

JUNE 13, 2013

12-2:30AM: unprecedentedly long text message conversation with [omitted]. maybe longest text message exchange of ever. it was like constant, like a gchat. okay. good. i'm thinking 'okay. good.' or 'okay. great.' as kind of 'brain hiccups' lately. the periods are part of it, when i think it.

3:51AM: tired. emailed rolling stone person links to all the mdmafilms event coverage/trailers/movies with corresponding 'page #'s where i think this happens in 'taipei.'" i said 'this is probably excessive' in beginning of email. made toast.

12:01PM: woke.

2:09PM: talked with mom, she finished 'taipei.' ate four small pieces toast. drinking coffee. having a hard time waking. need to go to lawyer's office.

do you people ever shake your head or sit up too fast or rub your eyelids too hard and you see black swarming glittery dots? they're really pretty. they move 'softly.' like soft…they're like drills. little spinning drills. anyone? *sparkly* it is key that you understand the sparkliness. like when cartoons 'see stars?' anyone?

mom said 'you are really slender, you lost a lot of weight.' she got a call from someone renting one of my dad's offices and i went to my room. we talked a little more about the book but i felt this fatigue thing…toast-driven fatigue…

i want to drive to mountains in frederick, md

i used to drive to frederick when i didn't feel so good

i feel okay today

i want to pick up papers from the attorney for the accident settlement

2:32PM: i'm listening to system of a down. the one where he's like 'why have you forsaken me.' so funny.

overheard mom say 'oh you're in aruba? in curacao? oh that's wonderful' on the phone.

4:08PM: mom offered me half her bagel. talked about the pros and cons of going outside. she left a little while ago to go to bed bath & beyond to get 'a toilet thing' for dad's office. forgot i'm having dinner with dad tonight.

feeling strange. answered ask.fm questions. have been reading about aliens on the internet. drank 12oz sugar-free red bull and maybe three cups coffee but feel only up to 'barely normal' levels of processing/functioning. looks like it's going to rain, there is thunder.

5:01pm: in car now. Guess I'm driving to Frederick. Attorney's office called, I called them back, coming in tomorrow. Ate 10mg adderall to improve mood. Receiving concerta shipment this week. Comforted by this, like this is my 'cushion.' Now looks like too much traffic going to Frederick. Now too much traffic in the new direction I'm going. I'll go to Towson.

5:24pm: I'm going to a goodwill I like in Westminster. Keep thinking about this ask.fm question I was asked, about how exciting and scary as hell it would be to have my consciousness reformed into a computer living forever

Eternal consciousness

I believe in that anyway kind of

Things I don't think people would think I believe in:

God

Existence of souls

Hm. Guess that's it. Sounds stereotypical or whatever but I attribute belief in both of these things to experiences with dmt and transcendental meditation. Also just doesn't make sense for those things not to exist, in some way. Person in jeep behind me just skidded to avoid collision. I'm in front of a jeep too.

I think of god as like 'my little buddy'

Like when I'm alone in my head there's also this other awareness

Existential awareness…has something to do with how I suddenly started existing…since I was a kid, have felt this. Like it's not just me in here

Could also be schizophrenic

I mean I know it's just me/my voice/ego/internal monologue in here

The thing I'm talking about is more of a feeling

Like I wouldn't be feeling it if I wasn't alive

Hard to describe

Aware I might be making this up as a 'coping with mortality' defense mechanism

So there's that doubt thing

Kierkegaard...the leap of faith thing...

Felt impacted by that essay in 2010 philosophy class

Crazy how much better I feel on just a little bit of adderall

The difference is astounding

Adderall: the difference is astounding

The difference: simply astounding

Make a difference: the adderall difference (a different difference!)

The adderall difference, by Stephen Elliott

God is just farming me out to...it's like, being paid by a pharmaceutical company. I'm an adderall ad paid for by god

Prove to me that's not true

I'm walking in to goodwill now

Also: what a difference wearing undies that don't fall down makes. Especially when wearing a skirt over them. What a difference!

6:11pm: I've seen like 10-15 'Alfred dunner' brand women's tops here. Someone is clearing out their Alfred dunner. Fantasized about replacing my entire wardrobe with Alfred dunner. Dunnering it up. Alfred: it's what's for dunner. I want to meet the person who wears exclusively Alfred dunner. Watch TV with them in their la-z-boy. Nascar. It would be a male, somehow. I don't know. Alfred dunner makes androgynous almost exclusively size 12 clothes, from what I can discern from this goodwill.

7:28pm: have been doing fast-paced fact-checking emails with rolling stone person. Exciting. Meeting dad for dinner

9:15pm. Going back to mom's to milk brain for June 4-June 6 elaborations.

8:15PM: mom made hot dogs and baked beans. they smell really good. she is watching monty python. showed her my goodwill bounty and tried to answer questions about the quality of furniture at goodwills to the best of my ability. ate last 10mg adderall and a little bit of noopept.

EVERYTHING I REMEMBER FROM JUNE 4, 2013 – JUNE 6, 2013 (CONT.):

i stayed awake all night working on the chris killen transcription june 4. ate adderall from masha without thinking about rationing, like, allowing myself to not ration, to finish transcription. tao gave me extensions on the deadlines. sent him the hummus thing around 7:45PM and the chris thing around 10:15PM. my phone was on silent and spencer had called maybe five times. forgot about alex seedman + spencer + willis excursion to beach. told willis i might be sleeping due to working on thought catalog things all night but then time kept going.

i think this is the night my juicer stopped working. talked with mom for maybe two hours and got off the phone around midnight. people at dad's office don't like how she decorates. there is one person renting an office who like, gave her an unnecessarily hard time about chairs. seems shitty. my dad makes the office really nice, he like, buys coffee and snacks for renters/ colleagues. my mom is decorating for free like it's a full-time job…and they're just chairs…i don't know. so. she vented to me about that, about this one person i know and like, who i could also picture throwing a tantrum about chairs.

june 5 i texted with mira about if we were going to the launch party, and that we'd figure out things about driving to baltimore for our reading the next day at the party. she said she's doing an internship at penguin books and works part-time. slept a little. i did laundry. there were three loads and i didn't have enough quarters. it was sunny. went to the non-pickles & pies deli to get change for $7 and the guy gave me $5. a woman by the counter said 'you never give me quarters.' the deli guy was the guy who told me i smelled nice the night i got thai food and talked to masha on the phone and it was windy and there was a concrete-fixer man in the doorway. he's always there. he's chill. encountered him day before yesterday also, he said he was falling asleep. easy/effortless communications. he gave me $5 of quarters. walked to chinese food place and got remaining $2. looked at menu for chinese place on the walk back to apartment. it was around 4:30PM. knew i should leave by 6PM to get to powerhouse arena by 7PM.

talked to mark while loading quarters in the machines. he was mopping the floor and advised me to use two dryers. he said 'does it smell like beer in here to you?' i said 'no, maybe it's my detergent though. because i wash my clothes with beer.' he laughed. i like mark. we shot the shit. felt like i wasn't the one doing the talking for me, someone else had stepped in. mark asked how my apartment was and i said the fuses blew out the other night and my fan and other lights don't work. he said 'oh, you just gotta flip the fuses, you got a fuse box on the wall.' i said 'i know, i tried...that's how it happened. the blowing out.' he said 'well i'll come up and take a look at it sometime.' this is the first time conversation felt difficult, explaining to him...the...it's even hard to type, what i just typed. 'knew' he wouldn't come up to check. asked him if he was the person who puts packages by my door. he said 'nah, that's the mailman. we have the mailmen do it. they put it up to your door.' i said 'that's so nice.'

it was getting later. remember considering ordering chinese food from the place. this day is very much colored in my memory with 'should i buy chinese food' and looking at my apartment with no curtains on the walls or sheets on the bed. looked at the menu for ciro's pizza also. think it was around 5:45PM when i walked back up to my apartment from putting the clothes in the dryer. realized i wouldn't be able to shower because i didn't have towels so i 'did' my toes and fingers, like, scraped the dead skin off my feet and rubbed a four-sided stick on my toenails so they'd get shiny. knew i was going to be late for the launch party which, at this time, i thought was a reading.

around 6:15PM i went downstairs to get mostly still-damp clothes from dryer. threw everything on the bed. blow-dried hair and changed outfit a few times, then used hairdryer to dry sweat from hair/being hot in the apartment. wore white dress i had only worn once, on new year's eve 2011-2012 at a motel with zachary, with black tights and a black belt and black high heels. thought 'high class hot girl from 'girls' whose dad is a newscaster in real life and isn't a character that much anymore.' nervous about [omitted] this whole time. this was part of why i was late, i think. nervousness.

left apartment around 7:05PM. really did get ready pretty fast, i think. realized i didn't know where i had left my car the other night (after coming home from michael seidlinger roof party around 5AM). jogged to the street and made eye contact with an older woman who said 'hurry up' and i said 'i will' quietly. walked up and down 118th-108th streets, looking for car. passed a zumba class and texted mira 'i don't know where my car is, should i just take a zumba class.' she and sam were at the [keep wanting to call it 'reading;' i was driving when i found out it was just a party] party already. it was 45 minutes away. looked up cabs in my area and didn't see any. followed a black cab-looking car down 113th st on the 'giving up' walk back to my apartment and my car was there. got in. drove fast. did small bump of heroin and gian texted to see if i had any and i said yes and that i was on my way and bringing it. mira asked if i had xanax for she and sam and that they'd pay for it. i said 'you can have it for free if [omitted]' and she said '[omitted].'

saw spencer and people exiting powerhouse arena when i turned left in front of it to look for parking. remember mira saying 'spencer and people left to go to some other bar' maybe three times throughout the night…seemed really funny every time, unintentional non-sequitur. parked on water st. nicholas texted that he was at the party and getting ready to leave and asked where i was. i texted that i was walking inside. this was around 8:30PM.

found mira and sam cooke pretty fast. i think…shit. they were outside. we were all outside. willis' NYU friend who works at powerhouse joined us. remember hitting mira and sam in excited frenzy and repeating 'is it just a reading' and 'what did i miss' and maybe 'where are you going now,' and them saying 'they just ran out of alcohol' and 'spencer and people just left to go to some other bar' and shrugging with these faces…i'm laughing… we were all on 'overdrive.'

inside: seemed chaotic. recognized a lot of people right away. saw gian right away and handed him hot pink straw and blue compartment drug container thingy with heroin in it and watched him disappear in the crowd. this became my 'thing.' i would leave conversations to say 'i want to find gian, he has my drugs.' i don't know if i told gian that. he was my 'out.' had funny inner dialogue about my frantic/illogical/insistent desire to leave conversations as soon as i'd start them, and gian's passive involvement. i felt like i was talking about him like he was 'tino' from 'my so-called life'—who i don't think really existed, the audience never saw tino. i repeated 'i need to go find gian, he has my drugs' to people a lot.

lost track of mira and sam after gian drug-turnover. remember sam saying a person was 'guarding' the alcohol and seeing the person standing on an upper level, deciding we'd all go up there to steal it, then suddenly being presented with nicholas and hugging him and introducing him to mira and sam, saying 'we worked at ukazoo together,' aware of mira and sam maybe not knowing i worked at a bookstore called 'ukazoo,' then they disappeared. talked with nicholas about how long we'd been at powerhouse. he said 'they just ran out of alcohol.' he said something i'm not sure he's comfortable with me writing about, but he seemed happy, and i was glad he was happy about it. he said something about an event next week or the week after, which i said i'd like to go to, and it was good seeing him the other night. he was walking away as this happened.

after nicholas left i started feeling what i'd feel for most of the night, until maybe 2 or 3AM—like i was in an episode of 'rocko's modern life' where rocko is falling down a tunnel and faces of supporting characters keep popping up to say nightmarish catch phrases to him. the bermuda triangle episode. i didn't feel like this in a negative way, or that the people that were 'popping up in my tunnel' were actually nightmarish…just…it was this feeling of out-of-control popping up. a feeling of looking around a lot. kind of like i was just tagged in 'tag,' like i was 'it' and it seemed like i would probably be outnumbered/swallowed and wouldn't be able to find another person to tag to make 'it.'

remember standing in line with marie calloway and rachel white to get my book signed by tao. had sort of 'sidled in' to the line. rachel said 'they're taking pictures for new york magazine, we'll have to get your picture' or something and disappeared for a moment. marie seemed happier than normal… talked about where she lives now and how powerhouse had just run out of alcohol and text messages and where i live now and jobs. think i asked if she was on drugs and she wasn't. rachel came back with kat sto[not going to look up on facebook how to spell], who i didn't know worked for new york magazine, approached me/marie in line. i think a guy behind me said 'are you marie' to marie, who looked at him, as this was happening. remember turning around a second time and seeing a man's face who said 'and you must be megan' or something like that to me and i said 'i'm megan,' and kat was there already…i think…shit. memory is deteriorating at this point. big time rocko's modern life. kat asked me for a quote about 'taipei' and i didn't know what to say. i said 'i liked it, great, really great.' she seemed to be asking marie or rachel for quotes. i interrupted her to say, 'no i have a better one, my quote is: 'he spelled my name wrong.'' she said 'that's funny. that's really funny.' there was a time where it felt like it was just me and kat and i was looking at her and thinking 'i know you from somewhere, what should i say' and maybe said 'facebook' or tried to pronounce her last name. marie and kat took pictures of the four of us in groups of three with their phones. kat said she wanted a picture of tao signing my book for the story, then gestured to a tall photographer who seemed to pop out of nowhere. she said he would be standing on a platform to get the shot of tao and i. i'm laughing thinking about this, like…remembering his face, happy non-sequitur friendly face and camera popping out of nowhere. the sensation of people popping up everywhere, out of nowhere.

approached tao. he asked a question about [omitted]. remember pausing and thinking 'the picture the photographer takes will be of this moment, where tao said that and i'm about to say whatever i'm going to say, i have a choice to lie right now' and mostly feeling nervous. i thought complicated things about tao asking the question right away. asked him how he knew and he said 'it just makes sense' in a dismissive way, like he had considered our interaction about this in advance, maybe. i answered his question. he said 'that's good, i'm happy for you.' i said 'i wasn't sure, but i thought you'd be okay with it' and he confirmed being okay again. he was writing something in my book while we talked.

508

he seemed confident or 'present' in a way that i didn't feel like it was hard to look at him. i asked if he was on drugs and he said he was coming down from xanax and molly and other things, maybe. he asked what drugs i had on me. i said 'heroin, xanax, adderall, molly,' and that i'd given them to gian. at some point i said a photographer was taking our picture for new york magazine, pointing to the area to the upper level area where he stood. distracted by people behind me in line and trying to see what tao was writing in my book. wanted to talk more. i think i said 'good job' a few times. tao said 'why didn't you try to convince [omitted] that i'd be fine with it?' and i said 'i wasn't sure all the way' and he nodded like 'affirmative: i have received information.' walked away.

IT'S 9:47PM I'M LATE TO MEET MY DAD FOR DINNER, RESUMING THIS AFTER DINNER…SHIT…SHOULD'VE WAITED TO EAT THE ADDERALL SHIT.

10:16pm: I DON'T APPROVE OF MY PHONE/GOODWILL UPDATE FROM EARLIER UPON READING IT AND OTHER THIBGS FROM TODAY SOUBDS LIKE IM JUST INDIRECTLY TALKING ABOUT THIS THING IM ABOUT TO SAY DIRECTLY NOW: I FEEL GOOD ABOUT MY RECENT WEIGHT LOSS AND I THINK I LOOK BETTER

DRIVIBG TO DADS NOW

ANXIOUS ABOUT HOW MUCH I SAID ABOUT [OMITTED] I MIGHT DELETE

MULLING THIS OVWR AT DINNER

RHE ANOUNT OF ANXIETY RIGNT NOW IS HIGH

ITS A LUTTLE BETTER NOW THAT I SAID THAT THIG DIRECTLY

11:17pm: dad gave me tour of entire office building. He offered me a beer and said 'slainte.' Driving to double t diner in separate cars now. Not looking forward to eye contact at dinner, always seems difficult, like even just now on office tour. The talking part is fine, just eye contact is hard.

11:32pm: have been seated. A man asked me if I wanted a drink 'or wait for company.' I said 'a Stella? Artois? Beer?' he said 'Stella?' I said 'yes please.' he said 'okay one minute.' a woman approached. She said 'can I get you something from the bar or are you waiting for company?' I said 'oh I think he got it already.' she said he didn't. I said 'oh okay, can I have a Stella?' she said 'Stella Artois?' I said 'yes please. The beer.' surprised she didn't ask for id, they usually ask when I seem anxious. She came back and said 'the beer, right?' I said 'yeah, thank you' and nodded my head.

12:45am: heart is pounding like it wants to escape from under skin. Bathroom thing. I said 'Jesus Christ.' The pee on the seat. Could not even pretend to pee. How could they leave it on the seat like that. Both stalls. And they saw me coming in, neither of them had finished yet. Horrible dinner talking bad bad bad shit. Now dad is taking forever in bathroom. 12:47. 12:48. Walked to waiting/sitting area. Outrageous…reverse psychology… lying…it's like a Richard Yates novel or story where you see them be this way and it's…you can just so clearly see why it's not working and how neither of them can stop. Then sometimes someone will want to stop, it seems like…and you identify with that person but you can see how the other person just wants to continue hiding in this dynamic, they don't know how to act another way.

Richard Yates would be able to either write down key points of dialogue or at dinner things that happened that made things bad, or maybe he just lived/experienced those things enough so he was able to totally invent new dialogue or scenarios or whatever but I feel too deep into it that I don't…I'm not able to detach enough to write about it right now, it feels too bad. It's like an actual mental block, like a white wall or something. In one of the 'children of the corn' sequels the main guy prevents the kids from reading his mind by picturing a wall or the ocean. That's what I feel like I'm doing right now. This is the most I can say about anything. I'm not saying anything. Currently feel instinctive 'I want to flee, I want alcohol or drugs' overtaking thing. Wave of 'I want drugs' against a wall. It feels protective or something, to want that. Like computer will overheat if you don't turn it off. It might be interesting to read the dinner conversation, I'm interested in reading things like that, wish I was a person who could push themself to not do the wall thing. It felt helpful to write this/'least I can do,' for now.

1:10am: parked at mom's. Am now at the level where I feel like I shouldn't have let things get out of control and me…just, I shouldn't say anything negative or argue at all with dad ever, I haven't earned that privilege, it's spoiled/entitled of me to argue.

Goddamnit but the thing I was saying was just…honest…I said 'it feels like you're telling me a parable' about this guy…then he wanted to argue and deny that there was anything similar about the guy and me. Just seemed fake. I said 'methinks the lady doth protest too much' and he said 'that means you think I'm lying.' I said 'I just didn't expect you to react with this grandiose denial of it.' after I said the parable thing he like…I don't know, it felt calculated. He was saying like 'oh no no. No. Never. I would never ever think you were like Ted, ever, I swear on my mother's grave [he didn't like his mother] and the bible and if I could I would slit my wrist right now to show you that in no way, that I'm aware of, do I think those things—or any similarity at all, really, between you two—I see him as this terribly self-centered person who'll take everyone down with him if he's going down, not like you at all—not about you at all.'

I don't know. Maybe I'm just imagining it and he's telling the truth. Really does not feel like it. I'm not exaggerating what he said, he said the mom's grave and bible and wrist thing and all the never ever's with this rehearsed-looking face and sarcastic tone.

1:21am: headache. Shit one more thing: what preceded what I just typed was a long monologue about how Ted had betrayed him and was hopeless and had 'zero interest in psychotherapy, zero insight, on the surface all the time' (dad repeated those phrases maybe three times each during mono-logue, all context points from previous recurring arguments we've had re: me not wanting to do therapy and not liking it, after having tried therapy and it not seeming to work). He said Ted was depressed and wouldn't leave bed for six months and his son who was three or four years old would walk by his room and say 'mom, is daddy seeping?' I said 'Ted sounds sad.' dad said something about how Ted was depressed but didn't have feelings. I said 'it feels bad to feel depressed, to have no feelings, I think depression is a feeling.' then dad said the 'zero insight' things. He and Ted were childhood friends and dad won't talk to him anymore because Ted got dad and his friends to invest in real estate before shit hit the fan around 2008. Dad thinks Ted is hoarding all their money because he won't return phone calls. I don't return phone calls either. That was another thing dad kept repeating, to emphasize Ted's shittiness: 'he never returns my calls.'

I said 'it just feels familiar, I can understand you wanting to talk about problems with me in this way, by telling a story instead of saying directly.' Dad did 'methinks the lady doth protest too much' things again. He said 'I would never do that, I'm not up to anything, I don't see any similarities between you and Ted at all and I'm truly shocked you would think that about me, I think it's bad when people don't say what they mean and I want to only say what I mean and not go around saying parables, I am not up to anything at all. I am really just so shocked you would ever think I thought anything was similar about you and Ted.' I said 'but there are similarities. I don't think it's bad, you're the one giving it bad connotations like 'up to something.' It makes sense to me that you or anyone would want to talk about something indirectly at first, I relate to that. There are similarities about Ted and me: I don't always return phone calls, I'm depressed and don't like therapy, you keep saying about the thing about him not feeling loved and that was an argument we had this spring that seemed to impact you. I understand why you'd think there are similarities, you're repeating all the similar things in a way like you want me to notice and it feels fake that you're denying all of this to the extent you are.'

3:05AM: it turned into another thing with mom. the thing with mom ended with me saying 'please can i just go away, i can't talk like this anymore' and crying. at some point i said 'when people tell me how much i mean to them i don't feel anything, there is just something wrong with me, i don't feel things when people say stuff like that, i feel like i'm in an empty room all the time but the room is me and i don't know how to get out.'

sounds crazy now.

mom said 'i just read this book ['taipei'] where you're doing a lot, a lot, a lot, a lot, a LOT of drugs and i worry that a person i liked is gone and not coming back.'

i said 'it's too late, i already did everything, i'm already different and i can tell, i'm sorry to be disappointing.'

the thing i was trying to 'drive home' was that i didn't want to say everything was okay about dinner because it didn't feel okay and mom was (she does this a lot/i understand/it's a nice thing to do) trying to comfort me and get me to say how it could be better.

the first thing she said when i walked inside was 'i talked to dad and i want you to know that everything. is. ohhh-kay' in overly calm voice, but i hadn't even said anything.

at some point when things felt heated i said 'i didn't even ask to be here, you guys are the ones who made me and all you want to do is fix me or hear me say 'everything is okay, i'm fine, i'm sorry, soon i'll stop being so messed up and you don't have to worry about me and i won't bother you anymore,' that's like operating behind every conversation like this or any time anything goes wrong, i don't get it, you just made me so you could fix me and i could say 'everything is okay, you did a good job, please don't worry."

shitty person, me.

i feel like the problem is me and not my parents.

512

the desire to not keep my mouth shut comes from a 'reaching'/stretching sensation combined with an 'about to jump off a cliff' sensation.

can see opportunities to keep my mouth shut.

near the end in relationships when i get discouraged i take those opportunities more and more and my ideas about the person become rigid/hopeless and i return to being alone.

so.

guess i have this to look forward to forever.

how do you be different, does anyone know.

people go to therapy for this.

maybe it will help to write this down.

does anyone know how to stop being the way you are.

is it always going to involve some kind of compromise, like, 'i wish i could do the other thing where i just act like how i am naturally but it doesn't work so i'll intentionally do something i would never do now?'

that would be okay.

does anyone want to be paid to tell me what to do…

follow me around and say 'do this differently, you do this other thing too much' (i'm unable to say what those things are because i don't know because i just act how i naturally act)…

4:21AM: ate 1mg xanax.

6AM, 9AM, 12PM: woke all these times and ate small pieces of carbs. hard to fall asleep again. felt UTI pain and took medicine.

1:55PM: woke and peed. mom said she wanted to go to the hotel resale furniture store to buy me a mirror and so i could see the place. she told me this while standing over me and patting my head while i was in bed.

2:02PM: attorney's office called. i said i'd be over there by 3PM.

2:28PM: texted matthew donahoo video of mom's apartment.

3:35pm: signed release forms for accident settlement at attorney's office. A girl named Elise came to the door. The doorbell was broken so I knocked. She said she went to 'Jekyll and Hyde' in NYC. I said 'broadway? The broadway play?' she said it was a restaurant where people in costumes approach your table. She guided me through signing papers. I got $6000 total but my hospital bills and attorney fees made it $3901. I said 'hell yeah.' she said 'you can't sue them again.' I said 'I don't want to, thank you though.' my mom got more money than me I think, because she went to therapy after the accident and had knee replacement surgery.

Stopped at a Carroll fuel minimart and bought monster 'lemonade rehab 20 calorie' energy drink and 16oz sugar-free red bull. Made video for Matthew donahoo. Mom called to say she'd be late to the hotel furniture resale store. Going to storage unit after store then dads office. Then back to NYC.

3:53pm: pulled into parking spot at 'solo furniture installer & liquidator hotel furniture installation and liquidation services.' waiting for mom. Listening to new pornographers.

5:11pm: texting with [omitted]. Meeting mom for lunch. I want an EKG or something to see if my brain is messed up. Mom bought me a sweet huge ass mirror and lamp. They look hotel style. Wish my entire apartment looked like a hotel. Feeling extremely lethargic/fatigued. Chugging sf red bull before lunch.

6:28pm: ate at la Madeline, a vaguely chain French restaurant amidst a confusing sprawling strip mall of ethnic food franchises. Talked more about 'Taipei.' I told mom about [omitted]. Ate salad and cup of soup and strawberries and iced tea and coffee. Still feel extreme mental lethargy. Something feels wrong with me.

7:59pm: back in car from starbucks. Before that, in reverse chronological order:

Walked in 'lilting, dust mote carried by the breeze' manner into Starbucks and greeted employee with sleepy confidence. Ordered large iced red eye for me and medium mocha frappuccino for dad. Pretty music was playing and the sun was coming through windows emotionally. Sat in a chair and waited for drinks. Felt like I couldn't stand when drinks were called.

Read my account of powerhouse launch party muumuu house tweeted, sitting in car.

Sat with eyes closed in Starbucks parking lot for maybe 20 minutes.

Drove for under ten minutes down route 40 and saw forest diner where I used to eat with dad is torn down, getting turned into a 'glory days' franchise.

Dad emerged from office and handed me $20. I said I'd go to Starbucks and return at 8 when his session was over.

Knocked on dad's door but could hear he was in session.

Dad called as I was leaving storage unit, I asked if I could poop at his office.

Loaded car holding in poop.

Cried.

Looked in boxes in storage unit and saw things from my old/childhood house which has now been foreclosed or something or maybe other people bought it.

Went around to back entrance of storage unit and cleared a path to the front so I could check if my books were there.

Books were not in the front or back of storage unit.

Front door lock to storage unit didn't work.

Pulled into storage unit.

Mom called to say to take the price tag off the mirror and to call dad.

9:12pm: driving back to mom's from dad's office. Went well. Sat and talked a long time about noopept and other drugs. Agreed we didn't want to talk about last night and we were both sorry.

9:38pm: driving from mom's to dad's apt.

10:39pm: I have a lot of drugs on me. Took a variety of what Google searches confirmed were opiates, seemingly hidden in vitamin bottles of dad's. Driving back to NYC now. Ate 10mg opana.

11:15pm: smoking clove cigarette I found in storage unit. Must be from 2005. Still 'works.'

11:34pm: peeing in rest stop. As I was writing that and peeing I thought 'I'm peeing my pants.' I really felt like I was and got confused and worried. Still feels that way a little. Funny twitter exchanges with gian.

JUNE 15, 2013

5:00am: met [omitted] in bay ridge. got drinks at two places. had sex in park by Verrazano bridge.

6:14am: ate bacon egg and cheese items and donuts with [omitted] at dunkin donuts on 116th st.

7:30am: had sex in my apartment. [omitted] washed my back in shower via grass rash from park. Ate Xanax. Fell asleep holding each other.

11:29am: woke. had sex. Two orgasms. Heheheh. [omitted] showered and helped me bring in mirror from hotel furniture resale store. Drove to his apartment, to meet his parents. Last night and this morning talked about 'what it is we're doing together, exactly.' established mutual unusual attraction and excitement. Bailed on lunch with his parents. Have been sending text messages back and forth about stuff we want to do together.

12:[something]–4:[something]pm: drove alone to Bedford L stop area. There was some kind of annoying street festival. Ate 60mg morphine. Bought green juice. Got a free iced coffee and tipped a dollar. Ran into Sam Cooke and his girlfriend on street. He introduced us. I thought 'she doesn't know why this is awkward but Sam and I do.' Told them I was sleepy and on morphine. Ate 1mg Xanax, half a bahn mi sandwich, and ice cream cone from pale yellow 'van heusen' ice cream van. From 'organic planet' grocery store, bought: three coconuts, three avocados, Dr. Bronner's rose soap, 'skin detox' tea, two pints van heusen ice cream, half pint raw cinnamon vanilla ice cream, candle.

6:00pm: driving home from Bedford ave area. Texted Chelsea and Mira. Made plans with Mira to go to tyrant books reading tonight.

6:37pm: lit candle in car. Feeling good.

7:33PM: back at apartment. put away groceries. snorted 30mg morphine and prepared things in bag for tonight. the new lamp looks good. mira didn't text that she'd left for reading yet.

7:36pm: driving to reading instead of taking train. Met 'Eddie' on the street. He had a USarmy flag on his bike and talked about believing in karma and the law, not like 'the lord,' the law, and pointed to the sky. Ate maybe 60mg morphine. Earlier ate a concerta to wake. Unsure if I like morphine.

8:01pm: ate 1mg Xanax.

8:03pm: made illegal u-turn. Stephen said they hadn't started yet.

8:32pm: about 20ppl milling around in tiny beer cigarette room. Saw Stephen and moon temple and theo then Lucy came in. Mira bailed. Peeing now.

10:57pm: talking w/moon walking to my car.

10:58-11:59PM: did not update.

JUNE 16, 2013

confused about how what i typed above happened on june 15.

JUNE 17, 2013

did not update.

JUNE 18, 2013

8:[something]AM: locked keys in car. zachery w. took picture, want to include video that was recording all last night. moon and theo are nice.

9:08am: driving home listening to rilo kiley.

9:41PM: things i feel comfortable saying: ate ambien as soon as i got home, woke around 4PM, bought ice cream and wine from places on 116th st, came back to apartment.

I AM DRUNK NOW I WANT TO JUST CHILL OUT AND NOT DO THE LIVEBIG THING RIGHT NOW, JULIET IS INTERVIEWING ME AT 11PM AND I WANT TO CHILL AND EAT LEFTOVERS AND WATCH NETFLIX TILL THEN.

THERE WAS A LOT OF FUN STUFF THAT HAPPENED WITH [OMITTED] THIS WEEKEND, THAT'S WHERE I WAS/WHAT I WAS DOING.

JUNE 19, 2013

12:01AM: somehow abruptly ended skype interview with juliet. no idea what happened. drank a magnum bottle of white wine and a vodka something. opened package from juliet and put on 'i <3 weed' shirt and made an emotional/embarrassing long video of myself rolling a spliff to the 'must be the colors and the kids' by cat power.

read 'charity' by joy williams and it became too hard to focus eyes on page.

ate an ambien before bed. ate leftover pizza from the other night when [omitted] and me ordered pizza and watched game five of the finals and didn't leave my room all day (june 16?).

10:03AM: woke and saw 'disaster zone' from muffin eating last night... muffin crumbs everywhere in the kitchen, powdered sugar, a plate with 25% of a mostly melted stick of butter and half a muffin and sugar on it. ate half an ambien and slept until maybe 2AM.

toasted and ate another 'chia muffin' from the 'free bag' from le pain quotidian (?) that a person gave away at reading. looked up nutrition facts. 300something calories. seemed 'better than i thought.'

looked at the internet and felt drifting thing...drifting...

read a little more of 'honored guest' could not sustain attention

felt bad about doing excess of 'don't be present: be asleep, be on xanax or ambien or weed' drugs and maybe effects of coming down from cocaine the night of the reading (june 17-18?)

watched shitty netflix movie called '30 blows' via wanting to see 'what normal people do when they live in new york in the summer'

tried to call mom...jesus. there were probably about 15 phone calls back-and-forth, total. my phone is doing this thing where i can hear the other person but they can't hear me. a woman named erika from AT&T called four times to try to put mom and i in touch. did not work. finally called her from google talk and we talked for an hour and a half. she said something funny, like 'i don't want you to be all alone thinking about dying at the end of the earth.'

texted with chelsea and made dinner plans for monday, and then have 'a day' saturday where we walk around PS1 and get drunk and i sleep over on her 'new twin sleeper sofa.'

texted with [omitted] who was making salmon and arranged to hang out at his place.

texted crissy that i loved and missed her.

12[something]-11:09pm: did not update.

11:10pm: driving to [omitted]. Three teenage boys running on the street. I put my key in the wrong car. Felt sinking thing thinking 'this is my street now, apartment in Baltimore remember that, Chelsea, soon you'll see Chelsea, this is your street, how is it this now'

Listening to Jeffrey Lewis

Have eaten maybe 60mg concerta to 'feel normal'

memorable things post-11:10PM:

circled around a cop and a popeye's more times than normal, looking for parking

texted with zachery w., made plans to do bing.com 'get $10 for photographing restaurants' safari thing friday

crissy texted back that if ever needed a 'break from the rat race' she was only a 16 hour car drive away. read that as i walked to the wrong address. imagined driving down to florida to hang out…bring my cats maybe…16 hours in the car. i miss crissy. would be fun to visit. in 40 years we'll probably be the only people left of our immediate family. i'll be 57 and she'll be 77

called [omitted] to say i was outside but that he didn't live where i was. my phone was doing the thing where i could hear the other person but they can't hear me

texted [omitted] same information

[omitted] texted me correct street address and i checked and it's what he texted in the first place too. sometimes some numbers look the same to me…or else i'm just not paying enough attention. numbers easily confused for me: two, eight, nine, six, four, five (especially eight and six, also i'm the worst at my eight's and six's tables) (also for the hell of it, letters easily confused for me [mostly confused about where they appear in alphabet, while working at a bookstore in baltimore. i'd be shelving books by authors with

names starting with these letters and i'd have to mentally say the alphabet: b, d, p, q, r, s, t, j, k, u, v, w])

parked near [omitted] and walked to address, looking around a lot

stood outside door to [omitted]'s building and texted i was here

heard someone say my name from maybe across the street and looked vaguely out into nothing and said 'yeah'

person said my name again and i looked up and it was [omitted] smiling smoking cigarette from fire escape window. he was wearing a hat. his face looks different every time i see him

i felt 'bouncy heart' and was laughing i think, surprised, said 'throw the ladder down to me, i'll climb up' or something

he said 'i'll buzz you in'

door buzzed for comically long time. thought 'good, he is prepared for my slow-motion door opening, he knows this about me already. maybe. do i open doors slowly? no, i just have a fear of getting locked in places, i move fast, he doesn't know any of this about me i don't think, he's just being considerate' while walking up stairs

his door was open. lighting in my memory is 'dusky.' duskily lit apartment. nice. safe-feeling. he showed me a video he made of me walking up to his apartment and him saying my name and me not knowing where to look. i said 'oh my god' and felt a big smiley thing and we were standing close together. would pull back my face from kissing sometimes and i'd be smiling and he'd be smiling. said little compliments and 'happy you're here' and 'do you want a glass of wine' things mid-kissing. had sex on the couch for maybe 20 minutes. took a break via sweatiness. after a few minutes of laying limply on each other and breathing similarly [omitted] said 'how about that glass of wine?' asked him what music was playing. he said 'the knife. this album's weird.' i said something about it sounding like the level of the ocean where there's just anglerfish with light-up things bumping into each other. later the music changed and i said 'more like dolphins now' and he said 'yeah, we've moved up several layers of the ocean, closer to the surface.' not remembering exact words.

JUNE 20, 2013

2:27am: [omitted] is making food. I'm not supposed to see what it is but I saw. Have been sitting on his couch drinking wine since sex. Feel calm and nice. Earlier [omitted] sat next to me carrying cigarettes and ashtray. I said 'let's make a bet, bets are fun.' he said 'okay, what do you want to bet?' He lit cigarette. I said 'one time Zachary and I bet each other a hundred dollars we wouldn't do drugs or drink alcohol. Then I lost after like, three days,' thinking something about how I was smoking an e-cigarette and how [omitted] had said he wanted to stop smoking, 'but that wasn't fun.' he smiled and made a face and said 'yeah, that doesn't sound like a fun bet.' i said 'let's bet we can't say the other person's name. The first one to say the other person's name loses. But like, I can say 'Megan;' you can't.'

Conditions of the bet we agreed on:

- loser pays $1.25 (via it's annoying to get change for $2)

- you can't ask the other person for change

- you have either three minutes or can go to three stores to get correct change

- can get out of the 'change thing' by saying the name three more times and making it $5 you owe the other person

Remember looking at [omitted] laying on couch from my upright sitting position. After a moment he said 'you know, I was thinking, it felt weird to say your name when I called to you from the balcony. We don't say each other's names.' I said 'yeah. It's weird to say your name too.' (the last time he was at my apartment I 'confessed' that I usually have to stop myself from calling him two names that are not his name before I remember his name). He said 'yeah, well I mean, you think I'm [wrong name #1]. And like, [wrong name #2].' I batted at him playfully and said 'you just look so much like a [wrong name #1]. It's not my fault.' I said 'the bet will be easy. It'll be a good reason to not say each other's names. We'll be good at it.'

A little later he asked me to read something aloud and it had his name in it and I reacted big like 'fuckkkkkkk' and we were laughing. Found $1.25 in my purse while he said 'three minutes, come on, three minutes or three delis, come on.' I used a fake-mad, 'aristocratically defeated' voice to say 'I have it. I have perfect change, here' and moved the dollar and quarter up his underpants, trying to maneuver into his asscrack. Unsuccessful, I think. This was good. Good stuff.

Read stuff on our phones for a while. He brought over maybe four poetry books and got excited and showed me parts of poems he liked and had forgotten. They were things I didn't think I'd like. Surprised I did. Seemed evident they 'struck more of a chord' with him than me but I liked them. They were funny/absurd. He is currently still making the food thing.

2:31am: he came over to couch/took a break from food thing and laid on me and we sometimes kissed and put pressure on different body parts in experimental 'trying to fit' yoga-like…unofficial pressing on each other/ finding comfy spots yoga. You hear the other person breathing and it sounds good and it makes you think about how you're breathing close to them, and you feel your torsos expand and contract in this…roiling…organism… with double-consciousness…but barely moving, like moving at 'century pace,' like you could keep the pace of what you're doing for centuries if you couldn't die.

2:33am: [omitted] said 'what time is it' I said 'it's two thirty-three a.m.' then we said things about Elliott Smith. Three minutes have passed. The album playing is 'new moon.' I said 'you know, 'new moon,' like, 'twilight?' you know 'twilight?' [omitted] looked busy with the food thing. He said 'I guess not. Sort of.' I said 'Stephanie Meyer? That thing?' he seemed big time distracted. Snort-laughed a little to myself typing this now, aware of myself not wanting to say the Stephanie Meyer thing at all but making myself further it to…like…socially painful extent…but it's funny, like an inside joke with myself, I do things like this 'on purpose' a lot I think. It's funny when the other person doesn't realize what's going on or they're just like, occupied with their own concerns and acting 'obviously, naturally disinterested in this obviously uninteresting topic brought to my attention by the usually otherwise benignly amusing or quiet Megan.'

2:38am: seems evident that I'm typing about things now, like when I take a break like now to respond, he can tell maybe.

2:40-3:[something]AM: sat at kitchen table eating edamame food thing out of cast iron skillet. [omitted] said he's been thinking about making this for 'months. months and months, since i first ate it at this restaurant. no, it must be years. a year and a half, i've been thinking about making this. i've been thinking about how to replicate the recipe.' talked about him writing a book, he said like, 'just think about how long it'd take me to write a book, if it took this long for me to make the edamame.' i said 'you just have a marination process. your brain is just like, where the stuff marinates.' talked about...here it is:

DIFFERENCE BETWEEN US:

- i like having all a lot of information available about myself on the internet. want to eventually have the most information about a person possible on the internet.

- [omitted] is private and sometimes makes comments like 'this is why i shouldn't have a twitter'/there is barely any information about him available on the internet.

NOT REALLY THAT DIFFERENT:

- typing all of the things i type about myself neutralizes their impact in my head...like i'll be thinking or obsessing about something and when i write it down i figure out 'no one cares that much, this isn't a big deal.'

- [omitted] seems to think similarly for reasons i don't think he'd be comfortable with me writing about but that i understand.

the 'not really different' thing is i think we both think a lot. overactive head things.

3:24am: Mark McCarthy. That is the name to remember. He is smoking and showing me books on his shelf and talking excitedly about them. I am feeling like an idiot

'I've never read Murakami'

'Me neither. Well. I started to read 'Norwegian wood' and I didn't...it didn't...but...' (trailed off as I typed this)

4:[something]-7:[something]AM: had sex in the dark then turned on the lights and i said 'yeah, better.' laid in bed and showed each other pictures on our phones. [omitted] showed me all the things on his old iphone. he was going really fast. kept asking questions to 'slow it down,' wanted to look longer at all the pictures, also thought his 'going fast' was cute and excited. started showing him all my tagged facebook photos and he said 'i don't know if i want to see that.' he's said things like 'i don't know if i want to read the liveblog, i want to just know you like this,' but he's read parts of the liveblog and other things i've written and 'taipei'...on the couch probably around 1AM he said something interesting about almost unfollowing my unedited twitter because of...jesus. going to paraphrase: 'that night when you got drunk recently, i don't know. it was like a tesla coil of this...it's this thing i like about you, your energy, but.' i said 'tesla coil? is that the thing in lightbulbs?' he said 'no it's that. you know it's this glass ball that has a blue light in the center and when you put your finger up to it all the blue light goes to your finger?' i said 'oh yeah, yeah i know those. he said 'well you know when you put both hands on it and it's like, it's all these blue lights going everywhere on the ball? they don't know where to go?'

INTERESTING....

during this time he also accidentally said my name. forget how. he gave me five quarters. earlier i had eaten 1mg xanax and he'd eaten a benadryl but we still felt awake. i said 'let's split an ambien.' then...hm. we ended up eating one ambien each, total, i think.

9:[something]-10:[something]AM: woke lazily. had sex. good. showered. [omitted] was going to be late. i said i wanted to sleep a little more then go to the library and he gave me keys and said i could stay as long as i wanted, then go back to rockaway park, or then meet up after work to watch game seven somewhere. i said 'i'll sleep and go to the library to work and hang around here until you get back.'

10:46am: drove [omitted] to the Q train. I hit a pothole and my car shook then a few seconds later [omitted] almost opened his door on man on a bike who said 'wake the fuck up man.' Parked two blocks from his place. Walking to his apartment to sleep a little more, then library. It's nice outside. I am happy.

FIRST FAVORITE THING I'VE SEEN TODAY:

> [omitted]'s face coming out of his white button-down shirt, standing still, watching the bike man ride away in the distance, face looking indignant but behind that something sweet and childlike and almost disappointed...unconsciously displaying some core level of emotion, like 'this must've happened before: the guy who yelled because of something i did and then he got away'...anger and ultimate resignation... there is a mouse in 'the Secret of NIMH' who makes this face. Big time endeared to him at that moment.

2:00pm: woke but was like nah.

3:57pm: woke. Want to get green juice and coffee and go to library. Read Chelsea text from last night and RSVP-ed to two google calendar events she made for our hangouts this week. Warm feelings about Chelsea, making the Google events. Chelsea. I miss Chelsea. Looked at pictures of her (ex?)

boyfriend on Facebook to make sure he wasn't dating anyone else because I'd rage against them…rage against dating anyone but Chelsea…

4:41pm: ate 60mg vyvanse. Bought large kale/spinach/cucumber/apple/ginger juice from juice place across the street. Jamaican music was playing. Walked to library and remembered wanting an energy/coffee thing. Walked to deli.

SECOND FAVORITE THING I'VE SEEN TODAY:

> older girl with black curly hair and two younger girls kicked a ball. man in neon orange 'jogging gear' neared them. the older girl kicked the ball into the man and he kept running. she looked at me with this dropped-jaw horror movie face and said 'oh my god' and i smiled and almost winked at her…wanted my smile to convey 'it's all good babydoll. you did good.' a family of four (two little boys, dog, dad, mom) walked the same path as the jogging man, opposite me. the mom seemed to see the entire thing and smiled at me the way i smiled at the girl.

4:44pm: hovering near line at deli now. Holding 12oz sugar-free red bull and a monster zero. The things keep happening:

THIRD FAVORITE THING I'VE SEEN TODAY:

> little boy puts a green Palmolive soap bottle on deli counter
>
> deli man says something
>
> little boy says 'that ain't $5.50'
>
> deli man says 'you want straws'
>
> little boy says 'i ain't gonna drink that' and disappears

6:42PM: have been sitting in library typing in/organizing liveblog. told [omitted] i would write an article. he said 'you should do that, write other things besides liveblog too.' i don't know what to write about. i don't like losing track of days. since i've been back from maryland it's felt like the same day and i'm never sure what day of the week it is.

7:10PM: [omitted] texted something funny about his name around 4PM. i haven't responded.

7:24PM: still sitting in library. no article dice. listening to 'colors and the kids' on repeat. the part where she says 'i could stay here, become someone different. i could stay here, become someone better.' oof. i don't know.

before i typed text in front of '7:24PM:' i had typed 'i think i have a problem with drugs.'

8:08pm: leaving library. Meeting [omitted] to eat before 9PM game. Wish I hadn't slept so much today and I didn't have plans tomorrow. Walking fast. Unsure where I'm going. He said to meet at [name of restaurant I thought was maybe fake].

8:14pm: the place was real. Real restaurant. Saw the sign for it and crossed street and he was standing outside with a plastic bag. Snuck up/ran to him and went 'AHHH' and 'hi' and we hugged and started walking to a liquor store. He said 'do you want wine?' I said 'yeah yeah, wine, I want a wine.' he said 'white? Cold? Maybe the cat I was talking about is here.' I said 'uh. The cat?' he said 'the cat I come here fo—' I said 'the cat! I remember. The cat. White wine, yeah. Cold.' then we were in the back looking at a fridge. He said 'should we get champagne?' I said 'champagne! Yeah. Prosecco.' All of this felt like a 'rising action' musical comedy number where the characters are acting determined yet unsure and like they know something the audience doesn't.

8:30pm: eating take-out at apartment. Jerk chicken. Have been hurrying, hurried pace. He said 'eight thirty, we have plenty of time.' I said 'but we should still hurry. Just because it's fun' and he looked excited.

8:38pm: now we're done. Finished food 8:33PM. One of us said that. He started streaming the game on his phone. I sang along to an '800-588-2300 empire' commercial and said 'I'm always going to know that.' Asked if he'd seen the eagle man commercial. Showed it to him at a commercial break. He liked it. Remembered 'lakers champions' video Nate and Seth and I used to watch and laugh and said 'oh there's another funny thing like that I want to show you later.' Started to describe video and said 'no wait, I shouldn't build it up, it won't live up to the hype.' he said 'the eagle man lived up to your hype.'

8:38-11:59PM: walked to bar to watch game. i bet him if the heat won i'd get to call him by his name again. he didn't really agree or disagree to bet terms. thought 'i'm being too [something]. too eager to think of ideas. no more bets for a while after this.' during the first or second quarter we stood outside and i smoked maybe 75% of a cigarette, said 'it's making my stomach feel weird, do you want it,' and he took it. happy to be there with him and everyone in the bar, all of us there for the same thing. said 'it smells of cabbage in here' a few times. [omitted] said 'shrimps.' i said 'a twelve-inch shrimp.' tweeted from unedited account. talked to people. bought six beers for each of us. when the game ended i cried a little and said 'imagine how they must feel right now, walking to their locker rooms.' [omitted] said 'i always forget that that's happening right now, they're doing that right now.' could tell i was hamming it up a little, but not disingenuously. we were walking and holding hands. this feels like a ben lerner-style confession.

i wanted to get another drink or do something to prolong the period before we were back at his apartment. felt restless. [omitted] expressed not wanting to drink more but wanting me to be happy. sat/leaned on a benched-in tree by an outdoor seating area. he pointed to a window and said 'see? they're putting the chairs up already.' i said 'that's okay, it'll be good to go back.'

i said we should race from where we stood to end of the block and back, separately, with the other person timing. he groaned. i said 'just time me, then.' he said 'no, just stay here.' i said 'no just please, just time me, i'll be right back.' he said 'okay.' ran as fast as i could, pretending i was getting chased by the nothing from 'neverending story' and [vague thing that wants to 'get me']. passed a man. the block was longer than i thought it'd be. jogged then walked defeatedly. [omitted] was holding his phone and watching. i did one minute 30something seconds. he said 'did you really run the whole way?' i said 'yeah.' he stood and said 'okay. i'm doing it.' i said 'even with the cigarette?' he put it out and said 'oh-hhhh, boy.' timed him. he ran faster than i felt like i was running. watched him shrink under street light shadows, then reappear full-size by me. i said 'one minute fifty-four seconds.' he said 'that's a good two hundred meters,' breathing hard. he said 'did you really go the whole way? to the sign?' i said 'yeah.'

it was hard for him to walk. he hadn't been wearing socks. felt guilty for making us run but that also he could've stopped.

at apartment:

remember him standing in the kitchen, taking off shoes and showing me his feet. skin was peeling off a toe and it looked red and bleeding underneath. both heels were also not so good. not in good shape at all. he talked about how his feet bones, from the impact of hitting the ground in a certain way while running, due to the shape of his arches, have started growing abnormally into 'spurs.' bone spurs. he was in pain. big time. didn't know what to do. we sat on the couch. i said 'oh now can i show you the other video?'

JUNE 21, 2013

12:35am: loaded 'lakers champions' video on my phone. he said 'i hate the lakers.' i said 'it's not really about that, just wait.' video started. he said 'oh no, he reminds me of this guy in high school.' i said 'it's not, he's not, don't worry.'

watched a little less than half of it. i was laughing a little and sometimes repeating lines and he was...not. doing those things. haha. i said 'we don't have to watch it, you don't like it, it's okay.'

argued. first argument. he thought the guy was taking advantage of the basketball fans in a mean-spirited way. i said i didn't think he was doing that and i don't think mean-spirited things are funny. he said 'he's acting. it's like 'jackass.' he just wants to show how stupid basketball fans sound.' i said 'i think he's making fun of himself more than anyone, if he's making fun of anyone.' he said 'he's definitely making fun of the fans.' i said 'you don't know though' [i also don't know]. he was in the kitchen. i said 'as a person who likes basketball and a person who likes to...um: i thought it was funny. also he must like basketball because he knows how to talk that way.' he said something about the guy being clumsy or unaware of how he's talking. i said 'no! at the end he like, repeats himself perfectly, he goes like, 'nn-nn-i couldn'ta said it, nn...n-better? without...? [exhales] uh, myself' twice. he knows what he's doing i think.' [omitted] kind of smiled. i was smiling too. he said something like 'yeah, but you and me and the guy, we're all in the position of, you know. we're aware of some things.' i said 'i don't like stuff like that, i don't like when people point out how stupid other people are so they can look smart. the thing about it that's funny to me is the language thing. he's pointing out how absurd language can be.' he said 'but he's doing it at the expense of these people, he's making them look stupid.' i said 'you're just having a personal bias, he just reminds you of someone you didn't like in high school.'

remember really wanting to 'hammer home' my thoughts about the video's pure intentions. i said 'i feel like the guy, like i don't talk well, especially about sports, i'm just saying a lot of nothing. like at the bar tonight when i said to the guy, 'we know who's gonna win it' or whatever. it's like this social agreement to say nothing sometimes, he's just making a video about that.' remember [omitted] emphatically saying something about how much the game meant to the fans and felt like i agreed. i said 'but even if it is that, like. what about that would even be bad though...i feel like anything can be viewed as funny, or just. not always. serious.' told story about acting school exercise where small groups of us went out on the street and stared/pointed incredulously at nonexistent thing in the sky to see how passers-by would react. he said 'yeah, but you were doing an experiment, it wasn't being filmed, no one could put it on youtube so there was no risk of anyone getting taken advantage of.' i said 'i'd like it if someone made a video of me like that and put it on youtube.' he said 'but you're okay with things like that.' made sense to me. felt like it was coming to an end around this time but i still felt interested in/wanted to be clear about...humor...what i don't like...i'm laughing, it's 2:59AM now, WITHOUT FURTHER INTRODUCTION HERE IS WHAT I THINK I SAID, OFFICIALLY STOPPING TRYING TO MAKE MYSELF NOT SOUND LIKE AN ASS oh my god goddamnit, goddamnit lol: 'so there's two kinds of humor: there's schadenfreude, which is when there's a plot to make someone feel bad... humor at the expense of someone's feelings...it's aggressive. then there's the other kind. which is about absurdity. i think. it's not directed at anyone, or it's directed at ideas or something, which is what i think the video is. i don't think schadenfreude is funny ever. like, looney tunes. i never thought that was funny at all, when i was little. i was just like 'why are they being like that, i don't get it." [omitted] seemed to kind of agree or...i think we were both losing interest in talking about this, maybe. he said 'you didn't even think wile e. coyote was funny?' i said 'no, not even. no. i just didn't get it.' i said 'mainly i just don't want you to think i think it's funny when people are made to feel bad or stupid, i don't like that.' he said 'i don't think you think that.' jesus. can't believe i'm still typing this. agreed. um. 'napoleon dynamite' was funny because it was sweet-natured and not designed to make fun of anyone.

what's funny about all of this is i'm sitting here now, feeling very serious as i'm trying to accurately recapture a now-resolved minor argument where i was feeling very serious about articulating why i thought a youtube video was funny, how i like being able to not take things seriously, and how stuff is funniest when it's not supposed to mean anything.

12:37am: 'no I need surgery,' walks away, 'I've been told,' walks back, 'I've been told I need surgery.'

12:39am: he is laughing from bathroom washing feet. I said 'use soap,' he said 'uh huh,' is now laughing maniacally. Recently established band aid situation: out of band aids. Prepared paper towels and offered to dress wounds, said 'my dad would bandage stuff when I was little, it felt good to have another person do it.'

4:07AM: applied makeshift paper towel bandages and he laid face-down on bed. tried to be careful but slipped a few times. remember saying 'you have to drink this whole thing of water before bed' and offering pain killers a few times, saying 'shit i'm acting like my mom, it can be annoying, i'm sorry,' him saying 'it's okay.' put on a t-shirt. had sex then went out to sit on couch (i'm not trying to be aloof/dismissive/detached/whatever it is people think i'm being when i write about how i had sex). put on big glasses mom said grandma could've stolen.

took pictures of each other. talked about [not comfortable elaborating, felt closer to him at the end]. went to bed. joked about how he hated the lakers video. i said 'that was the first time we argued, interesting.' he said something like 'you were just feeling strongly about something, it's okay, it doesn't change anything about how much fun it was to watch the game and do other stuff with you tonight.'

hard to sleep. at some point i ate 5mg hydrocodone and gave him a small amount of morphine.

4:08am: laid in bed in the dark. Talked about writing/liveblog. Felt annoying insistent urge to…jesus. I said 'I'm not all this one thing, will you read this, I don't know why I want you to.' He said 'I'd be happy to' and I texted a link to a vice article and he read it and laughed sometimes and I tried not to react and looked at my phone and felt fragile/shaky. Then it was over and I felt normal again. Gave him 'treasure hunt' back rub thing mom used to give me.

5:34am: can't sleep. He's snoring. Listened to Brian eno song on earphones. Didn't help. I am loud moving from the bed to living room. Ate 1.5 ambien units, 5mg hydrocodone, six beers, half bottle of champagne tonight.

10:30am: woke to hug/kiss from freshly showered [omitted]. Drippy. Nice. He asked what time I'm meeting Zachery in coney island. He is going to a party tonight. Asked if I wanted to hang out after party or tomorrow. He is having a hard time walking.

11:24am: did dishes. Felt latent embarrassment about asking him to read my article, like how I'd make my mom listen to me practice monologues before auditions in high school. He said 'I wanted to read it, that's why I read it.' It's bad when you ask someone to be interested in something, knowing 'real interest' only happens without prompt. Then you feel like you pressured the person to 1) be interested, 2) reassure you of their interest. Never works. Always bad. My fault. Why did I want him to read it so much right then. Real cringefest Boyle. NEVER AGAIN BOYLE.

Sitting on couch. Ate noopept, 54mg concerta. Not feeling effects yet. Going to sprinkle some adderall balls on tongue. Fuck.

11:46am: Zachery texted that he wanted to rest before coney island bing. com photo safari. I said I could pick him up whenever he was ready. Want to get green juice and walk around I guess…wonder how long it'll be…

12:05pm: did time + paper towel wasting thing. drew pictures of fish chasing fish on paper towel, cut them out with scissors, placed on his bed. I would leave things like this on second ex-boyfriend's bed. Like. Objects or drawings. He would leave in the morning and I'd make his bed and 'tuck in' a bottle of Windex or something.

12:17pm: at green juice place. The juice is being made. Feeling insane bad for some reason. Yesterday I felt good because I knew I'd go to the library then there would be basketball. Now I'm about to do a potentially fun social thing but I don't know when to expect it'll happen. Feel like I have nothing to say right now. No I don't know. It'll be fun. Lately my baseline/ waking feeling is several notches below the 'normal' line. I think most people naturally wake somewhere above the 'normal' line…like. Most people are plankton at the surface of the ocean and I'm something slow-moving and groaning and 'as yet undiscovered' in the bottom-middle area.

12:30pm: bought two 16oz sf red bulls and e-cigarette. Deli man said 'I smoke this. I try em all. You like this one?' I said 'yeah. I like how the smoke doesn't hurt.' he looked at me and I waved my hand over my face and said 'my eyes don't hurt.' he nodded like 'of course, of course' and said 'oh yeah, the smoke don't hurt.'

12:34pm: sitting in car to garner air conditioning for a minute. No ticket. Have to poop kind of.

12:38pm: affectionately thought of myself as 'clumbering lummox.' Chugging red bull and going to library to update this.

12:48pm: exited car. Have to poop badly. Ate remaining 20mg xr adderall because why not. Looking very 'this is the third day in a row of this dress' and 'unwashed.' found mascara in armrest and put it on. Kind of used it like eyeliner, dotting a line and blending black smudges. I feel happier walking around here than my neighborhood but I think it's just because the library is so big and nice.

12:54pm: calm assertive body guard-type man in tight t-shirt gave a 'whoa buddy, please slow down' arm gesture to a slowing and stopping van and I did the same thing way after it was appropriate for me to cross the street or for the man to still be stopped. Felt like 'Chimley, lord of the devilish pranking street elves.'

12:58pm: pooping big time stanky. Using the handicapped stall, which has a broken lock. Lady is next to me. While walking to poop locker started going on mental tangent about 'Chimley,' like...'the distressing discovery that one is, in fact, a Chimley' and 'widespread undiagnosed Chimley symptoms in the population, not to be ignored.'

What if there was a hell where the door was just barely locked. You could just always almost lock it, or when it sort of locks you don't feel confident it'll stay locked if you don't constantly stare at/tend to it.

Little girl is saying (typing as it happens): 'mommy can you flush it for me? It's so loud. Mommy when you flush it I feel it in my ears. You don't understand. It's so loud. Thank you mommy. Am I finished? Now you flush. I don't want to hear it. Mommy does it bite? Whoa. It's so big. Okay? Okay? The phone is ringing. Do you like it? Can I flush it? Do I press it?'

2:13PM: have been answering backlog of ask.fm questions. again. there was a period where these men were near me and it was irritating...they were like...i don't know. just...hovering. looking around with 'thought-heated eyeballs' at a hovering pace. heated eyeball hovering. one of them was across from me. he kept leaving and coming back and looking up from his computer to scan the room. i was typing hard for a while and forgot about him. heard a voice say 'is that bacteria?' looked up from typing and he was looking at my arm. i said 'no, it's a rocket.' he pointed lower and said 'no, that one. is that bacteria?' i said 'no, it's the moon.' he said 'what?' i said 'moon. it's the moon.' he said 'ah. a rocket going to the moon.' i nodded and pretended to continue typing. he said 'and now, what are all the ones on the other arm, the left arm?' i said 'just...a lot of stuff.' i was smiling and trying to be nice. he said 'like what? it's very colorful and pretty.' i said 'it's just a lot of stuff.' resumed fake-typing. he said 'does it have any meaning, to you?' i said 'no, not really. just stuff. stuff i like.' continued fake-typing. he said 'it's very colorful.'

MY HEAD WAS SCREAMING TYPING THIS, REMEMBERING THIS.

used bathroom. have been sitting outside at a table to avoid man and garner sunlight. haven't heard from zachery yet.

2:45PM: composed flaking text. goddamnit. can't not flake. can't not. cleaned out purse. can't find e-cigarette. i'm sitting at a wire table under a large umbrella. it looks like spain or somewhere european out here. a man in a yarmulke walked up to the man at the table across from me and said 'erin? hello? is that you?' got scared it was a 'rampant 'taipei' fan.' the seated man did not seem to know the yarmulke man, who was talking at length to him about a 'new media social networking platform.' the sitting man responded minimally. the yarmulke man may've said 'hey man' and not 'erin.' after a maybe two-minute uninterrupted monologue about the social networking thing, the yarmulke man said 'good talking to you brother, glad to make a contact.'

2:53PM: zachery replied with mutual flake text. made plans to do bing. com safari next week. ate 60mg vyvanse. might feel worse tomorrow, having eaten this now. shit. don't think about tomorrow. i'm not rationing well, my tolerance is down. this is shitty. i don't want to do this. it's all just so i don't feel as shitty right now. i feel shitty because of alcohol and ambien and hydrocodone from last night, maybe. my brain just needs to recover. i'm not giving it time. too late to. shit. too late. i'll just learn, this is what learning is.

3:07PM: the sitting man who was bothered by the yarmulke man now sitting in front of a salad. i can smell it a little. he's looking around peacefully, exuding 'i respect the aloneness of everything and of myself, i don't want anything from the world that's not already given to me, i am entitled to nothing.'

3:09PM: two women just sat at table, completing 'triangle of tables between unentitled alone man and me.' one woman is saying (typing as she says): 'my blood pressure is high. from the subway. i'm lightheaded, you know. i need to sit down and eat a sandwich. it's from the subway. i don't do well in [inaudible]. no. it's hot [laugh]. i don't do great in the heat. stay in the shade. i never just sit on the beach, i never just sit in the sun—never! well i never did but i certainly don't now. [inaudible] for-ev-er. and then i'll come out the water, i'll sit under an umbrella and read a book! i'm not a beach person. lie in the shade. right. i don't know about just lying there in the sun. dumb. just dumb. first of all, it's your skin.' she has quieted down. the other person sometimes encourages her malignant talking force with an inaudible question. perhaps the other person is worse than the woman. why do i hate everyone right now. hating everything. hate. shit. hating hard. 'you know, i'm dressed much cooler than you. you and my sister. you and my sister. it's not good. yeah. you know if you don't sweat it means your heart's not right. if you sweat it means your heart's not as efficient. it's not working as well. that's terrific. that's terrific! you go three times in a row? i must go [inaudible], i must. that's great. oh it's up[inaudible]? i have to make a commitment.'

nevermind i like her. i'm enjoying hating her. she is allowing my head to be occupied with typing her voice. she is okay. the only okay person. forcing herself…like…i don't even have to think about how to describe her, she's so strong. she's just talking. all i have to do is type what she's saying. i had to describe the sitting man. his demeanor. the woman is just going 'yamyamyamyamyam.'

3:22PM: cop has circled shark-like behind me maybe five times. very 'shark' of him, to do this. sun-hating woman and her inaudible friend took their traveling sideshow elsewhere. the exclusive street theater production of 'waiting for godot.' i was the only audience member. they meant it to be that way, this was all planned. now you're part of the audience too. this is progressive. i feel 100%…that this is what i like about art…or if there's a thing called art, it would be the scenario i just described, which now involves you. or. actually i don't know anything about art, don't listen to me. people are setting up instruments near the library entrance. unentitled sitting man who was bothered by yarmulke man has been replaced with 'bearded-yet-scabby-faced college student.' he has re-arranged his chair… it's like we've been seated facing each other, at separate tables. i can feel him smiling and looking around dopily but i'm not bothered, because he's…like. i'm laughing. he is my scallywag. a girl approached and he said 'i was s-ooo productive in there, yeah right!' i love him. my scallywag. it's 4:21PM. the instrument people are playing something loud and jazzy. it's. i can't take it. not going to last much longer. farewell, my scabby scallywag. my beloved partner in crime. my one and only bumbershoot. shh. shhh-hhh. i feel vyvanse, this was brought to you by vyvanse, you have just been subjected to a new kind of subversive advertising technique sponsored by vyvanse.

4:28PM: walked to library entrance, carrying macbook with opened lid and still-attached earphones. 'tossed' earphones over my shoulder as i opened the door. thought 'something about this is like a clumsy sidekick scenario. it looks like the macbook is my clumsy sidekick who i'm always dragging around but actually it's in charge, i'm the sidekick.' saw sharky cop preparing to make eye contact with me and initiated counter-offensive 'look important by dimming screen until it's blank' maneuver. closing the lid would've admitted defeat. like if the cop saw me doing that and i saw him seeing me do that, we'd both know i was a shifty lawbreaker up to no good.

4:58PM: opened bathroom door and stood behind two women in line. closed macbook lid and stowed in bag. this is how it happened:

first woman in line: [cautiously opens handicapped stall door] woman in handicapped stall: excuse me! what you think you're doing opening my, someone's—

first woman: sorry, sorry, the door was open, you didn't lock it

handicapped stall: the. lock. is. bro-ken. how do you not check, how do you not see i'm

first woman: and how'm i sposed to know if a fuckin door is broken or not? i'm not lookin around everywhere for your stuff, calm down, how'm i sposed to

handicapped stall: and how do you think it feels to be me, huh? [toilet flushes] getting walked in on, getting a door opened on me?

[third woman emerges from non-handicapped stall]

first woman: oh my god. it's not that serious, all that happened was i didn't see you in there, it's not that ser-i-ous, you actin' like it's all

handicapped stall: no! this is serious because of you, because here you are say all of this when if you just said 'i'm sorry, i'm so sorry to walk in on you'

first woman: i said i'm sorry, oh my god [walks to non-handicapped stall]

handicapped stall: excuse me but no you did not!

first woman: oh my god yes i did why can't this be over already?

handicapped stall: 'cause you started it, you started this, otherwise we wouldn't be talking now would we, this can be over and we can be smiling anytime, i didn't start this

first woman: OH

[quiet for a few moments, then skinny model-looking woman emerges from handicapped stall and avoids eye contact with woman in front of me in line, me, new woman behind me. woman in front of me walks into handicapped stall and someone exits middle stall and i walk in to that one to pee]

first woman: i can't believe that. she mad. she flippin' out, thinkin' it's my job to check if her shit's on the floor before i do, i don't even know new woman: [says something supportive that i forget. someone said 'princess' i think. new woman and first woman say a few things back and forth, then it's quiet]

me: [from stall] she was out of line, i thought

first woman: i know! she walkin' around actin' like that, thinkin' she can get away with whatever [door opens and closes]

me: [flushes toilet, walks to sink] out of line…

new woman: [exchanges eye contact/grins with me in mirror, walks to handicapped stall] and look what she left on the floor, what is all this toilet paper, what is this. this nasty.

me: i know, nasty

5:58pm: library closed. Walked outside and put bag on a table to look for phone and e-cigarette. Man with uncomfortably simultaneous soft and masculine affect approached me from behind. Sensed him there before I saw or heard him. He said 'miss? Scuse me, miss?' Shook my head 'no' and winced as I said 'hi' and walked away fast.

5:59pm: angelic-looking teen approached on my left, said 'scuse me, m'am? Your skirt's up a little, in the back.' touched dress and pulled it down and said 'oh boy, thank you' in Jim Carrey voice, aware of how my urge to disguise embarrassment was stronger than maybe non-existent embarrassed feelings.

6:12pm: sitting in car. Going to drive home now. Going to feel bad maybe. No I feel okay. Pulled on my dress a lot on the walk to the car.

7:19pm: parked. Do I want to go to pickles & pies now to get e-cigarette cartridge refills and energy drinks. What I want to do tonight. Man in a wheelchair pushed himself backwards with one foot. He took up the whole street. The whole middle, where cars go. Backwards.

7:25pm: still in car. Looked at instagram and felt paranoid and inadequate.

8:24PM: went to pickles & pies. got the stuff. walked to building thinking 'unable to be surprised…unable to be surprised [something]. wait that's not true. i wrote that i was surprised to hear [omitted] say something, i think. i wasn't really surprised though, there's just not another word for it. what was it that he said? maybe i was surprised. i'm simultaneously extremely able to be surprised and…the opposite of that.'

remembered being on mushrooms and walking towards my building with zachery however many weeks ago that was and saying 'hold on: i just felt like, how is this…this is where i live now? a few days ago i was at mom's. i live here. wait,' and him kind of like, vocally nodding, encouraging me to say more but i didn't know how.

remembered the retired MTA wheelchair man from colin's 'welcome to the building' dinner and saying i'd bring him smoothies. i haven't done it yet. i probably won't. vault containing semi-explored friendlier, selfless, extroverted version of myself sealing off. it feels like an actual sucking. i'm sucking something out.

it smelled like the ocean a lot.

watched a black SUV cavalierly reverse itself into garage of my building.

passed dumpster and remembered the fucking…mattress…still in my room.

inserted keys in second glass door and was stopped when a man exiting from the inside opened it. i said 'thanks' and smiled. the elevator was on the third floor. thought 'am i going to wait to go on the elevator with him: no.'

back/garage door opened and mark walked in the building.

i said 'hi mark.'

mark said 'hey megan. what's happening.'

something about his face fucked me up. he was looking at me like 'there has been a conference about what we should do with you. we have decided that action needs to be taken but you're safe for now. you are on probation.'

i said 'oh you know, just, you know. getting in. tired, i mean. i am. so, you know' heard mark say something to the elevator man and stair door close behind me.

oof

a real shiner…left a real shiner, that one.

remembered something about last night. starting foresee problems about myself. think they're correctable. i'd feel better if i changed some things. this is all self-imposed. maybe. actually am probably just saying that to convince myself i'm stronger and less impressionable.

fed cats, cleaned litter box, took out trash, made bed, organized piles of things and cleaned surfaces, all very fast. scooted around the floor on my knees with a hand-sweeper, saying 'oh my god' and 'shit' quietly.

something had escalated by the time i got to the bathroom and i was sweeping and saying 'oh shit, oh shit, oh shit' and stopped to sit on the edge of bathtub.

the inside of the bathtub is dirty.

i was looking at it and thinking about laundry and all the time between now and

shit

hyperventilating

actual

i'm going to stop right now

11:02PM: listening to 'untitled 1' by odd nosdam on repeat. i feel like i'm missing something, since i've been back at the apartment or maybe further back than that. not missing like 'not including,' missing like 'a lack; an active absence; something i don't remember losing but can feel the space it left.'

11:13PM: how is it so late.

JUNE 22, 2013

3:11AM: i'm not learning anything from the goddamned liveblog. i didn't start it to learn anything. i don't think. i lost focus again. simultaneously caring extremely much and extremely not at all about people liking me. at the 50/50 line about this. over time anyone/everyone will lose interest in me or die and there's nothing i can do. i can just keep doing this, or doing it in other ways. it's always going to feel like this. pulse is always going to sound like 'here i am, again, again, again, again, again, (…)'

copying and pasting 'again' 1,000,000 times would have the same effect of 1,000,000 other words.

STUFF THAT IS DIFFERENT ABOUT ME RIGHT NOW THAN ON MARCH 17, 2013:

* three months five days older

* live alone

* weigh less

* longer (redder?) hair

* use e-cigarette

* have been given two lamps, other things

* more certain about how i like to communicate

* more…i don't know. better memory. write more but maybe worse. more likely to doubt epiphanies/generalizations, maybe (haha)

* a little less interesting/less motivated/more depressed

* feel better overall i think/wanted to delete above thing as soon as i wrote it

* have given up on the possibilities for some things for myself (not bothered by/accept/resign to this, also open to being wrong about this/ changing drastically/[other unforeseeable possibilities])

* larger digital record of me (other things like this)

* sleep less overall but have slept more hours overall (other things like this)

4:00AM: drinking vodka club soda i didn't finish from the other night. petting alvie. shirley sleeping next to me on the other side.

4:12AM: did i mention that i have been given two lamps

two lamps have been gifted to me since march 17, 2013

let that be a lesson to you all

merry christmas to all and to all a good night

god bless us everyone

jack nicholson has never played santa claus but can you imagine?~!?!?! i mean...

received mental picture of jack nicholson in a sleigh superimposed on an ad for some kind of creamy 'morning food' as i typed ellipsis

people don't talk about how jim carey and jack nicholson are both...like that

do other people think they're like that

sweet i'm entertaining myself again

probably my favorite thing about the liveblog is that i think 'wiggitywiggitywhaaaa!' sometimes now

want to start thinking 'sccccrrreEEEEEEEEECCCHHH-ER-R-R-R-R-R-R!!!!'

is it clear what sound that is

do you understand

i'm not going to say what it is

now it's 4:30AM

entertaining myself in a lone MSword document, audience of me

cowboy...MSword cowboy...desert...desert imagery

i haven't said this: there was a letter from the apartment management building under my door when i walked in today. IT WAS A BED BUG WARNING. THERE ARE BED BUGS ON THE FOURTH FLOOR.

NOT SEEING ANYTHING ABNORMAL BUT...

THAT EVER-ELUSIVE WONDEROUS PRESENCE OF THE POS-
SIBILITY OF SOMETHING BAD HAPPENING BEHIND THE
SCENES!

SOMETHING I WANT TO TALK ABOUT:

I FEEL BETTER EVERY TIME I WATCH THIS TWO-PART YOU-
TUBE VIDEO OF DAVID LYNCH PREPARING QUINOA AND
BROCCOLI AND WAITING FOR IT TO COOK AND TELLING
THIS WACK STORY ABOUT SUGAR WATER AND COINS AND
COCA COLA AND A TRAIN

ALSO NO MATTER WHAT, HOWEVER STINKY I AM, IT SMELLS
GOOD

ALSO I HAVE NEVER SAID '

DAMN STILL TOO CHICKEN TO TYPE IT

ALSO I'VE LIED FOUR TIMES SINCE UPDATING THIS

NO I LIED, I'VE ONLY LIED TWICE

MORE LIKE 'WILLFULLY WITHHOLDING THE TRUTH FROM
YOU' THAN 'CREATING A FALSITY'

WAIT GUESS I'VE WILLFULLY WITHHELD A LOT OF THINGS

GODDAMNED [OMITTING]

LAUGHED A LITTLE

THE SOLUTION TO ANYTHING, HERE COMES:

PICTURED A MOSTLY EMPTY MOVIE THEATER SHOWING A
3-D MOVIE

JESUS

THAT'S THE FIRST THING I THOUGHT

SOMETHING HURTS ON MY TOE, SHOULD I LOOK

HUH

SHOULD I

I LIKE WHEN I'M ALL CAPS

THE FIRST DAY I EVER HUNG OUT WITH A FRIEND OF MINE WHO I MISS DEARLY AND LIVES FAR AWAY FROM ME…

(YOU KNOW WHO YOU ARE)

THE FIRST DAY WE HUNG OUT: YOU TOLD ME ABOUT HAVING LICE

THAT IS WHAT IS MAKING ME FEEL OKAY ABOUT BED BUG SITUATION

IF YOU ARE READING

YOU KNOW WHO YOU ARE

THIS IS OUR SECRET, THAT I'M TYPING ABOUT IT IN THIS WAY, YOU MUST ABSOLUTELY 100% KNOW YOU'RE THE PERSON I'M TYPING ABOUT IF YOU ARE READING THIS

DAMN I WANT MORE SECRETS LIKE THAT

HOW GOOD WOULD IT FEEL TO READ SOMEONE GIVING ME A SECRET SHOUTOUT LIKE THAT

VAST NETWORK OF SECRET SHOUTOUTS LIKE THAT

LIKE

ALL OF US YELLING SECRETS…ANONYMOUSLY…SO

BUT

GET IT?

HOW IT FEELS BETTER OR MORE SPECIAL OR SOMETHING?

IT'S LIKE A TREASURE HUNT

I'M DOING THAT FOR YOU, ANONYMOUS FRIEND

PERHAPS [OMITTED] ACTUALLY LIKES READING THIS STUFF, I DON'T KNOW, I DON'T THINK SO

EITHER WAY I'M STILL…HAHA…PICTURED FIVEISH BLEAK 'LIFE SENTENCE'-LIKE SCENARIOS IN RAPID SUCCESSION (DYING AS OLD LADY IN ABANDONED WAREHOUSE, DYING AS OLD MAN [???] IN ABANDONED WAREHOUSE, A LONG HIGHWAY IN THE DESERT, ME FIVE-TO-TWENTY YEARS OLDER SERVING FOOD AT A KITCHEN TABLE IN THE SAME

AD FOR 'CREAMY MORNING FOOD PRODUCT' FROM EAR-LIER)

MOM TOLD ME ONE TIME MY WRITING HAS A 'CRINGE EFFECT'

SHE SAID 'IT'S LIKE A CAR ACCIDENT'

MOM...

I'M LAUGHING...

I'M APING THE STYLE OF SHUTUPMOM.DIARYLAND.COM RIGHT NOW

JUST BECAUSE I'M WRITING IN ALL CAPS AND LISTENING TO MODEST MOUSE AND BEING

UNRESTRAINED

BOLD

BOLD BABY BOYLE COMING AT YOU

4:53AM

STILL HERE

OH SHIT I JUST SAW THE...

OUTSIDE IT IS TURNING BLUE

THE SKY, I MEAN

'TOO SOON'

OH SHIT IT'S THE SUMMER EQUINOX, LONGEST DAY OF THE YEAR

JUNE 21...ISN'T THAT ALWAYS THE LONGEST DAY...

ALWAYS GOING TO REMEMBER JUNE 21, 2004

SHIT NINE YEARS AGO

SHIT

OH MY GOD

OH MY GODDDDDDDDD

WELL I'LL SPARE YOU THE DETAILS BUT LET'S JUST SAY 'ME AND MY TWO BEST FRIENDS AT THE TIME FELL ASLEEP IN MY BACKYARD ON A DOWN COMFORTER AND WE WOKE UP AND IT WAS NIGHT OUTSIDE AND MY OTHER FRIEND TEXTED 'ARE YOU GOING TO SEE !!! TONIGHT AT 9:30 CLUB [OR OTTOBAR]' AND I FORGET WHAT I SAID BUT WE WENT INSIDE AND WATCHED 'MANHATTAN' AND THE ONE BEST FRIEND WHO I'D BEEN FLIRTING WITH AND HAD A BIG CRUSH ON AND I MADE OUT FOR THE FIRST TIME ON THE COUCH WHILE THE OTHER FRIEND WAS SLEEPING [MAYBE NOT THOUGH, BLESS HER HEART, I THINK SHE WAS PROBABLY AWAKE FOR THIS AND AT LEAST ONE OTHER SIMILAR EVENT, WISH I COULD GIVE SOMEONE THE EXPERIENCE OF...HONESTLY IT'S...I WANT TO GIVE SOMEONE THIS KIND OF TRUST? IS THAT WHAT I MEAN? TRUST? SILENTLY ENDURING THE MAKEOUT OF YOUR FRIEND BECAUSE...YOU WANT THEM TO BE HAPPY...YOU PUT YOUR COMFORT ASIDE...I WANT TO DO THAT...LESSER FRIENDS WOULD BE LIKE 'OH MY GOD I CAN HEAR EVERYTHING, ARE YOU SERIOUSLY DOING THIS IN FRONT OF ME'...MAYBE NOT. WAIT. THAT'S HOW MOST PEOPLE WOULD REACT I THINK. WAIT. WOULD THEY ENDURE...IS IT EASIER TO ENDURE OR CONFRONT... HUH? HUH? ANYWAY I WANT TO DO WHATEVER'S HARDER, WHATEVER OPTION IS HARDER, I WANT TO DO THE HARDEST THING FOR SOMEONE, LIKE WHAT THEY'D VIEW IS THE HARDEST...JUST...TO LET THEM KNOW...I'D ENDURE/ CONFRONT BASED ON WHATEVER THE PERSON THOUGHT WAS HARDEST TO DO, FRIENDS OR ROMANTIC PEOPLE OR WHOEVER: I'M AVAILABLE TO DO THAT. FORGET WHAT I'M TALKING ABOUT. HONESTLY FORGET. THE IDEA WAS TO SAY 'I'LL SPARE YOU THE DETAILS' THEN WRITE A REALLY DETAILED THING, I THINK I'VE ACHIEVED THAT, YOU GET IT, PUNCHLINE, OKAY DONE]'

THE PUNCHLINE IS ALWAYS FUNNIEST TO THE PERSON TELLING THE JOKE

IS THAT A PROVERB

A 'CHESTNUT,' AS THEY SAY?

A FEW DAYS AGO I LEARNED MY WALGREENS SAVINGS CARD IS ALSO VALID AT DUANE READE

ZACHARY USED TO SAY 'YOU OLD CHESTNUT' SOMETIMES

OUT OF NOWHERE…LIKE THAT…

HE'D SAY THINGS OUT OF NOWHERE

FUNNY INTELLIGENT PERSON

I WISH HIM THE BEST IN THE WORLD

I WISH EVERYONE WOULD JUST WISH EVERYONE THE BEST

NOT EVERYONE GETS ALONG EASILY, IT'S OKAY

WHAT ELSE IS THERE TO DO BUT THINK IT'S OKAY

WHAT ELSE IS THERE TO DO

YOU CAN GET SAD ABOUT IT

WAIT IT'S NOT LIKE THIS FOR SOME PEOPLE, SOME PEOPLE
ARE REALLY AGREEABLE

WAIT I TAKE THAT BACK

WHAT IS THE THING THAT'S LIKE 'NO TAKE-BACKS,' IT'S
FROM CHILDHOOD

TAG BACKS

'TAG, NO TAG-BACKS'

IS IT CLEAR THAT I'M WITHHOLDING RAGE AND FEAR ALL
THE TIME

DO PEOPLE READ THIS AND THINK 'LOOK AT THIS FESTER-
ING MOSH PIT PARTY OF ONE'

'WHEN IS SHE GOING TO JUST…'

YOU KNOW

DO YOU THINK THAT

I'M NOT REALLY LIKE THAT

VERY QUICK THOUGH, TO…JUMP TO…

CAN HEAR A TRUCK OUTSIDE

IS MY CAR GETTING TOWED

I HEAR AIR BRAKES AND AN ENGINE IDLING

SHIT

GOING TO MOVE CAR AGAIN NOW

BY HOOK OR BY CROOK

SHIT

BRB

6:42am: can see my car from here I think. Still going to move it. No Saturday-Sunday parking. Passed car with 'WWII: I SERVED' sticker and my face got hot and chokey neck. Walking parallel to truck making air brakes noises. Remember recently talking with someone about how the last scene of 'glory' makes me cry and they said 'me too, it's a real tearjerker' and I got excited and carried away with describing Matthew Broderick on the beach knowing he's about to fail and it's all been for nothing and the person was like 'wasn't the last scene a battle' and I said 'yeah, I guess this part this is right before it. The moment before the battle. On the beach. Matthew Broderick' and they said 'Oh. Yeah…' and I thought 'it's okay, I've been there, I've been where you are, you don't have to pretend to remember, how do I convey that non-verbally, I can't'

6:56am: SITTING IN OBVIOUSLY UNTOWED CAR NO TICKET HELL YEAH GETTING A LITTLE BETTER AT THIS

7:08am: moved it. Thought 'it's shitty of people to do shitty things to me. I'm shitty but at least I don't try to pretend I'm' and jumped via averting collision with fast-moving intense-eye-contact-making older man in a tucked-in t-shirt popping out of seemingly nowhere

Just exchanged mutually docile 'good mornings' with slow-moving man of around the same age. He initiated the greetings

Saw an even older man walking towards me and thought 'I'll be the first one to say good morning this time' and I was and he either didn't hear or ignored me

This would be an interesting study about race

What races do you think the men were

(The second man was black, everyone else was white)

As I was typing sentence before last a man of perhaps latin American decent and I stopped to greet each other at almost the same time

No early morning street encounters with Asians or Pacific Islanders or [other]

7:31AM: smells like wet dog in here. earlier i was angry at a barking dog. irritated now. no sleep. irritated because of no sleep mostly, i think. that's why i'm allowing myself to do this. i'm washing over space.

9:35AM: i like how soft kyle maclaughlin's voice sounds.

12:56PM: have been watching david lynch documentary things and 'twin peaks' and halfheartedly trying to sleep. tuned guitar. made a tuna mixture. cats seemed interested can-noise but not the taste of the fish. negative on fish taste. practiced saying something for an hour or so and decided 'don't say anything, or if asked, say you don't want to talk about it but you don't feel bad.' fantasizing about moving to montana with david lynch and having lots of kids.

1:[something]PM: ate 1mg xanax. drank maybe four vodka units over course of evening/morning/afternoon.

2:[something]PM: woke hungry. ate bite of frozen banana.

4:46PM: woke. texts from rachel and mira from last night. feeling shitty. hard to move but don't want to go back to sleep and don't think i could.

5:15PM: mom called. i could hear her but she couldn't hear me. called her on google talk.

5:39PM: got off phone. worried about how much i've said about [omitted], like i expressed too much excitement or...i don't know. messed something up. mom said to call back in ten minutes.

5:55PM: i don't think i'd be good for anyone right now. i mean, 'tuna mixture.'

6:00PM: sitting in bed. really just sitting. sitting. that's all. picking at skin. being mad at the beach and sunny nice day for being there just a few feet away from me and i don't want it. think i have a chemical probem. brain... chemical issue.

6:07PM: going to get my ass to petsmart. what should i eat. walt disney ate dog food when he was having a hard time in his 20's, i read earlier. hard to find more information on this. (to clarify: i will be buying wet food for alvie and shirley, not for myself). should i get fucking. chinese food. adult child. big baby boyle.

here's something nice: when i was learning how to talk…i'd have a bottle before bed every night i think, until i was maybe three years old or something. in the morning mom would be at the bottom of the stairs and say 'BOMBS AWAAAAAAY!!!' and that would mean i was supposed to throw the empty bottle down to her and i'd say 'BOMBS AWAAAAAAAY!!!!!'

7:04PM: ate last 10mg hydrocodone to 'be rid of it.' called mom back and left message.

7:06PM: mom called. emotional to listen to her talk, knowing we both knew i could hear her and she couldn't hear me. she said 'i keep thinking 'megan on the beach' and i love you, and anyway, call me back if you want honey, i'll hang up now.'

7:11PM: downloaded 'the elephant man' and 'the straight story.' might watch those tonight. david lynch mosh pit party of one.

8:26pm: walking to belle harbor steakhouse. Ordered spinach salad and cheeseburger deluxe. Passed a parked car playing 'the safety dance' by men without hats. The guy who took my order said 'and who'll be picking it up?' I said 'Megan.' he said 'Megan fox?' I said 'no, Megan Boyle, just regular.' he said 'well that's still good. Twenty minutes Megan.' I used google talk. Godamned phone.

8:33pm: I riffed my ass off with the phone man. Megan fox man. Conversational Olympics gold medal. Lost points at the end when he said 'you know what? I think Megan Boyle is hotter than Megan Fox.' I said 'well. You're a minority.' he looked like he might be not have been born not in the U.S. but I meant it like 'not many people would agree with your opinion.'

8:39pm: walking back to apartment. Stopped at pickles & pies to get ice cream because what the fucking fuck it. The conspiracy theory 'even the president, even kings, so much money they're all mafia' cashier rang me up. I love him. I said 'is it busy tonight?' he shrugged like 'eh, yeah, but doesn't matter, I'm just here some time.' I said 'Saturday night' and snickered and he did too. I said 'the moon is really big tonight, really pretty, you should go out and see.' he said 'end of the month. Biggest moon.'

9:[something]–11:[something]PM: watched most of 'the elephant man.'

11:20PM: [omitted] texted a picture of the paper towel fishes i left on bed. paused movie. the elephant man had just said 'i am not an animal, i am a human being.'

JUNE 23, 2013

12:30AM: continued texting. funny things. made plans for [omitted] to come to my apartment tomorrow/technically today. resumed movie. i liked the movie. felt bored sometimes. i feel like the elephant man.

12:3[something]–4:[something]AM: read masha's latest update about going to tao's reading recently. happy masha's updating again. read about joseph merrick (elephant man). watched three episodes of 'discovery channel: my shocking story.' one was about a woman who woke from a 20-year coma and started talking again. one was about a woman who was pregnant for 46 years. one was about 'the family who walks on all fours.' felt affected by the pregnant for 46 years woman. she was nine months pregnant and had labor pains and went to the hospital and they said she'd need a c-section to save her life and the baby's life. then she heard another girl getting a c-section and screaming and she got scared and ran home. she said 'i thought if i'm going to die, i want to be at home.' she was in bed for three days or something, i think, then she said 'and then i felt him go to sleep. i thought 'if he wants to sleep, i'll let him sleep." she adopted three children and they grew up and had kids and she had the sleeping baby in her the whole time. she was in her 70's when they removed the baby. felt preoccupied with 'was the baby alive when they removed it, could it have been alive,' until maybe the middle of the show. they take a long time to get to the point on 'my shocking story.' they said 'calcified mass' about the baby. 'calcified.' it had grown outside of her uterus, somehow. when she felt the labor pains she was actually feeling the baby running out of oxygen, the doctors said.

looked at ASMR videos. i can look at it for hours, trying to find 'the perfect thing.'

12:04–1:00PM: woke a few times. dreamed something about marie calloway and rachel white.

1:01–4:15PM: tried to sleep. watched ASMR videos. ate bites of ice cream. want to watch full documentary of jay-z youtube commercial. jay-z sounds like he's talking backwards sometimes, like the dwarf from 'twin peaks.' he does this reverse-exhale thing.

5:51PM: drank a monster 'absolute zero.' feel a little better. i didn't eat xanax or ambien last night to fall asleep, 'proud' of that. read 'a fan's notes.'

[omitted] texted. i want to do laundry before he comes…shit. shower and laundry. can it be done in mere hours. shit.

6:37PM: [omitted] texted he was going to get naked and rub olive oil on himself and stand in front of his air conditioner. i said that was a good 'tenderizing' method. made plans to get tenderized by him at his place tonight so i can impress people at a BBQ tomorrow.

drinking sugar-free red bull. might shirk laundry in favor of exercising.

7:04PM: ate noopept, b-vitamin, 27mg concerta. listening to alcoholic faith mission. updating liveblog, then wailing on my abs for ten minutes, then showering, dressing, leaving, etc. dinner with chelsea tomorrow. i'll go to the library after [omitted] and write until chelsea dinner at 7PM.

7:23PM: got caught in a looking-at-pictures hole. there are pictures of zachary from 2007-whenever i saw him last on this computer. tao and other people i know are in pictures. watched a video of tao and zachary walking around a casino. tao said 'have you ever been to any other buffets, not in casinos?' zachary said 'i've never been to any other buffets.' a few moments later tao opened a camera and pointed it at zachary and said 'what do you hate about black people,' grinning. matching his satirical tone, zachary said, 'i just think they're stupid' and they laughed. tao said 'oh shit, the police. let's film the police.'

8:36pm: I said 'Megan Boyle you are leaving this apartment at 8:20' in the shower around 7:50pm, knowing that would ensure I'd leave by 8:30 but allot for ten-ish minutes 'safe time.' sweaty hairline. Hair is wavy. Walking to car. I said I'd be at [omitted]'s by 9pm.

8:41pn: jogged four blocks. Can see my car. I have looked better. Eyelashes and sand and hair have entered left eye since locking apartment door.

8:56pm: texted I'd be there at 9:15

9:02pm: six or something miles away I got this fuck these red ass lights

9:04pm: sweating has stabilized. I'm listening to 'star guitar' by aphex twin on repeat. I like the video and the making of the video for this. I do the same thing with my eyes in cars that the video illustrates.

9:09pm: gmaps says 14mins with traffic holy hell keep recalibrating route good thing I didn't do the eastern parkway thing I almost did which now says 17mins I'm only three miles away I hate this shit

9:13pm: I'm on Atlantic ave now I think yeah

I always want that thing to be true from 'catcher in the rye' where he's like 'it doesn't matter if a girl is late as long as she looks good'

I haven't experienced that to be true

Modern day update of 'catcher in the rye' where he's like 'it doesn't matter if a girl looks good, it's always going to piss me off a little if she's late. She's not as hot as other girls, anyways'

I'm also always a little pissed off if the guy is late, so

9:19pm: on the road leading to apt now. A few hundred feet away. Love following the gmaps dot with my eyes as it follows car, it's like I'm the dot, makes me feel taken care of

9:59pm: he read updates.

JUNE 24, 2013

10:13am: woke to [omitted]'s alarm. we'd be laying/touching each other in some way and I'd fall back asleep easily. Heard him shower then move around in kitchen then watched him lean over me in work clothes to give little kiss and say 'bye.' Laying in bed now. Dark air conditioned room. Feels nice.

10:16am: moved car. No non-metered parking spaces. Car used to be in front of apartment, now it's 20 feet away. I have until 12:08 until I have to move car or add to meter I feel happy want to sleep a little more ate a mystery 2mg I think of Xanax.

12:04pm: added money to meter.

2:23pm: woke from Chelsea dream and wanted snacks. Kept sleeping and waking and confusing dream with her texts and not knowing where I was. Got in on grapes and some 'omega trail mix' thing from last night. The past two times I've gone to meter I've put on shorts and a shirt over the t-shirt I'm wearing. [omitted] has a lot of t-shirts from the 1980's that are falling apart. They're the best t-shirts. Think he's the first guy I've slept with who's offered me a t-shirt to sleep in, or is at least the first whose offers feel more like 'I want to see you wearing my old shirts' than 'I want to politely offer pajamas.'

Added money to meter. Was going to sleep more at apartment but thought 'get a grip Boyle' and went to coffee shop. They were cash only. I had a card. The girl said 'it's too hot for you not to have it. Here, we've been using napkins, just write your name on a napkin.' I did. She said 'oh no, you don't have to put your phone number too.' I said 'no, I mean for, thank you, it's just for credibility. For my credibility.'

3:43pm: ate 60mg vyvanse. Got green juice. Repaid coffee place. There were like 20 name-napkins on the wall. People just don't come back?

3:47pm: Parked close to library. Ate 27mg concerta. Walking to deli to buy sugar-free red bull.

4:27PM: pooped in an efficient, businesslike manner. library is crowded as hell.

5:13PM: WHAT I REMEMBER FROM LAST NIGHT 9:22PM – 2:[SOMETHING]AM:

- texted [omitted] i was outside and he texted 'will buzz.' door buzzed for almost entire duration i was walking up both flights of stairs. thought 'he either read the thing i wrote in the liveblog about noticing he held the buzzer for a long time the other night or...something else.' it buzzed a little 'toot' buzz when i reached his floor. he opened the door and was smiling and i thought 'this is different from the other night when he opened the door, my face looks different, it's reacting to his different-looking face, faces are showing...thoughts...or...' hugged and kissed. i said 'that was a nice long buzz, i like a nice long door buzz.' he laughed and said 'i thought you'd like that.' he was smiling... we were both smiling but it felt a little hard to look at him for as long as i usually do. seemed like he was also having difficulty maintaining eye contact. wasn't sure where to stand. he said he read what i'd written in liveblog about the door buzz...i think...around this time...something like 'it takes some people forever to get in, they miss the buzz.' i said 'oh shit, oh no, you read it' or something. then we were standing by the window and kissing, then i started spinning around in a circle in place and said 'i'm going to just be spinning now, okay?' then i stopped and we kissed again and i turned around and he held me from behind and said something about how high my high heels were. i said 'oh, they're just regular, regular style.' then he was sitting on the couch and i like... did a somersault thing over him, laughing and saying 'i can't believe you read it, no, you read it, you're not supposed to want, you read it, oh my god.' landed by his head. he said 'ow! ow! my hair' and i moved my knee. kissed him upside-down. established mutual hunger. he started making steak.

- sat at table where there was a thing to read. i usually sit on couch. he said 'want a glass of wine' and i did and he poured it and one for himself and brought it to me at the table and we kissed a little and he started making dinner.

- he said 'you'd like [thing on the table] i think, it's really funny' and i read it. was self-consciously holding e-cigarette entire time. i liked the thing i read.

- at one point i sat up from the chair and it stuck to my dress. he was standing near me and we kissed/embraced and he and said 'i know, they've always done that, i don't know why the chairs are sticky.' felt my head being 'behind his head' during embrace. i said 'it's good. it's the chair that sits back.'

- entire time he was making dinner: i read another part of the thing on the table, we talked a little about [would reveal his identity], long pauses, i said 'what did you think about what i wrote,' he said 'i didn't read all of it, i wanted to read it to see how the style compared to the vice thing' (remember him looking at me in an interesting way when he said this, knowing i'd written about how i wanted him to see i had different styles of writing, and that he'd probably read my uncomfortable description), he said 'i'm glad you picked up on the door thing and the man on the bike we never discussed, who was like 'wake the fuck up man.' i said 'oh yeah, the man. yeah, your face after him was really good, you were like [face + whaa noise].' felt self-conscious tunnel vision and heightened awareness of conversational pauses that could also be attributed to him making dinner and me not doing anything. i moved to the couch. he said something about an article about a man who ate 413 red lobster biscuits and got into a coma and i looked it up, tried to see if the man had broken the record or not. walked over to him and said 'oh. potatoes, boiling? boiling potatoes?' he said 'yeah, boiling!' stood back to back, touching his ass. returned to couch. loaded liveblog on phone, knowing it was at least four days ago, when the 'man on the bike' happened. i said 'i'm like, looking up...looking at the liveblog now, to read, uh. reading. to see. right now. if i said anything embarrassing.' he said 'what?' i said 'i'm looking at what i wrote to see if i said anything like, embarrassing. how much did you read?' he said 'i really didn't read that much. i just saw that muumuu house had tweeted a quote,' he looked at me, 'something about how you want to have the most—' i said 'the most information possible about myself on the internet.' he said 'right' and went back to cooking. i said 'so...what'd you think? about... uh...[snickering]...i feel like i want to read, like, sitting with you looking at it and like... interview...you.' he said 'what?' i said 'what did you think about... the parts you read?' he said 'well it's definitely. i liked it a lot. i really didn't read all that much of it, it was really just. i scanned it.' i remembered the thing he said about considering unfollowing my unedited account due to occasional intense emotional outbursts. a little later he said 'i was mostly, i was really fascinated by it.' i said 'what?' he said 'i thought it was...fascinating.' he was crouching by the broiler. i said 'oh. oh. good.' he said 'you like yours ra—' i said 'yes, rare, i like mine rare.' i said 'i've been worried i said too much about you, like. i went from not saying anything at all to just...saying everything except your name.' he said 'i don't think you should feel worried about that.' he said 'i mean, it might mean something to you and me, but i only think [person] would be able to maybe guess who i was.' i thought "mean something to you and me'...what does...it's evident that liveblog has changed something shitshitshithisthsthitttyshit. don't write this much anymore.' i said 'good. good.' some more time passed. i said 'i gotta say, i feel really weird, like, a little inhibited right now, knowing you've read it.' he said 'i was wondering about that. if it'd feel uncomfortable to you. i was theorizing.' i said 'so…what were you hypothesiz—what was your hypothesis?' he said 'well. i thought: she's either totally fine, you know, with exposing all of this, wanting to show all of this part of yourself—these private thoughts you're exposing, about a person, or maybe there was the possibility that you'd feel uncomfortable.' i said 'hm. i don't think i feel…i'd only feel uncomfortable if you like, read too much into…like, if you attributed too much meaning. to what i'm saying.' he said 'right.' some time passed. i said 'i sound a lot more insecure, huh? newly insecure?' he said something about not sounding insecure in my vice article. i said 'no i mean, like. in person.' he said 'well. yeah, you're definitely exposing a part of yourself that's not represented, normally.' i said 'yeah. yeah. but i mean. it's just, you know. thoughts.' some more time passed. i said 'i mean, i'm just always thinking stuff like that, thoughts like that, they're just always [fluttery gesture around head] going on. that's normal for me, what i wrote about.' time passed. asked him about 'weed moonshine' he said he tried at a party friday and he came over to the couch and told me about it. wanted to ask more about the party. i said 'i went to your website.' he said 'oh you did? what'd you think?' i said 'well. i mean you're definitely exposing a part of yourself i don't see normally, you know, it's definitey different than what it feels like to interact with you in person' and we laughed a little. talked a little more about the website. i said 'i feel like i should be helping you make dinner.'

THE REST OF THE NIGHT, BASICALLY, WILL BE UNDERREPRE-SENTED DUE TO NEEDING TO LEAVE LIBRARY IN 20 MINUTES TO MEET CHELSEA FOR DINNER:

- dinner topics: apartment was clean, broccoli vs. cauliflour, what dinner was made of/how he made/where it came from, what would people-meat would taste like, he doesn't like talking about gross stuff while eating, he thought he was eating too fast and apologized, i said 'don't apologize' then 'good, be sorry' in fake-dominant voice the next time he said it, i said 'when people eat too fast it makes me want to start talking about disgusting things,' he thought my dress was pretty and it had hearts on it and so did the one i wore last time, i said i thought they were polka dots and 'if you zoom out far enough it's polka dots,' teased him about finishing fast while i was still eating.

- sat on fire escape

- fire escape was fun. felt more at ease. he threw a cigarette down to a man. i suggested we play a game that's kind of like 'i spy' but you say... like you pick a thing you can see and say a statement about it. he was better at guessing my things than i was at his. we were laughing a lot. my last 'thing'...the last statement i said was 'this might be a mirage. it's full of water. it contains the color blue and the letters 'blue.' it was the design of his cigarette pack. it took a long time for him to guess. at the end of it one of us made a movement and the cigarettes fell onto the roof below us.

- had sex. bike fell onto bed. after sex i felt comfortable/normal again.

- i said 'we're still sweaty, even though the air conditioning is on.' he said 'i know. i should've chilled the room.' i said 'you chilled the wine,' then sang 'chill the wine, but not the room' to the tune of 'spill the wine' by war. he didn't know the song. i said 'it's an old disco song, i know you'd know it if you heard it.' looked it up on youtube on his phone and listened to it, eating a cold/frozen chocolate bar and drinking water.

- showed him the video of the guy twerking and he showed me a video of a news story of 33 high school students who got suspended for 'upside-down twerking.' he said he was going to learn how to twerk and would be able to next time i saw him. i said 'good' and like...kept moving my ass on the bed...i said 'i'm obsessed with twerking now.' i tried to twerk on the bed and he said it was pretty good. he went to the bathroom and i said 'i want to try the upside-down headstand kind' and when he came back i was doing it...kind of...this was good.

- agreed we wouldn't be able to fall asleep without sleeping aids. i said i didn't use anything last night and he said he didn't either. he said something like 'we have a hard time falling asleep together, we'll be up until like...' i said 'like four or five a.m.' he took benadryl and i ate 1mg xanax. he said 'i wish i had a movie or something, do you have any on your computer?' i said i downloaded 'the straight story'

- showed each other pictures on his phone + my computer

- other stuff...before i brought in the computer...nice time in bed. he said 'i'm wide awake.' i said 'i'm getting another xanax, do you want?' he said 'okay.' i said 'do you want a xanax?' he said 'yes, yes, good.' at some point he got up and rubbed his stomach and looked at it then me and said 'i'm hungry.' he said 'i have to make sure everything is in order before bed, everything has to be [something, i forget, felt like i understood...preparation for bed...when you don't really want to do something, you have to like…adjust everything so it's perfect].' i said 'okay. okay. make a food.' he went to the kitchen and i looked at pictures on my computer. he brought in a bowl of grapes. a little later he brought in a bowl of fried rice

- watched 'the straight story,' laying on each other. held computer on my lap

- he said 'i'm getting sleepy' and i said 'do you care if i still watch it' and he said 'no.' plugged in earphones and watched a few minutes.

7:04PM: no longer feel weird/nervous about the shit i wrote that he read, think it's fine. feel okay about writing this much too, i think. i think.

7:10pm: walking to car. Man with yoga mat just passed, saying 'oh yeah, the super moon, super full moon, that's what that is' with 'great gatsby'-like wealth and privilege and disregard for others.'

7:45pm: parked on berry and 7th walking to Chelsea at Vietnamese restaurant on bedford.

JUNE 25, 2013

4:18AM: chelsea rules the hardest of any dog, if you fuck with chelsea ever i will cut you

i keep smoking the goddamned evciggaret backwards and WHEN THE FUCK THIS MATTRESS GONNA GET OUT MY HOUSE

MY APARTMENT CLEAN AS HELL RIGHTH NOW YA'LLY I'M GONNA WAKE UP TOMORROW

AND BE LIKE 'WHO CLEANED MY APARTMENT'

WHOOPS

'WHOOPS' –TIMOTHY WILLIS SANDERS

LOVE 'WHOOPS'

SO ALL NIGHT CHELSEA AND ME WERE TALKING ABOUT HAVING SWAMP ASS

WHEN WE LEFT CAMEO I WAS LIKE 'IT'S WET, MY ASS IS DEFINTEY WET, CAN YOU TAKE A PIC TO SEE'

WE WERE LAUGHING REAL HARD

CHELSEA WAS LIKE 'IT'S NOT LIKE THAT, THE FLASH ISN'T ACCURATE, FLASH CHANGES EVERYTHING, IF I WERE TO JUST SEE YOU ON THE STREET YOU WOULD'NT BE ABLE TO TELL AT ALL'

I'M LAUGHING...WISH THERE WAS A DOCUMENTARY OF TONIGHT...WOULD BE WAY FUNNIER BETTER EPISODE OF 'GIRLS' BECAUSE LIKE...THE PEOPLE AREN'T...WE'RE MORE...LIKE I WOULD NEVER WANT TO HANG OUT WITH THE CHARACTERS IN 'GIRLS'

FEELING GREAT

GREAT NIGHT GREAT DAY WOW WOW MOTIVATED TO DO SHIT TOMROROW LIKE LAUNDRY AND HOT YOGA, HOT BIKRAM YOGA SOMEWHERE

I'M GOING TO USE THE TRAIN

BECAUSE

JUST

SHUT THE FUCK UP I DON'T NEED TO TELL YOU WHY

KOLIOOIORIUSEIJSISOEOIUER

LISTEN

YOU ARE IMPROVING MY LIFE, BY READING THIS

THANK YOU

SINCERELY

I THINK THIS WHEN I'M SOBER ALSO

THOUGHT THE THING I JUST SAID LIKE 20-40 TIMES TODAY

IT JUST FEELS GOOD TO KNOW I'M NOT ALL ALONE

I DON'T KNOW

YOU KNOW

YOU'RE HERE TOO

BABY

I DON'T KNOW

THANK YOU FOR DEEPLY REAL

BABY BABY BABY

ALVIE'S BREATH SMELLS LIKE A STRIPPER WHO'S BEEN TWERKING UPSIDE DOWN AT A FISH MARKET FOR LIKE 20 HOURS STRAIGHT

20 HOUR SHIFT

IT SMELLS SO GODDAMNED GOOD

LOVE YOU ALVIE

LOVE YOU SHIRLEY

LOVE YOU EVERYONE

1:00PM: woke and felt embarrassed about drunk update. realized i wanted to be awake shortly after eating 1mg xanax in misguided 'maybe i'll go to sleep again' effort.

4:50PM: have been watching 'drunk history' on youtube, texting chelsea and [omitted]. drank two 8.4oz sugar-free red bulls. ate maybe 10mg adderall xr. transferred money from savings to checking.

THINGS I'M GOING TO DO TODAY:

- 6PM yoga

- buy cat food/groceries from waldbaum's

- write about last night

- start vice article

5:10PM: sky suddenly darkened. wind is blowing curtains ominously. smells pretty.

7:31PM: walked on beach after yoga. the teacher was funny, real 'new york style.' maybe 12 people in class, mostly older ladies, one guy. got a two-week unlimited pass. hungry. it's 82 degrees and the sun setting. groceries. cat food. need to get a fan for apartment, or get air conditioner from the storage unit. hotter in here than it is outside.

9:52pm: in waldbaum's. Passed old man and smiled. Passed him again and he said 'peaceful, isn't it?' I said 'good night' like 'yes, this is a good one, I hadn't considered the possibility.' he said 'good night' like 'goodbye.'

10:04pm: have been walking leisurely and…something. Mournful tone to walking. Feel like I'm moving underwater.

10:35pm: paid, did self-checkout. Walked to between-stores area where you can see the skyline. City separated by the bay. Thought about my position on a map. Island is three blocks wide. You can see the ocean and the bay at the same time if you stand in this between-stores area.

10:42pm: crossed street to avoid interacting with smoking-by-door 'Megan fox' belle harbor steak house man.

10:55pm: remembered I forgot cat food. Gave cats treats. Poured glass of wine and said 'don't worry, I'll get it, I'll be right back.' Whatever I type sounds like I'm mocking myself. Depressed despite yoga today and Chelsea last night. Not really depressed. More guilty and calm…calmly resigning to…just…being me, the room I live in, memories, present circumstances, aging, all the people I've known, all the others. It's almost July.

11:24pm: still haven't left for cat food.

11:35pm: it's raining. They don't even like the wet food.

JUNE 26, 2013

6:11PM: going to yoga again.

JUNE 27, 2013

6:00AM: woke hungry. boiled 'no carb' pasta and heated leftover kale/ eggplant/tomato sauce i made night before last. ate 1.5mg xanax.

3:25PM: woke from dream about japanese airline. intense 'wish i was still there' dreams past few nights. keep remembering as if they actually happened. like would think 'oh yeah, that's like when the security guard started kissing me, when was that' then i'd realize it was just a dream and get sad.

ate bag of red grapes. drinking sugar-free red bull. listened to voicemail from dad. i said yesterday that i might be coming up today to get the air conditioner.

last night after yoga i sat on fire escape eating bowl of leftover kale/pasta.

watched an old man pushing a walker approach on the sidewalk to my building and eventually the ocean. he moved maybe a few inches per step, with long pauses between steps. his face was in a fixed position looking at the ground and his back was hunched. his shirt looked like it said 'oberlin.' he stopped for almost a minute by the alley. he turned his walker and started walking down the alley, where i've never seen people. got nervous he had seen me. could feel breeze on my ass as i 'dove' through window and onto bed.

read 'a fan's notes' and texted with [omitted]. listened to alcoholic faith mission and angerbird and missed zachary. right now we would be sitting at the kitchen table playing cards, maybe, after dinner.

i'm going to maryland to get the air conditioner i guess. back tomorrow.

hanging out with chelsea saturday. excited.

3:54PM: ate 27mg concerta, noopept, b-vitamin. pooped. cleaned cat box. has only been two days in a row of yoga but body already looks different, maybe just to me. arms are more toned/flat on my body and legs are...more continuous lines...a little smaller...lol...stomach is also flatter/shows ribs and hip bones a little more. i want to weigh 115-120lbs. weighed myself the other morning at [omitted]'s apartment and was 134 but had eaten a lot the night before. mostly want to weigh 115-120 because i felt healthy and like...limber...i liked not-worrying about how i looked in clothes. there was less 'tweaking.' hot yoga feels good, like i die a little in each class. after each pose you stand or lay completely still, like not even wipe your sweat. it feels good to know i can make myself stand still while my heartrate is freaking out and i want to breathe hard and drink water and wipe sweat. feel 'stronger.' during 'savasana' (laying down) poses between the floor poses (floor part starts maybe 60 minutes into the class) i have zero thoughts, i think. i just pick a dot to look at on the ceiling. i don't even need to blink because the air is so wet and hot and thick. it's like i'm in an eyeball. zero thoughts. feels so good. getting to have zero thoughts while your body feels attached to you…it feels 'loving' or something. a loving kind of discipline that's new to me, to experience.

4:21PM: statcounter in real life would just be staring at each other. walking down a street where sometimes you're the most 'stared at' person. sometimes people would stare at you for like, hours.

5:45PM: bought bag for old mattress at hardware store. the fucking. the mattress is out of here. it's about to be out of here. sweating a lot. while walking back from hardware store was smelled enthusiastically by two small dogs attached to leashes held by a girl.

6:22PM: now it is gone. i dragged it out to a dumpster. woman seated on a fold-out chair said 'you'n puttin' that out by there.' thought she might be a 'mattress authority.' i said 'yeah i'm just dumping it…over. here. mark said i could.' she said something hard to hear and laughed. i said 'oh yeah!' i tied the ends of the yellow bag and started back to the building. smiled at her and said 'hoo.' she was smilling. we said 'have a good night' at almost the same time. what she said sounded more like 'now that's it's good evenin's.'

6:23-11:59PM: did not update.

JUNE 28, 2013

did not update.

JUNE 29, 2013

did not update.

JULY 1, 2013

10:00AM: woke, saw clock.

12:06PM: woke, saw clock.

2:[something]–5:11PM: woke. swept apartment. pooped twice. ate 54mg concerta. drank two 8.4oz sugar-free red bulls, water. texted with danny landlord. talked with dad on googletalk via not-working phone. organized screenshots chelsea sent from june 29/30. i haven't laughed as hard as i have with chelsea these past two times than any other time in recent memory, it's like constant laughing…belly laughing.

5:13PM: i've been updating/writing pretty consistently since whenever i last updated but am undecided about including the actual text for reasons i don't feel like explaining. i'll know whether i want to include the actual text or not in a few days, i think.

QUICK SUMMARY OF EVENTS FROM LAST UPDATE UNTIL NOW: i drove to maryland, arrived at mom's and talked for maybe three hours, slept, talked more with mom, drove to dad's office to get storage unit keys, got air conditioner from storage unit, went to walgreens, drove back to apartment/arrived around 11PM, mark was at the door with a hand truck and offered to install air conditioner for me, i stayed awake until maybe 7AM and smoked pot and painted nails, ate 1mg xanax, slept, woke around 3-4PM (june 29), went to two delis and a liquor store, drove to chelsea's, chelsea made vegetable curry and we drank wine and put on 'trying to look like we're not trying too hard to look good' make-up and outfits, we went to three (i think) bars in greenpoint and sent funny messages to strangers on tinder and laughed a lot, got bottle of wine 'to go' at bar called diamond, i held onto metal bars gating an outdoor seating area and screamed at people sitting outside then chelsea and me stood and smoked e-cigarettes for a while and i convinced her to walked back to the area where i screamed to stare catatonically at the people, and we did…no one seemed to notice… laughing now…damn going to save details for later…continued to walk to a bar near chelsea and screamed 'DAD' at other people in an apartment, we were yelling 'where are you dad' and 'i need you dad' and 'dad we need to talk' and things like that on the way to the last bar, some guy stopped his car to ask me about my tattoos and i yelled something like 'my dad did them, are you my dad, i miss you dad,' asked bartenders if they'd play 'drops of jupiter' by train (inside joke-type song…goddamnit will write more details later) and we sang along and were laughing and all the other bar patrons left almost immediately, something happened that i'm not sure how i want to write about yet, chelsea made a box of pasta in the morning and we ate it and laughed a lot, chelsea's ex-boyfriend came over, i dropped chelsea off at a bar called commodore, drove back home, read 'frowns need friends too' and liked it a lot/remember thinking 'i can see some people reading some parts and having those parts wash over/confuse them but i think i understand what he means and if so then shit…creative…good way to say that,' watched episode of 'the office' where they go to chillis for the dundies and got goosebumps at the end, set alarm for 9:46PM, woke around 11PM, texted chelsea, ate 2mg xanax, watched two more episodes of 'the office.'

6:54PM: danny landlord texted again. can smell my sweatiness. yoga starts 8PM. might make it back in time. going to dress in yoga clothes and get the hell out.

7:18pm: made eye contract and smiled with young man wearing earphones repeating 'nigga I ain't worried bout nothin' on street. In car now.

7:22pm: texted 'on the way see ya soon,' started driving, a Judd apatow-like period of comic timing passed, Danny texted 'Ok' and phone buzzed/vibrated twice like it was saying 'o' then 'k.'

7:48pm: parked on 88th st.

7:51pm: standing on corner of 86th and 5th, texting with Danny. Told him where I was. He said 'ok' then 'I came there now.' I said 'great, I'm on the corner by citibank.'

8:16pm: Danny wanted to get a drink with me. I said 'I'm going to yoga, next time.' he said 'next time' and walked beside me. We said 'how's it going' twice. He veered off to peek into a bar and said 'we get a drink now, come.' I said 'no I really have to go, I told myself I'd go.' I understood maybe 30% of what he was saying as we walked to my car. He asked what kind of engine it had. I said 'regular, I think.' he said 'v-four? V-six?' I waited a moment and said 'v-four.' He nodded and said something about gas. There was a time when we were standing by my car and he was saying something about carrying things in a van…there was a better alternative to the van, it seemed. I nodded and tried to exude 'I understand that there is a better alternative to the van.'

9:43pm: sitting in car after yoga sweating ass off Jesus foggy window heart is still going Jesus.

10:44pm: texted with Chelsea and [omitted] while sitting in parked car. Had tentative but unlikely plans to hang out with [omitted] tonight and he confirmed unlikelihood. Graphic uncensored depiction of not feeling disappointed but still feeling interested. Graphic. Unruly. Out of control supportive calm feelings. Driving to Chelsea's now to shower and drink beer. Spontaneous ass hangout. 'Like what normal people do,' I thought.

JULY 2, 2013

5:42am: driving back from Chelsea's. She let me borrow her glasses, they are helpful. Laughed typing that. She also let me borrow a shirt and bra and underwear and her ex-boyfriend's christmas-themed 'house shorts' to wear instead of soggy yoga clothes. We sat at her dining room table and talked about the other night and...a lot...talked the whole time, from I guess around 11pm to now. Went to buy e-cigarettes and more beer and walk her dog around 1am. She made pasta with mushrooms and green peppers and I bought garlic hummus and pita chips. So happy Chelsea is in my life again. I've thought about her so much since 2010 or 2011 or whenever we 'stopped' being in each other's lives. She's been like, a beacon...like...'hold on, it's bad now but maybe you'll see Chelsea again someday.' People are always asking 'what's your favorite [anything]' and I never know the answer but Chelsea is my favorite person. I'm not saying that to alienate anyone. Every time I sit down to write about Chelsea I immediately want to say something like 'if you fuck with Chelsea in any way, I will seek you out and punish you.' Dog for life. At 4:15am I made a new 'note' in my phone that says 'nan madol.' it's an island she showed me. There are no people on the island. It's all ruins, ruined buildings. Wikipedia says it was used for 'mortuary activities.' one of us said 'what's a mortuary activity.' Chelsea said something about 'weekend at Bernie's' and wanting her corpse to be taken to nan madol where people can party with it. Chelsea said I could sleep over but I knew if didn't wake in my bed I would want to shirk liveblog/other obligations and prolong having fun. On cross bay blvd now. I should've stayed over and prolonged fun. I do 'shit of life' to-do list things thinking 'once this is out of the way, I'll be happier.'

6:29am: parked. Walking to apartment. Ate 2mg Xanax a few minutes ago. Listened to noemotion on drive back. Girl just opened door to stairs I'm now climbing. She looked professional and normal and smiled at me and said good morning. Unsure if she saw me for long enough to understand silliness of my outfit/accessories in contrast to her outfit/accessories.

6:36am: fed cats, cleaned box, peed. Stood at sink and thought about twitter. Seems like everyone is trapped in some building. Like. Trapped. How do I say this. People say interesting things about boredom but don't say the boring things they're actually doing, like 'fed cats, cleaned box, peed.' Should I be a flight attendant.

7:33am: typing on phone feels less serious. Xanax is working. Getting sleepy. Also hungry again. Gonna eat on these fuxking pita chips and hummus and wake with a hummus container on the floor.

7:34AM-11:59PM: did not update.

JULY 3, 2013

did not update.

12:05AM: last night i talked into computer camera for six hours 28 minutes and i've been transcribing the video close to non-stop since maybe 5AM. this feels sick. i like feeling focused on doing it but…interacting with the content…of it…in this way…i feel like i'm in hell, this is hell. getting to hell has something to do with the duration of…gradual sinking in of it…like hell sinks into you over time without you noticing, part of what makes it hell is knowing you let it happen. at first talking/transcription idea felt like an exciting ending or advancement to liveblog and then it was all i was doing and now it's now. sometime this morning i was thinking things like 'this is all i want to say, for anything, i don't have to say anything ever again, now everyone will know' and 'here is a new kind of novel where you can watch a video of every moment a word appeared in the author's head, you can know more about how it happened, text and video at the same time, maybe people can study it and find out where thoughts come from or something about time-travel.' previous sentence seems dark. like, very dark sensation comes with re-reading anything from the perspective of knowing what i now know about…i'm afraid to type 'myself,' i was trying to find another way to type it for like four minutes. it's going to help me to type this, after i type this i can think at least one person will have read it and imagined it like they were me imagining it and i don't know why that's comforting: i feel like every few seconds i'm waking for the first time in a jail cell and a cop approaches me and says 'last night you were involved in a car accident. you are the only survivor. you were driving and you were drunk. your parents and everyone you could've loved more were the passengers. your punishment is to live for 5000 years' and it's the same cop every time. waking every few seconds for the first time but it's the same thing every time. are other people…could other people do what i've been doing today and feel good? if this made people feel good they'd just do it naturally. think it takes me longer to realize when something feels good or bad. like i can do something that feels bad for a long time and not know it feels bad until way after most people 'get it.' also applies to good things. i don't fully know how good something felt until the next day or later. this is embarrassing. embarrassing horrific display of a person. i'm talking about what i did today and liveblog and me. horrific permanent display of 'look at me showing myself to you' and 'can you get me out of here.' think this is a good time to stop.

5:49AM: i'm cracking myself up still. partying with gmail drafts. relocate your party to gmail drafts: cuts costs (on something, probably!), password-protected (it's not a party if anyone else but you is invited!), reliability (great way to familiarize yourself with looking at your gmail draft screen!)

have been typing this in a draft to no one:

what if someone said this like a rap saying, it was a rap thing:

where are you right now

HEEEEELLLLLLLLLLLLLPPPPPPPPPPP

dumplings (code name for puffy part of nipple)

dumplins (code name for the smaller dots on dumplings)

gumplin turkey (code name for nipple head on a dumpling)

that's a really big bear! (that's a really big bear!) that's a really big bear! (that's a really big bear!) (would be a call-and-response with those whistles that...shit. i don't know what they're called. when i picture the sort of man-shaped giant things made of windbreaker material that shrink and grow and flap around in the wind—they're usually outside of like, mattress discounters, or like, brazilian parties—these whistles i associate with those things are in the background)

comcast bundle saves you more

800-588-2300: empire

sheeps (code name for semen)

i like some water / i like some meat / my cat's feet get loud when i sleep / oh no sheeps sheeps sheeps sheeps sheeps / oh no sheeps sheeps sheeps sheeps

frodo (just something people call out sometimes)

bumpy fish (code name for...i want to say 'bumpy fish.' 'bumpy fish' is a code name for bumpy fish. and maybe that's all you need to know)

(not a thing people would say but what if a whole rap crew repped jerry stiller extremely hard, like. to the point that jerry stiller gets restraining orders against them. they make a song called 'i'm sorry jerry' on album titled 'what jerry likes')

6:33AM: laying on bed with earphones in to block out air conditioner and cat noises. crumbs in the bed. sheet is bundled...how do i describe the thing i don't like about sheets...hm. it got to be this way from the motion of my body over time. it is fully untucked from mattress. it is 'free-floating,' kind of, between fitted sheet and comforter. usually when you buy a sheet it's folded and packaged in such a way that you can easily handle it during the trip from the sheet store to your house. then you unfold the sheet and shake it out and make it big…you give it a 'wingspan.' you spread out the sheet wingspan and tuck the bottom corners/edge under the mattress so it doesn't move around much while you're asleep. you do the tuck thing, i think—i do the tuck thing—to prevent my current sheet situation (free-floating bundle not spread to 'wingspan'-capacity). you want the sheet to be as flat as possible. 'flatness: it's a sheet thing.'

was almost 100% certain today's 12:05AM update would be my last update ever, but look at ol' grandpappy sheets.

i like people who know about 'sheetz.'

i don't like that the thing on top of me is called a 'comforter.' is a down comforter a 'DTC'…like 'DTF'…down to fuck…down to comfort…'DTC' looks like when people have monogrammed shirts where the middle initial space is actually filled by their last name initial (sounds crazy but it's true, my dad has those shirts), and normally their intials spell out 'CUM' or 'DOG' or 'VAN' but now that they have this new kind of reorganized monogrammed shirt their initials look like 'CMU' or 'DGO' or 'VNA.' why does my dad buy those shirts though.

JULY 5, 2013

5:50PM: [omitted] made .gif of me at beach

JULY 6, 2013

did not update.

JULY 7, 2013

12:00AM-11:00PM: did not update.

11:03PM: dinner at bar corvo: i said something about feeling good when i'm improving with a person, he agreed, i said 'i like to make lists,' he said 'i noticed' and laughed, i said the thing about tao and me working together for like four hours and setting a timer kind of, he said something re 'i don't want to do what you and anyone else did,' i said 'i also kissed tao and other people and i kiss you and i like kissing you so...' in playful voice. he got a pasta goat cheese dish and i got amish roasted chicken and didn't eat it all and he ate some of mine. he said his weight at some point. i said 'that's why i started yoga a few weeks, i thought i was gaining a few pounds and wanted to look good,' he said something under breath/interrupting like 'i didn't notice,' i said 'i notice more.' he said something around this point like 'i've been in relationships where i just forget and both people gain weight,' i said 'me too, i don't want to do that,' and food or drinks were placed in front of us. he expressed worry about being indulgent with me with drugs/alcohol/food/not sleeping/sleeping a lot but that those things were fun.

something about ice cream...weight...mentioning weight on the way to the italian place.

smoking cigarette

sex: starts on couch, ends in here

remember laying on bed recently and him saying 'your character [in 'taipei'] mentions weight.'

JULY 8, 2013

12:03AM: [omitted] naked opposite me in bed. i am wearing his shorts and blue t-shirt with holes. talked maybe 10-15mins. at 12:30 i am eating ambien and he is eating benedryl. at 12:50 if hard to sleep we look at internet. he said 'don't write this down.' i said 'okay.' i said 'i like to wear headphones when i work on things.' he said 'okay.' offered me a pillow and i said 'yeah yeah.'

12:26AM: he asked where i got 'moose.' i started calling him 'moose' in text messages. stretched and said 'huh? moose. i don't know, i just thought 'moose.'' he motioned for e-cigarette. i said 'it tastes different now, see? more electric. you'll see.' he grabbed my toe and laughed. i said 'you just… suckle on that one. that one is yours.' he made a 'suckle face.' i said 'just the tip.' he said 'the tip is the most intense part.' i said 'just the tip, just to see how it feels.' he said something about the tip. i said 'just the tip, for a minute.' he grabbed my toe again. we understand the joke.

12:33AM: wonder if he knows i'm typing this. going to focus on poem i've been solicited to write, for 'parlor.'

12:43AM: i didn't focus on poem.

12:11pm: moved car to underhill and sterling or prospect. another amben

3:38pm: hit snooze a few times. ate 30mg adderall. Woke last night to eat small amounts of ambien and Xanax. Bought and ate pint of red velvet cake ice cream, kombucha, sugar-free red bull sometime after moving car. He told me to sleep as long as I want but 'not too late.'

6:15pm: Pooped. Made [omitted]'s bed. Dad called but my phone is still broken and [omitted] doesn't have internet. Put pencils under crying paper towel monster I drew with a caption that said 'this is the last one…i promise…' brushed teeth. Refined paper towel drawing. Added more objects to pencils in its stomach.

Phone was dead by the time I reached area where I thought car was. Drank remaining half of kombucha and threw away. Found car on underhill by prospect ave. Sat in car with a.c. on to charge phone. Thoroughly cleaned car using 'say yes! To cucumbers' face towels. Cleaned tote bag so no more sand can damage electronics. Think my phone has suffered sand/beach damage. 'kid a' by radiohead played twice. [omitted] found it last night in binder of CDs from 2003-2005. The cleaning job is obscene. Clean ass honda.

Ordered large green juice from juice place. The guy said 'lemon?' I said 'yeah, le-mon' like Gucci mane. An infomercial was playing. A fatherly yet-likely-childless man in his mid-forties explained 'food isn't supposed to taste good, if it tastes good it's probably bad for you' while holding a brown square.

An older man with a washcloth under a bucket hat and a larger towel over his shoulder said something to people near me. He asked me about 'beating the heat' and said something like 'oh you got an energy drink, I got mine earlier.' I said 'you're smart, you have towels.' he seemed confused. I said 'under your hat, you got a washcloth, good idea.' he said 'oh yeah! Heat come out your head.' I said 'I know, that's where it comes out first, my head is like, ahhhh' and patted my head, grinning. He paused in a…the pause seemed 'grave' or uncomfortable. He said 'yeah, well.' he said 'you could do it too.' I said 'what, a towel on my head?' he said 'yeah! Why not.' I said 'yeah. Yeah I guess, yeah why not. Yeah like, a sweatband. A sweatband' and motioned where the sweatband would go around my head. 'sporty,' I said. He said 'there you go.' he was kind of following behind me the whole time and turned to the left, behind me, holding keys. He said 'alright m'am, you have a beautiful eve'nin.' I said 'you too' and waved meekly, knowing he couldn't see.

Passed a little boy on a bike passing man on a long custom-looking low rider bike. The kid said 'you need a bigger bike!' the low-rider man said 'me?' the kid passed. I said 'I like it. Low-rider. You got a low-rider.' he laughed like 'heh-heeee-hee-heh-haaaa.'

8:23PM: at library now. emailed with matthew donahoo and sarah. started working on poem for 'parlor.'

8:24-11:59PM: did not update.

did not update.

JULY 15, 2013

4:55PM: at brooklyn public library. i've been feeling like liveblog is overtaking my life in a negative way and is a source of anxiety and counter-productivity. mostly i feel a self-imposed sense of obligation to update and because of that i think i'm losing interest. what i just typed reminds me of a dynamic i've experienced in failing romantic relationships. i don't want to say 'i'm stopping forever' or 'i'm going to continue doing this forever,' i don't know what i want right now. will update august 1, 2013.

AUGUST 1, 2013

this is my third try at doing this 'cause i keep on...ending up rambling. today's august first, i said i'd—i would update the liveblog today, i don't feel like writing, it's six fifty-two a.m. i got...uh, i'm in...new york. i was in...my... in maryland, at my mom's. for some days. um. um. tonight—really briefly, what i've been doing—um. my friend jordan is visiting either tonight or the next...day...and he's allergic to cats, so most of tonight since i've gotten home i've been cleaning the apartment. um. i've be—i've been—[points to bottle] this isn't really coconut water. it's just water. [picks up windex]. i've been using this to kill—i left a lemon on my windowsill, a-nd...it was full of fruit flies when i got back. so, um. i don't recommend this way...of killing... bugs? because i think...this is...poison? um, because it kills them. but i-it, it is good, you demobilize them. um...and i think eventually like, even if you don't...smash them after you de-mobilize, they like. slowly kinda lose their...faculties, or something. they go on their own. i've been getting a lot tonight, i probably killed like twenty...or something, tonight. i can't believe there's so many, i feel like they're breeding. um. but i—where? where? where are they breeding? um. i'm pretty good at getting them with my hands.

i went...to maryland...'cause the guy i was seeing, who—i don't [nose laugh]—the 'omitted' person? um, that ended. i don't wanna get in...to... it, 'cause. i don't. wanna. give him the. satisfaction [laugh] of getting talked about, anymore, by me. it ended pretty bad. um. and. so i was hanging out with mom—i didn't do any of the things, in maryland, that i said i was gonna do, um. which were to, like. something with my phone. um. and print out, uh. applications for schools. [exhale].

so cleaning the apartment: that's what i've been doing...uh. [pause]. last night. [pause]. you can't tell how clean it is, 'cause i tried to show in anoth— that's the laundry, that i have there. right now it's a temporary...comforter, temporary, uh—my old one—'cause...the cats...peed...while i was gone.... so i u-uh, a lot—i shampooed—i was shampooing and blow-drying the... mattress, a lot. all the cat pee's out. i just don't wanna. um. i just wanna sleep with a mattress pad on it tonight. no sheets. um.

so i guess i'll show you—four minutes, is that kinda long?—[pause]. show you some stuff that's different.

[picks up picture] um, th-this? th-this. this? um. i...this is called 'fucked tuna.' there it—there he is. there's the other ones. i commissioned tao to make that, um. 'cause he made a similar one. for someone, and i thought. he gave it to me like really cheap. i really like the colors of it. and. um. just like, i like [close-up of picture] *that*, the...what's going on, with that [laughs]. um. it was really nice. of him. to do that, cheap.

um. bathroom...? is anything different in the bathroom? dyed my hair? in here? a couple weeks ago? i got a zit, it's like...the last...kinda...days... of my perio—i really, i—i just—you can't tell i-i, i just—i cleaned it. the apartment. i cleaned it really hard, tonight. um. did i say why? i forget if i said why. doesn't matter.

um. what else. let's get a variety of [nose laugh] shots. um, tha—i don't know, it's—it just looks really...clean to me. like, the surfaces. and then there's not much crap around anywhere.

um. oh—uh. [pause]. here [opens freezer]: i was disappointed to only find spinach, when i got home? 'cause i thought i had bananas, and i could make a green smoothie thing, tomorrow? guess i can't. [opens refrigerator]. here's the refrigerator situation, um. on the top shelf i have kimchi, raw, and red cabbage, raw. cat food, as usual. got some garlic. some hot sauce. um, i still have this chia mixture thing. i'm kind of afraid. to see what happens with that, and. under there—you can't tell, but i threw away the milk—i had milk—and uh, a bud clamato? thing? um...that...i got both of those with uh, whatev—'omitted,' or whatever [nose laugh]. it doesn't matter. um.

um, so i'm gonna show you this other stuff, now? really quick, about my mo—my mom and i talked a lot. i had a really good time. with mom. and i had a good talk with dad, today, too. [exhale]. mom gave me a lot of jewelry. for kind of a sad reason. kinda, uh. she thinks they're probably...she wants... me and my sister to have...some of her, stuff. before. she [whisper] dies, or something. um. so. she's into...um—i'll get into that in a second. she gave me, earrings, th-thes—she has a lot of nice jewelry. it's like, 'nice.' these are like emeralds, or something? and then, she let me pick out rings—i used to wear rings a lot. um. and, these i've always had, and i've felt a little weird about...wearing them just plain, um—this one's my grandma's engagement ring. and then, this one's my mom's...something...special. um, but i-i, i feel wei—like. a little like. it's not my 'married' finger, but it looks like i'm—i don't know. i don't know. i feel weird about wearing them. but i really like them. but i feel like it looks less weird. 'cause [laugh] i have...other rings, now. um, this one? it's a stone called like peridot, and. it's on mars, my mom said. they found it on mars. and then this one—this, is special, to me, because my mom watches the jewelry channel, a lot, it's—and, um. um.

knoxville tennessee or something—it's not home shopping network but it's like that, and. um. she ordered this. she orde—sh-she, she just bu—she likes the people on it, and. s-she has, all these like plates with like rocks and crystals and stuff on them, she. used to be into crystals, a littl—when i was little. 'cause she's like, 'they're—you should have them. they hold you onto the ground' or something and, other reasons, she has this whole thing about crystals. which i think is really cute. and she. so she gave me—she gave me this, which is like an old butter dish, they used to put butter in this. and these are all from the jewelry channel. they're all pretty...pretty! sparkly! just nice, you know—nice little...jewels—and she's like, 'just—just look at them sometimes. and think about how. pretty, they are. and, um. and feel nice.' so i'm gonna do that. it's funny to be talking about stuff like this like, 'oooh oooh, rocks! and stuff,' but. um. [pause] and like, stuff! like stuff, that she was like, 'you can't. give. anyone. any blowjobs, if you wear this,' [laugh] um, or, 'you can't have butt-sex,' [laugh] and...'you should start taking care of yourself' or, something, and. um. i-i, i don't—but i... like? doing those...things? some peop—i don't know, she was ver—uh, i. i don't—i don't know. um.

so anyway it's weird 'cause...it feels kinda cool, kinda different, to have those things. um.

i think that's about it. for what's happened tonight.

i ea—i ate, i have oxycodone, and i have xanax—i ate two milligrams of xanax, earlier, and...fifteen total oxycodone tonight, since [pause] around probably like, eight p.m. and i still. i'm having a hard time sleeping, a lot. [exhale] and...um. overall feeling...um. i was feeling pretty good, i was feeling pretty good. then the thing with, um. the person. happened. then i felt pretty bad, i've been feeling pretty bad. uh, since tha—that happened friday. today's wednesday—or thursday, now, technically—jeez almost a week. um. so. i don't know...if i'm gonna wanna update...liveblog, right now. for the next few days. 'cause i wanna be hanging out with jordan and stuff. and not thinking. and not wanna type stuff.

before...um...i g—part of my thing, part of my plan, when i stopped... doing...the liveblog thing, i was like 'i'm gonna write, uh, i'm gonna start writing articles. for vice. again. and 'i'm gon-na...apply...to s—to colleges,' and i...i sent in my fafsa. forms. for, colleges. um. but i really haven't done much of anything yet. um, and i thought i would. those were kinda things i wanted to kinda straighten out, er. or like, i'm gonna do research studies... or something. um [pause]. f-eeling in general...like i don't have anything... to say [laugh]. to...or con-trib-ute, to stuff. that was another thing with the guy. 'omitted' guy. he kinda has his shit together and i kinda don't. it seemed to not bother him but maybe it did. um, i don—i don't, actually i don't think—i don't know what it was, um. he seems more...kinda obsessed, with like...sex, than me...um....i could take, or leave...sex [laugh]. um, and he...did i say he cheated on me? i said it on twitter. he cheated on me. that's never happened to me in the, the um. [shows necklace] this is from coldwater cr-creek [laugh], um. never happened to me in the beginning, the beginni—like, the two months, 'beginning'—it's...happened at the end, when things are already bad, or i've agreed with the person, like, 'we're gonna see other people' and. and i-i, i'm pretty sure—uh, i don't know, i don't wanna get into...um...talkin'...shit—

days just keep going by, and then they turn into night, and then they turn into morning, and i'm up for all of it, and it sucks. um. and i'm...flaky... person [laugh] to hang out with, but then, so seems kind of, everyone, sorta...um, tolerated in this particular group of people that i like hanging out with sometimes? um. [pause]. i'm probably the worst, 'cause i'm not even good at emails or stuff. or, uh. or being...consistent, with stuff...or... anything. so...

i guess that's about it, um. [pause]. no matter what, it—it always feels a little better if the apartment's clean, if everything is really really super-clean, really—surfaces are all dusted and, um, laundry—it's just like...there's less cells, of. that person. here. uh [pause]. or, yeah. there's just less of it. um. this is really long. thanks for listening if you want. it's—here, this—let this...tide you...ov—i [laugh]—uh. i'm not gonna update for a few days, so...um...stupid, stupid stupid stupid st—okay, um. the end thank you for listening goodbye.

9:41AM: laid in fetal position on mattress pad. placed beanbag eyemask on forehead. realized i'm 'exhausted.' last night i asked chelsea if she wanted to get lunch today. haven't heard back yet. set alarms. covered eyes to block out light.

2:00PM: have been resetting alarms and hitting snooze. chelsea texted not long after i'd fallen asleep. ate 20mg adderall XR and experimented with sitting positions. phone rang twice. it was the numbers i don't recognize from buffalo, NY and wayne, PA. the last night i was in maryland, the wayne, PA number left a garbled 'mothman prophecies'-like voicemail. played it for mom. my room felt scary, because of its proximity to balcony window. remember pretending to 'naturally' shift posture of supine body as if already sleeping. it prompted mom to say, 'are you sleeping in here tonight?' i paused and said, 'no, maybe for a few minutes. i'll get up though, i have to leave at like, in the morning.' woke in the afternoon in her bed.

4:14PM: heard a crash. walked around opening cabinet doors to scare fruit flies. texted chelsea that i'd fallen asleep. asked if she wanted to hang out after danny landlord picks up rent around 6PM. texted jordan to see if he still wants me to send him a moneygram, if he knows his e.t.a.

mentally replaying details of the last night i saw [omitted]. mom said something like 'people can't go from despairing to feeling okay, getting angry is a way to jumpstart yourself out of wallowing.' he doesn't know that i know he lied. i figured it out. there wasn't time for him to shower between sex with the other girl and seeing me. he said they used a condom. i would've tasted or smelled the condom when i gave him the blowjob. succumbed to urge to text him something mean, followed by the shitty princess 'i'd like it if you didn't respond.'

i think shirley was the one who peed. four times on the mattress and comforter. hell ride.

5:16PM: loaded comforter and sheets in washing machine and walked upstairs. searched room for quarters. i need more quarters. wrote rent check for danny landlord, waved it to dry ink, folded in my back pocket.

walked to pickles & pies to get quarters, then buy groceries from waldbaum's for jordan's visit. thought 'he hasn't responded, the moneygram place closes at 9PM so i can't send him gas money after that, 9PM is coming up, he would've said if he needed money by now. maybe.'

chelsea texted that she was taking her ex-boyfriend out for a birthday dinner tonight, and that i should bring jordan to his birthday party tomorrow. withdrew $60 from ATM outside pickles & pies. $28 left in checking account. paid for e-cigarette refills with cash and asked for two dollars in quarters. cashier didn't seem to count change, handed me a lot of quarters. walked outside. it was raining lightly.

standing as if stopped on the sidewalk ahead, a figure in a black cape stared at the vacant storefront next to pickles & pies. walked closer and excitedly recognized olivia, my old friend and boss, under the cape. it wasn't her. the caped woman stared at the storefront like she had travelled hours and made great sacrifices to arrive at this spot, where she had been told a person would be waiting to give her further instructions, and the person still hadn't shown up. i thought 'maybe ask her if she needs help,' but continued walking. a few seconds later i heard a woman's voice behind me. the voice sounded upset. i thought 'it's the caped woman, she called the person who never showed up.' the further i walked, the louder and faster the voice sounded. heard 'your lies' and 'another two-thousand years of this shit.'

turned and locked eyes with the caped woman, who looked like she'd been directing boundless ancient anger at my head since i'd passed. she was following me. people on the street (man in basketball shorts, old person with a walker, two or three others i think) watched us with blank expressions. i focused my eyes on the distance ahead as i walked, and thought 'do people think i robbed her, she looks wealthy, do they think we're related, who looks crazier: me or her? she's yelling and wearing a cape: slightly crazier, maybe. should i say something to her, what would i say, 'two-thousand years of this' is funny.' the woman continued following me and yelling. turned in her direction and avoided eye contact as i smiled exagerratedly and 'twinkle-waved' my fingers in a way that, considering the rage i had somehow triggered in her, could've been interpreted as 'a tauntingly mischevious sign of the devil.' turned right into a post office parking lot, which is a short-cut to waldbaum's. thought 'this is where it would make sense for someone to stop following me, right? is she going to waldbaum's too? does she know about the short-cut? no one would see her beat me up, no one is ever in the post office parking lot.' pictured her beating me to the ground by a mail truck, then taking my wallet. i'd have to let the comforter air-dry. felt a little afraid. decided to keep my face forward until i got to waldbaum's. her yelling was fast but coherent. it sounded like she had been waiting to say these things for a long time. heard 'i know where you're from, you're from [something] township, you and your [something], you just think [something], that's all you do,' then after a few seconds, 'asshole.' that was the last thing. 'asshole.' it was quiet but i didn't want to turn around. two men passed. didn't think they made it in time for the 'asshole' but i still looked at them as if they saw, like, gave them a 'visual shrug' (combination of 'beats me' + 'get a load of this'). crossed the waldbaum's parking lot, anticipating the woman's face eerily silent and close behind me. didn't turn until i was close to the entrance. she was gone.

walked around waldbaum's putting kale, five oranges, bananas, cherries, two avocados, a cucumber, watermelon, lemon, lime, 12 cat food cans, 12-pack 8.4oz sugar-free red bulls, flour tortillas, sabra 'classic' hummus, and toilet paper into a plastic cage-like carton with handles. i wanted to go to waldbaum's so that 1) i could finally get a waldbaum's savings card, 2) i could use the self-checkout to buy condoms, and 3) if the self-checkouts weren't working, whoever rang me up might not notice condoms among the variety of things i was buying. i've only bought condoms once, i think, with my boyfriend at the time. the person overseeing the self-checkout saw us and said 'have a good night.' we laughed and joked about the 'good night' we were about to have as we exited the store.

walked to the first aid aisle to look for condoms. two women were in the aisle. thought 'they're onto me.' couldn't get a good look, but it didn't seem like there would be condoms. thought 'shit, that's right, condoms are an 'asking people' thing. they make the worst things 'asking people' things. [pictured myself asking pickles & pies employee for condoms]. all the employees know me, they can't know i want to buy condoms, then they'd know i have sex, i don't want to add that to our dynamic. they'd be less friendly and flirt more aggressively. maybe i'll just ask jordan to pull out. no, scary, you can still get pregnant, scary, out of birth control, scary.'

remembered duane reade. thought 'there won't be enough time to go to duane reade before danny landlord's 6-7PM window to pick up rent. he hasn't texted back either. nobody's texting me back. it's okay. karma. make jordan buy condoms maybe. maybe he has condoms. condoms suck. what if jordan shows up in a few hours without ever texting me back, did something happen, did he get in trouble, maybe his phone died, the comfortor will be in the dryer when he shows up, what if it still smells like cat pee, shit. no, it's okay.'

waited in a makeshift line at the customer service area where i thought waldbaum's savings cards were distributed. two older men were ahead of me in line. the first man was returning a large cylindrical container of pretzel sticks. he looked unhappy. after his transaction he looked at me and said 'alright, who's next' and i kind of smiled and bumped my head, wanting to convey some combination of 'that's nice please don't say more' and 'i am not next in line.' the next man wanted cigarettes. he said 'marlboro gold pack.' the customer service girl said 'lights?' he said 'no, gold pack.' she scanned the cigarettes, looked at him, and said 'reds?' the man said 'no, gold pack, marlboro gold pack.' she pointed and said 'these?' he said 'yeah.' she took the new pack, raised her eyebrows, and said 'these are called 'lights.'' the man didn't react in a way other than paying her. as he was paying i was preparing how to ask her for a waldbaum's card in a way that would equalize the man's ignorance about how they were called 'lights.' i would be the 'less-bad' customer, the spokeswoman for all 'lesser-bad' customers. thought 'this might not be where you apply for waldbaum's cards, but don't ask. she doesn't want to answer that. she's already answered that like 20 times today. approach the counter with certainty. maybe roll your eyes at the guy. create a sense of comaraderie. no, too complicated, she might not get it. plus it would seem disingenuous. plus it'd make her think more about you than 'this person wants a waldbaum's card.'' smiled and made eye contact with her. she looked like she was 'on her last straw.' thought 'no matter what i say, she's going to complain about this to her co-workers—more about the man than me—no, she doesn't talk to her co-workers. she doesn't talk to anyone. her rage is private. the unstoppable, silent, complaint-free, next level rage of a waldbaum's employee on her last straw.' i said 'h-iii. i was wondering if i could get a waldbaum's card?' she said 'here fill this out' in a monotone and gave me a clipboard. under the clip were a stack of empty application forms. i took the clipboard to the counter and penciled my information in the top form's blank spaces. felt a presence behind me. turned and saw a short smiling man, watching. stepped aside and gestured to him like 'go ahead, i'm not in line.' he said 'good morning' to the rage employee. thought "good morning.' it's almost 6PM. i like him.' didn't listen to their conversation but sensed the rage employee's waves of chronic frustration. stopped writing today's date below the words 'TO BE MARKED BY STORE PERSONNEL ONLY.' handed clipboard to the rage employee. thought 'there is no way she cares that you wrote the date where you weren't supposed to, no chit chat required, she is good, she wants as little from you as possible.' she poked three cards from a perforated piece of plastic, handed them to me, said 'there you go.' i said 'thank you.'

too many people stood in the self-checkout lines. i stood in regular line behind a woman 'carrying on' with the cashier scanning her items, many of which were chicken cutlets. the woman bewilderedly said something like 'the other waldbaum's.' i thought 'how is this related to chicken.' the cashier said things about 'the other waldbaum's.' the woman left looking overwhelmed. i put a pack of orange trident gum on the black rubber con-veyer belt. a man stood behind me in line.

cashier wordlessly greeted me and i said 'hi.' she said 'do you have a wald-baum's card?' and before i could say something stupid like 'why yes, in fact i've just gotten one—finally!—after all these months,' she saw it in my hand and scanned it. i bagged groceries as they slid down the conveyer of rolling metal cylinders. the last conveyer belt they'd ever know. first the rubber one, now this rolling one, then no more, forever, for as long as ye both shall live. swiped my card in the paying device, pressed 'credit,' resumed bagging. the cashier said 'fifty-one oh-six.' i stopped bagging. a glimmer of pessimistic hesitance peeked through the cashier's mostly blank expression. i said 'oh, it didn't run as credit?' the cashier said 'yeah but it only took twenny-eight dollars.' remembered seeing '$28' on the ATM screen. the man behind me wasn't buying more than he could hold. more people stood behind him. i said 'oh no, that's…can i—i'll just go the ATM.' the cashier said 'the ATM over there?' i said 'yeah, yeah, i'm sorry, this is embarrassing, i'll be right back,' looking alternately at her, the man behind me, and the faceless line behind him.

the machine worked the second time i swiped. withdrew $60 from sav-ings account. jogged back to the cashier and the people in line, most of whom seemed to be looking at me. thought 'shit, i could've said to cancel my order and waited until it was less busy.' handed cashier $60 and said 'i'm so sorry, this is so embarrassing.' my remaining groceries had been bagged. the cashier did things to the register. i said 'thank you, sorry again, embarrassing.' she handed me my change and either said something or looked at me like 'i understand, it's okay, sometimes money is hard.' as i exited the store i felt like a fraud, undeserving of the cashier's sympathy. embarrassed about overstating my embarrassment and guilty that i didn't feel more guilty about inconveniencing the line. wanted to apologize. not to the cashier, but something.

5:53PM: tried to evenly distribute weight of four bags on arms. purse and red bull 12-pack threw off balance. worried about not having enough money to fund jordan's trip. think he said it would be $400. still no texts from him, or danny landlord. damp air. dull hidden corners of bags kept bumping my legs, causing their handles to twirl and cut off circulation in small areas of my arm before unwinding and bumping another bag or me again. felt shitty, carrying the bags, anticipating washed comforter still smelling like cat pee, maybe more pee on the mattress, buying condoms, how and why i've depleted my savings account, how danny doesn't know the checks i'm giving him today will bounce, how i'll need ask dad for money, how no one has responded to my texts except the person i'd said 'i'd rather you not respond' to, how saying 'i'd rather you not respond' is pretty transparently self-protective and controlling and probably reads more like 'i'd rather not sound like a pathetic fragile loser who not only would rather you respond, would rather your response be extreme enough to erase the last time i saw you and the thing that's been happening in my stomach when i think about how it felt to push against the weight behind your skin or to watch your face change when you didn't know i was looking or the smell of your pillows or the drive to your apartment or that baseball game we never went to.'

saw a small gathering of people inside apartment building. walked in. danny landlord and mark were talking. everyone was smiling. i said 'hi, hi hi,' smiling really big. danny said 'i was waiting here for you!' i swatted him and said 'you didn't text me' in faux-scolding voice. everyone was just…smiling, laughing. snickered typing that. what was everyone so happy about. put grocery bags on the floor so i could get the rent check from my pocket. mark said 'you sure are popular today, huh megan?' mark has a way of… whatever he says kind of trails off at the end, or else he just doesn't move his mouth much when he talks, ventriloquist-style. i like it. danny said 'hey' again, like 'hey, here we are, finally!' i gave him a 'side hug' with one of my arms and said 'it's nice to see you. i'm sorry to keep you waiting, were you here long?' handed him the check. he said 'no, not long, don't worry' and his face matched. i put the bags back on my arms. danny said 'so hey, so how thinks working out?' i said 'oh good, great, the apartment's great,' looking at the bags. he said 'you got job?' continued bag focus and said 'yup, yeah, i'm going back to school.' danny made a noise with vague implications. i said 'yup. yeah, it'll be, yup. so, this spring. but i'm up for it!' mark and the other person were still talking. mark had been holding the elevator for mc the whole time. i looked at danny and gestured to the elevator and said 'well, gotta go put this away, i'll see you next time!' he said 'okay bye' and waved. i said 'bye mark, thanks.' mark said 'see ya megan.' i said 'bye' to no one in particular as the elevator door closed. pressed '2.' felt like i had just run a marathon.

put away groceries and killed fruit flies with windex. they like the sink. thought about putting away the laundry. left dad a long voicemail about the yelling caped woman and the cat pee and fruit flies. pressed a button and it was deleted. left another voicemail that was mostly 'i'm afraid the check is going to bounce again, i'm out of money, can you do rent?'

9:12PM: think the guy at the deli just gave me an amount of quarters that seemed like was 'enough' when i asked for eight. he's the guy who…it's hard to interact with him every time. there is always some misunderstanding.

which is all to say: i'm drying laundry right now and i am one quarter short. i don't think i ever want anything as much as i want one quarter when i'm one quarter short of a dryer load. i looked everywhere spare change could be in my apartment, i think. i had five quarters and the cashier at wegman's gave me a quarter too. there is no way that guy gave me eight quarters. going to the chinese food place to exchange two dimes and a nickel for a quarter.

9:32pm: I lied about the quarters. Have been lying about weird things lately. I had two dollars, I was planning on getting change for two dollars. Walking back from Chinese place. I only got change for one dollar. I didn't get change for the other one because felt guilty about lying and didn't consider that I could just delete 'two dimes one nickel' and replace it with 'one dollar' or 'two dollars.' I don't know what's going on. Stared at a package containing fist-sized mounds of dough wrapped in something that said 'almond cookie' as woman gave me four quarters. I brought the dimes and nickel in case I changed my mind and wanted to be a 'good Samaritan who does what she says she's going to do.'

9:39pm: the lady gave me a Chinese quarter I think. It did not work in dryer.

9:40-11:59PM: answered backlog of ask.fm questions. here i go writing things like 'backlog of questions' again. at some point dad called.

AUGUST 2, 2013

12:56AM: sam cooke texted that he and mira and gian were hanging out. planning to respond 'i'll come as soon as i finish answering this question or in 30 minutes.'

2:56AM: texted 'are you guys still partying.' still haven't heard from jordan.

3:38AM: made a fist around orange 30mg adderall while looking indirectly at an area of my bed to 'give eyes a resting place while brain decides.' thought 'maybe don't eat it. remember sam's (chelsea's ex-boyfriend) party tomorrow. you will be tired if you don't sleep tonight. [memory of reading chelsea's texts this afternoon and how the light looked]' and put adderall in mouth.

my apparent interest in being social and very likely tendency to flake out of social events is becoming predictable in a self-parodying kind of way. starting to get bored with this.

TO-DO THIS WEEK (AS IN FRIDAY AUGUST 2 – AUGUST 9):

•   do two social things you said you wanted to/would do

this will be too easy because i'm committed to going to sam's party tomorrow

two things, i want to do two things

two things...one week...

i want to make 'two things, one week' like 'two girls, one cup.' time-lapse footage of me over the course of one week, trying to motivate myself to do two social things i said i wanted to do, ending up sitting in different places in my apartment. the video is somehow more revolting than 'two girls, one cup.' or no, it could just be the same video. yeah it's just the same video. 'two things, one week' = 'two girls, one cup.' i'm aware of trying to sound like i did in the beginning of the liveblog. now i'm going to stop doing that.

THING I'VE NOTICED WHICH SEEMS TO BE A RESULT OF LIVEBLOG:

•   when someone asks me about the specifics of an event, i do something like 'mentally accessing library where my memories are stored,' which is...i'm just scanning a mental index of liveblog. the memory of typing something often comes before the memory of the event i typed.

4:07AM: this is the longest i've sat at this table. the table is helping with… something, i feel. nonspecific helper table.

4:10AM: wonder if anyone actually is a paid member of those websites that don't have real downloads of albums/movies but always want you to be a member. do those websites employ people? how does that work?

4:11AM: on the walk home from the grocery store tonight i thought, 'people i follow on twitter…people don't seem as interested in things… something used to feel more active, i used to feel aligned with something… where do you go to find interesting things…motherboard, htmlgiant, gawker, io9, wired…no one cares anymore, even those places…wait was htmlgiant one of those places…yyy-es…i think'

6:13AM: ate 800mg choline and 800mg aniracetam instead of more adderall. feel more alert than a few minutes ago. peed and turned on bathtub faucet for alvie.

6:34AM: have been looking for a way to re-download 'eskimo snow' by why? was surprised to see the name 'ben rosamond' in the comments section of a website that showed up on google. left this comment:

> 'ben rosamond
>
> damn
>
> ben rosamond from australia or new zealand maybe?
>
> it's 6:24AM and i've been trying to find somewhere to re-download this album periodically for the past few hours…have a new computer…this is megan boyle…gonna give up and buy again i think
>
> 2009 ben rosamond blast from the past
>
> hi, if you ever see this'

6:53AM: left this comment:

> 'damn didn't know you contributed to wefuckinglovemusic
>
> i can't remember how i know about wefuckinglovemusic or for how long i've known about it
>
> (i'm talking to ben)
>
> hi-ho, megan boyle still here

pictured continuously commenting on this thread in this manner until it becomes like 600k words long

would happen really slowly, like over the course of 40 years

bookmarking this page, maybe will do this

probably not

shit now it seems unavoidable

as i was writing that it seemed 'highly avoidable'

okay signing off for now,

megan

hi again, ben (do you remember me? can't remember if we've ever talked or emailed, i just know who you are, maybe from the BSG short story contest thing…maybe we were just commenting on things around the same time…)

okay signing off for now,

megan'

8:45AM: left these comments:

'ben, i remembered i've read a gchat between you and zachary german that involved me in a funny way for a few lines

haven't said anything about this album yet: i like this album a lot

2009 jesus…yeah that makes sense, that's when i first heard it

probably my second favorite why? album…'alopecia' first favorite…

this one has five of my favorite songs by them on it though ('this blackest purse,' 'into the shadows of my embrace,' 'against me,' 'these hands,' 'january twenty something')

i know the titles from looking at my phone, i just have those five songs from this album on my phone, i can't remember other songs (which is why i wanted to download)

the full album was on my old computer

afraid to sync my phone with this computer due to…i don't know

if i sync my phone with this computer my old stuff will be gone forever considering the spectrum of things that could happen to a person, 'losing my phone's old stuff' would not be that bad

actually it'd probably be good

have been hearing vacuum noises coming from somewhere in my building since maybe a little before i wrote my first comment

it's 6:46AM on a friday, why is anyone vacuuming right now

never understood how 'vacuum' is one of the most commonly misspelled words

in my head it sounds like 'vac-que-oom,' the 'que' and 'oo' transition easily/sensibly into 'u' and 'u'

the noise seems to be coming from above and to the left...opposite side of the hall as me...opposite/above...

they didn't have e-cigarettes in 2009

the person who invented e-cigarettes had yet to make their millions

i feel like my entire...everything i've done since 2009 has disappointed ryan manning

i associate you (ben) with ryan manning

same period of my life

i like ryan manning

he sent me an email recently that said 'what happened to you,' confirming my suspicions of disappointing him

he could've just been being friendly though

tried to think 'he's probably just being friendly' as i wrote response

feel like he will probably read this and...i don't know

i do seem pretty bad now

not too well-off

used to think something life-altering would happen to me when i turned [every age i'm about to turn]

currently sort of hoping no one reads this

or someone reads it and thinks 'who is this crazy person, she does not seem too well-off'

'well-off' feels strange to type, what does it mean exactly

sounds like it could've originated in australia or new zealand, like you, ben

it would be funny if you're not the ben rosamond who i think you are

is this…am i harrassing? 100% good intentions, just want to take a break from the other stuff i was writing

guessing 'well-off' means 'someone has left something, they are now 'off' that thing. since they've been 'off' mostly good things have been happening to them'

mostly good things have not been happening to me since i've left the things i've left

that sounds dramatic

think i'm just getting older

pretty sure my younger self knew getting older meant there would be less choices for me to have made

feels different to be living in a world of less choices/already-made choices

wonder what you are doing right now ben rosamond

'rosamond' sounds like 'a mound of roses'

pretty thirsty at the moment

sitting at a table

it says this is too long to post as one comment but i wrote it as one big thing

guess i'll split it up

okay signing off for now,

megan

it usually says 'tomhanks' when i comment on things but i don't feel like signing into the email i registered my old blog with that email is beckdoestherobot@aol.com

i used an aol.com email address for a long time

the first email on my yahoo account is from january 8, 2007

it's a picture of a 'pizza-billed platypus' from my best friend at the time

the second email is a myspace account confirmation from august 21, 2007

then there aren't emails until october 2007

how is that possible

in october 2007 i signed up for nanowrimo

then there are mostly nanowrimo emails

at 11:58PM january 5, 2008 i registered with dominos.com

at 12:03AM january 6, 2008 i ordered this pizza: 1 Large(14") Hand Tossed Pizza, Whole: Cheese, Extra Sauce, Green Peppers, Onions, Bacon, Jalapeno Peppers, Left: Extra Large Pepperoni, Extra Mushrooms, Tomatoes, Extra Diced Tomatoes, Right: Italian Sausage $10.99

that was one hell of a day

one hell of a five minutes

the pizza was delivered to my best friend at the time's dorm

we would order as many toppings as possible

i was a 'strictly cheese' woman before we were close

sometimes on saturdays my dad would bring home pizza and half of it would be topped with mushrooms and onions

for a brief period i thought mushrooms and onions were the most popular pizza topping

pepperoni was like, 'something that happens on people's birthdays, might be due to dietary restrictions'

it says this is too long again

okay signing off for now,

megan

people are talking in the hallway now

vacuum is still going

i used to say 'i'm sorry' when i meant 'i see that something i've done has upset you and i wish you weren't upset,' now i say it when i mean 'i also dislike what i did and don't want to do it anymore'

i was exaggerating about 'not too well-off,' was trying to be funny

feel mostly okay about things that've happened to me

not sure what i'm referring to anymore

forgot what this website was called for a moment, thought 'weheartour-blogspot'

think i'm imagining the vacuum thing, going to try turning off the faucet

turned it off, i was right

my cat likes to drink water from the bathtub faucet so i turn it on sometimes

i can't believe…all this time…not a vacuum…damn

learning new things every day

was getting pretty irritated at that vacuum person

vacuumer…vacuumaisier…vacuumassuese…

do you know the jay-z where he says 'i'm not a businessman, i'm a business, man'

for a while i tried to make something like that work but with 'vacuum and' and 'acumen' (not necessarily in that order)

i don't remember the song other than that line

it's possible i just know it from people quoting it

should i stop feeding my cats 'fancy feast'

they act like they like it but i'm pretty sure it's poisonous

my best friend's ex-boyfriend calls her dog 'the imp of the perverse'

the dog is a tiny chihuahua that vibrates almost constantly

its face is extremely expressive

i think 'the imp of the perverse' originated from an idea that the dog is the by-product of all the misery in the world, like technically its parents are all the pain and suffering in the world, that's why it is the way it is

it's funny if you see the dog

maybe

this might be strictly 'seeing the dog'-based humor

mild background fixation on if and how i'm disappointing ryan manning

wanted to do this partially out of a desire to not disappoint him

realistically i don't think he or anyone but maybe my parents thinks about/interacts with me enough that their experiences could be disappointing compared to their expectations

no, i don't know

getting a little carried away with this comment

it's going to be 86 degrees today

at the end of the day i will have eaten or not eaten a number of oranges but right now it's anyone's game

potentially five oranges could be eaten, i have five and do not foresee wanting more

smart money is on 'one orange will be eaten today'

anyone's game though…anyone's…

at this point…

almost afraid to stop doing this, what will i do after this

okay signing off for now,

megan

9:28AM: ate 5mg oxycodone for 'actual pain relief.' seeing less fruit flies. strange abdominal cramping. morning feels bad. to my right is a 30mg adderall 'just in case.' seems like jordan will not visit today. no word on the jordan front. 'the jordan front' sounds like an early 2000's math rock band. maybe screamo band. maybe opening for thrice this wednesday at power point live. all is quiet on the jordan front. would be funny if he showed up in a few minutes. wonder what's going to happen. i haven't unpacked from maryland or folded laundry or put clean sheets/comforter on the bed yet. shirley has not tried to pee the bed since yesterday. wonder what's going to happen…!!!!

9:36AM: sleepy. can't believe i'm allowed to live like this. i'm only going to want to stop living like this if i can stop thinking things like 'can't believe i'm allowed to live like this.' it's okay to be living like this for now…there is obviously…no other way to be doing it, for now, otherwise i'd be doing that instead.

9:45AM: whoa felt insane bad for a few seconds

normally would just leave that like it is, now going to try to unpack what felt bad exactly: i was looking somewhere between water container and sugar-free red bull. remembered i hadn't updated recently-made auxiliary twitter where i tweet everything i eat/drink with anything i've ingested tonight. started thinking about how having multiple/auxiliary twitter accounts feels dark, especially considering me doing liveblog. thought about how both men i've been close with since starting liveblog have not liked that i was doing it. tried to imagine updating liveblog 'or maybe a twitter' with this and felt…just…icky/dark. remembered things i've typed today and felt icky/dark about them, and that there was a time when i felt positive about anything i'd say in here. then felt sudden overwhelming flashback-type series of thoughts like 'what was different about me in the beginning of this, if i find out what it is then maybe i can get it back, i know i wasn't happy then but at least it wasn't now but that's the same thing i feel now.' remembered walking to the chinese food place to get quarters last night

what's with me picking guys who don't like the stuff i like then feeling sad when it's over

okay boyle that's dumb, don't do that anymore

how about you seal off your…just…

your romantic interest keg is tapped

who decided that when there's no more weed something is 'cashed' and when there's no more alcohol something is 'tapped'

wait 'tapped' means the alcohol just began

tapped an ass

want to make a to-do list, would that make you feel good? let's make a to-do list:

- mail matthew donahoo package

- fax car inspection document to insurance people

- read and write blurbs for chelsea martin & heiko julien books

- party with chelsea tonight

- print applications to schools

- eat something

- put away laundry

- put other comforter in dryer (maybe you can just let it dry though, won't it just dry?)

SHIT I FORGOT TO MOVE MY CAR SHIT GODDAMNED FUCK-ING...SHIT ASS...

well no sense in doing it now

no i should do it, what if they haven't caught me yet

i have 12 unpaid parking tickets. i looked last night. can they arrest me? what can they do...

i would let a cop beat me within an inch of my life if it meant i would never have to pay for or think about having another parking ticket ever again

or i could just never pay the tickets and not get beaten up

that seems to be the way this is going (knock on wood!)

1:13PM: killed maybe ten fruit flies in kitchen with windex. moved at a slower-than-normal pace and avoided 'wiping' until the end. it's unfair that flies get to rest but most fish have to keep moving or they'll die. there is a hair in my eye. ate 800mg choline, 1g aniracetam. felt more alert and less lumbering. did i say i had a hair in my eye? it's in my eye, the hair. wouldn't have felt able to form sentences a few minutes ago. bugs don't understand that everywhere is not 'outside.' i've thought this before, that everywhere is 'outside' technically. sometimes this gives me a vertigo-like feeling.

was david foster wallace's graduation speech thing called 'this is not a fish' 'this is not water'

slideshow of things that aren't water

i don't even know if that's the real name of the speech yet

oh, 'this is water'

haha

slideshow of every kind of water…the water cycle…wasn't there something about fish in his speech

the teacher who spoke at my high school graduation talked for over 30 minutes and people in the audience had bullhorn-like noisemakers and were booing her. then people had something to talk about after the ceremony. highly polarizing speech/event…the booing…she didn't know it, but she gave the liberty high school class of 2003 and their families/friends the gift of 'materiel for brief, less-awkward exchanges with people who happen to be standing near you in crowded auditorium lobby, topic is applicable to anyone there, even strangers and people you'd probably otherwise have very little to say to.' she also gave me the gift of 'memory that, in ten years and a few months, you can use to occupy yourself with the task of making into sentences for about 20 minutes in a liveblog about your life that you will feel 51% apprehensive and 49% indifferent about updating.'

the only thing i remember about her speech was her leaning over the podium and talking about a rabbit with a carrot on a stick/rope device strapped to its head

the leaning motion looks exaggerated in my memory, her head gets bigger and she makes dictator gestures…she was a small person…'fiesty'…fluffy head…

does it sound like i'm shittaking her? i'm not. she was one of my favorite teachers. i liked it when she did the thing before everyone graduated, i liked graduating high school

'i liked graduating high school'

why is that funny to me

three-minute youtube commercial featuring hundreds of celebrities making eye contact with the camera, earnestly saying 'i liked graduating high school.' you can't fast-forward it, you have to watch

it's for the global…'global help fund'

'global help fund' charity benefit gala evening, brought to you in part by CLGHS (celebrities who liked graduating high school)

too far…too far…went too far with it…

do i sound like i'm shittalking my parents…i'm not…did that thing earlier sound shittalky…shit

there's no way to change what you think, whoever you are, if you already decided something

2:04PM: dad left a voicemail from a number that isn't stored in my phone. in the first 14 seconds he apologized three times for being half-asleep when we talked last night. didn't know he was half-asleep.

trying to learn english at this age would be very hard.

3:27PM: administered another round of windex to fruit flies in kitchen. have been mentally referring to this as 'doing the genocide.' nostalgic for summer 2011 when i did a similar ant genocide thing at dad's place. had forgotten it also involved windex. fed cats.

stuff i thought while doing the genocide:

- respond to texts at 3:30PM in honor of 2:30PM, the one-hour anniversary of when you said you'd do that.

- 'all is quiet on the jordan front'

- the thing i do with the dry food. it's like, 'the retard rotator.' pouring the dry food from the bowl they don't eat from as much into the emptier bowl. why do i have two bowls. 'retard rotator:' shaking it up. a gruff dirty man in a wifebeater who only leaves his la-z-boy once a day to do 'the retard rotator' for his cats. he calls them 'retards'…affectionately? derogatorily? he like, yells 'ey you fucking retahds' so many times a day he doesn't even know what he's saying or who he's yelling at anymore. he and his cats equally don't know what he's saying. no one notices, it's like all the other noises in the room.

- what will you have to say to people at the party, all you've been doing tonight…you're doing the retard rotator on yourself, somehow. what does that mean. it means you like thinking 'retard rotator.' it's bad to say 'retard,' maybe i should stop.

- the flies like to hide in the hobby hole [vent above the stove]. someone would say 'hobbit hole' whenever i'd say 'hobby hole,' like they thought i didn't mean to say 'hobby'…it's 'hobby hole'…i don't know…it's always 'hobby [something].' the thing that makes it funny is 'hobby.' the reasons why something would be primed with the word 'hobby'... people with hobbies don't say 'hobby baseball rec league' or 'hobby trivia night,' those are just their hobbies. the only thing i know that's 'hobby [anything]' is 'hobby horse.' seems so insane. a 'hobby horse.' i'm not even sure what it is. i think it's that plastic horse thing that's sort of floating mid-air, suspended in this wire frame, attached with springs. they were around when i was little. i always wanted one of those things. you bounced on it. pretty sure that's not what a 'hobby horse' is...'hobby horse' is like, a name for a piece of wood...maybe... one of those weird nicknames that catches on...like 'dingy'...there are better examples.

- there is always something in my eye when i'm doing the genocide. always the past two times. the past two times i've done the genocide there has always been something in my eye. and that is a fact.

- should i take a break to write this down so i don't forget...no i'll just remember whatever.

- what if there was a little gnome following me around saying things like 'time is of the essence, m'lady.' would that be good? who even said 'time is of the essence, m'lady,' why do i know that, do british people say that? no, common misconception: people think british people say 'time is of the essence, m'lady' because the hobbits spoke with british accents in 'lord of the rings.' are there any midgets/dwarves who like 'lord of the rings' and prefer to be called 'hobbits?' where are hobbits supposed to be from. 'glendora.' if i thought more about this i could remember where they're from but i don't care. a little hobbit following me around saying 'm'lady'-type things: how would that actually be different than what it is now? a lot different. no, that's what...most people would probably be like 'oh that would be so good, i want that,' but think about it: in what ways would it change anything? it would probably be annoying. it would be, like, 'something to adjust to.' i would feel sort of uncomfortable, at first. what would we say when we weren't saying stuff like 'time is of the essence, m'lady.' what if there was a sexual dynamic. one of us would mention something about it and then it'd...something would be different. we could never go back to the time when it was unmentioned. also, people on the street would definitely notice. people feel more comfortable approaching strangers when their situation is obviously 'not normal,' people think it's more okay to comment on it. i might get less done/go outside less because of this. i would adjust to the thing of someone being around me con-

608

stantly. when i'm around someone a lot i start feeling annoyed with them. or no, maybe i'm always annoyed, i'm just more likely to tell the person about it when things are slowing down and we're familiar with each other and i'm starting to feel like i can predict things about them so it's getting a little boring. the hobbit would annoy me. i'd be like 'why are you doing this to me, why are you here.' maybe that passes. i've never gotten past that. maybe something else happens after the period of annoyance. it's probably just indifference. calm supportive indifference, ideally. so i'd probably just feel the same as now. it would be sad when the indifferent period would start...like after a certain point, somewhere between 'annoyance' and 'indifference,' one of us would try to do a 'last gasp of air' thing. we'd start saying 'time is of the essence, m'lady' to each other again as a weak kind of joke with these desperate-looking faces...making eye contact but then it feels too intense so we pretend to not look away really fast...sharing a silent awareness of 'what it once was'...probably each thinking 'i bet they're not thinking about 'what it once was' like i am. if they were thinking about it too, that would mean we'd be thinking the same thing and it wouldn't feel like this'...mutually preparing to enter the phase of indifference...but still, that wouldn't be very different from now. it wouldn't be too much to handle. it would actually probably feel kind of nice. comforting.

4:25PM: got carried away with hobbit thing, i didn't think all of that while doing fly stuff. two-hour anniversary coming up.

5:30PM: mom called. cut phone call short due to wanting to prepare for party.

6:03PM: recorded a video which started out as a critique of my body from top to bottom (forget if i've mentioned, i've been making videos periodically as i've been losing weight to see progress and note what 'needs improvement' and...just...i don't know, this whole thing is embarrassing a little, to me). had been thinking 'i'll stay up all night and then i can be 'zany sleepless person' at the party, i usually like myself more and worry less/feel less self-conscious when i haven't slept. started dreading party and dreading un-responded-to texts. ate 800mg choline, 800mg aniracetam and then 20mg adderall xr. talked in the video like...in this way, i've been doing...i've been making long videos of me talking, which i almost rarely re-watch. just feels nice to think 'something 100% nonjudgmental is listening to me (even though it's not really listening, it doesn't really 'need' to be listening for me to get the effect i like from it).' ate an orange. seems very unstable, the 'making of' this video and the things i talked about, even though i can't remember most of what i said. just...the fact that a person would want to do this. gotta stop getting down on myself about stuff like this, it just makes it worse (aware of repeating myself...i think). concluded it was okay to not go to the party or respond to texts, i could tell chelsea in person or email her that i'm 'in a dark place' and not wanting to be social, feel like she would understand. still seems shitty of me. i don't know. for most of the video i'm just wearing a bra and underpants. talked about a lot. covered a lot of bullshit topics. haven't watched all the way through but i'm pretty sure i'm talking almost constantly, or like, maybe taking 30-90 second breaks. i was thinking 'you're always thinking, just transition the thinking into talking, make there be as little transition as possible from thought to language.' early-on in video i noticed that in this, and in other videos, i'll get distracted and leave a topic or story mid-topic/story to focus on the distraction, which leads to more distractions. a 'reoccuring theme' in this video was...jesus this is hard to type. hard to figure out words. i wanted to allow myself to get distracted by [whatever] and then eventually go back and finish all the things i started. think it worked, i finished all or most things. felt interested in doing this at the time, like 'this will be a documented example of the nonlinear way thoughts bounce around in my head, seems sort of like what happens in novels, things keep reoccurring, with a novel you know the author is intentionally making things reoccur but when you're just thinking/talking it feels like you're not in control of the reoccurring, but it's the same thing.' cried less in this video than the six-hour video from july 2/3 i started to transcribe. at some point shirley peed on the mattress pad and i yelled and freaked out at her, like made her smell the pee and said 'no' sternly. then, on a website, i read that cats don't under-stand negative reinforcement, they just learn to be afraid of who/whatever yelled at them. felt like the worst person. bad. actually i took longer breaks towards the end, during 'cleaning cat pee' time and 'nurturing shirley and giving her treats so she'd feel less afraid' time. removed peed-on mattress pad and replaced it with a yoga mat and sat there. shirley acted cautious and like she wanted to be left alone.

sometime during the video it became august 3.

AUGUST 3, 2013

12:00-3:[something]AM: somewhere around here in the video i stopped filtering thoughts before talking, video became me narrating inner monologue looking at the internet. dressed in clothes i was wearing before video. looked at CDs of old pictures, AIM conversations, diary-like text documents from 2004-2009. downloaded iphone app called 'anxietymint.' heated two flour tortillas on my stove and spread hummus on them and filled them with raw red cabbage. remember noting this is the first thing i've eaten, besides the orange, since the eight cashews on july 31.'

3:[something]-7:45AM: ended video accidentally, 'for the best.' ate 10mg oxycodone. my bed doesn't feel like a bed because it's technically in the kitchen area. decided to make the table and bed switch places. first i measured the bed with the long side of 'pop serial 3' (a little more than five 'pop serial 3's), then measured the space i thought it could maybe fit (a little more than four 'pop serial 3's). moved it. the leftover/hangover length seemed negligible. swept and mopped floor. this will be helpful for shirley, she will see the bed in a different place and maybe not want to pee on it. how do cats decide where to pee.

dressed in neon orange shorts, t-shirt, gray hoodie, glasses, flip flops to move car. expected to see a ticket. played 'anxietymint' game on the walk. there was no ticket.

6:30PM: woke.

6:30-11:59PM: going to type rapidfire style what i remember:

- called mom and talked for a long time

- thought about more thoroughly washing peed-on blankets and things soaking in the sink

- looked at internet

- there was a block party downstairs that [omitted] and i had talked about attending. there was also a reading on michael seidlinger's roof. the reading was rescheduled for today. i was going to read at the first, non-rescheduled (just...scheduled...haha) reading but cancelled and i think other people cancelled too and there was rain and the whole thing was cancelled. felt guilty about not responding to michael's facebook message but like, more of a latent guilt, because it didn't actually feel like days had gone by where i hadn't answered it. i just knew they had.

- read mira's and willis' tweets about the reading

- enjoyed looking at apartment from the perspective of 'new bed place-ment' a lot…like…just sat, looking at stuff

- colin knocked on the door to say he was moving out tomorrow. he asked if i wanted to hang out downstairs with 'a bunch of us.' i said i wanted to order food and didn't feel social. this was around 10PM, i think. he offered to come by again in a half an hour to see how i felt then. i said 'i mean, i'll probably be eating.' he said 'right'—not in a hostile/resentful way, just like 'i understand.'

- ordered seaweed salad, salmon/avocado/cucumber roll, shrimp tem-pura roll, spicy scallop roll from o'sake (which, according to google maps, is 0.3 miles from me but i got delivery to avoid interacting with people at the block party)

- food came fast

- texted with willis and made plans to hang out at the beach on mon-day (aug 5). felt solid about plans, like 'yes, there is enough planning, neither of us will flake, i want to go to the beach more before summer ends and hang out with willis, this is a great opportunity to do both of those things'

- colin knocked on my door again as i was unpacking. he had a friend. he's told me about the friend, reggie. they met during hurricane sandy. reggie said he was hiding in his closet reading bible verses during the storm. that's how colin found him. colin told me where he was moving and i said 'oh i go the library near there' and he and reggie looked surprised in a way that surprised me. colin said we should hang out if/ when i'm around there and i believed him. he is a good person i think. reggie too. once we were talking i liked talking. stood by my door and talked with them for a few minutes, feeling some kind of…it was similar to the vestigial guilt about michael's facebook message i didn't respond to. like 'i was never there, so how can i feel regret,' but still. i don't know. felt sad that colin was leaving, even though i think our last long-ish minimally awkward conversation was in may, at his 'welcome to the building dinner' with the ex-MTA wheelchair man and the fancy food student from the fourth floor. colin gave me a newspaper where he was quoted, saying something about rockaway park. he said 'i want to give you this' and showed me the page where the article was before handing it to me. i looked at it. he said he and reggie were going to a bar soon. i said i wanted to stay in, my food had just arrived. he said it would only be for like, an hour. i said 'i'm really feeling kind of [noise like 'eeuurruh' with 'icky face' and 'vague hand movement'].' he seemed to understand. it felt good to just say i wasn't feeling like going out. sat in bed and realized it's normal to say 'i don't want to go out tonight, i don't feel social.' that is a perfectly normal thing to say.

- think i ate xanax and watched TV. yes. i did that. i watched the news.

AUGUST 4, 2013

12-3:[something]AM: ate more xanax. watched 'stardust memories.' paused it near the end so i could look up youtube reviews of ben & jerry's ice cream so i could decide what flavor i wanted before i left apartment, to minimize 'standing around deciding' time at deli. i don't think i decided what i wanted, i just left after maybe 30 minutes. bought and ate a pint of 'chubby hubby.' pretzels were crunchier than i remembered, they are doing something new to the pretzels to keep them crunchy. it had freezer-burn but i didn't care.

3:[something]AM-7:14PM: remember waking a few times to walk around or pee then almost immediately return to sleep.

7:15-11:59PM: going to type what i remember doing rapidfire style:

- woke and wanted to take a walk on beach but 'seemed too hard,' then started to become dark.

- took pictures of my room with the sun hitting the crystals hanging in my window, which make rainbows on the wall. they used to hang in our old house when i was little. mom let me have them. sent pictures to mom to see what she thought about new furniture arrangement.

- called mom after sending pictures. mom didn't like the furniture rearrangement at first but by the end of the phone call she was saying, 'it really does make more sense for a bed to not be in the kitchen.' remember describing to her, with childish urgency, how it felt like there were three main rooms: the 'walk-in' room (contains records/books/record player), the bedroom (contains bed, mirror, closet, bathroom), the kitchen (contains kitchen table and kitchen). we talked for a little over than an hour i think. i asked her to tell the stories behind all the jewelry she gave me. seemed like she'd get sidetracked, talking about their value, which depressed me a little. i was reminded that she wanted me to have them in case i need money after she dies, and that she'd think i'd ever even want to sell it—that some part of her may have thought it could come to that, for me, someday. remember saying 'i don't want to hear about that, i'm never selling any of this, it's too sentimental, i just want to know the stories behind them' or similar things whenever she'd start talking about how much the jewelry could be worth. she knows a lot about gemstones. she used to write a newsletter about gemstones. she would go to jewelry auctions, to 'cover' them, for a newsletter. mom did the sweetest things with her life. she had her own newsletter, they paid her to travel around the world and write about it. other things. she worked in the ticker tape room. all while having my sister...jesus. mom is a very strong person, i think. wish i could've been her friend for all of her life.

- this is hard, honestly seems like the same day, all the days since august 1 or 2 or before that.

- turned on TV and watched 'locked up' and 'the office' (new furniture arrangement makes TV feel more inviting, i've been watching the TV every night i think).

- remember this feeling of 'it's okay, it's sunday night' that didn't make any sense.

- periodically wondered if jordan was still coming, i think, or if i had hurt chelsea's feelings by not responding to her text and not showing up at the party before she left america again.

- made and drank kale/watermelon smoothie.

- ate around 100mg morphine slowly, first 60 then 20 then 20, not feeling much.

- watched the 'seinfeld' where george and jerry pretend the limo at the airport is for them and george's name is 'o'brian,' then it turns out o'brian is a nazi.

- continued feeling minimal morphine effects but wanted to feel something else. tweeted that my tolerance for all drugs i currently have other than weed seems too high for anything to be 'worth it,' asked if i should buy beer or smoke weed. 'weed' won. smoked in kitchen.

- remember thinking it'd be funny if someone did a wailing heavy metal guitar solo of 'the happy birthday song,' like really wailing, wailing hard...winning pulitzer prize for wailing.

- walking from the kitchen to the bed, i felt a strong wave of paranoia/ anxiety. stopped walking and grabbed counter. face felt hot. tried to discern what i was anxious about, which in itself caused anxiety. seemed like i was mostly anxious about 'what is happening to my body.' vision started blacking out in patches that looked sparkly at first, then became dark, then i couldn't see the room at all, it looked like my eyes were closed. thought 'this is it, you did it, morphine and weed and nootropics, this is what finally does you in.' probably fully blacked out mid-walk back to the bed. i had walked from the bed to the kitchen to get my phone 'just in case' i needed to call 911 (didn't factor in phone is broken or that i probably wouldn't know if i should call until after i woke, which might not happen) before laying down. found bed by slowly walking a distance and 'pawing'/lightly kicking the air. felt completely blind as i walked. laid down. thought 'do not go to sleep, you will not wake from this sleep.' unsure how i stayed awake. vision slowly returned and i felt sober.

- first thing i wanted to do when i became more awake was have sex/look at porn. looked for a while but it kept seeming gross or...i don't know. something about seeing the bodies while touching my body. couldn't do it, but not in a 'damn i missed out on something good' way. it more like, 'no onions on mine, thanks.'

- smoked a little more and watched netflix movie, 'the bachelorette.' it was horrible but comforting, like 'here is your outlet to the world, this is what the rest of the world does, maybe.' sometimes thought what i didn't like about kirsten dunst and her friends were because i was stoned. smoked while watching too, i think, due to not thinking i was stoned enough to think the movie was funny or interesting. still did not seem funny or interesting. got obsessed with picturing the 'making of' documentary of the movie, how it felt like a dollar store or something. walking around in a dollar store. all the cast members going to their trailers quietly and it's never sunny enough to look sunny but it's not cloudy either, it always looks like 3PM on a sunday. just. walking in and out of trailers. dollar store. seemed extremely bleak to think about this as i watched the movie, like how porn was unappealing when i thought about my body, but the movie was still comforting to watch and almost...like...idly concerned with its own bleakness...in a way that seemed uplifting...like a forgotten documentary about some man four people knew...laughing right now, at ellipsisesessess.

- ate four tortillas heated on the stove with hummus spread on all of them: two plain hummus, one hummus + raw red cabbage, one hummus + avocado. ate entire avocado with lime and salt and most of a 'personal-sized' watermelon i didn't use in smoothie.

- don't remember falling asleep (around 3AM according to web history, i think)

- woke around 12PM. remembered this was 'willis beach day,' i had told him to come around 2 or 3PM. didn't feel like doing anything. felt overwhelmed with mental and physical sensation of depression, body/thoughts both heavy and hard to move around. thought 'no more weed ever again. it's always like this.' the lights were off in my apartment. discovered all the power was off.

- texted mark about the power being out.

- discovered, via twitter, that tao had eaten a large dose of mushrooms last night, deleted his twitter, facebook, tumblr accounts, and threw out his macbook due to being 'posessed by aliens.' thought 'sounds about right.'

- willis texted that it wouldn't be a good day for the beach and i agreed. made tentative plans to hang out with his roommate at their new apartment tonight. said i wanted to 'get stuff done' before that.

- mark texted he'd come see about the power around 4-4:30PM.

- willis texted that i should come over because they were making a chicken thing.

- read large chunk near the end of 'the remainder' by tom mccarthy. recommend this book. i feel like the guy in it, kind of. he's awarded 8.5 million pounds from this car accident settlement, doesn't want anything with the money, then at a party he's bored and goes to the bathroom and sees a piece of plaster on the wall and all of a sudden has this sudden unplaceable eidetic memory/image of himself in an apartment he spends his money physically reconstructing. he just rec- reates his memory of this thing he's not sure why he remembers... highly recommended.

- the lights came on around 5PM. texted mark 'woohoo! you did it, thank you!'

- mark came up to check my electricity. someone was doing repairs in the building earlier and remembered to turn everyone's electricity back on but mine and another person's. mark did things to the stove. then the stove worked. we talked about cats mostly, i think. when he was by the stove, i saw that there was no way he could not see the things in the sink, so i said 'oh that stuff in the sink is my pre-laundry soak pile' and told him shirley peed. his cats pee too. he said they recently got a kitten. i said i wanted it if he didn't. meant it at the time. felt easy to talk with mark, he's a real...he's got a real 'gift of the gab.' a lot of... shit. i don't pay enough attention to remember. they're kind of like wisecracks. have thought for a while that mark is 'onto me' but now... seems okay. not sure what he'd be 'onto,' other than shitty embarrassing life i seem to be 'hiding from' more than 'living,' how would he be 'onto' that. he left.

- mark brought up his daughter and the kitten. the kitten was named 'gary.' i asked why that was his name. he said 'i don't know, we left it at [relative]'s house and when we picked it up it was 'gary.'' i said 'that's good.' his daughter said something negative about spongebob. gary walked around the apartment cautiously, which seemed to sur- prise mark. he said 'where's your other kitty?' i said 'oh alvie? you've never seen him i don't think, he hides from people.' mark always seems surprised when cats act like cats. it's funny. i gave gary treats. gary is a maine coone. he is six months old. mark and [forget daughter's name, will just call her 'mark jr.'] and gary partied with shirley and me for probably 20 minutes. alvie hid. at some point i felt comfortable 'pull- ing out the big guns' and said, 'you know ernest hemingway? this was his favorite cat, maine coone cats. he called cats 'love sponges.' does gary have a fifth toe? alvie does.' mark jr. held gary and the three of us looked for his toe. mark jr. said 'i can't t-ee-ll...' i felt the back of his foot in the toe spot and said 'yup, he's got it. fifth toe.' mark said he went to ernest hemingway's house and saw the cats. i said 'oh cool,' and tried to remember where in illinois the house i walked by was, that i thought was ernest hemingway's. he said 'yup, key west. saw some of the cats.' he was kneeling by the door. i said 'florida. nice.' he said something about seeing the house while 'on tour.' i said 'you were on tour?' he said 'yeah, yeah, you can take 'em, we toured the house.' i said 'oh, i thought you meant on tour like, you know, 'on tour'' and made 'rock n roll face/hand gesture.' mark said 'well yeah, i mean it was a tour of the house.'

- forget how i fell asleep or if/what i used to help me do that.

AUGUST 6, 2013

3:30PM: woke.

7:52pm: loaded laundry and coins into dryer. Have been thinking 'you live on the beach, walk on the beach, do stuff there, soon it'll be winter.' Got e-cigarette and phone from room and walked along the shore, at first trying to not get wet, then standing in place calf-height in the water, letting it flush in and out with me in the middle. Not many people on the beach. A few men were fishing, they had put a pole in the ground. Two or three were sometimes lifted off the ground by parasail-style kites. An oyster shell bumped my foot in the water. Tried to hold onto it with my toes. The tide pushed something that looked like a turtle back and forth. It was upside-down the next time I saw it. Definitely a turtle. The waves washed it on the sand for a moment and it walked confusedly. I walked away. A fishermen said 'is that a turtle? You should've picked it up.' I said 'oh I didn't know if it was supposed to be there, you know, like 'sea turtles?'' He said 'we got two of them already.' I thought something negative about turtle fishing. Waded into the water with him. He said 'that's a fresh water turtle, fresh water. There's probably a lot more, we keep finding them.' He picked it up and 'presented' it to me. Its head and limbs were retracted into its shell. He said 'look, there it is.' I put my face close to it and pointed almost close enough to be touching it and said 'aw look it, turtle.' The man's friend said 'we should give it to those ladies, they took the other two, giving 'em to a pet shop or something.' The men yelled 'hey!' and 'hey ladies!' to a small group of women. I pointed and yelled 'turtle!' Felt like the three of us were 'in this' together. Turtle alert squad. Look out, pet stores. The women were almost where the sand meets the road. They stopped walking and turned around. The first man said 'whaddya wanna name it, you wanna name it?' He was smiling incredulously. Felt like I had just been 'tagged.' I looked at the retracted turtle head and said 'uh. Kenny.' The man laughed and said 'Kenny?' He looked at me like I had just said a maybe inappropriate inside joke, a 'too soon to make this joke' joke. I said 'yeah, Kenny, see ya later Kenny.' The man laughed and jogged to the women, now walking towards the water. I looked at the other man by the fishing pole stuck in the ground. I said 'you don't think it's a sea turtle though, do you?' He said 'nah, no way. There's probably a lot more where that one came from.' I said 'why is it there?' He said 'I don't know,' looking in the distance, 'they just keep showing up.' My body was turning away. Could feel myself looking for an 'out' to the conversation. I said 'well, good luck, hope you find more,' unsure if more turtles were what he wanted to find.

Walked to apartment building. Approached one of the parasailing men. The kite lifted him maybe three feet off the ground. Felt 'on a roll' from the turtle interaction and said 'that looks like fun.' He said 'it is, you pull this lever here, see? When you want to release, see?' I extended my arm noncommittally, feeling 'expected to' do this. He said 'wanna try?' I said 'yeah' and grazed the main handle-stick, which he pulled away fast. He said 'oh no no, no, no. Very dangerous. You need harness [patted his harness]. A man, he try? It lift him up over traffic and drop him, eh?' I said 'oh no.' He said 'no, no. No, you need lessons. I'm professional, see. You need harness like me. You learn how to do it, see? You don't just do it.' I said 'can I take lessons from you?' He said something about a service called 'guide tours' or 'kite tours' and pointed to the other two men with parasail kites. He said something about Brooklyn. I asked if I could take lessons from him. He said 'from me? No, Brooklyn? There is a female, female teacher in Brooklyn.' I said 'and it's called 'guide tours?'' He said 'yeah, just look up, you know? The guy over there, he knows. Ask him, over there, he knows.' I pointed and said 'I should ask him?' He said 'yeah he teach. But I give discounts, I give cheaper deals to you' and smiled. I smiled and didn't know what to say. He said 'ask that guy over there, he knows.' I said 'okay, I'll just ask him, thanks' and I walked to the other two men. Both wore harnesess, one held a parasail kite that sometimes lifted him a few feet off the ground. Couldn't discern which man I was supposed to ask. Stood and watched them from at distance close enough to make me feel like I was stalking them deviously. Stalking with ill-intentions, perpetrator, 'getting off on this' somehow. It was like if they were sitting behind me at a café and I knew they could see me not-so-subtley playing their YouTube channels full-screen at full volume, from a chair where I sometimes turned to grin 'non-threateningly' at them. The man in red didn't react. The parasail took the other man away. I said 'excuse me, do you give lessons for that?' The man in red looked at me then looked away as he mumbled something like 'no, no lessons, this is just my friend.' I said 'oh, he told me to ask you' and pointed vaguely in the direction I came. The man in red said something I didn't understand, looking left and right, mostly at the ground. I said 'sorry, I'm sorry,' as I walked towards the road. I don't know where I was looking when I said that but it wasn't at him.

8:17pm: in waldbaum's now, buying laundry detergent. It's going to take more than one wash to get this smell out of towels and comforter. The Shirley pee smell is gone but bedclothes have been soaking in the sink for three days and there is this moldy smell.

8:24pm: smelled two versions of a Downy product you can add to your washing machine to make things smell nice. My current stinky things 'need it.' Have been trying to decide between the two scents via imagining how they'll smell combined with the detergent I usually buy, how the smell of 'just washed' things combines with my sweat or cats or dust or time or whatever and makes 'new smell.' Seems like either Downy product will create an odd smell. Odd but not bad. Better than moldy. Withdrew $40 from ATM so I can get change for a $20/more quarters for laundry.

8:28pm: in line. Cashier said 'who's the cookie monster in the house' to man in front of me. He said 'nah, no one, just three for six bucks.' She looked at him funny. She said 'who's gonna eat all that?' He said 'it'll get eaten.' He has a black cloth urban outfitters bag. He is definitely over 50 years old.

8:33pm: asked for eight quarters with my change. She did it without questioning. Surprised. She bagged my things. I said 'thank you thank you' in an accidendally breathy, distracted voice and she said 'you're welcome you're welcome' in the same voice. Felt nice. I passed Candy at the self-checkout station as I left. The day I stopped liveblogging something happened with Candy that I thought 'shit wish I could've written about this.' I'm walking back to my building now. Going to save typing the 'Candy thing' for inside. I heard Candy's voice last night from the aisle across from me and felt endeared to him. Candy feels like my 'buddy.' He's the only person here who…I can't explain it, I don't think. Candy walking to his van as I was sitting in my car typing about him the night I avoided the party. Candy's van driving away playing traditional-sounding Mexican music. Candy scanning my things at the self-checkout.

8:39pm: passed an old woman in sunglasses and 'nice clothes' holding a plastic bag. She was just standing there. Motionless. She burped.

8:49pm: removed things from dryer and reloaded in washer. Used downy 'no stink' product. Walked to third floor by accident, typing previous sentences.

10:49pm: Shirley peed the bed again. Walking to deli to get baking soda, vinegar, hydrogen peroxide (doubt they will have this) and paper towels.

10:56pm: glanced at 'cleaning stuff' aisle. Walking back to waldbaum's. Third time today I am a waldbaum's-bound clown.

11:12pm: walking back to apartment. Bought hydrogen peroxide, baking soda, white vinegar, 'oxy-clean' product. Candy and the girl who gave me quarters (she's also the girl who once stopped me from paying in the self-checkout so she could use the 'store bonus card' since I didn't have one, then scanned my stuff on the fourth of July when I was with [omitted],

I like her, she's quiet and doesn't move her face much, has an affect of 'peaceful resignation to a life she'd rather not live but has long given up on changing') were standing by the self-checkout area. They were saying things about other cashiers going home. Hope this shit rids Shirley and Alvie and me of the pee smell. Rides us out of the pee smell. One-way ticket out of the pee days. I think she peed because I was gone for something like four days. There was still food in the 'extra food' dishes I left but…I don't know. Annie used to pee everywhere too. Why are cats always peeing on my stuff. It would be so nice if everyone just peed where we're supposed to pee.

11:45PM: at apartment now. here is what happened with candy the night i stopped liveblogging:

i was the only customer, i think. it was almost midnight. they had closed down the self-checkouts. candy was scanning my things. in the produce section, i've noticed, before they mist the vegetables, they play a variety of audio samples. sometimes it's 'thunder,' sometimes a few seconds of 'singing in the rain,' sometimes 'rainforest.' the rainforest sound happened. candy said 'what is that, is that a bear? i always think it's a bear.' i said 'i don't know, do they make noise?' he said 'yeah they make noise! that's the noise they make!' i said 'oh no.' he said 'i'm just afraid there's a bear back there, you know, it's gonna run out here and tear it all up! tear the place up, run out and eat me!' i was smiling really big. couldn't tell if he was serious. i said 'you think it could eat you?' he looked shocked. he said 'yeah! have you seen those things? they're huge, huge paws.' he demonstrated the paw-size with his hands. i said 'oh whoa, whoa.' he said 'i'm just worried it's gonna come running out, when i hear that, you know?' i said 'yeah. yeah, you never know.' he said 'they're huge, those things! grizz-el-y bears.' it was quiet for a few moments while i paid. i picked up my bag and said 'well, i think you're in luck, i don't think they like the beach.' he smiled and we made eye contact and then i knew he had been joking. candy. love candy.

AUGUST 7, 2013

12:54AM: used old towel to blot vinegar/peroxide/bronner's/baking soda 'peeodorizer' on bed. now i just have to wait for it to dry. staying up all night, i think, to work on this and maybe (let's not kid ourselves: 'definitely not,' but cute idea, boyle, nice try with that 'maybe,') other things.

taped rainbow lights under kitchen counter. now kitchen look like a 'hot spot' in one of those 'not for tourists' guides. zagat-rated for sure. zagat kitchen. the zagat kitchen: simply unforgettable, rainbow lights will blow you away.

still probably have a suspended license, 12 unpaid parking tickets, count-less un-responded-to emails and texts, a more countable number of late packages to mail, no direction in life, no motivation to write things other than this, nothing to offer as a friend or romantic partner, mattress full of cat pee. two parents who seem to like me a lot, though. also i have rainbow lights, let us not forget the rainbow lights, an integral facet of this up and coming hot spot.

remember sometime around when i moved in, after i got the bed, saying something to mom like 'it feels good to have a bed now. it really makes a difference: stepping out of a bed. i feel like i live in an apartment of a person who has their shit together. someone who has their shit together would live in a place that looks like this.'

2:54AM: at 8PM i'm answering questions from the @altcitizen twitter account re my interview they posted today (that i did in april sometime) and anything else people want to ask. someone on twitter asked me what my room looked like. just took pictures of apartment, going to make a little flickr album…i don't know, i'm aware that by doing this i'm 'wasting time' but i still want to do it and what 'time' am i 'wasting' anyway. my life is a giant accumulation of time-wasting events. the wasting cancels itself out, since it would be the same thing if it wasn't 'wasted,' like how it's the same thing if you followed everyone on twitter or no one. ate 30mg adderall before juliet's email but only feel mild effects. thought my two days off would've done something.

3:04AM: eating 60mg vyvanse to 'test' tolerance, to see if it's just adder-all-related. going to want more adderall before the twitter question-answer-ing. i can't find brandon gorrell's response to my 'considering soliciting brandon scott gorrell for advice about getting out of depression' thing. it was on the muumuu house tumblr, which is now deleted, due to tao's 'alien possession while on mushrooms' the other night. remember reading and thinking 'i think i understand, wish he used specific examples from his life.'

i tried re-reading this entire thing a few days ago and only got about four days in. originally i just typed everything…like even stuff like 'i want to be a female cat sam pink forgot to spay and i back into a q-tip he put vaseline on.' i stopped doing that. think i got in a mentality of…i don't know. this started feeling less private. it used to feel like a game i was playing with myself, that other people were watching, but that didn't matter. when the [omitted] person wanted to be omitted…something happened around there. or before then, maybe. i'm going to go back to including everything. okay. here we go. everything from this point on will be 'everything' again, until i forget and restart. NO FORGETTING. too many things to remind myself of, though, it feels like, regarding…everything…things i type in here and other duties. that's just a way to rationalize not including everything. why would i want to do that. okay stop doing that. ate the vyvanse, here we go.

3:22AM: keep typing 'PM' instead of 'AM.' not new. dreading looking out this window and seeing morning light. not new. they say it'll be cloudy and rainy tomorrow. not new. why can't i just pause it so time keeps moving but for me the sky always looks like night.

listening to 'the peter criss jazz' by don caballero on repeat. masha seems to have mostly vanished from the internet. in an email to juliet i said 'wish the internet was just another state, like everyone on the internet at the same time would automatically be in the same physical location.' imagine the party. it'd be a party for like, a week. then we'd all be like 'oh, okay.' maybe. maybe. new people would keep joining the party.

POINT OF ANNOYANCE:

i said something to [omitted] about why i wanted to keep doing the live-blog, like 'yeah but i'm doing it longer than anyone else has.' he said something like 'i don't know about that' and showed me the tumblr of this girl he dated. it was just a tumblr. someone's tumblr. i don't know. she just… her thing wasn't 'consistently updating/writing the events and thoughts of as many minutes and hours of the day as possible,' it was like, 'reblogging stuff i like, sometimes posting pictures or writing accounts of things that happened, but not attempting to say everything.' remember him saying something like she had prefaced her blog with a similar thing as me but… it was just a sentence…it was like, 'i'm going to use this blog to blog' or something. i'm bitter about this because…i didn't like the way he'd talk about girls he dated…i think…didn't like being compared to this girl…feel like i'm doing something more than just…i don't know…it's stupid, this is stupid…didn't like that he saw me as doing the same thing as her…er, was more surprised that he thought i was doing the same thing than…because i know i'm not…i don't know…seems obviously very…bothered by him not acknowledging the…i don't know. he was never that supportive of me doing this or interested in my writing in general and i don't know why that bugged me but it did. STOP WRITING ABOUT HIM NOW. i feel the vyvanse i think. keep getting whiffs of the formerly peed-on comfortor that didn't dry all the way which is now sort of moldy-smelling, draped over the chairs next to me. annoyed by this. annoyed.eres.reoersjs.

3:46AM: can hear footsteps of the person who lives above me. they are usually awake when i am. hours most people are sleeping. the person is me, i think…like…me ten years from now…some kind of time warp is going on…

when zachery w. and i ate mushrooms in may, we had an ongoing conceit about 'what if all the apartments in my building were actually just my apartment at different times.' it got complicated. wish i had written this part down. the building across from me was…something about empathy… it was where people incapable of empathy lived or something. it was a factory maybe. shit. he made that part up, i wasn't completely following that part. seemed interesting though.

6:06AM: LIVEBLOG: FOR ME, NOT YOU, REMEMBER. not really though. this would be different if i didn't think people were reading. i think. would it? no, i don't know.

6:13AM: peed. left just enough toilet paper on the roll for 'one more time.' one last go-around on the wheel of glory. 'can't be mad at me for leaving just this much, because there is Just Enough left for next time.' defend-able in a court of law. restraining order. eventually getting a restraining order against the insane future me who thinks i had left less than what was required to pat away those final little piddle drips. you really don't need to use a lot of toilet paper. this is a lesson in conservation. leaving Just Enough is benefiting all. unicef. peace corps. alissa milano's sincere face looking into the camera and imploring, 'one rotation of toilet paper. what if that's all it took?' then it's replaced by a slow-moving slideshow of impoverished chil-dren's faces with big sad eyes holding cardboard tubes, some of which still have little white strips of paper attached to the adhesive, then a voiceover, 'one rotation of toilet paper every time. that's less than twenty squares a day. what if someone told you that's all it took? that's all it would take to save a child in need.'

in all fairness, to 'future insane me who thinks i had left less than required,' i really did leave the bare minimum. in fact, would put money on me starting a new roll the next time. especially if it's a you-know-what (a poop!!!!!!). no question…i mean, no question at all if it's a you-know-what…

it's funny when people call anything a 'you-know-what.'

want to start calling normal things 'you-know-whats.' like 'don't worry mom, i'll be sure to lock the you-know-what on my way out.'

9:44AM: the sky is cloudy, just like they said it would be.

10:44AM: ate 20mg adderall XR. down to five 20mg XR, three 30mg IR, one 60mg vyvanse. going to want more soon. peed. i peed one other time since mentioning the toilet paper—i used the Just Enough i had left (mostly out of 'i told you so') and started a new roll. the pee i just peed was wiped with the paper of a crisp new roll.

if a cat pees or poops in the box i've been scooping it into the toilet right away. i'm here, so why not…you know…the least i can do. the least i can do is helpful. every time.

every time you guess something correctly you should get a point. the points can go towards anything you want. i think. i haven't figured it out yet, how the points will work. it's just a way to pick up bonus points. catch-all. like when your 'health points' are down and you have cancer, if you can correctly guess if the nurse will pause before she pronounces your name or guess the color of the shirt of the next person who walks by or guess what vegetable they'll bring with dinner…i don't know. you should get something. even if it's just a little sign by your head that says how many points you have, and like, an index of your 'best wins.' you can guess more points for guessing harder things. like a few days ago…shit. i forget this completely. no i don't, it was with my mom. i guessed it was 78 degrees exactly. at the last minute i changed from 81 to 78 for no reason. you should get something for that.

i'm officially going to start 'getting something for that.' will keep a tally of points i earn. it's going to start with a tally. then i'm going to make my million dollar iphone app…once i can correctly guess how to write code… now that would be something. damn. feel like there are definitely people out there, very successful rich people, who have gotten everything they have just by guessing. no. maybe just a few people. less than i would think, actually. probably no one. think that's in 'sirens of titan,' someone gets rich because he discovered a code in the bible or alphabet that corresponds to the stock market. maybe there already is a points system. the illuminati knows about it. damn this seems real to me. maybe i'm onto it by…i'm discovering it the way the first illuminati person discovered it…maybe they can tell… they're listening, maybe…CAN YOU GUYS TELL I FIGURED OUT THE POINTS SYSTEM, CAN I BE A MEMBER OF YOUR THING NOW? i'll write a report…i won't use ellipsis in the way i just used them and will limit or restrict using the words 'thing,' 'something,' 'like.' willing to limit 'seems' if you think it'd be a problem, but would rather not restrict completely (given the nature of the paper i think you'd want me to write).

if i got in the illuminati here are the only things i'd want, this is all i'd ask of them:

- to get my car insurance situation taken care of

- to get a new york license so i could get the car insurance situation taken care of

- to un-suspend my license (70-75% sure it is) so i could get a new york license so i could get my car insurance situation taken care of

- to pay my parking tickets so i don't feel like a criminal when i go to see if my license is suspended so i could get a new york license so i could get my car insurance situation taken care of

- for someone to fill out college applications for me (or give me a job or money so i won't have to go to college)

- for the lawyer person to send me the accident settlement money already (or give me a job or money so i won't have to use accident settlement money)

- for someone to fix my phone

- for shirley to stop peeing the bed

- would like a garbage disposal and a printer and a juicer that works (luxury items, can wait)

i think that's all. looked around my room and checked to-do list several times to see if i'm missing anything. illuminati probably can't get me other things i want that aren't on the list.

while i'm at it, might as well just…i'm really pushing my luck, but:

- would like a device that gets all the crumbs off my feet before i put them into bed. like a suction…thing. self-wiping floor. you just peel off a new floor every few hours. it would peel off in that way plastic covers for certain electronics peel. it's a very special kind of 'peeling,' the peeling i'm talking about. like you want to put it back on right away just so you can peel it off again and hear the peeling noise and feel how light and flexible the plastic is. my dad leaves the peels on his things, drives me nuts. imagine peeling a floor. your entire floor. i'd get chills. i just did, a little. 'the illuminati floor peel.'

3:21PM: THINGS TO DO BY 11:59PM TODAY:

- mail packages for matthew and juliet

- shower

- do twitter thing for alt citizen article at 8PM

okay. little steps. it's okay, little steps are okay, remember. they are still steps. the least you can do. tomorrow you can go to fedex. wait, it makes more sense to just make one trip to fedex ('real reason' is to fax document to car insurance people). hm.

REVISED LIST FOR TODAY:

- i'm going to think about it. 'thinking about it' deadline is 5PM. i have to decide if fedex happens today or tomorrow by 5PM.

rationally…the faxing. shit. the faxing involves a phone call, which should happen at fedex, and my phone says 'no service' and won't make/receive calls…asking to use the fedex phone with no sleep and thinking about 'i have to be back by 8PM to do the alt citizen thing'…shit, too stressful.

that was easy. fedex will be another day.

had been sort of entertaining the idea of 'getting away from it all' (haha) in maryland and…okay be realistic. be real do real talk real style no 'but i was thinking, but…'

WHY SHOULD YOU GO TO MARYLAND:

- the people at the at&t store know you and it'll be easy to get your phone fixed.

- kenny knows how to re-wire lamps and your floor lamp is broken and it'd be nice if it wasn't.

- can use the printer at mom's house for college applications.

- can go through the storage unit and organize what remains of your stuff so dad doesn't bug you about the storage unit anymore.

- can get your health insurance card which will help you when you get that new gynecologist whenever that magical day may be.

- the drive feels nice.

- change of scenery and it feels like you belong there.

- get to party with mom.

WHY SHOULD YOU NOT GO TO MARYLAND:

- there are at&t stores probably everywhere in new york, all qualified to fix your phone.

- shirley peed on the mattress the last time you were gone.

- the last two times you've gone you haven't fixed your phone or printed things like you said you would. you just partied with mom.

- might be good for you to stay in the same place for two weeks. your apartment/neighborhood might feel a little more familiar if you were here more often.

THESE THINGS FEEL MOST IMPORTANT:

- getting phone to work.

- getting away from here.

- staying here to see if that helps this feel less like a place i want to escape, more like 'when i want to escape, i come here.'

so sort of at a stand-still. will probably end up going to maryland tomorrow. yeah. here's my big dream: waking at 9 or 10AM naturally and feeling refreshed, making a little hobby stop at the neighborhood fedex before chugging down to maryland, either arriving before the at&t store closes OR arriving after, having a nice dinner and talk (oh man, if you get there before 7PM you could even go to a YOGA CLASS!!!!) with mom, going to sleep before 2AM without drugs, waking naturally and refreshed around 9 or 10AM on friday, get the at&t store to do their business to you, drop off broken lamp at [location to be determined], bring dad a coffee at his office and maybe talk or go to dinner, then make your merry way back to your favorite beachside hidey-hole.

that'd be okay. that'd be good, if i did all that.

3:49PM: ate 800mg choline, 1.2g aniracetam, 400mg phenethylamine. i started eating similar amounts of these things daily a little more than two weeks ago. that's not what i wanted to talk about.

as i was spooning these powder thingies onto my tongue and chasing them with water here is what is was thinking:

if someone who's won the pulitzer prize had to live inside me for a day… it'd be. hm. then they would know what 'hard' is. can i make that funny? sounds too 'mad'…or…complain-y…it's just not funny. the hard thing is when the easy things feel hard because not only do those things feel hard, most people do them with ease, which could mean or not mean any number of things about you, but it does seem reasonable to conclude 'there is something dysfunctional about this person,' especially if there are no real reasons for you to feel this bad. your basic needs are met.

i wasn't thinking that. i wasn't thinking the 'basic needs' thing. i always want to say 'i know people have it worse than me' stuff when i complain, to create a guilt/blame-free buffer zone. but that's just the same faulty 'comparing myself to masses of people' thinking which is what initially makes me feel inept and that, if i'm viewing rationally, doesn't make sense to do. i don't know how to stop thinking things like this. how to stop getting in the way of myself.

before i went into the basic needs buffer-zone, the point i was trying to make, which…whatever, here's the point: no matter what, any solution that is offered to me by anyone, or that i invent on my own, i will find a problem with that solution.

6:01PM: ate 30mg adderall. moved to bed. sitting on dried baking soda pee-cleaner mixture. the adderall is just making me feel 'normal.' i got caught up in the problem/solution thing. why do i feel pressure to stop doing stuff like that…stuff i get distracted by…hm. interesting. the pressure to stop makes me want to keep going.

glad i saved all my 'i think it's empty' e-cigarette cartridges for a time like this. do not feel like buying new you-know-whats.

i can feel my boobs on my stomach when i sit like this.

6:05PM: highlighted everything i've written from that last sentence until the text directly under 'august 2, 2013.' it says it's 21,765 words. seems impossible. what the hell.

6:11PM: walked around saying 'where's the shirley' and 'where's the shirley we all know and love' and things like that. found her under the bed. don't cats hide when they think they're going to die? shit. should i take her to a vet. shit. she's probably just spooked by the baking soda. now she's sniffing around the bed. spooked. spooked by baking soda, classic. oldest trick in the book. wanna know a surefire way to spook a cat? wait for them to pee on your bed, then rub baking soda on the pee. gets 'em every time. spooked to high hell.

6:12–11:59PM: signed in to @altcitizen. answered maybe four questions. mostly tweeted with one person about funny hypothetical situations involving tom cruise. felt aware of concurrent 'three-hour only' online premiere of adam humphrey's and zachary's movie, 'baseball.'

AUGUST 8, 2013

12-2:03AM: have been gchatting with zachary. laughed aloud a few times. craving being in the same room as him. surprised to hear he and ex-girl-friend live together and don't have sex....seems complicated...it's probably not though, for them. i could be a dick and say something about his pre-diction that i might find 'true love' in 'some alternative arrangement.' ate 10mg oxycodone.

2:24AM: read first few pages of 'adam's summer purgatory.' it makes sense that adam is canadian. in my sixth grade textbook there was a picture of people playing basketball indoors, captioned 'canadians: they do what americans do, with slightly colder weather.' it was confusing. no one had told me about canada, though. ate 5mg oxycodone.

shirley peed the bed twice. 12th bed pee since i've been back. the last two pees don't smell. there is a small amount of baking soda left in the box i bought yesterday. 'from vancouver,' i wanted to add. feeling the humphreys influence. the unmistakable canadian influence of a humphreys gone wild. its first taste of freedom. adam is a nice person.

here are some things i thought while brushing caked baking soda off the bed, sweeping that from the floor, picking at hair in my eye, scooping terds in trash because the toilet is clogged due to too much toilet paper filled with cat pee:

do i sleep on the comforter tonight? the other comforter is still drying. probably still contains pee. smells wet. if i lay on top of the dry comforter i will put the pee/baking soda spots face-down so it's harder for shirley to smell her pee and i don't wake covered in pee. no, if they're face-down then the pee will be on my body kind of. no, the sheet. no...there's pee on the sheet. the top sheet? yeah einstein the top sheet too. i could take off the mattress pad. so much work. one side of the mattress pad has four large pee stains and the other side has five or six but which side is better? the side with the most stains...most of the stains were already there, but both sides currently contain recent pee. below the mattress pad is the mattress: weighing in with four pee spots. pee. pee. PIDDLE PAD. SHIRLEY'S DELUXE PIDDLE PAD BEACH BLANKET BONANZA! TELL ALL YOUR FRIENDS, THE EVENT OF THE SUMMER, IT DOESN'T MATTER WHERE WE PEE!

i hate anyone who has pets that don't pee on their bed. i hate them and i hate their pets.

how can parents do this with cats and dogs and babies all at the same time. scared if i ever become a mom i'll find out 'the secret' my parents were protecting me from, which is that it is not fun to have children, but if you don't tell them you love them they'll turn out really bad (and sometimes they turn out bad even if you do tell them, as my parents have likely discerned by now).

i understand shirley's 'it's okay to pee anywhere' attitude. i have that too, humans pee everywhere. they just put a toilet wherever they want to pee. i wasn't around for the toilet invention and i couldn't build one on my own. like, i couldn't just invent a toilet. there's no way i would've known what to do after i invented the toilet. there would be no toilets today if i had invented the toilet.

oh cool i'll just feed you guys and give you water so you can drop some stank terd and pee where i sleep, and then later maybe you'll stand just far enough from my hand so that i can almost pet you and when i pet you you start moving around out of reach oh okay okay okay. so here we are in this apartment where i bring us food to eat, we poop and pee, sit mostly alone, and sometimes we make noises that startle each other and we all jump and freak out. that's what we've got going on here. that's our thing. huh. okay. admittedly i was a little more enthusiastic about giving you attention when i wasn't sleeping in your excrement. just one of those things about me. i know, i hate it too. it's like how some guys have some freaky opinions about what you should do to your pubic hair. i'm like that guy, i'm the pubes guy…i just…it's a quirk of mine, a neuroticism, this 'learning to accept that i am now sleeping in excrement.' i downloaded something that's supposed to help. it's an app. the app is supposed to help me with this.

to let a 23-year-old person like i was adopt cats…no, it seemed like i had hope back then, i get it. plus there are just so many cats. what else are we supposed to do.

what do other people around my age do when a cat starts peeing the bed. what do other people my age do, in general? do they live in like, warehouses? lofts? is there a lot of newspaper on the floor from art projects or whatever, do the cats just pee on that? no, no. that's not 27. that's like, 18-25. guess i missed out on that. never seemed like anyone cleaned at those places. huh. 27-year-olds live in places with refurbished kitchens. they have small business start-ups. or something. they're married. not like how i am, they're like, pressured…they experience pressure to 'settle down.'

huh. i don't know if i'd like that. i can't do something like that right now. the small business thing. there is this air of 'things are calming down but they're still exciting and i'm looking forward to whatever adulthood has in store for me' about people my age. definitely not me. think my air is like 'can you tell i sleep in excrement, that is, when i sleep, i mean most of the time i'm sitting in my bed but that's not really sleeping, do i look awake to you, too awake? am i too awake? i'm sorry i'll go lie down, thank you for your time and consideration.'

3:11AM: the band 311 is really funny. i lit a candle. currently obsessed with 'does it smell like poop in here.' i'm having the adderall or no-sleep thing of…it feels like there are little hairs in my eyes. as i was tweeting from alt citizen i experienced the 'neon spinning spherical turtle shell made of tiny shifting geometric patterns and if i look close, stuff that looks like the outlines of rice kernals which i used to think were my rods and cones.' i get this around the 36-hour 'no sleep' mark, i've noticed.

earlier in the bathroom while picking at a maybe nonexistent hair i thought 'richard yates didn't like himself very much. he or someone like him said something like 'if people relate to what i'm saying, that is bad. people who are doing well should not relate to this." feels strange to think about someone reading this, relating to it.

3:12AM–11:59PM: i don't remember most of what i did. things i'm pretty sure i did:

- ate 2mg xanax

- stood mattress upright against wall and used carpeted cat tower thingy to prop it up so there would be no shirley pee when i returned. broke part of bed frame doing this.

- walked to pickles & pies for e-cigarette cartridges.

- man named paul approached me on the street as i was walking to p&p. it went something like this:

  paul: hey how're you doing?

  me: okay.

  paul: you live around here?

  me: yeah pretty close.

  paul: oh nice. hey i'm paul, what's your name?

me: hi paul, i'm megan [shakes hand].

paul: where you headed?

me: pickles & pies.

paul: cool, cool. hey can i get your number, you wanna get a drink sometime?

me: i don't think so, no, sorry.

paul: it'd just be a drink [something i forget]

me: no, it's not going to...no, i'm feeling pretty depressed and antisocial lately

paul: [concerned face] what do you do?

me: uh, nothing, write. writer.

paul: oh cool, writing, that's cool. hey can i just get your number?

me: [had started walking faster than him] no, really, knowing me lately, i'm...think...it's not going to happen, i don't feel like...i'm like, depressed, i'm...it's...[gesture around head] solitary confinement.

paul: well okay, okay. here, how about i just give you this [hands me business card] then. just in case, alright?

me: okay okay sure okay.

paul: i live right over here on one hundred seventeenth

me: oh cool. have a nice night.

paul: you too megan, gimme a call.

- got two slices cheese pizza from slices & ices
- moved my car from beach 113th st to an 'it's okay to park here on fridays' zone three blocks up on my street
- ate 2mg xanax

AUGUST 9, 2013

12-3:[something]AM: used 'free' coupon to watch 'oblivion,' a post-apocalyptic tom cruise movie. tweeted with person who i was tweeting funny things about tom cruise with during altcitizen q&a.

3:[something]-7:00AM: was afraid of looking at liveblog and averse to typing during this time. googled my name. an argentinian article came up. seemed hard to focus on one thing/completely read one website. ate 2mg xanax. was going to eat .5, then thought 'fuck it.' 6mg xanax total, tonight. saw naked reflection in the mirror. lighting looked okay. recorded a video of parading my naked shitass buffalo bill 'silence of the lambs' style. things are looking 'unwashed' and 'spiney.'

haven't weighed myself for about two weeks. [omitted]'s scale said 129.4lbs. pretty sure now i'm less. hate myself when i write shit like this but whatever, it'd be in my head if it wasn't words. yuckmaster buffalo bill. rubbing the lotion on its skin or else it gets the hose again. actually no, i shouldn't hate that. i want to weigh less and it's happening so i should feel good about that. i do. a little embarrassing to think about other people knowing this about me but…nah. nah. okay not embarrassed anymore. is there any person who has never thought about their weight or how their body looks? anyone? anyone? IF THAT IS YOU AND YOU'RE READING THIS: HOW MUCH DO YOU WEIGH AND WHAT DOES YOUR BODY LOOK LIKE? HAHA MADE YOU THINK HAHA HAHA.

recorded a video of typing an email response to rachel white, who had emailed a few weeks ago asking me if i wanted to participate in a gallery/reading/art show event she's organizing august 30. she suggested for my part of the thing, i would be liveblogging in front of a video projection of me liveblogging. seems funny. potential to repulse maybe 15 people. decided to not send the email right away via 6mg xanax/sleepless/potential incoherence.

watched ASMR videos to fall asleep.

woke a few times. remember eating an orange and a banana.

1:[something]PM: woke and didn't want to be awake. think i just laid there half-asleep and dreaming for a few hours, or just like, in a very light sleep.

3:46PM: saw 3:46PM on the clock.

3:58PM: looked for e-cigarette, phone, computer plug for what felt like 30 minutes. fed cats. shirley is acting weird and hiding. worried about pee situation. alvie stood on the litter box and vomited, then he like, dug at it and sniffed it and looked like he was going to eat it.

4:15PM: ate 800mg choline, 1.2g aniracetam, 600mg phethylamine and drank a zero calorie monster. jordan emailed. he's having some kind of insane money crisis and his parents are kicking him out of his house. going to moneygram him $300 remaining in savings account. jordan's hell sounds worse than mine. he has a job at least...at least...shit. a few days ago he emailed that he still wants to come to NYC but things were complicated and i understood.

4:47pm: walking down apartment building stairs. Smells like weed. Pee-proofed (I think) bed using mattress maneuver from last night. Wearing shorts bought in 2010, didn't fit until summer 2011, and are now a little baggy. Ate 20mg adderall xr before leaving. Having eidetic flashbacks to dream last night, involving trying to save three kittens and their mom. One kitten and the mom were missing an eye. Someone was moving into an apartment on the first floor but it wasn't my building. I kept climbing up and down a fire escape to take the kittens up to an empty apartment on the third floor where it was safe. Buttercup was there. We were looking at the apartment, empty except for cats, and saying 'it seems small, way too small.' At ATM now.

5:10pm: withdrew $300 from savings and walked to Duane reade. They're playing the song that's like 'there's a hole in my heart that can only be filled by you' that makes me feel like a sad empty dollar store. You use a phone to do moneygram things. I spelled and said Jordan's name twice and each time the woman repeated 'gordan' back to me. She said I need his middle initial. I said 'does it really matter?' She started to sound irritated and said 'yes, the name must match the person's official ID who you're sending it to.' Wanted to say 'it's Luis or Francisco or something, sounds Spanish.' I said 'I think I know it, can I think for a minute?' She said 'mmhmm' and after a few seconds put me on hold. I hung up the phone. Looked to see if my phone picked up wifi. No dice. Asked cashier if I could use cash. Couldn't picture how the cash in my hand would get to Ohio. Another customer approached. Cashier said 'I think so, yeah' and paged the manager. I looked at the customer he had started to ring up, said 'I gotta find out a middle name, I'll be back in like ten minutes.' Cashier said 'cool,' picked up the store phone, said 'cancel.' Currently walking up stairs to apartment. Still smells like weed. Feel like I'm going to pass out.

5:18pm: sitting on toilet. Out of breath. There's a new email from Jordan in our email chain. Since I blacked out the other night I've been periodically feeling faint and like I need to lay down but then that kind of makes it worse. Used toilet paper to wipe Alvie's vomit from floor, then dropped the clump of it in toilet.

5:35PM: sitting on floor. listening to 'what that was' by majical clouds on repeat. waiting to hear what jordan's (or 'gordan's,' as he is known in certain moneygram circles) middle name is.

6:01pm: descending apartment building stairs. Jordan is at the grocery store where money should be sent. Worried this isn't going to work. It's going to work. Got that middle name in tow: 'Julio.' Me and Julio down by the Duane reade moneygram station. Wish Jordan was here. Dreading apartment re-entry. Feels like the bleakest place…solitary confinement headquarters…in a bad way.

6:05pm: put phone in pocket and waited to pass a man standing by a van to write this. Forget what I wanted to write. Remembered as I was typing 'what I:' I don't feel effects from adderall anymore.

6:25pm: when I said Jordan's middle initial was 'j,' the moneygram man said "j' as in 'Jordan?"

There was a $23 service fee. I had $2. The cashier said the whole thing had to be in cash. Tried Duane reade ATM several times but it didn't read card. Ran to pickles & pies ATM three blocks away and withdrew $60 from checking and ran back. There was a line. Female cashier waved to me and I waved and smiled. She said 'just step over here' and I walked to the moneygram phone. Female cashier asked who I was sending money to. I said 'Jordan Castro.' Male cashier said 'that's me!' I said 'oh my god, Jordan! I haven't seen you in so long, you look so different!' We laughed. Female cashier handed me ~18" receipt with reference number on it. Then everything was good. I thought 'let's push my luck while I'm at it.' Asked her for quarters in exchange for $3. Said 'I have a laundry…situation…' She wordlessly laid out little stacks of quarters then said 'here you go.' I said 'woohoo thank you.' She smiled and I walked out the door.

6:41pm: walking up stairs to apt. Winded.

6:46pm: Jordan emailed that it all worked out sweet ass hell yeah. Emailed back that this gave my day purpose…also things about wanting to get pounded by him…heheheh…damn want Jordan sex bad right now. Picturing him at grocery store receiving money and feeling happy, I was able to provide help for a good person, this is making me feel better, I am less wasteful. Surge of horniness. This is funny. Feeling horny due to these circumstances. Genuine horny…thing…imagining Jordan at my door and like, grabbing him, making out, damn. Hehhegehheheheh. Laying in bed with Jordan, 'reading the newspaper,' I thought. Haha. Both of us in 'smoking jackets' or fancy bathrobes, side-by-side on the bed with our legs extended after sex, holding newspapers, noncommittally quoting the stock market.

7:33PM: chelsea emailed something very sweet and thoughtful and funny and emotional. she is in curacao. fucking. so happy chelsea is in my life. wish everyone could know chelsea, or have a person like chelsea in their lives. people like chelsea make me want to keep going.

took pictures of myself in bathing suit from freshman year of high school. it smells like chlorine. it has always been tight around the waistband part. still gathers/bunches at waistband a little but all in all, not bad. not bad shitass. have always wanted one to have one of those inviting gaps between my upper thighs. why? so, uh…so the guys know…so they can more clearly see 'where to put it'…i guess? no reason really. i have achieved inviting thigh gap. inviting thigh gap achieved. and just look at where's it's gotten me. 'woohoo.'

took down 'pee prevention fort.' did 400 crunches, chewed 30mg adderall IR with incisors, opened fridge and a 12oz sugar-free red bull and zero calorie monster drink fell onto floor. opened the red bull over sink and tried to drink the fizz to help wash down adderall.

alvie just had a hilarious scare with my earphones. i haven't showered since august 1. this might be a personal record. my friend alec and his two friends are visiting NYC this weekend and i said they could stay at my place. forgot it was 'weekend' already. sent him a facebook message saying he could stay and that i've been feeling bad and it's all seemed like the same day since sunday (day of his last message to me). he responded a few minutes ago with something very sweet and empathic that…damn. don't want to type it all, just want to respond.

9:20PM: wrote a long emotional response to alec's message which basically said 'here's how to park, this is where i live, i want to be alone tonight, i want to see you and have you stay over tomorrow/however long you want to visit.'

10:04PM: just going to insert 'abandoned' now, in parts where i thought i'd write more and stopped.

10:05-11:59PM: abandoned.

AUGUST 10, 2013

1:08AM: keep losing my goddamned e-cigarette batteries. keep. keep losing. stood to look and got dizzy. heart beats faster when i stand up. in a rap it'd be like: 'heart beats faster when i stand up [noise that goes from low to high, like when something 'powers up' in a game or something shit why do i know this sound, it's like 'd-oooyyyyyy-ing?']' then the beat drops.

1:51AM: bought 'turns turns turns' EP by majical clouds from itunes. think it's actually 'cloudz.' shit. i always forget um. the main idea of this, liveblog. which is that…nothing is permanent…or something. i think the main idea was to feel like things were more permanent/i had more agency. er. i don't think permanence was addressed. i completely forget my introduction to this. the prelude…i'm laughing…'prelude to a liveblog'…one of keats' uh, lesser-known…very rare…you can only see it if you do a tour of his house, it's like, in a journal that's kind of falling apart, they keep the journal in a clear bulletproof plastic case…bulletproof…it needs to be…you don't need to know why it needs to be bulletproof, it just is…it's not even open to the page with 'prelude to a liveblog,' because that part, he actually…um. he ripped it out before he died, actually. he was too ashamed.

people think a poem about a 'grecian urn' is like…[something]…but a lot of those same people think what i'm doing is [something else, bad]. i don't know that to be true. this is just a feeling i have. i'm laughing. what the hell am i trying to say. peace b witchoo keats. bummer about your name being almost the same as 'yeats.' bet that gets you rolling over in your grave.

wonder how many poetry M.F.A.s' first exposure to keats and yeats was 'cemetery gates.' 'oddly enough' i knew about keats and yeats a few years before i knew about the smiths (or knew…that those names were mentioned in a song i knew by a band called 'the smiths').

people don't really talk about the smiths much, in contrast to a period in my life where some of my close friends were into them.

i like them. i like morrissey. what the hell is with morrissey. what is that thing. gotta love him. i have told msword to stop capitalizing 'morrissey' three times but it keeps doing it, i feel like that's morrissey's fault, he's doing that. gotta love him. what a polarizing fellow. morrissey and DFW: polarizing. that means they're doing something right, i think. think i feel a default interest in anything that seems polarizing due to not really knowing what i like/want…interested in things that cause strong feelings in people...no, not accurate, i'm not interested in religion or politics. also i know what i like/want. i think. mostly. shit i don't know. what i'm doing right now is...i'm trying to make up an idea about myself. i think people do this easily. they're like 'hey, i'm [this thing].' guess i did make up an idea like that: 'hey, i'm...i don't know.'

whew!

3:22AM: chewing 30mg adderall IR with incisors. alvie made a nasty stank poop. laid one hell of a grecian urn.

5:20AM: hearing voice of [omitted] in my head saying 'is the liveblog getting in the way of other ways you could be being productive?' not his voice. it's not my voice. voiceless thing. wish my inner monologue had a definite voice. sometimes i remember people's voices or like, if i'm tired or zany/lighthearted i'll 'hear' a voice pop in. going to try to discern the voice of the thing doing the thinking...the baseline voice of that thing...i don't like when people say 'voice' when they talk about like, 'the voice of this story.' i'm not talking about that. er. kind of. you could say i'm talking about that i guess. what i'm wanting to talk about is the actual...if my inner monologue could speak the way i can talk, how would that voice sound. you would think 'it would sound like my talking voice,' i bet. but no. when i hear a recording of my speaking voice it's never like 'oh yeah, that's me.' they showed this really well in 'being john malkovitch,' when someone is inside the malkovitch and looking through his eyes and his voice is sort of muffled and vibrating. contains more bass.

WHAT VOICES MY INNER MONOLOGUE SOUNDS LIKE (IT'S LIKE A COMBINATION OF THESE, IF YOU COULD COMBINE THESE THINGS INTO A NEUTRAL VOICELESS THING WHICH IS ALSO SOMEHOW ABLE TO TALK):

- john arbuckle (surprised that's the first thing that came up. john from 'garfield.' haha)

- daria (monotonous qualities more than sarcastic qualities)

- batty from 'fern gully' (voiced by robin williams jesus...i'm just listing these as they come up)

- keep picturing an inhumanly beautiful faceless slender man who is like, just out of reach, who kind of wants me to touch him but is content with—'being wispy,' i thought

- the 'ringo' character from 'yellow submarine' but not british

- when i'm crying sounds like a dialogue between 'hal' from '2001' and the shoe from 'who framed roger rabbit' before the evil guy lowers it into the vat of liquid that destroys cartoons

- why are they all cartoons…what the hell…interesting…

- goldie hawn (felt pressured to think of an actual person, think my speaking voice just sounds like her)

- the voice my friend brian and i used to do when we'd 'do the voice' of my dog, lady (kind of like the 'belly voice' jerry seinfeld would want to 'do' to his girlfriend's belly when she was sleeping)

6:17AM: oh great it's morning again time to turn out the lights…almost… shit. no, not going to sleep. will be zany sleepless megan around alec today. everything will be fine. but then, even if it's not? still okay.

1:29PM: don't want to talk about it. goddamnit. haha. haha. like nelson. wish my keyboard would make a sound like nelson going 'haha' when i'd type. or like. just sometimes. random intervals, to keep me guessing. having weird period-like cramping again but it is way past my period and no way i'm pregnant.

have been listening to 'what that was' by majical cloudz on repeat since sometime last night. sad pretty song. sad in the dollar store way but it's not like a dollar store, not depressing. it like, has the yearning of a dollar store. the quiet forgotten yearning of a dollar store.

which is all to say: this is why i think dentistry is scam. fake industry. totally made-up. what, your teeth are going to fall out? seriously? come on you just wanted to be another kind of doctor and they hadn't invented 'tooth doctor' yet, come on. jig is up. fake ass 'd.d.s.' jig is up. you know it's just 'd.d.s.' because they were still in the process of figuring out how to spell 'dentist' and gave up. that's like if i was 'megan boyle, a.a.s.d.f.a.d.f.a.d.f.s.d.f.' in fact that is me. that is what i am, that is my suffix. i am a special kind of doctor. i specialize in helping people find the best angles to tilt their heads. fuck you this is important. tilt specialist. licensed certified full tilt specialist, a.a.s.d.f.a.d.f.a.d.f.s.d.f. if you think this is bullshit, fine. just don't come crying to me when that far-right corner of your ceiling suddenly disappears from your peripheral vision.

1:37PM: i don't feel like going back in time to talk about how a few nights ago i 'went all out' and bought a lot of carbs. have not even mentioned that i've eaten a box of cereal since then. oh my heavens.

shit i want to do laundry before i see alec. also showering: major issue, must address. major. oh my heavens. alright guess i'll get this shitshow on the road. here we go. heavens. my heavens.

wait before i do that, i want to…

IMPORTANT THING:

- it doesn't help to write to-do lists in this.

1:47PM: how are people so uniformly relaxed about whether there's a comma in four-digit numbers or not. how has there been no authority about what this should be, officially. how is this, of all things, something we haven't 'figured out yet.' this is what ended up undecided for so long. all this time. slid through the loophole. no one cares. in 500 years people are going to type like 'e;oiweu w pwe sdsp lp;l brbr.' i don't care about that, actually. it's just a comma, chill out. the number is still at least 999 whether there's a comma or not. all is good. all is quiet on the comma front.

2:31PM: cats seem to have lost their taste for food that is not the mechanically separated and poisonous, i think, fancy feast. fancy feast makes 'appetizers,' which are smaller and more expensive and feature upscale packaging. they are just like, fish. like a can of tuna, but probably not tuna, and in a vacuum-sealed plastic tray. cats hate 'em. they have clearly lost their appetite for the real fishes. what have i done. my son my son what have ye done.

2:49PM: i'm afraid to update this. just. afraid. what the hell is my life. i'm devoting my life to this thing. think i've made it impossible to 'call me out' on anything regarding being a shitty wasteful person. if anyone ever says anything like that to me i'll just be like 'oh, you must have read my liveblog.' it would be a sick person who'd want to pick on a person as sick as me. it would be like having sex with someone in a coma. who is related to you. you sickos, i know you're out there. actually it'd be nice if someone would…kick my ass…somehow…show me a better way to live…better ways to think…feel like this is something that needs to be demonstrated to me. i am open for beatings or harshly worded anythings.

6:23PM: need to get more cat food plus shower plus laundry goddamnit i just want to be on a porch drinking mountain dew with a little something else in it and…seems like that's all…all i want…yeah. should i eat one of the last adderall to keep me going, or what. what the hell. the stuff about worrying about getting 'called out' seems like my dad, so great, now i know that, so great. great. sometimes people try farming. should i let the cats roam free and try to work at a farm. free cats back into the ocean… where all the fancy feast in the world awaits them…the fanciest of feasts…

wouldn't they be happy? in the ocean? that is an awful thought no no especially because shirley has been good with her peeing all day. will it ever be back to normal…need 'life adderall' to get me back to 'normal'…will i even feel the effects…mountain dew on a porch…a little something else in it… when can i go home though, do i ever get to go home at the end of this…

7:26PM: swept and mopped. thought i wouldn't be able to do it without eating phenethylamine or an opiate. opiates will make me more tired. don't want to eat adderall. imagined trying therapy again. would be a struggle to leave apartment. then the talking, explaining context. i'd be smiling like the last time i tried it because i'm always smiling because things don't want to hurt you as much if you're smiling. it would take forever. i would be a smiling idiot for like four months, saying 'well, you know, i guess it's just a slump.' imagine not doing that, like going in, allowing my face to be like it is now with no muscles tensed, shaking therapist's hand, saying 'i'm going to try something different. i'm going to try not smiling or bullshitting with you at all. i have not done this before.' then six months or something later when i'm…i don't know…when it's not like this, the therapist would say 'i knew it, i knew from the minute you said you didn't want to bullshit me: this one would not be like the other hopeless cases. congratulations, you've made it to the other side.' she would hang a photo of us in her waiting room. in the photo our arms would wrap behind each other's shoulders with the casual, natural interdependence of two people steadying their balance after running a marathon. the other therapists would have initially mixed feelings about the photo, but pretty soon similar photos of themselves with patients would cover an entire waiting room wall, under a banner of cut-out letters spelling 'greetings from the other side!' between stacks of magazines on a nearby table where there would be a little upright plastic apparatus proffering free 'tickets to the other side: simple time management strategies for jumpstarting your progress in therapy' pamphlets, that would open to a page with the heading '1. STOP SMILING, YOU'RE NOT OKAY!' opposite a page with the heading '2. SAVING THE BULLSHIT FOR THE OTHER 23 HOURS OF THE DAY,' and thoughtful tips under both. my therapist would keep a framed copy of our photo on her desk, to remind her of the success story that started it all. the picture was taken right after we finished the first draft of the pamphlet.

got lightheaded when i'd bend over swiffering. remembered someone saying something like, 'don't worry about it, there are plenty of idiots out there in the world who would really like you.' it wasn't that exactly. i don't remember when it was said. it was just a lot of stuff like that. they were jokes i think, but also true. remembered sometimes people get hospitalized for 'exhaustion.' sounds good. it would feel bad to be there though, what they would think of me, isn't 'exhaustion' just politically correct code for 'drug problems.' maybe i have a drug problem. a lot of my problems do seem centered around drugs. the hospital staff would know about 'people like me.' they would have biases. they would be required to do a bi-monthly training workshop about tolerance. it's part of the job. the older hospital staff wouldn't even think biased thoughts anymore. partially because of the training, mostly because they would've seen too many people like me and it wouldn't matter anymore.

get a sick little annoyingly symbolic thrill when i see less of myself in my reflection. i like seeing more of me that's not there. the least i can do is make it go away a little. make a little less of it a little more every day: the least you can do. stood in front of mirror for 'daily inventory session' of what remains of me from yesterday, as if my mental report of this would be directly sent to some forensics lab, which experts would analyze then send back to me, so finally i could know 'what happened to the body' and get some sleep. case closed.

7:59PM: brushed hair. a lot fell out. typing/saying 'seems interesting' or 'seems funny' after anything makes you sound like 'don't worry, i'm in control.' a lot of the time when i say it i think i mean 'don't worry, it feels worse when someone is worried.' i don't like it when people have answers to everything but i'm like that too. most of the white parts of my eyes are red. i've been wearing bathing suit all day. all night. no reason to not wear other clothes. a lot of how i'm feeling right now is probably due to not sleeping for 31 hours and adderall leaving body. this is a miserable existence. thinking about what drug to eat to prepare me for the shower. jesus christ. how will i respond to alec. i want to see alec. i want a beer or something. i would fall over, maybe. maybe the e-cigarettes are making me feel faint. should i not wash my hoodie as a souvenir of this smell? the smell is really something else.

8-11:59PM: abandoned.

12:46AM: responded to alec's message after i'd resigned to 'a depressed night of not responding.'

12:57AM: feeling better. tweeted with tao. debated ordering pizza. listening to the 'hole in my heart that can only be filled by you' song from duane reade yesterday. dollar store song. ate 1mg xanax for motivation to shower or do laundry and walked around, pausing arbitrarily but with 'doom intervals.' have been wearing bathing suit from freshman year of high school since last night. red light, rainbow lights, and soft yellow light are on. it feels nice. ate 5mg oxycodone. wonder how tao is watching 'oblivion.' on phone? he is in the UK without a computer. clicked on a 'these horses have better hair than you' link. they did.

[unsure]-4:[something]AM: read 'frowns need friends too,' feeling comforted and sometimes laughing. watched 'the office.' ate 1mg xanax, avocado with salt and lime, and what remained of a bag of 'pirate's booty' cheese puffs it seemed like i had hidden in a cabinet. at 2AM i saw alec had responded to my message at 1:30AM saying we could hang out if i picked him up in bed stuy now. hadn't showered yet and felt sleepy, said i was going to stay in.

10:[something]AM: woke and saw clock. thought 'great, up early, i'll sleep for another ten minutes.'

1:37PM: woke. feeling groggy. alec and his friends are driving back to rhode island tonight, i just read in a new message. he asked if i wanted to come too.

2:49PM: ate half a 'personal-sized' watermelon, 800mg choline, 1.2g aniracetam, 800mg phethylamine. driving to rhode island at 6PM. 'personal jesus' by depeche mode is playing in my head only it's 'your own… personal…melon.' this sometimes happens when i think about 'personal-sized' melons.

3:17PM: before leaving: buy cat food, e-cigarette cartridges, shower, pack clothes. shit. packing. gonna get moving with this.

5:57PM: two women walked behind me as i walked from pickles & pies to waldbaum's. one said 'i got a grandson that's 18 years old. pshh, i ain't got time for this!'

saw a gold cube on the ground in the post office parking lot. it was near where the woman in the cape yelled 'asshole' at me. picked it up. think it's a bouillon cube. cube of bouillon. considered putting it back, in case a homeless person wanted to use it in their food, then thought 'no one will ever see it. this is my cube.'

in waldbaum's a dad-looking guy pushing a shopping cart said 'what kind of soda does shannon like?' someone said 'sprite.' he said 'i won't get sprite then.'

the girl i like, candy's friend who used the 'store card' for me and doesn't move her face much, was monitoring the self-checkout line. when i passed her to exit the sun was hitting the back of her head and she was smiling at whoever was talking to her. it was nice to see her smile.

fed cats, washed dishes, laid out extra food and water, packed clothes in a hurry when i got home around 5:45PM. sweat a lot while doing dishes. took off dress. removed sheets and things from bed, put comforter and pillows in closet, and stood/propped mattress upright against the 'cat tower' to prevent pee while i'm gone. still seems like there will be pee. looks like some of the pee from the mattress pad has sank into the mattress. going to do a cleaning/scrubbing bonanza when i return and throw away mattress pad.

a package with no return address, which looked 'internationally sent,' arrived a few days ago. have been 'afraid' of it. it was hydergine. i had ordered it a few weeks ago. it's used to treat dementia. invented by the guy who invented LSD. ate half a tablet before i left for p&p and waldbaum's. seem to be…sweating more. i don't feel like i need caffeine. feeling better than yesterday, like, baseline mood is better, but that could just be circumstantial. ate other half of tablet a few minutes ago. 'we'll see.'

6:08PM: alec said i should leave around 6:30PM. asked juliet if we could reschedule our final video interview for tomorrow or later tonight. gonna write directions and get this shitshow on the road.

8:07pm: think about how many people would kill themselves if they knew they could see how people would react to their death. I would definitely do that. Then I'd probably get bored and want to be alive again.

Listening to Barr. Stopped at CVS for uti pain medicine. Sometimes I'm really moved by Barr. He seems really intense, maybe, to hang out with. I feel like we 'get it' and probably have the same sense of humor, but I wouldn't be able to stop myself from arguing with him about things he feels more strongly about than I do. He reminds me of Zachary. The music thing Zachary did, Fishkind, was like a funnier version of Barr.

Picked up bag of 'unreal'-brand candy. It's candy without corn syrup and preservatives and hydrogenated things. There are three kinds: fake snickers, fake Reese's peanut butter cups, fake Milky Way. Got the Reese's kind. Who the hell eats milky ways. I did when I was little. Have a memory of running in a field after...I think my parents just parked so I could run or something. I was always wanting to run everywhere. It was in a grassy area of parking lot, in my memory, where I ran and my dad said 'time to go' and I said 'can I have a Milky Way?' He said there was one waiting for me in the car. It was in the car. It was a 'Milky Way Dark.' That can't be right. Warped memory. I like the warped one better.

Get goosebumps/tingles when I listen to Barr. Haven't listened to this in a long time. Sometimes I like, laugh/cry, not a wet cry. Before I started writing in this I had done that, I was laughing and crying and said 'what the fuck' about the last song on the album.

8:26pm: missed exit on 687 turning around. Using written directions via broken phone. Passed nytmes building. The breakup song is good, I like when he goes 'catharsis is real.'

10:10pm: slow traffic on 95. Passing building that says 'one stamford forum.' Looks misspelled. Stopped for gas and to ask for directions earlier. Think I'm in Connecticut. Hope Alec and his friends also encountered traffic. Before I left I thought I had lost phone and quickly accepted that. I wouldn't even try to get another one. Life without a phone seems fine. Maybe better. I like not feeling reliant on gmaps for directions, it's like an adventure, nature hike.

AUGUST 12, 2013

1:48am: driving to gas station. Arrived at Alec's a little before 1am. Was driving up and down his street a few times looking for his house. Knocked on door and rang bell and walked around porch. Left him a note. On my way into city, saw a building with a decorative neon red design that looked like another language. Alien language. What if that was my spaceship and I missed it.

I'm in Rhode Island. Haha. What am I doing in Rhode Island. Rhode Island Rhode Island everywhere and not an Alec to answer his door.

1:49-6:46AM: bought 'krave' brand disposable e-cigarette from shell station. drove past motel 6 exit several times, listening to 'take ecstasy with me' by magnetic fields on repeat. didn't feel bothered by missing exit, enjoyed driving. checked into a la quinta inn around 3AM. talked with the girl behind the desk. she said she'd been playing games on her phone, didn't even realize what time it was. i said i've always wanted her job. she said it was fun except on fridays and saturdays they get a lot of 'motel 6 drama' and cops come. i asked who causes the drama and why. she said 'they just come over here, already fighting. or they don't want their rooms to be transferred.' she said there was a free continental breakfast starting at 6AM and that she'd be awake for it. i said 'i don't think i'll be up' in vague fatherly-joking voice. got the feeling we were friends. considered asking if there were any 24-hour food places around here and if she wanted me to bring her anything. i said 'i'm just gonna, go, um. grab my stuff from my car.' she said 'okay.' when i walked back in with my stuff she was there. a man who looked like the guy in new orleans who tao and i asked if he thought darth vader would die in the new harry potter movie asked the overnight check-in girl for change. she said she had it. made brief eye contact with both of them and maybe waved as i walked to the vending machine area. didn't seem to be anything good in the vending machines. the guy approached the vending machine area and stood by me and said 'hi.' i said 'hi' and walked away.

looked at dunkin donuts website in my room. the dunkin donuts by me closes at 4AM. considered driving there, seemed too hard. sent apologetic facebook message to alec, thinking he had maybe thought i would arrive earlier and had maybe heard me knock and ring the bell but was upset that i was late and didn't want to answer. said i understood if he didn't want to hang out tomorrow but if he did, to contact me, and that i felt okay and was staying at a la quinta inn. emailed juliet that i could do the interview now. got t.g.i.friday's 'cheddar bacon potato skins' bag from vending machine. spent a long time deciding between cheddar cheese combos and the t.g.i.fridays thing. was surprised to see email from juliet on screen when i returned to room.

3:30-6:46AM: talked with juliet. considering going to AA meetings in brooklyn. juliet said there were a lot of attractive people there. near the end of the conversation i asked what was the thing that made her want to get sober. she said she was surprised that she did, that it seemed like a bunch of coincidences lining up. agreed that anything that ever happens to me that 'stays' is due to…just…like, 'feeling right.' series of coincidences. something like that. we talked about god and men we like. it's now august 20, i'm doing retroactive update. i like juliet a lot. she's coming to NYC at the end of october. told her she and scott (my 'parents') should move into colin's empty apartment across the hall from me and feed me soup using feeding tubes. juliet is good. will miss talking to her on skype. think it was hinted at or said outright that we both liked our talks and would like to talk more. ate 2mg xanax.

7:10AM: decided to take advantage of free continental breakfast. overnight check-in friend said 'oh, you're up.' i said something politely meaningless, smiling. another girl was at the desk too. walked to 'the breakfast room,' where many people were seated, mostly alone. two TVs were on. two teen-age-looking girls holding styrofoam containers circled the belgian waffle station, taking turns talking in a kind of call-and-response conversation led by neither about whether their pizza and chicken wings 'would be enough,' to eat. seemed like they'd never decide. walked to the carb-toasting station and stood beside an old man in a tank top with big lips and a 'fishy face,' who seemed to be waiting for something in the toaster, built to toast four things at once. i asked where the knives were and he silently handed me his knife, gave me a chivalrous nod, and looked away. cut semi-pre-cut bagel in half using plastic knife and placed it in toaster. looked around the room a lot. didn't know where to look. everyone seemed to be furtively redirecting their gazes to an arbitrarily wide variety of points at intervals suggesting a collective heightened yet noncommittal awareness of fulfilling their roles in a situation they'd regrettably involved themselves. wondered how long i'd have to wait for my bagel to toast. the fishy-looking older man was turned away from me, looking at the TV. thought 'lucky him, he has the TV to look at, but if i try to look at the TV he's in the way and he might 'feel my eyeballs' looking at him and think i'm staring at him.' found the area where plastic cutlery was stored. brought the fishy man a knife and he said 'thank you' and resumed looking at the TV. filled a styrofoam cup with hot water and a chamomile tea bag to bide time. people seemed to be 'watching me,' i thought, because of my outfit (platform wedge sandals and 'old lady' polo shirt and pink shorts). returned to toasting station. bagel still not toasted. got a banana from the other room, closer to the check-in desk, to bide time. when i returned to the toasting station my bagel was done but the fishy man's muffin still wasn't toasted. said a few words with him about the toaster seeming broken. i said 'you should try my side, i think your side is broken.' he nodded slowly, almost graciously. i liked him. thought he was probably a trucker. i said 'have a good morning.' he said 'you too darlin'' or 'you too, sweetie.' was surprised at whatever term of endearment he used, and felt warm about him and our quietness. took two things of philadelphia cream cheese and walked back to room.

ate bagel while watching 'the office.' knew i'd feel sad when the bagel was over.

9:55AM: woke to aggressive door-knocking sounds. voice on the other side said 'you have to check out by 12PM.' i said 'i'll just pay for another night.' the voice said 'you have to call the front desk.' barely remember calling front desk to do this.

11:02AM: woke to door-knocking sounds. it was maid service.

4:17PM: alec had sent a facebook message around 4AM. he apologized and said he had fallen asleep. thought 'he definitely ignored my knocking on purpose. no. it's possible that he didn't. he would, though. maybe. i would understand if he did. there's no way to tell for sure, i think he'd say he didn't if i asked him in person. whatever the reason, it is okay.' i called him from the hotel phone. he was at a café with a friend. i said i'd meet them in 30 minutes.

parked across from the café. talked with alec and his friend, alexandra, for a few hours. i liked her a lot. alec and alexandra are going to brown university this fall for masters programs and moved in early. one of the first things alec said was that he tried to call my room at the la quinta inn after he saw my facebook message, but the check-in woman said no one with my name had checked in. i thought 'shit, he thinks i lied.' i said that was really weird. we talked about how it was probably a legal issue, they're not allowed to give out information about who's staying at the hotel or something.

talked for a long time about woody allen and fellini movies. also another movie about hannah arendt. remember trying to access my 'hannah arendt: what you know about her' file in my brain and could only think of something funny zachary said and an essay i remember not enjoying reading in a women's studies class i dropped after something like two weeks, my first year at depaul. the movie seemed good. hannah arendt wrote an essay about how the 'evil' part of the holocaust was that people who didn't seem outwardly 'evil' were nazis. remembered this after alec and alexandra talked about it...don't think this is the essay i had read. the movie was about how hannah arendt's friends turned against her and called her an anti-semite after she wrote the essay.

sometimes felt 'dwarved' by how much alec and alexandra knew about things...movies/culture things...like i wasn't sure what i could contribute to the conversation if i talked. felt like an imposter a little bit, talking to them, like 'how can they not know i'm not smart, somehow they aren't picking up at how i'm an imposter.' alec said something that struck me. it reminded me of how my parents sometimes talk in a 'richard yates-y' way where they think they're concealing something. alec was talking about a woman in a fellini movie who...i forget. alexandra liked the movie. the movie is about a woman with some degree of clairvoyancy. think alec was saying something like she was self-involved and unaware of her craziness. thought he was like, saying a parable or something, about me, that he might think of me as similar to his interpretation of the woman in the movie, based on our recent interactions and me seeming flaky or depressed and self-involved and maybe losing some kind of awareness. the thing alec was saying about the woman didn't seem related to other things, and alexandra wasn't agreeing or disagreeing. i hadn't seen the movie. alec said something like 'i'm sorry, i don't know how i got to talking about that for so long' at the end. felt embarrassed and wanted to make a joke, like i wanted to say 'i get it i get it, the woman in the movie is kind of like me.' also thought 'this isn't about me at all, i'm projecting/being crazy and overthinking.' we talked about keurig cups, funny things about the future, reading 'star charts'/astrology, ways to make coffee, google glass, i think...there were funny things i'm now forgetting. we developed a running joke type thing about 'buying and selling,' like, financial jargon. forget how that happened.

something about pace university, that's where alexandra went and where colin went. we talked until it was dark and alexandra wanted to go home, via not having a bike light yet. alec asked alexandra to text him when she got home and she said she would, and had forgotten to last night due to her roommates talking, and alec said 'i figured that's what happened.'

alec asked what i wanted to do and i said i wanted sushi. neither of us knew the area well. we went inside to use the bathroom. the bathroom was a 'one-holer,' behind the employees-only area. i went first. a girl usurped alec's spot in line, surpassing the employees-only area. i stood by alec and we kind of shrugged and laughed about the girl and talked about pooping. i said 'i like your shoes.' alec had 'business shoes.' he did not like his jeans.

we asked the lady who i bought iced coffee from (the coffee was poured from a 'narragansett' beer tap thingy…the lady was older and danced as she poured it…felt aversion to her, kind of, but also endearment) if there were sushi places. she said she had just moved back to providence and wasn't sure. the girl left the bathroom. alec asked if he could leave his backpack (large black jansport, i think, which was surprisingly light in contrast to its size and 'turtle shell'-like protrusion) and i said 'yes.' my phone was picking up wifi so i checked email. jordan emailed that he had been arrested. alec emerged from the bathroom and the female coffee lady was standing next to a younger male employee, holding a white bag of sushi leftovers. the male coffee guy said the name of a sushi place.

8:26PM: alec and i walked to a shell station and i bought 'krave' brand e-cigarette starter kit. interacted with the shell station cashier with like… grandeur, i keep thinking. bravado. rapport. i knew what to say and i said it. paid and left, vaguely in the direction of the sushi place neither of us remembered how to get to, sometimes making noncommittal statements about how 'it must be one way or the other.' alec asked about e-cigarettes. i said i liked them more than regular ones and have no desire to smoke regular ones anymore. he said 'that seems mature, a sign of maturity' or something like that. gave alec a regular-flavored 'krave' e-cigarette and smoked the menthol one. alec said i seemed taller and i said something about my shoes. he asked about the shoes, the decision to wear high heels. i said something like 'i've just liked them lately,' not wanting to talk about how my recent wearing of high heels has been partially due to a pattern of dating men as tall as me or shorter, or taller than me but who didn't like high heels, and feeling like my 'high heels incentive' is stereotypical. alec said he thought he had a spine tumor and i said something about a bump on the top of my spine, that's always been there, and he moved to feel it and i put his hand on it. i said 'it's always been there.' asked him where he felt pain and he said it was mostly an all-over kind of tension and maneuvered my hand to an area on his spine. i said 'it's probably not a tumor.' he said it was probably not real, just due to anxiety.

passed a hardware store with an intricate window display. alec said something about the display. i said 'it doesn't seem real, it looks like an art thing' and sort of walked backwards for a minute, thinking if alec followed we would look at the display again. shortly after this we saw the sushi place. asked to be seated outside. looked at the menu, sensing both of us doing the thing where you look at the menu without reading it, you just like, 'absorb' it at first, because there's so much information. said things about what we wanted to eat. i held the paper 'sushi list' and asked him if he liked salmon, eel, other things/if he had preferences. he said he didn't. felt anxious about the waiter appearing. i said 'do you just want me to pick a bunch of things from the list and we'll get appetizers or something?' alec said 'yes, you seem to know much more about this than i do,' which i felt i didn't. alec said 'do you think it'd be okay if i got beer from somewhere and we drank it here?' i said 'probably yeah,' and looked at the menu to see if it said 'BYOB.' it did. i said 'yeah that'd be fine, it's BYOB.' we talked about appetizers. decided to get shrimp dumplings and seaweed salad. alec asked about beer again, seeming unsure. i said 'it's BYOB, they say it on the menu, it'd be fine.' felt like he left for beer still uncertain about it being 'allowed.'

8:50PM: the waitress brought one set of chopsticks. i said 'one more set.' she said 'one more?' i said 'one more, for my friend. two people.' she said 'two people.'

notable things i remember from dinner: alec said he hadn't read 'taipei.' felt surprised and asked him why. he said he doesn't want to read things that make him more depressed…like he is wanting to read things that make him happy lately, a lot of which are classics, i think…think he said 'dickens'… something about how depression or writing depressed things folds in on itself and becomes…jesus. i forget. we talked about how we first met and he asked if i knew he had a crush on me for a little bit, in baltimore, and i said 'yes.' he asked how i knew and i said 'when you asked to spoon me that night.' he said 'you asked me to spoon you!' remember this…specifically another way…snickering right now…i could've asked him to spoon me though, now that i think about it. remember the night it happened, his 20th birthday, the day before we took a bus to new york and stayed with his friend ryan for a few days, walked around brooklyn a lot and i bought sandals and shorts, then i met jordan and mallory for the first time with tao at pure food & wine and we ran around times square, then i cat-sat for zachary at his apartment in brooklyn while he was on vacation with his then-girlfriend, jamie, who has been living with him at the same apartment since sometime this summer. alec and i did a 'power hour' on his porch in baltimore the night of his 20th birthday. the only other 'power hour' i had ever done was on my 20th birthday too. regarding the spooning: i remember thinking 'it's possible that we could have sex but i feel platonic, maybe spooning would be okay,' something about a hand…thinking 'it's okay if he holds my hand, i like alec' and wishing i felt romantic things.

after dinner i drove us to la quinta inn so i could check out. a new person was at the desk. she said my room was good until tomorrow morning, and said i could keep my key, in case i decided to come back. alec said 'we should give the key to a homeless person' and i said 'yeah, yeah' and felt interested in doing that. idea dissolved quickly, i think, but i forget how.

we decided to put the beer at alec's apartment and go to a bar called 'the grad [something].' looked at the receipt the check-in person gave me, in a manner that reminded me of how my dad looks at checks at dinner. he will like, stop everything to make a display of how he's examining the check. he has a story about why he does this. his dad was poor but was somehow friends with a rich man who was involved in building the new york city subway system. when they'd go out to dinner with the rich man, he would examine the receipt—like, really give it a good up-and-down, really consider how much money everything cost. then my dad's dad started doing that. then my dad started doing that. i usually feel annoyed when my dad does it, like he's 'performing an examinination of the receipt' rather than examining it, and felt myself being annoyed with myself as i did it in front of alec, wanting to 'prove' to him that i in fact, checked in last night, i wasn't lying. alec and i looked at the receipt. i don't think the receipt said what time i checked in, so it was possible alec still thought…um…in my mind, it seemed possible for alec to think 'megan probably didn't leave new york until very late last night, which is why the check-in person said no one under 'megan boyle' had checked in, megan probably just checked in a few hours ago, so she could have an 'alibi." alec pointed out the top of the receipt, where it said 'margaret matlock.' we said things about how that was probably why they didn't connect him to my room. felt relieved but also like alec probably still didn't believe me/thought i checked in right before i came to the coffee shop or something. the only thing i lied about was not reading his facebook message he sent at 4:30AM. i saw it after the interview with juliet but felt committed to staying at la quinta for the night and didn't feel like hanging out or calling him at 7something in the morning, was a little suspicious about him being asleep when i knocked and then waking at 4:30AM, knowing the previous night he had been up late and it was possible that he had just…ignored my knock…out of spite/intolerance of me being flaky the past few days and inconveniencing him by not having a phone (i understood and didn't resent him for any of these possibilities or variations on these possibilities).

walked into alec's apartment. noticed a light was on inside a room with a closed door. used the bathroom and put down my stuff. think we were talking about alec's roommates, who he met from craigslist. alec said something about not liking nintendo 64. there was a n64 game console on the ground. he emerged from a room and noticed the light on in the room with the closed door and said 'oh shit, do you think he heard' and we started whispering as we left the house. i said 'you didn't say anything bad, you just don't like nintendo 64.'

walked around the 'young/college' part of town. joked about how people say 'urban' but mean 'black.' passed an urban outfitters. made jokes. talked about johnny rockets. the part of town…seemed depressing, something about its smallness and affluence and 'who it seemed to be built for/who would enjoy it,' and the people i was seeing mostly through my peripheral vision. a girl with wig-like red hair and a union jack shirt and maybe a boyfriend passed alec and me. alec said 'did you see the union jack shirt' and i said 'yeah, it's bad here.'

the bar was on the brown university campus, in the basement of a campus building. it was cool. you had to go down stairs that reminded me of stairs at my high school. it looked like the bar in 'twin peaks.' there were maybe five rooms, and an oddly-placed glass display showcasing a large skeletal or tooth-like sculpture made of what looked like balsam wood, 'eating' a can or plastic bottle of soda. the bar was empty except for a table of loudish people who left shortly after we arrived. we sat on a couch, side-by-side, but something seemed bad…even though the view from the couch was where the bar most looked like the 'twin peaks' bar and i thought i'd like it. the couch was silver and plastic and sparkly. i said we should move and we did.

before midnight i think we'd had two or three drinks, each. i drank vodka club sodas and alec drank beers i hadn't seen before.

AUGUST 13, 2013

12–2:00AM: sat at the bar. drank four vodka tonics and two negronis. alec ordered a new kind of beer every time, i think. he suggested a beer. can't remember everything we talked about and am unsure if alec would feel okay about me saying everything i do remember. we caught up on a lot of things. life incidentals. i vented about [omitted]. alec had read 'the remainder' and liked it. we were talking intensely about a philosophical aspect of 'the remainder.' remember thinking 'when alec first met me i was studying philosophy and had things to say about philosophy but now i forget everything, i wish i knew more.' alec said his friend anto, who i'd met last summer and liked, reads my liveblog. anto recently told alec, 'it doesn't seem like megan does drugs for fun.' he responded, 'sounds like you 'get' megan.'

exited bar and walked on street. asked alec if he wanted to split 10mg oxycodone and he said he did. i yelled something like 'I'M ON DRUGS, I HAVE DRUGS' at a cop car. then we said things like, 'who lives in that house, someone must live there.' we passed a pizza place. alec said he'd like it if i wanted pizza but he didn't want any. i wanted something. didn't want to be the only person eating pizza. we stood outside the pizza place. alec said there were chips and hummus at his house and…haha…the tone of this part of the conversation was funny, like 'wartime decisions.' a lot of me asking short questions about the specifics of the chips and hummus, alec giving one or two word answers, me nodding with a concerned face and looking at the sidewalk, maybe pensively touching my mouth or chin, receiving enough information to declare the 'big decision:' 'let's just eat chips and hummus,' resuming walking, alec saying 'are you sure,' me saying 'yes, it'll feel better.' by the time we got to his house i decided 'i want to turn around to get pizza' but then realized where we were and walked inside.

wanted one aspect of the food to be hot. thought it'd be better if the hummus was hot. 'fried' hummus in olive oil in a frying pan. the frying made it really mushy. we were laughing a lot during this. laughing in the kitchen, eating the hummus. i mostly ate it with salsa, i think. there was a soggy chip in the salsa. drank the beers we had saved from earlier. ate several mini-hershey bars that had been sort of vulnerably arranged in a strange graph-like pattern on the otherwise empty kitchen table.

brought a handful of mini-hershey bars to alec's room. alec said 'i want to see you eat that when we listen to limp bizkit.' listened and sang along to limp bizkit and other numetal things, then the goo goo dolls. got in a maybe 30-minute fake argument about how we couldn't be friends because i was in a relationship with alec's dad. we were being really serious, like, acting. improv. yelling. alec was hiding in a box and i hid in the closet. wish i had video. it felt actually kind of cathartic, via...i think i was only able to fake-argue like that due to real-arguing like that...it felt good to make fun of it.

laid in bed and read parts of 'the remainder' to each other. can't remember how this happened, but at some point we kissed briefly and i said 'no, i can't.' think we spooned. felt similar to the time we spooned in baltimore, like 'i wish i was romantically attracted but i'm not.' usually if i feel... er...i don't know. usually i don't stop myself from something sexual when it starts, even if i know i'll feel bad after it, but i was glad i could stop because it seemed like it would negatively effect the friendship. or. i'd feel guilty if we had sex and he had feelings for me, and wouldn't be able to ignore the guilt because i like him too much. ate two or maybe three ambiens and gave alec one and a half.

2[something]PM–11:27PM: alec woke me once but i was too sleepy. we had plans to walk around the RISD museum with alexandra at 3PM. alec woke me again, saying something like 'do you want to shower?' i said 'no, i'm fine.' the shower thing was repeated...walking around...groggily...alec said 'sometimes some people like to shower in the morning, i don't know, i didn't know if you wanted to do that.' there wasn't enough time for me to shower, i thought, even if i wanted to. i felt inhibited. alec had been up for a while. i wasn't sure how to act. felt like the thing i wanted to avoid by not doing sexual things had already...it was just there, i wasn't able to avoid it. some kind of tension. i didn't want the tension. gave alec choline and aniracetam. he requested 'less than [i] usually take,' in a way that stuck out to me. i think because normally people i'm giving drugs to don't specify the amount of drugs they want. if an amount is requested, i think it's usually for more than less drugs. i ate the amount i usually eat. alec said 'it's making me feel groggier i think.' i said 'shit...'

i drove us to a coffee place, where alec went inside to buy coffee for alexandra and me and i stayed in the car, before picking her up at her house. when alec returned to the car with coffee we said things about directions, then something i forget, then it was quiet. i said 'i wish we had been filming the argument last night, it was so funny.' alec said 'it was,' and something about how it was better or more special, that there wasn't a video.

parked on the hill outside alexandra's house. noticed a 'butter colored' lion sculpture on the porch. i pointed and said 'look, butter lion.' alec looked in the direction i pointed. i said 'it's the same color as the staircase last night, butter color. lots of butter here. rhode island.'

i paid to get into the museum and students got in free. alec said something funny about…like as soon as we got our 'clippy shirt visitor tags' he said something about a nearby pole, like 'so what aspects of this, uh, er…what aspects should we be taking note of, here?' we walked around a log cabin-like area with desks, pretending it was art.

the museum felt like that part in 'ferris bueller's day off' where they walk around the museum. the first painting i saw was a giant bright red neon opitical illusion-type painting. stood close to it and went 'whoa.' read the plaque about it. i forget what the plaque said. alec approached me, still looking at the red thing, and said 'look at this.' it was a painting of impressionistic grayish brown splotches. think the plaque said something about the holocaust. i pointed to a splotch and said 'so what's this part, is this part anne frank?' alec said the red painting was anne frank, actually.

alec and alexandra joked around but also had informed/interesting things to say about art. i mostly had 'potty humor' or 'durr…i like it' things to say about art. we walked around an exhibit about 'the dandy.' it was cool. it was mostly outfits, standing headless and mannequin-like, donated or purchased or reconstructed from some 'dandies.' i liked seeing how big the people were, like truman capote and john waters. i didn't know there was an official thing called 'dandy,' or that so many people fell under the category of 'dandy,' but it made sense. there was a drag 'dandy' woman from the 1920's i felt interested in…small picture of her with a bald head… head cocked to the side, not smiling, arm on her hip…a big white space before the frame…wrote 'claude cahun' in iphone. couldn't tell if i was sexually attracted to her or liked something else about her. the plaque said she wrote things. think it said 'surreal.' alec and alexandra came up to me and i said 'she's cool.' they looked. we talked about how people in the olden days probably stood for pictures expressionless, slouched with hands on hips, because it took so long to take one picture and they wanted to be comfortable.

broke away from alec and alexandra for an amount of time. read a lot of the plaques. a woman was showing alec and alexandra a picture on her phone from the opening of the dandy exhibit. the picture was of a 'real life socialite,' dressed like scarlett o'hara. the woman was really excited. alec was asking her a lot of questions. i liked the woman so much. she had an accent but i couldn't tell what it was. she was smiling and so excited about the exhibit and other paintings. she liked andy warhol. when we were at the exit to the exhibit, the lady said 'you know the wicked witch of the west?

andy hunted her down for eight years, tried to get her picture for eight years. and she finally let him.' i said 'from 'the wizard of oz?' she said 'yes!' i said 'the actual person?' she said 'yes, the wicked witch! that's his picture of the wicked witch,' smiling really big. she said they had a warhol painting that wasn't included in the dandy exhibit. alec said 'it should've been.' the way she said it, how he said that, and her reaction felt like if alec had said 'your son was a brave fighter. he should've come home to you. i will always remember him.'

after the museum we walked around providence. walked downhill on a sidewalk made of asphalt, with a lot of potholes. felt a little preoccupied about food...or just like, wanting something...i kept saying things about 'the sandwich place' near where we parked, but didn't really want to eat there and dreaded feeling 'sandwich stomach,' and sitting in the place (it had a trendy name, like '[something] fat sandwiches,' a black storefront, and what i imagined...i don't know...felt like i could 'smell' the atmosphere of crumbs on tables and 'artisan soda').

walked by a plaque that said 'built by john updike.' someone said 'it must be a different john updike.' someone said 'no, he could've built it, the famous john updike.' things were said about the building (the first floor was some kind of restaurant or furniture store, i think). i took a picture. alec said something like 'do you want a picture? i want a picture of you guys, you guys, come on, picture time, john updike.' alexandra and i stood by the plaque. wasn't sure what to do at first, then one of us suggested we make the 'dandy posture.'

decided to take spontaneous road trip to newport, RI. alec said he wanted a sugary 'nasty' gas station-type iced coffee before the car ride. pulled into a dunkin donuts. got coffee coolattas. alec and alexandra got small coffee flavored ones and i got a medium mocha. alexandra said something about pep boys and alec told a story about his friend prank-calling pep boys. could tell it had been funny in the moment, but probably funnier to see than hear, and that alec probably knew this. got some kind of second-hand enjoyment from this...like...relating to the situation of telling a 'you had to be there' story. it was just as good for me, i think, because of the feeling of relating.

driving in newport, on the main drag of town, i saw a dress on display and said 'i want that, can we go buy it?' parked in a lot one block up from the store. alec said something funny about dads. he said 'should i bring my jacket? it might get cold.' i said 'you can wear my cardigan, it's for guys and girls.' looked at alexandra, who said i could call her 'allie,' and she was smiling. there was a 'newport conceit' going on. seemed like we were regarding newport as a bizzare and slightly offensive spectacle in this faux-entitled, travel channel 'tourist show about tourists watching tourists' way.

the three of us entered the store with the dress. i found a medium on a rack and bought it without trying it on. alec was being really funny with the cashier. sometimes alec goes into 'tim and eric show presents: woody allen' mode. he was asking the cashier questions about the appropriateness of certain things. she was responding minimally. i was trying not to laugh. he said 'thank you for letting me stand in your store and look at your things' earnestly and she kind of rolled her eyes and smiled. so funny.

alec said 'i want to buy sunglasses' and we walked around a sunglasses store. i couldn't tell if alec really wanted them or not. he said 'guys, should i buy oakleys? should we all buy oakleys?' i said 'yeah.' i tried on sunglasses with frames that looked like martini glasses. allie and i were mostly talking/joking about who would buy those sunglasses. kept picturing a guy on his yacht, going 'party time.' alec seemed maybe seriously interested in buying sunglasses, and was walking around the store in a way i felt i walked around the RISD museum earlier when alec and allie had things to say about paintings that i didn't.

walked to ben & jerrys to use the bathroom. employee gave directions to the public bathroom, inside some kind of mall with an antique store we'd just passed. there was a gathering of middle-aged women standing outside the bathroom. one of us asked if they were in line. one lady said 'i don't know, it's for both men and women, but there's a guy in there right now.' the door was open. a man's voice from inside the bathroom said 'you can come in, it's unisex.' allie and i walked in. the man was peeing in a urinal. i peeked over the top of a stall and watched allie walk away as the man said something like 'there's a spot if you know how to use a urinal.' exited bathroom and allie entered. heard atonal, single-note piano noises coming from the hall. alec was standing at the piano. the lid was mostly closed. he said 'i'm playing my song.' i started playing 'heart and soul' and he said 'oh that's an actual song.' i couldn't see the keys. alec must've walked into the bathroom and allie came out. we talked about the urinal thing and looked at a mounted black-and-white photo of about 60 people sitting and standing in lines. the picture was from the 1940's but i forget when. it was captioned '[something] clam bake, [date].' i pointed at a group of three darker-skinned people and said 'they probably had to cook.' allie and i looked mostly quietly at the picture, sometimes pointing at the funny expressions of people not-yet accustomed to the idea of photographs. alec came out of the bathroom. he said 'you're still here!' we said things about the antique store/mall containing the bathroom, how strange it seemed that it was in business. there was a telephone booth for sale. i said 'the first iphone.'

walked on a dock, behind a man and child. allie said 'yeah let's put our feet in the water.' at the end of the dock, some kind of sign adverstised a tour or ferry. inflatable boats were tied to the dock. alec or allie said the inflatable boats take you to your yacht. there was a little debate about if we were allowed to be walking on the dock. i said 'ey, this is public property over here, we're walkin' ere.' we started saying variations of 'ey this is public property over ere' to each other. it was really funny. felt aware of the man and child passing us, and seemed to disappear at some point. alec and allie stood at the edge of the dock. the light was really pretty. i said i wanted to take a picture and i did. allie took out a cigarette. alec said he wanted a cigarette and i gave him my e-cigarette, then allie gave him a real one.

walked in the direction of the street. the man and child who had been behind us were somewhere ahead, by a parking garage. a cool-looking 1980's honda scooter in the parking garage seemed to interest alec and allie a little more than me. thought 'i could take a picture of this but…no.' alec said 'my friend [anto i think] has a scooter, it's so cool.'

we kept yelling 'ey this is public property, ey!' and 'i'm walkin 'ere, ey!' and things like that as we walked.

we got focused on finding lobster rolls. followed alec into a candy store where he was being…hilarious…jesus…asking the people about lobster candy, if they sold lobster-flavored candy, where to get lobster rolls, saying how good the candy store was and how he wanted to recommend it to people. the candy store employee gave complicated pictoral directions to a place called 'the lobster bar.' alec was egging them on, kind of, like repeating the last thing they'd say…in a funny/non-antagonistic way…shit. thought 'he's not paying attention to directions.' but he had been.

passed a sign that said 'dropkick murphys.' i said 'dropkick murphys' and pointed. no one looked. i was glad because i didn't have anything to say. stopped to ask a guy with black slicked-back hair and tattoos, about the 'lobster bar.' he was sitting by a pedi-bike. the tattoo bike guy gave similarly detailed, pictoral, landmark-based directions. thought it was funny how people in newport…this is how they give directions, this is the newport way. thanked the guy and kept walking.

approached a shopping peninsula, where it seemed like 'the lobster bar' might be. a teenage or slightly older than teenage guy playing a guitar, leaning against a wall. aimlessly said 'do they have…a punk scene…is newport 'punk," to minimal response. saw a sign for 'the lobster bar.' briefly sat at the bar and ordered beers, which came in plastic cups, then hostess seated us at a table where it was pretty and the sun was setting. noticed unusual green lights and transparent floating orbs in the water. pointed out lights to alec and allie. waitress took our picture.

alec asked the waitress about the green lights. she said 'oh, we turn them on. we're in charge of the lights. we turn them on at night, you know, for the effect. it looks different at night.' alec was making 'smooth' conversation with the waitress. she said she gets to take a lot of pretty pictures at work. she moved to get her phone, then gestured or said 'i shouldn't do this, i'm at work, i'll get in trouble.' one of us said 'no, show us.' she passed around a picture and she said she wanted to submit it to a contest. alec said 'you should.' i said 'yeah, do it, you should do it.'

people took pictures by our table. got 'obsessed' with taking pictures of a man who looked like werner herzog, standing near our table with a professional camera. alec stood in the 'herzog zone' so it could look like i was taking a picture of alec. herzog man seemed hilarious to me. herzog stood behind me, alec took picture.

the waitress returned and said something about an appetizer they don't serve anymore. alec said 'why not?' she said 'they just couldn't get it right this year. they kept trying.' alec said 'thank you for telling us.' the waitress said 'yeah a lot of people here, they'll say [made a face] 'we're out of that,' but i like to tell it like it is. they just couldn't get it right this year, i don't know why.' alec said 'that's good, i appreciate that kind of honesty.' she said 'yeah i won't lie to you.' alec said 'thank you, i won't lie to you either. ever.' i said 'yeah thank you, i won't lie either,' smiling at alec. i ordered seaweed salad and a lobster roll with fries. allie ordered a lobster roll (comes with chips. there was…things were said about this, i think mostly between alec and the waitress). alec ordered clam chowder. surprised that was all he wanted, especially after 'the grand lobster roll hunt.' things were said about…how i had eaten seaweed salad last night…the seaweed salad they brought was really big.

had a somewhat involved conversation during dinner about humor and what makes things funny. allie talked about the part in 'crimes and misdemeanors,' i think, where a character says 'comedy is just tragedy with timing.' i tried to paraphrase a schopenhauer quote about humor, that i think is something like…'the most tragic/problematic/important/serious-feeling things are the source of most humor, the ability to view serious-seeming things as funny is intelligent (or something), and people laugh as a reaction to feeling some degree of dissonance about a situation/topic.' i did not do a good job of paraphrasing now or then. when i said it aloud it was probably something like, 'well there's that thing schopenhauer said…um…how all serious stuff can be viewed as funny…that's kind of why it's funny…or it's just as…like the most controversial things are also the most laughed at… but then there's that other thing, the two types of humor, the mean kind and the other…funny…um…the second type…what freud said [mumble/ trailed off].' somehow felt like i was annoying alec during this conversation. he left for the bathroom and i asked allie if he seemed annoyed and she said she didn't know. we talked more about the humor thing. allie used the bathroom. i said 'am i annoying you? i'm sorry if i'm being annoying, was something annoying about the humor thing?' to alec. he said 'no, no, not at all,' not looking at me.

we asked them to split the check. there was an error with my check. i had ordered the most food and made a miscalculation and there was $15 left over. seemed tense. i told the waitress to charge me an additional $15. something felt different. felt myself go into 'kamakaze sensitivity mode,' where i interpret everything as 'the people around me are not having fun and it's my fault.' used the bathroom. walked past gigantic 'farm' of maybe six 15'-long lobster tanks that i saw, and wanted to look more closely at, when we entered the restaurant. wanted to take pictures. the tanks were filled with about eight inches of water. lobsters and 'anonymous,' dis-placed-seeming fish crowded together in small clumps. the ceiling was very high and unfinished, with large dusty industrial pipes and vents. saw alec and allie in the distance, taking pictures of their faces inside a cut-out area of a giant plywood painted lobster. people were gathered under a tent nearby, watching a band play covers of john mayer-like songs. allie took a picture of my face inside the lobster. i said 'that's so good, facebook, send it to me, new facebook pic.' she did things to her phone. felt people 'putting up with me' as i emailed the picture to myself.

keep thinking 'something seemed different.' we left the lobster bar and walked destinationless, saying things about how we felt full but we could get ice cream. allie and alec talked about harry potter. alec said 'i'm only talking about harry potter so much today because the last time i was in newport i read [one or all or a lot of] the harry potters.' i saw a storefront with a sign that said 'scrimshander's scrimshaw.' thought zachary would think it was funny. i don't know what a scrimshaw is…just, 'scrimshander's scrimshaw,' that would be funny. stopped to take a picture. alec and allie continued walking. wondered how long it would take them to notice i wasn't there. 'a long time,' i thought. i moved closer to the window of the scrimshaw store—some kind of gift shop selling things that seemed too disparate to be parts of a theme, or maybe all of these things were 'scrimshaws.' felt something complex, watching the people inside with the boat figurines and kites and glass objects, knowing none of us were really looking for anything.

didn't see alec and allie for a moment. they were maybe half a block ahead on the sidewalk. it looked like they'd only recently stopped walking. i waved and smiled, jogged to them. i don't think any of us mentioned what happened. i didn't feel bad about it, just something. i did it, i made the thing possible, the thing i felt. they were still talking about harry potter a little, i think. alec pointed at a candy store and said 'maybe there'll be fudge samples' and we walked inside, where people who looked like families milled around. no free samples. i stared at a box of head-sized pastries labeled 'elephant ears.' alec said 'should we just buy a thing of fudge, a big thing?' i said 'yeah, let's do it, let's get fudge!' alec said 'or elephant ears?' i said 'no, not that…' a man and a boy approached the elephant ears. the man was giving the boy a lesson about pastries. i said 'let's just buy fudge.' alec and allie were exiting the store.

i said 'i want ice cream.' alec said 'i saw a place called 'kill ones' earlier that had ice cream. it looked like they'd have free fudge samples too.' passed crowded ben & jerry's, which i felt indifferent about, but alec and allie seemed averse to standing in line. someone said 'should we ask the ben & jerry's people where 'kill ones' is?'

walked into a subway. it was hot, they were 'baking bread.' the sandwich-makers were busy with two customers. felt eyes looking at us. we were just standing there, saying things about how hot it was, not ordering. i stood a little closer to the employee zone. made eye contact. alec asked if they knew where 'kill ones' was. more people looked. alec said 'it's an ice cream store? we're looking for ice cream.' an employee said we should go to ben & jerry's.

walked into a gelato store. the employees were helping a gathering of mostly small upset children. the gelato was all sorbet, no 'ice cream' kinds. alec or allie said 'it must be miserable to work here,' within earshot of the employees. i said 'yeah it's really bad in here,' also within earshot. someone said 'why did we come in here?' i said 'i saw it earlier, i thought it'd have the creamy kind.' someone said 'this is all sorbet.' i said 'i know, let's go.' walked out as a group and looked at a picture on the wall, signed 'andy warhol.' we looked at each other and made 'seinfeld'-like faces and said 'andy warhol?' and 'oh, andy warhol.'

allie walked into a new age-themed accessory shop, with a sidewalk display of tapestries and incense. alec followed allie briefly, then returned outside with an employee following him. alec asked about 'kill ones.' the employee used a different pronounciation of 'kill ones' and said it was in the opposite direction. allie came out. she said there is a certain kind of rosemary incense she likes, which only some stores have. i asked what it was called. she said 'i don't know, i just know it when i see it.'

talked about 'blue velvet' while walking to 'kill ones.' allie hadn't seen it. alec said 'let's go back and watch it at my house.' i said 'do you have it? the movie?' he said no, he had amazon prime, which gives you free shipping, and offered use of his account to allie and i. he said you could also watch movies with it.

we found 'kilwin's.' it was in a stripmall-type arrangement of stores across from the lobster bar. there were a lot of little colored lights, a lot of lit-up things, little hills or something. as we crossed the street alec said 'i feel like i'm in disneyworld,' (i thought 'me too, he said it right, this feels like the parade at the end of disneyworld [which i had forgotten i'd seen until that moment, i think]) 'like i'm watching the parade at the end of disney-world.' i said 'me too, me too. it feels like that exactly.' entering kilwin's, we talked about people who would go to disneyworld—then newport, rhode island—to save their marriages.

no fudge samples were available inside. many people milled around but not many seemed to be in line. i stood in line. alec and allie were elsewhere. i asked to try a few samples of ice creams, didn't really like any, but ordered turtle cheesecake and chocolate peanut butter in a waffle bowl. felt shitty. it was $7. i snickered and said 'you guys aren't getting anything,' which souded more like an antagonistic observation, or maybe question, than the deadpan jab at myself i had intended. wanted to continue on, like, 'don't even think about getting a bite,' but it seemed like i was the only person interested in or aware of what i was saying. alec seemed...i wasn't sure what he was doing at first. he picked up a box of chocolate covered cherries. encouraged him to 'do it,' thinking i was either encouraging him to buy or steal the cherries. he said 'no, i don't want to steal from them.'

i was mostly behind alec and allie as we walked to the car. they were talking about bob dylan. allie likes bob dylan a lot. felt happy to be occupied with 'eating ice cream, not talking for now.' we approached the parking lot. finished giant bite of the waffle bowl and people seemed impressed. remembered telling alec earlier that he could wear my cardigan if he got cold, and how he had been periodically mentioning feeling cold since the sun had set. thought 'say something? no.'

alec's phone died. allie said we could use her phone for directions home. whenever this conversation happened, sometime at dinner i think, alec and allie said things about not knowing how to work gps on their phones very well. felt really full from the ice cream. started driving without knowing where to go, not really caring where i'd go, confident that 'we'll end up home somehow.' allie and i found the way to the highway around the same time. sort of bickered with alec about radio stations. he switched stations fast. i kept saying 'i want to hear 'blurred lines,' let's see if it's playing any- where.' my 'thing' became saying 'this isn't 'blurred lines.'" i liked bickering, was either laughing outwardly or inside the whole time. alec said 'okay, let's find a radio station where you don't try to make funny comments or complain about the music.' allie was quiet in the back for most of the ride. alec started dancing to a song i didn't know. felt annoyed by the way he was dancing, and annoyed at my annoyance.

arrived in providence. allie said 'this is my street,' and i missed the turn, distracted by thoughts about whether anyone remembered we talked about watching 'blue velvet' tonight. alec said something about pep boys. i said 'fucking pep boys' and fake-scoffed. turned on allie's street and parked by her house. remembered 'the butter lion.' i said it was really nice meeting her and she said something nice back. alec said something long and funny about hanging out again soon, which she reciprocated, waving goodbye as she walked across the yard. waited for her to open the door. she had said something earlier about the lock being funny. alec said 'yeah we should wait until she gets in.' allie approached the passenger-side window and said 'you guys know how to get home, right?' alec said 'yeah, yeah, thanks' and i said 'oh yeah, yeah, i think we can figure it out.' she said 'okay, see ya,' smiled and waved, walked inside.

didn't really know where i was driving but had a feeling it was close. alec asked what i wanted to do. i said 'i think i want to go home actually.' he seemed disappointed. i said 'my cats, and also i know if i don't...if i go back tomorrow it'll be harder for me to get things done, but tonight i'll have a night.' something felt different.

alec tried to look up directions on his ipad. i said 'i can just reverse the stuff i already have, it's fine.' he said 'no, no, here, you should have direc- tions' and changed something on the screen. i said 'no it's okay, i'll figure it out.' felt that i was leaving quickly and that he wasn't happy. i hugged him lightly and said 'thank you for letting me stay, it was good to see you, i had fun, this was like, rejuvenating mental thing, for me, thank you,' which i wanted to be more true as i said it, feeling some irreconcilable fault in me alternately fight for my attention and hide from it, wanting to be anything other than myself walking towards the door. he said 'i'm glad that's what you thought about it.'

11:28pm: 'baba o'riley' playing on radio. Stopped at Walgreens for energy and e-cigarette. This song gives me chills, the end. It ended. Feel full and sick. Distracted by wanting some drug that doesn't exist yet.

11:43pm: 'chantilly lace' by the big bopper is playing. Happy Zachary memory song. He'd play it sometimes and we'd sing along. So funny. It never wasn't funny. His face. 'A ponytail. Hanging down.' Sometimes imagined he was affectionately directing parts to me, like 'ain't nothin in the world like a big eyed girl.' But my eyes aren't really that big. And we both knew it. Especially towards the end. It sounded like the big bopper knew it too, towards the end.

AUGUST 14, 2013

12:42am: Alec said something funny about a song being Elliott smith earlier. Listening to Elliott smith now. I'm most attracted to depressed hopeless people with no futures who don't like me much. Not because I think 'oh I can save you,' because I'm depressed and hopeless and don't care about my future and don't like myself. I don't think either thing I just said was accurate, but...you could say those things are accurate...looking at my life...I guess.

'Put down that mouse. You can come see rare Mexican wolves.' –billboard feat. picture of wolves that I just passed.

1:15am: listening to mix-cd from 2004. Scream/sang along to bright eyes and q and not u. Was really into q and not u for a period. I like their drumming and how often every song changes. A lot of different sounding parts in each song. I was so young when I made this cd. 18 or 19. I am only 'the older age you can be in a year' from October 15-December 31. Every year. So I always seem a little younger. Have probably seen q and not u play more than any other band. Aloha or q and not u. I miss old me...little happy drug-free show-going shithead...with funny male friends...before I had sex with all my funny male friends and so I liked all of us more...'I guess this is growing up'-blink182

Now radiohead is playing who the hell was I Jesus. I like when he goes 'ill laugh ubtil my head comes off' and 'this is really happening' in this song, forget what song is called, remember like, waiting on those parts to come up...waiting to relish in those parts of the song, so I could sing along with 'thom yorke' eyes. Thom yorke should start a newspaper called 'the Thom Yorker' big bucks in that get on it googly eyes!

1:27am: now 'admit it' by say anything is on. Did anyone else like say anything? Forgot I was into this stuff, my 'can't do it' quoting friend and I used to drive around singing along to this stuff.

Taking back Sunday holy shit

Having emotional moment

2:27am: a little lost. I don't know what road this is, near Jamaica ave, which I know from Pizza Hut/taco bell das racist song.

2:58am: walking to apartment have to pee badly.

2:59–5:31PM: don't remember what i did.

nothing i want to do really.

if anyone reading has thought 'there is a crucial error she is missing, something would be better if she knew/did [whatever] differently' and you think i'm not aware of the thing, please tell me. if you want to be anonymous you can ask say it on ask.fm. if you want. anything would be appreciated, any thoughts. that sounds…i'm not…miserable…not trying to be funny either…just stuck or something, i don't know. michael scott.

5:33–11:59PM: don't remember most of this. think i started recording acapella cover of 'take ecstasy with me' by magnetic fields. ate an amount of oxycodone or xanax or both.

AUGUST 15, 2013

did not update.

AUGUST 16, 2013

5:35PM: have been watching slow accumulation of pigeons gather outside my window, perching in an ominous line on building across mine. seems like they're about to watch a public execution.

AUGUST 17, 2013

9:36am: there was a ticket on my windshield. Was looking forward to getting a medium coffee coolatta with no whipped cream the whole walk to car. The coolatta was my main reason to leave bed. The promise of a coffee coolatta. Can smell the ocean. Thought 'I'll just walk a mile along the ocean, why don't I ever do that' on the way to dunkin donuts. In elevator to my building now. Exiting elevator. Getting the coolatta to prolong wakefulness/laying in bed to watch 'the office' and probably not wash the cat pee sheets is funny. I asked for $2 in change from the cashier at dunkin donuts. Encountered some inane mutual confusion. Ended up grinning and saying 'laundry' a few times at the end. Pretty sure cashier didn't understand me.

9:43am: the coolatta is making my stomach hurt. Third coolatta of my life. The other two were 'mocha coffee coolattas.' This one is a 'coffee coffee coolatta.' They were all mediums. I endorse the coffee coolatta product.

10:27AM: have mostly been watching 'the office' the past two days. wanted to look at [omitted]'s okcupid profile this morning but seems like my account is suspended. zachary's account was still signed in on firefox. found a number of annoying discrepancies between what [omitted] chooses to say on his profile and things i know to be true about him.

10:52AM: gchatted with zachary about coolattas. forcing my coolatta interest on the innocent. sent him the link to [omitted]'s okcupid profile. we got into shittalky stuff, quoting the profile. i was laughing. without knowing who [omitted] was, zachary picked out stuff i thought was funny/interesting/like 'what the hell is this' about the profile. was surprised by um. his ability to see things. i'm not surprised by that actually, i know zachary sees stuff. observant sensitive intelligent person. the surprise was more in hearing another person notice the things i think i can ignore about people and like, privately conclude 'no one else would notice this, i'm being too picky/overly sensitive, i should be grateful that anyone wants to get to know me' about. have re-read our conversation maybe four times. felt 'intense,' all the times. considered including in liveblog but i'm already drawing more attention to [omitted] than i feel good about doing, by including this at all.

11:09AM: zachary asked what his job was, which is part of the funny thing, why he wanted his name to be 'omitted' in this originally. i said the job. zachary said 'lul' twice. looked at profile pictures again and felt shitty. remorseful something. like 'he isn't a bad person' and '[picture of him reading this on his phone and...].' i don't think he'd even want to read it though. the cheating thing just seemed like his way of indirectly breaking up. he could've said 'i don't want a relationship right now' or 'i don't want a relationship with you after all' but this way it like, 'sealed the deal.' like maybe some part of him knew cheating on me would be a way to get rid of me forever. there would be no break-up conversation. just...obvious. obvious action. i would be the one who would end it. he still got to have sex with this girl. i'm just the other girl who ended it. he didn't even have to do any work to end it. the only work he had to do was to have sex and lie. he didn't have to be involved in this at all. have imagined him thinking gradually, like, 'i don't like megan as much anymore, she eats lobster messily, she wants to talk about dreams, she seemed upset by [something vague about dreams or memory and tom mccarthy book he recommended that he couldn't remember well], she's too sensitive, she isn't as ambitious as me, she doesn't know people in 'my industry,' she does more drugs than me, she doesn't know how to cook, she shares too much with the internet, she does not seem to like dogs as much as me, she's always going to the library and 'working on stuff' but she never finishes and then i come home and oh great...just...there she is on the bed, she was more interesting when she was a character in a book, she says socially inappropriate things, she is kind of 'intense' with the crying and the reading and the things she read were a little 'intense,' she likes karaoke, we are at different points of our lives, she wants to talk about all of this, she can see i'm becoming less interested and i don't want her to know,' and wanting to end the whatever-it-was but he couldn't think of a 'safe way 'out'' and by cheating...it was like he could still be...like, 'all the best, so sorry, i feel so bad about this, i never meant for this to happen, all the best, please drive safe' but secretly he's thinking 'yesssssssss!!!!!!' partially think that due to. um. the night that it happened, he had sex with the other girl and didn't tell me for a few hours and i had started sucking on his penis that had just been in this other girl yuck yuck yuiuck red glitter on his penis and he lied about using condoms (we had been drinking). i wasn't as drunk as he was, but still. if zachary and i were arguing and drinking and i'd want to drive to maryland or something, he wouldn't want to let me do that. he'd get very insistent. he'd be like 'don't do this, don't drive drunk, it's stupid and dangerous.' but [omitted] seemed relieved when i left. he texted 'so sorry, please drive safe' or something like that. something bureaucratic. the 'please drive safe' seemed striking. like he had planned it. i don't know. i know he didn't plan it. er. i don't know, he could've planned it, i don't know. why did that strike me so much. 'please drive safe.' bureaucratic. i remember foreseeing this becoming an issue early-on, the bureaucratic thing. we were at a party with an 'important person:' a regular person who seemed to be pretty blatantly behaving in a way like they thought they were 'important,' doing things that would probably upset their family, that they thought they could get away with doing, because of their 'importance.' [omitted] was like...really buying into it...like, celebrating this person's acting in these ways. i understood why—the person is successful and could probably advance [omitted] in his whatever-he-does someday. i don't know. i might be misjudging the person. but anyway—just. i don't know. the way [omitted] was acting. it was like the world stopped for this 'important' person, who sometime after the departure of, he said he thought we would've had a regrettable threesome with, had my interactions with the person gone differently. i didn't think that would happen, but i felt a distance, thinking 'he thinks this could've happened.' neurotic distance. when i told him i didn't like how the 'important' person was acting, he reacted like this was unheard of and scandalous. it was like i had informed a devout baptist of the fact that books about satanism exist, as if satanism itself could shake the foundation of baptism–which means it's equally or more powerful than baptism, which means some part of you knows the thing you're so devout about is weak. a devout baptist who feels so threatened by topic of satanism that to them, a world that capable of holding multiple belief systems is a world largely abandoned by its creator, whose attention must now be fought for by his now-ignored chosen people, in addition to their already longstanding fight against the evils that somehow exist within his creation but are not of it, which threaten his flawed yet flawless design. cool thing to devote your life to, smart guy. cool criteria of 'importance,' cool guy. closed-minded. i didn't like that. i started noticing other stuff like that...like, little niceties... disingenuous stuff...inconsistencies in his conduct i probably would've otherwise ignored. he'd bought his apartment something like a year ago, for example, and leaning against the wall were frames he still hadn't found pictures to go in or gotten around to hanging. maybe this was due to the forgivable laziness of a busy life, or wanting his surroundings to look the way he wanted but not yet knowing what he wanted, but i don't know. maybe it was a metaphor for the life of someone who could never commit to the things he found important, because deep down he knew the important things wouldn't give him the time of day either. maybe they could, though. but not to someone who has already decided they can't.

11:57AM: ate 400mg choline, maybe 1g aniracetam, 200mg noopept. realize that acknowledging 'i noticed this stuff about [omitted] that i didn't like, and i noticed it early-on' means my choice to continue being with him was similarly disingenuous as the things i'm describing about him that i didn't like. here is how i have rationalized this: maybe i'm learning to trust my instincts more. i wasn't being disingenuous by dating him, i liked him a lot, at the time. i also disliked stuff, just like with anyone i've ever dated. but then how do i know what to focus on in the future...should it be the 'liking' or 'disliking'…it'll be based on the situation, i guess. i'll just know what to do then. i'm more informed now. maybe. probably not.

12:13PM: started feeling nauseated and dizzy during last paragraph, like was thinking 'maybe you should just lay down and close your eyes,' which quickly turned into 'maybe you should stand over the toilet.' vomited a lot. think it was the coolatta. coolatta and nootropic blend of nasty. stomach started feeling queasy drinking the coolatta. when no more stuff came out i was just like, dry-heaving. did maybe four dry-heaves. then a little more stuff came out. 'the very bottom stuff.' it tasted different. more acrid than the humble coolatta beginnings.

brushed teeth. blew nose in sink. nose has 'that puke smell.' comforted by my assumption that most people know 'that puke smell.' chest feels tight. as i was brushing teeth i thought 'you are becoming an insane ranting dislikable person. if you post the rant about [omitted] you are further alienating yourself from [end thought]. insane dislikable ranter. you don't even update the liveblog regularly, people know they can't count on you. slowly chasing away all people with your insane dislikable rants about how you're insane and dislikable. counting this. if you write this down, that 'counts' as part of a rant i think, furthering your…the bad thing that you are…'

i'm more awake now, no longer dizzy. unsure if i'm poisoning myself with the nootropics. coolattas are maybe more poisonous than drugs.

3:35PM: still gchatting with zachary. i'm having fun. emailed him a picture of alvie pooping and looking at me. email subject was 'alvie taking a tip from his ol pal holong' (holong is adam's cat, he stares at you when he poops), email body was 'it's briney bitch.'

5:43pm: walking back from sushi place. Have been gchatting with Zachary this whole time. Here's what happened on the way out of apartment:

- saw bike in hall, considered taking a picture for Zachary

- opened door to stairway. Said 'hi how are you' to man doing stuff to a box on the wall. I said 'fios?' He said 'time warner.' We decided something pleasant about each other, it seemed. He started walking down stairs just far away enough to be 'too far to hold the door for,' but close enough that it also would've seemed appropriate to hold. Thought 'don't hold any doors for him, you decided holding doors is stupid, remember? Stick to your guns. You'll never see him again. Except when you come back inside [too late all doors already closed]'

- thought 'you really are an anomaly, Boyle, walking around with the coconut oil on your hair and the neon orange shorts.'

- picked up sushi

- could tell I was staggering a little as I entered station wine & liquors. Selected large bottle of white zinfandel from fridge. Cashier who always acts suspicious of me predictably asked to see my ID. Handed him 10% off coupon. He said 'alright.' When I grabbed the bag he handed me he said 'you got my finger.' I didn't understand. He said 'my finger, you can't take my finger.' I let go of the bag and laughed and apologized. Still didn't feel his finger. Exited saying 'I'll use that coupon next time'

5:55pm: took picture of bike in hall and emailed Zachary.

6:44PM: just ended gchat with zachary. what a charming funny person i got to know. still get to know. great. 'still.' haha. when i type in the liveblog as if it were my best friend or me or a diary or something, that's how talking to him felt. so much love in my big stupid heart for that guy.

6:51–11:59PM: ate sushi. continued gchat with zachary. laughed a lot. drank a bottle of wine. tweeted picture of cat pee stains. the pee shape resembles australia. i sleep on the pee-free side, on a yoga mat. recorded video of myself screaming to a desaparacidos song in my closet.

AUGUST 18, 2013

6:52AM: woke in a strange position from vivid dream that felt two or three days long, about a tsunami. couldn't remember where i was for a long time. left leg is numb. looked at the internet.

8:00AM: woke with a feeling that something had been watching me sleep, or i had been taken to a parallel universe and maybe not delivered back to the one where i belong. something about the wall is scary. i don't want to face the window because it looks too bright, but having my back to the wall feels vulnerable. reminds of the scary face i saw out my window when i was little, and am sometimes afraid i'll see again. the face is kind of like the dumpster man from 'mulholland drive.' just pictured the face and it had a body. this is the first time it's had a body. definitely the same face. it's like a hulking body in robes, too tall to be a person. couldn't shake feeling of… just…that something had been implanted in me in my sleep, which is why my thigh was numb, and the scary man had been involved in this.

1:35PM: woke from another vivid dream. felt less scared. emailed mira. we're meeting at the bareburger on 3rd ave at 8:30PM. going to get a freaking coolatta.

2:14pm: bought medium coffee for a man standing outside dunkin donuts. His name is roi. We shook hands and he said 'r-o-i, roi.' I said 'm-e-g-a-n, Megan' a few times. He said 'okay.' I said 'okay' and let go of his hand.

8:03pm: walking to car. Sam will be at Bareburger too. Ate 800mg phenethylamine, 1.2g aniracetam, 4.5mg hydergine. Feel like I'm about to vomit and I'm being watched and my execution is soon. Eerie. Feels like my dream last night, the same amount of vividness.

8:11pm: second vivid dream involved photo session by train tracks, double-date with Michael Scott. Billy Joel was talking about the song 'big shot.' We were standing by a table with no chairs, waiting for something.

8:14pm: large area of back left thigh has been numb since waking. Left forearm keeps twitching.

8:15-11:59PM: got lost. stopped at a CVS for directions, then walked across the street to a deli where i saw something that looked like a payphone and was, gutted. asked the cashier if he knew where i could find a payphone. a man handed his phone to me and i thanked him. didn't know how to work phone. called mira to say i'd be 20 minutes late. parked on

35th ave. saw mira and sam sitting outside at a table with a centerpiece of onion rings, a beer pitcher, and glasses. sat beside mira and ordered 'chicken pickle' sandwich.

after dinner we bought three bags of cocaine, $40 each, and $20 of xanax. i had eaten 2mg xanax before dinner. my nose was congested. there was a somewhat laborsome process of…laughing right now, why was this so hard…seemed like it took forever for sam and i to find the bathroom. why didn't we all just go at bareburger? sam went somewhere and mira and i went to walgreen's so i could buy nose spray. then i had to pee. sam said i could pee at a pizza place. mira texted her drug dealer while i was in the bathroom. when i walked out sam and mira were…i forget where. they knew my phone wasn't working so they wanted to wait for me. sam bought beer. remember mira saying 'you bought beer?' and sam saying 'yeah, i thought we'd have beer.'

sat on a raised-curb area, sharing a 24oz coors banquet in a paper bag. there was some uncertainty about which of the drug dealer's 'henchman' would show up. a man appeared and mira scampered to him. the man looked like a someone who fixes computers for a living, or works at best buy. forget what sam and i talked about. stopped being able to see mira at some point.

walked to my car, which a cop car had parked near. a group of three australian women were taking pictures by the cop car. i said 'did you guys get arrested?' and they started talking to us as they followed us to my car. nobody was in the cop car. the australians were vacationing with like, eight people, staying in some kind of vague hotel operation…thing…outside of which i was parked. they were talking without much prompt from mira and sam and me. they were funny. they just kept going. one of them said 'oh come on, these people want to go' about us, shortly before their husbands showed up. their husbands were just like them. the australians. they wanted us to go to australia.

AUGUST 19, 2013

12-5:00AM: at sam's apartment we snorted three baggies cocaine, three mollies split into three lines, 'parachuted' 800mg phenthylamine twice, ate unknown amount of xanax and i think a little ambien. near the beginning, i spilled beer and immediately started 'cleaning'/sucking it up from the floor with my mouth. at some point we decided to change clothes every time we did a line. a garfield costume became involved. some time ago, sam's friend ralph gave him a garfield costume. so good. we went outside and took pictures in a park. i wore the garfield body and mira wore the garfield head. remember wanting to exercise, run instead of walk, and rally the group to do crunches when we got back to sam's. mira and i gave each other 'airplane rides' on sam's bed. threw out my back and did something to my right ab muscles that is only starting to not hurt now (aug 26).

after first 800mg phenethylamine we started talking in 'the voice,' similar to how tao and i would sometimes, on MDMA, mimic the speech of 'intellectuals' on podcasts. one of us would say something, someone would disagree, then the first person would say 'that was a test, i was demonstrating the effects of [whatever],' then someone would say 'that's amazing, the way you did that. i feel so connected to your strong beliefs.' wish i had been recording a video. sam recorded a video of mira and i saying 'marxism' and 'feminism,' which i uploaded to youtube with the title 'TEDTALK: FEMINISM AND MARXISM.' asked mira and sam to draw a tattoo for me.

~2:30PM: woke to mira entering sam's apartment with a bag from pathmark. talked about how we still felt like we were on drugs but unsure what. mira had bought bagels, cream cheese, hummus, and a tomato. she toasted two everything bagels. i sliced the tomato. spread cream cheese and topped it with tomato and salt and pepper. we sat and talked at the kitchen table for an amount of time, mostly about what we remembered from last night. discussed plan to get tattoo somewhere in midtown when mira and sam get off work tonight.

gps worked on phone via sam's wifi. got lost on the way home and stopped at a starbucks. ordered 'substitute coffee coolatta: mocha light frappucino with shot of espresso.' asked man how to get to woodhaven drive. got lost a few times.

~6:00PM: got gas from the wave station by me. tried to buy e-cigarette refills but my card wasn't scanning. checked ATM. nothing in savings account, $12 remain in checking account. ate 1mg xanax.

parked and called mom about coming to maryland tomorrow to fix my phone. she was upset that she hadn't heard from me in so long. upset about other things too. remember saying 'can you please stop yelling at me' and i think crying at some point. she said it wouldn't be good if i came to maryland tonight because dad was coming over to talk about money. i said that was fine. i remember saying something like 'if you don't want to see me it's okay, i just want them to fix my phone at the place where i got it so it'll be easy, i can just drive down and leave really quick, you won't even see me.' she said dad told her i was spending $1000 a week, which i am absolutely nowhere near close to spending. tried to calm mom. dad seemed mostly upset about things on my bank statement from rhode island. dad has a tendency to exaggerate or fabricate things when he feels 'wronged.' think he was just upset about me not responding to his emails, going to rhode island, forgetting about him visiting me today. felt shitty about forgetting his visit. forwarded mom emails from dad. sent him a long email apologizing for forgetting his visit. this is embarrassing to me.

ate two units of ambien. emailed mira and sam that i was out of money, that jordan said he'd pay me back thursday, and i was transferring what's left in my paypal to my savings, so couldn't do the tattoo tonight but would like to another time.

gets blurry around here.

stood in line at pickles & pies, to pay for toilet paper, 'late night snack' ben & jerry's ice cream, white cheddar cheese puffs. thought 'my total must be under $12.' outside it was dark. woman near me yelled into a phone about not knowing where she was. she kept repeating 'pickles & pies,' and something indicating she thought the person on the other end of the phone was supposed to pick her up and had maybe left her there. exchanged looks of 'what is there to do' with cashier, who in early june said 'you can't trust anyone' about the government, who i talked with on the 'super moon' day, who recently sighed and smiled in a world-weary way when i asked how he was, answered with a word in another language he said meant 'marvelous' and that he viewed life as, no matter what, always being okay.

smoked weed in kitchen. dipped cheese curls in hummus. ate the ice cream. watched episode of 'the office' where pam gives birth. felt uncomfortable about babies, pam having a baby, the idea that the baby had been in her and that now everyone was talking about it. looked at porn and tried to masturbate. felt distracted by pam's baby. felt like there was nothing i could do or want to see or say. clipped and painted toe and fingernails. felt like this was the only 'safe'/neutral thing i could do. anything else would lead to a downward spiral of negative thinking.

AUGUST 20, 2013

12-2:22AM: alternated between 'the office,' porn, trying to download 'bridesmaids.' searched 'eating cheese puffs with hummus' on youtube, to feel less alone.

3:29AM: smoked more weed.

3:37AM: looked at porn.

4:30AM: i don't remember orgasming or masturbating, but i could've. turned off lights except for battery-operated push-button 'star projecting' night light by my head. curled in ball, facing light.

1:12PM: woke. watched 'happy hour' episode of 'the office' and laughed hard at things, unexpectedly. ate 20mg adderall XR, drank zero-calorie monster. emailed with mira and sam. heard a crash coming from closet.

6:25PM: talked with mom on googletalk. driving to maryland tonight, getting phone fixed tomorrow.

6:57PM: got out of bed with the plan to eat another 20mg adderall and take a picture of the tattoo mira and sam drew for me. poured 'dried bits of wet cat food that had been soaking in water so their dishes would be clean' into toilet, clutching e-cigarette. cleaned litter box. a fly has been hanging out in the bathroom for a few days. used to try to kill it but now consider it 'my buddy.' it flew around excitedly as i scooped cat poop in the toilet. flushed toilet. it clogged. did 'the retard rotator' on the cats' dry food and split a can of wet for them. turned on 'main lamp' and 'red lamp.' took picture of tattoo. pill box contains maybe .75mg xanax, 1.5 units ambien, 60mg vyvanse, 20mg adderall xr. sat on bed and took pictures of toe/fingernails. plugged phone into computer. placed adderall around 18" to my right.

7:03PM: alvie is crying. said 'adderall' using tone of voice i used to say 'alvie.'

8:04PM: 20mg adderall XR is on back of tongue. zachary gchatted me. the drawing i made in march with mira, sam, and sam pink fell off the wall. swallowed adderall. earlier i scanned all the videos on my computer...have so many hours of shitty footage of shitty videos of...shitty...depressing. jesus. too much. considering posting all of them somewhere, it's probably like over 48 hours of footage of depressing me rambling depressedly. had forgotten about a video i made of myself july 16, in [omitted]'s apartment, like...cheerfully showing things to the camera, saying 'this is what you do when you're at the apartment of the person you're dating and they've just left for work,' seeming happy and lighthearted.

10:59PM: peed. ate small spoonful choline, large spoonful aniracetam. have been elaborating on rhode island stuff. it feels good to remember it. the last time i was in maryland, my mom gave me a heart-shaped rose quartz stone. she said 'i know you probably think it's crazy, but i really believe this stuff has mystical properties, rose quartz—if you just hold it—will you promise me you'll just hold it sometimes?' i said 'i don't think that's crazy, rocks are just stuff, like people. we're all made of stuff. i'll hold it.' she said 'just put it in your pocket, okay? and feel it sometimes?' i said 'i will. i'll hold it.' she said 'the thing to know about rose quartz is, well, it's said to bring positive energy about love. matters of the heart.'

later she asked me to pick out rocks/crystals in her apartment that i liked to take back with me. she said 'you need a talisman. that is what i feel.' i said 'that's funny. i need something, i'll take anything.' i asked her more about what she thought crystals did. she said 'well, you know that crystal store in ellicott city? i went into it one day, oh, whenever it was that grandma was moving here. i was really nervous about her moving here, you know. and i just…i was there, i went into the store for some reason, and as soon as i walked in the man said to me: 'you need a talisman.' i was drawn to these stones, which he said were called rose quartz. and i really feel that this—this—that this is something. crystals. it never hurts to think you can bring magic into your life, and that i know.' i said 'definitely, definitely.'

asked if i could have a spherical pink crystal. she said 'now, that? that is really something. that is something, that you were drawn to that one. it's also rose quartz, and there's a story—um. i gave that very crystal to your sister when she was going through a tough time, romantically, and then she gave it back to me. actually just a few years ago. she had met [current boyfriend's name] and she thought i could, well. you know. it'd be good if i had it again. so your choice, meggie, that's really interesting.' i said 'that is interesting. that's weird, that i'd pick that one. it looks like a planet, i like how it's like a planet. are you sure you don't need it?' she said 'yes, yes. this is the one for you right now, it's your time to have this one now.'

when i returned to my apartment i knew where the crystals were for a while—had held them the night of august 2, probably. they get hot in your hands. after i rearranged furniture i couldn't find them. thought they were probably lost forever, but the day i had the long gchat with zachary i found them in my jeans-pocket. i hadn't been looking for them. since then, i've been keeping them close, like, either in my hands, hoodie-pocket, or purse, if i'm going out. i sleep beside or on them. i don't know if this is doing anything. they feel good to hold. they are heavy.

AUGUST 21, 2013

1:18AM: just spent maybe…oh i don't know, definitely not a long time, but certainly a length of time searching for an .mp3 of 'baba o'riley,' bought it for $1.29, scrolled down itunes to 'the who' where—you guessed it—there are now two 'baba o'rileys.'

how the hell can i do anything else right now. who even cares. no one wants to read this much from a person. what do i mean by 'this much.' what do you do with a person, any amount? fuck all of you. there is this much of a person here and none of you want it. at least now i know. fine. or. i don't know. no one wants it who i want to want it. or if they want it i don't know about it. i want more adderall or caffeine. should i just eat the fucking adderall. one left? i'll…more is coming…'for more is always coming'… great…goddamnit. i was supposed to drive to maryland tonight. i still want to do that. i'll arrive at mom's house early in the morning. it will be light outside. will feel so shitty. running low on the things that make me feel better and put me to sleep.

will someone adopt shirley? themeganboyle@gmail.com

serious inquiries only…please…please inquire…

i love shirley so much but the person i am right now can barely muster up the energy to care for itself, let alone another living thing.

i think shirley only started peeing on the mattress because i was gone for several days, but now the mattress smells like her pee so she just…goes there for fun…i don't know. have also thought it's territorial. she started peeing on zachary's mattress in november 2011, but i don't think she did before she met me. think she peed the bed a few times at the philadelphia apartment. she and alvie fight a lot. they seem jealous whenever i give the other one attention, but shirley especially. like it should definitely be just one cat…shit. goddamnit. why is she peeing like this. nobody cares. i'm the only person who cares and i don't care enough for any of us to get fixed. if you want sad…i don't know.

2:06AM: i want to buy e-cigarette refills and a caffeine and take a break and drive this shitshow to maryland.

2:36AM: i made a poll called 'WHAT DO YOU WANT MOST FROM ME.' i will do the thing that gets the most votes. please email me or go here:

http://polldaddy.com/poll/7336288/ and vote. keeping this poll open. here are the results, as of today:

- vice column (would be updated weekly or bi-weekly) [RESULT: 3 votes]

- liveblog (would continue updating for my whole life, would be more consistent w/updates) [RESULT: 10 votes]

- novel (would contain things from liveblog, would want to focus everything on writing/editing this for 6-18 months [i.e. stop liveblog, no articles], would want to get an agent and a book deal where i have enough money to live without another job or help from my parents until i write another book, would continue to support myself financially this way until i die or think of something better) [RESULT: 27 votes]

- disappear from the internet (would delete everything i can delete, would write in private if i wanted to write, would not publish anything on the internet ever again) [RESULT: 3 votes]

- nothing [RESULT: 4 votes]

- novel + vice column + other writing things [RESULT: 13 votes]

- I want you to stop doing drugs forever. Get clean. [I DIDN'T WRITE THIS, RESULT: 13 votes]

- i want you to be happy forever [I DIDN'T WRITE THIS, RESULT: 9 votes]

- love [I DIDN'T WRITE THIS, RESULT: 5 votes]

- Be my best friend [I DIDN'T WRITE THIS, RESULT: 6 votes]

- I want you 2 live sumwhere w/ beach + ppl u love [I DIDN'T WRITE THIS, RESULT: 6 votes]

- i want to get you to a nunnery [I DIDN'T WRITE THIS, RESULT: 1 vote]

- I want liveblog but book+agent prob better 4u [I DIDN'T WRITE THIS, RESULT: 1 vote]

- ur balls in my face bbz xooxoxo [I DIDN'T WRITE THIS, RESULT: 6 votes]

- Happy forever but also the liveblog [I DIDN'T WRITE THIS, RESULT: 5 votes]

- relationships with other ppl [I DIDN'T WRITE THIS, RESULT: 1 vote]

- love u megan [I DIDN'T WRITE THIS, RESULT: 3 votes]

- whatever u want i dont know [I DIDN'T WRITE THIS, RESULT: 3 votes]

- hi megan, i think ur wonderful! stay creative!!xxx [I DIDN'T WRITE THIS, RESULT: 5 votes]

- happy 4ever/liveblog/novel/do drugs w me [I DIDN'T WRITE THIS, RESULT: 4 votes]

- peace of mind 4 u bb [I DIDN'T WRITE THIS, RESULT: 4 votes]

- Other [RESULT: 3 votes]

thank you.

2:54AM: i said i didn't want ot do this shit and now i'm tryig nfocufgio-sugnsrkkrsglharwthl;twrh;ltwe

fucking

why won't it save the post

huh

HUH

UNIVERSE IS TELLING ME SOMETHING?! IS THE UNIVERSE ANSWERING THE POLL FOR ME?!!??

OFTEN THINK 'THE UNIVERSE IS TELLING ME TO _____' AND A LOT OF THE TIME I END UP DOING THE WHATEVER-IT-IS MOSTLY BECAUSE IT FEELS 'RIGHT' BUT...

WHAT I'M TRYING TO SAY:

THE UNIVERSE IS VERY EXTREMELY VERY VERY VYER VYER VYER RARELY RARELY IF EVER BUT LIKELY NEVER DIRECT OR FORTHRIGHT

I WOULD LIKE VERY MUCH TO BE RULED BY A TOTALITAR-IAN...FUTURISTIC...I DON'T KNOW, ALIEN SOMETHING...

JUST ANYTHING WHERE I KNOW EXACTLY WHAT IS EXPECTED OF ME, I NEVER HAVE TO MAKE A CHOICE AGAIN

PEOPLE WHO TALK ABOUT FREEDOM ARE RECKLESS

MY SCALP IS TINGLING WITH ANGER AT YOU PEOPLE

YOU GODDAMNED RECKLESS ENTITLED PEOPLE WANTING TO MAKE CHOICES BECAUSE 'OOOOOH MY CHOICES MAKE ME THE PERSON WHO I AM' WHICH IS WHAT, WHAT ARE YOU GODDAMNIT, COOL CHOICES, LOOK AT YOU

ANYONE WHO THINKS THEY'RE…I DON'T KNOW

ANYONE WHO IS PROUD OF WHO THEY ARE IS PROBABLY SOMEONE I NEVER WANT TO TALK TO

ANYONE WHO IS DOING ANYTHING OTHER THAN TRYING… HUMBLY…JUST…TRYING IN THIS SHITTY WORLD…TRYING…

NOT DOING

DOING SUGGESTS 'I'M MAKING CHOICES'

THE ONLY PEOPLE I LIKE ARE CHOICELESS

IT'S NOT A CHOICE

IT'S NOT…

NO DOING THINGS IS FINE, I TAKE IT BACK, I JUST WISH I FELT CONVICTION IN MY CHOICES

WHAT I MEAN IS IF YOU'RE PROUD OF YOURSELF AND HAPPY TO BE ALIVE PLEASE NEVER TALK TO ME UNLESS YOU ARE CONSIDERING ADOPTING MY CAT BECAUSE I'M SURE YOU ARE A LOVING PERSON, AS ALL OF YOU PROUD HAPPY PEOPLE ARE, YOU REALLY ARE, I HAVE MET A LOT OF PEOPLE WHO DON'T SEEM TO HAVE THE SAME PROBLEMS OR SENSITIVITIES AS ME, THESE ARE MOST OF THE PEOPLE I'VE MET, A LOT OF THEM ARE VERY NICE, I AM BEING SINCERE

I DON'T GET WHY HALF…MORE THAN HALF…UM

I UNDERSTAND WHY LIKE, LESS THAN TEN PEOPLE RELATE TO MY BOOK OR MY WRITING, BASED ON WHAT I KNOW OF THOSE PEOPLE

THE REST OF YOU?

BEATS THE HELL OUT OF ME

I AM BASING 'BEATS THE HELL OUT OF ME' ON THINGS PEOPLE HAVE SAID TO ME OR ASKED ME TO DO OR…I DON'T KNOW…INTERACTED WITH ME IN ANY WAY, THAT IS NOT THE WAY THE LESS THAN TEN PEOPLE HAVE INTERACTED WITH ME

SEEMS SO DIFFERENT FROM THE WAY I LIKE TO DO THINGS

BUT THE STUFF I'M…THAT I WRITE…OR WAHTEVER…I FEEL LIKE IT'S VERY BASED ON 'THE WAY I LIKE TO DO THINGS/ THE WAY I THINK'

YOU PRECIOUS LESS THAN TEN PEOPLE

YOU HAVE NO IDEA

YOU MAKE ME WANT TO KEEP GOING (I DON'T KNOW IF THAT'S A GOOD THING)

THE HOPE THAT THERE WILL BE MORE OF YOU

ACTUALLY I JUST COUNTED, THERE ARE TEN EXACTLY

I AM THANKFUL TO HAVE MET THIS MANY, THAT YOU ARE OUT THERE, THANK YOU FOR BEING OUT THERE

ARE THERE MORE

I'M NOT SAYING THIS TO ALIENATE ANYONE

I'M SAYING THIS BECAUSE I NEVER GET TO SAY IT

NEVER ALLOW MYSELF TO SAY IT BECAUSE I'M AFRAID OF ALIENATING ALL OF YOU PEOPLE WHO SEEM TO HAVE NO QUALMS ABOUT ALIENATING ME

SHITTY

ALL OF US ARE SHITTY

YOU ME THE LESS THAN TEN PEOPLE ALL THE REST OF EVERYONE THE WHOLE BIG WRITHING DUMP OF SHITTY-NESS YES EVERYONE

EVERYONE BUT MOM

HER TRAGEDY IS THAT SHE THOUGHT I WOULD NOT BE SHITTY

EVERYONE SHOULD LEARN FROM MY MOM

DAD TOO, KIND OF

IT IS TRAGIC HOW THEY THOUGHT...I WOULD...JUST... CONSIDERING EVERYTHING...PEOPLE...THE WORLD... WHAT WERE THEY THINKING

I'M SORRY

I'M SO SORRY TO EVERYTHING

3:25AM: shirley jumped on the bed and sat by alvie's head and he was laying and raised his head so he could lick her head and for one moment everything was okay. i didn't think about anything else. it just filled me.

4:14AM: gathered laundry, put out extra food for cats, put on 'frederick barthleme' shirt from tao via 'in case i die this will be a funny shirt to die in and it will get people to buy frederick's and tao's books maybe.' laying on mattress. responded to gchat from zachary. we've been riffing about [omitted]'s okcupid profile. looked at the profile. he added something about wanting 'great sex,' not just 'casual sex.' yuck. just another person out there. doing doom. not just 'casual' doom, 'great' doom. making little doomsdays. laying doomsday turd. preparing to shit all over whatever unlucky toilet comes his way. doesn't even know that's what he's doing. i know there is someone out there for him, probably hundreds of someones, but how is it that they're all stupider than me. they are...but. how are there so many stupider than me. i'm so stupid. it's funny. haha. who will my next person be. will i be too stupid for them or will they be too stupid for me. back hurts. ate amounts of choline, aniracetam, three tylenol. tired. i don't want to see the pickles & pies employees seeing me at 4AM, buying energy drinks.

i want to live on a ranch in montana where all i have to do is make babies with some stupid guy i love and who loves me and we get to play with the babies and eat food and watch movies and jeopardy every day and all of us get old and die and there are no banks or car insurance or drugs or parking tickets and the internet burns down and shirley never pees the bed again for as long as we both shall live.

4:50AM: there are more than less than ten of you. i didn't factor in certain things.

5:39am: going to Duane reade instead of pickles & pies. At traffic light. Windows foggy.

5:45am: bought e-cigarette, sf red bull and monster zero from Duane reade. Card didn't scan. Guy said 'i'll just have to do it manual.' 'Sorry.' 'That's okay, give me something to do.' Liked him.

5:51am: Can't believe [omitted] would change that he wants 'great' and not 'casual' sex but would neglect to change 'body type: thin' to 'body type: 'average,' 'athletic,' '[maybe just omit this part].'' Unless he's lost at least 15lbs in three weeks. He looked good to me but would not call him 'thin.' Girls looking for 'great' sex must be disappointed when they meet him in person, if they expected 'thin.' I'm being nasty right now I don't care. If y'all don't like my lyrics you can press fast forward.

7:47am: stopped to pee at Clara Barton rest stop. Parked in front of abandoned yellow stuffed bear with a price tag still on its ear, perched atop a garbage can. Seems endlessly…just…endless. Saddest thing. Endless. Not really the saddest thing. 'Up there,' though. I'm peeing now. Pee smells dehydrated. I am sucking through this e-cigarette hard. Can feel I've almost depleted it. The only brand that 'pulls' hard enough for me is called 'logic.' Smoking a 'blu' brand disposable. Should've sucked it up and bought refills from pickles & pies instead of subverting familiar employee interactions at Duane reade.

7:51am: thought 'I want to be in love' and pictured myself here, in stinky rest stop stall, bent over iPhone, having finished peeing for some time now, and laughed through nose. Here I am, world!!! At your service!!!!! Human toilet having a precious moment on a toilet toilet!!!!!

There was this porno video my friends Seth and Matt and Lindsay and me used to watch. It was an inside joke. The girl has a toilet seat on her neck and the guy is saying 'you bad little toilet' and 'it's never enough for girls like you, is it?' and 'bad toilet! That's a good toilet.' We would quote it to each other a lot and call people 'bad toilets.' My heart is like, fluttering remembering this, I loved 'bad toilet.' The thing about it though…I didn't think there were actually men in the world who'd orgasm from that. It was too over the top, not even sexual. Oh how young I was. I've never said 'bad toilet' exactly but Jesus Christ the things I've said and done.

Putting in a request, for my next person: it can't be someone who would call themselves 'obsessed with porn' or likes humiliation porn or anal sex. It's just. Um. As open-minded as I like to think of myself as being…think I don't want to do stuff like that anymore. Unless…I don't know. If they were similar to me in ways I thought were more important and like, doing the '[whatever sex thing they want to do]' would make them happy and I didn't doubt other things about our relationship, then. Yeah. Guess that'd be fine. I'd prefer us to like the same things sexually though.

7:57am: inserted two quarters in coin slot and cranked the knob of a vending machine labeled 'treasure chest.' Thought 'hope I get something cool, I want one of the cool things.' Got a ring. Put it on. I don't know what the 'cool thing' would've been. Wandered around sunoco travel mart, looking for e-cigarettes. No cashier. Heard voices coming from somewhere I couldn't see.

7:59am: sitting in car now. It looked stolen, for a moment. The sad yellow stuffed animal is still here. 'Still here, as it ever was.' Now people are sitting at the picnic table.

8:07am: sang along to 'sympathy for the devil.' The part I know best is the guitar solo. Tongued potential cavity. Upper left molar. Second from furthest back. It is foggy but sunny outside.

8;18am: I've only had anal sex with two close friends and [omitted]. I feel like I want to have anal sex with like, hundreds of men now, so [omitted] doesn't think he's special. There is something raw and unexpected about typing this. He dated me and had anal sex with me and now I am a girl he 'really felt something real, sweet girl, had genuine feelings for her.' He'll say that to the next girl, like he'd say things like that to me, about girls he's dated. 'Sweet girl, had genuine feelings for her.' Why does 'sweet girl' kill me like that. When he'd tell me he'd told people we were dating, a lot of the people seemed to know who I was. Seems so shitty. Leveraging knowing a person as shitty as me to have sex with some other shitty person. How do I take that back? Can I take back knowing...him...no. I don't know what would help. Making him watch me have anal sex with younger more attractive men. Men I've been in relationships with and want to be in relationships with. Getting it real hard. Skypeing all his co-workers and friends and yelling secrets about him while someone passionately has sex with my ass and other parts, and [omitted] is just there in the background on a chair or something. Fuck that guy. 'Not just casual sex, great sex.' The [omitted] way. The thing I'd be doing to him would be called 'omitted style.' His sad empty whatever-it-is where people's hearts usually are. Omitted. It is fitting that he's 'omitted.' Perfect. Would suggest a legal name change if not for the text message it'd require, and all the government employees inconvenienced by paperwork for a person who never needed to be there anyway.

I'm aware of being dramatic right now. I've been restraining myself from typing things like this for weeks. Will be interesting to put this out there.

Think I would rather be known as someone 'insane, emotional, advisable not to fuck with' than 'kind, reasonable, empathetic, forgiving.' At this point. At this moment, 8:28am August 21, 2013, that is what I want. I'm just upset and this will pass.

Do not fuck with me.

Enough of people thinking they can fuck with me.

Go ahead and try. I have nothing to lose. Do not fuck with an emotionally unstable woman with nothing to lose.

Go ahead and tell everyone about sex with my asshole. No here, I'll do it for you.

I shit out of my asshole every one or two days. Your dick has had particles of my shit on it. So. Joke's on you. Why do I feel this way about this.

The most hurtful thing said to me was a long text message from an ex, harshly critiquing my body.

I hope [omitting this part as of August 26, 2013]

[omitting this part as of August 26, 2013]

Haha.

Nothing to lose.

[omitting this part as of August 26, 2013]

Wanting to 'beat' rage by pretending I don't feel it.

It feels so bad.

Nobody in my corner, not even me.

Everyone wants something from me and when they get it they're done and so that means it's over.

I am stupid enough to allow it to happen and I do it too.

Not anymore, fuck that, no one gets to fuck with me anymore.

Fuck with me and get hurt.

Want to be known as the DMX of emotional...something...

Only to people who hurt me on purpose.

I consider 'just not thinking, in the moment'/'not considering how I'd feel about something you're about to do, like lie or have sex with others if we've agreed to be honest and monogamous' to be 'hurting me on purpose.'

I don't know maybe not though.

Tired of thinking 'I'm responsible for everything that happens to me,' sometimes I'm not, I don't get to choose everything but I get to choose how I react but I'm tired of choosing to react by keeping quiet and accepting/ moving on. I will always get to the 'accepting' part.

There is a part in between that I ignore but maybe part of my problem is ignoring that part as much as I do.

I've never felt anything like this, that I can remember, that I feel right now.

Corner-reversal, now 100% in my corner.

No one else is.

Someone needs to be if I want to stay alive.

I feel most 'in control' when I'm saying 'I accept this and move on.' This is a survival thing, I think. It's not completely genuine.

There is always this hot moment before accepting though.

Do not allow myself much time in the hot moment because it is a little scary, the hotness.

I think I could do very terrible things, I have the potential to go absolutely insane with rage, I have raged out on myself as like, a substitute 'host body' for the rage.

Most violent things I've done to me: three suicide attempts (12, cutting wrists & pills: 17, pills; 26, cutting wrist & pills), scratching my arms/ skin in arguments until there is blood, picking at face and back until there is blood weekly to daily since 2002, a few months in 2006 where I'd get drunk and drive to see 'if it happens this time,' a few sprained ankles as a kid from intentionally falling or not stopping myself from falling so I could get out of gym class, making myself vomit, guess you could say my lifestyle/ drug habits aren't healthy but are less outwardly violent. Feel stupid for saying all of these things, like. I'm not bragging, just wanted to make a list to see if it was as bad as I thought and it wasn't.

9:40AM: arrived at mom's. smelled it. the smell of it here. saw her sleeping and tried to silently place keys in the dish. it smells like so much. it's something kind. i'm crying. i can't take it. how someone…the way…just getting to see that she's bought groceries. all of the names of products. an 'heirloom watermelon.' i can't take it. what is going on with me. i can't say it well now. i'm crying. she's too good of a person to know me. i'm the unlikely winner of a reality TV show contest, they just said 'you finally got it: the prize,' and now they're showing me all changes to come. that's what it feels like to be here right now and to smell it and see the groceries and there is cold water in the fridge and so many things in the fridge and boxes of 'kind' bars and all the pretty things she's collected over the years, the things she'd say 'look at all the pretty things' about and the little me she carried would repeat 'pitty sings,' the light she leaves on all the time because of how it looks coming through the slats of the trash room door. it's like i'm out of jail. i can't believe this room. she put the dragons on my bed. no one else in the world would think that much about me, to do that. something like that. nobody.

9:41AM–8:59PM: abandoned.

9:00pm: mom is excited about her 'droid' phone. Told her I'd buy her a box of 'kind' bars and 'harvest bread' from whole foods.

9:51pm: whole foods was closed. Driving around beltway.

10:24pm: parked at wegman's.

11:04pm: still sitting in car. Ate 10mg oxycodone. They should prescribe it as an antidepressant. It makes me calm and gracious and view things like the wegman's sign as benign and gossamer-y. In the distance a 90's-sounding r&b song has been playing on repeat. Earlier a man with a bandana on his head sang along in a falsetto while he loaded a car. Wanted to blow him a kiss. Car is smelly like my shoes and perfume. I feel oily but like…how the oil in parking lot puddles reflects a rainbow sheen…like, dreamily/foggily spinning. Back and right-side torso muscles hurt. Think I did something to it the other night when giving Mira an 'airplane ride.' Have been sitting here since like, 10:24pm. I can hear crickets. It is hot and stale in this car but it feels nice. Feels like the song 'drinking in l.a.' by bran van 3000. That was one of Zachary's and my 'songs.'

11:11pm: guess I'll go in now.

11:50pm: bumbled around store. Bought surprises for mom and smoothie materials. 'Mr. Blue sky' by elo and a plinky Gwen stefani song played.

AUGUST 22, 2011

12:[something]-2:[something]AM: arrived home from wegman's. talked with mom, helped her with her droid, painted nails, ate leftovers, watched old SNLs.

2:[something]-4:[something]AM: watched 'crazy stupid love' with mom and talked/joked a lot during it.

4:[something]-9:[something]AM: looked at internet. 3mg xanax, 20mg oxycodone total. looked at ASMR videos.

4:[something]PM: woke.

4:[something]-11:59PM: abandoned.

AUGUST 23, 2013

did not update

AUGUST 24, 2013

3:11AM: watching 'the office' in my room. waiting for 'newman's own' pizza to bake.

5:16pm: walking down stairs. Driving to inner harbor whole foods.

5:21pm: sitting in car parked in whole foods parking garage. Bought 'blueprint' green juice. Nostalgic for summer 2011. Kenny (guy who lived with his girlfriend, my dad, me) is at dad's office. He lives in West Virginia now.

5:31pm: I didn't even really want the green juice. Just hanging around here for…I don't know. I don't want to go back to New York. Dad is off work 6. Driving to his office to say hi. None of the music I have feels right.

5:36pm: car with 'Baltimore rock opera society' bumper sticker passed on the right. Passenger and driver inside. Imagined them listening to queen or something.

6:03pm: Mom said I could come back whenever I wanted.

6:23pm: met a pregnant patient of dad's. Eyes watered while listening to her talk cheerfully about due date. Now she is behind me at traffic light. Slammed on breaks. It was yellow but I could've gone.

6:31pm: radio dj said 'I heard you like roller coasters.' Girl said 'I do, a lot.' Dj said 'have you ever been on a stand-up roller coaster?' Girl giggled and said 'no, I haven't.' Dj said 'well we're gonna change that.' He sounded kind and old.

6:39pm: Parked at petsmart.

6:52pm: the cashier liked 'Benny and the jets.' She asked if I wanted a bag for three items.

6:58pm: stopped at Walgreen's for e-cigarette. Woman behind me in line said 'well that was a very nice, uh, how do you do' as I left. Feel horrible. Have eaten 10mg oxy, 10mg Vicodin today.

7:03pm: ate 10mg oxy. Fleetwood Mac playing on radio.

8:11pm: at pretty futuristic Delaware rest stop. Accidentally parked car (only needed gas but going to 'run with this' and use bathroom). Smells like chicken in here. Have been listening to dancehall radio station and feeling happy but it's not coming in clearly anymore.

8:13pm: two pennies on floor of bathroom stall. Picked them up, putting in pocket currently. I lied, they were in my pocket by the time I typed 'them.' Distinctly remember sitting in this stall for like, a long time… tweeting something, maybe…years ago, maybe.

9:35pm: ate 1mg Xanax. Have been listening to 'drinks after work' by Toby Keith on repeat for maybe an hour. It came on the radio and I googled lyrics and bought it before it had ended.

11:11pm: ate 1mg Xanax. Want McDonald's badly. Shit I gotta feed cats before me. Gian texted. A gian event has popped up. Gotta pee. Hope there are no piles of doom awaiting in apt.

AUGUST 25, 2013

did not update.

AUGUST 26, 2013

6:00AM: woke. ate amount of ambien.

2:00PM: woke. ate 30mg adderall.

8:18PM: drove to UPS, mailed package for matthew donahoo and returned broken phone. fed cats, sat at table. sent a long emotional email to juliet, who had emailed the interview she's transcribed from our skype video sessions. she had said she voted on 'novel + vice things' on poll and that the liveblog has become a 'big hentai monster' and i should stop, and i agreed. going to shower now. averse to my negative rant about [omitted].

10:10pm: driving to Sam's to hang out and smoke crack. Am somewhere near queens, maybe. Looking for 70th st. Have recalibrated route several times. Feel bombarded with information from street signs. Feel micromanaged by gmaps. Listening to 'drinks after work' by Toby Keith on repeat. Just got whiff of someone's cigarette from car next to me at traffic light. I don't know what Sam's job is. What if I never ask. Doesn't seem to matter. Toying with idea of never knowing what Sam does for a living. Passed green sign that said 'triboro bridge has been renamed RFK bridge' and thought 'great sign, great, tax dollars at work, thank you' on autopilot, like, warming up for conversation.

did not update.

AUGUST 28, 2013

did not update.

did not update.

AUGUST 30, 2013

did not update.

did not update

SEPTEMBER 1, 2013

8:58PM: drinking miller high life. sitting in bed. trying used e-cigarette cartridges to see if they're empty. watching 'into the abyss.' waiting for sam to arrive. just returned from pickles & pies. walked behind a man using what i thought was a wheelchair, but was an elaborate walker device. there was a mattress with a 'pillow-top' label on the corner of 117th and rockaway beach blvd. smelled awful when i passed. it was there last night too. people in clown wigs, on bikes, gathered on the corner by pickles & pies. saw a lot of people but the street felt quiet. foggy. eerily foggy. fireworks exploded in the sky while i walked to apartment building. for the first time since my interview with the apartment 'committee that screens potential tenants,' i saw the three dogs in the window of the house with the screened-in porch. the dogs were standing almost motionlessly, staring in the same direction. somewhere there is a picture of this. didn't take another picture tonight.

walked behind a smallish man carrying two plastic bags. from a distance he looked close to my age. imagined he lived in my building. maybe he worked in the city. he was someone like me, maybe, we had each been keeping our existences secret this entire time. the dogs barked at him. when i passed, one dog walked away, the middle dog continued barking, and the third dog and i made eye contact. slowed my pace so the plastic bag man wouldn't feel obligated to hold the door for me. tried to remember what i had imagined would happen when i'd move here. beach parties. something. i probably didn't know then either.

used apartment key to open the building door. through the glass, watched the plastic bag man join maybe two others, waiting for the elevator. one of the others was the ex-MTA employee in a wheelchair, who i told i'd bring smoothies, and had believed i would, the night of colin's 'welcome to the building' dinner. heard the familiar click of the door's weight closing behind me. approached group closely enough to recognize plastic bag man: the 'fancy food student' from the dinner. made eye contact with MTA wheelchair man as he reversed into the elevator. we said 'hi' quietly, kind of sorrowfully, overlapping the word at intervals suggesting neither of us meant for the greeting to be heard. focused eyes on one of the plastic bags. remembered they both lived on the fourth floor. i didn't get on the elevator.

For their consultation, wisdom, and support—without which this book wouldn't exist—I would like to thank Giancarlo DiTrapano, Adam Robinson, Nicole Caputo, Zachary German, Jordan Castro, Nicolette Polek, Sam Cooke, Simone Campbell-Scott, and Pamela Sue Dutton Boyle.

Megan Boyle was born October 15, 1985 at 4:14PM.
She lives in Baltimore, Maryland.